I0592736

The Pentagram Woman

by

K Mc Vere

1

March 27ᵗʰ, 2017

Jane Smith waited patiently near the front desk of the hospital lobby for Dr. Bishop to finish reading a paper attached to his clipboard and acknowledge her and perhaps smile down at her and shake her hand and finally after all these years say the words she had imagined him saying while alone in her bed listening to the whisper of starched uniforms passing in the hall.

In the beginning, there had been only five words. Five very important words – *We have found your parents*. When she lost faith in hearing those words, she chose seven new words which helped her sleep at night. After all, the number seven was a lucky number. Her knees shook a bit as she waited for him to look up from his clipboard. *Say them*, she thought in a fierce whisper as she looked down at her feet, *say the words: You are officially released from Ward Eight*.

Moments. Maybe seconds passed. Patience. What were a few minutes compared to years and years of pretense? She kept her hands demurely clasped in front of her, the fingers relaxed, her entire body relaxed, mind blank, as blank as a smooth creamy piece of writing paper. Hold on. Maybe not? Maybe a little animation might be good, perhaps curiosity even? Yes. Good idea. Look around, pretend to be interested in your surroundings.

Look up at the ceiling, around the room with its white walls and white tiled floor and magnificent windows pushing back the dark while dumping loads of sunlight into the room. The most appreciative in the room were the audience of potted plants. They had to be, all their foliage paid homage to the sun. Some of them were gigantic members of the congregation nearly brushing the vaulted roof with their greenery.

Yes, it was easy enough to gaze at the plants and the light and the beauty of the outdoors. It was more difficult to be interested in the comings and goings of the humans: the strollers, the pacers, and the sitters, the ones fidgeting in their seats waiting for a family member, some sipping coffee and staring off into space: some whispering, most reading magazines or surfing the Internet. That woman though, the one in the corner hiding behind the gigantic Fiddle Leaf Fig appeared to be terrified. She probably was thinking that someone from work or the neighborhood might pass the hospital windows and mistake her for a patient.

It might be 2017, yet, people were still fearful of psychotics. No matter how sophisticated and urban you might be – in the back of your mind you're thinking, "Oh my god, this is a loony bin, a booby hatch, the bughouse. This is where they keep the crazy ones in the rubber rooms, the ones that when they are released pass you on the street and scream at you with spittle inching down a quivering chin. Yes.

This is where the crazies commit hallucinations, urinations, and flagellations. This is where they tie you to your bed, put you in a straitjacket, and pump you full of anti-psychotic medications. It's all their fault. All they have to do is get back into their right minds. Yah, their right minds. Which right would that be again?"

Jane Smith looked out the window at the frozen world with bare trees and snow and people covered in warm jackets and knitted caps. Such a windy place, Chicago. She would be out there soon, one of those people rushing purposely by someone's window having a place to go, people to find, and perhaps, if lucky, one or two people to kill.

For a few seconds, she examined the coat slung over her arm. It had been a gift from the redheaded one, the human with the freckle problem, a slender, bony one. Don't say human. Not even in your head. Saying such a thing implies your crazy. Female. The redheaded female with the tight smile, her face contorted most of the time as if she smells something bad. Why had she given her such an expensive parting gift? People were funny. Oh yeah, that's right. She'd forgotten the true story behind the coat. So many stories to keep track of.

Dr. Caleb Bishop handed his clipboard to Jason Michaels his shadow, his special student, the man who would one day take over his practice; or no, perhaps Jason would move on to bigger and better things, bigger and better psychiatric hospitals. Who knows? Who cares? Perhaps Michaels cared although Jane thought him incapable of caring or of having any doubts about his rightness in the scheme of things.

In order to be a person who cares, one has to have some doubts about the future. Michaels didn't appear to have any doubts or reservations about his prospects. He knew for a fact he would go on to bigger and better things. They could have been father and son – Dr. Bishop and Jason Michaels – two peas in a pod, two bookends, the way they interacted with patients and the staff and their associates, the way they talked to her, eyes clinical, judgmental, rehearsed words spewing from their lips.

Thirteen years of Dr. Bishop and his entourage: his nurses, his students, his patients. Thirteen years spent in Canal Critical Care and Recovery Hospital, in other words – stuck in purgatory – either in the Critical Care Unit or the Recovery Facility. The Recovery Facility was a smaller building with ten floors.

Why they put the psychiatric unit on the eighth floor was anyone's guess. The doctors referred to the psych ward as the Jung Ward while everyone else called it the 8-Ball Ward. A lifetime of surgeries, sympathy, sweet talkers, and stink bugs. Oh no. Visualize a blank sheet of paper. No lines, just blank. Wait . . . better yet visualize two huge dots separated by white. Go into that white center and stay there.

Bishop stepped closer to her. She looked up. Big mistake. His face grew larger and larger, so large she feared his face would take over the room. She had to look away. She hated when that happened. She wanted so much to look him straight in the eye, to appear confident and ready to greet the world. In her head, she counted to ten forward and backward listening to his voice droning on and on ad nauseam.

"Jane. I know you're eager to get out into the world and experience life first hand," he began clutching his clipboard under his armpit as if it were a baton, "but in my opinion, you are just not ready for the world outside these doors. It's 2017 and so much has changed since you were a child." While Bishop continued to extrapolate on the dangers of the outside world, Jane rose to her feet and nodded politely toward both men. It was her custom to ignore Bishop's words and instead pay attention to his body language. Actually, her intense focus on facial movements, body positioning, and vocal tones from anyone in her vicinity had become an instinctual habit, her way of assessing the dangers around her.

Just as this gift had saved her so many times in the past, her awareness of Bishop and his clipboard saved her from a serious eye injury. The man had this weird habit of greeting people with a stiff bow and an air kiss toward an imaginary cheek which reminded her of the courting gestures of penguins. When he moved in close the sharp metal attached to his board nearly poked her in the eye. Seconds before the impending peril, she stepped back her heel connecting with the chair behind her.

Bishop never noticed continuing his diatribe about her vulnerabilities without pausing. His intern's alarmed expression coinciding with an ineffectual grab for Dr. Bishop's arm at the same moment Jane Smith's heels hit the chair. The sound of the metal chair's legs screeching against the tiled floor turned heads in the lobby. Only Bishop remained clueless to the near miss.

Familiar with Bishop's obtuseness, Jane nodded politely toward both men and felt her face assume the expression she had been practicing for weeks in front of the bathroom mirror. The expression she finally settled on conveyed a dash of hero-worship and a sprinkle of excitement. She kept the expression fresh as Bishop wound down his monologue, ". . . but I also want to assure you that if you ever need to talk to someone you can call me at any time. I've asked staff to include an address book in your personal belongings. It has several helpful contact numbers on the first page if you should ever need to reach us."

Determined to appear as normal as possible Jane made herself look up into his face and was relieved to discover his face remained the same size. She glanced at Jason and his face also remained normal. Feeling a bit more confident, Jane made herself smile remembering to smile with her eyes because humanoids were hardwired to recognize fakery.

For the benefit of his student and the witnesses in the lobby, Dr. Bishop continued his current charade of professionalism. A week earlier, things had been totally different. At the time, they had been alone in his office. In the past, she had dreaded those intimate interviews mainly because he had been such a consummate bore talking over her, interrupting her when she tried to speak and ironically blaming her for an inability to shut him up. She supposed he had gotten used to the Cabbage and Tomato Jane Smith, not the emerging new Jane Smith.

This time she came to his office ready to open up and let him see the real Jane Smith. It was a meeting-of-the-minds, a virtual reality meeting-of-the-minds, a combination mesmerism and Spock mind-melding experience. Their talk finally penetrated Dr. Bishop's shell of authority and confidence. She'd been brutally honest with him. He'd kept her under lock-and-key for far too fucking long. Her status as his chief guinea pig and unusual test subject was now at an end.

Fifteen years ago, she had trusted everyone, thought anyone wearing a lab coat and carrying a clipboard must be a genius, must be a god, someone who just knew what was wrong with her and could fix the owie like magic. Jane could be excused for her naiveté – she'd only been six years old when she met the other kind of medico, the one with the dead eyes who poked her and stabbed her with needles and looked right through her as if she were a fascinating specimen on her busy surgical table. Her victims (those still able to speak) called her Harpy of Death or Butcher Queen. It took Jane's body years before it stopped flinching whenever she saw a lab coat.

Her earliest new friend, a very wise older woman who called herself Tessa Mourning Dove explained to Jane about these opposing forces in the medical community and helped her reconcile her horrific past experiences with her current situation. Tessa assured Jane that only a handful of people calling themselves doctors were monsters and urged her not to tense up when she saw someone wearing a lab coat. Ana tried to educate Jane on the most notorious of pain-givers and death-dealers by going back through history remembering the worst of the worst, but Tessa shut her up before she got to some guy called Mangle or Mengala.

Over the years, Jane realized there were more medicos than Mengalas in the world. Knowing that this monstrous woman was still alive and probably doing unspeakable things to unsuspecting and innocent people, Jane resolved to find the demon woman and expose her vile experimentations to the world. Or maybe for the good of mankind, she'd just end the filthy creature's life.

For thirteen years while at Canal Critical Care, the medicos soothed her with kind words, wiped away the blood and dirt, stitched her wounds, washed her body, offered her food and drink, gave her drugs for pain and pills for sleep. She'd needed those years to rebuild herself and prepare for the journey ahead. Those medicos had known what was best for her, using everything the medical apparatus had to offer in order to accelerate the healing of her body and her mind.

Dr. Bishop claimed healing her body had been easy but healing her mind would take much longer. She didn't believe anything that came out of his lying fat mouth. He was a mediocre doctor and a parasite who from the beginning of his career had claimed his wife's strategies and other medical professional's brilliant ideas as his own. He had to be sued by several psychiatrists before he stopped publishing their ideas and claiming them as his. He was the worst kind of blood sucker, a person who had never had an original thought his entire life, yet, found all sorts of sneaky ways to get noticed by his superiors and claim other people's ideas as his own.

She knew better now. Oh yes, those plastic surgeons, the good ones were really – really – good, and the skin grafters, and the physical therapists, and the nurses, and all the little people she had to admit were fantastic at their jobs and knew what they were doing. And that first shrink, she had been one fine woman, one excellent human being.

Thank all the goddesses of the earth, the fire, the sea, and the sky including the great goddess of them all for creating such a fine human being as that woman. When she first arrived at Canal Critical Care, it had been Jane Smith's lucky day to have landed a shrink like Dr. Angela Bishop. Jane would never forget Dr. A's soothing voice and her kind eyes. Also, Jane would never forget all the nurses who had come and gone, the ones who urged her to eat and the ones who took the time to read to her. And now she had new friends, friends the hospital knew nothing about and these new friends had her back; they would not betray her. They were as motivated as she was to see this project through.

A man's voice interrupted her memories of Dr. A. Momentarily annoyed by the rude interruption, Jane returned to the present and concentrated on what the outside voice was telling her. "I've notified Mona of your arrival. Here are the directions to her place. She'll be of invaluable help to you, Jane. You remember our conversation about Mrs. Lawson. She lives in Idaho. You said you wanted to see the ocean. Drop in on Mona before you enter Oregon. She's on the way to the coast. You will stop by and see her, won't you?" His question sounded more like a command.

"Oh, Lawson. Yes. You mentioned her before."

"I'm sure she'll be delighted to see you. And she can help you acclimate to the outside world much more quickly than if you tried to do so on your own."

"Thank you, Dr. B. I'll stop in and see her."

His face registered annoyance while his voice remained neutral for the benefit of the people in the lobby, "I hope you'll do more than just stop in. She's willing to provide a home for you and assist you in your recovery." When his pager went off Dr. Bishop frowned. Then as was his custom, he motioned for his assistant Jason Michaels to take over. Inwardly Jane sighed shaking off her growing irritation and impatience. Such a fuss. Michaels, new to authority touched her arm and beamed at her as if she were some sort of child. His ignorance astonished her.

Last night the staff had given her a going-away party. Everyone had wished her well. She had been touched by their concern. Dr. B wasn't there. Jane suspected no one had remembered to ask him. After all, over the last two years, she had only seen him a handful of hours. The unsung heroes of the Eight Ball Ward were her true healers of mind and body. Jane allowed that perhaps Dr. B had a crushing load of nutcases to deal with at other hospitals. She'd gathered over the years that he had precious little time for even his own family. He was a busy, busy, busy fellow.

In that awkward moment as Dr. Bishop focused on his cellphone and Jason Michaels looked uncomfortable, Jane had an epiphany. What was she doing just standing here in the lobby with her thumb up her ass? She'd been set free. She could leave this place any time she wanted. She had the upper hand. Instead of farting around waiting for someone to dismiss her, she would take the initiative. She did so without delay extending her hand to Jason Michaels which consequently disarmed him just enough for him to buy into the self-assurance act. He accepted her hand. His hand was dry and cool to the touch. They shook hands briefly as she said, "Well, thanks for all your help. Goodbye and tell Dr. B I'll keep in touch. Take care now."

Without waiting for Michaels' response, Jane marched toward the swinging lobby doors and stepped outside of Canal Critical Care and Recovery Hospital. She threw her new coat over her shoulders, held her leather purse between her knees, then stuck her arms into the sleeves of her red blazer. Once she had the matching knit cap snug on her head, she took in a deep breath of fresh icy air. Free at last. Free at last. Thank God, I'm free at last.

A moment of shame washed over her.

She had no right to speak those words. Those words were not her words to say. A face rose up from the depths of her mind, a familiar face with kind brown eyes and dark skin like midnight. With her heart pounding madly inside her chest, she looked around desperate to escape the memory.

She would not make the same mistake again. Three years ago, she'd been released from Canal Critical Care on a temporary pass to a halfway house. Unfortunately, she'd been caught breaking the law and bounced back to the 8-Ball Ward and Dr. B. This time, she was prepared. Back then she had been a hopeless case unable to focus for even a minute.

Now she had friends to back her up and keep her moving forward. Her friends were her best advisers. They told her how to present herself to the monitors on the ward and personnel at the duty stations, and especially the cleaning staff who were Dr. Bishop's eyes and ears and never far away. Her friends showed her how to look and act and cautioned her when her tongue started wagging. She outwitted them all with her incredible acting talents; too bad only she knew it was an act.

After months of debate, yesterday morning the Big B reluctantly agreed to sign her release papers having been pressured by the hospital board and Jane's case worker. This time she was released for good. Everyone agreed she was ready for the outside world. She had been a child when she was first discovered. When her parents never came forward to claim her, she became a ward of the court. Dr. B's wife Dr. A, as in Angela Bishop, and many other medicos did their best to tease out, rouse, sometimes haul up those lost memories of her tragic past. They were unsuccessful. Dr. B came along and tried some of his remedies as well without success. It was eventually decided by all to wait until she was older and hope that time would heal her mind's wounds.

Fuck brains.

Idiots.

Douche-bags.

Vaguely she remembered the first time she walked through the hospital doors by herself with all she possessed in one small suitcase. At that time, she'd been given a bus pass and a map of the city and had been told to find the half-way house on her own with only her wits to guide her through Chicago's busy streets. If she didn't show up at the half-way house by five o'clock that day, her case worker would assume she was a runaway and contact the authorities to pick her up and return her to the 8-Ball Ward.

It had been the best and the worst month of her life. Visiting the shops and the grocery stores, losing herself in the library with free access to the Internet, buying clothes with her first real money, and most of all, her first time eating a Royal Pie loaded with beef, chicken, veggies, and all sorts of foody goodness was the most incredible, the most quad triple awesome experience of her life.

She had made some mistakes. Sorry, sorry, everyone, she thought to herself and tried hard not to giggle. She couldn't remember that last day of freedom much and wondered if the troglodyte in the room next to hers had been lying just to get rid of her. On visiting days, the troglodyte's fat smelly toad of a father would tease her about her butch haircut and playfully try to rub her head. She managed to avoid his touch each time he moved in on her personal space. Even standing a few feet away Jane could smell the rankness of his breath.

Her last day at the half-way house went badly, very badly. She wasn't as quick on her feet during their final encounter. Because she preferred to eat her meals in her room, she happened to be carrying her tray with a dirty plate, an empty glass, and a fork down to the kitchen when she met him on the landing. He tried to give her a bear hug. The encounter resurrected something ugly she had thought she'd extinguished forever. Trogolena claimed she'd attacked her father with the fork in order to maim him. She missed the artery in his neck (which in retrospect worked out well) and instead stabbed him in the chin.

Never mind, never mind. Water under the bridge. She would be twenty-two in July. Her birthday had been chosen by the staff – July 14th Bastille Day. That was the day she had arrived at the 8-Ball Ward after spending nearly a year in intensive care. Irony was not lost on some of the staff. After all Bastille Day was about independence and freedom from oppression and here Jane was a prisoner of her body and her mind in a psychiatric ward.

Once all was explained to her about why the staff chose July 14th as her birthday and she learned more about the events that took place on that day, the dullness that had been her daily experience vanished and she discovered a new interest. She read everything she could about that day and decided even if she did discover her true day of birth, she would still celebrate July 14th as the day of her rebirth and the day of reckoning for those faceless ones who had left her for dead.

On Bastille Day, only one of the Royalist's garrison died in comparison to the many who died to bring down the symbol of brutality and injustice. When Jane learned about Bastille Day, she asked for books about that momentous time in French history. She read Alexandre Dumas' Count of Monte Cristo five times identifying passionately with Edmond Dante's struggle to free himself from his prison on the island of Chateau d'If. He was a prisoner for thirteen years. Jane had been a prisoner in the Canal Critical Care and Recovery Hospital for a bit longer.

Yesterday she'd been prettified by the staff and later in the evening given a combination birthday and going-away party. The party was short lived when one of the patients had a hissy-fit and destroyed Jane's room because all the attention was on Jane Smith and not her. Jane didn't mind the interruption. She was glad to have the spotlight off her; and in compensation for the breakup of the party, she now owned a brand new beautiful coat and stylish purse and some lovely untraceable cash. Of course, she also had the monthly government checks deposited into her bank account. As one staff member reminded her – "Even if you don't remember your name, you have parents who contributed to social security and disability. You are entitled to those benefits."

The whole incredible year had been a miracle. The first few months at the halfway house when she had her miracle moment and then the rest of the time on the Eighth Ward had been a time of preparation. She hadn't told anyone especially Dr. B about her revelatory moment while at the halfway house. And when she was arrested then returned to the hospital, her friends did not desert her. They stayed by her side through the painful days and nights always providing her with useful tips on how to survive.

So did the nurse on duty the first night back inside the Recovery Facility on the 8-Ball Ward. Her name had been Alice Rathburn. The redheaded nurse had been the only staff member to suggest strategies for dealing with Dr. B and his entourage. She had said, "Watch me. See what I do, Jane. Listen closely. Let them believe they're right in some things and the things you don't agree with keep to yourself." Jane had watched her and noticed how the staff treated the redheaded nurse differently than the other patients. And when Mrs. Fitch informed Jane that the redheaded nurse wasn't a real nurse, Jane simply laughed and said she had known all along.

The rest of the 8-Ball Ward were not to be trusted; yet, even though the silly redheaded wench had passed herself off as a nurse wearing a stolen set of scrubs, Alice had given her good advice. This time Jane watched how the doctors and orderlies and nurses behaved toward each other instead of worrying about what the patients might be up to. She parodied the so-called sane humans and discovered so much about the professional staff from watching them interact with each other.

At times, the masquerade could be a bit nauseating as she witnessed the false good-cheer, the exuberant compliments, and the careful speech especially those long-winded narratives chock full of medical jargon: "patient, case study, MMPI, CPS, EEG, PTSD, labs, rad reports, medically necessary, behavioral controls, DSM," and the oft used word "variables." Her pet peeve which even now made her jaw tighten was the greeting every morning between the occupant of the nursing station and the on-call doctor, "No acute events overnight, Doctor."

The one she hated the most, the one she wanted to stuff back down Bishop's throat was his overuse of the word "kiddo." So, what if she couldn't remember her name or her past? You would think he'd know the fake name the staff gave her at least? Or the one his late wife had given Jane the day Jane arrived on the Eighth Ward. Why hadn't he respected Angela Bishop's name for Jane? Jane had liked being called Rose. Every time Bishop called her kiddo she wanted to rush at him screaming and tear his eyes out. Instead Jane swallowed her rage and imagined herself walking out the lobby doors and onto the streets of Chicago one fine day.

Her first bit of acting had been sloppy, but eventually she caught on, learning how to separate her inner dialogue from the art of acting. The secret was not to say the first thing that sprang into her head but rather choose an effective compliment supplied by her trusted friends. After thirteen years at Canal Critical Care and Recovery Hospital, moving from one floor to the next, from surgery to postop to psych, Jane had accumulated several new languages, the language of polite society and the language of medicine and psychiatry.

After many years, she decided polite society's language was a big fat bore. Her personal favorite would always be the secret code words used by the professionals. Although, with the implementation of (EHR) the electronic health records system, medical professionals rarely recorded insulting lingo anymore. So sad. There goes another era, just like patriarchy and sexual harassment. Place heavy sigh here girls. Everyone knew the omission of written medical secret code words was because of the doctors' fears of a sudden epidemic of lawsuits. "Epidemic. Ha-Ha. Very funny, Ana." The only place the lingo is still alive and well is in staff rooms, in whispered conversations between staff members or when staff think you're asleep.

In the past, Dr. B had been called the Butcher, even though he technically wasn't a surgeon. Now they call him the Black Cloud Doc while a few of her favorite lab techs were lumped in with the rest of the Blood Suckers. Happily, though, Jane was no longer the Bunny Boiler;

Alice Rathburn had been crowned Bunny Boiler which meant she was as bat shit crazy as that chick in the movie who stalks Michael Douglas.

For years Jane searched for the meaning behind the euphemism Bunny Boiler. Little clues staff dropped in her hearing and her temporary stint in a halfway house, as well as, a secret viewing of the movie educated her on the meaning of Bunny Boiler. Jane never could see the connection between Alex Forrest and herself. She wasn't sexually obsessed with anyone on the Eight Ball Ward and didn't find any of the men attractive. No, she just wanted to get the hell out of Dotty City.

When she'd been younger she had spent most of her time in the Cabbage & Tomato Ward. Everyone felt so sorry for her back then, most of them pretty sure she wouldn't last the year. Then as she improved the staff started calling her Rockalena. Cute. When she started seeing a psychiatrist they started calling her Amnesia Lisa. They didn't realize she could hear them even while in an induced coma while vacationing in the Cabbage & Tomato Ward. Or did they?

Who cares? That's the past. Shrug off the nasty energy and suspicion of that place and move on. She was nearly free. She couldn't consider herself really and truly free until she was at least outside of Chicago. This morning, instead of swallowing the pill the nurse gave her Jane fake swallowed it and later stuck it in her hidey hole along with all the others nearly a year's supply worth. It had been her plan all along to re-gift them to the redheaded nurse who now wanted to be called Rachel. Rachel could do what she wished with them. She could distribute them out to her "patients" or keep them for herself. The patients didn't mind a bit of spit and slobber on their meds. Fun times. In dee-dee do da.

A flock of new interns and nurses swept past Jane and Jane stepped onto the grass and waited for them to enter the hospital. She didn't recognize anyone. Jane looked down at her feet. She was wearing sensible black pumps today. Then she saw the black nylon backpack. It had been a gift from the staff. While eating a piece of German Chocolate cake, Alice Rathburn had leaned over and whispered in Jane's ear, "The coats not from me. I just took it from the nurse's locker room. I guess the owner of the coat must be on another floor. Hee-hee. Guess what Jane? You're a liar and a snitch and I would never give you a present."

Jane's new friends (not the redheaded Alice Rathburn) had advised her to tell Nurse Tallman about the stolen coat. When Jane handed over the coat Nurse Tallman pushed the coat back into her arms and explained with steely eyes, "Ignore Alice. She's just upset that you're leaving. The coat is our gift to you. It was a gift from all of us."

Jane practically ran toward the waiting taxi. All she owned she carried over her shoulders in her black nylon backpack: two pairs of jeans, a sweater, three cotton shirts, and an extra pair of comfortable shoes. The fair for the taxi had been provided by Nurse Tallman and the money for a hotel for three nights had been the staff's contribution. No one had asked Bishop to offer up any cash. Somehow, they all knew she would have burned his contribution. A wave of grief washed over Jane as she thought about Dr. A. Angela Bishop had been such a kind, sweet, gentle person. Everyone on the Eighth Ward loved her. Jane remembered their first meeting, "What shall we call you? Jane Doe doesn't fit you. What would you like to be called?"

Jane had considered Nancy Drew or Drew Barrymore or Michele or even Betty Crocker anything but Jane Doe. Then she remembered the flowers Dr. A brought to her room and how excited she was to see them, smelling so wonderful and looking so gorgeous and she told Dr. A, "I am Rose." It took her another day to figure out her last name. When the nurse's whispered among themselves about the poor little girl with amnesia, she knew they were talking about her. Only in the night did she forget to forget. Something kept her from telling the staff or the mind-peepers that she knew her real name and what had really happened to her all those years ago. It was her secret. Secrets were empowering.

Until she was sixteen Jane had been called Rose by Dr. A and the staff. Then Dr. A died of breast cancer and her husband took over her caseload. Rose instantly disliked him and when he called her Rose, Jane nearly puked. There was something about him she instantly disliked. She refused to be called Rose by him and thereafter by everyone. It didn't really matter. The high turnover rate at the hospital meant people rarely stayed long enough to know you or remember your name. In a hospital people aren't people anyway; they're charts and blood types and numbers on doors.

Some of the nurses who had known her back in the day still called her Rose and she didn't mind. But eventually Jane had a breakthrough and rediscovered herself and for a few years she would only accept the name Leona. That had led to intense therapy and eventually Jane realized that her future belonged to the not-knowing of things. A few more years passed before she and Dr. Bishop had their final private talk and she had her awesome discovery. Enough with the acting performances and the fake sweetness, she was more than ready to be the pentagram woman. Her first act as the pentagram woman had been to teach Bishop a lesson in manners.

She supposed her frankness had been a bit over-the-top. Yet, in retrospect as she reviewed their last therapy session together, she had to conclude, in all fairness to herself that he had managed to pull through the agony of the meeting-of-the-minds without screaming or running out of the room. Okay, so maybe if she were honest, she might have shared a few too many significant memories with the pompous boob. And maybe he'd overreacted to the horror bits and the pain bits and especially the gross bits. She couldn't be sure since no words passed between them during that one and only pentagram swap. "I'll share mine if you share yours, Dr. B," she remembered saying to him with a smile. He was so eager to share his own childhood trauma, he threw professional caution to the four winds.

"Fair enough," he said. "Well, I remember my most frightening moment, it was back when I was five or six. I'd been playing in the front yard and my mother was inside washing up the supper dishes. It was a beautiful summer evening. I remember…

So, to quickly wrap up, I'd gotten myself lost you see. Couldn't remember how I'd gotten so far away from home. And boy was I scared – truly scared. Well, it seemed like it lasted forever walking round and round and not recognizing anything, but I was lucky enough to bump into a nice policeman and we got to talking and he eventually figured out where I lived."

Every so often she would nod her head and smile encouragingly and when he was finally done, she leaned in and padded his hand, "Oh gosh, that's sounds awful. Okay then. So. Is it my turn now? It's my turn. Yes? Let me see. Which one should I share? Oh. I know. Come closer Dr. B. I don't want anyone else to hear this."

When Dr. B leaned in close with a hand on each of his knees, Jane rested her small hands on top of his hairy knuckles and closed her eyes, "It was after the big move. They had to ship us across country in a long-haul semi-truck. We were two to a coffin." At several points, he jerked wildly trying to break the connection. She held on even tighter. Who knew she had so much strength? It was her intention that Bishop experience several key moments via skin, bone, muscle, nerves, sight, sound, touch, hearing and the ever-loving suspense of not-knowing kind of nightmare, the kind of nightmare moment when your body refuses to wake up and the ugliness and pain just keeps on rolling. She went for a true high-definition cinema style living color with an added dash of sensory realism.

An hour later Dr. Bishop left her room barely able to walk. Jane saw very little of him for the next few days. On the second day, she began to worry that she might have overplayed her hand. Then she received her answer in a visit from Bishop's new intern Jason who said cheerfully, "Well Jane. It looks as if you'll be leaving us soon. At times like this the usual response would be – so sorry you're leaving, we'll miss you – but since leaving the Eighth Ward is a positive sign; I'll just say, good luck to you and (no offense) hope not to see you again. Ha. Ha."

Jane looked out her taxi window and watched the hospital recede from view. No emotion. Not even a tear. Home – it was not. She faced the front and her new future recalling with a smile the last thing she said to Dr. Caleb Bishop on that special day before he ran out of the room. "Now, you can really and truly appreciate what being scared feels like, huh? Thanks for not throwing up on me."

Fifteen miles from Canal Critical Care, Jane handed the taxi driver two twenty-dollar bills and stepped out into the fresh Marsh air. When her ears began to ring and her head swim she knew she had only long enough to get into the hotel, register, and get to her room before the dam broke. She had her identification cards ready and her photo id which told others and her that she was officially Jane Smith. And just the other day, she had been given her Social Security card.

Before she lost consciousness, a memory returned. She was eleven years old. It was 2 a.m. and the nurse's station was empty. She had barely recovered from her sixth surgery and the final skin grafting procedure. Five years on the Eighth Ward granted her unprecedented freedom. She was the staff's mascot allowed access anywhere. That night she rode the elevator to the 10th floor, found an empty office, opened the window, and crawled out onto the ledge.

Her idea was to vault into the air as if jumping off a diving board. Even in the early morning hours the intense heat of the day rose up to greet her. Her bandages were soaked with sweat. She could smell the residue of exhaust fumes and burnt rubber from a multitude of vehicles, hear the fire trucks and police sirens warning drivers to get out of the way and above it all see the full moon ablaze in the blue-black sky above her.

She spoke to the sky, "I'm not here anymore. I'm out there. Not now. Not yet. Eat the dirt and die. No, we can't yet. Just do it! No! We don't go there. I forbid it. No dirt here. There is air to breathe here. See the sky. See the ground. It's not time yet. We have work to do. Eat the dirt, you, stupid fuck. Let go."

Just as she tensed her legs to vault off into the air, Tessa spoke, "Don't do it honey. Don't let them win. Are you gonna let those rat bastards get away with this? Are you gonna make it easy on those soulless devils? Don't. There's always a better way." Jane's arms were quivering from the effort to hold onto the ledge. She stepped back inside the room, her legs collapsing under her. She knelt on the floor clutching the windowsill. For a long time, she rested her chin on the sill and stared out the window contemplating the moon as she waited for her body to stop shaking. A voice she did not recognize told her, "You have to fake it until you make it."

Years before, she'd had no access to her limbs to do what everyone wanted her to do – die. Back then the doctors put her in a coma so her body could recover. No one had been pestering her with questions. It had been like living in limbo between heaven and hell. She'd wanted it all to go away. Her body refused to budge. Her brain kept churning out dreams and memories.

She managed to challenge the nightmares and while in a coma make plans. It would take great courage and lots of money. She could do it. She had the talent. In a coma, in all time zones and all possible presents and futures, she could multitask and eavesdrop. The staff and the visitors provided her with excellent insight on the stock market. Sometimes, they even had useful advice on how to make money and keep it.

Her attempt at self-murder was because everyone asked her annoying, damned idiotic questions. Nosey bastards. Nosey fuck-faces. She found a way to escape their constant nosiness. She'd almost ruined her great manifesto – do onto others as they have done onto you. She had Tessa to thank for rescuing her from a tragic dumb-ass mistake and Frankie to thank for her brilliant list of twenty ways to obfuscate and confuse the peepers. Sometimes she cried, sometimes she laughed, often she deflected or accused or planted crazy, contrary ideas in the medicos' heads.

What a chore pretending to be insane. What a relief to be free.

2

March 25^{th,} 2001

March 25th, 2001

Constance Ann Wade, born Constance Ann Kearny, a baby-boomer and educated, successful woman, known to her students as Professor Wade, known to her sons as Mom, and to her niece as Aunt Connie tittered on the edge of the butte the toes of her hiking boots poking out into air; below her boots, she measured at least two miles to the bottom. Was she brave enough? Could she just step out into nothing but air and hope to die? And as a bonus, perhaps she could die gracefully? Was it even possible to die gracefully?

No. It was not possible.

She had to admit the facts. Facts were facts. Everyone knew what happened to a body when the body dropped from a great height. Instead of beautiful Juliet draped tragically on the ground below; she would look like a squashed peach left too long in the sun. By the time anyone discovered the mess at the bottom, she would have become a snack for every passing coyote and critter in the Owyhee Mountains. She stepped back. Curious and exalted, she peered down again appreciating for the first time the savage wonder of living.

What had she really seen earlier this morning? A woman jumping off the cliff and falling to her death?

No. Not possible. She must have been dreaming. It had to have been a dream. No one could survive a fall from up here. And she couldn't see any evidence at the bottom of the cliff that anyone had fallen. Everything looked the same as it had the night before. She must have been just on the brink of waking and seen an eagle or a turkey vulture flying overhead, and as with dreams, she must have incorporated the bird of prey within her dream-world.

Below Succor Creek moved like a snake: sexy, slow, and secretive. She wanted to be like the waters of the Succor Creek. She wanted to take her time about getting to places, see the countryside with her whole body, keep her secrets to herself, and march through the seasons without apology. From her perch, so high above the creek, the world seemed to make sense. Then she thought about what she had to do today, and she was afraid again.

Remembering the scene last week with Professor Krutcher made her wince the way her hands had beaten the air like Ophelia on speed. Not a pretty sight. How far would she stoop, before she succumbed to crawling on her belly for that man? Why hadn't she spoken up sooner, told him off the moment she knew, done anything but act like a weakling fearing she would lose her chance at tenure? She had no trouble arguing with her students. Professor Krutcher wasn't even handsome. He was a toad, an ugly nasty toad with a vicious tongue.

The man had nothing to do with her discovery. Yet. He's getting all the credit.

The bastard.

She'd found the clue in Underwood's letter. She'd discovered by meticulously going through Underwood's correspondences with his family back east, a juicy piece of information about his relationship with one of the indigenous women from a Columbia tribe near present day Cascade Locks, Oregon. In his letters, he'd confessed his love for one of the women and his family had been shocked that he would ever consider marrying a heathen. So, it was no great leap to put the clues together.

The Columbia woman trusting Underwood's declaration of love had betrayed the whereabouts of the foreign woman even though the foreigner had saved her people from the white man's disease. Underwood had written that he and his soon-to-be wife were on a journey traveling south to meet with a Piute woman where ancient pine trees grew atop a summit. He also mentioned the medicine woman would be taking them to a beautiful lake in Mexican territory.

As if to tout his own horn, he mentioned an arranged meeting with the famous G. K. Smithers who would be traveling through the Mexican territory in his one-of-a-kind light-weight steel carriage pulled by six sturdy mules. Underwood assured his parents their journey would take only a few days even though the trip was nearly eight hundred miles as the group would begin their journey by water and trade their canoes for horses for the remainder of the trip.

Once she read Underwood's description of his journey especially the words: eight hundred miles, in Mexican territory, atop a summit, and the part about a beautiful lake, she had an approximate time in history and a good idea where Smithers and Underwood's expedition would end up. Her conclusion, after examining the maps for Oregon, Idaho, and Nevada was that Underwood planned to meet Smithers in Ely, Nevada and together they would travel to Cave Lake. Cave Lake was a sacred place. The Shoshone and Piute women would never have willingly taken white men to a sacred site.

So, Constance was forced to search through a multitude of historical records for other clues as to why the women would have escorted these men to Cave Lake. Then she found the evidence she needed. The indigenous people of the Great Basin believed an evil creature had taken possession of their sacred site and hoped the white men would have the power to chase the evil creature away. It had taken her months to discover so little and the idea of all her hard work wasted on such a piece of shit as Krutcher made her furious.

Her belly grumbled reminding her she had had nothing to eat since the day before.

In a high clear voice Constance addressed the whistle pigs, the coyotes, the birds of prey and all the little critters including pixies, fairies, and water sprites of the Owyhee Canyonlands, "Give me a sign. I want out of this hell hole. I want my life back." Her words echoed through the canyon and back to her. The sound startled the birds resting in the cliff face opposite. It felt good to scream, to shout, to go crazy. Only two months left, and summer break meant a trip to London and a visit to the British Library. She could deal with her students, office politics, and grading papers for just a little bit longer; and then she would be free.

On the cliff face across from her, birds darted in elliptical patterns as if unable to figure out where they wanted to go, the majority just following the leader who clearly did not know where he wanted to go. Constance could hear Succor Creek below, the water rushing through the canyon spilling over rocks and sand and circumventing sage and willow. The muted colors of the high desert in pale shades of yellow, red, and green soothed her. Her annoyance with the world began to fade.

The light blue sky reflected in the waters of the Succor Creek complemented the lighter greens of the sage and the willow growing along its' banks. The colors washed over her, her eyes lighting on umber and ochre, sienna and cinnamon, slate, and silver with the mint of winterfat and softwood sage abundant. When her eyes rested on a flowering plant, it was like seeing a rare sapphire on the riverbank.

Reluctant to leave but aware of her inner alarm clock ringing quietly inside her head, she turned away from the scene below and started back to her Jeep. She picked up the Navaho blanket bunched up at the foot of the camp bed and tossed it inside. When she reached for her sleeping bag, she noticed the collection of bugs crawling on top. Disgust mingled with dread made her more vigorous in her attempts to rid herself of nature. She shook crickets and tiny ants off her sleeping bag as if she were shaking the world clean and with a shriek which echoed off the cliffs tossed the bag on top of the Navaho blanket without bothering to roll it up.

A thought unbidden popped into her head: *It took guts to walk up to him when you were afraid. You did what you could to make things better. It's not your fault they're cowards and chose their reputations over the safety of the students.*

She looked around wondering if someone snuck up behind her.

She heard the voice again, the voice inside her head: *Yes, it took guts to confront those foul creatures.*

3

May 25ᵗʰ, 2001

Summer would be here soon. And with summer would come – warm weather and bare skin. Oh, yes. 2001. Oh, yes. 2001. A good year for him. Last year had been ho hum, so, so, but this year would be different. This year would be mucho, mucho better.

Ray Millhouse waited patiently for the fat woman to move away from the peaches. He needed time to select his peaches. They had to be fresh, but not too fresh. He hated those wrinkled ones. They had to be just right, so that they tasted just right. He would give her another minute then he would leave and come back later. But she finally moved. So relieved. To have the peaches all to himself. Yes. He looked down at them with anticipation, his eyes glistening with delight. So many to choose from.

Inside *Around the World Pawn*, Ray could see Leland messing about with the cash register and preparing to open the shop, but Ray chose to ignore the old geezer. After all, he had only a few precious minutes to look over the produce before making his choice. Ray heard someone pounding on the window from inside and ignored Leland. God, why can't the greedy old bastard leave him alone just for one fucking minute?

Leland Ansel stood watching Ray Millhouse for several minutes thinking nothing in particular. Time. Yes. Time would take care of that little problem. He walked back to his cage and the safety of being enclosed in tempered glass where not even the most dangerous of crazies with an assault rifle could get to him. He resumed his work ignoring the bum pounding on the front door. He would open the door at nine o'clock precisely. No sooner. No later. He still had five minutes to double check his figures before opening for business; but before he dropped his eyes to the columns in his book, the bum outside his shop turned to speak to someone. Leland noticed the scars.

He jumped off his stool and hurried outside hoping to catch the bum before he disappeared. As he cupped his hand over his eyes to screen out the blinding light from the west, he noticed Ray standing on the street corner watching the preschoolers crossing the street their teacher and a few mother-volunteers directing them toward the daycare down the block. The lead teacher smiled pleasantly at Ray and the children looked up and waved. Ray ignored the women, even the slim, young mother with golden blonde hair and tasty thighs. No Ray was absorbed by the children. Ray watched and watched them and waved and waved. Fucking idiot.

Irritated with Ray, Leland's voice rang out more sharply than he had intended, "Hey, Ray. Do you plan to work today or not?"

Ray took his time turning his head. He waited until the last child disappeared around the corner then decided to face Leland. With an uncharacteristic attitude of disrespect Ray stuck his hands in the pockets of his brown corduroy slacks and deliberately took his time returning to the shop, strolling toward him oh so casual as if he were on holiday, even pausing at the pawn shop door to breathe in the morning air. Smarmy Bastard. Leland experienced a momentary shock. When Ray insolently brushed passed Leland to slip through the door, Leland suppressed a strong urge to punch the fuck in the lower back. The kidney area would do the trick.

As the bell jangled, Leland stared Ray down and it was Ray who dropped his eyes first and hurried into the shop without a word. While Ray had been salivating over the children, Leland had pulled out his cellphone busily searching in his address book for Dr. Winter's private line. As Leland pressed the phone to his ear and listened to the ringing on the other end, he watched Ray saunter inside the shop with his hands on his hips as if he had no clue what to do next. When Leland heard her voice, he slipped back inside the shop and relocked the door.

"Yes," she said curtly obviously having recognized his cellphone number. Something had pissed her off. It was none of his business and he really didn't give a damn. As long as she continued to pay him, he would continue to ignore her disrespect.

"How old is too old for you?" Leland asked. "Hurry up. If I want to catch him, I'll have to leave now."

"Have you been sniffing glue again? They're no use to me over sixty-five," she said and without another word hung up.

Dr. Violet Winter slipped her cellphone back in the pocket of her white jacket and stood beside her patient's bed, absently padding the man's hand. Beneath all the bandages she knew that a miraculous transformation would soon take place. It would just be a matter of time. Of course, there would be blood. The blood would need to be measured and tested. The patient groaned through swollen lips. A minute or two passed.

Violet checked the man's vitals then looked down and saw the patient open his eyes. The look. Oh, yes, that familiar look of trust. It sent a jolt of joy through Violet. So much pain. Yes. Pain was part of the process, the initiation into a new self. But she was here. She would take care of everything. She said as much to him, "You're recovering nicely Terence. Lay back and rest now. You need all your strength. Don't worry; I'll take good care of you." She wished her Spanish speaking patients understood her as well as this man. It would have made her task so much easier.

Leland threw his phone on the counter and glared at Ray's back. For a moment he seriously considered taking the pervert up to his hunting lodge and throwing him into his meat locker. No more insolence. No more sneaking behind his back. The man's appetites didn't bother Leland so much as the thought that one day the idiot would do something really fucking stupid. Yes. He had talent. The old cows loved him. Even the young cows. They saw his pretty face and his big blue eyes and would do anything in the hopes he'd get in their pants.

On the pretense of appearing busy, Ray fetched the duster from the back and wandered around the shop swiping half-heartedly at the objects on display in front of the big picture window. Leland returned to his stool behind the counter and stared through the bars at the SOB; and as he pretended to be absorbed in his bookkeeping, he began forming a plan, a fitting end for his insolent soon-to-be former partner. He used a blank piece of scratch paper to manifest his plan into future action.

If Ray had had a soupçon of sense, he'd be tuned in to Leland's displeasure and prudently stop pissing him off. Leland's thumb ached. He looked down aware he was clutching the morning's mail too tightly between his thumb and fingers. He made himself relax the muscles in his arm, then his wrist, then his fingers and finally his thumb. He sifted through the mail throwing the junk mail to the side.

The letter from the lawyer sent waves of rage rushing through his body from his stomach to his head nearly blinding him. He took several cleansing breaths to calm himself down. After a few minutes, his heart resumed its normal rhythm. He looked up and searched for Ray until he found him off to one side peeking out the window. Ray's avid eagerness calmed Leland. The freak anticipated another flock of children marching passed the shop.

"Ray," Leland shouted.

Unbeknownst to him, Ray jerked guiltily unable to hide the twitch of a slender shoulder, though he made a point of taking his time crossing the room. Leland had to grab the arms of his chair or his hands would have wrapped themselves around the freak's neck and choked that smug self-satisfaction off his pretty-boy face.

"I need you to do a little work for me tomorrow."

"Why? It's a Monday. The shops closed."

"Not here but at my house."

"I already told you I don't do any heavy lifting. My back is bad."

"Now you and I know that ain't true," Leland said and gave Ray the eye.

Ray blushed, a little smile appeared on his pretty face, "Well that's different. That's recreation."

"I'm inviting you over to meet my neighbors. We'll go have a talk with them about this little problem we have. I just need you to butter up the old cow, his wife."

Ray looked constipated, "I don't know. I had other plans and I don't want to break them."

"The cow's got a daughter," Leland said watching in amusement as the rat sniffed the bait. "Her name is Kallan Dilys Fremantle and she's just six years old. You'll like her. I just know you'll like her. Her parents call her Dilly and that she is – she's a dilly of a deal. Funny, huh?"

4

May 28ᵗʰ, 2001

It wasn't until nearly three months had passed right after the grades were posted and she left the university for summer-break that Constance met someone she thought might become a friend for life. And of all places, she met her in the town Constance hated the most – Las Vegas.

The way people drove in Las Vegas shattered the little confidence Constance had left. She'd driven for nearly five hundred miles stopping only for gas and a quick pee before continuing. Her back ached and a tension headache throbbed between her eyes. Her brief stop in Vegas was not for love of gambling or the Vegas nightlife; no, she was here out of obligation – to stop at her mother's apartment to be sure the villagers weren't set to run her mother out of town with pitchforks, torches, tar, and feathers.

Constance pulled into a nearby gas station and squinted at the small screen of her cellphone. At first her tired eyes rebelled against the switching of perspectives – from panoramic wide screen in technicolor to microscopic flat screen in monochromatic. She unclenched her hands from the steering wheel and with trembling fingers managed to press the correct keys: contacts icon, group, family, then #5 in her list.

Her sons were first for obvious reasons followed by her current significant other, a distant cousin, and ending with her mother, the last on her list – for a damned good reason too. Rather depressing to think she had only five numbers in her family group. Her grandparents had died when she was young, she had never known her father, and she was an only child. Oh well, her work contacts were numerous; they made up for her lack of family.

After several rings her mother answered in her usual impatient voice, "What now? You lost again? For Christ's sakes Connie you turned off the freeway nearly two hours ago."

Resigned Constance said, "Yes Mom. I guess I'm lost."

"Well, where the hell are you? Give me the address. I'll direct you."

Constance realized too late that she was screaming into the cellphone, "I damned well don't know where I am. If I knew I'd be there by now. Holy Jesus and all her saints." Then she noticed with a rush of embarrassment the man in front of her pumping gas. He had turned to stare at her startled by her loud voice. When he realized she wasn't being robbed or raped or set on fire, he shot her a dirty look, probably under the impression she had been shouting at him to hurry up, so she could move forward. Constance looked away from him and locked her doors. Just in case.

There was an accusing silence on the other end of the line. Constance leaned back and rested her throbbing neck on the headrest. She counted to ten then heard her mother say, "You don't have to shout at me. I can damn well hear you. I'm not deaf."

"Mom, I'm going inside this gas station and get directions to the nearest hotel. When I know which one, I'll give you a call. We'll have dinner near the hotel. Okay?" "I'm not driving at night. Are you crazy? You can get murdered walking around this town at night."

"Then why do you live here?" Constance asked ignoring the fact that she'd asked the same question many times before and continued to get the same answer every time.

"Mom. Mom, are you listening?"

"What you said hurt. I'm hanging up now," she said.

"I'm going to check into a motel. I'll call you later. Alright?" Constance asked and when there was a stony silence on the other end; Constance hung up too tired to deal with her mother's emotional blackmail. With a twinge of shame, Constance knew she had orchestrated the situation to avoid spending the night trapped in a tiny apartment with a narcissist who loved to hear herself pontificating on subjects she knew nothing about and didn't bother to research.

As Constance pulled up to the pump and climbed out of her Jeep, she heard her mother's voice in her head, "You're such a bore. Always with your nose in a book. Boring. Boring. Boring. That's what you are. Now me; I'm not a loser. I'm fun, fun, fun. I always find fun things to do. Never a dull moment when you're with me. Everybody tells me that."

An hour later, Constance checked into the High Desert Motel and called her mother's number. Constance got her voice messaging service instead and with a slight catch in her throat gave her mother the name of her motel and her room number, then left the cramped motel room to find a diner wondering how she would be able to sleep in a room in which the carpet smelled of decades old urine. She wasn't too crazy about the neighborhood either, but her stomach was growling so loudly she couldn't wait any longer. Two blocks south of her hotel she found a family restaurant offering cheap beer, limp salads, and every imaginable pizza combination. She ordered a pizza to go and waited impatiently until the pizza was cooked and boxed up.

Out on the street while balancing her pizza box and separate smaller box of salad, she heard retching sounds and turned to her right just in time to see a man with a straggly beard, dirty plaid shirt, and limp, dirt encrusted jeans throw up near a clump of mistreated arborvitaes. What amazed Constance was his ability to hold onto his lit cigarette and the neck of his bottle of Jack Daniels while throwing up.

Constance averted her gaze from him and hurried toward the curb waiting anxiously to cross the road, afraid any moment the guy would lurch in her direction and ask for loose change or something even more lurid. Then she noticed a woman leaning into the window of a green Buick. The woman had stiff bleached blonde hair with an excess of frizz due to an abusive ratting regime and to add to the misery wore a tight short skirt and high heels that made Constance wince with sympathy for the woman's poor feet.

Something the man said made the woman laugh. That gravelly voice and husky laugh like a man's coming from such a tiny woman turned heads. It was obvious the way she was dressed that she was a hooker. In the 16th century hooker meant something altogether different. On any other occasion Constance would have giggled at the thought of this woman stealing bedclothes from an open window with a hook attached to a long pole. Then again, when a person knew no better way of life how could she blame her?

Constance tried her best to ignore the two and waited impatiently for modern technology to give her permission to walk across the damned street. The cars just kept whooshing past her blowing exhaust and dirt in her eyes. When she tried to wipe her eyes with the edge of her shirt, her fingers fumbled over the pizza box. The pizza box fell out of her hands. Constance moved to retrieve the box from the street.

Someone shrieked, "Stop." Constance froze. A motorcycle swept past her missing her by inches. Constance watched the biker drive on without stopping or apologizing then looked down at her crushed box of pizza and felt an overwhelming urge to chase after the motorcyclist and beat him to a pulp.

Constance turned her head in time to see the prostitute's relieved expression and impudent wave. When the guy inside the Buick leaned over to open the passenger door for the woman Constance realized two important facts: the woman would be gone for good and she didn't deserve such a miserable, degrading life. Constance found herself opening the back door and jumping inside the stranger's vehicle to the astonishment of herself, the driver, and the woman. Before anyone could speak Constance blurted out, "You saved my life. My God. I could have been killed and you saved my life. I can't thank you enough. If there is anything I can do for you, I will. Just name it."

The prostitute looked at her prospective client. Her client was studiously examining something interesting out his windshield. The prostitute twisted around to face Constance. Between words she snapped her chewing gum with a hard-jawed strength and energy Constance admired. After studying Constance for a few seconds with a curious eye, the prostitute laughed and shook her head in disbelief, "And I thought I'd seen it all. Guess what lady you're nearly at the top of my list of weirdness."

As if she had known him all her life, the prostitute asked the John, "What do you think honey? You think she's an egg short of a dozen?" Under the circumstances, the man seemed unnaturally relaxed with his hands resting lightly on the steering wheel of his gas-guzzling vehicle with its 1970s plush interior and extravagant leather seats.

When he spoke, Constance was surprised by the softness of his voice, "If your friend's coming along for the ride, you'll have to split the cost between you."

Constance ignored the pervert and his capitalist blindness that attributed everything as a commodity to be bought and sold – even a woman's body – and instead, she concentrated all her attention on the woman, the woman that had shown her a moment of kindness. In her life experience, kindness was rare. Kindness was as valuable as diamonds.

"My name is Constance, Connie Wade. What's yours?"

The driver never looked back at her as if embarrassed to be caught doing something so perverted and illegal. She should hope so. The prostitute said, "If I tell you my name will you get out and go home?"

"Well, I guess so; but I thought we could exchange phone numbers and I could maybe treat you to dinner or something."

"It will cost you fifty bucks for one night with me honey. Can you afford it?"

Constance hoped she wasn't blushing, "I meant as a friend not as, ah, one of your, you know."

The woman looked at her from a pair of serious brown eyes. Even with all the thick mascara and black eyeliner and startling green eye shadow, her eyes appeared kind. When Constance thought they softened she began to relax. She seemed like a really nice person. The woman glanced at the man in the driver's seat then smugly away as if he didn't count. She seemed pleased to have two people fighting over her. He glanced at the prostitute as if sizing her up. He seemed to have come to some sort of conclusion, at least Constance thought she saw his reflection in the rear view mirror smile, then he resumed his contemplation of the cars whizzing up and down the boulevard. Constance made a point of not looking at him again.

The prostitute shrugged her shoulders and said, "I'm called Frankie and that's all you need to know. I don't have a card but if you've got a pen and paper, I can give you a number where you can reach me. Will that do?"

Constance searched through her purse for a pen and paper and said, "I know it's not my place to judge anyone. Believe me I've done some really stupid things in my life. But because you've been so kind to me, I just want to return the favor. This life you're living, well, it must seem as if this…thing you do is the only answer; but honestly, there are so many opportunities just waiting for you to explore. For one thing, you could go back to school," Constance ignored the man's snort of amusement. She continued, "There are programs that can help you get back into school and find the career that best suits your interests. Please think about it. Think about how different your life could be if you chose a different path."

The woman shook her head in wonder, "You don't know shit about me, yet you think you can just come up to me when I'm working and interfere in my business? What gives you the right to be holier-than-thou, huh? You don't know me. You don't know anything about me. And I don't need your help, lady. So just get your ass out of this car and leave me to my business."

The man looked up with renewed interest and instead of turning his head to look at Constance chose to look at her from his rear view mirror. His eyes seemed familiar, eyes so opaque they appeared to lack light or liquid. Frankie's sudden change of personality hurt Constance more than she would have imagined a stranger could hurt her. When Constance opened the door to climb out, the car shot forward. Astonished Constance fell back onto the seat still holding onto the door. She considered jumping out at the next intersection; after all, he would have to stop some time.

But as the car moved further and further away from her motel, she began to wonder why the lights seemed to be cooperating with him. He weaved in and out of traffic like a crazy person. As the sun set beyond the hills and buttes surrounding Vegas, streetlights began to pop on one at a time. A bug smacked into her cheek. Constance felt her check swell up and wondered if she'd been stung by a bee. She was allergic to bee stings and feared she would end up with a chipmunk cheek soon.

Frankie glanced over her shoulder at Constance and frowned. Constance heard her say to the driver, "Hey, don't think you can get two for the price of one. The chick in the back can negotiate her own deal. Do we have an understanding? Hey, I'm talking to you, asshole."

The Buick executed a brisk right-hand turn into an empty parking lot where a disused car repair garage stood abandoned with only boarded windows, weeds, and trash blown in from the streets substituting for landscaping. The most gorgeous man she had ever seen moved away from the shade of an old maple tree pulling a little girl behind him. He had thick dark hair and blue eyes. He was over six feet tall, lean, and yet well-muscled from his tight-fitting t-shirt to his tight-fitting jeans. At first, she assumed the little girl must be his daughter. She heard the driver say, "Get in the damned car Ray. I don't have all day."

"There's someone in your backseat," Ray said noting the obvious as he bent over to look inside the car at Constance. A closer look revealed a bored, handsome man with a petulant mouth and empty eyes. His blue eyes, so absent of life, generated the beginnings of uneasiness. Her sudden discomfort circulated in her stomach like bad shrimp. In the searing heat of a summer afternoon she shivered as if freezing. The little girl rubbed her eye with her free hand and left a fresh track of dirt on her face. She looked hot and tired and scared.

"She's leaving," the driver reassured his friend.

"I'm not leaving unless this woman leaves with me," Constance told him in a quivering voice feeling her cheek swell to the size of a hard apple as her stomach turned over once again. "And I'd like to know whose child this is." She realized too late that her remark was one of the dumbest things she had said yet in a marathon of dumb things. Pretending ignorance or jumping out of the car and running for her life or even running down the street screaming for the police would have been smarter.

In the past when she blurted out what she was thinking, she would receive swift punishment. She waited for the blow. The blow did not come. A calm stubbornness settled over her. She gripped the seat and the door handle afraid they would try to throw her out of the car. She would not leave until she got an answer. She refused to run away from what she suspected was soon going to turn very, very ugly. The child was so frightened, she refused to look up from her intense contemplation of the asphalt.

The next few minutes would determine all their fates. Nothing would make Constance leave the car now – absolutely nothing.

Frankie had been appraising her customer's friend Ray and the child with him and said, "What the fuck is going on here?"

"And you bitch about my poor choices Leland," Ray sneered shaking his head sadly while opening the car door. "Come on Dilly. Get in and I'll take you home." And when he opened the car door and shoved the little girl inside a shot of alarm played along Connie's spine.

"Forget this shit. Take the batty lady in the backseat if you want her and give me five bucks for my trouble," Frankie said making motions to leave. While Ray made himself comfortable beside the little girl, the driver had been crouched over searching for something on the floor of his car.

"I'll pay you for the extra company," he said in a breathless voice his big belly getting in the way as bent over. He might have been looking for his wallet.

Interesting how no one had bothered to answer her question about the child. Obviously, there was something terribly wrong. Constance considered screaming then looked around and realized uncomfortably that there was no one near enough to hear her screams not even a passing pedestrian.

"No way. I don't do orgies, ass . . .hole," Frankie said throwing the car door open and preparing to desert Constance and the frightened child who took one glance at Connie's face and tucked up close to her. Constance put her finger to her lips silently signaling for the child to remain quiet. Kallan was smart enough to understand and closed her eyes pretending to sleep. No one seemed to notice their exchange. Ray was staring out his open window obviously bored and impatient. He had his right arm hanging out the window and proceeded to drum his fingernails on the car door.

Constance put her hand in her purse with the intention of getting her cellphone out and calling the police. A strong arm shot out and grabbed her wrist squeezing painfully until she let go of her purse. "Let's see what you got here?" Ray asked in a censorious tone reminding her uncomfortably of her least favorite second grade teacher Mrs. Connors.

Time seemed to expand and contract unfairly; first it slowed down for the driver so that he could find the item he needed under the seat then it sped up as Constance became aware of how isolated they were from witnesses or anyone who could alert the police that a kidnapping was in progress. It seemed to take forever for Frankie to say her piece and move into position to desert them. It took no time at all for Ray to search through Connie's purse, find her cellphone, and tuck the phone into his fanny pack. During the whole miserable moment, Connie had also debated on whether to jump out of the car and drag the child after her to the nearest police station.

But what if he was a relative? She would become the kidnapper. And how far could she get? Ray was physically strong, twice her size and twice as mean. When she looked at Ray he looked so normal albeit magazine model normal. He was someone's uncle or brother, definitely someone's son or grandson; and whatever she might suspect, she would look foolish if she were wrong. She'd been wrong before. The time in the airport when she told the airport attendant she suspected the guy in the blue blazer carried a gun and might be a hijacker and he turned out to be a U.S. Marshall, she'd been truly embarrassed.

It was late afternoon. In the west the sun was dropping behind the trees. It was still blistering hot. And the interior of the car only added to the airlessness and heat. It must be the heat. The child was just hot and tired. This Ray guy had probably taken Kallan, his niece or maybe his cousin to the park across the street and now they were headed home.

Connie tried feverishly to remember her mother's stories about the family tree, tried to remember the names of all her mother's relatives, relatives Connie had never met because her mother had managed to fight with all of them wondering if one of them had had a son called Ray, but her brain kept sending alarm signals up and down her spine saying "Get out. Get out. Run. Run." She ignored the signals and pulled Kallan closer to her side. Kallan wrapped her skinny arms around Connie's waist and held on tightly.

Frankie swore under her breath. Her right foot touched the asphalt of the parking lot. But before Frankie was clear of the car, the driver straightened with something in his hand. Only in the movies. This stuff happened . . . only in the movies. Not in real life. Not here. The sickening crack of metal against bone made her wince in sympathetic pain. Then she saw spots in front of her eyes.

Oh God.

A child screamed.

5

November 3rd, 2003

Mom would have been amazed to see so many people milling about her tiny house. The furniture though clean was eclectic; in other words, nothing matched. It was their grandmother's pet peeve that Mom had no sense of taste, color, or organization. Grandma believed furniture should match. Only a man or a hippy or one of the ignorant poor used substitutes for the real thing, substitutes such as outdated fake wood stereo speakers for end tables and cardboard boxes filled with books covered in old towels as coffee tables and even worse piling books up against the wall and letting dust collect on them.

Before her disappearance, Mom had had plenty of money to pay a carpenter to construct several fancy bookcases or go to the best stores to purchase tastefully matching furniture, but she had chosen not to remodel or buy new furniture because she preferred to buy secondhand because she had always been a fierce believer in going green in every way she could – also as an excuse to piss Grandma off.

Mom would have been uncomfortable with all these strangers in her house (well, not strangers) most of them were friends and/or academic associates from the university. In fact, the dean of the archeology department, Krutcher was in Mom's study at this very moment, a study which had been Brent's bedroom before he moved out. Supposedly, Dean Krutcher was offering his expertise in valuing Mom's academic papers: her journals, research, maps, and collection of artifacts.

In Brent Wade's opinion, the rush to clean out his mother's possessions during a post-funeral reception seemed tasteless. His brother Chris didn't seem to mind. According to Chris, the inventory had been his idea. Brent didn't think so; it was clear Krutcher with his over eager attitude and predatory search of the room had planted the idea of doing a quick inventory straight away while the guests were busy in the other rooms.

With his arms crossed and held close to his chest, Brent could hear the mourners in the front part of the house milling about sampling the tiny cakes and coffee and murmuring condolences to his grandmother. Instead of joining his grandmother in the center of the vortex of grief, he chose to keep his eye on Krutcher. He leaned against the door-jam and watched them pawing through her things. Chris was sitting on the floor with his legs crossed pulling out folders and objects in a series of boxes Mom usually kept in the study closet.

Dean Krutcher sat in Mom's leather chair sifting through papers, occasionally commenting to the room at large, "The library might find these interesting. That one looks promising. That one you can keep for sentimental reasons if you like or simply toss. It's outdated . . . This is interesting. Where's the sticker for this one? I'm sure the university would accept this one as a donation, but we need to know where she obtained it for our archives."

The sight of them poking and prying into his mother's personal belongings and life's work made Brent sick. This morning at breakfast the moment he had opened his mouth to ask Chris for help, he knew he'd made a colossal mistake. He should have been smarter, waited until after the service, waited until Grandma and the others had gone home and it had just been the two of them in Mom's house. He knew his brother hero-worshipped Krutcher and should have known Chris would jump at the chance to show off Mom's academic papers, artifacts, and other treasures.

Chris had inherited a love of history and old bones from their mother while Brent preferred engineering. So, the idea of asking for Chris' input into their mother's life's work seemed logical. Brent had assumed his brother would recognize if something she had dug up or one of her journals might be valuable enough to donate to the university or keep for future generations.

After all his brother had nearly completed his undergraduate degree in anthropology and planned to continue toward his Master of Applied Anthropology. Yet for all of Chris' book smarts, his brother lacked the savvy to know when he was being conned. Didn't he wonder why Krutcher hadn't bothered to attend the memorial service at the university this morning when the Lookout Room had been packed to overflowing by former students, staff and people who had known her by reputation?

The memorial service had been arranged by Connie Wade's former colleagues in the Anthropology Department and a few of her former students as soon as the Idaho Statesman reported the findings of the judge for the Wade Missing Person case. The judge determined "death in absentia" based on her reputation as a leading and well-respected faculty member at Boise State University, who had been of sound mind and body previous to her disappearance.

Adding to the summary decision had been eyewitness accounts of her last few hours in Las Vegas which concluded she had been neither suicidal or inebriated. To clinch the decision had been the fact that over the last two years no funds had been removed from her bank accounts. Instead of the usual waiting period of seven years, the judge declared Constance Wade's "death in absentia" and permitted her heirs to take control of her property and abide by her Last Will and Testimony.

It had been Grandmother's constant hectoring which led Brent as the eldest to give in to her demands to end the vigil that one day she would find her way home. Brent hated to give up, but he knew deep down inside his mother, if she had been alive, would have crawled all the way home from wherever she was if necessary; therefore, unless she was a prisoner in some madman's basement, he had to conclude she must be dead. The memorial service had taken place at the Lookout Room in the Student Union Building which could seat 136 people comfortably. Brent and Chris had stood by the door and greeted each person who entered the theater. Dean Krutcher had claimed to be out of town.

Yet when Chris called Krutcher after the memorial service when just a few select friends, family, and former students had been invited to their mother's home for a private reception, Dean Krutcher miraculously arrived on their doorstep twenty minutes later. He hadn't bothered to make excuses for not attending the memorial service and had simply nodded acknowledgment of Brent's presence as he opened the door. Krutcher proceeded to call his brother's name ignoring the mourners in the room and upon sighting Chris by the study door marched toward him without a word to anyone.

Brent remembered his mother's favorite Krutcher joke about how Krutcher was the kind of person who would ignore the dying man on the ground if he spotted an Indian arrowhead near the body. And here Krutcher was in their house and Chris in his grief and pride in Mom's contributions to the field of anthropology couldn't put the series of events of the day into perspective. Even if Brent had tried to explain his misgivings about the man, the fact that Mom and Krutcher had been rivals and Mom had been on the short-list for the Dean posting would not have swayed Chris' opinion of Krutcher.

According to Chris, Dr. Krutcher was a link to their mother. Krutcher spoke the language of anthropology and shared Chris' love of history and discovery. Or so Chris thought. Brent was convinced otherwise. Brent's shit detector was telling him that Krutcher was a publicity junky, a shallow, lazy idiot who'd climbed the ladder of success with a bit of luck, a whole lot of bullshit, and by claiming credit for the accomplishments of others.

And then Brent remembered something he had been told at the memorial service by one of his mother's teaching assistants. The thought cheered him up a bit. Dr. Krutcher wasn't his brother's current advisor and wouldn't be in the future because somehow, someway, Dean Krutcher had received a major grant by an unspecified donor and would be on sabbatical for a year somewhere in northern California. By the time Chris needed an advisor, Chris would be at the University of Chicago finishing his degree and well away from the man's predatory clutches.

As far as his mother's family, there were four of them: a second cousin Sheila who was the grandchild of Mom's great-aunt and sent holiday cards and occasionally an email when a special event occurred in her life, who at the moment was sitting on the couch looking at her plate probably wishing she was a million miles away; Grandma, of course, was sitting in the best chair by the fireplace being consoled by some of Mom's closest friends; and then there was Christopher and him who made up the last remaining members of his mother's family.

Really shitty, he thought, only four people who truly missed and mourned her; well, make that three, he wasn't sure about Grandma. No, that was too cold. He was sure Grandma mourned her too. It was just hard to tell. Grandma's sister's children would have been at the reception like a shot if they'd been alive. They would have arranged everything. They would have scoured the western half of the United States looking for her.

Tragedy struck everyone that year. It seemed as if 2001 had been a tragedy not only for everyone in the United States, but also targeted his family with a vengeance. Brent remembered many summers spent at the Quintus Rose Ranch learning how to ride and floating down the river. His mother's cousin Cara Rose and her husband Benjamin Quintus Fremantle had died in a terrible fire at their ranch around the same time his mother vanished never to be seen again. What had baffled the authorities was the fact that Cara and Ben's child Kallan had never been found. Her parents had been found in their bed. It was assumed Kallan would also have been asleep when the brushfire, encouraged by high winds, set the woods behind the house and the back of the house alight. In a matter of minutes, the place was ablaze and Kallan's body was never found.

He thought a lot about Kallan. She had been a few years younger than Brent. She had been such a quiet, sweet little girl with big hazel eyes and dark curly hair.

A surreptitious movement to his right made him turn his head. A voice only he could hear urged him to pay attention. He shook his head wondering if he was hallucinating. He returned to the present situation feeling a jolt of energy coursing through his body. Maybe he should cut off the caffeine and eat something instead?

The oddball mourners in the house like the neighbors would have made Mom furious if she'd known they were slipping in unannounced and unwelcome, walking among the bereaved, touching her stuff, milling about among her furniture, judging, always judging, and worst of all listening with their glittering exalted eyes to family gossip and Grandma's continual wet gasps filled with unshed tears.

Brent remembered all the years Mom complained about the neighbors. Yet she could have sold the house and moved somewhere else easily enough. Why had she put up with them? He watched Dick Grueber shove his way through the press of people. He looked familiar. Where had he seen him before? There he was in his gray pin-striped suit with his long oily black hair hanging down to his shoulders. No. He wasn't someone Brent knew. He just looked annoyingly familiar all dressed up with his long face pale as a hairless dog and his gangster body pressed into an innocuous suit that belonged on someone more cerebral.

Dick Grueber's lack of manners did not surprise Brent. English pushed his way through the mourners without apology heading for the dishes of food arranged on the kitchen table. Brent suspected the guy was after Mom's silver tea service. The guy kept staring fixedly at the tea service and picking up the delicate cups examining the markings underneath. Brent kept an eye on him. Then Brent saw Beatrice Kiben, the holy terror of the neighborhood trot into the kitchen with the blank look of a Rottweiler. Luckily, she stayed only long enough to dump a tuna casserole on the kitchen table and look at Brent with her cold black eyes and say, "My condolences," before disappearing into the crowd.

It was the third day of November 2003 and Mom had been missing for two years, three months, and two days. A garbage man found a bag full of her clothes in a dumpster at a trailer park in Lake Havasu,

Arizona. The coroner couldn't identify the blood as hers but the hairs on the lapel matched the hairs on the brush the police found on her dressing table. And then an elderly couple while waiting for their corgi to finish his duty on a lonely stretch of desert road in New Mexico stumbled upon her cellphone.

The last call she made was to Grandma shortly before checking into the seedy motel. The front desk's night duty cashier later testified to the police that he had seen her standing across the street just before dark arguing with a hooker in front of the pizza restaurant. He thought the two women might have known each other; otherwise, he told the cops – why would they be arguing with each other?

The next day, housekeeping discovered his mother's suitcase in the room assigned to her. No one at the motel thought twice about a middle-aged woman leaving her personal belongings and her vehicle behind; not even a week later, when the suitcase still sat in the manager's office waiting for its owner. No one thought twice (as per motel custom) when the manager donated the suitcase and its contents to a nearby charity, nor did they question the removal of his mother's vehicle by a towing service. The police later impounded her car. Her personal belongings were long gone by the time the police got involved. And the police only got involved because Grandma kept calling them insisting her daughter was an upstanding and responsible citizen and would never just simply take off for no good reason.

Brent didn't learn about his mother's disappearance for nearly two weeks. He'd been hiking the Pacific Crest Trail. When he returned to Idaho, his brother Chris had just gotten back from Vegas having spent the week questioning people around the motel where she had last been seen. He and Grandma canvassed every building along Nellis Boulevard starting at the Air Force Base and going door to door all the way down to Desert Inn Road beyond Grandma's apartment complex having traveled nearly eight miles and hundreds of stops along the way.

Brent grudgingly admitted, even though his Grandma could drive him to distraction, as the most stubborn, cantankerous person he knew, she was the only one in the family who refused to give up. Even after Chris had spent the week questioning clerks, cashiers, maids, bankers, waiters and waitresses, and anyone on the street who would slow down long enough to look at the flyer, Grandma continued the search long after Chris had returned to Boise and college.

Every day when Grandma left her apartment, she would make a point to stop people on the street and show them one of the dozen flyers she kept in her car. Yet no one recognized or remembered the woman in the flyer. Even so, Grandma continued to drop by the motel and the pizza restaurant to pester the clerks and waiters. She would ask them if they remembered anything that might be of help and they would shake their heads sadly and tell her no. She kept it up until those jobs were taken by new people and there was no one left in Vegas who'd been present at the time of his mother's abduction.

A sane person would accept the evidence and move on. He couldn't and when he'd asked the authorities if they could do more, they gave him pitying looks and negative responses. Without a body, his mother was in limbo. She might be alive perhaps a prisoner locked up in a basement or perhaps she was dead and buried somewhere out in the New Mexico desert. He would rather believe she had died quickly and painlessly than die a slow agonizing death in some hellhole with a psychopath.

Once the reception wound down, his mother's former students having left first, Brent was grateful when his cousin Sheila volunteered to drive Grandma back to Las Vegas. Grandma hated airplanes. Brent couldn't have managed the trip trapped in a car with grieving Grandma, even if it had been only a mile. Her insistent talking would have driven him insane. He knew it was the drugs. She'd never been so long-winded until she discovered this new doctor. She must be higher than a meth head on a three-day binge. If he'd had to drive her the five hundred miles home, he might have been ready to kill himself just for a moment of peace and quiet.

Sheila must have been thinking along the same lines because before she climbed into her car, she leaned over and whispered in his ear while Grandma continued to ramble on about getting to a hotel before nightfall and how she was thirsty and hungry and wanted to take the freeway. Sheila's calm voice whispered in his ear, "Don't worry about your Grandma. When we get to Vegas, I'm finding her a new doctor and making sure the doctor tests her for prescription overdose. You take care Brent. You've always been so levelheaded. Your mom would be so proud of you."

They hugged quickly as Grandma's voice rose to shrill crescendo.

An hour later, Brent sat across from his brother Chris at his mother's kitchen table and both were aware of each other but unwilling to look at each other. The house was finally empty of guests. Krutcher was the last to leave carrying a box Chris had donated to the university. Brent hated to see the shithead taking anything from the house. His arrogance as he sauntered toward the door and nodded his head curtly in their direction made Brent want to jump up and take the box away from him.

It was just the two of them in her house now. All the family mourners and neighbors were gone. Brent looked up from the contemplation of his coffee cup and stared at his mother's refrigerator. All those post-it notes. He lost his composure for a moment and tried to hide his grief from Chris.

Brent heard Chris' chair skid across the floor. He looked up in time to see Chris stomp away. Mom's old cedar floor buckled and shook until Chris reached the front door and threw it open. Then the floor steadied. From the other room, Brent thought he heard gasping as if someone were drowning.

The slamming of the door sounded like a thunderclap in the tiny house. Brent heard the refrigerator turn on. He listened to the humming until everything inside went peaceful. She wasn't dead. Someone had made a grave mistake.

6

November 4th, 2003

"I'm lying," Ana Evans said aloud to the others in the pitch dark, a dark where their bodies and the spaces they occupied had become one organism, an organism that shifted together when legs cramped, or blood congealed. Kallan ignored her pain and concentrated on Ana's voice. Ana had a compelling way of speaking, her words carrying far and in such soothing tones. Kallan loved to listen to her speak her thoughts aloud. Kallan believed Ana spoke to them all because they all needed her words of wisdom now – especially now.

"Isn't it fascinating? Just think on it. Our conception of God and the Devil is still just as primitive as were our ancestors. Even today our conceptions of these beings require us to imagine what God and the Devil look like and what they are doing; in other words, God and the Devil rely on us to make them real. We should forego them. We don't need them. They are a distraction from the principle issue here. Praying may help our reptile brains – I mean give us a moment of peace anyway. But then we wake up and look around and reality returns and we are devastated.

I'll give you an example. See here, I'm in the process of capitalizing both words: God and Devil," she told them. "Here is the word God. Do you see it? And below the word God here I am writing the letters for the word Devil. You cannot see me writing the letters in the air but some of you can imagine me writing the letters in the air; and others of you probably just don't give a shit what I'm doing. Well there you have it – praying is just as much a distraction as listening to me and imaging me writing the words God and Devil.

As Epicurus was believed to have said, Is God willing to prevent evil, but not able? Then he is not omnipotent. And so on and so on. I'm sure I've quoted him before. You all know the rest. But what you don't understand is the real contribution of Epicurus. Even though there is no God to rescue us, we must not despair. We can choose kindness over brutality, sacrifice over survival, and justice over injustice. In the grand scheme of things, the law of averages is on our side. One of us, maybe two, even three will survive, survive this nightmare to testify to the world what is happening here."

In the dark, Kallan couldn't see Ana clearly; yet, her imagination took over, and she saw in her mind's eye Ana drawing the letters for the word God and the letters for the word Devil in the air and she could imagine Ana in her enthusiasm brushing her fingers against the rough beam running across the crawl space above their heads.

Some of them ignored Ana and her philosophizing about demons and angels because they were frightened by the few who were no longer in their right or left or any kind of mind. One person who no one had ever thought of as crazy was showing disturbing signs of trauma. While Ana lectured, the person most of the group depended on for practical advice had suddenly become an unknown quantity.

The words Frankie spoke were unfamiliar to Kallan. It wasn't Spanish or French. Not really, although sometimes the language sounded romantic. Then Kallan realized she was listening to Latin. Yes. Frankie was praying in Latin. Where had she learned Latin? Kallan wished she would stop. Praying or speaking in a foreign language was a mistake. The consequences if someone upstairs objected would not be good for Frankie or any of them. Frightened by the rising tension all around her, Kallan crawled over to Connie and tried to cuddle up close to her good side. Connie remained oblivious to them all and unmoved by Kallan's presence.

Between Frankie's prayers and Ana's lectures Kallan thought the voices would cut right through the cinder block walls. Connie was so quiet lately. She just stared at the floorboards a few feet away from her nose and Kallan could see from the faint light sifting through a loose board how Connie's eyes still shined and how her peaceful face expressed an inexplicable joy. Connie stared at the hole in the wood above her head with an intensity that made Kallan wonder if she'd come up with another plan.

Kallan turned to the others and whispered, "Shush. Please be quiet. Connie's sleepy. Let her sleep." But the others ignored Kallan just as they ignored Ana and Frankie. None of them would listen to reason. They were too scared. No one had a plan, a sensible plan of action. Connie had had one once.

From above, Kallan heard the familiar tread of heavy footsteps, those big feet in their soft canvas shoes and the way they squished as if the feet inside the shoes were all sweaty and dirty, as if the wearer were squishing bugs with her bare toes and hard heels. Kallan heard a child crying. It was time to disappear, time to hide inside that big black hole in the wall, time to plug her ears and curl up to Connie's warm body.

Connie remained unmoved. She had slipped away again.

Kallan wanted company. Even though she knew she would get in trouble, she spoke to the shadow in the corner, "Guess what Terrence. I dreamed I was a black man, once. There was a mob, an angry mob of white folks pulling on my clothes, my neck, my arms, trying to drag me back and kill me. I ran and ran. I ran faster and soon I was running so fast I was flying. They kept coming. They grabbed at my ankles. I had big black feet, strong feet; and I kicked those angry mean people away. I kicked them all away. Then I flapped my arms and I rose higher and higher in the air and soon I was flying over the tree tops and the buildings, flying straight to my old school and my old house. Do you hear me Terence? What do you think of my dream?"

One of the women spoke up, terror in the syllables, "Shut up and go to sleep Kallan."

Terence's voice rumbled in the air, "Why would you want to be a black man?"

"I don't know. I just was."

Tessa spoke up, "Color has no meaning in the dark. The only thing that matters is that we're alive and that we want to keep on living. So, stop your crying everyone. Do you intend to live down here forever? I don't. I want the sun on my face."

7

Present Day

Along Willow Creek we sat and discussed our plans. Well, more accurately Acacia did all the wishful-thinking, anticipating a glorious end to it all, while Leona cautioned us to be realistic and ruined the effect by breaking into sobs that wracked her body. In the meantime, Ana insisted on more data before embarking on the proposed journey. We tried to ignore Eve, but she would occasionally wiggle and moan and make herself a nuisance, so we allowed her the chance to say something. No surprise she insisted the body get its reward. Frankie interjected her soul into the mess and somehow out of the odds and ends of the dialogue a plan began to take shape.

Acacia drowned out Leona's sweet voice, "Fuck that noise! Caution my ass. Timidity has been our watchword for too friggin long. It's time to imagine the deed done. Totally done. You got to immerse yourself in the vision and by God things begin to happen. I know about this shit; I'm telling you. And when it's said and done, you know what I'm gonna do? Oh yeah. First, I'll yank out all his hair. No. No. Better yet I'll yank out one hair at time with my fingers then I'll tie him outside near a nest of nasty wasps. Then I'll pour grease in his hair and sprinkle pieces of meat all over his body. Let him suffer I say. Let him suffer."

Simultaneously, Ana and Eve spoke.

"You can imagine all you want," Ana broke in. "But a good plan calls for research and thoughtful analysis."

"Kisses would hurt him more," Eve said. "Rubbing up against his body and licking his face would make him scream."

"I would be sick, sick just being in the same room with Leland," Leona cried. "Don't make me do it. Please. Let's think of something else to do. God will take care of him. You'll see. What comes around goes around."

"I'm not talking about ugly smelly old Leland," Eve said with a gasp. "I'm talking about Ray Millhouse. He's so cute. I love his body."

"I hate to hurt your feelings...Dear...but Ray Millhouse is only interested in children not a young woman like yourself; no matter how pretty and sexy you might be," Ana said with a condescending air of someone who knows a little bit about a lot of things. "He'll only be

45

repulsed by you. No amount of saltpeter or drugs or deprograming can stem that man's urges – not even a lobotomy."

"Fuck y'all," Acacia said. "This handwringing and second-guessing crap is all bullshit, a colossal waste of precious time. I'm sick of y'alls timid pea brains. Monsters get away with their crimes every god-damned friggin fucking day and live long fruitful lives and die safely in their beds. Even itty-bitty babies know it. It's the goody two-shoes chicken hearted ass-wipes with their caterwauling that keep the story going and the story is pure garbage – the bad guys will get theirs in the end – horseshit.

The bad guys want you to believe the stories so y'all ignore them and let them keep on making mischief and misery. They're playing with y'alls minds. Retribution is right here and right now and we're gonna miss our chance if we don't get off our asses and get going. We get us some AK-47s and lots of ammo and we lay in wait and shoot them all to hell and back. The rest of you – don't listen to Leona's bullshit. She's just a freaky Looney Tune."

"Stop it Acacia. I'm sick of hearing your potty mouth. You could care less about fucking anyway, so why use the word? You think it makes you sound tough? Huh? Tough isn't a dirty mouth. Tough is flexibility and tenacity," Frankie said in a calm voice that sounded oddly soothing even though her words came from a throat gone raspy and hard from too many cigarettes and shots of cheap whiskey.

When she was especially upset, Frankie's voice reminded them all of a rusty metal gate squealing in protest when opened. "No, we're going about this all wrong. Think money. Think about how we can hurt Leland through his pocketbook. It's simple really. All we have to do is find out where he banks and take every damned dime he has. I have other ideas too – lots of them. We could ruin his livelihood. We could sneak into his shop and rob him of all his merchandize or we could burn the place down to the ground. Then we could go to his fancy house and burn that down too. That way we won't have to expose ourselves to the public. Rest easy ladies; we won't become a circus side show. I promise you."

There was a moment of silence as everyone contemplated Frankie's crazy, wild, dangerously risky idea, and in the silence, the sounds of the coming night met them on the banks of Willow Creek. They could hear a few miles away a lone vehicle slowing down for the four-way stop on Graveyard Point Road and then accelerating as it turned onto U.S. 95 South. Nearby they could hear birds chattering in a magnificent old oak tree, the only large tree growing near another strange structure, a mound about eight feet long and four feet tall made of rocks and dirt covered in stubby sagebrush and wild grasses. They could see bushtits racing from one sage to another. Resting up against the mound was a rock. It reminded them of a big old walrus sleeping on a beach. Its black and gray backside was splotched with white as if centuries of bird droppings had penetrated right into its tough hide.

Frankie turned to Ana for confirmation, always uncertain when she used an unfamiliar word, "The word is tenacity right? Tenacity is when you hold on and don't let go or when you stick to something no matter what? Right?"

Ana sighed, "We've been making a lot of noise but making little sense so far. Yes. Yes, Frankie you've used the word tenacious accurately. Let me interject once again a need for more data. Sure, we can go straight to the source. We have his address now. We've mapped out our destination. But we may just be heading into a more elaborate trap. You know that a sure sign of insanity is when you do the same thing over and over again in the hopes that the outcome will be different. Think about it. We've been back twice. We've circled the block so to speak and still the same outcome; still they are free and doing their dirty work. We need a plan, a really good plan."

"Well Frankie's plan will backfire," Leona said quietly staring down at her skirt and in the process hiding her face from the scrutiny of the others. "Because there's the insurance. She forgot about the insurance. So, we rob him or burn down his shop and home. All he has to do is cash in his insurance and rebuild."

Tessa spoke for the first time, "I've never been a fan of revenge. Revenge usually backfires on the perpetrators. Yet doing nothing is equally bad. Something has got to be done and like Acacia I'm in agreement that it must be sooner rather than later. It's frustrating that the doctor is so well known and well liked; and rather ironic, that we are in this state of being that nobody is going to believe us even if we speak the truth. So please, stop arguing amongst yourselves and come up with a plan. I liked Ana's idea about renting an apartment close to her home and keeping an eye on her comings and goings. I think the more we know about the doctor's habits, the better plan we can come up with."

"You all is so smart, Granny. I sure do agree with y'alls advice 'bout the simplest plan beings the best plan. Though I'm not so enamored wit the one you are telling. Oh no, no ma'am," Acacia argued in a simulacrum of a sweet southern woman's exaggerated antebellum drawl. "We all will just be wasting our damned time skulking around, peering behind bushes, tiptoeing here and crouching there and we'll end up getting caught by some frigging cop or some nosey neighbor. Let's just go in there with guns blazing and blow a hole between their eyes and leave the assholes to rot. Yeah, I say rot, let um rot in their gross body fluids until the stink raises up the neighbors."

"Acacia, think for a minute. That's just as complex as my idea," Ana retorted in disgust. "We'd have to steal a gun because those gun shops all have surveillance and the police would track us down. How are we going to get an AK-47 anyway? Be realistic. What about when we have the AK-47? How are we going to conceal something like that? How would we get close enough to her without having her recognize us? Your plan would surely fail."

"What's all this SHE shit? You know who I'm after. I'll get the big guy first and the little shit last," Acacia retorted mimicking sighting down the barrel of a rifle.

A quiet voice broke the unhappy silence, "How about one of us befriending her maid or her cook? Then that person would relay information to us about her comings and goings. Then we can pick the moment when she's alone and vulnerable and all go in and take care of her."

"I don't know, Leona," Ana said.

Leona jumped to her feet and threw out her arms, "Well, how about impersonating a doctor? That would be easy for you to do Ana; you're so smart and all. You could read up on the latest medical procedures and call her and suggest lunch or dinner. Then when she invites you to her home, you let us in and we all take care of her. Wouldn't that work?"

Acacia groaned, "Oh y'all are seriously fucked! Don't you realize that's gonna take more time. Ana would have to go to school. I'm talking medical school – maybe eight years or more for Christ's Everlasting Sake and that could take forever. We don't have forever . . .you idgits."

No one spoke for a minute or two dismayed by the disintegration of their dream. In the distance, they could hear traffic and near by a hive of bees settling down for the night. Then Tessa asked in a censorious voice, "All of you seem to have decided that ultimately she deserves to die. Is that what the real outcome will be? That we are trying to figure out how to kill them all?

If that is so, then I warn you – there will be consequences. We're free right now. After fifteen years of hell, we are finally free to go anywhere we want. We have the money too. We could get on a plane and go anywhere. We could live our lives in peace somewhere tranquil and beautiful."

No one responded for the longest time. The silence made them all uncomfortable.

Tessa's laugh sounded strained even to herself, "I use to think I had all the answers. I used to think I would never, ever, harm another living creature. Now I'm not sure what I'd do or what I'm capable of doing."

Acacia jumped up and started pacing back and forth kicking small stones out of her way and gesturing wildly with her hands, "I know what I can do. Just like I said before, I get a picture in my head; I see the asshole lying six feet under and it's all good. Forget this sentimental shit. He, least of all, deserves our pity. Remember what he is."

"But she's worse," Leona reminded Acacia. "She's far worse and you know it. How many people has she hurt since we've been in hospital? It's been fifteen years. They're were twenty – maybe twenty-five of us back then. How many more do you think she has experimented on? And why him first anyway? All he cares about is money. We could just as easily bribe him to kill her."

"I've discovered over the years that my best ideas come to me when I'm not even thinking about a problem," Tessa reminded them. "And usually the answer is so simple I wondered afterward how I could have been so dumb not to have thought of it before."

"I still think it's a friggin mistake having Leona in charge. I've managed to get us here without screwing things up," Acacia said with an undercurrent of threat behind every syllable.

"But Leona had the dream," Tessa argued. "And it's gotten us this far. Tell us the dream again Leona."

Leona hesitated as she tried to remember. It had been years ago. Even the few seconds after she had woken from the dream the details had become a bit fuzzy; the telling always brought back new details though. "I saw myself entering a shop. The sign above the door said *Around the World Pawn*. When I entered the shop, the door shut behind me and I couldn't get out. I was scared. Here I was, trapped in a strange place and it's so dark I can't find the door. The worst happened next when I heard someone pacing outside the building. Through a side window I saw this dark shape; it could have been a man or an animal, maybe a bear; I don't know for sure. It was moving from window to window.

Then I see this middle-aged man standing behind a bullet-proof plexiglass window and the room is cluttered with junk for sale. The man is wearing a baby-carrier. You know one of those contraptions parents carry their babies in that hangs in front rather than behind. But what's odd is that there's no baby in the carrier. The empty pouch is just dangling from his belly. He sees me and glares with these cold brown eyes.

And in the backroom which I imagine to be filled with shelves full of junk, I hear a child crying. I see the baby wrapped in a filthy blanket on one of those shelves among broken toys and old appliances. I try to get to the baby; then from nowhere this huge creature rushes at me. I fall to the ground and I can feel his hot breath on my neck. Then I wake up."

Frankie clears her throat, "But what about your drawing Leona? I didn't recognize him. It wasn't Leland. He was too good looking to be Leland (that fat ugly suck-face) and the guy wearing the baby carrier wasn't Ray either."

"Oh, my friggin dingo dog from hell!" Acacia snorted. "We are gonna look like . . . I don't know. Just imagine. Come on simpletons. Can you see us running here . . . running there . . . running everywhere like some dumb-ass whistle pigs and never getting any closer to finding the SOPs. Don't cha know what happens to whistle pigs when they cross the road?"

"You and your son of a prick," Tessa laughed. "Too bad it didn't catch on."

No one noticed the sun gradually setting behind them. They continued to sit by the creek wading their feet in the cool water, looking up into the canopy of willows above them and digging their fingers into the dry sandy bed beneath them, some searching for warmth, some for answers. It wasn't until sunset that the women decided to move on. The group chose Leona to be their spokesperson. She did have the uncanny ability to read faces and even anticipate people's intentions.

Acacia disagreed loudly with the group's choice, but Tessa's comment final silenced her grumbling. "In a few hours one of us will be

50

entering a strange new town and meeting new people. Leona has an endearing quality about her that puts people at ease. She is the best person for this job."

Ana spoke up just before Leona moved to leave. "Have some self-control Leona and avoid using your talent in front of strangers. Just remember, there is no heaven or hell, justice comes from us. It's no good imagining that when bad people die they'll end up paying for their crimes in hell. Heaven and hell, god and the devil are just distractions to keep the real criminals from getting the punishment they deserve; we must be the ones who dole out justice. So, it is up to us to take care of them – all three of those oozy riddled pustules."

"Isn't that what I friggin said already?" Acacia complained throwing her hands up in the air.

Leona barely suppressed her growing excitement. Soon she would be free to see the world and meet new people. She hadn't been allowed to drive for months and she was eager to climb behind the wheel of the car and take off without being constantly monitored or criticized for talking crazy.

They were all relieved to find the Ford Taurus still parked by the side of the road near the abandoned farm house. Earlier the women considered bunking down in the two room shack circa 1907. After one curious glance inside though, Acacia noticed the rotten floor boards and gaping holes in the roof and communicated her opinion with a mocking snort; Eve squealed in disgust when she saw the termite infested joists; Ana her eyes traveling over the bare walls shook her head in horrified concern; Tessa stared in awe at an impressive beehive in the corner between the rafters.

Everyone agreed the meadow surrounded by locust trees near the creek would be far more practical a place to spend the night than the farmhouse. It was impossible to imagine, for even one night, stepping inside the farm house much less sleeping in the ruins.

The group decided to make themselves comfortable down by the creek and when Leona tried to follow them Tessa turned and gently pushed her away, "Since you're leaving early you sleep in the car and keep an eye on it." Leona watched as Ana and Frankie between them guided Tessa away from burrows and hardwood sage and onto firmer ground. From a distance, Tessa might have been mistaken for a child, a child tenderly guided by her parents through a dangerous patch of terrain.

The reality once face-to-face with Tessa was a shock when those shrewd brown eyes, so sharp and knowing, without warning assessed you and found you wanting. Everyone made the mistake of underestimating her. It had been Tessa their jailers underestimated. She had had a plan all along and kept her plan to herself, knowing there was someone in the group who was a spy, a spy who was relaying information to their captors. Tessa fooled them all, and because of her knowing ways, she saved the six of them from a living hell.

Long after her friends disappeared into the copse of trees, Leona stood by the side of the road and contemplated the gathering night. No such thing as streetlights, stoplights, marquees, or neon signs in the countryside. When the dogs started to bark, Leona got nervous. No, those weren't dogs. Maybe they were coyotes. Or maybe wolves? Afraid for the first time in a long time, Leona reluctantly turned and started back toward the car.

She climbed inside the backseat and made herself a make-shift bed using Ana's fancy red silk cape as a buffer between her body and the cold plastic lining. She used Frankie's wool blanket as a coverlet and Eve's fleece-lined coat as a pillow. The backseat of the Taurus wasn't any more comfortable than the hard ground but at least she had something between her and the coyotes? Or was it wolves? By the coldest part of the predawn hours, Leona seriously considered ripping off the cold vinyl just to feel the warmth of the stuffing along her face and side.

In the early morning hours, she woke still feeling tired. She climbed out of the Taurus and ran across the meadow to find her friends. A chorus of voices some sleepy some bright and cheerful greeted her as she drew closer. They were near the embankment. Tessa was handing out food from the basket and the ice chest. Frankie was washing her face in the cold creek. Ana had a book on her lap and was engrossed in the pages. Acacia was on the other side of the creek fishing with her bare hands and cussing up a storm. Eve could be seen moving from around a huge boulder adjusting her skirt.

Once Leona laid the wool blanket on the ground near Ana and accepted a piece of cheese and slice of bread from Tessa, her tiredness returned. Unlike the others she had not slept well at all. Leona woke feeling cold. When she sat up she realized that the others had let her sleep the entire day away. Beyond the foothills, the sun was setting. Her face felt hot and she supposed she would have a miserable sunburn as punishment for her laziness. They should have been mad at her, but they seemed to understand. Acacia even kind of smiled or what passed for a smile – a sort of grimace. Tessa broke the silence, "It is really time for you to go now honey. We can't hide out here forever."

As Leona moved away from the group, she couldn't help but look back. The sun dropped behind the mountain and spread its warmth upon the foothills. In contrast, the meadow began to merge with the night. Leona picked her way through the sparse meadow with its sad collection of scraggly brush and tough grasses, aware uncomfortably of the vastness all around her. At that moment, she feared so many things, getting lost in the vast open spaces all around her, space that stretched for miles where acres of fallow fields rolled on and on.

She especially feared meeting a cow right now. What would the cow do to her? Would it try to eat her? She remembered the day before when they found themselves soaking their tired feet in the creek near the road. She didn't remember how they had arrived at that spot, but she did remember seeing the fields beyond the creek and her panic only subsided when she located the Taurus tucked away near a small copse of tired and thirsty trees.

The memory of miles and miles of farmland with the occasional poplar soaring above the flatness like a lonely sentry at attention made her shiver. So much space. A person could walk for days and never meet anyone. A person could die out here. Take your pick – heat exhaustion in the noon day sun or hyperthermia on a cold and windy plateau. Acacia had laughed at her fears and told her all she had to do was holler and some farmer would come out of his barn and tell her to get off his land.

Leona turned back for one last look. She thought she recognized Ana's shadowy figure under the willows. She waved. Leona heard Ana call out, "Don't forgot about Mrs. Lawson. Dr. B will be suspicious if we forget to visit her. Be careful and drive safely, Leona."

Leona threw her words over her shoulder feeling her heart beating rapidly in her chest, rapid with excitement and a tinge of dread, "Don't worry. I won't forget. Be safe. I'll be back, I promise." The words made Leona lightheaded. She managed to find the road in the gathering gloom and with real gratitude leaned against the car for a moment. Her words had brought on a moment of panic. She'd made a promise to someone else once – again unfortunate words which had provoked a series of terrible events and ended so much worse than she ever imagined.

Leona climbed behind the wheel of the Ford Taurus. Out of habit she glanced in the rear view mirror to make sure there was no one behind her and laughed at herself. Who would be parked behind her when she was surrounded by acres and acres of fallow fields and wild grass and an abandoned farmhouse? Something about her face in the dusk seemed odd. Leona leaned closer to the mirror and noticed with shock how her eyelashes were dripping with a heavy application of black mascara. The look startled her so much she nervously glanced over her shoulder as if she thought someone might be hiding in the backseat of the car.

The backseat was loaded with suitcases and shoes and on the floor, there were a jumble of empty pop cans, beer cans, potato chip wrappers, a collection of tea bags, and other much worse unidentifiable food stuffs. The others must have taken everything out of the trunk and put it in the backseat. What a mess; I'll have to clean it out before it gets so bad I won't be able to see out the back window. Leona tried to laugh and all that came out was a high-pitched cackle. She forced herself to smile at the image in the mirror. She hardly recognized herself.

Amongst the debris, she found Frankie's cold cream and several tissues tucked inside her makeup case. Leona proceeded to carefully remove the mascara from her eyelashes, the bright red rouge from her cheeks, and the purple lipstick from her lips. As she dabbed and wiped the color off her eyelids and cheeks and lips she murmured, "Really Eve, your jokes are getting a little old."

Once Leona felt presentable, she glanced out the passenger window and squinted through the smudged glass trying to see if Eve might be standing by the willow chuckling to herself at her good joke. Leona thought she saw a white arm raised in farewell. It had to be Eve. Leona excited and scared had no energy left to be mad at Eve. Eve's joke had been motivated by playfulness, not malice. Eve could be clever and fun and sexy and silly. Leona envied Eve's gregarious nature.

Knowing her friends would be upset if she dawdled any longer, Leona waved to them all then turned the key in the ignition. It would be pitch black soon. Getting lost on these back roads would be a disaster. Driving at night was bad enough in itself much less wandering up and down deserted roads with only the headlights to guide her. Besides she needed to find a hotel room quickly and make the necessary phone calls. With her purse next to her thigh, Leona pulled out onto the dirt road.

Once on the paved highway, she squinted at the milepost signs and searched for a sign that would tell her where the nearest town might be and how far she had to go. A moment of doubt assailed her, and she wondered why the group chose her to drive. She hated to drive at night and the glare from passing car lights made her nervous. She tried to shrug away her fears. Well, the group had chosen her. They believed in her. She just had to believe in herself and all would be well. She turned on the radio. The grating voice screaming about the devil made her wince. She twisted and turned the dial until she found a nice soothing channel. The New Age music rolled through the car relaxing her taunt muscles and twitching jaw.

When she noticed the sign cautioning her to go twenty-five miles an hour she was surprised. Where had that come from? Then she saw the buildings a few yards ahead and realized she had been in the small town for a few minutes and never knew it. She must have missed the sign announcing the name of the town while searching for a better radio station. Obediently she slowed down and coasted along the main drag. There appeared to be only one main street.

She searched both sides of the unlit street for a likely hotel and absently noted the shadowy shapes of homes. They appeared to be abandoned, some of them looked as if they had neat lawns and gardens but most of the yards were full of rank weeds. These yards included cheap lawn furniture, old tires, forgotten mowers, and rusty cars as lawn ornaments. Leona thought of Dada or Postmodern Art with its attempt to shock and annoy the viewer with its lack of respect for the petite bourgeoisie. Well, maybe not intentional Dada or Postmodern Art; after all, someone might need that toilet seat or that push lawnmower.

Most of the homes were simple shingled sided wood homes, a five-room floor plan: a living room, a kitchen, two bedrooms, and a tiny bath. In the past that's all people really needed. The houses were like sentries guarding the town's past and perhaps some unpleasant secrets hid behind the walls as well.

With relief Leona reached the intersection. The town seemed to shut down at sunset. Creepy. The only sounds she could hear were cars whizzing by on the highway about three miles back and another sound she couldn't quite identify. There were hundreds of them singing in chorus. Then an old memory surfaced of her grandmother on the porch one hot July night telling her the sound she heard were the Mormon crickets rubbing their legs together warning people that the following day would be hot.

That was a memory, a real memory! Leona tried to see the woman's face in her mind's eye. Nothing came, just the words wrapped in an idea thrown forward into the present by the mind. She nearly ran down a man weaving across the unlit road and had to brake suddenly. She watched him stumble his way into one of the boxy houses on the other side of the street.

A voice inside her head which she thought might have been her old 5th grade biology teacher said, "Sorry but your grandmother was wrong. They are katydids and the males are rubbing their front wings to woe the females. They feed on dandelions and sagebrush..." She shut the voice down as the voice moved in to lecture mode.

Leona feared this town had no hotel. It wasn't until she'd driven a third of the way through town that she noticed a billboard announcing *Lucky Sage Motel.* A car honked angrily behind her and she realized that she'd been so busy looking at the billboard, she'd forgotten to check for oncoming traffic. Once she was safely parked near the motel's office, Leona turned off the engine and sat for a moment behind the steering wheel until her hands stopped shaking.

Now she had to go inside and pay for a room for the night. Determined not to blow this opportunity Leona climbed out of the car and marched toward the office fully prepared to be assertive. After entering the lobby and noticing the woman sitting behind the counter Leona relaxed. No need for assertiveness here. The woman with short gray curls and big brown eyes smiled up at Leona with genuine delight and affection. Amazing. Even more amazing, the woman looked to be smaller than Leona. Leona smiled back with profound relief and managed to fill out the little hotel card and pay for her room with cash without saying anything that might annoy or unwittingly shock the old lady.

On shaky legs Leona left the office and searched the numbered doors for her room. Number Seven, a good number, a lucky number. The rooms were connected like one huge horse shoe. She found the design comforting, a sure sign of future luck to come. And when she reached number seven, she touched the horseshoe nailed to the wooden door for additional luck then entered the room and threw her heavy satchel and purse onto the closest queen size bed.

By the time she'd showered the grit off her feet from Willow Creek and dried her hair she was ready to make her phone calls. Ana had made the necessary arrangements. All Leona had to do was call the number written in the notebook, the one stuffed somewhere in her purse. Ana had chosen the notebook in Helena, Montana from a tiny bookstore crammed between a laundromat and a diner. The notebook was rather frivolous and expensive. Its four-inch wide, six-inch long hard cover had a design of library shelved books on the front and back and gold filigree curls and tails along the binding. The first three pages inside the notebook were filled with names and phone numbers and one in-particular had been circled in red. That was the person Ana had asked her to call immediately.

It took Leona a frustrating fifteen minutes to figure out the motel's phone system and she had to use one of the precious credit cards to call long distance. Leona heard a pleasing male voice reciting a prescribed message, "I'm not in now but you may leave a message at the beep. If you need the main office of Ogden House Publishing, please press two; otherwise, our hours are nine to five Monday through Friday. Thank you and goodbye."

Leona hated to leave messages on impersonal recordings, but she'd promised the others, so she spoke hurriedly into the receiver, "Hello Mr. Grover. I'm a friend of Dr. Evans. She wanted me to let you know that she will be in your town soon and would like to set up an appointment the middle of the week preferably in the morning. You can leave a message at this number." Leona read the number out of the notebook next to Ana's name and finished the message with a wheezy. "Thanks, and good bye."

With a soft sigh of regret, she dropped the phone in its cradle and lay back on the bed. The call reminded her of Ana. She jumped up with a startled oath and grabbed her car keys and the room key. Ana would be furious if Leona left the briefcase in the trunk all night in a strange town.

After Leona had successfully moved the car closer to her motel room and extracted the briefcase from the trunk, she locked the motel door and proceeded to get herself ready for bed. There was really nothing else to do. Even though it was only eight in the evening, she figured she would be less likely to get into trouble if she just got ready for bed and did a few deep breathing and meditation mantras.

As she got ready for bed, she thought about her friends. The thought of them made her smile. They all knew modern entertainment infuriated Frankie. Frankie referred to television and social media as bloodsucking timewasters. Unlike Frankie, Acacia loved action movies claiming she got her best ideas from the martial-arts sequences as well as nifty survivor tips from the intricate ways the heroes escaped capture.

Eve, well, Eve enjoyed her romances, her mysteries, and every so often a tastefully crafted porn flick. Ana and Leona, they preferred quiet contemplation with a magnificent view and a nice cup of tea. Unlike the younger generation, Tessa could spend hours at her needlepoint her nimble fingers creating great art. It was a standing joke with Frankie that watching Tessa work was more therapeutic than any sleeping pill.

As for herself, Leona enjoyed watching people, preferably somewhere secluded where she could sit and sip a latte, bite into a delicious croissant, and observe the interactions between groups. At those times, she felt like a spy gathering valuable information which would ultimately protect her friends and might even save her country from a potential threat.

Like a hero in a thriller, she listened in on private conversations and when she overheard really juicy stuff, it was the highlight of her day. Years ago, she'd had an epiphany – the juicy stuff she thought she was hearing wasn't coming from her ears, but from an unknown source, maybe from electrical currents from their brains to her brain. Instead of hearing conversations like everyone else, she'd been absorbing private thoughts along with the dialogue and converting the two into one. Somehow, her brain was able to synthesize the private and the public and make sense out of the two.

From a very early age, she'd wanted to know what people were honestly thinking behind their public masks. And then one day she could. She didn't know how she did it; all she knew was that she could. Unlike Frankie's philosophy that making money would keep her safe and secure, Leona believed knowing what others were thinking would keep them all safe and secure

Belatedly she remembered Frankie's request and had to rush about the room searching through luggage until she found Frankie's address book, a simple black leather cover with Frances Margaret Stewart inscribed in gold leaf. Leona made the phone call. When the woman answered, Leona jumped. She'd expected a recording.

"Underwood and Sturm. How may I assist you?" the woman asked.

"Well, I'm calling on behalf of a friend who wanted me to leave a message with Bob Underwood."

"Yes. And what might that be?"

"Ah, Ok. Tell Mr. Underwood that Frances Stewart will be in San Francisco on the 23rd of September and a one o'clock lunch is acceptable."

The transformation in the woman's voice surprised Leona, "Frances Stewart? You're a friend of the writer Frances Stewart? Oh. Wow. Would you do me the great honor of telling Ms. Stewart how much I love her books? I can't wait for the next one. This is just incredible. I'm talking to someone who knows Frances Margaret Stewart."

"Well that's great. I'll let Frankie know. Anyway, did you get the message?"

"Of course. You tell Ms. Stewart not to worry. I'll relay her message to Mr. Underwood pronto and I promise never to reveal her nickname. Zip. Zip."

"Well, goodbye then."

"Is Ms. Stewart there? May I take just a moment of her time?"

"No. She's not here. But I'll relay your sentiments," Leona said and then before the woman could gush any more she dropped the receiver onto the cradle. The ting echoed in the quiet room. Extraordinary. Leona tried to imagine Frankie as a celebrity. No. Not possible. Frankie – an A type personality better suited to a boardroom or a high-powered lunch with the ability to micromanage everyone within her orbit wasn't Leona's idea of a celebrity. Or was she? What did she know about real celebrities anyway? Maybe she would have to buy one of Frankie's novels and read it. She wished she had one right now. The silence fairly shouted at her.

The parts of Leona that she could see in the mirrored section of the wall behind the television, a series of panels splashed with swirls of imitation gold reminded her of an old movie, something from the '70s or '80s and the sight made her oddly uneasy. The image that looked back at her, an image emerging in bits and pieces – a head she didn't like, a neck she did and then when she stood up, a thin person she didn't recognize made her want to cover the mirrors with one of the thin sheets on her bed. She froze in the act of turning on the television feeling someone standing behind her. The ache in her neck forced her to move. She made herself walk toward the mirrored squares and as she drew closer she saw green eyes and dark thick eyebrows. She liked her eyebrows and her dark eyelashes and even her eyes.

Although, the mascara Eve had piled on her lashes was a shameful waste of money Leona thought now that she had managed to scrape off most of it with several applications of cold cream, a warm washcloth and plenty of water. And to her astonishment, Leona kind of liked her skin too, no blemishes or wrinkles.

How odd a sight. The foreignness of her face made her uncomfortable. The only part of her she hated was her nose; her nose was too thin. It reminded her of pictures she'd seen of witches. Out of habit, she ignored the nose and concentrated on the other parts of her upper torso. Her hair needed cutting. It looked all jagged with black spikes springing up everywhere like tiny Martian antennas. What must the desk clerk have thought of her? A Goth girl? Oh, so nineties.

A film of white blocked her view of herself for a moment. She blinked thinking she had gotten some of the cold cream in her eyes. She rubbed her eyelids gently, opened them and then looked into the mirror again. The uncertainty passed. There was nothing wrong with her. It had just been an exhausting day.

For a few seconds Leona seriously considered doing something she had never done before - searching through her friends' personal belongings. Why not? She was less interested in Acacia's duffel bag because while moving her stuff to get at other items in the trunk, she had fingered the bag feeling only soft things which meant underwear, jeans, grungy tank tops and most likely smelly socks. The items from the other containers looked more interesting. Frankie's celebrity status might mean a wad of hundred-dollar bills or diamonds or a Swiss bank account? When Leona discovered the combination lock on the briefcase she was miffed. Fifteen minutes later she was furious. In a desperate last attempt, she tried Bill Gate's date of birth wasting precious time by searching through Frankie's calendar to find the date. Frankie had outwitted her again. It had been a stupid idea anyway.

The strange surroundings and ominous silence compelled Leona to do something she rarely did – she turned on the television for comfort. The motel room was no bigger than her room on the 8-Ball Ward but there was a world of difference between this room and her old room. She reminded herself of the nightly rituals of her old life, how there had always been someone out in the hall or at the nurse's station. Instead of never having a moment's privacy or the freedom to come and go, here she was on her own for the first time in her life, here she was now, free as a bird, free to go anywhere in the world and do anything she wanted to do.

Outside her motel room there was only darkness and silence. No one walked past her door recording personal shit on her clipboard for every nosy idiot to see or wake her up from a sound sleep in the middle of the fucking night to check her vital signs or drug her some more. Oh yeah. This was going to be nice. She just had to get used to the quiet that's all.

It was the ordinary everyday things that could drive you bat shit crazy. And she'd forgotten her other pet peeve, there was no one driving by her motel room making a hell of a racket like the orderlies sometimes did when they raced down the halls pushing a gurney. The sound of the gurney's wheels and the metal parts banging away meant a patient had misbehaved and needed some time in solitary. She hadn't realized until this moment how accustomed she'd become to the noises from the 8-Ball Ward.

She should be grateful for her present circumstances. Yes, she was. Upon further reflection, she was grateful indeed. She had plenty to be thankful for now and she owed her new freedom and new bounty to her new friends.

Interrupting the silence, she said, "Bless you ladies, one and all."

After brushing her teeth, she lay back on the pillows, both anorexic and lumpy. She tried to focus on the television. It was unpleasant being in a strange town sleeping in a bed, thousands of strangers had slept in, strangers doing god-knows-what on a mattress which might or might not be teaming with bedbugs and other nasties, in a room where the walls were probably home to mice and spiders. Yes, and just as terrifying was the idea that the only thing between her and an intruder was particle board and a flimsy chain.

Yet the idea of sleeping on the floor disgusted her. The carpet, a once upon a time yellow shag circa 1972 contained some suspicious stains and dismal bald spots. Even the family pet would probably turn up her nose at such a horror.

She missed her friends.

The remote for the television turned out to be annoyingly difficult to operate just like the phone. Once she got the hang of the device, she managed to find a movie that wasn't a bloody horror flick, porn, or slapstick comedy. The movie was about an Irish immigrant living in America. The young woman's creamy skin, lilting Irish brogue and deadpan expression inexplicably annoyed Leona. Was she annoyed because the Irish lass' problems seemed trivial or because Leona couldn't identify with the protagonist's desire to live in America? Why would anyone want to live in America, the land of covert apartheid?

From her earliest memories, Leona had longed to visit the United Kingdom and discover her roots. Someone in her past (long before the 8-Ball Ward, maybe even before her abduction) had put the idea in her head that her ancestors were from the British Isles. Instructed carefully by her friend Frankie, before she left the Canal Critical Care and Recovery Hospital, she insisted on getting copies of all her medical records. For weeks Dr. B ignored her verbal requests until she threatened to sue him and the hospital.

When he and his intern delivered the box filled with binders, she found medical records going back to the very first day she had been discovered in a remote area of Montana near the Canadian border. The records included observations by the paramedics and emergency staff and all subsequent surgeries over the years. In addition, there were numerous case studies which recorded her psychological profile and interviews with the Bishop team.

An unexpected surprise to her was the results from a DNA test taken in 2005. No one had asked her permission or even mentioned the DNA test. She learned she was 100 percent European and had no genetic defects. Unfortunately, or fortunately (depending on the persons Leona talked to: staff, physicians, psychiatrists, her case worker, even her secret friends) the test was a dead-end as far as discovering the identity and whereabouts of her parents. Either they were dead or had never contributed to the popular testing sites on the Internet. Dr. B suggested she upload her results to one of the popular DNA sites as a way of finding cousins or maybe aunts or uncles. After more than a decade of being Dr. B's favorite test subject, the idea of sharing anymore of her fluids with strangers made her want to vomit.

Before Leona fell asleep she thought about her friends (not the patients or staff at the Recovery Center) they had never been her real friends. Like her the 8-Ball Ward sheltered prisoners of circumstance, prisoners forced to live among strangers, forced to adapt to their surroundings and forced to get along with each other. Her real friends were friends by choice, five women she trusted with her life. She sent each one of them a prayer filled with love and friendship hoping they were spending the night somewhere dry and warm.

8

Navan Keys walked into the bar and grill called the Woolly Man. She'd discovered the rather offensively named establishment purely by accident. The Woolly Man was many unpleasant rough dusty hot miles off I-84, a place somewhere in eastern Idaho where only the locals dared to venture. Most of the locals drove around in 4WD vehicles which made a hellava lot of sense. They had no trouble traversing the washboard roads unlike her Ford Taurus which had squealed and shrieked the whole way. Only much later did she discover the naming of the bar and grill had nothing to do with overt racism but was the Nerin family's inside joke.

The Nerin family were interested in all things archeological – Woolly Mammoths and ancient artifacts. Many years ago, the family commissioned a local artist to create the sign explaining carefully why they had chosen the name Woolly Mammoth Bar and Grill. He had been a terrible speller. Later to fix the gaffe, the youngest member of the Nerin family Quincella Nerin created the image of a wooly moth man digging in the desert surrounded by bones. Her artistic effort ended up as an etching on a cedar plank which the brothers attached below the sign. But everyone in town called the bar and grill the Woolly Man and the name stuck.

As Leona closed Woolly Man's screen door behind her, she noticed the two men first. They were sitting at a booth close to the door. They were the most beautiful creatures she'd ever ogled outside of Hollywood. They were both long and lean and wearing loose blue jeans with short sleeved t-shirts. They had several maps spread out on a table between them as well as empty beer bottles and bowls which had once contained chips and salsa.

The man who faced the door appeared to be the oldest person in the room with his butch cut and a sprinkle of gray hairs. He might be in his early thirties. She couldn't be sure because all she could see was the top of his head since he was absorbed in scribbling in a black leather-bound notebook while the other man dictated numbers which Leona recognized as GPS coordinates. The stenographer must have forgotten his glasses because he had his nose practically touching the page. The younger one seemed to be getting his coordinates from a screen on his smartphone. His voice sounded positively smug. Even the way he sat with his back ramrod straight on the cushioned bench radiated smugness.

Although he sounded like a poser with his occasional lapses into a British accent when he pronounced "latitude" and "longitude," he seemed to know his subject well. She'd already decided he was smart; yet, the mixture of Oxford English and Idaho drawl irritated her. Even though the way he spoke seemed out of place amongst simple folk, she guessed him to be an educated person and she quickly decided he was better educated than anyone in the room including herself. His choice of words and arrangement of sentence structure, his degree of confidence in using those words, and his general air of hauteur marked him as having had at least eighteen years of education.

Not only was she convinced he was well educated (maybe even a genius) his voice – a soft baritone simultaneously soothing and sexy sent shivers of delight up her back. Oh, the body was a traitor – sneaky and cruel. She hated herself when she let her guard down.

The educated one with the sexy voice had a long torso and an efficient way of moving; although his fashion sense – as one way of decorating his beautiful body – made her want to laugh. She swallowed a betraying giggle and her body, at odds with itself paid her back by forcing air along with the salvia down her throat. With a throbbing throat protesting its abuse, she managed to make her way into the room without choking and tried not to call attention to herself. Fat chance.

As she moved to the center of the room, she could see more details about the occupants of the bar and grill noticing the educated one's long shiny black hair tied back from his face with a piece of leather string, the leather looping through and around the thick strands of his hair in intricate folds. He couldn't have braided his hair by himself, could he? Why do men waste so much time on their appearance these days? Was this a reversal of gender conformities? For a moment, she wondered if she was experiencing one of Alice Rathburn's romance novels where all the characters were gorgeous and dressed in revealing and historically inaccurate garb.

When he turned to glance at the waitress, Leona noticed with a sudden lurch of her stomach soaring eyebrows and high cheekbones. Oh My God! He did look tasty. She also noticed that he wore a pair of leather sandals on manicured feet and a necklace made of hemp around a lean handsome throat. Everything about him was so perfectly proportioned from his tight buttocks to his long lean legs. Such perfection seemed unnatural and rather disturbing. Most disturbingly were his eyes – the color of new grass in the spring. Such eyes belonged to a pale red head but instead stared out of the face of a black Irishman with a perfectly proportioned nose and skin the color of caramel.

At first, she assumed he might be of mixed parentage perhaps an Irish mother and Native American father then she noticed his hands and the pale skin behind his ears. A Caucasian male masquerading as a persecuted and marginalized member of the first Americans seemed more suited to the 1960s than present day. Hum. His tan likely owed much to his occupation.

Such beauty and artifice brought out the snot in her. From the first flush of lust and awe followed disgust; and as she continued moving toward the center of the room, she conjured up feelings of outrage to offset desire. Maybe he lived off rich old ladies or was an unemployed parasite with a poor drudge of a wife who braided his hair in the morning and worked all day to keep a roof over his head? Or maybe he was a trust-fund brat who chose his current style to piss off his parents?

By the time she had finished thoroughly trashing him in her head, she had convinced herself he no longer mattered. Then his eyes lit on her and Leona's heart raced. He knew! He could read her mind. The appraising intelligence in his eyes forced her to reassess her initial impression of him. Grudgingly, she had to admit he appeared to be smarter than she first thought not just book smart but the kind of smart that could sniff out liars.

The waitress called him Luke.

The man across the table from Luke looked older, older not just because of the gray at his temples but because his eyes were sad and seemed to have seen so much more unhappiness than anyone else in the room. Luke's stenographer kept his dark hair cut short and as a testament to the universe's perversity he happened to be as equally gorgeous as the other man. There was a family resemblance, but they were not twins as she had first thought.

The stenographer had startling blue eyes with thick black lashes. When he lifted his beer to his shapely lips and glanced up in time to see her pass his table, a flush of embarrassment mixed with pleasure ran through her body from her tingling scalp to the soles of her feet in their oversized army boots. His blue eyes decorated with gorgeous dark lashes and brows were so penetrating that Leona forgot to look where she was going and tripped. She blamed the boots. They were too loose. The flowing tie-dyed silk skirt was hers, but the boots belonged to Acacia.

Before the man could reach out to prevent her from falling on her face, she counteracted her fall with a little dance step and the straightening of her spine then continued walking as if nothing had happened even though her face felt as if she were standing next to a roaring fire. She made her way through the bar and grill passing empty booths circa 1950s and small café tables trying to get as far away from the men as possible.

The men went back to what they had been doing before she entered the room. She heard Luke say, "Did you get the coordinates down correctly? Hey over here Zak. I'm over here. Zak, you listening? I'm talking to you man. We need those coordinates to triangulate our position. I don't want to be digging test wholes when I'm eighty."

"42.8626° N, 112.5784°W," Zak snapped slamming the notebook shut, "The Buhl Woman was discovered in 1989 – by accident. A road crew found her remains. That's all archeology is these days Luke, amateurs finding artifacts while not looking. I'm done with this chicken shit side show. Go ask Mom to be your personal assistant. I've got things to do."

Luke responded to Zak's anger with the appearance of composure belied by a sneering tone, "Dear brother. There is no need for you to embark on a useless trip to town when I have gone to the trouble for you. I've taken care of everything."

"Butt out of my business, Luke."

"No need to distress yourself unnecessarily dear boy. I've been perusing the wares of that establishment for several months now and I do believe I've made some head way with the proprietor. Don't look at me like that. I'm not betraying you. Why wouldn't I go in there? It's where artifacts are pawned. And one of these days, I might get lucky. Some stupid schmuck might just pawn something really valuable."

"Screw it," Zak said fiercely. "You aren't looking for something to buy; you're trying to sell something. Whatever it is, it better not belong to me. Anything for a buck, huh? You'd sell Mom for a crummy buck, wouldn't you? That's the kind of dirt-bag you are."

"I am hurt, baby brother," Luke said holding his hand to his heart feigning shock.

"Get real Luke. You're about as emotionally intelligent as one of your fossils."

So, Zak was the younger one. The graying temples must be fake or a genetic disorder, maybe he'd used food coloring; it seemed to be the current rage. People were so odd. Why would you want to look older? Time is so short anyway. The average American male only lives about seventy-five years and a few years less if they're poor. Their angry exchange made her regret her decision to come here. She should have chosen the meeting place instead of letting Mona Lawson dictate the time and place.

Leona needed physical and mental space between her and the people in the room (the two men especially) a safe distance where she could observe them as if she were a member of an audience witnessing a live play on stage. With distance, she could gather up her dignity. Her cheeks grew hot imagining the angry one getting up from the table to start a conversation with her. She wouldn't know what to say.

All her life she had been on the outskirts of the likes of them watching under cover of books and thick glasses and silence as the parade of pretty people laughed and joked and made love to the world expecting love in return. Even when she managed to rid herself of her glasses, she'd never had the skill or style to talk to pretty people. They were as foreign to her as aliens from another galaxy. Now that she no longer had thick glasses to hide behind she felt exposed and vulnerable imagining them judging her and finding her wanting. She would have no words to fight against such an assault on her psyche and her dumbness would be seen as weakness.

"Zak, you want another?" the waitress asked impatiently with her eyes staring off into the distance as if she could care less that the two most gorgeous men in the place were sitting only inches from her.

"Yeah and bring us more salsa."

"I'm not your slave; go and get it yourself," she said strolling away with a shake of her head. "Talk about a lazy ass male with delusions above his station."

In a silent prayer, Leona wished both males would up and leave the place. She didn't want them present when she met Mona Lawson for the first time. Dr. B had probably told Mona all about her. There was no such thing as privacy anymore. People these days over share too damned much. The kids at the half-way house called it TMI – Too Much Information. Maybe the world was starting to get fed up with listening to personal tragedies from other people's sad sick lives. Wait. No. He couldn't. Her records were sealed. If he revealed anything about her past, she could sue him and the hospital.

She should have just said "fuck you doc" and kept on driving west.

Part of Leona's prayer came true. The one called Zak got up from the table with a grin and disappeared into the kitchen returning with a bowl of salsa which he unceremoniously dumped onto the table nearly spilling some of the stuff on the pages of the notebook. She noticed the scar above Zak's right eye and wondered how he had gotten it. He looked like the kind of man that relished a good fight. Or then again, he might have gotten the wound in an inane way perhaps falling off his ten-speed in junior high or tripping over his big feet as an adolescent nearly poking his eye out on some innocent object minding its own business.

While the men bickered, she made herself comfortable in a corner of the room where she hoped to be close to what little light penetrated the gloom inside the bar. The spot she chose was beyond the pool table and near a side door. There was also a big window where she could look out at a field of dry grass and a few humps which might have been burrows. There was also an old rusty truck sitting on blocks near a long disused outhouse.

Her shoes, two sizes too big, slapped against the bare rough boards of the bar floor as she tested the bench seats on either side of the table, first the one where she might have her back to the room, then the other. She chose the bench facing the room, so she could see the enemy coming. She hated it when people crept up on her unawares. The bench was cold and lumpy. She made do by slipping off her sweater and using it as a cushion then set her cracked leather satchel between her and the wall. Only after she found a firm spot on the bench and a footrest on a rung of the table leg did she finally find the courage to look around.

The young black woman behind the bar, the waitress dressed in a pair of tight blue jeans and skimpy tank top approached her table with a pencil and pad ready to take her order. The waitress' face could have been her fortune. She had the sculptured nose, high cheekbones, and pouting lips of a model, as well as a size two figure, ramrod straight carriage, and long legs. Threes, all in threes again. Bad luck. Leona rubbed her aching forehead and told herself to shut up. No more connections. No more superstitious nonsense. Think four, four is a lucky number, the earth number signifying the four corners of the earth and the four primary elements: water, air, fire, and earth.

Leona desperately searched for two more features to describe before the woman noticed her and came over to take her order. She had to cancel out the negative energy she'd just conjured up. Soft skin. No. She had no idea if the damn woman had soft skin. Blemish free skin. Ah, yes. No, wait. No zits that she could see. Don't think about zits. Zits and shit. Shit the woman was nearly at her table. Big feet.

No! Think positive. Must be a positive adjective. One more for the three and the three. Then she'd have four features linked with another four which would total eight which would be lucky indeed. Hands. Before Leona would accept the menu from the woman she had to describe her hands. She stared at the woman's hands until her eyes were in danger of falling out of their sockets. Long, shapely hands with manicured painted fingernails. Nice color. That shade of cinnamon matched her eyes.

Just as the men were far from average, Leona realized the waitress was also unique. But like all beauties, she had the familiar centerpiece of beauty, the triangle of wide forehead, high cheekbones, and well-proportioned chin. Leona had expected a different type of person working in such a place, a person willing to venture into a rundown shack like this with its smudgy windows, flies circling the spilled beer, gouges left in the table by the drinkers, and the smell of greasy burned bacon pervading the air would more likely have suited some tough biker chick with tattoos and a badly healed knife wound somewhere on her puffy white bellied body, or . . . a poor fatalistic female routinely smacked around by an even dumber boyfriend.

Idiot, she thought to herself. None of those overdone limp stereotypes were true. People were too complex for stereotypes. Leona acknowledged her unconscious prejudices with a deep sense of self-recrimination. She was better than that. She blamed her lapse on fear. Fear made a person crazy, crazy enough to misperceive situations and imagine others as the enemy. To see truth objectively, she just needed to open her eyes and look at the world without prejudice. She chose that moment to really look at her surroundings.

The Woolly Man Bar and Grill was so off the beaten track she had had to drive at least five miles around and up and down the peaks and valleys along a stretch of dirt road where cattle crossed when they felt like it, a snake tried to bite her front tire, and a jackrabbit jumped out from a nearby bush where she'd squatted to pee. Yet the stereotype of such places conjured up images of grizzled old men with crazy eyes and tobacco dribbling from the corners of their gin soaked lips – not these three extraordinarily beautiful people. These three belonged on the red carpet in Hollywood, not of all places, among the snakes and rocks and dust of the desert, miles from a decent coffee house or five-star restaurant.

The silence had stretched on too long and once again Leona found herself exposed to other people's sudden discomfort. The waitress had been waiting for a response from her, at least an acknowledgement of her existence and Leona had been too busy searching for lucky signs. With a wary eye, the waitress handed her a greasy menu and said, "We stopped taking breakfast orders ten minutes ago but there might be a little leftover Spanish omelet if you're interested."

"That sounds great," Leona said forcing an airy detachment she did not feel as she handed the menu back to the woman making a point to look her straight in the eye without flinching. A person appeared in her line of sight behind the waitress. She ignored the person and focused on the waitress in front of her. She had been aware of the waitress from the corner of her eye picking out important details such as height and beauty, but she had not really taken the time to see the sweetness and the intelligence in the eyes and in the kind smile. The last thing she noticed was the tag stuck on the woman's tank top, a white packing label with the name Quinn scribbled in barely discernable green magic marker.

Just because Quinn should have been on a runway instead of this sorry-ass place did not mean that she was a disgruntled employee or a cheap whore waiting for her sugar-daddy. No. This child, yes, still a child with her baby fat cheeks and fresh unblemished skin had an inner knowing and sweetness Leona liked. It had been a long time since she had trusted anyone especially a stranger.

"Is there a town nearby?" she asked the waitress. "I'm sort of lost."

"Yes. Woolstone is only two miles northwest of us," she said with a puzzled look. "You had to have passed through it to get here. The road," she jerked her thumb over her shoulder, "dead ends about five miles south of here at the Canby Ranch."

"You said Woolstone? I don't recall a sign announcing the name of the town," Leona said trying desperately to remember if she'd driven through the town. She must have been daydreaming or the town must be so tiny she mistook it for something else.

"Oh sure. There's a sign. Unfortunately, the locust needs a trim and you probably couldn't see the sign."

"Do they have a gas station? I don't recall seeing a gas station."

"Yes, but it's not on the main road. You have to turn left just before Drummond's Market then you'll see the gas station."

"Oh. Great. Thank you."

Before Quinn turned away, Leona forced herself to ask her most pressing question, the question she really meant to ask, "You wouldn't happen to know Mona Lawson and where she lives would you?"

"Who?" Quinn asked her beautiful brows lifted in puzzlement.

"Mona Lawson," Leona repeated.

Quinn shouted over her shoulder, "Hey Mom. Do we know a Mona Lawson? This lady wants to know."

Leona had been so preoccupied by the men she hadn't noticed the woman standing behind the bar. The woman held her head erect and had the most startling white hair Leona had ever seen. This woman had more confidence than most, confidence enough to let her graying hair grow naturally without resorting to hair dyes or pampered visits to a beauty parlor. Her silky white hair had been cut short and lay neat and close to her perfectly shaped skull. Her eyes were the most brilliant shade of brown, especially with the sunlight shining through the window and accentuating the flicks of gold in them. Then everything clicked into place and Leona realized with a sort of thrill that the three beautiful young people in the room must be her children.

Even with the dusky look of many sleepless nights and morning hangovers around her eyes, the woman's incredible beauty shown through the crowfeet and the slight indents near her full lips. Like her daughter, the woman had a razor thin body.

"You know her Quinn. She comes in here all the time. The birdwatcher," the woman said watching her daughter's face for signs she understood and when she didn't find what she was looking for added, "the tofu sandwich lady."

"Oh her. Yeah. The one who orders the tofu turkey sandwich and hold the tomato but don't forget heavy on the cream cheese," Quinn said as she turned back to look down at Leona. "She rents old Mabel's house in town. You had to have passed the house on your way here. It's the gray one with the wagon wheeled fence and the gemstone wind chimes on the porch. They make quite a racket on windy days. But the sandwich lady loves the noise. Says it drowns out the voices." Quinn's chuckle reassured Leona. It was a friendly sound as if the absurdities of people were something she expected but did not fear.

The sexy young males ignored the conversation flying back and forth across the room and only looked up from their maps when a middle-aged man with long straggly salt and pepper hair exploded from the kitchen wearing a dirty apron and carrying a bag of garbage. He glanced at Leona and stopped dead in his tracks. His sweet smile unnerved her. All of a sudden, she was scared. He reminded her of a gargoyle. He had a broken nose and wide Slavic cheekbones with an unfortunately overlarge jaw and broad forehead. All his proportions were out of whack. His head looked too large for his small stature and his ugly face didn't fit with his beautifully muscular lean and tanned body.

He dropped the garbage bag on the floor near his boots and just stared at her. The man with the scary eyes the one called Zak spoke to him sharply, "Nate. What is your problem? Don't you know it's impolite to stare?"

Nate ignored him and strode over to Leona's table. Unconsciously Leona tried to make herself invisible by dropping her head and hiding her eyes with her hair and her hands. She heard him say from above her, "Where have you been all my life sweetness? God-all-mighty you are one stunning piece of art."

Leona covered her face with her hands and started praying he would go away. She heard the woman behind the counter say, "Nate. I need your help over here," and in a harsher tone. "Now please." Leona heard the man walk away. A young woman's voice overshadowed the older woman's gentle remarks to Nate. Her voice sounded close. It grew louder. Leona jerked realizing Quinn had been whispering in her ear. The unexpected proximity disturbed Leona even more. She tried to squeeze herself into the splintery dry wood of the wall at her side.

Quinn whispered, "Are you alright honey? Don't be upset with Nate. He believes in speaking his mind. And don't worry about him bothering you. You just tell him to buzz off and he'll leave you alone."

Ashamed of herself, Leona dropped her hands in her lap and with superhuman effort lifted her head. But when she made contact with Quinn's eyes and recognized the pity in them, Leona looked away, "Sorry."

Quinn's laugh shook Leona. Had she said something funny?

"Why are you apologizing for Nate's whorehound ways? It's not your fault he's so damn horny all the time. Besides you must be used to it," Quinn said with a thoughtful look as she studied Leona's face. An uncomfortable couple of minutes passed with neither of them speaking. Eventually, Quinn shrugged as if to say "whatever" and walked away.

Leona stared at the tabletop trying to figure out why this young woman chose to flatter her unnecessarily. Another misreading? Evidently this kid was just as phony as everyone at the hospital. At the Recovery Center, the staff use to pull that crap on her too. They would claim that even at her worst she looked better than many runway models.

Leona knew their compliments were a trick. Her friends knew better too. It was all a scam. The type of crap manipulators used to get a person to like them. After the first surgery on her face, she'd spent years avoiding mirrors; and when she was forced to look at herself, she would take only a nanosecond to make sure she didn't have a booger in her nose or sleep in her eyes. Otherwise, she didn't want to watch the parade of unfamiliar faces after each successive surgery and especially buy into the magic elixir of flattery.

The first time she heard a nurse say, "Oh Jane. It's like a miracle. Normally it takes years to erase the signs of morbidity and trauma in severe burn cases. I'm just amazed. Most people must go through numerous laser treatments to achieve these results but not you. You must have the most remarkable healing powers." Once Leona turned fifteen all surgeries to mend her broken face and body stopped. The staff claimed her bones were healed and her burns and cuts were invisible. She knew different.

But why would the waitress lie? Leona had no delusions about herself or her looks. She had stopped hoping long before she hit puberty. Teenagers were cruel but at least they were honest. And now another disappointment, now another misreading. The kid had seemed so sweet and kind and most of all honest. And why did strangers like Nate stare at her as if they thought she knew Santa Claus personally? She didn't come bearing gifts or life changing prophecies. She was a nobody.

There was no such thing as a grand scheme, a divine god looking down on them prepared to reward the good and punish the bad. No, it seemed that the bad prospered and died comfortably in their beds while the good truly did die young. In other words, people were no better or worse off than dogs or cats or wild beasts searching for a warm den and a full belly. And when humanity ultimately destroyed itself – no matter – something else would come along and take its place.

The waitress' beautiful siblings had stopped talking. Even the woman behind the bar and the man called Nate paused to turn toward Leona and Quinn. Leona sensed a new tension in the air. She did that to people – made them uncomfortable. She supposed she should look up and try to make light of the situation. Nate disappeared inside the kitchen and returned with a tray.

As he headed toward Leona's table, she cringed wondering what further comment he would think up to humiliate her. Nate ceremoniously dropped a plate of eggs and Canadian bacon and toast with a big glass of cold milk in front of her and with a courtly sweep of his arm and a bow said, "Bon Appetite Sweet Cheeks," ruining the effect by glaring in the direction of the silvered-haired woman as if challenging her to criticize his words.

Leona gazed at the big glass of milk in awe. It had foam on the top and reminded her of the way milk used to be. She drank the milk down in one gulp shuttering with delight at the feel of the cold liquid sliding down her throat and hitting her stomach. The men watched in fascination as she plowed through the eggs and bacon and toast. Her hunger took command and superseded their rudeness.

The tall one with a romantic desire to be marginalized stood up and wandered over to her table. (His name was . . . shit . . . It was on the tip of her tongue . . . Luke . . . yeah. It was Luke). He stopped beside her table and said with a pretense at casualness, "I know you from somewhere? Don't I? You're a student. Yeah. Of course. BSU? I'm right aren't I?"

"I went there once, a long time ago," she said.

He chuckled, "Right, a long time ago, like maybe a year or two at most," then threw over his shoulder. "Hey Zak, she used to go to BSU." When Leona glanced up at Luke the intensity of his stare made her self-conscious. She tried to hide her face with her hair and heard him say, "So what was your major?"

"Secondary Ed," she lied as she finished off the last of her eggs and sensed a sudden disinterest. Even though her major disappointed him, he persisted with the cross-examination as searching for something specific. What could be so important about her time at Boise State University?

"Where have I seen you before," he said to himself and for the benefit of those in the room. Leona waited patiently while those satyr looks produced delightful chemistry inside her body. Her hunger now satiated, other parts of her were awakening. But those feelings were only for private nocturnal moments. She suspected her friends and their conflicting thoughts were to blame. Alarmed she did her best to stomp on them and realized he was still talking.

"Had to have been one of my anthropology classes. Yeah, you took a one hundred level anthropology class, am I right? Huh? Had to have. Sure. I used to be a TA for Dr. Mason, but fieldwork is what I do best, so I left BSU. I'm on my own temporarily. No funding, mind you, but some day with the right contacts I'll find a patron. My name is Luke Nerin by the way and over there is my brother Zak. Quinn is my sister and that's my mom Jule. What's your name?"

"Navan Leona Keys. Everyone calls me Leona," she said accepting his hand reluctantly unable to control the need to look down because looking up and up at him hurt the bone fragments floating around in her neck. Someone had told her once loose particles of bone floating around in the body are normal. The idea frightened Leona. Bits of bone swimming around in the blood and fluids of the body. No. Never. A stabbing pain in her eye made her groan. Self-inflicted. Too much negative thinking. The last thing she heard was a crack as something heavy hit wood.

When Leona woke, the light nearly blinded her and the heat from the sun beat down on her head hot and full of anger. She found herself sitting in a chair in the parking area just outside the Woolly Man staring at the dirt beneath her feet. Someone had his arm around her shoulders. His tone was deceptively soothingly in contrast to his words which were nasty, not what she had expected from him, "How do you know all this? Only a few people know. Don't say anything more troublemaker or I'll shut your mouth for good."

A paradox. Shut her mouth when explanation might save her. Better to ignore the linguistic inconsistency. That sounded like something Ana would come up with – linguistic inconsistency. Try to say that ten times without stumbling. She swallowed a giggle which turned out to be bigger than she thought and hurt her throat, a throat threatening to explode her breakfast in their faces.

Afraid to look directly at Luke, Leona lifted her head and stared at the parked cars wondering if anyone else had overheard him. From the corner of her eye, she saw the older woman called Jule. She thought she heard her son Zak pronounce his mother's name "my kali," as if his mother was his personal Hindu goddess of destruction and of life. Well…why not? The day couldn't get any weirder, could it?

It was obvious the woman belonged to Luke especially around the eyes and the mouth. She stood with her hands on her hips and stared down at Leona as if gazing at some worrisome spot on her floor. Oh yes, she was Luke's mother the one he introduced as Jule. "Luke leave her alone. I'll deal with this problem. You go back inside and calm your brother down."

Regret bubbled up from the black abyss of her thoughts. Then confusion took over. What had she said? She had gone and said something profoundly stupid and now these dangerous people were going to do her some unspeakable harm. Her obligatory visit to Mona Lawson at Bishop's request receded from her agenda. It was imperative to find a way out of this place and as far away from these angry people as she could get. She'd said something truthful which had alarmed them.

Were they bank robbers or cattle rustlers or modern-day highwaymen preying on innocent tourists? They would tell her eventually, perhaps just before they slit her throat. What scared her the most was her reaction to the thought, a leap of excited anticipation at the thought of dying. No more suffering. No need for revenge.

Leona studied the objects within her view. Anyone with any sense at all would have turned around the moment they saw the beat up dusty old vehicles with gun racks in the back windows and hunting dogs drooling all over the vinyl seats, especially after reading the angry sometimes obscene stickers slapped on fenders. Leona noticed one sticker which confused her: a boy pissing on the words – Boise State University.

Hum. This place, this limbo of desert between civilized towns was probably the breeding ground for people like militia groups and serial killers of all ethnicities and perversions. Then she remembered her family's bumper stickers and was forced to admit her own prejudices. When had she become an elitist snob?

The woman knelt before Leona, her hard-good looks and steely expression made Leona shiver in the warm sunlight. "You bloodsucking blackmailers are all alike. So, you got a talent for making trouble? Let me tell you right now, I don't believe in that mumbo-jumbo New-Age shit. So, don't waste your time. You hear me. Don't try it on me or any of my family. I have no patience for skinny bitches like you. What'd you do, go ask a bunch of my neighbors about us? Do some snooping at the courthouse; maybe, checked up on us through some loser friends of my ex-husband? Or do you know my ex-husband's new wife? Did she put you up to this?"

When Leona's legs began to shake, she knew she had to do something. If she let the fear overtake her, she'd never get away. She had to be cunning. "Whatever I said I don't remember. Please. I'm not trying to con anyone. I swear. It's my neck. It's got something to do with the bone spurs in my neck. That's what the doctor told me. I guess I can pick up things the way radios pick up signals."

The woman grabbed a hunk of Leona's bangs and jerked her head up. Pain shot down Leona's neck, down and down, right to the small of her back. The woman's eyes were the color of petrified wood from an ancient oak. "There were things you said that I didn't even know. Who are you?"

"Nobody. I'm nobody. Honest."

Both turned at the sound of the screen door squawking. Nate burst out in his usual wild style with his long hair flapping in the breeze and his short legs eating up the distance between them in. "Holy shit, are you friggin crazy? You want to get sued? Leave the girl alone."

Leona puzzled over his description of her. Was he being serious or just figurative? Nobody had described her as a "girl" for a long time, not for the last thirty or forty years anyway. *Oh, this was not good, go away, please go away*, Leona thought pushing the panic down and ignoring the urge to call in the cavalry. In her preoccupation, Leona missed the first half of Nate's speech, "No sense in letting everyone know our personal business. Get her inside and talk to her. Those damn pawnbrokers are just thieves in disguise. And Leland is the worst. He hired the sick shit. He's the one you should be angry with."

Leland. A thrill of angry excitement nearly burst from her lips in a cascade of words, words which would have ruined everything. Wait. Not yet. Nate could be talking about a totally different Leland. What were the odds of these people knowing Leland? Zero. Then she remembered Nate saying something about a pawnshop. Of course. Of course, it all made sense. Life really was a never-ending reboot of absurd coincidences.

Jule got up close to him. Even though she was three inches shorter and slighter than Nate, she stood belligerently close and seemed much more intimidating than the man, "Smoke, this dirt-bag tried to blackmail us. Remember that. We know nothing about her and, yet she comes in here and says the things she says, private things, stuff that only we know. She's either one crazy-ass bitch or a cop or part of their sick fan club."

"Forget Ray for just one second, will you? This girl has nothing to do with him. Did it ever cross your mind that maybe she is the real thing; maybe, she has some of that ESP we all hear about these days. You know what I mean? There are a few people who really do have it. I know. I met one once."

"Most of them are cheats; they're just good people readers," Jule spat out before marching back to the Woolly Man.

Leona knew exactly what Nate planned to say in response. "Just the kind of person who might come in useful to us," he said to Jule's back as he helped Leona stand.

Zak and Luke were sitting at the bar sipping their beers. Zak ignored Leona. Leona sensed a familiar bemusement mixed with horror. She should be used to people's shocked and disgusted reactions after one of her episodes. Instead the confirmation of his loathing and fear plunged her once again into that dark place she hated to be. Nothing she did would make her life secure again. Nothing she said or did would make the demons go away. Leona had been doing what she did best all her life: placating people. She writhed in shame at her pitiful need to be loved. And as usual her desire to please only turned upon itself and made people even more afraid of her.

Desperate to get the past out of her head, Leona glanced around the inside of the Woolly Man wondering how she'd known Zak's dark secret. Of course, she'd probably intuited much about him from the name of the bar and grill and the maps strewn about the place. The men's interest in archeology probably stemmed from their father's interest in rocks. What did they call those people? Rock hounds, yes, a father who lived in Quartz, Arizona and sold rocks. Wait. No. Quinn's father lived in Quartz, Arizona and sold rocks for a living. Quinn's father was black. He was small and wiry, his ancestors the Bantus of Central Africa. How did she know all this shit? How could she possibly know Quinn's father lived in Quartz, Arizona, or anything else about him?

And what of the other parent, the father of the Nerin brothers? He lived in Montana and had a wife Debra and three young children and? And then the truth dawned upon Leona why Jule looked so angry and sick. Leona sensed the Nerin brothers didn't know the truth. Jule had kept silent to protect her sons. Leona shut her eyes. Were these memories real or made up? Were they anecdotes told to her years ago?

While the women had been crammed inside the small car like old socks in a cardboard box, someone had mentioned the minute the car reached Idaho that the landscape looked familiar. Evidently, one or several of them had spent some time in Idaho or maybe had family in Idaho. None of this situation made sense. It wasn't supernatural. The memories belonged to the others. Please don't say anything about them. Especially not them. Wash the truth away. See the river and the truth tumbling down the rocks and far away. Let the truth trouble someone else.

When she opened her eyes, Leona remembered what she'd said to Luke and Zak. She had warned them to stay away from graves. But she'd meant a different grave site, not the grave they wanted to dig up. Young people were always dreaming up risky projects. She'd seen Zak reading an article in the Archeology Review about the discovery of a particularly rare find – a grave of a warrior woman in the steppes of Russia.

The article had given Zak ideas, ideas about the indigenous people who used to live near Willow Creek and had wintered in the caves near Woolstone. Zak wanted to check out the mounds two miles from the Woolly Man beyond Willow Creek with a half-formed wish that perhaps the distant ancestors of this area had buried their warriors close by. Such a discovery, Zak believed, would make the Nerin brothers respected members of the fraternity of archeologists.

How had she known about the mounds anyway? Why did Woolstone seem so familiar to her? And this bar called Woolly Man – who could forget such a name? The name Nerin sounded familiar too. Not only had she conjured up Zak and Luke's secret from thin air, she had seen the ugly moment which had nearly ruined Zak's life. She must have been there. No, she couldn't have been. Someone inside was telling her she was wrong about a few things but mostly right about the rest.

Now that was a paradox.

Little did Zak know, but he had been a very lucky kid. Most of Leland's victims never had the chance to run away. She wasn't some freaky medium able to speak to the dead. In reality, she was probably more like a receptacle of other people's stories, a sort of living anthology of several family histories – five of them – as a matter of fact. That had to be the explanation for her uncanny accuracy.

From the corner of her eye, Leona took a quick peek at Zak watching as he sipped his beer and stared at the counter while ignoring his mother's thoughtful gaze. Another clue as to how Leona had figured out what the men were interested in. In fact, she'd seen Zak in the process of turning the page of the magazine just as Nate brought her a bowl of chili with chopped onions and wedges of thick cheese on top. The sour cream nipples were exactly the way she'd seen them in her vision. But then again maybe she'd seen a similar bowl being carried across the room and handed to another customer?

She looked around the room and realized there were no other customers, nor had there been any other customers since she'd first entered the bar. There was a perfectly rational explanation for her knowing all these things. She'd probably figure out the how when the truth no longer mattered. She had pissed them all off, not just Zak or Luke. What had she said? There were times when she couldn't remember anything afterwards and times like now when she was scared to the point of peeing her pants and seemed to catch thoughts the way a master fly fisherman might catch a rainbow trout.

Jule's thoughts gave Leona a major headache. There was such heat and anxiety in her. She exuded a mother's fierce protectiveness and paradoxically a profound disappointment – all toward her children. She would protect them even against the truth and perversely would end up hurting them because she lacked faith in their ability to handle adversity. Cleaning clean glasses and wiping an already clean counter then recounting the cash in the cash register seemed to unleash some of the residue of emotion buried behind Jule's tight smile and watchful eyes.

Nate sat down on the bench facing Leona and watched her eat. Leona looked down at her bowl. She was disappointed to discover that there was no bowl in front of her; Nate had simply handed her a glass of water. There had been no chili; therefore, there had been no real physical signs that she could have used to figure out the truth. She accepted the water without looking into his eyes. When he didn't move away, she made herself sip the water. She was extra careful placing the glass on the table worried she might make a noise and bring everyone's attention back to her. Nate had to lean forward to hear her say, "Thank you."

His closeness frightened her. "No, Mr. Nate," she whispered politely trying to tell him to back-off. Overcome by a rush of lava inside her belly, she held her stomach and her mouth.

From far away, she heard him say, "It's not Mr. Nate, just Nate, a name my Pop gave me. My friends call me Smoke. My last name's Cooper . . . My Pop was," he stopped talking the instant her mouth opened.

In a voice nobody recognized, she began to talk, "It isn't Zak's fault. It's Leland's fault. He's a monster. He uses people. He knew what Ray was like when he hired him. But that was years ago. I'm forgetting. Wait. Not 1994. I'm talking about 2001. In 1994, Zak was Leland's victim, but Zak kicked him good and hard and hurt him bad."

The woman's lips stretched into a wide fierce smile, "Yeah. Good for you Zak."

The smile disappeared, "So Zak got away; he was one of the lucky ones. And his mother fought fiercely for him. That's the key to success, that attitude is important. Not to let the shame overshadow your life, blaming yourself, and wanting to hide the shame from your neighbors. That's the key. Expose the monster; bring him out into the light."

The woman's eyes opened staring at nothing in particular, "I know you think I'm some sort of psychic, but I'm not. I probably read about what happened somewhere; maybe in an old newspaper or on the internet. It's a matter of public record. The child's name was omitted, I'm sure of that. I just guessed all this because Zak mentioned *Around the World Pawn*. You see. Easy-Peasy."

"Nobody mentioned the pawn shop's name," Luke told Nate.

From beyond her table Leona sensed them on the move. Bodies were coming closer sucking up the air, making the bubble around her stifling hot with its gathering ugliness. The Nerin family moved in wanting to catch every word. She tried to stop the flood because the words were for Nate alone. It was too late. She tried to mouth the words, but the voice needed to be heard. Inside she writhed in frustration then an overwhelming fear engulfed her and with the wash of blood from her brain down to her groin her body experienced a series of spasmodic orgasms. Unable to stop them, she griped the edges of the table with both hands, bent her head to hide her shame, and let them take over her body, all the while knowing that the words would mask the secret.

The voice grew harsher and louder, a decoy for what was really going on, "Hey there, Smoke. I know you. You're Nate Cooper. Do you remember me? Probably not. I knew you years ago. You were a student of mine. Oh, your beautiful hands, I remember your hands so well. It was Talent Day. Students were allowed to show off their skills on Talent Day whether they thought of themselves as artists, writers, dancers, or musicians. You played the guitar and sang, sang so beautifully too. I do recall you were obsessed with breasts. Any girl in the room, even an old lady like me caught your eye. I mean our breasts caught your eye. Your eyes would just light up at the sight of a big breasted girl."

A different voice broke through and took possession of Leona's vocal cords, "Don't forget *Around the World Pawn*. Who gives a shit about school days long past? The 1990s are over. This is the 21st century and time is running out. Don't forget Leland is an evil prick. He is an evil douche bag of a man and no one seems to notice his crimes. Twenty friggin years of pedophilia, white slavery, kidnapping, and murder and you have the nerve to reminisce about some stupid Talent Day?

Idiots.

Fuck-brains.

What are you all doing – playing with your toes or cleaning out your navels? Get with it. Punish this a-hole. If you don't; I will. Someday I will. Someday the world will know how evil he really is and the one that pays him; she's just as bad. No! She's worse, much, much worse. She's supposed to be decent, but she's filthy. She's a smelly-rotten soul who must be removed from the human race."

The compulsion which had overtaken her abruptly seized its control over her limbs and her mind. By the time Leona had finished speaking, Nate was on his feet and staring down at her as if she'd grown an extra head on her shoulders. Zak and Luke had backed off in embarrassment for their old friend, stifling their discomfort with giggles, their giggles drowned out by Jule's loud and angry admonishments for everyone to shut up. All of them were staring at Leona now with identical expressions of horrified curiosity as if she were a grisly victim of a ten-car pile-up. Jule walked over and touched Nate's shoulder, "You alright hon?"

Nate's benevolent expression returned. Beneath the surface something burned brightly behind Nate's eyes, unseen by the others, but neon to Leona. He was furious. Leona had effectively extinguished his pity. She straightened her shoulders. Pity was the last thing she wanted from anyone. Then the tingling in her belly started all over again and the flood of words expelled from her mouth once more though she tried her damnedest to swallow them.

She heard herself say, "I really wish there were a hell. I really, really do. I want there to be a hell, so that Ray and his kind burn there for eternity. But most of all I want science to figure out a way that the Rays of the world cannot be born or that they are caught early and the nasty part of them cut out. I'm so sorry Zak, so sorry you were one of his victims too. I wish." Leona drew breath and tried to choke back the flood, but her throat burned, and her stomach rolled with waves of nausea when she tried to stop. Wetness ran down from the corners of her eyes and from her nose and landed salty and gooey in her mouth.

"What fills the belly better than heat? I have this habit now of munching on cookies or crackers or something and then taking a nap. I'm a baby again, sleepy when my stomach is full. I fill my belly with food and dream lustful dreams. That is how I live now. I used to smoke cigarettes as a way of filling my belly, only my belly would be full of smoke and my blood swimming with nicotine. I did everything I could to prevent the emptiness and loneliness from rising to the surface of my psyche strangling me with the truth. The truth that no matter how much we fill our bellies with food, sex, and babies we are still isolated from each other and can never truly share the same experiences. We can tell each other stories, but even the stories are lies. And those stories become their stories and so on and so on until the kernel of truth dies. I'm ready to daydream now. I know it's an escape and I don't care."

No one moved. Leona heard a fly battering against the screen door. She empathized with the fly. She too wanted to run, run as fast as she could to the nearest quiet motel room and hope to never see another expression on anyone's face as the one that played across Zak's beautiful countenance. One moment his cheeks were aflame the next white as snow. Before the shock wore off there were suspicious tears in his eyes.

The giggling stopped. For a nanosecond Luke looked ashamed of himself for his juvenile outburst. Then his face relaxed into its customary sarcastic disbelief. He was the first one to move toward her as Zak headed for the door. But Zak didn't get a chance to leave because his mother moved faster. Zak switched gears and walked towards Leona's table shoving Luke aside. He gazed at her with a bewildered expression.

"Please don't be mad Zak," Leona tried to say. "It just comes over me sometimes. I don't know where it comes from. It can't be true. It's something intangible, something outside me that wants to cause mischief."

Zak brushed past his mother and disappeared around the corner. Leona heard a door open and shut ending with a bolt sliding into place effectively locking people out and locking the occupant inside the room. Jule followed him and Leona heard her banging on his door. "Let me in Zak. Let me in please." Jule smacked the door a couple of times, then gave up and stood listening. A few minutes passed. The door opened. Leona heard Jule slip inside.

Leona felt sick at what had happened, not sick enough to puke, just sick enough to worry that she wouldn't be able to control the spasms. She'd only experienced the spasms twice in her life, once with Dr. Bishop in his office and once alone in her hospital room in the wee hours of the morning. Her new friends had been supportive and understanding; in contrast, Dr. Bishop pretended a clinical detachment he did not feel. After her outburst, he changed his mind about committing her for another year. Instead, he set in motion her early release from the hospital. A few days later he suggested she go see his former patient Mona Lawson.

She still wondered what she had said to Dr. Bishop to change his mind. Before the outburst he had ignored her requests claiming they were a classic example of female histrionics while also making up excuses why she couldn't be discharged. One of her favorites was his claim she was detached from reality. She knew which one of them was the crazy one in the room; and it wasn't her. Since no one had come forward to claim her and the police had no clues as to her identity much less nationality, he had taken on the responsibility of her care personally citing charity and love of humanity as his reason for keeping her a prisoner.

She had seen through his lies. She knew that his real aim was to use her as a case study for his own glorious research into the weak female brain and how his techniques would someday cure PTSD as well as a number of exotic mental illnesses he'd been creating in the long sleepless nights. Over the years each new nurse arriving at the ward would be given Leona's back story: how she'd been discovered by a couple of Canadians portaging their way home and life-flighted to the nearest hospital which was in Ely, Minnesota. That she had been found on a small island in the Boundary Waters between Minnesota and Canada.

The nurses were also told how she'd woken up while in the helicopter and when the EMTs questioned her said an angel with long dark curls and brown eyes had saved her life, that the angel rescued her from a burning building and carried her across the night sky then left her on the front lawn of the hospital. The nurses were also told she'd created this fantasy as a way of shutting out the truth. Once she arrived in the Emergency Room at the Ely Hospital, the doctors soon discovered she had burns over eighty percent of her body. The local police claimed she'd been beaten, doused with gasoline, and nearly burned alive.

That wasn't what happened. That story was made up. She didn't understand why they would fabricate the crime committed against her. Years later she decided people needed lies as a way of keeping their brains from burning out with so many unanswered questions pinging around in their empty shitty heads. She knew different. The angel had been real. The only medical and historical truth the nurses and staff were told was that when Leona entered the Critical Care Unit the doctors immediately placed her in a coma to help her mind and body heal.

Thank you, coma. Thank you, amnesia.

No sense in reliving the past while awake – that was just masochistic; after all, her nightmares made sure to keep her up to date and were relentless in rehashing all the ugly moments. Yet she had to be grateful for those spasms. If not for them she might still be a prisoner of the Eight Ball Ward. Leona turned to those left in the room. Quinn had backed off to hide behind the counter. She was busily straightening stuff under the sink and wiping imaginary spots off the glass window. A chip off the old block. Luke kept staring at Leona, staring so intensely she wondered if his eyes would fall out of their sockets and land on his shoes. Luke walked over to his sister Quinn and bending at the waist whispered something in her ear.

Leona watched them from beneath her eyelashes. Luke was easy to figure out; he was smart and analytical with a slice of narcissism which made his sexiness even more dangerous. She flipped through the images in her head of him interacting with his family followed by his questions to her and winced at some of the chilling examples of his zealous ambition. Luke really was obsessed about discovering a rare and wondrous archeological find which would make the world stand up and take notice of him at last.

Zak, on the other hand, she saw only the one unhappy image from his childhood and could see no more. From what she could figure out with her own two eyes – Zak was a beautiful man who avoided the limelight by deliberately making himself look grungy and dirt poor, who had a hair-trigger temper, and seemed too sensitive for these backwoods, small town life, and crude surroundings. He seemed more comfortable as a loner hiking in the desert, turning over rocks, digging holes to find arrowheads and rusty bits of metal that might be from pilgrims on the Oregon Trail. And if he discovered something truly amazing, he seemed like the kind of person who would be at odds with himself, knowing in the back of his mind, he should offer the find to a museum yet reluctant to let go.

Zak had left – not because of the attempted rape in his past and his family learning the truth from a stranger but for another reason. Why? A moment of shame washed over her. She wished she could go back and unsay everything. Then she understood. It was ironic really. Luke should be the atheist in the family with his analytical approach to everything but now she was convinced Luke believed in the supernatural.

When Leona had had her seizures, which included bits of historical fact confirmed by those present in the room, Luke had been vibrating with smug excitement realizing his secret suspicions had been confirmed. Zak, when confronted by her seizures was so disgusted with everyone in the room, he had had to leave, afraid his temper would get the best of him. He believed her seizures were an act and she was a phony grifter trying to get money out of them all.

Luke turned his back on Leona and pretended to be disinterested in the spooky female with the ventriloquist act knowing very well the impression he made on people, his beauty and agility was something he took for granted. He liked his hair long because the style exaggerated his height and leanness whereas his brother Zak preferred his hair short and spikey which Zak believed made him appear older and more menacing. Leona had an unreasonable urge to laugh out loud at them. Men were just as vain as women.

After nearly twenty minutes of peace and quiet while also being carefully ignored by those left in the room, Leona began to relax. Maybe they would leave her alone now? She was just in this stupid bar to meet Mona Lawson to placate Dr. B and maybe have something to eat before moving on. She figured her eccentricities and weird voices would be the topic of conversation by this family for many months to come but eventually they would forget about her and figure she was just one of those poor pathetic homeless crazies everybody tried desperately to ignore.

When Luke took off Leona was surprised by her reaction. She watched as he marched out of the bar, watched with a sense of loss and regret. From outside she heard another door opening, a heavier door made of metal. Car doors don't sound like that anymore. She connected the sound with her childhood, a heavy door opening, a heavy door belonging to some sort of muscle car.

Then she remembered when she first arrived squeezing between a Camaro and a truck feeling the heat radiating off both as if she were making her way through a gigantic incinerator for dinosaurs. The truck had so much gray primer along its heaving flanks, it reminded her of a poor old rhino napping in the sun. She had tried unsuccessfully to avoid touching either vehicle and still managed to get a streak of mud on her sleeve.

Appreciating the coolness inside the bar, she listened to the sound of the creaking of old hinges again as Luke closed the Camaro door. Luke's return surprised her; somehow, she'd expected him to drive off into the sunset. Instead he walked inside carrying an old Navaho blanket in his arms and walked straight up to her with a nasty glint in his eye. When he dropped the blanket in her lap, she just stared at him unable to think clearly. For a tingling moment, she wondered if blanket-tossing was some sort of ritualistic invitation to have sex in this part of Idaho.

"Here, tell me something about the person who owned this blanket."

"It doesn't work that way," Leona said.

Luke leaned toward her, his hands resting on the table, his nose nearly touching her nose. She could smell the beer on his breath and his musky underarms. It was a clean smell not sweaty and nasty. My God, she thought, even his smell is erotic. That isn't fair. She had an overwhelming urge to kiss those full lips. He sensed it and smiled wickedly.

"You do this for me and maybe I'll do something for you in return."

A fly crawled across Navan Leona Keys' hand, but she didn't move. They were alone in the room. Quinn had disappeared. Leona could hear Quinn clomping up the stairs to the second-floor rooms in her heavy platform shoes. No, she told herself, they call them wedges now. She pulled the blanket towards her and closed her eyes.

She saw the people in the bar from her perch near the ceiling looking down upon them with intense hunger. She pushed off from the beam to circle the room capturing objects and prey with her keen eyes. The space expanded to include the outdoors as walls fell away. She could see the tops of trees and rooflines. Sometimes she saw the Woolly Man, sometimes a dark road. She hated endless spaces and darkness.

A single image refused to go away. It was blurry. She should be tired of the process by now, but she knew that if she were patient enough the dusky quality would miraculously sharpen, the shapes would become people and furniture or maybe a landscape she could identify. She fingered the fold of the Navaho blanket on her lap. Cashmere meant expensive, affluent, pampered. Sturdy wool meant cold harsh winters and hardworking people. She was happy to be close to something which represented pragmatic resilience.

Many people prized the Navaho blankets. This blanket she knew intimately. It was the main reason she'd traveled two thousand miles from Chicago to Idaho. And here she was in Idaho in a quaint western town with a bar and grill reminiscent of a bad Hollywood movie with the bonus of an erotic young male offering her a sex substitute. Just like that, serendipitous, an offering from the gods, an offering made by a gorgeous male with a hard body she so wanted to press against. This gift meant she didn't have to go traipsing all over the damn place asking Mona Lawson dumb questions about Leland, *Around the World* and Indian artifacts.

Here was the blanket – a familiar friend. Joy surged up her spine spreading throughout her body. The blanket lay on her lap and covered the tabletop. She moved her hands along the fabric thinking about the woman who used to own it. Was her DNA still clinging to the threads of the blanket even now? What about the rest of them? She pulled the blanket closer to her face smelling the old wool.

Collective insanity. Leona swallowed a giggle. It hurt going down.

Like magic the memories came back to her. Leona fingered the rough surface and the fold down the center. She could feel something crusty in the fold, some spilled food that had hardened. The blanket smelled of sour milk and sweat and ground-in-dirt. This blanket had been loved to death not just by her. The idea of that other, that most special other loving this blanket, holding this blanket as if holding a life preserver made her heart race in anxiety for her.

Something else landed on the Navaho blanket. It was a metal object; the point of a spear maybe. She refused to let go of the blanket yet with her left hand she explored the spear. "It's been in our family for several generations," she heard Luke say somewhere above her head and then he paused and addressed a person standing across the room. "It's alright Quinn. I'll keep an eye on the bar. Take a break or something."

"No. I'll stay until Mom comes back. You're too busy acting like a jerk. Why don't you leave the poor girl alone? Can't you see she's scared?"

Luke ignored her and said to Leona, "This artifact has been in our family for several generations. It's the head of a spear, I believe from at least a hundred years ago. It was found not far from here by my great great-grandmother. Can you tell us anything about it? We need to find the original burial tomb. We need a place to start digging and we want to find the rest of the objects that go along with this spear. Do you sense anything yet?"

Leona heard a door open and two sets of footsteps, one lighter most likely Jule Nerin followed by a heavier tread in clomping boots most definitely belonging to Zak. Leona refused to open her eyes and see disbelief, disgust and/or hate in theirs. A desperate need to separate herself from these hostile people in this unhappy room washed over her, preventing her from returning to the blurry photograph in her head.

Then she remembered the blanket and her promise to the others. She used one of her old tricks, a silent prayer Terrence had taught her as a method of escaping the present and returning to the in-between. Her body relaxed, and she went as far under as possible. It was safe here. The others welcomed her home.

Jule Nerin hid behind the bar wiping down an already clean dry counter. She needed to do something with her time. No normal person just sat there staring off into space and damn sure not for nearly an hour. She glanced at her daughter. Quinn had finished her chores and since there were no customers and hadn't been for the last fifty minutes this crazy woman was sleeping with eyes open, Quinn proceeded to apply new nail polish to her fingernails. Jule looked across the room at her sons. The sight of them made her proud. Her children were beautiful and normal. They were normal and clean and pure. Their offspring would be healthy and strong and intelligent unlike- Jule doubled over surprised by her reaction.

The screen door slammed, and a voice announced to anyone interested, "I've arrived at last. Anyone feeling up to some Cordon Bleu? I'm starved."

The spell broke and the others in the room shifted cramped legs and arms. Jule threw the dust rag under the counter and moved toward the bottles of beer. Quinn jumped off the barstool and wandered toward the jukebox. Luke lifted his arms and leaned back stretching his long torso. Zak sitting across from him at one of the tables threw back his chair, stood up, and wandered over to the window to make sure Nate hadn't parked too close to his Camaro.

The only person in the room who hadn't moved nor so much as twitched when Nate burst through the door was the crazy female sitting at the table in a trance in the farthest corner of the room. Her table was near the window with the hanging plant of Wandering Jew's purple and green leaves tickling her hair. The leaves were beginning to curl into themselves slowly dying from neglect. No one had noticed for weeks until today. Quinn itched to water the plant wishing the customer would finish her phony psychic mumbo-jumbo and leave the bar.

The strange woman remained unmoved by Nate's grand entrance. With the sun beating down on her dark head, the woman called Navan Leona Keys had been sitting frozen and stiff on the bench seat staring off into space like a mannequin in a shop window, the Navaho blanket in her lap and the spear lying on top of the table. The only parts of her moving were her fingers over the blanket and her lips as she murmured words Quinn couldn't catch.

Luke sat at a table nearby with his laptop open and his hands poised on the keyboard waiting for her words as if waiting for God to speak. "I didn't get that last bit? Was that 2001? This all happened in 2001? That name sounds familiar. She taught at BSU. Holy shit! Professor Wade disappeared around that time!" he exclaimed in an excited voice.

The crazy clairvoyant stopped stroking the blanket and without warning something dangerous entered the room. They could all feel the change in her. A foreign expression crossed Leona's face. Even Nate paused in the act of moving toward the kitchen and stared at her. The shy nervous woman who had entered the Woolly Man was gone. In her place was someone cold, hard, and calculating.

Those sensitive enough to appreciate the transformation were shocked. Zak jerked up off his stool feeling a sudden need to protect his brother. He reconsidered his move when the foreign look vanished from Leona's face. Embarrassed by his reaction, he settled back on the barstool feeling sick to his stomach. That wasn't natural. How had she done it? Not even the greatest actor in the world could pull off something so creepy.

Nate nearly dropped his packages. When he again looked across the room, he relaxed recognizing the crease in Leona's forehead as she concentrated on her task and the sweet dreaminess of her expression returned. Quinn had had her back to the tables as she busily blew on her newly painted nails, so she missed the peculiar transformation of Leona's sweetness overlaid by a mask of murderous calculation.

Those who had been present in the room when the psychic struggle began were unintentional voyeurs, unable to look away the way people were fascinated by a car accident or circus sideshow, a thing both horrifying and singular. They were compelled to watch the crazy female caress the blanket and whisper nonsense because the sight was outside their normal experiences. They listened to her talk about camping in Succor Creek National Park and were chilled wondering how she could change the tone, cadence, and vibrancy of her voice so easily.

Instead of speaking in her usual soft breathless way hesitating between thoughts, Leona was now speaking in a clipped assured manner with a clarity of purpose unlike the young woman, where every word was a precise rendition as if words were second nature to her reminding each of them of past teachers, lecturers, and a few rare extraordinary politicians. The voice was a public speaking voice. It sounded strange coming from Leona's lips. It didn't fit with her age or personality. Most of the listeners realized the voice belonged to a much older woman, most likely middle-aged, a mature sophisticated highly intelligent woman with a variety of interests. Leona, who looked as if she was in her early twenties couldn't possibly know so much about music, art, literature, history, and archeology.

As the performance ground on the people in the room grew more uncomfortable. Some of them were downright disturbed; others were more skeptical. Nate gave Leona high scores for her acting abilities. Zak wished she'd stop making a fool of herself. Quinn thought the whole experience was hilarious and wished she'd remembered to bring her cellphone downstairs to record the event because none of her friends were going to believe her later. Jule Nerin wished she'd thrown away all the boys' comic books and paid more attention to the garbage they watched on television. They could be atheists and yet believe in ghosts and mediums and freaks like this nut – how was that possible?

Zak moved about the room restlessly wondering when the woman would wake up and tell them something concrete. He needed some answers. He needed to be doing something productive not sitting here twiddling his thumbs. He looked across the room at her again. The girl was pale and skinny with black hair shinny and soft and cropped to just below her chin. Her bangs touched her closed eyelids and along her right cheekbone a few strands of hair curled towards her lips, the ends still wet. He'd thought his blue jeans loose enough until the erection made him bolt for the bathroom.

A part of Leona sensed a shift in the energy of the room. From above the room, Navan Leona Keys looked down at herself. She was sitting at the table fingering the blanket. She noticed herself sucking strands of her hair. A bad habit just like her other bad habit of chewing her nails until they bled. Her closest and dearest friend had cured her of nail biting. She remembered his kind black face and his gentle words, "Are you feeling insecure? Is that why you chew your nails? Why do you think that is?" Leona had found a new habit to cultivate; now she sucked her finger or her hair or any object available, most often pens or pencils. Her friend was Terence. She smiled remembering his face and then she began to cry remembering he was dead.

9

The crying brought Zak rushing back into the bar. It had been an earsplitting high-decibel cry. He assumed a child had been injured. When he looked around the room, he realized the same actors were on the stage: the woman Navan Leona Keys was still in the far corner her hands clutching the Navaho blanket, her eyes shut pretending to be in a trance; Luke, at a table nearby was frantically writing in his notebook; and Quinn was busily flitting from potted plant to potted plant watering the neglected and mostly dead vegetation. Unlike the others, his mother had her back to the room doing something industrious behind the counter.

The sound was a primitive wail of grief and pain, so primitive that most adults would come running expecting to find a helpless child in need of rescue. But there was no child in the room, only four adults. His brother and mother seemed unmoved by the crying. The only people affected seemed to be Quinn and himself. He wanted the crying to stop. But this was no ordinary situation. This wasn't a child who could be picked up and rocked and bribed with candy. This was a grown woman, a stranger to them all. Then he got a look at her face. He froze unable to move any further.

Quinn dropped the watering can on the nearest café table and moved toward the girl. Jule rushed out from behind the counter and grabbed Quinn's arm preventing her daughter from reaching the crying woman, all the while shaking her head and saying, "She may have you all fooled but not me. This is an act. She's trying to manipulate us." As if Jule's words had been a caution to them all, everyone returned to their respective places and waited.

The only person who seemed oblivious to the strangeness of the situation was Luke. He was too busy marking the moment in his notebook to even look up. Eventually the crying stopped. Zak would never forget the stranger's transformation, the moment when a child's face superimposed itself onto Leona's face, a child with big green eyes, a pug nose, and chubby cheeks. Later, he would assume what he had seen was a trick of the light. It was late afternoon and the sun was beginning to set behind the foothills surrounding them. It must be the light. There were many shadows in the bar. It was an old building with old glass windows and the gathering gloom was playing tricks on them.

In the silence which seemed to go on forever, something new and frightening entered the room. They all saw it: Luke, Zak, and Quinn. Even Luke saw it this time. He looked up from his notebook sensing a strong presence. A different person had taken over Leona's body. Equally as disturbing as the previous one, this new persona looked wrong on all sorts of levels: an aged infirm woman looked about the room with a calm acceptance of the room's occupants as if the sight of all these people staring at her did not surprise her in the least. How Leona managed to convey this new persona without contorting her body into the appearance of someone with the curved back of osteoporosis or head tremors or the spasmodic dysphonia of a raspy quivering voice was a miracle.

A creeping trickle of revulsion permeated the air. Some who were sensitive enough to recognize the wrongness of a young woman speaking and behaving as if she were a decrepit old woman turned away from the sight hoping by ignoring the stranger's crazy behavior, the crazy would go away. It did not.

The crazy began to talk, "Your mother is afraid. It is understandable. Many people are afraid of what they don't understand. But she's wrong about Navan. Navan isn't here to manipulate or con anyone. Your brother Luke seems to think Navan can help him find the whereabouts of an ancient burial site through some hocus pocus spiritual mumbo jumbo crap. He truly believes Navan can communicate with the dead. Well she can't. No one can. Professor Wade is not here. She is long gone and at peace. She can't help you find your legacy. Go back to the tested and true methods of research and excavation. You don't need the occult to find what you seek. Leave this poor child alone."

Zak glanced over at his mother. She appeared to be preoccupied with drying the inevitable shot glasses and staring off into space. Only the occasional grimace revealed that she had taken in the woman's words and did not like the gentle rebukes. Unlike his mother, Luke was transfixed by Leona's performance. He had dropped his pen and was staring at Leona with his mouth slightly open; his eyes took in every gesture and word with a sort of gleeful wonder.

Then Zak turned to see Quinn's reaction. Quinn sat at the bar sipping from a tall glass of clear liquid filled with ice seemingly bored out of her mind while flipping through her favorite fashion magazine without really looking at the pictures or reading the articles. It was in the twitching of her shoulders that he recognized his sister's discomfort. At the end of each sentence, Quinn would physically try to shake off the bizarreness of hearing Leona talk about herself in the third person using the vocabulary of an older generation while chastising their mother.

Admiration leaped up in his chest at the sight of his sister's smoky skin and long black hair cascading down her back with those braided metal doohickeys clinking together whenever she moved. Just as an artist will focus intensely on the person or landscape he wishes to represent on canvass, Zak, with nothing else to do with his time focused on Quinn. He knew without even knowing how he knew about the core of strength at the center of her being. She'd been born with it. She had never doubted herself or been interested in self-reflection like other girls. Zak admired her strength and the easy way she moved through life. But her style wasn't his style. Just sitting back and watching life go by had never appealed to him.

Like the boys, his mother had chosen to name Quinn after the Greek word *nereid* which was a reference to *one from the sea*. Nereids were the daughters of Nereus, the old man of the sea. They were young and beautiful. And supposedly there were fifty of them. Quite an achievement for an old man. Hard to imagine even a rich old man fathering fifty daughters. But that's Greek mythology for you – over the top and narcissistic as hell. And after a childhood of being force fed family legends, he was hardily sick of hearing about their fantastical family history. It was all crap.

In Zak's family, the naming ceremony became a tradition, when the first female descendant immigrated from Greece to America in 1824. Her first act upon landing in the new world was to change her surname to Nerin and refuse to answer to any other name. She'd been a widow at sixteen. The tradition was passed down from generation to generation with the women in the family formerly changing their surnames. A few male descendants rejected family tradition but overall most of them raised on the stories of their illustrious heritage chose to officially change their surnames when they reached sixteen.

Jule Nerin chose to bypass the sixteen-year mile marker and instead made the name official from the moment of her children's births. Nerin had been written down on all their birth certificates without any objections from David Guy (Zak and Luke's father) or Parker Youngblood (Quinn's father). Jule Nerin's husbands had been willing to give up patriarchal tradition for some ridiculous family legend. Zak had learned the hard way that the stories families told each other often sprang from unmet desires, irrational fears and/or hubris. Even as a child, Zak had thought his mother's obsession with finding Amara seemed frightening in its illogical intensity.

He remembered as a child the nightly ritual. Mom would tuck them in and recite the oral history of their family. It was never written down and always the same. She never deviated from the narrative or added to it. Every night she would sit in the rocking chair near their beds reciting the story that had been told to her by her mother and her mother's mother and so on from the first official Nerin immigrant (who probably made the whole thing up anyway) with the expectation that each generation would carry on the tradition and tell the story to their children.

"Here is our story. Listen carefully children. In ancient Greece our ancestor Ocypete, one of four hounds owned by Zeus which the Greek people referred to as a harpy and her sisters called Swiftwing lived in a cave on Crete with her family. Unlike her sisters, Ocypete was curious about humans. It was her habit to fly alone at night over villages observing the mortals as they rested from their labors. She had so many questions to ask them:

Why did their young take so long to grow?

Why did they live in puny homes?

Why did their hair grow white and their backs grow crooked?

Why did they bury their dead?

Years passed and Ocypete grew restless. She no longer trusted her sisters and Zeus. Her sisters could be just as capricious, cruel, and unyielding as the Gods. As the middle sister, she struggled against the bonds of her older sisters and the temper of Zeus. She wanted to be free to fly anywhere in the world and to do anything she wished without first having to beg her sisters or Zeus for the privilege of doing what came naturally to her – soaring above the clouds and swooping down from the sky like an arrow killing her prey cleanly with one stroke of her deadly claws.

One night, flying over an island near her home, she spied a young man pulling his small craft up onto the beach. Curious she circled the sky above him and watched as he lit a fire and began to cook a roasted lamb on a spit. Even in the sky the scent of roasted meat tempted her. Yet Zeus forbid her from interfering with mortals unless the mortal had disobeyed Zeus' laws. For several nights, she flew near the island and saw the young man cooking his supper and drinking his wine before a roaring fire. On the third night, she could no longer contain her curiosity and hunger; she descended from the sky and broke bread with him.

He was so handsome and kind that after several weeks she fell in love with him. They met many times on the shores of Crete. Ocypete kept her love for him secret. Eventually the young man confessed to her that he was Aiolos, the son of Poseidon. It was too late for Ocypete for she was with child. Everyone knew Zeus was a vengeful master and he would not take kindly to his brother's son falling in love with one of his hell hounds.

Zeus punished the lovers by taking Ocypete's child away from her and bestowing the child on a mortal family. Aiolos was banished to the depths of the ocean by his father Poseidon and changed into a creature who crawled on the bottom never seeing the light of day or the sky above until Zeus and Poseidon agreed that he would never betray the Gods again. Zeus granted Aiolos lordship over the winds giving him an island of his very own. During his immortal life, he married a beautiful woman and had many beautiful children by her. Even today, he lives a happy and free life, remaining as handsome as ever, never growing old and never experiencing pain like us.

The family Katsaros (meaning curly haired) raised the little girl as their own and when she was of age to marry, arranged for her to marry a wealthy son of a neighbor Alexis Sikaz. They called her Adoni (she who fights dragons) and no one in the village knew that she was the child of a demi-god and a harpy. She never exhibited the physical appearance of a harpy or the powers of a demi-god. But when Adoni and Alexis' child was born she had tiny protrusions on her back which over the following years became fully functional wings and when extended reached two feet beyond her finger tips.

In half the time of a normal mortal, her chubby arms, legs, and baby torso evolved into the voluptuous body of a fully-grown woman. Her mother insisted she hide her webbed toes and retract her long sharp black claws – lethal tools for tearing apart prey – when out of doors or when humans were near. Every morning, Adoni bound her daughter's chest in strips of linen and wrapped her entire body from the neck down in a sheet. When her daughter began to crawl, Adoni insisted her curious and wayward offspring wear tiny boots made of leather her mother had sewn with her own hands even though Greeks preferred to wear sandals or nothing at all on their feet.

For months, her husband saw only his daughter's head covered in reddish gold curls. One day, Adoni entered her dressing room to find her husband bending over their daughter's cradle and unwinding the sheet. He looked up from his work to say over his shoulder, "I heard her crying. Look at her. She is burning up. Sweat is pouring off her little body. She is too hot in this sheet. You are making her suffer unnecessarily." Upon seeing for the first time his daughters clawed feet and lifting her up to find the budding of downy wings protruding from her shoulder blades, Alexis Sikaz banished his wife and the creature she had tried to pass off as his child from his villa and the village.

He soon remarried the widow of his neighbor. Banished from her home and her village, Adoni, in defiance of her husband's claim that her daughter was an abomination, named her Amara (meaning beautiful) and Katsaros for the family who had accepted them. She returned to her adopted family who revealed to Adoni her true heritage, that she was the offspring of Ocypete, and Aiolos was her father, the son of Poseidon. To learn more about her heritage, Adoni traveled to Crete and found her mother Ocypete. Ocypete begged Zeus to forgive her daughter and granddaughter asking that he make them human so that they might live among the Greek people.

Zeus forgave his favorite hound Ocypete and hid her granddaughter's deformities from mortals. He warned them to never forget to give thanks to the Gods and to the sea and always to worship the old ways. If they forgot to worship him, Amara would be turned back into her true form. Because the women were born of a demi-god and a harpy they did not grow old or die of old age like humans. Their heritage condemned them to travel from town to town, reinventing themselves in each new place. They discovered they could be killed when Adoni fought a dragon and the dragon slashed at her arm with its claws and she nearly bled to death. They could never marry for fear humans would discover their secret and put them to death.

Through the centuries, Adoni worshipped the Greek Gods and gave thanks to the sea. Her daughter Amara, on the other hand, ignored her mother's warnings and neglected the Gods sure that her beauty would overwhelm the men she met and make them her slaves. When she fell in love with a British sailor and ran away with him to his home on a cold island and then took passage on a ship to America, she came face to face with Zeus' cruel punishment of those who ignored his warnings.

The sailor returned to Greece the following year and confronted by Adoni admitted that he had killed the creature in his bed and only after she lay dying did she turn back into Amara. He claimed he had thrown her overboard in the middle of the night. The sailor had been on the ship HMS Discovery captained by George Vancouver and when the captain discovered he had hidden Amara on his ship, he set them both ashore. The stowaway and the sailor boarded the ship Columbia captained by Robert Gray. It was on the Columbia that Amara woke to find her lover stabbing her in the chest.

When Adoni pulled out her weapon to plunge the blade into the sailor's heart, he begged her not to kill him and claimed to have seen natives of the Americas pull Amara's body out of the river. From the ship, he could tell that Amara was still alive. Adoni plunged her blade into his heart anyway hating him for taking her beloved daughter away from her and for admitting that he had tried to kill her. Adoni set out for America determined to find her daughter. Five years later in 1796, she landed on American soil.

She traveled west and searched for her daughter and over the years met several men and had children with them. Unlike her daughter Amara, her children did not live forever. Several died in infancy and one son died in battle. She returned to Greece determined that if the children showed signs of the curse, she would kill them herself. Her ten children obeyed the will of Zeus and before Adoni died she was the matriarch of forty-seven grandchildren and two hundred and five great great-grandchildren. When her children were old enough to fend for themselves, Adoni left them knowing the gossips would wonder why their mother never got any older. Three of the youngest great-grandchildren immigrated to America. Adoni while fighting for Greek Independence (disguised as a man) died in Moldovia when an Ottoman arrow pierced her heart.

Our family chose to remain in America in the Pacific Northwest and search for our ancestor Amara Katsaros. Even though we must journey every year to the ocean to give thanks to Zeus, we live in the desert with the expectation that one day we will find Amara and return her to Crete where her body belongs."

And once the tale was told, their mother ignored their questions, turned out the light and left the room leaving them to discuss the story then later argue amongst themselves as to the truth of it. Back when they were young and impressionable, they never questioned the truth of it. But when they reached their teens and were generally more skeptical, she grew more taciturn and stubborn refusing to listen to their counterarguments.

With a bit of snooping, Zak discovered their family story sprang from an ancient grudge, a loss of imagined power and a desire for revenge against a neighbor from the old country. His research uncovered the fact that the Nerin's nemesis had long ago died without any direct descendants. The whole stupid family obsession was seared in his memory – forever - by the antics of his Aunt Esther. At the time, he'd been about nine years old and on an excursion to the mall with a few friends. Aunt Esther volunteered to be their chaperone and drove them to the mall. For most of the day, they ran in and out of shops on a spending spree, ate lots of junk food and managed to get Aunt Esther to buy them a few cheap toys.

Their last stop had been to the ice cream parlor and while sitting at a booth, Aunt Esther proceeded to regale his friends with Nerin history. She told his friends the Nerins were direct descendants of Poseidon's mortal children and went into great detail about how such a wondrous thing came to pass. His friends went home and told their parents Zak was a member of the royal family. They got a British Monarchy and a Greek myth mixed up and thought Zak was the great great-grandson of the Queen of England.

So, over the years, from Jule's mother, grandmother, great grandmother, and as far back as the women wanted to believe the story, the children had been christened Nerin and the women had insisted their husbands either change their names or allow the mothers to legally change their children's surnames. Thus, the matriarchal line had continued (according to his mother) for nearly one hundred and ninety-three years. It had been his mother's fondest wish that once Amara was discovered, the family would return to Greece and find the temple on the island of Delos and give thanks to Poseidon.

Nuts, he thought, he would do no such thing. They were all bloody-ass nuts.

Zak glanced at Leona, the one Luke believed might have an answer to their family prayers; the one he was beginning to suspect might be more like a slobbering-spider-eating moron in a black and white vampire movie. There she was with the babbling mouth that needed to be filled with words or food or whatever the hell someone like her conjured up from her sick brain. He was completely and unequivocally mortified – embarrassed for his family and furious at being associated with the woman and a party to the whole messy stupid drama.

He'd couldn't help his reaction. It had been happening to him since he was a kid. Whenever someone said or did something in public that was crazy, a wave of embarrassment would wash over him for that person and for himself as a witness to the mayhem. Because invariably there was always mayhem. Right at this very moment, he itched to slap her out of her playacting and get the real story of why she was in their bar asking about Mrs. Lawson the Loony Tune Lady.

Was he any different than his mother? He tried to imagine explaining his family history to outsiders. Everyone would think he was just as crazy. Crazy was his mother and the women before her and this poor orphan sitting in a trance in front of him channeling the spirit world, so pale, twitchy, and Gothic reminding him uncomfortably of a sexy Romani (what his mother's generation called gypsy), a Romani with perfect breasts and haunting green eyes. No, this Romani wasn't crazy. She probably really believed in her spirit world. The real crazies were the members of his family especially his brother Luke. Quinn was the exception – the only sane one among them.

The old woman speaking through Leona had stopped talking. Zak looked over at the stranger who had entered their place of business and turned them all into voyeurs. He relaxed recognizing the sweet quiet expression of the young woman they knew as Leona. Her eyes were still closed but she seemed to be herself again.

The drone of Nate's voice in the kitchen, the clank and clatter as he threw pots and pans around and kicked the stepladder out of his way, all contributed to a sense that normalcy was returning to the Woolly Man. Quincella had chosen another sappy song to play on the jukebox and Luke had managed to move himself over to the pool table. When Zak realized what he was listening to he sighed in resignation. Usually when the customers were in the bar they got to choose the song but when it was just the family, the women decided what to play. When Zak wanted to listen to his favorite music he went back to his trailer and cranked up the stereo.

His sister's choice fit the gloomy atmosphere. Zak knew musical tastes were determined by many different factors and just because Quincella was half Greek and half African American didn't mean she automatically loved soul music or hip-hop. She'd never been much interested in soul music, hip-hop or even Greek music all that much. She grown up in the Woolly Man Bar & Grill listening to country, rock, disco, and a lot of Greek and Irish ballads. With all those choices, his sister preferred folk or Scots Irish ballads. He never did figure out why.

He'd rather walk a mile on rusty nails then listen to country music and Irish ballads. Like his sister, he was a nonconformist. He preferred heavy metal – give him Zeppelin, ZZ Top or Jimmy Hendrix any day.

Kelly Clarkson's song *Addicted* floated through the air and made him wince. If he had to go through another afternoon of crooning females boohooing, he was going to puke. After twenty minutes of silence from the crazy female and as Luke knocked a few pool balls back and forth, Zak wandered toward the imposter and sat down opposite her. She had her eyes open. He watched as she gazed at something beyond his shoulder, her expression haunted by some terrible sight. He scrutinized her carefully for any sign that she was aware of his presence. So far, he couldn't see so much as a flick of the lid or a fluttering of the lashes. She seemed oblivious to everyone in the room.

The screen door protested violently at the assault on its old hinges and several new people entered the bar. Zak glanced over his shoulder. Two men stood by the doorway. One of them carried a dirty green duffel bag over his shoulder. The other one carried fishing tackle and a fishing pole. Zak glanced at his watch. It was nearly supper time. No wonder Nate was hungry. The men sat at a table across the room near the wall where they could observe people and still be able to talk privately. Quinn took their orders. The men glanced at Leona then away as if they'd seen it all and weren't surprised by anything that happened in this place.

Zak considered kicking the woman with his boot to see what she might do. He changed his mind figuring his brother would just get pissed off if he woke up the female Svengali and messed with the family's chance of finding their lost ancestor.

Instead of sitting around collecting dust bunnies, they could be doing something useful two miles from here and maybe get themselves noticed by the Archeology Department in Arizona. Zak had some clues. So why not just follow those clues and find the grave? He had a pretty good idea where it would be. Zak glared at his brother. Luke was too busy daydreaming and knocking the balls back and forth across the pool table to notice Zak's angry stare. Every so often Luke would look up and survey with clinical interest Leona's trance like state.

The twitchy sensation returned. Unable to contain himself any longer, Zak jumped up from the table and left the Woolly Man. No one stopped him. His mother and sister were used to his abrupt comings-and-goings and his inability to sit still for long. Luke never even noticed Zak leave, he was so deep in his own thoughts.

In the desert, just before dark the landscape of sagebrush, rock and cheatgrass will turn to pale yellows and greens. It is an eerie landscape then. Sounds seem magnified and smells are more intense. The temperature drops a bit and all sorts of nasty annoying bugs choose this time of day to leave their hiding places and torment the living.

As he stepped off the porch, the butte in front of him and the mountain peak to his left appeared to hunch their shoulders and draw closer to him. Their dark heads blotted out the fast fading light. When on his digs, sometimes the sudden darkness would surprise him and leave him stranded standing by a hole he'd been investigating unable to see his hand in front of his face, much less what waited beneath the soil. But today, today the cloud passed by and the sun shone down upon him, its intense light baking the top of his head. He lifted his face to the sun and stood by his baby's metallic blue gleaming new finish and equally awesome shiny grill enjoying the warmth and the solitude.

He would rather be driving down some highway going as fast as he could with the wind whipping his hair and the landscape flying by listening to Zeppelin on his CD player. Or just as good, he would rather be hiking through the mountains searching for signs of Indigenous habitation discovering artifacts along the way. It annoyed Luke no end the way Zak had the knack for finding arrowheads. The trick was to keep your eyes open at all times just the way their ancestors used to track big game. Zak liked to follow this bit of sage advice with an insulting observation and tell Luke to stop tripping around the damned desert daydreaming and maybe he'd find an arrowhead or fossil himself.

Until the drama inside the Woolly Man ended, Zak would have to twist in the wind and wait. The last two hours seemed like eternity. He decided to check the Camaro's oil and the air pressure in the tires and wash the dust off the windows. A renewed sense of purpose lightened his mood and the day didn't seem such a damned waste. He pulled out his tool kit from the trunk, opened the hood of his silver 1969

Camaro Z28 and started cleaning the excess oil and dirt off his engine and radiator. There wasn't much to clean.

Everything gleamed. Yes. The way an engine should look, clean enough to eat off. He'd spent every penny and five years of hard dirty work restoring the Camaro to its original luster and speed. The doors had been a bitch to take off and put on. He'd had to bribe Luke into getting his hands dirty. Luke preferred staring at a computer monitor all night chatting with strangers and researching harpies, Greek Gods, and explorers of the Pacific Northwest. He learned very little about harpies and a whole lot about Greek Gods and famous explorers.

Zak heard rocks rolling down a hillside and the panicked squawk of a killdeer followed by an unnatural silence. Without giving anything away, he continued to unscrew the radiator cap while his body tuned into what was going on to his right. Absently, he noted the level of the radiator fluid and checked to make sure he had the proper concentration of water and antifreeze.

After five minutes and no sensation of anything out beyond the Woolly Man, Zak relaxed. It had been his imagination. He returned to the task of wiping the excess antifreeze off his engine with the intention of checking his brake fluid and air filter next. His friends thought his pampering excessive. But then again, they didn't have a 1969 Camaro in mint condition with the hidden headlights and the shiny chrome.

He heard something to his right panting shallow and fast. The mumbled growl and grunt finally convinced Zak an animal was foraging nearby, a big mammal from the sound of it, larger and more dangerous than a simple rabbit or rodent. The sound came from the vicinity of the shed as if the animal no longer feared discovery.

Zak stepped away from the engine and looked to his right wondering what kind of animal would be bold enough to come up to the bar and sneak around their property. He moved forward, careful to watch his step and make as little noise as possible on the gravel. He managed three steps before the animal shot out from behind the shed like a streak of black powder. It was sleek, black, almost hairless with no tail. *Holy Shit! What was wrong with its ears? What was it? A panther? No, not around these parts; maybe a feral cat? Hell no. A hairless wolf? Come on.*

As Zak tried to figure out what he was seeing, the creature jumped over tall sagebrush and into the tall grass then disappeared beyond the garage into the safety of the willows. He heard the splash of something hitting water and knew the animal had to be near the creek behind the building. Without a moment's hesitation, Zak raced after the animal, his heart pumping wildly, the excitement and fear sending waves of adrenaline through his body and making his head feel as if it might explode. Then he stopped. He had nothing to shoot it with, no way of protecting himself. He ran back to the Camaro and grabbed his gun from the trunk just behind the spare tire. He considered running inside to tell Luke. No. Luke had to keep an eye on their guest.

He tracked the animal to the creek but saw only his own prints in the dirt along the banks for nearly a half mile. Evidently the creature had made his way north by way of the banks of the water attempting to obscure his tracks from the hunter. What kind of an animal was smart enough to do that? Zak sat on a mound overlooking Willow Creek and searched the area watching the tall sage for any sign of movement. Whatever he'd seen, it was long since gone or hiding in some nearby burrow.

It might have been a dog, maybe one of those hairless dogs or nearly hairless dogs. It ran like a greyhound but had the body of a cat. He was sure it had to be feline. Zak returned to the shed and investigated the ground trying to understand what had attracted the animal to this spot anyway. There was no food lying around. Mom didn't keep pets or chickens or anything that would be an additional mouth to feed. Having to feed the hungry hunters, fishermen, and infrequent tourists was enough for her.

A foot beyond the shed behind a large gnarled bit of desperate sagebrush, Zak found a hole where the creature had been digging. Ten minutes later, he'd managed to uncover several bones and a skull. They were small bones, not small enough to be a prairie dog or whistle pig but maybe big enough to be a jackrabbit. He knew he held a skull and a femur and the rest he would have to determine later.

Lots of jackrabbits around. It definitely wasn't a whistle pig. The bones had to belong to an animal about the size of a domestic cat or medium-sized dog. Zak feared if he just left the bones in the hole, the animal would return and take them away before Luke could study the remains; so, Zak took a picture of the grave and the bones with his cellphone, then found a box in his trunk where he kept his extra motor oil. With his gloved hand, he placed the skull, femur, and smaller bones carefully in the bottom of the box.

Just to be sure, he sifted his stick around the hole in case he'd missed something. It looked to him as if some predator had dragged the animal to this spot to munch on while listening to a ballad about sappy love from his mother's jukebox. The idea amused him. As he carried the cardboard box full of bones toward the house, he changed his mind. Quinn would shriek in horror at the sight of the bones and his mom would make him take it back outside anyway.

He stood with his hands on his hips, debating whether he should store the box in the trunk of his car then remembered he had all his expensive tools in the trunk. He decided to leave the box in the backseat and show Luke his find later. In any case, the creature he'd seen would find (if it returned) that its prize was gone. Zak played with the idea of returning the bones to their original site just to smoke out the animal. Why? Most likely he'd frightened it away for good.

Zak respected wild creatures – this one in particular. Any animal that had the balls to walk up in broad daylight and start digging where humans lived either had to be loco or incredibly brave. He decided it was brave. Somehow the fervid nature of the beast, the sounds it had made digging, the way it had managed to get close to the place without being detected awakened Zak's curiosity. Its tenacity and stealth reminded Zak of the way human's behaved. The animal's behavior confirmed his suspicions that wild creatures who were losing their habitats were adapting by becoming crafty urban hunters.

When he reentered the bar, he realized he'd only been outside for about an hour. It had seemed longer. The girl was still in a trance fingering the artifact. Her head was tilted slightly to the right as if listening to something beyond the four walls. Zak chose to sit at a table near the door where he could see the shed from the window. He sipped his bottle of beer and flipped through the pages of his notebook. Some of the pages were yellowed from age, others brand new. The leather cover had been a gift from his father. Even though Zak no longer had any respect for the man, he had chosen to keep the notebook anyway. The notebook was a sentimental reminder of his childhood and burgeoning desire to be an archeologist.

On the leather, an artist had stitched the figure of a mermaid in gold thread with lovely breasts and long beautiful reddish blonde hair. She rested upon a map of the continents of the Americas and in gold script the major rivers, lakes, and oceans had been written in Spanish. He'd stared at the mermaid so often he no longer saw her. In the beginning, she'd been his ideal image of womanhood. Now his tastes were more eclectic. He preferred young brunettes with beautiful bodies to match their beautiful minds. They had to be smart. He'd tested the dumb ones and had no patience with them, unlike his brother Luke who had indiscriminate tastes and would bed anything that moved. Well, not just anything; they had to be breathing.

Zak chuckled and looked up in time to see Luke staring at him suspiciously guessing based on past experience that Zak's amusement was at his expense.

Outside the window something black streaked past Zak's peripheral vision. Zak leaped up and ran to the back door. Luke threw down his pool stick and followed. Once outside Zak stopped in his tracks, spun around, and put his finger to his lips. Luke frowned in annoyance and shrugged pantomiming "what the hell's up?" Zak waved him away furiously and turned to face the shed considering several hiding places. Directly ahead of him rested the skeleton of his grandfather's old 1956 Chevy Bel Air bleeding rust onto the cheatgrass and dandelion-choked ground. Zak moved cautiously toward the Chevy thinking the animal was hiding behind it.

Inside the Woolly Man, the inhabitants were oblivious to the antics going on outside. No one noticed Leona get up from the table and follow the Nerin brothers outside. Quinn and Jule were busy attending to the fishermen and Nate was in the kitchen preparing dinner for customers. The Nerin brothers never saw her creep down the steps and circle the Woolly Man in the opposite direction. She managed to flit across the dirt road without being seen and hide behind a large willow tree growing along the bank of the foothills.

On the butte above the Woolly Man Bar & Grill, Terence Frederick Hunter watched two tall skinny young men creep out of the side door of the bar and serpentine toward the '56 Chevy; the rougher looking one was running and midway dropped down to the ground to crawl on his belly toward the Bel Air while the other one dressed like a pot smoking hippie crouched and stared in bemusement at the crawler. Terence heard the hippie whisper, "What are you doing Zak?"

The one called Zak turned his head and put his finger to his lips. The hippie stood up. Zak frantically gestured for him to stay down. The hippie shrugged and returned to his position by the porch. Zak grabbed a dead tree limb on his way around the front grill of the '56 Chevy. He rose to his feet holding the tree limb up as if he meant to brain someone with it. He peeked around the grill, looked right, then looked left and finally with annoyance straightened to his full six feet two inches. The other guy stood up and strolled over to Zak with his arms crossed examining the ground for clues.

Terence wondered what the Sam Hell those two idiots thought they were doing. Woolstone had been his home for nearly fifty-eight years and he'd never seen grown men behave so childishly as if they were playing cowboys and Indians. They were too old to be playing games. What difference did these strangers make anyway? More importantly what was he doing here? There were days when he couldn't remember from moment to moment what he'd been planning to do or why he was in a particular town or on a lonely highway in the middle of the night. Must be all that damn weed he'd smoked as a teenager. Then he remembered what he was doing on the butte above the Woolly Man Bar & Grill.

He'd come here out of instinct, an instinct both irrational and overwhelming. A need to come home, home where he felt safe and loved. With grief in the wake of his journey, he had only one desire – to find her as he had promised and to return her to the people who loved her most. But she was gone. Someone had stolen her once again. What he had found behind the shed had not been her. It had been that other thing, the thing the Butcher Queen had created. The poor creature deserved to be at peace. God had had nothing to do with this monstrous act. Only a human could think up something so perverted and evil. Someday, the Butcher Queen would be punished. Someday, she would live out her life in hell tormented by demons. He was convinced it would come to pass.

The bent-up frustration of losing her once again and finding only evidence of the Butcher Queen's latest abomination returned to plague him. He rose from his hiding place cautiously and with muscles tensed slipped down the butte unnoticed. The boys were too busy arguing with each other to be aware of him, so close he could smell their sweat and fear.

"I tell you I saw it running behind the Chevy."

"It? Describe this – it."

"Don't act so damned superior Luke. You saw it too. I know you did."

"I saw a black dog, a big black dog."

"Screw that. You did not. Quit your lying. It was tailless and looked more like a jaguar or cougar except for the ears. You think there's any chance a black cougar would be around here? Maybe. But it didn't have ears like a cougar. It had ears like a man."

"You're hallucinating Zak. I told you to lay off that damn shit. It will make you crazy."

"I haven't had any pills in months. I know what I saw. It was an animal, some kind of freaking animal running on all fours with paws and sharp teeth. I've never seen anything like it before."

"What was it doing?"

"It went behind the shed and started digging something up, but I must have scared it away in time. It ran off. I chased it for a bit but lost its trail. When I returned, I finished digging up what was buried behind the shed. I'll show you what I found. It's in the Camaro."

He heard the men speak, but their words had no meaning for him. He wasn't interested in other people's problems. He had plenty of problems of his own to deal with. In fact, he'd had this unexplainable unfulfilled problem for far too long. By the time he'd reached the bottom of the butte, the two were standing near the Camaro. The man called Zak had opened the driver's side door and reached into the backseat to pull out a cardboard box. The other guy named Luke peeked into the box and shook his head, "Looks like it might be a jackrabbit, a young jackrabbit I'm guessing."

"Are you sure Luke, because it resembles something else to me?"

Terence thought this would be his best opportunity to run across the dirt road and hide behind the shed. But before he could make it across the road, he heard a vehicle in the distance heading his way. He managed to hide behind the willow in the shallow ditch before the black Volkswagen swept into view and sailed past him spewing gravel and dust in his eyes and mouth. He had a sneezing fit.

No one heard or noticed.

The Volkswagen made enough noise to drown out anything he might do. The sound reminded him of one of those hot busy summer days when everybody had the same idea – mow the lawn and trim the hedges and with the rattling, sputtering and metal whining, the neighborhood would be engulfed in racket. But eventually those lawns would be manicured, and bushes would be trimmed, and a blissful silence would return before dusk.

Terence shook his head. The motion only made his vision blur. He lay down behind the trunk of the willow and tried to collect his thoughts. There had been a time when everything he did and thought and said had been lucid, had purpose, and had given him a feeling of strength and comfort. Nowadays, he just longed for a good nap and some peace and quiet. But he had a pressing need to finish what he'd promised he would finish. He was doing this for her. They'd agreed to do what they could when the time was right. His time had been right for far too damned long now. But he couldn't let her down. Not today. Not ever.

Terence watched Zak and Luke walk up to the Volkswagen and greet the guy struggling out of his low seat. The Volkswagen Man handed Zak a metal detector. Terence remembered the days when he used to go out with his metal detector and search for lost treasure. When they were fresh in love, Sally would come with him on his hikes through the Sawtooth Mountains. His obsession with treasure hunting took up most of his free time. He remembered those egg salad sandwiches Sally used to pack for him and the crisp sweet pickles. His mouth began to water. He was hungry, hungry all the time now.

The only thing that extinguished the hunger was what he saw around him and his need to keep his secret safe. Terence forced himself to pay attention to what the three fellows were doing across the road. The boy Luke reminded Terence of his youth, the time he snuck off to San Francisco and saw all those hippies wandering the streets. That had been 1968 or was it '69? Zak, on the other hand, looked relatively normal for this neck of the woods. Neck of the woods, Terence thought with amusement, glancing around worried someone might have heard him. Where had that idiom come from?

The willow he rested under was the only tall tree for miles around. Then Terence scrutinized the young fella climbing out of the Volkswagen. The boy looked constipated and confused. His hair hadn't seen a pick or a brush for days and sprang out of his head like a porcupine's quills, only a porcupine with frizzy sometimes curly quills. The ends were black, and the roots were bright yellow. Terence blinked several times to be sure he was seeing the boy in the right way.

He watched the boy take something out of his pocket and press the thing to his eye then look down into the box Zak pushed toward him. With astonishment and gathering uneasiness, Terence heard Zak say to the boy, "I found these bones buried behind the shed. What do you think they might be Professor?" Terence listened with all his body and soul. Their problem had become his problem.

The Professor sighed, "Quit calling me that Zak."

"You're smarter than any professor we've ever had; so, don't be so damned modest," Zak said. "What do you think huh? Luke thinks this is just the bones of a jackrabbit."

The wind gently stirred the long bangs of the willow. A strand dangling just above his head tickled Terence's scalp. Terence jerked. Then he relaxed realizing it had just been the hairy touch of a leaf. For a moment, he'd thought someone had crept up behind him. Uneasy, he decided to move in closer to the boys. No one noticed. Now out in the open, exposed to the hot sun above and the creepy crawly things below, Terence realized his error and slunk back to the willow.

A memory stirred, a memory of crossing Succor Creek near the valley of cliffs one day. There had been birds above him dancing a minuet amongst the cliff faces. He remembered feeling the hot sun on his back that day. Then he looked down into the cool moving water of the creek and the image he saw in the water frightened him. He bolted onto the other side of the bank then broke into a blind run, running as fast he could to get away from the truth.

The groan of a car door opening and closing brought Terence Hunter back to the present. He froze behind a pile of wood. The Professor looked up from his examination of the contents of the box and pronounced in a loud authoritative voice, "The femur and the skull are human. You see the indentation here on the top of the skull. That's the crown, a baby's crown. The two plates were beginning to meet in the middle here. So, I'd say this child must have been approximately ten to eighteen months old at the time of his death."

Her death, Terence corrected the porcupine boy.

"No frigging way," Luke said. "There is no way these bones are human. Look at the jaw. This is not the jaw of any human I've ever seen," Luke said, emphasizing his point by running his finger down the jaw. "It's clearly not human."

"But the crown suggests a human skull and there are many reasons why the jaw might be deformed."

"Have you studied Zoology?" Luke asked prepared to fight all night if necessary.

"No."

"I rest my case," Luke said throwing up his hands.

Zak closed the box and started to walk away, "You guys can argue all you want. The only way I'll know for sure is through DNA testing."

"You got the money for that Zak?" his brother asked. Zak ignored the question and dumped the box in the backseat of his Camaro.

Terence moved quietly by the Camaro appreciating the fresh coat of paint and sleek lines. It was a rare sight in these backwoods – a 2 door, silver 1969 Camaro 302 Z/28 with SS-350 manual transmission. Few homes around here had safe places to keep such a rare car. It would drive him crazy to be constantly worried about someone scratching the gleaming finish or spilling ice cream on the seats. A man can't have a Camaro and also a wife and kids.

While the men continued to quarrel, Terence crossed the road unobserved and without much effort made his way toward the back of the building. By keeping to the tall grasses and the occasional sagebrush, he managed to find a hiding place under the back porch. He could hear the jukebox music and the drone of voices inside. Once or twice, someone laughed which startled him but eventually the sounds merged with other sounds, sounds both familiar and strange. In all his fifty-eight years, he had never had much time to listen or sit quiet and contemplate the world around him.

Now as he looked about him taking in this time and this place, and even back when life meant little, he had exercised the fine art of listening and at this precise moment listened with his entire being. Over the years, his hearing had become acutely precise, so precise he could hear the beetles munching away at the locust tree beyond the old Chevy Bel Air. He could also hear the colony of ants just on the other side of the shed tunneling new freeways and nests. He wondered if he concentrated hard enough would he be able to hear clear to the town of Woolstone. The town was about two miles away? Would his wife Sally be in the kitchen cooking? Could he reach her before he lost his way again? Impossible to know.

It was the nothingness he feared.

Terence heard Zak walking toward him. The other two were walking toward a set of trailers parked on the other side of a meadow near a garage. That boy Zak is stubborn. He's like a terrier down a hole determined to find the rabbit and drag it home for supper. From Terence's perspective under the porch in semi-darkness, he could see the boy's boots. They were steel-tipped leather boots worn so long the creases were yellow. Yet the bootstraps were new.

Zak stood with his hands on his hips and contemplated the view. He examined the garage first because the door was open and there was the possibility that the creature might be hiding inside somewhere. His mother's precious 2-door red 1968 Ford Mustang convertible was parked in the middle of the garage to prevent any of the customers or occasional boyfriends from parking their vehicles next to hers. There were a couple of garbage cans set inside a receptacle he'd build for her with boards encircling the outer edges. The cage kept the stray dogs and coyotes from tipping the cans over and rooting inside for leftovers.

The barn had seen better days; yet, the barn looked more natural with its gray aging wooden shingled walls than the new beige aluminum garage. The barn hadn't seen a pig or a goat or a cow for years, nor were there any tools or farm vehicles parked inside. Instead there were rocks stored in the barn, every damn rock that Quinn's father had ever collected in his lifetime, rocks from as far away as Canada and as close as two feet away. Rocks collected and stored in every conceivable spot in the barn from the hay loft to the stalls. Rocks and more rocks. Rocks everywhere.

Quinn's father had up and left seven years back but the rocks he left behind. Mom hadn't bothered to do anything with them. She insisted that Parker would have to come back and drag them out himself. Zak supposed the rocks would still be in that barn when he was ninety and Parker was long dead because Luke sure as shitola wouldn't bother to cart them away and Zak sure as shitola didn't want to have to go through all of them and decide which ones to throw away and which ones to keep. So there the rocks slept waiting for a crazy rock hound to come by and take them all away.

Zak supposed he'd been standing in the same spot for five minutes or so and nothing had moved yet. But to be sure Zak wandered over to the garage and stepped inside, looked around, then wandered out. He heard the front screen door open and close from the direction of the trailers and Luke calling his name, but Zak ignored him and moved toward the barn.

There were rocks piled in wheel barrows, boxes, old five-gallon plastic paint containers, even his old toy box. He recognized a few of the rocks especially the picture jasper which he liked the best. Luke liked the smoky quartz crystals and the shiny stuff, the malachite. Mom had gotten so sick of rocks that the sight of one anywhere near her made her sneer with disgust. Yet the rocks remained in the barn. She could have sold all of it to that old man years ago, the guy down the road. He'd even offered her five hundred dollars for the lot.

A sound like an animal crawling on its belly startled Zak. He spun around and tensed listening with all his senses on fire. A minute passed, and nothing happened. He relaxed. I'm getting twitchy in my old age, he thought. He wiped the sweat from his forehead and looked around just to be sure. He supposed a creature could hide behind a few of the tall sage nearby but otherwise the land was flat for miles and only dipped occasionally where old creeks still lay.

Zak was getting hot and angry. Time to leave off hunting and see if the crazy one was awake. He walked around the Woolly Man one more time wondering if he'd really seen that funny looking creature or just dreamed him up because of the woman inside. It could have been a cougar, a black cougar. A jaguar or a cougar sort of had human looking heads. And with his ears flat against his head, yeah, a cougar's ears might resemble a man's. Yet the image persisted of a big black jaguar with human ears, a chimera: part cat, part man.

As he lay still contemplating the dirt under his nose and waiting for the terrier to loose interest and go inside, Terence remembered his beloved Sally. Egg salad sandwiches and pickles. Scorching summer nights down by the creek giggling and making love. Winters inside wrapped in blankets and snuggling. Yes. Those were the best memories. He liked to bring them out every so often and relive them one by one.

Unbidden the memory of how everything turned ugly rose up like bile from an upset stomach. He and Sally had wanted a baby so much. They had tried for years and time was ticking away. Soon it would be too late for them. They had maybe a few years at most. The thought of Mona raised the hairs on the back of his neck. He let the fury wash over him in waves of hate. She had been their neighbor, a peculiar woman who made both of them uncomfortable, even when she wasn't present. Every time they went outside to water the grass or plant or play, they felt her scrutinizing them from behind her curtains or sitting back in the shadows. He and his wife Sally tried to be kind but the intensity of Mona's fetish for snooping was like a wave of heat scorching the very air they breathed.

They found excuses to build a tall fence and plant arborvitae along the fence, so she couldn't stare down into their backyard and watch them from her second story bedroom window. They found excuses to plant cactus and yucca in the front, so they didn't have to water and be exposed to her hungry eyes. Over the years, they became resigned to her snooping and on most days totally forgot about her.

That had been their biggest mistake, Terrence believed, having all too much time these days to relive the past in its every wrong turn.

Mona Lawson must have been furious at being ignored. One night, she showed up at their door and refused to leave until they invited her in. Sally, bless her sweet soul, felt pity for her and allowed her inside. Terence remembered Mona handing him a piece of mail. "The mailman dropped this off at my house by mistake," she said in her gravely midwestern accent. The letter was from the adoption agency.

"Mail carrier. They're called mail carriers now," his Sally corrected their neighbor.

"Oh sure, mail carrier," Sally said absently her intense focus directed at Terence and Terence only. It was her habit and had never varied, not even once in fifteen years. Mona would scrutinize his face and body as if she were trying to capture his image in her long-term memory for posterity. Whenever she bumped into them (which wasn't often if they could help it) she would ignore Sally and stare at him with undisguised hunger. When the fine hairs on his body registered danger, he tried to convey his concern to Sally. Unfortunately, Sally had her own devils to deal with when it came to Mona Lawson. Her jealousy for the woman was irrational. Terence had no desire to touch Mona much less bed her. She was a repulsive, irritating female who stuck her nose in other people's personal business and had no filters, no borders, no emotional intelligence what-so-ever.

He should have realized something was very, very wrong that day. He'd known for years she was sweet on him and did his best to avoid her. There was a time when Sally felt sorry for her too. On that day, Mona unmistakably vibrated with urgency and seemed more desperate than ever. Something had changed. He'd been wondering what the catalyst had been which provoked her into stepping outside her comfort zone to go to all the trouble of conning them into that fake clinic. She'd stolen their mail. He was convinced of that. But would she have done so on her own? Mona didn't have the smarts, or the craftiness required for implementing such a devious plan.

They should have moved away, moved to Boise, moved anywhere to escape her foulness, but Sally had family in Woolstone and wanted to stay near her mother. So, they had been trapped in the small town for years – Sally nursing her mother and Terence working as a handyman doing all sorts of odd jobs, sometimes having to work outside of town. If they'd just waited a year. If they'd just said no to the woman that day and kept on telling her no for a year, they could have been free, free of Mad Mona and the town.

"I couldn't help but notice the name on the envelope," Mona said. "And I just wanted you to know that I know someone who could help you. She's a genius. She knows almost everything about everything. I went ahead and called her, and she said she'd be happy to talk to you about your situation. She just opened a clinic in Twin Falls and she'd be happy to examine your wife and maybe find someone who could help. She knows everybody in the field of infertility."

"Well, I don't know," he remembered his wife saying glancing in puzzlement at the woman. He could read on his wife's face her futile attempts to conceal her distaste for Lawson's bluntness. It was an effort for both of them to keep their faces neutral and speak calmly after so many years of being spied on by the woman. She was like a plague of craziness infecting everyone she encountered.

Terence finished his wife's thought, "That's very kind of you, Mrs. Lawson, but we haven't made up our mind yet."

Pointing at her chest, Mona addressed him, "You remember Terence that I'm a retired nurse? I wouldn't steer you wrong. I promise."

If only they had run, run as far away from Mona Lawson and Woolstone as they possibly could without having to immigrate. He had sensed trouble the minute Mona walked into their home. And the trouble just kept on keeping on. Eventually, his wife gave in discouraged by the news from her own physician. Mona's genius doctor recommended a colleague and Sally had treatments and dutifully took the recommended shots and the pills and still nothing happened. Then the clinic found a surrogate willing to have their baby. They harvested his sperm and Sally's egg and inseminated the surrogate – for a price. They had to take out a second mortgage to pay the young woman.

For nine months, they experienced a joy so complete it would only be possible in heaven. And then the joy turned to grief and the grief to nightmare. He should have known something wasn't right when the doctor insisted the young girl have the baby at the clinic instead of the hospital. He should have known something was wrong when Mona Lawson offered to assist the medical staff. How could a retired nurse practice medicine? Was she even a nurse? They wouldn't let him into the delivery room. He and his wife had barely known the surrogate, having only met her a couple of times: when she was introduced to them at the coffee shop, the time before she was inseminated with the fertilized egg and when she was near term. And when the day came, and they arrived at the clinic ready to take the baby home, the doctor told them the baby had died along with the surrogate.

They'd been waiting for hours sitting in the lobby drinking coffee and tea, anxious and excited, everything at home ready for the baby's arrival. They had the baby's car seat set up and plenty of diapers and bottles. In the clinic's spare lobby with its blank off-white walls and eerie quiet he got up to get a magazine, stumbled and wondered why he felt so tired then noticed how Sally moments ago had rubbed her forehead looking so exhausted. He should have known something wasn't right. He should have grabbed her arm and run outside and climbed into their car right there and then.

And then a stranger came out and told them the baby had died. Just like that. It was all over. It wasn't over for his wife, his sweet fiercely protective wife. She was grief-stricken and angry; and when she got angry, she said what was on her mind, ignoring the danger around her. She told the doctor she was going to call the police and have them investigated. She voiced her concerns about the whole situation, even letting them know she'd been doing her own research and people were telling her nobody conducted fertility clinics in such a haphazard fashion. And he remembered Mona and some big guy in blue scrubs coming out of the back room. Before the door closed, he'd heard a baby cry. Sally heard the baby too.

Sally tried to push Mona out of the way. Mona slapped her. Terence remembered going for Mona and the orderly grabbing him and the doctor injecting him with something. He woke in a strange bed with

Mona bending over him saying, "I'm so sorry Terence. We had to do it. You were acting so crazy."

"Where's my wife?" he remembered shouting, his voice raspy and hurting. It had been late afternoon when they heard the baby cry. It was dark now, perhaps the middle of the night. He discovered later they had sedated him for the entire week.

"She's right next to you dear. She's at peace now," a stranger told him. And when he turned his head, he saw his Sally just before the orderlies took her away.

And Mona, he remembered her bending down and murmuring in his ear, "Poor thing. She had a heart attack. It was the grief, I'm sure. Don't you worry. I'm going to take good care of you. And your baby is fine. They don't know. So, don't say anything to my aunt. She'd be so mad with me if she knew. It's our secret. Ok? Baby Jessica is doing just fine, sweetheart. You'll see her soon. She's safe with me. Now you go to sleep. Sleep now. You need your strength."

He didn't want to think anymore. He just wanted to sleep and forget.

Leona thought about running for the Ford Taurus and getting away from these crazy Nerins then she remembered she'd left her leather satchel in the bar under the table. The satchel had her car keys and map inside. She would have to figure out a way to get back into the bar without being noticed. Peeking through the window, Leona saw Zak standing by the table she had vacated. He lifted one end of the Navaho blanket (as if she might be under the table) looked around the room then dropped the blanket back into place.

Jule Nerin called to Zak and he walked toward his mother still turning his head from side to side as if searching for someone. Leona had no doubt he was looking for her. She ran back to the side door and slipped into the bar without being noticed. Her luck held as she made her way to the door labeled Ladies and slipped inside. There were two-bathroom stalls. She hid inside the one closest to the door and sat down on the toilet seat to wait.

10

In 2007, Luke turned twenty-one. While in Stanley, Idaho experimenting with speed and other illegal paraphernalia, he met a woman who told him that her husband was a retired detective with the Vegas Police Department. Luke remembered the red head with a shiver of revulsion. She was so drunk she could barely sit on her barstool, "He just left the damn thing on the kitchen chair. What was I supposed to think? I thought it was something he'd dug up from the garage in those old boxes of his. He used to collect the nasty things.

I swear, it was just a misunderstanding. Boy was he pissed when he came home from work and found I'd given the blanket away at my garage sale. It was just an old blanket I told him. How was I supposed to know it was evidence in a kidnapping?" the red head shouted over the noise from the jukebox nearly breaking his eardrum.

Without warning she started to weep, big huge tears mixed with black mascara which dribbled down her fat cheeks and joined the dribble of snot from her left nostril. It was all Luke could do not to rush out and leave her to her misery. But when she mentioned the Navaho blanket which was evidence in the case of the missing BSU professor Constance Wade, he knew he had to stay and listen.

"Who did you give the blanket to?" he asked.

It took several precious hours for him to get the facts out of her. She'd lied to her husband telling him she'd sold the blanket to an unknown young couple, but in actuality, she'd given the blanket to her neighbor, someone she'd been seeing behind her husband's back. She was afraid the guy would reveal the affair to her husband and her husband would kill her. It took all of Luke's ingenuity and three glasses of Scotch to learn the name of the man.

Once Luke knew who had the blanket, everything else made sense. He drove home plotting how to steal the blanket and then he thought of his brother and realized that fate had stepped in. A gift had been handed to the Nerin family without their knowledge, a gift to be discovered at the proper moment. How blind could he have been, Luke thought, amazed at his stupidity? Luke found his younger brother Zak in his trailer lying on the couch. Unable to contain his excitement, Luke shouted out, "That blanket of yours. Where is it?"

When Zak pressed his lips tightly shut and scowled at his brother, Luke rushed down the hall and burst into Zak's bedroom. He stood on the threshold of the room dismayed and dispirited. It would take days to sift through the piles of junk. Luke itched to wrap his hands around Zak's throat and throttle him, "Where is it Zak? You wouldn't leave it in this stinking mess. Where'd you hide it?"

"Why do you want to know?" Zak asked suspiciously.

"What was the name of the pawn shop where you stole the blanket Zak? Come on. This is important," Luke said.

Zak walked towards his bed and threw the pile of dirty clothes onto the floor, "I told you before, I rescued the blanket from Leland's filthy paws. Why do you care? Did you hear something in town? Wait. You couldn't have. The cameras were fake. And the ones in the front were turned off. I made sure. You think I'm an amateur or something?"

"No. Don't worry about that. Everybody knows Leland's a crook. Why would he keep the blanket and the pipe hidden away if they were honestly come by? They're valuable. More valuable than he even knows. Guess what Zak?"

"I'm not selling um," Zak said with a stubborn look. "I don't care who you owe money to or what scheme you've come up with this time."

Deep down inside Luke knew there was no such thing as coincidences. Luke was meant to have that blanket and discover the truth and much more significantly to find the burial site that would reestablish the greatness of the Nerin family.

"Let me see the blanket Zak. Please," Luke asked. "Come on."

With excruciating slowness, Zak got up and walked toward the cupboards above his bed. The blanket was the only piece of material in the room which had been folded neatly and put away. This one bit of neatness in a room of mess was typical of Zak. When Luke moved to take the blanket vacuum-sealed in its plastic case, Zak jerked the object out of his reach and tossed the blanket back into the cupboard. "It stays with me. And if I find out you've taken it, you'll pay. Maybe one night when your asleep I'll drag you out into the desert, stake you to the ground and pour honey all over your body. Then I'll walk away and leave you to the ants. Or maybe I'll just beat the pretty right off your fucking face."

Luke had no trouble believing his brother's threat. He'd seen the frenzied fury of his brother's sporadic rages before. It was an ugly sight but effective. When in those moods, nothing short of a bullet could stop his brother. The last time Zak got into a fight was when a guy hit on their sister Quinn. Only when the fight ended did Zak realize he'd fractured his own wrist.

The serendipity of Zak's burglary and the confession by a cop's wife meant the Nerins were getting closer to their goal? The Navaho blanket's association with Wade, the best treasure hunter of all time seemed to suggest they were moving in the right direction. Yet months had passed with no significant discovery or sign they were getting closer to their goal. Just yesterday he'd been so despondent he'd dumped all his notes and maps in a suitcase and shoved them under his bed prepared to forget about the Nerin family legend and move on to another project. Then this morning before the Woolly Man was even open, he'd answered the old rotary phone his mother kept behind the bar and heard a woman asking for crazy Mrs. Lawson.

"This is the Woolly Mammoth Bar and Grill or Woolly Man as we like to call it. We are not a personal answering service. If you need to reach Ms. Lawson, I suggest you try directory assistance."

"What's your name young man?" the woman asked in a voice which reminded him unpleasantly of his days at Oxford when even the staff turned their nose up at his American accent and drab appearance.

"Duke of Brontë," Luke said smirking into the mirror behind the bar and standing at attention as if he were the famous naval officer.

"He's been dead for a long-time smart-ass," the woman said. "And you are no navy captain that's for sure. An officer and a gentleman would never talk to a lady in such a boorish manner. So, listen here young man I want you to relay an important message to my cousin. If you see Mona tell her Violet needs to speak to her immediately. No need to write it down. You're an Oxford man after all." Without giving him a chance to speak, he heard the click as she disconnected. The dial tone was the final insult.

As his mother entered the room carrying several bags of ice, he slammed the phone into its cradle and said, "What a royal ass snot licker. I wish she'd just sod-off the bloody planet."

"Hey there," his mother admonished him. "Don't be taking your annoyances out on Grandma's phone."

"Some old biddy ordered me to give Mad Mona a message. Who does she think she is? I told the old biddy we weren't a personal answering service."

His mother handed him the bags of ice, "Put these in the freezer for me honey. Don't worry I'll speak to Mona. She's too cheap to buy a cellphone, so I'll tell her she has to pay me twenty bucks a month for the use of our phone and she'll stop giving out our number. Even twenty bucks is too much for her. She'd rather walk a mile in a blinding snowstorm just to save herself a few pennies. Idiot woman."

"Oh, has the scarecrow done this before?" he asked.

"Mona's got some rich relative in Oregon. She brags about this woman all the time; how smart she is and how rich and that everybody in the medical profession thinks she going to be the bigger than the guy who discovered penicillin. I think her relative is working on some new drug that will keep us all young and beautiful. She's some sort of plastic surgeon and works mainly on Hollywood stars. Rich. Filthy rich according to Mona. Sometimes she even helps reconstruct people's faces. I've never heard of her, never seen her on television like those other celebrity doctors. I'm pretty sure it's all bullshit."

"Well if she's so rich, why doesn't her rich doctor relative take Mad Mona off in her private jet and leave us the hell alone?" he asked. It was as he turned to leave he felt a chill of excitement run up his back. Whenever something really good was about to happen to him, he'd feel a rush of excitement run down his spine, as if his body recognized the significance of the moment before his brain caught up with the news. It had happened just before the mail carrier delivered Oxford's acceptance letter and just before the discovery of the Buhl Woman's skeletal remains.

With adrenaline pumping through his body, he ran to Zak's trailer and after an hour of intense negotiation managed to persuade Zak to let him examine the blanket. He assured Zak that the blanket needed to be aired once in a while to prevent degradation. In retrospect, it was astonishing how these series of coincidences were happening one after the other. This morning before Leona entered the Woolly Man, he'd been staring in wonder at the handmade, obviously very old, Navaho blanket, a blanket which contained the DNA of so many former owners, both ancient and more recent.

It was equally awe inspiring to consider the symbolism behind the Navaho blanket, the craftsmanship and history of the Navaho people and then to connect the intertwining of the Wade and Nerin families with a common goal. He was convinced Constance Wade had been looking for something more than just evidence of Smithers' expedition.

She had been following in his footsteps searching for the existence of Amara.

Somehow Professor Wade must have learned about the Nerin family legend and Luke suspected the "somehow" was through his Aunt Esther. Aunt Esther had been famous for shooting her mouth off to anyone – even total strangers. Constance Wade might have heard from someone who had heard from Aunt Esther about the existence of a harpy who had been rescued by the indigenous people at the estuary of the Columbia River. Or maybe she had read oral histories of people who had woven into their own creation stories the story of a woman with wings and claws? Maybe she had even found Smithers' collection of letters from missionaries all over North America and decided to do her own investigating?

His brother thought he was jumping to conclusions and Professor Wade had simply been looking for evidence of Smithers' expedition. "There is no conspiracy, Luke," he remembered his brother saying. "It's all in your tiny brain. Professor Wade was a professional. Unlike this family, she wasn't a nut job."

It dawned upon Luke how Zak's hoarding and his passion for archeology had conspired to benefit the family. With Zak as its guardian, the blanket had remained in its present state for months cocooned in a sealed plastic bag, untouched, unmolested by housewifely interference. Not only had Zak protected the bag from their mother's cleaning frenzies but also preserved the blanket in its near original condition. Yes, a few hands had contaminated the blanket since Dr. Wade's disappearance: the police, the cop's wife, and Leland Ansel, not to mention Zak himself. Yet. It could have been so much worse. The blanket could have been sold to some stranger at the garage sale in Stanley and been lost forever. Instead, the blanket was now in their possession. And that was good news. Hopeful news.

There might be rotten food on forgotten plates under Zak's bed and in his sink, but as long as one valuable object remained in pristine condition, luck was still on their side. He remembered being so irritated with Zak for stealing the blanket. Now, he was beginning to realize how valuable the blanket was to them all. The blanket's incredible journey wouldn't end in a trailer. The blanket was going to show them the way to Amara. And once they found Amara's grave, they were going to enjoy the prosperity promised to them by their ancestors.

And now the Navaho blanket Zak had protected all those months ago had served its purpose. When Luke entered the Woolly Man with the Professor in tow, his eyes went immediately to the table where Leona should have been. Panic leaped into his throat when he saw that she was gone. "Hey? Mom? Where'd she go?" he called out. Both his mother and Zak turned to look at him. Zak was the first to move. In three strides he was standing beside Luke. They heard a toilet flushing then water running as someone inside the women's bathroom turned on the tap. Less than a minute passed before Leona came out of the bathroom and returned to the table she had occupied for the last hour. She sat down and touched the Navaho blanket then looked across the room at the people staring at her.

Those who had been staring started moving again. Leona took a sip of her warm water, rubbed her forehead furiously and frowned. She raised her right arm in the air and gave the Nerin brothers the bird, "Stop looking at me. It's rude. Just go away and leave me alone." When the brothers turned away and made themselves comfortable at the bar with their backs to her, Quinn noticed Leona's shoulders relax. The weird girl dropped her head in her arms. She might have gone to sleep or just pretended to sleep. No one in the room knew and they couldn't do anything about it anyway.

An hour passed, and Luke's impatience mounted. He carried his beer back to the table near Navan Leona Keys and watched her sleep. If Luke looked away from Keys and concentrated on positive thoughts only, any minute now Keys would open her mouth and say what he needed to hear. He knew instinctively that she would guide them to Amara. Dr. Krutcher had used Constance Wade on several of his digs and boasted she had an incredible spatial intelligence, so incredible he claimed she could walk across the Sahara Desert without a guide or a compass.

"Come over here and have something to eat?" his mother demanded of Luke. Luke turned in time to see his mother turn off the television on the shelf above the bar.

He glanced at Keys and remembered a watched pot never boils, so he got up from his table and carried his beer to the bar.

"What are you thinking about so fiercely honey?" his mother asked, setting a bowl of soup and crackers in front of him. "I thought you were going to break a blood vessel staring at the female."

He looked back at Keys. She was still oblivious to the occupants of the room and probably the world itself.

"I was thinking about certain key people who might just make our family famous," he said leaning in and speaking in a muffled voice so that the fishermen couldn't hear. "You know Krutcher had been lucky to find Wade because she enhanced his career when she led him to what remained of G. K. Smithers' archeological expedition. You remember me telling you about G. K. Smithers?"

"Maybe," his mother said. "I don't recall. Sometimes you talk so much I tune you out."

"Yes, well thanks, Mom," Luke responded absently familiar with his mother's brutal honesty. "He had been the son of a steel manufacturing tycoon and wanted to replicate the achievements of the great archeologists of his time. Rather than travel to Egypt and deal with the capriciousness of local authorities and languages, he decided North America would be a far friendlier and more accommodating area to explore. But his ideas were as fanciful as his taste in transportation. He commissioned the creation of a unique kind of carriage constructed of light weight steel; then, he hitched mules to the carriage, mules which were capable of traveling in all types of weather and in all types of terrain."

"What does that have to do with Krutcher or the missing woman. What did you say her name was again?" his mother asked as she pulled out her ledger and began recording the receipts for the day. Luke, used to his mother's multi-tasking, didn't care if half her mind was on the accounts and the other half on what he was saying. He just needed someone to bounce his ideas off and hope to come up with some sort of a plan. He would have preferred talking to Zak, but Zak was in a piss-ass mood lately and would be useless right now anyway.

"Well, they're all connected you see. Krutcher and Wade are archeologists from this century and Smithers was an amateur archeologist from the mid - 19th century. Let me start from the beginning. Alright with you?" he asked.

His mother nodded.

He continued, "I'll go back to the early 19th century. You see, originally G. K. Smithers had been interested in finding out if the bedtime stories he had been raised on by his Irish mother were true. Even though his father was of English descent and an extremely practical man, his mother raised him on stories about the perilous journey of Saint Brendan who crossed the North Sea and discovered paradise. She convinced her son that Saint Brendan deserved to be called the first European to discover America, not as the history books claimed that Christopher Columbus was the first to arrive in the North America."

His mother looked up from her ledger, "What? Columbus didn't discover America? You're joking, right?"

"Well. Ghee. How do I begin? Scientists are now pretty sure Vikings were the first to discover America. In 1960, archeologists found copious amounts of evidence in Newfoundland that Vikings had been the first to land in America at a place called L'Anse aux Meadows. But there's always been this other rumor that perhaps Europeans discovered America much earlier. Five hundred years earlier. Let me give you some background on these guys."

"Who? Krutcher, Wade, and Smithers?"

"Ok, forget about the team at L'Anse aux Meadows. It'll just confuse you anyway. Let me tell you about Smithers first. He is important to our family, really important," Luke glanced over his shoulder to be sure the fishermen couldn't hear him. "Smithers, by accident or design discovered evidence of Amara's existence."

His mother's reaction reminded him of his father's hunting hounds when spotting their prey. She froze, her muscles quivering with excitement, her full attention on him, the ledger completely forgotten.

He continued, "Smithers' father sent his son away to school in England to cure him of his fantasies about Saint Brendan. G.K Smithers spent three months at Oxford and left in disgust. His ideas about the founding of North America had been ridiculed by his professor and some of the students. He returned to the states and applied for admission into Harvard University. After graduating with high honors, he became a dual member of both the British Archaeological Society in England and the Archaeological Institute of America. When Smithers returned home to take over his father's business, he found the job tedious and hired a manager for his father's foundry. G.K was convinced that Saint Brendan had discovered America before Columbus.

To prove his theory, he and his wife collected stories from missionaries in Iceland, Newfoundland, Nova Scotia, Maine, and New York asking for creation stories and/or folktales from indigenous people. He had hoped to hear of an Irish monk who landed on their shores named Saint Brendan. None of the responses he received fit the description of the famous Irish monk. But there was one story which caught his fancy. It was a tale told by a missionary from Oregon who lived in a place called The Dalles near the Columbia River."

His mother interrupted him, "I know about The Dalles, Luke. Don't talk down to me because I never finished high school. Remember, we've been to The Dalles. We've been to Multnomah Falls too."

"Mom, just let me get this out," he told her and tried to continue but Quinn showed up and sat herself down beside him to listen. With both women eyeing him intensely he tried to collect his train of thought and start over, "Those indigenous people who survived the near decimation of their numbers from smallpox and measles spoke of a magical beast who had wings like an eagle and the body of a beautiful woman. She was known as Amara. They told the missionary of how their ancestors revered her because when they grew sick, she nursed them back to health. She could not save them all yet compared to the other people of the Pacific Northwest battling the white man's diseases most of Amara's patients survived.

She stayed with the people of The Dalles for several years and then left them one day without a word. An eyewitness swore he saw her jump off the cliff, spread her wings, and soar through the air like a great eagle. He watched as long as he could as she traveled east. Their people never saw the white woman again. Yet her story has been passed down from generation to generation. They believe she was a great medicine woman sent by the creator to save them from the invaders.

Unfortunately for our family, the original letter sent by the missionary was never found. Archeologists and historians as well as Smithers' descendants searched for the letter and any documentation which would collaborate the tale. Had Smithers simply lied about his reasons for searching the Pacific Northwest? Why would he go to so much trouble and expense based on a rumor anyway? And why would Krutcher and Wade try to find his lost expedition? They must have discovered something important.

It was all fantastical. The idea that Saint Brendan and his seventeen monks survived a journey across the sea in an open boat isn't as fantastical as Smithers abrupt departure from his original purpose. Even though the journey had been replicated in the 21st century by Mr. Severin and four of his companions, I still question why Smithers, an amateur archeologist would switch gears from Saint Brendan's epic journey to an obscure reference to a mythical Greek creature and then spend all those years searching for evidence of her in the Pacific Northwest. It seems suspicious.

He must have discovered something even more compelling to risk his marriage and all his wealth. He spent time in Washington, Oregon, Idaho, and Nevada recording creation stories and folk stories along the way, searching deserts, mountains, and canyonlands for evidence of the harpy's existence. His wife left him and returned to New York. And two years later, Smithers and his companions disappear never to be heard of or seen again, until Professor Wade discovered his burial site.

It must have been sweltering inside that contraption. Smithers may have been mad, as archeologists and others claimed, but at least he'd acted upon his dreams rather than sit back and do nothing. By the time Smithers turned fifty-five, he had spent most of his inheritance and his wife's dowry searching for Amara. And then in the spring of 1846, Smithers led one last expedition. His wife had long since left him. A year later, his wife reported his disappearance. No one had the time or money to search for the missing man."

His mother and his sister stared at him for several minutes. Quinn punched him in the arm and said, "Why have you never told us this story? How long have you known? Does Zak know?"

He rubbed his arm and got up from the bar stool, "We've known for years. We just didn't want to say anything to Mom because she'd tell Aunt Esther and Aunt Esther would tell everybody including the newspapers and we'd be a laughing stock and our reputations would be ruined. You get it now? What I told you is just between us. Understand?" He looked at his mother and his sister for confirmation. His sister shrugged and jumped off the stool as if she no longer cared about long dead archeologists. His mother studied his face with an uncomfortable intensity.

"Don't worry, I won't say anything to Esther or anyone else. And I'll make sure Quinn doesn't say anything either."

When his mother started to look at him as if he were some kind of genius, he walked back to his table near Keys and sat down with a fresh beer to take notes and watch her closely.

Luke heard the story of Smithers' expedition as a freshman in Professor Wade's class and his first reaction had been betrayal. In his experience hard work and dedication led to greatness. But here was a story of someone who had been dedicated yet forgotten until an amateur journalist spoofed him in a book about eccentric Quixotic people who lost everything in their crazy search for unicorns, mermaids, Big Foot, and most particularly in Smithers' case – a mythical Greek creature called a harpy.

The tale of Smithers' fruitless travels and pathetic death still haunted Luke's dreams. Would his history parallel the same ridicule and disgrace? A person's reputation in the field of archeology was everything. Even the slightest hint of improper practices or false claims could end a career.

In 2007, after encountering the cop's wife, Luke realized Leland must have known the value of the blanket and must have been ecstatic to have been handed such a valuable item at little cost to himself by a woman who had no idea what she was giving away. Luke was sure Leland dealt in stolen goods. A week after his encounter with the cop's wife, Luke wandered into Leland's shop in the hopes he might find something linking Leland with the blanket or some other valuable artifact.

He found a map instead. It wasn't even period, just a reproduction of a map. It was the initials sewn in gold thread on one corner that made his heart race. Dr. Krutcher had testified that Constance Wade had used a similar map to keep track of her exploratory digs.

For barely five minutes, Luke fought with himself over what to do. It was in this pawn shop that Zak's childhood had ended in such an ugly way. As the older brother, Luke should have wrung Leland's neck for the sicko he was, but he knew revenge would only hurt his brother. Over the years, there had been many occasions when he wanted to punch the smug smile off Leland's fat ugly toad of a face. He looked the pervert in the eye and said, "Where did you get this map?"

Leland didn't so much as blink, "Some guys came in here years ago. They told me they were brothers. I forget their names. Their mother's body had been discovered. You know . . . the one that worked at the university. It was her sons that pawned most of her stuff. I got a couple of lamps and some other junk I've never been able to move."

It took all his self-control not to rush up to the fat bloody bugger of a frog and shake him good. Luke managed to say, "You're talking about Professor Constance Wade. Are you trying to tell me Wade's children pawned their mother's possessions? I find that hard to believe. Before I buy it, I want a receipt for this map with a detailed description of the provenance."

Several minutes passed as Leland considered his request. Luke remained calm. Leland looked back at him with cold calculating eyes and without a word pulled out his receipt book and began writing. Clearly here was evidence that Leland (the wart on the ass of the world) had pawned goods from a grieving family; yet, if Luke went to the police and exposed the man's criminality over the Navaho blanket and this map, he would get his brother into trouble as well.

Besides the police would confiscate the blanket and Luke would have no leverage. He considered going to Professor Wade's sons with the blanket and the map and explaining how he had obtained them. He even thought about asking if he might have access to their mother's field notes as a way of discovering clues to her death. But realistically he knew he couldn't do any of it because revealing the reality of the blanket would mean everything would come out – the cop leaving a valuable piece of evidence in his home, the cop's even dumber wife giving the blanket away at a yard sale to her lover; and most importantly, his brother exposed as the kid who stole the blanket.

What a shitty situation, he thought. He wanted to do right by everyone, but circumstances prevented him from ratting out his brother. Luke fervently wanted to know what Wade had left out of her published book referencing her discovery of Smithers' expedition. Maybe what hadn't been recorded was evidence of Amara? The news would have ruined the reputation of the team: Dr. Krutcher, Dr. Wade and their three graduate students. Maybe Krutcher had disposed of Constance fearing she would reveal their real reason for the dig? If so, that might mean Krutcher had Amara's remains.

His ruminations were too fantastical. If Krutcher had really discovered the remains of Amara, he would have called all the local news stations and recorded the whole thing for posterity. Something else was going on. Too many people important to the dig had disappeared or died.

Here it was the year 2017 and Krutcher was nowhere to be found. Back in 2004, he'd gone on his famous sabbatical for two years and no one had missed him much. Two years and two months later, his sister contacted the police worried something had happened to her brother. Her last postcard from him had been in 2004. The university had expected to hear from him but believed he had chosen to retire early rather than come back to teach. And by 2007, he was officially pronounced missing.

Could life jerk Luke around anymore: Dr. Wade possibly dead and Krutcher missing, two people who might have knowledge he dearly needed in order to find Amara – what were the odds of that happening?

After all his rumination about whether to go to the authorities, Luke chose to remain silent and bought the map for a lot less than the asking price. When he walked out of the pawn shop with the map and a letter supposedly proving provenance, he couldn't shrug off the sense that he was just as tainted by avarice as Leland.

Trying to shake off the memory of his abysmal hour, Luke picked up a pool stick and shot the eight ball into the right-hand corner pocket so hard the ball ricocheted off the wood frame and flew into the air then bounced onto the floor. His mother frowned at him. Luke shrugged and forced a smile to his lips. Unable to resist his apologies, his mother returned his smile.

Luke had to look elsewhere for his ancestor. The Smithers' notebooks had been reproduced by graduate assistants of the department for the edification of the public. Before he went missing, Krutcher had included an appendix, field notes, and pictures in his last book. But Luke found his most fruitful information at the university library in special collections transcribed from the actual Smithers' notebooks.

Luke found the cramped writing difficult to read but after a week of study, he finally came across the information which had been carefully excluded from Krutcher's book. Krutcher's painstaking erasure of Smithers' ideas annoyed Luke. The old fart had probably never had a romantic notion in his entire life. No wonder he hadn't found anything of significance since the Wade discoveries.

Smithers' notebooks had given Luke hope, especially the sentence that stated: *I am on the verge of finding her at last!* Smithers had described his meeting with an old Piute medicine woman who claimed to know where the harpy rested. Smithers had written of his intention to follow the woman. But the succeeding notes had been disheartening.

The Piute woman had died along the way and the location of the harpy's grave had died with her. Luke tried to brush aside the memory of Zak's snide remark when Luke had mentioned the entries in the notebook, but the words echoed inside his head jeering at his hopes of finding the bones, "If I were a hungry dispossessed Piute, I might lie and tell some stupid rich guy what he wanted to hear just to get a nice meal and a warm bed."

Without his family's knowledge, Luke went to see the site of the Smithers' dig for himself. He had to backtrack and start in Ely, Nevada then follow the directions included in Krutcher's book which showed where Wade had located the Smithers' artifacts. When he was there, on the spot, he shook his head in admiration at her remarkable intuition and skill. In contrast to the beauty of Cave Lake, the site of Wade's discovery was a desolate place and there were no clues left which might suggested history lay beneath his feet.

Luke had had to check and recheck his maps because when he surveyed the land with his naked eye nothing looked disturbed, nothing appeared to suggest a dig had ever occurred; and only after he carefully counted off the necessary steps from the dirt road to the site did he locate the spot where the dig took place. Anyone else would have walked by and never known that dozens of people had been sifting through the soil and carting away artifacts from this spot. But there were signs if one looked closely enough: loose soil, unnatural mounds unlike animal burrows, and a flat much-trampled area where he guessed the team had set up their sifting tables and other equipment. He even found a piece of orange rope which archeologists use to cordon off an area for excavation.

Usually people leave their mark upon the land. Not Wade. After Krutcher left for New Guinea and Wade had finished photographing the site and cataloguing the artifacts, she must have refilled the holes and raked the ground smooth carefully returning the land to its former state. Luke stood on that site with the mountains behind him and an incredible expanse of land stretching for miles everywhere, barren, and hot and magnificent. He stood there thinking about Smithers and imagining what Smithers had found.

As if he were performing a benediction to Smithers and Wade, Luke ceremoniously opened Krutcher's book, a book Krutcher dedicated to Constance Wade after her disappearance (ironic since Wade had done all the work anyway) and read her meticulous notes which catalogued the findings: two sets of hinges from what might have been the stage coach doors, a steel container the size of a steamer trunk loaded with digging tools and a nicely persevered leather satchel found in a special compartment beneath the bottom of the trunk; and in this compartment, Wade and the others found the most valuable discovery – Smithers' notebooks, notebooks which recorded all of Smithers' past expeditions.

And Wade's streak of luck continued when during the second week of the dig, a student stumbled across the skeletal remains of three people. A few months later, forensics identified the bones as belonging to two males and a young female. The bullets in the bodies of the skeletons answered the question as to what had happened to G. K. Smithers. Nothing else had survived the harsh environment of the Nevada high desert though. Any wood would have long since rotted away or been carried away by people who needed the material more than the dead.

Most likely feeling threatened, Smithers must have hastily buried his most precious possessions in the experimental holes he and his team had already dug before being set upon by his murderer or murderers. There were plenty of outlaws and vagabonds roaming the desert in those days. History was gearing up for a major war between the United States and Mexico over the territory of Nevada. In 1821 Nevada belonged to Mexico. After the Mexican War in 1848, the new territory belonged to the United States. It didn't become a state until Lincoln's presidency because most of the people of Nevada were anti-slavery. Ironically the murderers must have buried Smithers and his companions in the test holes still left open by their excavation.

What intrigued Luke the most was the identity of the female on Smithers' expedition. Who had she been? She wasn't mentioned anywhere, not in any newspaper articles of that period or in Smithers' notebooks. Krutcher had assumed the other male to be Smithers' cousin Matthew. Could the woman have been a relative of the old Piute medicine woman? No. God. He was overthinking this. Forensics had already determined the unknown woman had been Caucasian. Maybe she had been a family member? Or perhaps one of the ladies of the evening Smithers took with him? It would not surprise Luke if Smithers had commissioned a prostitute to come along on the expedition as an extra pair of hands to cook and clean for the men.

All signs seemed to suggest that the Smithers' expedition and the Krutcher/Wade expedition had been doomed from the beginning. It was as if bad luck followed anyone who tried to discover if Amara really existed. Was this evidence of Zeus' will? Would he and his brother experience the same fate?

Unbidden, a sharp bark of laughter erupted from his throat. Embarrassed, he glanced around the room to see if anyone else had noticed. No one was paying any attention to him. Keys remained stiffly upright in her seat with her eyes shut. Her face looked so tranquil that the rational part of him pitied her. She must be seriously damaged to allow this craziness to continue. Yet another part of him wondered if she was evidence of an evolutionary process going on in homo sapiens sapiens. Perhaps the Greek myth of Cassandra the prophetic daughter of King Priam was a harbinger of things to come? Or was she channeling something else – maybe knowledge of or a relationship with Dr. Wade?

Were there others like him, their rational side warring with their superstitious nature? Dr. Wade had never had any doubts. She believed in Darwin's theory. Her mantra was always "if it can't be replicated using science or proved with empirical evidence, chuck it in the spiritual bin." So here he was searching for a logical explanation for his family's fantastical legend. To please both his mother and Wade he decided there had to be a rational explanation for the existence of Amara. After all some babies were born with tails while others were born with long hair all over their bodies. Were these children examples of an earlier evolutionary era?

If Constance Wade had lived, she would have made a phenomenal archeologist. If . . . what am I saying, Luke thought, shocked at his own doubts? Of course, she's alive. She has to be alive. They never found her body. That woman in New Mexico could not be identified. The police were too busy with more recent disappearances and murders and other crimes to keep on searching for a woman who didn't want to be found. And later of course, by a fluke, Luke discovered why the police investigation had come to a sudden halt. They had ended the case because they didn't want the public to know that their detective was too stupid to put evidence somewhere safe instead of leaving it lying around in the garage for the wife to sell.

Luke shook his head free of the cobwebs of the past and turned to stare at the girl who hadn't moved in nearly an hour. Even if someone slept, the sleeper would inevitably twitch or readjust position. The fact she had barely moved in all that time was another clue she was the real thing. Luke was convinced this woman would lead them to Amara. He had an instinct about these things. He kept his thoughts focused on the girl before him. Open those sweet lips wench. Open those sexy eyes and sweet lips and tell me what I need to know, he urged her silently.

Professor Squirt passed Luke on the way to the toilet and Luke kept his eyes on the floor so as not to reveal his jealous resentment. Zak erroneously assumed he and Andy were friends. Nothing could be more untrue. Everybody thought Andy was such a damned genius. Hell no, Luke thought. Andy was no genius. Anyone can memorize a book and regurgitate the contents. Real genius came from imagination, inspiration, creativity, and so much more. Professor Squirt hadn't a clue how to think outside his books and his laboratory. Unlike Squirt, Luke had the imagination to do something really spectacular with his life. And Luke knew damned well the skull Zak found was from a rabbit. They had more important puzzles to solve than some horrifying carnival sideshow. A human/rabbit hybrid was just too creepy to be real, while an infant/rabbit hybrid was over the top grotesque.

He looked up in time to see Zak slip out the door again.

Feeling antsy himself Luke shifted from one foot to the other, stretched his arms up in the air, and finally decided he'd go bonkers if he stared at clairvoyant-girl any longer. Impatient with the silence and state of inertia, Luke jerked the screen door open and stepped outside trying to take a couple of deep breathes to calm himself. No one noticed his abrupt exit. Keys or Leona as she preferred to be called continued to finger the blanket with her eyes closed. He had been watching those eyeballs of hers moving side to side as if she were in REM sleep which a cynical person might think a sign of fakery. She wasn't faking. No one, no matter how desperate would sit still for an hour and thirty-five minutes just to impress strangers or try to whittle money out of them.

It had been stuffy in the bar. He breathed in the fresh air and noticed Zak circling the shed. He didn't want to know what his brother was up to. Luke stood on the porch with his arms crossed and waited for Zak to finish marking his territory. No, Luke realized, Zak was looking for something, the chimera he claimed he'd seen. Luke needed privacy and a place to step away from all the drama. As he walked toward his trailer, he fished out his cellphone and called his mother. She answered on the first ring.

"Yeah," she said.

"I forgot something at the trailer. I'll be back in ten."

"Why is this woman still sitting at one of my good tables taking up space? Huh Luke? Why is that? I've got a business to run here. I don't need any of your weirdoes ruining my reputation. If she isn't out of here in another hour I'm going to wake her fake ass up and throw her out. You hear me Luke?"

"Mom. Listen. This woman might be able to lead us directly to Amara. You understand now I'm serious. She could have all the answers. Please. Just let her be."

"An hour ago, I thought you might be on to something. Now, I don't think so. You've got to be kidding me? Is this one of your elaborate jokes?"

"No. I'm serious. Just give it another hour. Please keep an eye on her and if she wakes up before I'm back jot down everything she says. Come on Mom. Do this for the family for Aunt Esther. Or if not Esther for Adoni. OK?"

"Another hour of this shit? I thought I'd beaten your freaky father out of you boys."

"Beaten? When did you ever beat us?" Luke asked with a laugh as he turned off the main dirt road onto a private road which led to his trailer. Zak's trailer was in front of his. Luke had to step over old car parts and other debris in his brother's front yard to get to his own trailer. Luke stared at the canopy of camouflaged mesh across the top of Zak's trailer and shook his head in amazement. Zak had been fourteen and in his GI Joe phase when he covered the trailer with camouflage against imaginary enemies from the air. Then the camouflage had served to protect his trailer from imaginary government conspiracies. The camouflage was here to stay and would stay until it rotted or blew off or his mother decided to get rid of it.

Once Luke stood on his property, he looked over his shoulder and saw the Woolly Man Bar & Grill from his stoop. A movement caught his attention and he looked toward the barn. He saw his brother come out of the barn and turn and stand with his hands on his hips staring fixedly at something inside. Luke did not want to know what he'd found.

"I beat you plenty," he heard his mother say in his ear.

"Yeah you go ahead and impress the customers with your toughness Mom," Luke responded with a chuckle. "Just do me this favor and call me when she wakes up, OK?"

"If you're not back here in ten minutes I'll be calling the hospital and asking them to come take this looney-toon away. See you in ten."

Luke stuffed his cellphone in his shirt pocket and glanced around his property. His grandfather had gifted the property to Luke and his brother. Luke and Zak chose to share the five acres equally. Luke glanced at the proximity of Zak's trailer and frowned. Zak had deliberately moved his trailer up close to Luke's. At first his younger brother's admiration had been flattering; now, Zak's nearness felt more like an aggressive attempt to take over all the available space.

Unlike Luke who enjoyed solitude, Zak needed people around him all the time. And with that thought Luke was reminded of another habit of Zak's that annoyed him. Luke marched over to the offending item and swept the candy wrapper up in his clenched hand. He was getting sick and tired of picking up after Zak. There was nothing worse than seeing garbage on the ground. He hated it when people trashed the desert leaving their old pop bottles and beer cans and junk behind. It was a filthy habit. Couldn't they see that it was filthy and wrong?

Zak should have known better; after all, he worshiped the outdoors. Once inside his trailer, Luke threw the wrapper in the garbage and realized belatedly that Zak would never abuse his body with candy. Zak ate only pure food untainted by salts, sugars, butters, or preservatives. He hadn't gone vegan at least; but he was close enough to drive Luke crazy sometimes with his whining about the nasty things they added to food at restaurants.

Luke noticed the sandals first. They were lying on his brand new burgundy Italian leather armchair. He nearly gagged at the thought of someone's smelly shoes resting where he planted his butt every evening. Luke grabbed the broom out of the tiny closet near his elbow and slipped the stick end through the straps of the sandals. The offending objects dangled above his chair for a moment as he tried to decide where they belonged. He opened his trailer door and tossed them in Zak's front yard. Then he rehung his broom carefully in the closet and proceeded to investigate the rest of his home. The flush of the toilet startled him so much he forgot to duck under the Caribbean oak ceiling fan in his kitchen. The whirling blades nearly took out his eye.

Practically everyone in the Woolly Man heard Luke's angry bellow. Only Quinn was interested enough to investigate. She shot out the side door and ran across the field. When she burst into Luke's trailer, she found him dragging a woman along the tiny hallway into the kitchen. Quinn had never seen the woman before. Evidently neither had Luke.

"I don't give a rat's frigging ass if you are a friend of Zak's. This is not Zak's home. This is my home and I want you out. Now! Get dressed and get your sorry-ass-butt out of my house."

Both women winced at the volume and passion in Luke's voice. Quinn had never seen his face so livid. Even though Luke had never brought a woman home to meet the family or shack up for the night and Zak liked to joke about Luke's lackluster libido, Quinn knew for a fact her brother was heterosexual, although, she had to admit his heterosexuality could be beyond quirky and sometimes into the weird.

That time in Las Cruces, New Mexico when she volunteered to help on a dig and there was that woman with long blonde hair and red finger nails. Quinn would never forget that day. No, of course, Luke wasn't a homosexual, he was just compulsively tidy and well-organized. This woman of Zak's looked as if she'd been blazing a trail through the Mojave Desert. Her skin resembled old leather. It was almost the color of cedar. She had a long mane of brown hair that dangled down to her skinny ass and the blonde highlights on top looked as if she'd applied them with a paintbrush. She had thick fingers which one might mistake for a man's hand and those fingers were in the process of pulling a pair of tight blue jeans over a pair of red bikini underwear. Her tank-top left nothing to the imagination either.

It made Quinn feel better to know that there were women in the world even smaller breasted than her. While the woman finished dressing, Quinn could hear Luke pulling out dresser drawers in the back bedroom and slamming cupboards over his bed.

The woman shot over her shoulder, "I didn't steal anything if that's what you're thinking. I just needed a place to crash that didn't smell of stale beer and rank garbage."

Luke appeared at the end of the hall his color much improved. "I told you to get out. Now get."

"Where are my damned shoes? I need my shoes."

"I threw them outside."

"What an ass," Quinn heard her say as she brushed past Quinn and left the trailer. She paused before closing the trailer door to ask Quinn, "Do you know where Zak is? He said he'd be back in a minute, but it's been hours."

Quinn considered lying but decided Zak could do his own lying, "He's over at the barn."

The woman tried to smile but the smile never reached her eyes. She looked miserable. So why had Zak chosen her? She was completely unlike his usual women. She was so much older than any of them. No amount of hair dye could disguise her age. She hadn't been in the bar last night either; Quinn would have remembered her. Where had she come from? There was a sort of buried sweetness to her, but she wasn't the kind of woman who had the desire or skill to befriend other women. She reminded Quinn of someone desperate to call attention to herself, desperate to find someone to love her; yet, when she found that someone, she would throw him away. Quinn recognized the addiction to suffering and all the sudden felt sorry for her.

Quinn watched as she tripped her way around sagebrush and rocks trying not to break her neck in her high heeled sandals. And what about Luke's Las Cruces' woman? Where had she come from? Where did her brothers find these losers? Quinn tried not to think about that blonde with the red nails, the Canadian slut looking like a two-bit hooker who happened to be the representative of the bank financing the dig.

And there she had been in her dubious glory lying at the bottom of a test hole with her legs spread in a place the former occupants a hundred years ago used as a dump. This hole happened to be a community dump where not only early pioneers left their trash but Native Americans indigenous to the area had been leaving their trash for decades.

Archeologists with all their education sifting around in hundred-year-old garbage dumps seemed crazy to her. Quinn had tried to understand.

And when she needed more answers she went looking for Luke and unfortunately for her and her future mental health found him on top of a woman wearing a fake wig, a blonde wig which spilled out on

140

the ground around her face in long tendrils reminding Quinn of yellow snakes. Then she recognized the woman. She was that Canadian chick with the red nails and pointed nose. Those red nails were raking her brother's back now, and the nose was stuck up in the air like a snorkel breaking the surface of the water as she writhed in imitation of an orgasm.

But even through the heat of Quinn's embarrassment, Quinn could recognize a fake orgasm when she saw it. And there beside the writhing bodies lay an aqua marine sequined piece of clothing. While her brother pumped away as if his life depended on his orgasm, Quinn realized that what she was looking at was the bottom half of a mermaid costume. Quinn's discomfort with her own horny reaction dissolved at the sight. Men were sick bastards and her brother sicker than most. And the Canadian slut opened her eyes and saw Quinn staring down at them from above. She shrieked, and Luke froze. He refused to turn his head and see who stood watching them. Quinn walked away.

All that week, Luke avoided looking directly at her. It wasn't until she had packed and one of the volunteers offered to take her to the bus depot in Las Cruces that Luke spoke to her. He looked her in the eye searching. It was at that moment Quinn remembered the good in Luke. She had Zak and she had Luke. They were her only family. There were no others, no cousins, no fathers, just the three of them.

And with memories of Luke and Zak defending her honor at school, teasing her ruthlessly, making a tree house for her during the long summer days when they could have been out with their friends on dirt bikes or swimming in the canal, those memories extinguished the ugliness of the last five days. She forgave him and did her best to forget.

"I haven't the words, Quinn," Luke began staring down at the dirt beneath his fingernails. "I haven't even the excuse of inebriation. It was a momentary madness. Someone told her I like mermaids."

With a flush warming her cheeks, Quinn realized who that idiot had been. She had told the Canadian hussy about Luke's secret obsession. She remembered the day the suits came to watch the digging and Quinn had seen the banker in her tight-fitting skirt and stiletto heels and watched in amusement as the woman minced her way across the uneven ground making a beeline straight for Luke. But Luke, as usual, had eyes only for the objects he could find beneath his trowel and his brush. And when the banker couldn't get his attention, she decided to pick Quinn's brains assuming Quinn might be a rival. What the banker didn't know was that Quinn wasn't a girlfriend or curious tourist but had volunteered to work on the dig and happened to be waiting for the lead archeologist to tell her what to do, the lead archeologist who happened to be her brother.

The banker had approached Quinn with one of her professional smiles and outstretched hand and Quinn accepted the hand without thinking. In an attempt at female camaraderie the banker had asked, "You know that man over there, the gorgeous one with the long black hair?"

"Sure, he's the lead on this dig," Quinn admitted, wondering why she had been so forthcoming with this stranger she already instinctively disliked.

"You think he might be interested in dinner some time?" she asked staring at Luke as if he might be on the menu.

"Not unless you had scales, fins, and hair down to your ass," Quinn said.

"Excuse me?" she said with a frown.

"You figure it out," Quinn had said in parting not liking the avarice light in her eye or her assumption Quinn was a rival.

The high-pitched squawking of a killdeer startled Quinn into the present. The killdeer strutted on the ground about three feet away from Quinn and Quinn guessed that her young must be somewhere nearby. The killdeer would sacrifice herself to lure the enemy away from the nest perhaps dying for her future offspring. The thought made Quinn even sadder than she had been a moment ago.

Sacrifice reminded her of Navan Keys which seemed so odd. Leona had a vulnerable quality which some might mistake for weakness. The intelligence was there in her eyes, eyes that were used to assessing, analyzing, studying, and making conclusions. The new-age clothes didn't suit her personality at all. Those eyes were full of wisdom as if she'd lived several life times. Quinn knew deep down she would have liked this woman, if they had met differently. But now, now things were different, and the stranger made her brothers crazy which Quinn hated. Weird how Quinn wanted to protect Leona from her brothers and their self-centeredness and simultaneously protect her brothers from the secrecy and strength of Leona.

Quinn stepped outside to let Luke vent in private and stood on the stoop watching as Zak's one-nighter weaved her way cautiously around sage, rock, and loose sand. Once she startled a jackrabbit and let out a shriek when it bolted away. Moments later she walked right into a huge spider web. Quinn chuckled under her breath. Watching people was better than watching television. There that lady was slapping away at her head and peeling sticky strands of spider web off her shoulder while the killdeer made such a racket defending her nest.

Watching the city girl was as much fun as watching reality television. People were hilarious. They really were. Zak hadn't seen his girlfriend yet, but the girlfriend stopped when she saw Zak. The woman reminded Quinn of a Labrador Retriever sighting its prey. Quinn thought about whistling to warn Zak then changed her mind. Once in a while, the guy needed to fix his own problems. The woman changed course and called out to Zak, her voice registering unhappiness and inevitability. Obviously, she didn't expect much from Zak. Maybe she wasn't so dumb after all.

Uncomfortably at the outcome and rather sad for them both, Quinn went back into Luke's trailer. Luke passed her without comment and dropped onto his overpriced armchair. He said nothing, just kept staring off into space. Quinn thought about asking his advice on whether to leave school but the expression on his face warned her he would not be in the mood for confidences. He had the best chance of persuading Mom to let her pursue her real dream. Why did she have to go to college if she planned on making millions as a model? She could wear all those wicked clothes and travel to exotic places. It just didn't make sense to go to college.

Quinn left Luke to his masticating thoughts. By the time she had crossed the field and entered the Woolly Man her mother was ready to leave. Disappointed at having to forgo all the passion and drama taking place, she listened unashamedly as Zak argued with the barfly outside. Some people might relish escaping Luke's simmering rage as he took shelter in his trailer and Zak fending off a lovestruck woman, but not Quinn. She was loving every second of her brothers' discomfort. About time.

Then Quinn discovered Zak had managed to charm Jule once again and she was too late to change her mother's mind. Jule had already offered the barfly a ride back to Boise. What the hell? Now pissed at her mother for giving in to Zak, Quinn was ready to leave and maybe she'd never come back. Why should she? Her brothers could commit murder and Mom would still find a way to turn herself inside-out to rescue them.

Before anyone could officially get in the damned car and drive away, Ms. Keys opened her eyes and looked around the room. So of course, Mom had to wait and hear what she had to say. It was weird how one phone call could bring the cavalry. The back door and the front door flew open almost simultaneously which was amusing really.

Luke looked at his brother as they both met in the middle of the room. Luke thought about the Nerin Genealogy which had been in their family for decades. He considered asking his mother for another peek at the huge leather-bound tome which included every ancestor for the last two thousand years. Soon what he learned today might be the next chapter in the family's fortunes or the end of the Nerin family legend. Whatever this stranger told them would mean the genealogy with its intricate cover and its onion skinned pages etched with gold-leaf would symbolize either success or failure. What amazed him and made him shake his head in wonder was that his damn family didn't even see what was right under their frigging noses.

He saw again the front cover of the genealogy in his mind's eye. The artist had imbedded letters in the center filled with real gold which spelled out the name Katsaros in Greek. Upon opening the history, the first image to appear on the left-hand side was the carefully detailed portrait of the woman's face drawn in ink and embellished with arsenic, copper, insect bodies, and lapis lazuli. His ancestors had used what was available at the time. His mother protected the dangerous mixture of colors with a sheet of wax paper to prevent the possibility of damage or poisoning.

On the right-hand side of the genealogy was the full-length drawing of the woman's face and body. She had been drawn on her side her head turned to look at the reader, arm resting on her hip and shapely legs slightly bent as if she lay resting on an expensive leather couch. The full-length portrait had always intrigued him from the time he was a little boy to this momentous day. He remembered his mother making sure no one was a witness to the book's contents not even in the privacy of her own bedroom. Neither of her husbands had been privy to the existence of the book.

His mother showed him the family ledger shortly after his thirteenth birthday when they were alone in the bar. She had locked the doors to make sure they were not interrupted and carried the genealogy in her arms as if she were holding a newborn. To this day, he has no idea where she hides the genealogy.

"Here she is Luke," his mother had said to him, carefully setting the cracked leather-bound book down on a clean counter and with a gloved hand opening the genealogy to the first page.

He remembered staring down at the image of Amara Katsaros' beautiful face and the Greek symbols that weaved through her long auburn hair. He heard his mother say with reverence. "Someday we'll find her again; and when we do, we will no longer fear hunger or want nor man or beast. We will be invincible. Once again we will live forever like gods." Then she closed the book and turned it over and showed him the drawing on the last page. It was an exact replica of the first drawing except the artist had added on her shoulder a reddish gold wing and the suggestion of another wing beneath. He had included on her slender feet talons protruding from her toenails; they were the color of ivory: sharp, curved, and deadly.

Luke had grown up believing Amara could resurrect their family honor. And now, now they were so close. He was convinced they were closer than ever.

11

The word of the day: limbo. She knew that state of being. She'd experienced limbo before as in the border between the divine and the tortured. The dictionary said the word meant – "the abode of unbaptized but innocent or righteous souls, as those of infants or virtuous individuals who lived before the coming of Christ" or "a region or condition of oblivion or neglect." More accurately perhaps for her current condition, she was in a "state or place of confinement." All three definitions applied to her in one way or another from her birth to the present day.

Well, perhaps not so much the part about innocence and righteous souls. She was hardly innocent, definitely not righteous. Anger rose up inside Leona and nearly choked her, an anger mixed with a sense of betrayal that churned her stomach into hot acid. And look what happens to the innocent and the righteous. Her anger was the catalyst that sharpened the picture in her mind's eye and brought the foggy image into focus.

It was night but there was a full moon. Its light seemed preternaturally focused on a particular part of the desert. It was winter. She could see their exhalation frozen for a moment in the air, particles that had traveled through their bodies and were now free and floating away. How vivid the image was in her mind's eye? She saw three figures crawling their way out of the earth as if they'd been buried alive. The unexpectedness of the vision frightened her so much she jumped away to a happier time. She saw herself sitting on a sandy beach watching the ocean waves roll in and behind her she could feel the forest thick and cold. A force inside fought back. Frantically, she tried to brush away the images leaping over each other pushing and shoving their way to the forefront of her conscious mind. She wanted those images, those memories to stay buried, but they kept popping into view without warning.

So far there didn't seem to be any point to what she was seeing. The farm was in a valley surrounded by hills and mountains. The only distinctive object in the entire landscape was the gigantic Catalpa tree near the farmhouse; otherwise, the view looked similar to most any other view in farm country. Then Leona saw the kids playing in the front yard under the Catalpa tree and she recognized one of them.

Leona had to look away fighting a searing pain in the back of her skull. She'd recognized the slim girl the one with the long curly black hair. After several deep breathes she relaxed her muscles fearing she would pass out or be sick. A man hollered to the girl. Leona blamed her nausea for the sudden blackness. Maybe it had been a mistake to offer her services to these greedy opportunists. They didn't care about her — all they wanted was to be famous in the world of archeology for rediscovering something someone else had already found. They were grave robbers. They were dangerous.

She heard a familiar voice say, "Don't let them get away with it Leona."

Panic seized her. She recognized the signs. She was going to have a meltdown if she wasn't careful and she would end up back at 8-Ball Ward or somewhere even worse.

Leona's body felt hot one moment cold the next. A stabbing pain shot up her arm. A different voice, a soothing voice whispered in her ear, "You're not alone, kiddo. Don't be afraid. Remember, we're here for you. Anything you need just ask." Leona relaxed. It seemed like an eon before she could regain her momentum and concentrate once again. When the new vision flashed before her eyes, she felt overwhelming gratitude. Here. This one felt right. The sensation of fear washed over her. She made herself hold on. The others needed her now. She wouldn't let them down.

She saw the inside of a cheap hotel room. Beyond the door was a bed. All she could see was the foot of the bed. And directly in front of her was an old stuffed recliner facing a television chained to the wall. The television was propped precariously on a homemade shelf in the upper corner of the room between the ceiling and the wall. There was a man sitting in a recliner. A chunk of his long greasy brown hair was missing. Right there in the back of his skull, the bald spot looked as if someone had come along and yanked the hair out by its roots. Otherwise someone had cut his hair in the mullet style of the late '80s or early '90s.

The image wavered for a moment. She pressed her hands together to keep herself from jumping out of her chair and running from the Woolly Man. She wanted to see more. There was more. Eagerly, she surveyed the room picking up details that might pacify these guys, so she could ditch them and be on her way. She noticed a cheap dresser made of pine covered in faux wood with a ghetto blaster resting on its surface. Closest to her she could see dirty green mini-blinds and several cheap prints in plastic frames on the wall. Motels used to hang oils done by local artists. Not this motel. This motel wasn't interested in atmosphere or the discriminating tastes of its clientele.

What was so odd about the whole image was her perspective. She analyzed the perspective and realized what she was seeing was what someone would see if he or she was lying on the hotel bed. She looked down and focused on the bedspread. She saw the Navaho blanket folded neatly at the foot of the bed and beneath it a motel bedspread. The pattern on the bedspread resembled one of those spotted cats, a leopard maybe or cheetah, the ugly yellow spots next to the brown spots made her sick to her stomach. She looked· away and realized she wasn't the one looking away or feeling sick.

She wished the man in the recliner would turn around, so she could get a good look at his face. The television was on. Two men in leotards were wrestling in a ring. Both wrestlers had hair down to their asses. Of course! Men looked manlier with long hair. Leona suspected wrestlers and wrestling fans were really just history's oppositionists. Everyone claims the reason for wrestler's long hair is all about amplifying the action in the ring for the poor-cusses in the nosebleed section? Maybe.

But there might be a more ancient reason for men to prefer long hair. The Greek Gods supposedly wore their hair long and the assumption was long hair granted men strength and virility. Medieval royalty if given a choice preferred a noble death rather than the humiliation of cropped hair. Everyone knew cropped hair meant you were a serf. Unless, the man chose a vocation in the church and became a monk.

Otherwise, anyone with cropped hair was immediately recognized as a low person. Expectations changed during the Roman Period when Caesars and Senators wore their hair short. What about those Barbarian Hordes in the north? Do wrestling fans think of themselves as barbarians? How about King Charles and his courtiers who wore their hair long or covered their heads with fake wigs? Hum. Wrestling Royalty? How about male buns today? Are men signaling to the world their conservative or liberal beliefs?

Why was she ruminating about something so silly? Was it because Zak wore his hair short and Luke wore his hair long? Luke didn't wear his hair in a male bun. Common sense told her to get the hamster off the wheel and concentrate on the job.

While concentrating on the man in the recliner, a brilliant thought came to her. Of course! It all had to do with display. The wrestlers were displaying their youth, health, virility, and strength to potential mates. Simple. Just like heavy metal bands showing off their skills with a guitar or male singers with their voices, wrestlers were showing off to the women in the audience. Born peacocks, everyone.

The fans screamed for their favorite and broke her reverie. She concentrated on the scene playing out inside her head. Then Leona saw small feet, the feet of a child. She realized with a cold shudder she was seeing the room from the perspective of the child laying on the bed watching the man watch wrestling on television. As the image began to fade, Leona tried to see the child, tried to call out to him or her wanting a name or a location, anything that would pinpoint the child's whereabouts in a historical context. Her voice refused to obey. She heard a high-pitched giggle from the man and a whimper from the child – then the image was gone.

Leona waited patiently for the vision to reappear. She hadn't had time to really get a good look around the room. She needed more time, more time to catalog the details, perhaps pinpoint the date more accurately. There were thousands of cheap motels all over the western half of the United States. Most cheap motels ended up abandoned or bulldozed for new development. If she could just know the year when those two people were in that motel room she might be able to backtrack and learn the name of the man who had been in that room with the child.

Desperate to hold on to what she had seen she recited the most important details silently to herself, unaware she was simultaneously mouthing the words. Luckily for her no one was paying attention. She was sure if she recalled as many details as possible she could pinpoint the decade, maybe even the year when the event took place. Plus, she might even be able to pinpoint the location of the motel based on the furniture, the clothes and anything else that made the motel room, the man, and the child unique. A voice whispered in her ear, "We've got it Navan. We'll keep the memory safe for you."

When she tried to go back to the motel room to see more, she hit a wall. Yet scattered and sporadic would be flashes of gray in a corner or a streak that reminded her of lightening. For a second she saw the outline of a pentagram in thick white fog. It was like nothing she'd seen before. It had six points instead of the usual five. The tips of the points were rough looking as if a dull blade had left slivers of metal along the rims.

The lines of the pentagram began to move reshaping itself until there were only five points. Words began to appear above each point and stopped when a word wrote itself in the center of the pentagram. The word *loft* hung above the top point and in a clockwise motion proceeded the words: *andi, jörðin, vatn, eldur.* In the center of the pentagram was the word *viska.* The only word she recognized was loft. Yet grouped with the other words she was pretty sure loft meant something different than "an upper room." The language might be Scandinavian. She would have to do some research. Maybe the words were clues to where she might find the child?

The pentagram faded away and she was left with the impression of the sun hitting her closed eyelids, a wallpaper of flesh colored pulsating light. No new images replaced the pentagram and no matter how hard she tried she could not get back the vividness of the motel room. Nothing else came to the forefront not even the usual faces that sometimes popped into her mind at the most unexpected moments, faces which would gradually grow bigger and bigger until she could see every tiny gross detail down to the smallest pimple or the ugliest nose hair.

In defeat, Leona opened her eyes at last.

Jule sat where she'd last seen her – at the table closest to the kitchen barely an arm's span away from Leona. Jule sat with her arms folded on the surface of the metal café table staring at Leona, her heavy-lidded eyes nearly shut; every so often her head would nod forward, and she would jerk herself awake with an effort. Leona heard a chair screech against the dry neglected wood floor and saw Quincella cross from the bar toward Leona's table. Before Quinn had reached her side, Leona was fully awake and prepared for a barrage of questions.

Doors burst open. People swooped down on her from every direction. It was as if some silent alarm had gone off. Belatedly, Leona realized Quinn must have text her family. Leona jumped not knowing which way to look. Zak came in from the back door and Luke from the front. They met in the middle of the room and stood staring down at her. Nate pushed the kitchen swinging door aside. The first sensation that hit Leona was an emptiness that ate right into her back bone. The emptiness grumbled, and everyone heard her stomach, but it was Nate who did something about her hunger.

"Sweet Cheeks needs my special aphrodisiac," he said punctuated by the sound of the kitchen swinging doors slamming against the walls. Pots and pans were shoved aside. A head collided with a hanging pot. Nate swore and something metal skidded across the room and crashed into a wall. Leona saw a bowl full of chili with chopped onions and thick wedges of cheese on top. But that wasn't all; she also saw two white dollops of sour cream that reminded her of nipples artfully arranged on either side. Nate must be horny, Leona thought. A giggle caught in her throat and nearly choked her. Zak slapped her on the back, slapped her a little rougher than necessary with the full force of his arm. Leona hunched her shoulders and Jule cleared her throat, her signal for Zak to knock it off.

Zak slid onto the bench seat facing Leona and scrutinized her from top to bottom, his expression clearly skeptical of her competence wondering what she had discovered and planned to say to them. Luke slid in beside his brother Zak, his expression reserved but compassionate as if he knew a little something about pain and suffering. He had no idea, no idea bigger than a mosquito's ass about pain and suffering. He'd been spoon-fed love and attention all his damn life, first from his parents, then by his brother Zak, now his half-sister Quinn. Luke was loved by all. From the lack of scars on his face, arms and hands, Luke had never experienced the usual childhood bumps and bruises.

Which wasn't the case for Zak. From the few signs she could see Zak had scars, childhood accidents perhaps. Was the one on his hand due to his own clumsiness? He had dark hair and startling blue eyes like his black Irish father; Luke had his mother's warm Greek good looks and hazel eyes. They were both tall, but Zak had more muscle and girth. They had long legs and slim hips and striking good looks. Dangerous. Very dangerous. Leona did her best to push the image of naked men out of her head. All that work to fish up a vision had left her hollow inside. Her stomach made the worst possible noises; Quinn at the bar across the room, chuckled.

Leona blushed and dropped her head. Then she realized how ludicrous it was to be embarrassed by the rumbling of her empty stomach when she'd just spent unknown hours in a metaphysical fog most likely with her mouth open and her tongue hanging out. She might even have drooled a little like she did when she was really tired and woke to find her pillow wet. My Ass, she corrected herself. Horrified that she had been prey to all sorts of indecencies and stares from strangers, she glanced surreptitiously around the room especially concentrating her gaze on Jule to see if the older woman's expression gave anything away. Jule looked tired and annoyed.

Before Leona could open her mouth, Nate returned with a bowl of chili just the way she'd fantasized the food would look so many hours ago. She was hungry enough not to care if the men stared at her while she ate. Nate even provided her with crackers. With a startled oath, Zak took the Navaho blanket away from her. He was probably concerned she would contaminate the valuable artifact with her uncouth eating habits. He folded the blanket with exaggerated care, wrapped it in a linen bed sheet, and placed the artifact back inside a vintage navy-blue foot locker. Without a word he picked up the foot locker. Everyone heard the heavy screen door screech as he carried the foot locker outside followed by heavy boots crunching on gravel as he walked away.

Five minutes later Zak returned. "What kept you?" his brother asked. Zak didn't bother to answer.

As Leona began to eat, the brothers moved to sit at the bench opposite her and waited impatiently for her to finish her chili. She set the spoon down and looked into Zak's eyes. She'd hurt him the most. She hoped by giving him as much information as possible, she could receive some sort of forgiveness for what she'd blurted out in front of everyone.

"All I could see was a cheap motel room and a man sitting in a chair. He was watching wrestling on TV. He had this big bald spot up here like someone had yanked a hunk of his hair out with her bare hands. It looked nasty. But I couldn't see his face. There was someone on the bed, someone wrapped in the Navaho blanket watching him. I couldn't see the child. All I could see were the feet. I also noticed the print on the wall above the television set. The print was a primitive landscape of a lake and a cabin and a man fishing in a tiny boat. Not primitive good but primitive amateur bad. Oh, and on television, they had text streaming across the bottom of the screen. It had to do with something called 911. So, what I saw happened on or shortly after an event on September 11, 2001."

Zak made no secret of his disappointment. Luke, on the other hand, seemed surprised. He opened his mouth to say something, but Leona was no longer paying attention to them. She'd noticed something moving in the room, something that shouldn't have been there. She had promised to leave Leona alone. She heard Luke ask, "You said *someone yanked his hair out with **her** bare hands*. How do you know a woman did it?"

Leona saw the harpy out of the corner of her eye. Her spoon clattered to the floor. The people in the room receded into the darkness and all she saw was the creature, the harpy come to life, a harpy just like the one she'd imagined from mythology; only this one breathed and smelled and made sounds and it was perched on the barroom counter, perched like some predatory bird but as big as a full-grown woman and as malevolent as only a woman in the throes of an insane rage could be.

The woman's face had a pale antiquated beauty and her dark opaque eyes dug deep into Leona's soul. Her curly black hair flowed over her shoulders and down her back between her wings. Where there should have been fingers, she had claws, claws that had a grip on the edge of the counter like a vise. Leona tried desperately to focus only on Luke's face, to look only into his eyes. He appeared oblivious to the harpy's presence. When the harpy moved, as if in preparation for flight or to strike with those long, lethal killing-claws, Leona lost all her composure.

Instinct prompted her to move, to get out of the path of the avenging woman. She'd made the harpy mad. She'd done something wrong. What? What crime had she committed? What terrible thing would make a god send his watch dog to bury her once again in the cold ground? She was going to die. The harpy would swoop down and take her straight back to the grave.

12

Someone slapped her several times. Someone else threw a glass of water at her. She felt the liquid slide down her forehead and dribble down her chin. Another person picked her up and dragged her out into the sunshine. Leona woke just as the sun was beginning to sink behind the butte on the other side of the road. The butte looked familiar. She'd seen that water tank before. Then she remembered where she was. She sat up and Luke made sure he was the first one to lift her up into his arms. Zak followed close on their heels.

"You finished having hysterics yet?" Luke asked as he carried her back inside the bar. Luke plopped her down on a nearby barstool and held her shoulders, squeezing her arms until she cried out. He loosened his hold only after Zak punched him in the shoulder.

Leona glanced around the room and realized with real anxiety that the women were gone. And so were the fishermen. Even Nate had deserted her. Luke's fingers hurt her cheeks as he forced her to look at him. She didn't want to look at him. She didn't want him to see what she'd seen.

"Who is this – she – that's going to take you down to a living death? Huh? And why were you apologizing to her anyway? Is this all an act? Because if it is, I'll tell you straight it's a bad one. You're going about it all wrong. You got to do all the hysterical shit up front, give the suckers a little info to wet their appetite then you wait for the money. So, this – act," his gesture encompassed her entire frame in an attempt to belittle her performance, "doesn't make sense. All you've gotten so far for your troubles is a bowl of chili. A bowl of chili? Get serious. You're wasting our time."

Leona saw Zak wander toward the jukebox, an expression of distaste adding lines around his mouth and nose. As if he were cold, Zak settled near the window where the sun's rays beat a bright warm path through the pane of glass. He crossed his arms and watched them, watched in particular his brother Luke with puzzlement in his eyes.

Luke continued, "Although I must say, I kind of like the way your eyes glaze over. That's good, very good."

Zak chimed in, "And the way she's got you all worked up and pissed off Luke. That's good, very good too. Maybe Oscar worthy huh?"

Luke let go of her face and threw over his shoulder, "She's too naïve and stupid to be a con artist."

Leona rubbed her aching cheeks and stared down at her trembling hands.

"We got a time period," Zak said quietly. "And it's easy enough to check her facts. She mentioned Vegas, something about Acacia's ride. Acacia is a tree and I don't think she means the tree in Greece. Maybe we should go to Vegas. Maybe that's where we'll find our answers."

"There are probably hundreds of acacia trees in Vegas? Or maybe none? Then what? With nothing to go on, what do we do? I think we should take her with us," Luke said stepping back and examining Leona with interest.

"You want to add kidnapping to your resume?" Zak asked.

Leona slid off the barstool. Luke stopped her from leaving by clamping a warm hand on her shoulder. His hands moved to her waist, the fingers of each hand nearly meeting. As if she were a child, Luke hoisted her back on the barstool with ease. "Hold on a minute. You're not going anywhere until you've answered a few questions."

She glanced at Zak. Zak was frowning. Leona was afraid to look into Luke's eyes. She was afraid to look at him, period, in case he sensed the power he had over her. His chuckle made her sit up straighter. She forced herself to look him in the eye.

"I see things sometimes. Dr. B says I just need to ground myself in reality and stop reading so much and watching so much television. He says it's a modern day problem. He says I've got too much imagination for my own good. I guess I'm alone too much. I don't get out anymore because things like what just happened tend to happen when I'm in public. Well, actually it's been getting worse, sort of a split between the real world and the dream / fantasy world. You know? I guess what I'm trying to say is that I'm . . ."

Luke interrupted her, "Nuts?"

"For your information, no. Dr. Bishop says I'm as well adjusted as anyone else in today's society. In fact, she says my biggest problem is my sensitivity, that I'm too sensitive and too squeamish for this cruel world. But you see she's from a totally different generation. She's even older than my generation. Did you know she used to work with Holocaust victims back in Tel Aviv?

Yes. She did.

And during the late fifties, all the way through the sixties and seventies, she worked with them. She's an expert in her field. I mean that's what the nurses tell me. I didn't believe the stories. I mean it took a long time to trust Dr. A, but eventually I did. She was so sweet. I miss her terribly. She died years ago. She's nothing like," Leona stopped so abruptly she swallowed air and choked.

Luke slapped her on the back a few times and when she kept her head down, he bent over and peered into her face with a degree of enthusiastic curiosity which was unnerving. The expression on his face showed conflicted intentions.

When he finally spoke, the oddity of his expression in combination with his words made her wonder who was the real crazy person in the room. "So, you're a nut job," he said with a smile. "I thought so. You've been talking a lot of garbage so far. First Dr. B is 'he' then Dr. B is 'she.' Great. I think you've wasted enough of our time today. So, you mind translating your gibberish for the rest of us," he said venomously. "And make it quick because I have no more time to spare."

"You implied that I'm nuts and I'm telling you I'm not. There are two Dr. Bishops. They were married to each other until Dr. A, that is Angela Bishop to you, died of cancer. The current Dr. B is alive and well and in Chicago. He signed the papers releasing me from the hospital months ago. He is a leading expert in his field and if he says I'm perfectly sane then I'm damned well sane."

"Which is it going to be, Dr. A or Dr. B? Ghee. Now you're confusing me," Zak said grabbing at his hair and pretending to tug.

Leona looked across the room at him and said, "You haven't been listening. Dr. Caleb Bishop is Angela Bishop's husband. Dr. Caleb Bishop is Dr. B and Dr. Angela Bishop is Dr. A. Angela died some time ago. Dr. B took over her practice. He's a poor substitute for Dr. A, but that's how the world works. The good die young and evil lives forever."

No matter how you slice it, sounds like nuts to me, Zak thought.

He watched as Luke stepped back and crossed his arms holding in his anger, "I get that part. I get the part about Dr. B as a psychiatrist. What I don't get is why you needed to be hospitalized in the first place. What'd you do that was so egregious the shrinks had to lock you up for it?

Nowadays, it would have to be a very serious offense. Anyone, even someone diagnosed with a mental disorder can just walk out any time after twenty-four-hours. Did your family commit you? Or did the police find you making a nuisance of yourself in public and put you in one of those places for your own safety?"

Leona slid off the barstool. Zak noticed how Luke forced himself not to touch her. Zak approached the bar. She backed away from them both as if they were some sort of creepy predators. She looked toward the front door. Someone had propped the outer door open with a rock allowing the breeze to circulate through the screen door into the hot room. She looked away from the front door with a guilty expression then toward the bathrooms. It was as if he could read her mind. She was looking for an exit and wondering if she could outrun them. When she moved into the center of the room and paused with a bewildered expression on her face, Zak felt a stab of pity.

He couldn't stop looking at her. He saw the long neck and the way the pendent made of picture-jasper nestled between her breasts. The peasant top had gone from crisp white to dusty beige and the material was so worn that he could see her nipples through the fabric. With an effort he looked into her face and then away, uncomfortable at the change in her expression from sadness to a sudden extinguishing of hope. His eyes focused on the swirling pattern repeated over and over on her India cotton skirt.

The purples and greens were making him dizzy. He noticed her feet and paused in surprise at the unexpected sight. She had on a pair of army boots, boots too big for her feet with the tops untied and the leather folded down exposing the inner lining. The whole effect made her ankles look even smaller than normal more the size of a child's.

His eyes traveled back up to her face. Yes, she was standing in the center of the room, so thin, so pale with those tragic eyes. He had an insane urge to comfort her. Why? She could be a Borgia? He remembered his reaction when Luke plopped her unceremoniously on the barstool. He'd been jealous. She'd looked like a little kid. He couldn't get those sad eyes out of his head. He looked at the floor, at the wall, at anything but her, afraid he might start beating on his brother. Luke pulled up his sleeves as if he was preparing to dig a grave.

Zak was beginning to worry about Luke's uncharacteristic behavior. He usually ignored women, unless he was horny. Most women were just dumb animals to him. But not this one. Around her Luke acted nervy, cross, sarcastic, even cruel sometimes. Something about her made his brother itchy under the skin. Zak's insides were telling him he was infected as well. The woman made him just as edgy and off center.

Before Luke could move to touch the woman again, perhaps set her down at a table and interrogate her some more, Zak pushed him out of the way and leaned forward. He spoke in a voice he only used with frightened animals, "We don't want to hurt you. We just want to understand. You never did finish your chili. Come on. Sit down at the table and I'll make you a fresh bowl. Please. Nobody will hurt you. I swear. We just want to talk."

"Then what happened to your mother and your sister and Nate? Where did they go?" she asked.

"Mom took Quinn shopping for school clothes in Twin. And Nate is sleeping right now. He's in charge while Mom's away. She'll be back later."

"Today?"

"Yeah," Zak said and watched with relief as the woman moved toward the table and sat down. Zak glared at Luke and Luke stared back then shrugged in resignation. Zak began to wonder why Luke wanted so badly to find an excuse always to be touching this woman. While Luke fetched Leona a bowl of chili, Zak sat down at the same table and faced her squarely tired of the games and the drama. He wanted facts. The best way to get the information he needed would be to treat the lady with kindness.

"What's your name again?" he asked.

The woman glanced at him and frowned, then said, "Navan Keys. Call me Leona."

"Let's start over. OK? Don't worry; I'm no longer pissed off about what you did earlier. I guess you can't help yourself sometimes. Anyway. Hi Leona, I'm Zak Nerin and the guy in the kitchen is my brother Luke. The Navaho blanket," Zak threw his thumb over his shoulder in the general direction of where his Camaro was parked outside, "I found in a pawn shop."

"You mean you stole it from a pawn shop," Leona corrected him.

A rush of anger mixed with embarrassment prevented him from thinking of an appropriate response. God, she was aggravating. "Yeah, I stole it. So, what? It needed stealing. It didn't belong to the guy who got it anyway. It belonged to the police."

"So why haven't you returned it to the police?"

The bang of the restaurant doors hitting one another and the sight of Luke coming out carrying a bowl of chili gave Zak time to formulate a response. Luke dumped the bowl in front of Leona and said, "Eat up. It's good and hot."

Zak jumped up, "Luke thinks everybody eats with their fingers like he does. Hold on a sec." When he returned he handed Leona a spoon along with several wrapped restaurant crackers. He sat down across from her. Both men waited until Leona had dipped her spoon into the chili, blew on the hot beans and pieces of steak, then popped it into her mouth. They could see that the first taste surprised and delighted her. She shoveled the rest in like a trucker who had to make up lost time on the road.

While she ate Luke talked, "Some of the things you've said today are too close to the truth to be a hoax. But all this garbage about mullet heads and cheap motels and living deaths doesn't make sense. Are you trying to tell us that the blanket belongs to some guy from the 1990s?"

Leona paused and set her spoon down, "I notice you don't want to talk about the harpy? I think I know why."

"Knock it off," Luke shouted. "If you're trying to extort money from us, just look around. Do we look like we've got money?"

Zak jumped up and pulled Luke out of his chair cautioning his brother, "Listen Luke you're out of line. You may have her all wrong. Step back. I mean it."

He turned to Leona and asked, "Why do you think Luke doesn't want to hear about harpies?"

The woman looked up into Zak's face and then toward Luke, "He thinks he's a man of science. I'm assuming from his conflicted attitude that he's uncomfortable about the whole pseudoscience of second sight; yet, another part of him really wants to know where the Navaho blanket came from and believes I have the answers. And me talking about harpies is making him uneasy. I get it. So, I'll stop. It's just an old nightmare I keep having. Ok? Can we get back to the original question?"

Both men returned to their seats and waited for her to speak. She rested her arms on the table and said, "I saw three visions."

"I thought you said you were cured?" Zak asked.

"Dr. B says I'm perfectly fine. I just need more rest and time to mainstream."

"What?"

"You know, go back into society and interact. I've never been good at talking to people anyway. I prefer my own company."

"You said visions," Luke interrupted. "What sort of visions?"

When the woman began to talk Zak made notes on the order pad in front of him.

Leona described her visions in as much detail as she could remember. What was striking was during her soliloquy specific details were beginning to surface. Some of them she relayed to the men, others she kept to herself. No sense in telling them everything. In any case, she couldn't be sure which details were accurate or just a manifestation of her need to placate these men. At first, her instinct was to trust these details.

She remembered what Angela Bishop had said, how talking sometimes helped to clarify events and could generate repressed memories. At the time, Leona had been suspicious. So, she'd made up lies to explain her past and her wounds. The wounds were healing, and Dr. B had had no right to mess around in her head. Waves of anger washed over her. While the brothers stood in whispered conference by the kitchen, Leona road the anger closing her eyes and doing her best to stifle a scream. The memory was so vivid.

Dr. A had clasped her hands between Leona's own knowing she hated to be touched. Her words surprised Leona, "One day you'll tell someone what really happened. You will trust again and find that special person. I'm sorry it wasn't me Jane. I know Jane isn't your real name, but we can't be calling you all the different names you dream up every day. We have names for a reason, to help identify us to ourselves and to others. So, I say again, once you find someone you can trust, you will tell them everything and the telling is the beginning of healing."

"Keys? Hey, Navan Keys are you ok? Where'd you go?" Luke asked with false cheerfulness that didn't fool her.

Leona looked down at her bowl of chili. She only had a few more spoon's full to go. "I was just trying to remember if I'd left out any details."

"So, what I'm gathering is that the Navaho blanket ended up on some farm where they grow corn and where this boy Scott liked to ride his horse. You say you saw a 1956 Chevy. What kind of Chevy?"

"I don't know. I don't know that much about cars. It looked like my," Leona stopped herself in time. "Ah... old boyfriend's Dad's car. He was always working on it, restoring the paint, the chrome bumpers, the interior, you name it. It had those little windows in the back and the big steering wheel. You know those old fat cars from the early 1950s."

Luke leaned back and rubbed his forehead, "I know. But was it a convertible or a standard? Did it have white wall tires? Help us out here. Give us more specific details. How about the license plate? Did you see it?"

Leona tried to remember. She'd only had a few minutes to really look around before the boy took off on his horse. The house had been more interesting to her. She'd given him all the details she could remember about the house. Why wasn't that enough? Surely the house would be easier to find than the car?

"I didn't see the plates. Sorry," she said. "But really what does it matter since the blanket ended up in that motel room anyway." She ate another bite of chili and watched Luke lean back, cross his arms holding them tight to his chest, a contemplative expression on his face. He didn't bother to explain why he wanted to know more about the Chevy.

Zak leaned forward the order pad in his hand, "None of this makes sense. You say in your vision you saw the Navaho blanket on or around September 11, 2001. Yet that blanket was discovered in a dumpster in Vegas in July of 2001. It was in police custody for..." then he grunted in surprise. Leona watched as his brother poked Zak in the side. Evidently, Zak was revealing too much information.

"Let's not get confused by minutia right now," Luke warned his brother. "We need to remain focused on the key details – the motel room and the man."

Zak had been staring at his hands. He looked up. "The interior décor of the motel sounds familiar to me."

"It would," his brother said sarcastically.

Zak ignored him, "It'll come to me. I'm sure I've seen that bedspread before. The jungle-look. Where was it?"

"You've been asking me lots of questions and now I've got a few for you and I want a straight answer," Leona said trying to appear tough which from their twin expressions of amusement did not pass muster.

"The blanket looks antique. I'm thinking at least a hundred years old," then she looked Zak in the eye. "And I didn't see you steal this blanket, I just guessed you did because you don't strike me as a collector of antiques. Now I want to know what's going on, why are you so interested in this blanket? And don't give me a story about your interest in old things. There's more to this than you're telling me. Maybe you'll tell me Luke. What's going on?"

Luke glanced at Zak then away. From the shaking of Zak's head and his annoyed expression Leona assumed Luke was going to give away a major secret.

Zak groaned when Luke said, "I'm looking for someone. She went missing in 2001. She was a professor of Anthropology. This blanket belonged to her. It turns out that the dumb cop who was supposed to send the blanket to the crime lab for testing left it in his garage and his wife thought it was junk and during a garage sale sold it to a neighbor. Well, my brother a few years back saw the blanket and, and, well, he decided that the blanket didn't belong to the crook who owned the pawn shop and he took it. Guess who her neighbor used to be?"

The Nerin brothers noticed first off how the woman's eyes were doing funny things. Navan Leona Keys was no longer looking at either of them instead she stared curiously toward the door. Zak had the feeling she was trying to see the Camaro. Something she saw turned her expression from curiosity to comprehension and finally to horror. The struggle continued for several seconds and finally ended when she looked up and around the room as if seeing the room for the first time.

The person sitting opposite them began to speak and both men strained to hear her realizing at the same moment that the voice speaking to them sounded different, sounded like someone else's voice without Leona's northeastern inflections or dreamy quality.

The voice reminded them of an older woman's, someone who had lived long enough to have experienced difficult times and all sorts of people and knew how to weather them all, "I'm glad you don't steal any more Zak. I can understand why you might want to hurt him though. Yeah, I can guess who the neighbor might have been. Leland Ansel, the pawn shop owner. I see what this is all about now. He recognized the blanket and snatched it from the unwary policeman's wife and tried to sell it in his pawnshop."

Both Zak and Luke turned as the screen door screeched and the outer door of the Woolly Man Bar and Grill flew open. Leona or whoever the woman was sitting across from them ignored the new arrival. Zak recognized the customer.

"You mind closing the door Mrs. Lawson. You're letting in the flies."

Mrs. Lawson glanced up at him then around the room, her thin, bony, wrinkled face devoid of expression. When her gray eyes lit on Leona, Zak noticed her sudden excitement although she continued to stand on the threshold with the damn door still propped open. She ignored Zak's reminder to close the door.

Mrs. Lawson was emaciated, all sharp lines and wrinkles. She must have been around five feet eight or nine inches but only a hundred or a hundred and ten pounds. The color of her skin reminded Zak of old leather, a cracked yellowish-brown kind of leather. She had long yellow fingernails and when she smiled, he could see that her dentures no longer fit so well. She had a nasty habit of licking her dried cracked lips repeatedly and wiping the spittle from the corners of her mouth.

Luke moved toward Mrs. Lawson as if his proximity to her might force her to step forward and enter the room. The old woman squinted at Leona in the far corner and said, "Is there a Jane Smith here? I was told I might find her in this place. Is that you Jane Smith?"

Leona spooned some chili onto her cracker and popped the cracker into her mouth. She washed the chili and cracker down with a swallow of milk. Zak took Mrs. Lawson's arm and tried to escort her into the room. Mrs. Lawson slapped his hand away, "Stop that damned you. I can move fine without your help."

Zak threw up his hands and settled himself down on a nearby barstool. Luke moved to the corner of the room with the window on his right and the jukebox on his left and the wall behind him. Once Zak knew he could see every nook and cranny of the Woolly Man, he relaxed. The first thing he noticed was Luke's odd behavior.

His brother's attempts to appear nonchalant were backfiring. When he leaned his shoulders against the wall he misread the distance and nearly fell on his ass and when he righted himself looking around to see if anyone noticed, Zak looked away struggling to hold back laughter. To make matters worse his brother attempted twice to cross his arms without success before finally giving up. Then Zak realized why his brother was acting like an idiot. His brain couldn't process normal motor control, because he was too worried about the women. It was comical watching his brother's eyes darting back and forth between them like a sport's fan might watch a tennis match.

Cheerfully, Zak watched the drama unfold.

Lawson appeared to know Leona, yet, Leona acted as if Mrs. Lawson wasn't even in the room.

The younger woman licked her spoon clean.

A bee flew through the open door. Mrs. Lawson remained unmoved.

Zak considered dragging her inside then changed his mind when the old lady began to chant, "Regna terrae, cantata Deo, psallite Cernunnos, Regna terrae, cantata Dea."

Zak and his brother exchanged looks. Zak stood up prepared to remove her from the bar. Before he had a chance, Leona dropped her spoon in the empty bowl with a clatter of cutlery and stood up in one fluid motion her shoulders back and her expression unreadable. With an economy of movement Leona slipped her leather satchel over her head. The strap lay snug on her left shoulder and traveled between her breasts the ends cinched through copper rings. As she moved, the satchel swayed seductively against her right hip. Her face remained impassive as if the antics of this stranger shouting out Latin verses seemed run of the mill.

"Kingdoms of the earth, sing to God, sing to Cernunnos, Kingdoms of the earth, sing to God," Mrs. Lawson translated. She continued in Latin, her voice getting louder with each sentence, speaking so loudly she could probably be heard in the next county. Throughout her performance her eyes remained tightly shut.

Over the drone of Mrs. Lawson's chanting, Leona spoke in a forceful and confident manner, extraordinarily without having to raise her voice once, "Thank you for the chili. It was delicious." Without ceremony Leona moved toward the door. Then unexpectedly she veered from her intended path and stood in front of Lawson. She cocked her head to one side as if listening to a familiar tune, a smile playing on her lips. Sensing something off, something dangerous in the air, Zak tensed.

Mrs. Lawson was the taller of the two and even though she might be wiry and a couple of decades older, the sheer intensity of her personality should have made her the dominant female in the room.

Yet it didn't.

Zak tried to understand what his eyes were seeing. He thought he'd figured Leona out – he'd seen women like her many times in his life – gentle, introspective, quiet females who went out of their way to avoid confrontation. Her actions so far were completely at odds with his understanding of her type. Leona could have left the bar through the side exit and avoided Mrs. Lawson completely. It would have fit with her personality type.

Yet she didn't.

In fact, the back way out was even closer. Instead, she chose to confront the old woman. She could have murmured some polite drivel like "pardon me, excuse me" and no one would have thought less of her. But no, Leona chose to stand in front of her waiting patiently while Lawson ranted on and on. It took a moment for Lawson to realize someone was standing close by. Leona stepped even closer. Mrs. Lawson opened her eyes.

This time Leona joined in the chanting and together the women recited the prayer in unison. Long after the insanity of the next five minutes was over, Zak remembered how beautiful their voices sounded ringing through the room in perfect harmony. He thought he recognized the sobriquet "infernal adversary" which everyone knew referenced Satan, the Evil One, Beelzebub, Father of Lies, and his particular favorite – Serpent of Old.

Even though Leona had to crane her neck back so far she looked like a bird waiting to be fed, she did so with a studied insolence. The air vibrated with aggression eager to unleash itself upon its enemy. Zak had met people like her before – both men and women – who happened to be small, but were as fierce as badgers capable of drawing blood before their adversary could blink.

Lawson's eyes opened, her gray eyes widening at the sight of the young woman standing so uncomfortably close. To the casual observer the tableau appeared to be a meeting between family members a beloved grandmother and a long lost granddaughter catching up after many years apart. The witnesses in the room knew nothing was right about these two. Even the familiar smells of spilled beer and onion rings had been replaced by a disturbing odor. At first he thought he smelled moldy cheese. No. Then he knew. No wonder his heart pounded like mad in his chest.

There was no fire; yet, he smelled burning flesh.

Lawson's litany stuttered and finally stopped. There was silence in the room for the first time. Lawson's gray eyes widened as she took in the young woman. The young woman who hours before had seemed so gentle and kind, now watched Lawson's face with an uncomfortable intensity not even bothering to hide a condescending smirk. Leona opened her mouth and out came the rest of the prayer, "Aradia ipse fortitudinem plebi Suae. Benedictus Deus, Gloria Patri, Benedictus Dea, Matri gloria!"

Nobody moved. Nobody spoke. Before Lawson had time to retaliate, Leona invaded Lawson's space by stepping forward deliberately provoking the older woman into a fight. Simultaneously, Leona's voice dripped sarcasm as she shouted out the final lines of the prayer in English – so loudly and so fiercely – that the words bounced off the walls and rang in everyone's ears long afterward, "Arad is the strength of His people. Blessed be God. Glory be to the Father. Blessed be the Goddess. Mother of the glory!"

"Mother of the glory!" Leona repeated in a passionate battle cry throwing up her arm with her hand clenched in a fist. And then she began to laugh. Her laughter was carefully crafted, filled with bitterness and a bone deep hatred. The hatred aimed at Mrs. Lawson found its mark. The expression in Lawson's eyes reminded Zak of a puppy desperate to understand its master.

Luke saw the exchange between the two women differently. He thought Mad Mona appeared menacing hovering over Keys' tiny body like a gigantic vulture ready to pounce and tear its prey apart. He recognized the Prayer of Exorcism and was offended by Lawson's rudeness to their guest. Her prejudices against outsiders and her ridiculously parochial mind made him furious. Just because Keys dressed like a goth girl didn't mean she was intrinsically evil. Then Keys began to mimic Lawson's prayer in a voice and manner completely unlike the woman he thought he knew and he had to quickly revise his first impressions. He made as if to move forward and stopped when the young woman spoke.

"What did Dr. B tell you about me Lawson? That I'm a demon? A witch? Maybe a psycho?"

Mrs. Lawson stared mutely at Keys transfixed as if the girl had horns on her head and wings on her back.

Navan Keys watched Mad Mona with clinical curiosity and Luke heard her say, "Even if I was any of those things, I don't think an exorcism will fix me or protect you. It's just words, just a bunch of dumb-ass man-words. If you stand in the eye of a tornado can words save you? Or if a tsunami comes crashing down on you, will repeating medieval baloney make the nasty waters go away? Huh? Huh, you silly old troglodyte? What's wrong dear – the devil got your tongue? Oh, stop me. That's too funny."

Even though Mrs. Lawson could look down upon Keys, Luke knew which one of them was the more dominant female. Amazing! Who would have thought? The shift was so dramatic that Luke was stunned for longer than necessary unable to grasp the implications. He could only gape at the transformation.

Keys wasn't the same woman. She appeared physically similar, the hair, the eyes, the nose, the mouth, and all the parts were the same, but they moved differently. She stood with her shoulders erect and legs slightly apart as if prepared for a fight. She exuded confidence and strength in every line of her body, in her face, in her muscles, and especially in her eyes. Even the color of her eyes had changed. Luke swore they looked cobalt and ready to tear a hole in anyone dumb enough to get too close.

"Don't be afraid of me Mrs. Lawson. I don't bite," the woman in Navan Keys' body said. "Not yet anyway. Your time is coming. Should I call you Mrs. Firebug? You do love a good fire, don't yeah?"

Mrs. Lawson stepped back, her eyes growing large with terror, "I'm not so sure bout that Mz Smith. How many you know about?"

Keys laughed, "Say again?"

"I was told to come talk to a Jane Smith and help her with her little problem but you ain't Jane Smith."

Luke moved forward for the first time, "She claims to be Navan Keys. At least that's what she told us, but she likes people to call her Leona."

Mrs. Lawson never took her eyes off Keys as she explained her presence in the Woolly Man, "Doc B told me you was coming to ask for my help. He said you'd had a breakthrough but still had some questions."

The woman they'd come to know as Leona walked around Mrs. Lawson as if the old lady wasn't even in the room and without a word left the Woolly Man. The woman Lawson thought was Jane Smith stepped out into the blinding white light of high afternoon. Mrs. Lawson spun around so fast she nearly fell on her face. Luke was close enough to catch her and help her out the door as everyone piled outside to watch what the young woman would do next. Mrs. Lawson wasn't ready to be ignored and shouted after Jane Smith, "I can help you talk to the others, maybe get a clearer idea about what's been going on, maybe lift the curse."

The stranger who may or may not have been Jane Smith glanced over her shoulder at Mrs. Lawson and frowned in disbelief, as if Mrs. Lawson were the crazy one, "What makes you think I'm cursed?"

"You got some blank spots in your life, don't yeah? You got some missing hours, maybe even days, huh? I know all about that. You wonder what you'd said to folks, what you done. The part that's the worst is when you find out," Mrs. Lawson hesitated and then rushed toward the woman, bent down, and whispered in her ear.

The younger female backed away with a crafty look in her eyes and said, "How far is it to the nearest town?"

Luke stepped off the porch and walked toward Keys, "I'll take you wherever you want to go."

Zak tried to stop him. Luke brushed him off and walked up as close as he could get to the young woman. He made sure to touch Keys' shoulder in passing then deliberately turned so that he stood only inches from her, blocking her escape.

"She doesn't need a lift from you Luke," Zak said shoving Luke aside. "She came in that," he said pointing at the lime green Ford Taurus parked near the end of the road.

The woman calling herself Navan Leona Keys examined the Ford Taurus with skepticism as if she didn't believe Zak. A few seconds passed before she moved. She surprised both Nerin brothers by marching away from the Taurus and heading in the direction of the dirt road.

"Hey where the hell do you think you're going? Listen to me; it's several miles to town on a hilly bumpy dirt road," Luke called out. There was no response from her, not even a twitch of the shoulders. It was as if, for her, none of them existed.

The three of them watched as she crossed the road and climbed the butte. Every step she took was determined and effortless, even though she looked silly wearing a silk skirt and army boots with her heavy satchel banging against her hip. Zak watched her navigate the narrow winding path with her eyes alert to obstacles on the ground and her arms bend to give her balance. He could see her slim pale neck and the way the wind played with her black hair.

At one point a gust of wind shoved her backward lifting her skirt into the air and he could see her slim shapely legs and white panties. He heard Luke suck in his breath and saw his face turn several shades of red. Zak expected a major tantrum from his brother because the woman had the nerve to ignore him but there was nothing but silence from his vicinity. Mad Mona started hopping up and down and screaming, "The Lord can save you. Come back Jane Smith. I'm here to help!"

When Zak looked for Leona again, she was nearly at the top of the butte. Then he heard Old Paint's door open and its engine start up. Annoyed Zak looked up and saw her disappear over the rise. Did she imagine she could walk all the way to the nearest town through that rough terrain, in those damn shoes? He anticipated a sleepless night tracking her down and dragging her back to the Woolly Man. Luke would be no help at all.

13

Acacia T. Pierce made quick work of the rough terrain, keeping as close to the cow path as possible while stepping over brush and rocks in her way. It took her ten minutes to get to the top. She could see down below a handsome man with close-cropped dark hair standing with his hands on his hips staring up at her. Another guy who resembled him a little and looked like an extra on the set of a western with his moccasins and long thick black hair braided into a queue had been standing in front of the hunky guy, but after watching her decided to move.

With his braided queue bouncing against his lean back as he ran, he reached the old rhino truck and jumped inside. She was too far away to see the Moccasin Man's expression, but the look of the other one, the one unmoving, the cute one still watching her from the porch of an old rickety building that might have come straight out of a western with its sagging roof and bleached cedar siding was a different story. She couldn't tell what he was thinking which intrigued her.

She enjoyed the view, especially the view of him, the way he stood at such elegant ease, all long lines, and lithe muscles. Then he decided to move, and she appreciated the sight even more, the way he moved with unhurried strides his long legs eating up the space between where he was and where he wanted to go, and especially the way his eyes sized up a person so carefully, all his instinctive abilities and intellectual strengths told her enough, enough to know he would be a challenge to tackle head on.

It was his solid center she admired the most. Speed was attainable with plenty of exercise and practice but persistence and the mental ability to block out pain – that took skill – and in the end, was more crucial. The idea of fighting him made her stomach flutter with anticipation and paradoxically with dread. There's the danger, she thought, imagining herself failing. She'd never done that before.

Only a few years ago, she'd dug up from somewhere deep inside herself an extraordinary fact. When she imagined an outcome, the outcome happened exactly as she wanted. If only she'd discovered this ability sooner. With the help of a personal trainer at the hospital (on the sly and unbeknownst to the staff) she found a way to sneak outside the 8-Ball Ward and attend the martial art studio a few blocks away. Ten years of intensive training honed her muscle memory to effectively defend herself and dispense major damage on her opponent. She had practiced most of the fighting moves of Aikido, Taekwondo, Karate, Judo, even a little Jiu-Jitsu until she could perform the moves without hesitation.

And as if all roads led to self-defense, one night she bumped into a Filipino at the studio who happened to work in the Recovery Center's laundry. He was practicing in the dark, warming up before executing his moves. She'd heard the beating of sticks against wood and slipped inside to watch. It took her several weeks to convince him she was ready to learn Escrima, a martial art practiced in the Philippines. She loved the sinawali moves and knew this martial art was just right for her.

Even if her opponent was taller and bigger, she could bring him down with the Kali sticks. But she hadn't been ready until her mind and body were one. And what helped the most was this new feeling, a feeling that she wasn't alone. There were others watching out for her, protecting her, guiding her. With encouragement from her new friends – anything was possible.

The anger (never far away) which had been nibbling along her backbone for years burst forth. She was free now, free of modern constraints, eager to dole out some old-time justice. Then she spotted the old bat with the pile of hay on her head masquerading as hair. It was quite a shock to see her still alive and well and meddling in other people's lives on behalf of the Butcher Queen. She considered climbing back down the butte and breaking the old bat's skinny neck. No. Not yet, not with witnesses watching her every move and recording the event on some ass-wipe's cellphone. Her time would come.

Some day they would meet again – guaranteed – because where Acacia was headed she knew the old bat would follow. What did they call her in the bar? Oh, yeah, it was Mad Mona. Acacia began to laugh, her laughter carrying her voice far and wide echoing back at her from obstacles in its path. The handsome one shaded his eyes and looked up at her. She smiled down at him and waved. Standing atop the butte with a sharp wind at her back, Acacia had a panoramic view of the rolling hills and valleys beyond. She realized a person could get lost, truly lost in such a place. It was an exhilarating thought.

From all four sides – north, south, east, and west – she could see the range of mountain peaks. Behind the place she had just left, beyond the faded wood and peeling paint of the Woolly Man ran a river along the base of a cliff face. The only way to get over that cliff would be to climb, and it would require the right equipment. She dismissed the idea and turned around. To her right were more mountains and a valley below.

In the valley, she saw a tractor. The monster machine creeping along with dust flying out behind and a barely discernible geezer inside the cab (probably listening to country western music and chewing on a cigarette) was gouging out the earth in preparation for planting. She knew she would either have to cross the mountains which meant tracking up and down them or choose a safer route walking the dirt road that led away from the Woolly Man. Unfortunately, if she chose the dirt road she would have to go back down the hillside and fight her way passed the brothers. She didn't feel like hurting anyone today.

The sound of the rhino truck climbing the butte surprised Acacia. Evidently, she had a more pressing problem. She turned and watched as the truck crested the rise. The sight of the gray menace eating up the turf like a rhino snorting and pawing the ground amused her. It looked so old and tired she figured no one would want to steal it much less gut it for spare parts.

Yet the truck had made it up the butte without falling apart or rolling back down the side. Amazing. The truck cut through the loose soil over the ridge and spit rocks back down the hillside. Then the rhino topped the ridge by some miracle and swayed to a stop. The man behind the steering wheel cut the engine and climbed out. The creak of the heavy door irritated Acacia for some inexplicable reason. How could anyone be so careless as to let their vehicle get into such a state?

"Haven't you heard of WD40?" she asked Moccasin Man.

As he started toward her with a determined expression on his handsome face, Acacia shifted position in preparation for her first move so that her strongest support fell on her right side. She heard him say, "There's about fifty miles of nothing between our place and the Interstate and if you were to get lost you might be wandering out here for days. Are you just plain stupid or what?"

As he stepped closer and moved to reach for her, Acacia chose to lean forward instead of opposing him. He took hold of her arm prepared to drag her toward the truck. She used his energy as momentum and pushed forward and with her left foot tripped him then knocked him to the ground with her clenched fists. It only took a second and he was staring up at her in mild surprise. He still didn't know what he was up against – the idiot! Acacia resented the man's surprise.

Still disbelieving what had happened to him, the man struggled to get to his feet. Acacia tried to drive her foot into his throat, but he rolled over seconds before her boot landed. While he was busy avoiding her, Acacia turned and ran toward the vehicle, her satchel banging painfully against her hip. What the hell did Leona put in there? Rocks. Before he had time to get to his feet, she was already inside the cab. The engine turned over without a fuss and she put it in drive and eased her foot on the gas.

The rocky uneven ground didn't allow for speed. The man had no trouble catching up with the truck. He looked so silly running alongside waving his arms and screaming at her to stop. But when he tried to reach inside the cab to grab the steering wheel, Acacia lunged at his bare wrist and bit down so hard she tasted blood. She heard him clinch his teeth and suck in his breath. The pain must have been intense. She felt him relax and at that moment opened her mouth and with her left fist punched him in the throat.

He fell back in shock clutching at his neck as if he feared his head would fall off. From the corner of her eye, Acacia saw him drop to his knees. As she pressed down on the accelerator, she glanced in the rear view mirror and saw the man holding his throat with both hands.

As the truck bumped and crashed down the butte jostling Acacia around like a wild ride on the Zipper at the fair, she noticed another man pulling his keys out of his jean pocket and climbing into a Camaro. Acacia hit her head several times on the metal roof but maintained her grip on the steering wheel knowing if she let go the vehicle would overturn. She bit her tongue once on the way down while the driver of the Camaro took several precious minutes fumbling with the ignition key.

By the time Zak got the engine warmed up and was on the road in pursuit of Leona, Luke had managed to stagger to his feet. He was grateful no one had witnessed Acacia's brutal attack and his undignified decent especially the tumbling and falling on his rear-end. When Luke finally landed on solid ground, he was just in time to see Zak's Camaro fly by spitting loose gravel and dust in his wake. Luke cupped his hands and shouted, "Hey Zak, you bloody idiot. It's only got a couple of gallons of gas. She won't get far." His brother kept on going too preoccupied with the hunt to hear him.

Zak saw his brother in the rear view mirror but ignored Luke's cursing and continued to pursue the carjacker. He had no time to pick up Luke and from what he could tell his brother wouldn't be much use anyway. Luke was bent over holding onto his knees. The guy was out of shape. That little jaunt down the butte shouldn't have made him puke up his supper. Embarrassed, Zak looked away from the sorry sight of his brother puking and concentrated on making the curves without plunging down a ravine.

The old truck's backend weaved madly from side to side in the loose gravel and nearly turned over around one sharp curve. The Datsun coming in the other direction plowed into the soft side of the hill to avoid being rammed by the truck; and when Acacia glanced in her rear view mirror she saw the Camaro try to swerve to avoid the Datsun which now blocked the road. The driver of the Camaro turned the wheel hard to the right toward the ravine. The Camaro skidded to a stop, the right front tire meeting air, until with a kick of gravel and dirt the muscle car inched its way back onto solid ground. At this point, the road began to descend, and the truck picked up speed.

Acacia had an unobstructed view in her mirror of the man in a fine rage hitting the roof of the Camaro with his fist. There was no water flowing in the creek below only large boulders and several thirsty tenacious willow trees. For a second, Acacia considered stopping to lend her assistance then realized her compassion would only place her in jeopardy.

Better to be prudent and put as much distance between her and those white slavers. They were too strange and unpredictable for her liking. And they had no right to detain her. Any court in the land would forgive her for carjacking once the jury understood what had happened. They might just lock up the whole bunch of them for kidnapping and attempted rape.

After several winding turns, Acacia glanced in the rear view again and to her astonishment saw a plume of dirt behind her. She couldn't afford to relax her vigil. It might be an innocent motorist, but on the other hand, it might be the white slavers. She pushed her foot down on the gas. The truck bucked forward with a rattle of pistons and a trail of black smoke from the exhaust pipe.

The road forked, and Acacia took the one to the left, the one with potholes and overgrown sage. In a few places sage had managed to grow right in the middle of the road. It was a narrow winding trail ascending a good-sized hill. She spotted a secluded area full of blackberry bushes, one impressive willow and several quaking aspens. The truck bumped and lurched onto the side of the road and down the bank into a shady area among the trees. To her left, she could hear water running over rocks. She supposed there was a stream somewhere close by.

With her heart still racing from the chase and the fear of getting caught, Acacia turned off the engine and sat for a moment listening to the sounds around her. She heard birds quarreling in the willow and the distance cry of some poor creature. The door creaked alarmingly when she opened it. She tried to shut the damn thing without making any noise. Then she heard the whine of an engine. In the time it took her to take two steps toward the road, the driver had already been and gone leaving only a trail of dust in his wake. It must have been the Camaro, either the Camaro or the other guy's partner in some barfly's vehicle.

Rather than start up the truck and head out, Acacia chose to wait a bit. She was glad she did because not ten or so minutes later she spotted a familiar Ford Taurus being driven by a stranger, a man with gray sideburns and mullet hair wearing a cook's apron. He was being followed by an extremely well persevered middle-aged woman in a blue van. The cook drove forty around the corner and accelerated down the steep descent swerving along the washboard road. The Taurus hit a rock embedded in the road and flew into the air for a second then landed with a crash back to earth. She heard the female bellow "Damnation!" and the squeal of her brakes as she tried to avoid hitting the Taurus.

Crouched near a pretty bush, one she thought might be a Syringa with some of its beautiful white flowers still in bloom, Acacia watched as the Ford Taurus navigated the next tricky part of the road, the forty-five-degree ascent. The Taurus seemed out of place in this landscape, only four-wheel drive vehicles and ugly rhinos belonged here. As she walked back to the rhino, she realized that the only way the Ford Taurus could have gotten this far is if the mullet man inside had Leona's car keys. And the only way he had Leona's car keys was because he also must have Leona's leather satchel. The cook was no better than a stinkin' thief.

In fact, the two of them, probably the whole damned family were nothing more than thieves preying on innocent bystanders. It would give her great satisfaction to muck up all their pretty faces. Acacia looked down at Leona's satchel which dangled from her hip. She lifted the leather flap and peeked inside. She didn't recognize any of the objects inside. A rising tide of rage overwhelmed her for a moment.

When she stopped shaking, she yanked the satchel off her body and dumped it on the bench seat of the truck. The contents spilled out: a large black notebook covered in unfamiliar writing, several pamphlets, a medical kit, compass, trowel, tape measure, a bunch of small yellow flags, pencils, sunglasses, bandana, and gloves. The satchel must belong to the friggin brothers. She would put her money on Moccasin Man.

They thought they were so smart. What they didn't know was her friend Leona kept an emergency wallet on her person at all times. Those freaks didn't have anything of value really, just a rented car, fake identification, and about twenty bucks. Acacia tried to recall if Leona had left any incriminating notes or other paraphernalia in her satchel. No. Just some mascara and gloss for her lips. They couldn't possibly learn anything from the items she'd left behind. It had been smart of Ana to mail the briefcase and its contents to the publisher and Frankie to keep her suitcase at the bus depot in the next town.

Relieved, Acacia jumped into the truck and began searching the glove compartment for something that might help her. She found five parking tickets and one speeding ticket, as well as an expired proof of insurance card. He also kept a comb, an electric razor and cologne in the glove compartment. A lady's man or maybe he lived in his truck, probably slept in the cab outside the Woolly Man. Under the seat she found empty vitamin bottles, several snack wrappers, a plastic container full of junk mainly smooth stones, what looked like bone fragments, even a rusted piece of metal she couldn't identify. The metal might have been a coin, but she couldn't be sure.

Acacia finally found something useful, several maps stuffed in the side pocket of the passenger door. There were three maps: one for Idaho, Montana, and Oregon. She unfolded the Idaho map and searched for Woolstone. For the longest time she couldn't find the damned town.

She had to find Pocatello first. It was along the I-84. That was the last city she remembered before Leona insisted on driving. Acacia remembered driving from Chicago through the states of Iowa, Nebraska, and Wyoming via I-80 E and I-55 N to avoid the toll booths.

If she had had her way she would have drove the entire night without stopping – twenty-one hours or more. The others insisted on a stopover in a cheap motel. She remembered continuing the journey the next day and stopping for gas in Pocatello. In Pocatello (conveniently after Acacia had pumped the gas, checked the tires, and washed the bugs off the windshield) Leona instigated a temper tantrum because she believed she was the only person capable of finding Mona Lawson. Why in a bug's ass did any of them need to talk to that crazy old bat? To reminisce? For the sake of politeness? How stupid. Put a bullet in her head and move on. They were free now, free of Dr. B's micromanagement; and much more importantly, they were free to carry out their plan.

Acacia's index finger followed the I-84 searching either side of the line for a town called Woolstone. Finally, she found the town, south of a place called Twin Falls which was about a hundred miles or more from the capital city of Boise. Well maps could be deceiving. She could be much further away from her rendezvous than she wanted to be. Acacia decided it was safe to continue. She started the engine. Nothing happened. For a moment she panicked. She pumped the gas pedal a couple of times then turned the key in the ignition. The truck roared into life. What a tin can piece of shit! With reckless haste she shoved her foot down on the gas and backed the truck out of the embankment.

Clods of dirt flew up in the air and a small stone hit the trunk of a nearby tree. It was more difficult turning the truck around on the narrow road than she'd anticipated. She didn't want to end up sliding back down the embankment. Hot and swearing by the time she managed to face the right direction, she skidded onto the main graveled road that descended into a green valley full of farms. Woolstone, Idaho must be in that valley.

Acacia looked to the west and watched as the sun began to set behind a particularly spectacular range of mountains. As her eye traveled along the curve of the mountain range, Acacia could see a pattern, a resemblance to a female sleeping on her back with her nose in the air. A burning cloud sailed over her sleeping form. Her mouth appeared to be congratulating Acacia. Acacia took this as a good omen and concentrated her attention on the road and stepped on the gas. It would be dark soon.

A sign warned her to slow down. There was only one main road in the small town of Woolstone, Idaho population two hundred and forty-seven. Acacia drove twenty-five miles an hour. When she drew near a mom and pop store called Drummond Market, she recognized the silver Camaro parked at the only gas station in town. In her haste to leave, Acacia didn't notice the street light change from green to yellow. By the time she reached the light, it had turned red. She stepped on the gas and raced through the light.

If she'd waited for the light to change, the man might have come out of Drummond Market and spotted her. She couldn't risk it. No one honked in outrage or gave her the finger. In fact, few people were outside, just the odd young person lounging against a wall waiting for something exciting to happen. Most prudent people were inside in their air-conditioned homes waiting for an evening breeze to cool the sidewalks.

Acacia glanced back in the rear view mirror and saw him come out of the store loaded down with bags. No doubt he'd chosen junk food. He dumped the packages on the passenger side and backed out. With her heart racing, Acacia turned right and slipped into a nearby alley. The alley was too narrow for the truck to be able to turnaround. She had to drive through the alley to the street at the opposite end and circle back to the main road. She decided to park the truck behind a trailer which she later discovered was the police station.

She waited a few minutes until she thought the Camaro Man had had time to leave town or returned to his shack in the mountains. As she sat in the truck with her hands on the steering wheel watching the main road, all her senses on high alert and prepared to flee at a moment's notice, she thought about the crazy Camaro Man with an odd mixture of annoyance and admiration. She was pretty sure the guy wouldn't give up. He reminded her of those zany terriers fixated on the hunt who ignored hazards and madly dashed all over the place aroused by the scent of the prey. She might have to use his self-destructive instincts and irrational persistence against him.

It was with a twinge of regret, she decided it was better to get going in the opposite direction and as far as possible from him. No sense in circling the block hoping he would disappear down the road. She had to do something. She fished the Idaho map out from under the seat and

178

looked again. She found I-84 west on the map and as her finger followed the line she noticed the interstate was a straight shot through Idaho into Oregon and beyond. Yet she needed a safer way out of Idaho; this shit-can of a truck couldn't handle the speeds on I-84.

Another possibility was US-93 into Twin Falls then west onto US-30 past Curry, Filer, Buhl, and Hagerman which looked as if it ended at a place called Bliss. The name sounded hokey. If she'd been superstitious, she might have decided on a different route. Bliss for some and maybe Hell for her. No. She would risk going to the town of Bliss. Once there she could continue onto I-84 for a bit until she reached Cold Springs Road and Exit 114. Off the busy interstate she would make her way on ID-78 west in Elmore County to Pothole Road in Owyhee County where she would end up at the Snake River Birds of Prey Sanctuary.

It was a good plan. On the back roads she could slow down and enjoy the scenery. Her only dangerous area would be Twin Falls where she might be spotted, and the Camaro could easily outrun her. It would have to be Twin Falls then on to the Bird Sanctuary. The others wouldn't like the change, but she had no other recourse – she had to ditch this turd.

And if the rest of them were pissed – so be it; they could sleep in the back of the truck or find a cheap motel. Once they were safe, anything was possible. She knew her objective and now it was time to go; parking near the police station this long was dangerous. She might have already attracted unwanted attention. Acacia backed out of the alley and took the main road through town again.

When she came to a tarred road, she spied the silver Camaro parked near an orchard. The smug fart stood by the side of the road like a cop watching for traffic violators. Furious, Acacia found a driveway where she could turn the truck around and proceed southeast. A few miles down the road, she wondered how she could get to Oregon without having to drive all the way through Nevada and California first.

She pulled out the map again and discovered she could avoid the fart's roadblock and get to Bliss another way. She could take Airport Road and Washington Street south and end up in Twin Falls where the traffic and the different exits would mean the fart would need someone at every street corner watching for his brother's truck. After a false start, she found Airport Road and followed the map. She kept an eye out for the Camaro. Once she saw the posted sign declaring to curious motorist they were in Buhl, she began to relax. In just thirty minutes or so she would be on I-84 and long gone.

Twenty minutes later instinct told her to pull off the road. She found a dirt road and drove down it until she noticed a place she could park without obstructing traffic. She made a U-turn and pulled over to the side of the road with an unobstructed view of the highway. She turned off the headlights and leaned back against the lumpy leather seat contemplating the darkness. She couldn't see much so she closed her eyes and tried to relax. She was confident the heavy throb of a muscle car's V-8 would warn her Camaro Man had figured out her ploy and was – like a terrier – attempting to run her to ground.

And when he caught her – what would she do? A thrill ran up her spine at the thought of finally getting the chance for full contact with an unfamiliar opponent. She would know for the first time if previous take-downs had been honestly won or her teachers had been humoring the crazy female with the death wish.

After an hour, with an odd sense of disappointment she realized Camaro Man had lost her trail. She started up the truck and drove back to Twin Falls. It didn't take long to find a motel with a vacancy sign just on the outskirts of town. Before paying for a room, she pulled her right boot off and took out the wad of money inside. She counted out five twenty-dollar bills. "Nearly a hundred dollars for a motel room and a meal seems ridiculously excessive. What do they think they are – the Taj Mahal?" Tessa said. Acacia looked in the rear view mirror and saw Tessa sitting in the backseat.

"It's not safe for you here," Acacia told her in the sternest voice she could muster, "Someone might recognize you. Please Tessa, lie down and be quiet."

"Oh, you silly child. I've been taking care of myself for more years than you've been on this earth. And I know this town like the hairs on my chin."

"Not funny Tessa. Just do as I say."

"Fine dear but be quick about it. I'm bushed."

The shop was still open at seven o'clock that night. Leland Ansel's cold face flashed before her closed lids. She opened her eyes, but his image wouldn't go away. She remembered entering the door of

Around the World Pawn expecting Ansel to look at her with shocked recognition. He'd looked up alright, but his look had been speculative as if he were going over in his mind his stock and what might interest her. She wandered around the store for several minutes trying to calm down. Her hands itched to grab his ears and slam his face into the counter.

The years dropped away, and she heard the man say again, "Well, I'm asking seven thousand dollars so don't be jewing me down. You're getting a good deal and you fucking know it. Instead of one, I give you three used bitches. So, give me my cash."

With those words reverberating in her head, Acacia pretended to search through the used music CDs and movie DVDs on a carousel. She considered her options. The blonde wig she wore felt hot and itchy and the thick mascara on her eyelashes had begun to burn. The other people in the pawn shop were too busy deciding what to buy or worried about their pathetic possessions to notice her.

There were at least five other people in the place. She'd chosen that precise moment to enter because she wanted to blend in but once inside the place, she asked herself: how can I blend in when I'm wearing tight red Capri pants and shoes that make my feet hurt? She looked ridiculous. Frankie was an idiot to have thought this outfit would be an excellent disguise. Her outfit and makeup and wig fairly screamed – look at me everyone, I'm a slut.

Even though Acacia longed to be wearing comfortable blue jeans and a pair of hiking boots, she had to admit Leona had been right all along. Her extraordinary gift for untangling mysteries and predicting the future were all coming true. Even if this dump wasn't the right shop, the next one might be and after seeing the creep in this place, she had a feeling the day was going to end well for her. He might not be the one, but he looked as if he needed a good beating. She really wanted him to be the one. No more perverts and pawns. No more traipsing back and forth between states. This was a time for celebration.

All of them were present. They could see the shop through Acacia's hidden video camera and hear the sounds coming from her earpiece. They could see the man sitting on his stool behind his self-imposed prison bars watching the customers eyeing his merchandize. The emotions churning inside her body were similar to the way the combination of beer and tequila made her dizzy and nauseous. It wasn't an effort for Acacia to push the excitement back down into the emptiness, back into its proper compartment. Everyone agreed the plan was too important to fuck up now with drama.

Acacia sensed the imminent end of their journey and anticipated with relish the moment when she would finally be able to exterminate this cockroach. If their plan had been a mistake, Leona would have warned her. Instead Leona remained quiet and watchful and Acacia took her silence as a sign of their impending success.

It was Acacia's job to check out Leland Ansel's security and figure out how to break into his shop later that night. Frankie had suggested stealing the phone bills and the idea made sense. But the more Acacia wandered around the place counting the number of hidden cameras and the bars on the windows and the plastic bulletproof fortress Ansel sat behind, she realized that breaking into this place would be tougher than she'd first anticipated.

Back in the hotel room, after Acacia had washed the evil stench of Ansel's place off her body she made a suggestion to the others. But no one volunteered, not even Eve. Evidently even Eve had her standards. In the middle of the night Acacia had a brainstorm. She jumped out of bed and dressed quickly then slipped out of the hotel room. The pawn shop was only three blocks away. In the alley she found what she was looking for and knew instinctively Ansel would be too crafty to leave incriminating evidence just lying around for anyone to find.

Then she noticed the back door to the pawn shop. It was an old wooden door with a brand-new deadbolt. She had to laugh. Of course. The guy was a cheap shithole which meant the front was just for show. All the special security measures in the front: the high-tech cameras, security alarms and blinding lights might frighten off lazy burglars but not her. A laminate door composed of chipboard and fake veneer which has been exposed to rain, snow, and searing heat for years and years might as well be a crepe paper banner. Acacia inspected the door carefully. There was a feeble light fixture above the door emitting barely enough light to see by. She took a step closer. The animal on the other side of the door went lunatic barking and growling and throwing himself against the barrier. Ooh-wee, he so wanted to take a chunk out of her.

Acacia left the alley and returned to the front of the shop. She searched the street and noticed on the corner a convenience store. After returning to her motel room for the necessary ingredient, Acacia returned to the alley and stood before the pawn shop door with her offering. Dr. B's medication would come in handy after all. Why had Leona even bothered with the leather satchel when everything she needed was in her boots? Acacia laughed at herself. Oh, yeah, now she remembered, she'd forgotten to tell the others. Poor Leona didn't know about the money or the drugs.

Acacia prepared herself by taking a deep breath. Two more deep inhales of cool night air and she was ready. She held the can of hair spray in her right hand and dropped the T.V. dinner seasoned with sleeping powder with her left, her mind replaying the image of herself leaping into the air and kicking the door down. She added one more detail to the picture – the door splintering in two. The weakest part of the door appeared to be the bottom half. Sun and wind and rain and mud had peeled the old varnish off the surface and revealed the warped cheap particle-board beneath.

If she were to run straight at the door, leap into the air, and with all her strength kick the bottom she would punch a hole in it. She saw the hole in her mind's eye. She remembered just last week, seeing her fists break those boards. She'd started with a quarter of an inch-thick piece, then an inch, then two inches. She'd broken them with the side of her hand, with her knuckles, and the thicker boards with her foot. She graduated from two-inch boards all the way up to four without even so much as a paper cut.

The intellectual side of her wanted to understand how such a feat had been possible. She ignored that part of her brain. Analyzing a situation to death would be a great waste of time when she could be practicing and imagining beforehand and building up her muscles and the skin around her knuckles and her feet. An equal force was important as well as a balance between energies – two solid objects colliding.

It was getting late. Acacia shook the doubts away like brushing off a fly and reexamined the door. The door looked to be no more than two inches thick. With her flashlight, she peered at the ground, pleased to see soft dirt. In fact, as far as she could see, she noticed the dirt and weeds and occasional tuft of grass growing behind the building. She turned the flashlight on the door once again and directed the light down to the foot of the door, absently noting the dog's frenzied attempts to get out and perhaps go for her throat. Maybe if she waited long enough the dog might get his wish, especially the way the cheap pine splintered and moaned with every swipe of the dog's claws.

Five more minutes passed and still no sign of a cop. Having spray painted the one and only camera in the alley which she found easily enough because Leland had attached the camera to the brick wall four feet away from and above the door. No need for a ladder either. All she had to do was climb onto the dumpster next to the building and crawl up onto the roof. Coming up behind the camera had seemed like the logical choice. Even if the police watched whatever type of video the camera recorded, all they would see would be a recording of a hand encased in a tight fitting gray leather glove holding a can of Aztec Dawn enamel spray paint.

Acacia imagined punching a hole in the door with her powerful legs and feet and the dog wiggling out of the hole and lunging for her. But he wouldn't get a chance to chomp down on her throat because she would point the hair spray at his nose and squeeze down on the button. The spray would momentarily surprise him, and he would whine and back away then she would drop the plate of food and entice him into eating the contents.

The moment had arrived.

Acacia took several deep breaths and filled her lungs and stomach with air. She said her magic words and opened her eyes. She stepped back and ran toward the door and leaped using both feet like a battering ram. The soft dirt cushioned her fall.

The door remained in its previous condition. Without recriminations or tears Acacia backed up once again and leaped toward the door. She heard an ominous cracking and smiled. It was the fifth kick that finally splintered the bottom half of the door.

Up until the moment the German Shepherd tore his way through the hole, everything had gone as planned. The feel of his sharp incisors tearing through the flesh of her right ankle sent shock waves through her system and galvanized her into action. Instead of spraying him with the contents of the can, she stupidly began to beat him over the head with the metal cylinder. The weapon might as well have been a towel for all the good it did. When he backed up as if to spring for her throat, instinct took over. Everything happened so fast, she had no time to think, she simply did what she had to do. If she had thought about the consequences, she probably would never have gone through with it.

The Shepherd lay motionless at her feet. Maybe she had killed him. His skull looked normal though. She stood above him feeling the blood trickling down her right leg and replayed the events of the evening so far; how she had replaced the image of his head with the image of her practice boards and imagined herself breaking the board with her fist. Yet if she'd really crushed his skull, there should have been blood and brains all over her shoes. She must have knocked him out.

A sick sensation washed over her. A long time ago, she'd loved dogs. She still loved dogs. Now was not the time to mourn. She would worry about him later. Now she had to act and act quickly. She looked around desperate to find some place to hide the dog's body. Then she remembered the dumpster. The Shepherd must weigh more than a hundred pounds. Don't think about weight. Concentrate on the end result she told herself. She wasn't aware of anything but the image in her head.

The surge of adrenaline coursing through her body made his weight seem insignificant as if she carried a child in her arms. With tears burning a path down her cheeks and droplets falling onto her neck, Acacia picked him up, all one hundred pounds of him, walked the three feet to the dumpster, and tossed him inside.

Instead of the squishy thud she'd anticipated, she heard the crackle of plastic. Precious seconds passed as she tried to figure out what was wrong with this situation. She stepped onto a five-gallon plastic container dropped near the dumpster and peeked inside. The Shepherd was lying on a bed of air-filled bubble sheets (hundreds of them) and underneath the bubble sheets were many rolled up sections of carpeting each tied with lengths of heavy duty industrial-strength twine. Her first reaction – what a lucky dog! Her second reaction – even if he was lucky, he was still unconscious.

If circumstances had been different, she would have figured out another way to get inside the pawn shop. If only the damned dog had taken the bait. Everyone liked dogs. What other creature bonded so passionately with humans as did the loving dog even when they were subjected to all sorts of indignities and cruelties? It made her sick to think she had ended its life. The Shepherd had been protecting his master's property; she couldn't fault him for doing what came naturally.

Acacia wished she'd been able to take the Shepherd with her to administer a much-needed intervention to turn him back into a loving companion. Now she had another reason to hate Leland Ansel, another reason to smash in his ugly toady face. So, when she crawled through the hole in the door and rose to her feet, she rose on shaky legs with a stomach that wouldn't stop turning over in peril of sending her dinner up her esophagus and onto the concrete floor. She had no time to throw up or pass out. She had to move quickly and get the job done.

With an effort she forced herself to look around. There were cheap metal shelves running the length of the back room from wall to wall with only a few feet separating each section. The shelves contained a mishmash of portable merchandize from kitchen appliances to video equipment. Hardily any light penetrated the dirty glass from a small window at the far end of the room. She was glad she'd brought her heavy-duty flash light with her, otherwise, she would have been tripping over boxes and other junk left on the floor. The storage room was a hoarder's wet-dream with only a narrow passageway amongst the piles of bins and boxes and plastic bags reeking of desperate attempts to keep poverty at bay.

She made herself move through the smells and sights of other people's misery toward the front of the building, her ankle throbbing as she hobbled down the narrow hallway and into the next room which was a cramped office. The room was furnished with metal file cabinets, a small desk and a leather chair. On the desk was an old black rotary phone and a current year calendar. She tried to open the desk drawers, but they were locked. She tried the file cabinet drawers. They were locked as well.

With time pressing, she abandoned the office and moved toward the front of the building. The hallway cut to the right and ended abruptly at a door. She opened the door and entered a room encased in bullet proof glass. It extended from the counter to the ceiling with two small cashier windows allowing the owner to do business without exposing himself to an irate customer. On the other side of the glass, she could see the display room. A barstool with a cushioned seat in black vinyl was tucked under the counter. The counter was made of cheap pressed-wood with an imitation wood laminate on the surface. And the card table in the corner with its matching chairs looked as if it had been fished out of a landfill.

Also on the counter were neatly stacked forms and a pen attached to a chain. Ghee, the guy was so cheap he even believed people would steal his pen. She shoved his cushioned stool away and searched the open shelves below the counter. The room included a laptop, an empty cash box and an old-fashioned steel heavy duty safe. Acacia found the combination to the safe taped to the underside of the card table. She opened the safe. The safe held an empty cash box. Acacia closed and locked the safe and returned the paper to its hiding spot.

The absence of family photos or paintings or plants or anything with color and intimacy, even a halfhearted attempt to make the room personal, corresponded with her memories of Leland. Yet he was a neat freak. Maybe too neat. Acacia made careful note where everything had been placed so as not to disturb the order of the room. Leland had the same freaky sense of neatness as someone else she knew, and he would remember if the pencil had been left on the desk by the sharpener or in the empty coffee can.

What difference did a little mess make? The back door looked as if a hoard of hungry termites had thrown a party for all their relatives. Idiot. She had to make it look like a robbery as if the burglar frustrated with the shop's cheap crap chose to tear up the place. Or? Why bother.

It took her nearly twenty minutes to find anything significant. The bills were filed in a green hanging folder marked "bills" in the cubby under the laptop. And the bills included copies of phone charges as far back as two years ago. Once the front desk area with its bullet proof glass had been methodically examined and nothing worth her interest was found, she moved back down the hall to the tiny office with its metal filing cabinets. She discovered a scanner/copier and fax machine behind the desk. The clock on the wall warned her she didn't have much time. It took a few precious minutes to get the copier warmed up and another ten minutes to make her copies of the most recent phone bills then return them to their proper folders.

Evidently Leland Ansel did keep money on the premises. She found the money in one of several boxes piled beside the copier. She took all his spare change, nearly two hundred dollars plus the ten dollars in coins. She also confiscated a pearl handled switchblade and book of stamps from the desk drawer. Before leaving the shop, Acacia stood beside the dumpster and held her breath and listened with her ears straining. She heard movement and a whining only a dog in pain can make. The whining hurt her ears more than if he'd howled. But as she hurried away from the scene of the crime, she was relieved to know that the Shepherd was alive.

In a gas station bathroom, she examined the teeth marks on her ankle. She had a series of nasty looking puncture wounds which circled her ankle and when she removed the dried blood from the wounds they began to bleed afresh. She'd had the forethought to buy ointment and bandages and proceeded to nurse herself. The only good thing to come out of her fifteen-year incarceration at Canal Critical Care and Recovery

Hospital was the medical training she picked up watching nurses working on the loony-tunes.

It was a good thing the gas station bathrooms had been accessible near the pumps; it meant she didn't have to go through the brightly lit convenience store where she would be recorded on video camera and anyone curious enough might notice and wonder why there was blood on her boots and blood on the cuff of her pant leg. Acacia had chosen a small gas station on a back road where people still trusted each other and there was very little foot traffic.

No one bothered her as she slipped into the bathroom and took care of her injuries. Barely fifteen minutes later she was back in the truck and on her way. Then she thought about the spray can. The convenience store clerk might remember her. There even might be video of her purchasing the can? So, what. Did she really give a bug's ass? Not really. What she planned to do in the next few weeks would make what she had done tonight seem trivial in comparison.

Down the road a piece, at a competing gas station she stopped and bought a bottle of aspirin and an iced coffee. Anything stronger would have been noticed. She longed for something to kill the pain but knew if she tried to buy liquor she would be scrutinized and remembered. Unfortunately for her she had a baby face and few people would believe she was twenty-one. Even with her brand-new license, there would be questions. What's a kid like you doing so far from home? What sign are you? You don't look twenty-one? Do you have any other proof of identification?

An hour after taking two aspirin, Acacia was forced to pull off the main road and park in a quiet spot. She turned off the engine, found an old blanket from the backseat and laid down to rest for a moment. She convinced herself she just needed twenty minutes and then she would continue her journey. She set the alarm on her cellphone for twenty minutes.

A dog barked in the distance and Acacia woke with a startled oath. Gradually it dawned upon her she was in Luke's truck. She pulled out her cellphone from her pants pocket and belatedly realized her phone was dead and needed a charge. She had no idea how long she'd slept. The truck's uncompromising bench seat hurt her ass. Swallowing the acid taste of annoyance, Acacia thought about going back to sleep, but didn't like the idea. She would be vulnerable to attack especially out here at night in the open in a strange place unable to see much beyond her hands in this pitch darkness all around her.

And what about the creepy crawly things out here? She could hear them flying and scuttling and crooning and doing all sorts of nocturnal stuff such as killing prey, eating prey, and shitting prey. The birds were kind of cute, but not the snakes and spiders; she loathed snakes and spiders and mice, and she didn't have the energy to deal with any of them tonight.

After a while fighting an overwhelming tiredness, she fished in the glove compartment and found a flashlight. Before using the light, Acacia started the engine. She pointed the beam of light at the dashboard to check the gas gauge. It read full. She was grateful to the man for being such a sensible guy and filling up. A clock would have been nice. She had no idea what time it was, nor what day it was. And what did it matter? She had eyes. She could see that it was dark outside, too damned dark to be stumbling around trying to find a place to pee. She would hold on as long as possible.

Acacia waited a few more minutes before starting up the truck. Her plan was to get off the back road and take the highway. Maybe she would head for Nevada. To reach Highway 95 south, she had to drive back toward a town called Marsing. Long before she reached the marker for Highway 95 South, she noticed the lights of the ION truck stop on her right. And when she pulled into the truck stop to fill up and go to the bathroom, she passed a Ford Taurus that looked remarkably like her former vehicle. It was parked beyond the lights of the station as if the driver had planned to spend the night in it or might be inside the ION station.

Before she could go much further she knew she'd have to figure out how to get some money and pay for the rest of the trip west. Truckers frequented truck stops and supposedly truckers were notorious for picking up stray women. Maybe she might find herself some willing victim, someone she could lure into the dark and relieve of his wallet. Acacia had no compunction about preying on men. She was beyond caring if she ended up smoking the devil's pipe. Tonight, she needed money. Tonight, she needed to get her ass to Oregon and end this journey for good. The committee had agreed to the plan. She would be the one to get the girls to their destination if it meant sleeping with the rankest, ugliest, nastiest critter she could find.

The ION truck stop seemed to be the ideal location for her get-rich-quick scheme. She considered swapping the truck for the Ford Taurus and decided to risk pulling into the gas station and parking behind a semi. She made a point of going inside the station to pee and purchase a bottle of water mixed with young green tea leaves and other supposedly healthy ingredients. What had happened to just plain water and regular food? While she did these ordinary chores, she looked for the two men chasing her. Neither one happened to be inside the ION store. Evidently, the man who owned the truck had abandoned the Taurus and drove on with the other guy.

Acacia bought a snack bar she would later throw in the trash, especially when she read that the third ingredient in the snack bar included corn syrup. This temple would not be polluted. Once outside, she walked quickly toward the Taurus and glanced inside. The windows were rolled up and when she checked the doors they were all locked. Behind her, customers were filling up their vehicles at the pumps. Even though she stood in semidarkness, she remained cautious. She discarded the idea of breaking into the Taurus.

Calling attention to herself would be a mistake. And regretfully, she knew nothing about hot wiring vehicles. Only in the movies did the heroes and heroines have such idiosyncratic skills as picking locks, hot wiring cars, and hacking into computers.

An hour later, Acacia found herself in McDermitt, Nevada. When she tried to turn the steering wheel of the truck to enter the parking area of the nearby truck stop, the wheel refused to budge. In fact, the truck refused to move any further. She turned the flashlight on and looked at the gas gauge. It still read full. She tapped the glass. The needle refused to move. She tried to restart the truck. Nothing happened. A car behind her began to honk. She rolled down the window and gestured for him to pass her. The dork kept honking. Finally, she climbed out of the truck and marched up to his window.

"Didn't you see me telling you to go around? What's your damned problem?" she asked the man. He must have been no more than twenty years old and still had a bad case of insecurity. His woman puffed on her cigarette and stared out her window ignoring them both.

"Move your truck, Lady. You're blocking traffic," he said, as if he hadn't heard her.

She leaned forward, "Are you listening to me, asshole. I said move around me. Go on. Back up. It's real easy. Even you could do it."

"You being smart with me?" he asked shoving his car door open and struggling to climb out. Why did people ask such stupid questions? Of course, she was being smart with him.

Before he could get out, Acacia shoved the door closed and grabbed his hand and pushed the wrist backward. He cried out. She knew the pain would be excruciating. And all he should be thinking about right now was the pain and have no energy to punch her with his free hand. He tried to pull away but that position only made the pain worse. His girlfriend let out an earsplitting scream and flicked her lit cigarette at Acacia. Unfortunately, the burning cigarette bounced off the inside of the car roof and landed between her man's legs.

"Shit. What the fuck?" he screamed.

While his girlfriend rooted around between his legs looking for the cigarette and the man bellowed in pain, Acacia heard the girlfriend say, "Hold on Simon. Quit wiggling. I got it. See Simon. See Honey. I got it."

Acacia let go of Simon Honey's hand and stepped back hoping he would get out of the vehicle, so she could really do some damage. Instead, he leaned back and nursed his sore wrist. The woman leaned over Simon Honey and threw her lit cigarette at Acacia. Dumb considering, they were at a gas station, Acacia thought. Acacia stepped back, and the cigarette landed by her boot. She stomped on the lit end and turned away. As she started walking back to her vehicle she skidded to a stop when she heard a car door open. The female marched toward Acacia with fury in her eyes, her high heels digging holes in the concrete.

"You slimy little slut. You think you're so tough. Let me show you tough."

By this time, they had an audience. A few people had paused as they came out of the store to watch the cat fight. There were no police yet. Acacia watched the woman and sensed a crowd forming. She had another danger to her left, a pair of overeager knights in rusty travel trailers with tobacco and beer stained t-shirts were headed her way.

"Leave the lady alone," one of them said.

Acacia wondered which "lady" he meant. Evidently it wasn't her. The lady in question marched toward Acacia, all five feet skinny ass of her ready to do battle. She had the look of someone who enjoyed speedballs and long nights in front of a stove. Her teeth must be ground down to nubs by now. Every muscle on her face twitched. It was tragic. Acacia spread her legs two feet apart and planted her feet firmly on the ground bracing for the impact to come. She waited for the woman to make the first move. Ms. Barfly paused finally noticing the crowd eager to see a cat fight. Suddenly the fight left her. Embarrassed at all the attention, she started walking back to her man and his vehicle and said, "Simon sweetie, are you OK? I'm sorry about the cigarette."

Acacia turned toward the rubbernecks. "Hey, I need some help pushing my truck out of the way here. I've run out of gas. Any of you mind helping?"

Two men came forward with smiles and nods. They looked hungry, poor, young, and kind which made her instantly suspicious. After they helped her push the truck into the gas station lot beside an empty pump, she regretted her first impression and searched the truck for some money. But they shrugged away her offer to pay them and instead reset their backpacks on their shoulders and walked toward the highway with their thumbs out waiting for a ride.

Acacia noticed how the other people, people one would expect to come to the aid of a stranger, with their well-fed and pampered attire, mostly couples driving brand new cars lost interest in her once the fight fizzled out. They avoided her eyes as they returned to the pressing business of pumping gas and buying lotto tickets. Then she saw the two in the shadows and how they moved forward only when the others drove away. She was alone outside the gas station standing by a full pump without the cash to pay for the gas.

Unlike the hitchhikers these two men were middle-aged and drunk. One of them looked as if he'd been born with a taste for bitterness. The other looked like he had money, money he probably got from the misery of others. He wore a shiny gold belt buckle with some kind of insect trapped in the amber, oh yeah, she recognized the scorpion. She'd seen similar ornaments in Mexico and remembered the initiation rites performed by Mexican boys in which they would lie down in the desert and wait for scorpions to crawl on their faces. The final rite included biting off the scorpion's head. How sweet.

The guy with the scorpion belt buckle and the beer belly sauntered over to her with his beefy fingers outstretched. She shook his hand and surreptitiously wiped his scent and sweat off her palm and onto her skirt. He noticed and frowned. She didn't like the way the other one stared at her breasts.

When he turned to face the skinny guy behind him, Acacia surveyed his backside in awe never having seen such a wide ass as his before. He could have moved the truck with his ass alone. But curiously neither of them offered to help her. Both men now appeared to be slipping and sliding their way toward a major crime, maybe theft, maybe rape. Acacia forced a smile. Smiling hurt. She supposed Wide Ass had the same affliction.

Just before she moved toward the store, she grabbed her head and cried out, "Oh damned, I forgot my purse." She returned to the truck, climbed inside, and pretended to search the glove compartment and the floor of the truck for an imaginary purse. When she came up for air, she noticed Wide Ass standing at the darkest corner of the store watching her and the cars. She leaned over the steering wheel and pretended to be despondent.

Wide-Ass watched her for so long she got tired of pretending and sat up. His unblinking stare was beginning to annoy her. When she leaned back against the seat cushion, she noticed the flashlight on the floor. She set the flashlight on the seat beside her. She kept the man in her sights and held the flashlight between her fingers feeling the cold metal handle.

It was a nice big heavy flashlight. At any other time, she would have been grateful for the truck owner's forethought in choosing such a handy innocent looking weapon. Wide Ass dropped his head. The dark baseball cap obscured his features and the yellowish light from the gas station cast his figure in shadow.

Several options occurred to her. She could go inside and tell the clerk she'd run out of gas and lost her purse. Or she could slip away and try to elude the man who was now stepping off the stoop and heading her way. Even before he spoke she knew. It would have been grand to encounter a guy interested in just helping a stranded female without wanting anything in return. This guy hadn't done anything to help her; yet, the way he lurked in the shadows and watched her made her realize he was more than just horny, he was dangerous.

Too bad that knights in shining armor protecting maidens in distress only appeared in children's stories. Although those earlier knights of the road had surprised her with their chivalry. Her knights in the rusty travel trailers had offered to help her get the truck out of the way, even offered to give her a lift, yet, they too were long gone now.

"You a cop? If you're a cop, you got to say so," he said, then walked over to her window, planting his hands on the truck roof as if he planned to stay in that position awhile. He bent his head to see her face more clearly, "And if you're a hooker, I'm not interested. I like my women clean. So, what are you?"

"Do I look like a cop? Get real. And I'm not a hooker," she said. "I'm just broke. And whether I'm clean is none of your damned business."

"That so," he said.

"If you aren't willing to lend me some cash for gas then go away mister. I'm not interested in SOPs," she said and tried to push the door open.

"What'd you call me, bitch?"

"An SOP – you know – a son of a prick."

"Is that how you pay me back, huh, by insulting me? You ungrateful slut."

"Pay you back? For what? You haven't done anything for me but creep me out."

"Time somebody taught you some manners, Missy."

"Move your fat ass away from my truck, mister."

"Or what? You'll pee your pants. Go ahead. I'd like to see that."

The man refused to budge. Someone had to come out soon. Where were all the people a minute ago? They'd stuck around to see a cat fight? But didn't stick around long enough to rescue a maiden in distress. It was just her luck. Most of them were probably long gone. Even the skinny one, Igor to this Frankenstein had probably slunk away sensing trouble. But there was the clerk inside the store. She could see him standing behind the cash register making a point of reading a comic book. Even Simon Honey and his girlfriend were long gone having paid their dues to the consumer-god.

Instead of getting bored and leaving his prey, Wide Ass looked around as if he didn't want anyone to see what he planned to do next. Acacia had long ago lost her fear of danger. The worst that could happen had already happened, anything else would be anticlimactic.

Acacia's present view made her nauseous. The shakes began with the thought of being trapped inside the cab. The truck was parked close to a metal garage near a strip of grass, so she couldn't get out the passenger side door either. It was all wrong. The truck was parked in the darkest corner of the gas station away from the lights and people. She'd been set up; even the knights of the road had been pawns in the game. How amateur not to have noticed.

Heat rose up from her belly and spread throughout her body: her arms, legs, even the tip of her head. Beads of sweat broke out through the pores of her skin drenching the back of her neck, her forehead, her armpits, and the flesh behind her legs – all her parts were pockets of itchy liquid. To rid herself of the suffocating heat, she had to do something. She needed fresh air. Yes. She must remove the obstacle blocking the fresh air.

Without conscious thought she picked up the flashlight resting by her leg and grasped the cool handle with both hands. Taking a deep breath, she exhaled and shoved the handle into the belly blocking her view. Wide Ass grunted in surprise. With the weight of her shoulders, she shoved the handle of the flashlight into his belly again and this time he staggered back. Before he could come at her and pin her inside, she kicked the door open and spilled out onto the asphalt.

Once she was outside the vehicle, she took a few precious seconds to orient herself. She clambered up onto her feet. Her relief at being free made her gasp for air and all the energy coursing through her body made her legs tremble. Her vision blurred. She tried not to panic. She knew from experience that all this shit would balance out in the end. She'd just overreacted; her body was confused by all the conflicting needs inside her head, the needs wanting to go in different directions. How could a body do anything sensible when part of it wanted to flee and the other to fight and still another to curl up under the truck?

Unexpectedly something swooped down upon her. Her lack of preservation, all screwed up over the years left her lethargic when she should have been alert and prepared for action. Most people would have flinched or ducked to avoid the blow. She was intimately familiar with pain and accepted the blow gratefully. The force of his fist meeting her shoulder sent her flying into the truck door. Instead of falling to the ground and screaming and crying as the average person would do when someone beat them, she started to laugh, a sort of gasping laugh full of salvia and snot running down her nose. Not snot. Blood maybe. She couldn't help but see the whole mess as particularly hilarious.

No matter where she went or what she did, inevitably she would attract the wife beaters, rapists, and misogynists. She had a talent, a real god given talent for attracting the truly screwed up fuck-brains. It must be something in her sweat or the scent she gave off, something that said, yes, here I am, I'm your punching bag, come work out your frustration on me, do your worst.

She imagined the sight they must present. A gruesome kaleidoscope of childhood movies flashed across her mind. She was Jack getting her head dented in and ribs broken by the Giant while one of Snow White's merry dwarfs sat inside the gas station and sipped his coffee and read his comic book. Unsporting, terribly unsporting of the mean old giant. Unfortunately for her, no one witnessed the fight or if they had, they had made the choice to remain inside the safety of the store, far from the ruckus.

Cowards, she thought. The world was full of cowards. She stopped laughing. The anger surged up, that familiar, beautiful anger she'd nurtured for the last five years.

The man stopped hitting her and stared as if she'd sprouted elephant ears. Dumbo maybe. She wished. Then she could fly away and escape this duffer. Her laugh turned into a gasp. He stepped back and looked confused. It was just the two of them outside under the yellow light cast by the gas station lights. Occasionally white eyes would appear out of the blackness along the freeway with a whoosh of motors and tires on pavement then become angry eyes blinking away the uncomfortable sight of a woman lying on the ground. And soon the angry eyes disappeared around the curve of the road.

In the cloudless sky the stars shown down upon Acacia and reminded her of the others. They were depending on her to get them to their destination. They depended on her to fight for them. So even though her shoulder throbbed, and her hip ached, and she felt as if her foot had grown two sizes too big, she struggled to untie her right shoe. The switchblade had been pressing against her heel for far too damned long. She took it out, flipped it open, and then threw it. His high-pitched scream satisfied her immensely.

Pleased with her aim, Acacia slipped her foot back in her oversized shoe then struggled to her feet. "I wouldn't try to pull it out if I was you, especially in that location. Just a little lower and I could have made you a castrato." The giggling started up again. That hadn't been her. Not her? Indeed not. She wouldn't be so crass as to laugh at another human being's suffering. But he wasn't human. He was the Giant. The irony made her giggle the more.

The man grabbed the handle of the switchblade and yanked it out. The blood flowed down his thigh and he dropped to the ground landing on his face.

"I told you not to do that. Now see what you've done," she told him shaking her head sadly.

She watched the blood spread out from beneath him. Lots of blood. Too much blood. But she hadn't hit any major artery she was sure. And if no one came out, he would be dead soon. She'd always wondered what it would feel like to kill someone. Now she would know. She struggled to her feet and watched the blood pooling like spent oil. In her ear she heard a familiar voice shouting at her.

Instead of running away she moved forward straight at the Giant and rolled him onto his back.

When Acacia swam up into the light of consciousness, she found herself sitting in the truck facing the store. The truck had been moved next to the phone booth. And between her fingers she held a piece of paper. She looked down at the receipt in her hand and tried to focus on the print. She pondered the receipt, a receipt for fifty dollars of unleaded gas. Was the receipt hers? When had she bought gas? She searched for the flashlight and found it nestled in the crevice of the bench seat.

There was something else in the crevice of the seat. She pulled out a wad of twenty-dollar bills. From behind her she heard men's voices. Someone pulled aside the darkness and stepped into the florescent light severely annoyed at the way young people could be so rude at times. In the rear view mirror, Acacia could see Tessa's snow white hallow of hair surrounding a sweet wrinkled face and the way Tessa's gentle watery blue eyes watched the ambulance with relief, apparently happy that the man had found help in time. Acacia, on the other hand, was mightily disappointed in the outcome.

"Too bad it wasn't a hearse. We could have saved the world a lot of misery tonight," Acacia said.

"Keep a civil tongue in your head young lady or we're all in trouble," Tessa said in her familiar gentle voice.

The paramedics were shutting the doors of the ambulance and climbing inside to take their passenger away. "Good riddance," Acacia whispered. Tessa sighed in resignation. A face popped into view so close to her open window the sight nearly made her pee in her pants. The face looked sturdy and sane. The man held his motorcycle helmet on his hip and she assumed from his attire that he was a cop. He stood before the driver's side door and looked down at her.

The policeman's concern puzzled Acacia; she expected to be thrown out of the truck and handcuffed by now. She heard the wail of the ambulance as it raced its passenger to the nearest hospital.

"Ms. Pierce, Mr. Michaels says you saved his life. He's grateful for your assistance by the way," the policeman said while his eyes searched her face. She didn't care for his scrutiny. The right side of her face was beginning to throb. Belatedly, she realized her right side was in darkness.

By morning, she would have a nasty bruise running from her eye to her chin. Acacia discovered that before the ambulance arrived, Tessa managed to talk some sense into Mr. Michaels. She held the wad of paper towels to his groin and lectured him on his rude habits. The towels, as she recalled, had come from the windshield washing dispensers, the ones most people used to wipe off excess fluid from the squeegees. The towels were dry, maybe not all that clean, but they were dry.

Frankie was the one who knew the most about Mr. Michaels (which wasn't his real name anyway). She actually enjoyed reading the Wall Street Journal and recognized him straight away. While they waited for the ambulance and the police to arrive, Tessa warned him his reputation would be seriously at risk if the other board members of his company learned about his nocturnal hobby.

His attempt to look like a biker in his leather chaps and helmet couldn't disguise the pricey wristwatch or the expensive ring on his fat finger. Rape and battery were serious enough charges that he might even end up in jail for a few years. The rich rarely paid for their crimes though. "Yet," she told him. "You never know what might happen in the court of public opinion."

Looking up into the cop's face, Acacia tried on her best smile and said, "Well tell him it was no trouble. I'm glad I came along when I did." She remembered Tessa's lecture about not revealing too much to strangers and hoped he wasn't going to ask for her address. She couldn't remember the address on her identification.

"You didn't see who stabbed him?"

"No. Sorry. I didn't. He must have left before I pulled in."

"If we have further questions, we'll be in touch Ms. Pierce."

"No problem Officer. Can I go now?"

"You can go ma'am. Luke Nerin confirmed the loan of his truck and told me to tell you, he'll be talking to you soon. We've got your phone number and address. No need to stick around. Be careful driving now. There are plenty of deer crossings along this stretch of highway."

"I will. Thank you," she said in her sweetest voice as she started the truck and backed out.

Acacia managed to drive a few miles before a headache forced her to park on the side of the road and give in to sleep. So, the cop had called the owner of the vehicle and Luke Nerin had lied. Why would he lie? The idea that he might have told his brother where to find her made her nervous enough she considered stealing another vehicle. But at this late hour, there were very few vehicles on the road.

Tessa who had been in the backseat and hadn't spoken once when the cop showed up must have gotten bored for the last couple of hours and woke Acacia with her monologue about her amazing kids at the Chicago School for Gifted Children. She'd loved those kids. Unable to have children of her own, she'd poured all her love into teaching.

Acacia straightened up and looked around the cab and out the window wondering where she had ended up this time. She soon discovered that she and the truck were miles from the gas station and Wide Ass. She remembered the fight and Tessa's quick thinking. She also recalled that after the fight with Wide Ass, Tessa reminded her she'd stolen a bunch of money from Leland Ansel's pawn shop and stuffed the bills behind the seat cushion.

Had she deliberately forgotten the money just to pick a fight with Wide Ass?

Acacia managed to drive another fifty miles before the truck ran out of gas a second time. Unfortunately, two mistakes conspired to ruin Acacia's plan of getting safely away from the Nerin brothers. The first mistake was in forgetting the satchel back at the Woolly Man and the second was in choosing the dumb-ass truck as a means of transportation in the first place.

By the time she figured out that the instruments on the dashboard were more decorative than functional, she decided she would just have to drive as far as she could with whatever gas was in the vehicle. She soon realized that not only did the speedometer, gas, and water gauge not work, but the heater didn't work or the windshield wipers.

Basically, the only part that did function on the truck was the engine and not all that well either. She didn't think anything was seriously wrong until several vehicles on the highway began to pass her and she noticed that the drivers were sneering. Of significance was the moment a KIA passed her and the woman inside gave her the finger. Evidently a KIA had more power than the truck and the truck had difficulty running uphill at anything above fifty miles an hour.

The last sign she'd seen had been the one that informed motorists they had twenty miles left before reaching Winnemucca. At the gas station in Jordan Valley, the clerk had told her the nearest town would be Paris, Nevada. Close to the Paris, Nevada border before the truck lost all momentum and she could no longer turn the wheel, she decided to find a place to park the piece-of-shit, dumb-ass, useless trash heap of a vehicle.

She pulled off onto the shoulder of the road before the man in the car behind her ran her off the highway. As she climbed out of the truck, she saw a vehicle slowing down around the curve she had just coasted down. She stuck her thumb out. Too late. She recognized the vehicle and the driver. The silver Camaro pulled over to the side of the road in front of his brother's truck. No place to hide now.

When the man climbed out of his car, Acacia considered several options and discarded the most ludicrous ones first. She might be able to run down the road screaming bloody murder in the hopes a motorist would stop and help her or she could run into the desert to hide behind a thorny bush or some cactus, maybe that tall sage or that big boulder. Or, if her luck held, she could tumble down a ravine. Overall, her choices were shitty and the only other one would mean a fight. She'd already had her fight for the week. Unlike Wide Ass, this guy looked lithe and flexible. He might do some real damage.

There was an easier way.

While the man took his time examining the rusty old truck for dings-and-dents — as if she could have done any worse damage to the worthless piece of crap — Acacia made the difficult decision to surrender for the greater good. Gentle voices and warm hands pulled her down into the womb of forgetfulness. An eager recruit swam to the surface, tingling with excitement at finally meeting the man face to face. Maybe this man would prove to be the one.

Jule Nerin stood by the Woolly Man door and watched Luke with a furrowed brow. She held one of Quinn's suitcases in her hand, waiting impatiently for Quinn to come downstairs with the rest of her luggage, more than ready to get her daughter away from the trouble she saw on the horizon. Luke acted as if nearly getting himself killed was no big deal. The woman had tried to run him down. She was a menace. And why couldn't she call the police? She'd almost called them while in Twin Falls. After all, the woman had threatened her family.

Now all she wanted was Quinn safely in her college dorm room, as far away from Woolstone as possible. Then she'd dump Zak's "date" off somewhere along the Interstate and make her walk the rest of the way home – the slut. At this very moment, Zak's "date" happened to be sitting in the backseat of Jule's vehicle with the hot sun roasting her already smelly body. With her nose in the air as if she smelled something foul, Jule watched her son Luke and her best customer Mona Lawson deep in a heated conversation at a booth in the far corner of the bar.

Mondays were always slow. It was the only day of the week Jule had the chance to really get her chores done and here she was waiting on her daughter and listening to the two in the corner discussing the nut case who had nearly murdered her son.

Luke Nerin sat across from Mona Lawson and plied her with another scotch. When she gave him a suspicious lift of her bushy gray brow, he told her the drink was on the house. "This guy Dr. Bishop asked you to keep an eye on Jane Smith and help her adjust to her new life. Is that right? And you're sure Jane Smith spent most of her childhood in a psych ward?

I don't know; I don't buy it. Nobody can keep you locked up in a looney bin against your will these days. There are laws, you know. And multiple personality disorder? Come on. Get real. Maybe gullible people bought that crap in my Granny's day, but this is 2017. The APA just loves these exotic mental illnesses; they give shrinks a real rush. Did you know the DSM used to include homosexuality as a mental disorder? In 1974 that all changed. And today, very few people think the LGBT community are insane. Maybe too styling for my taste, but not insane."

Luke paused glancing at the older woman sitting across from him, belatedly realizing, she was of a generation which had grown up vilifying homosexuals. He changed tactics, "I have a minor in psychology, so, I know of what I speak. Well, maybe you wouldn't agree about the homosexuality part since you're ah, um, well, never mind. But I tell you the DSM is a load of garbage. It's way too easy to diagnose someone based on cultural biases and personal prejudices. You know what I mean?"

After an uncomfortable few minutes of absolute silence, Mrs. Lawson spoke. With her chestnut brown eyes attempting to bore a hole in his brain, she said in a monotone voice, "No. Don't know what the hell you mean cause you don't know it like I know it. My doctor calls it MPD and she says it's also called DID. I can't remember what that last one stands for, but my doctor is a good doctor and she knows her stuff, so smarty pants, you just listen up and I'll tell you what you want to know and then I'll be on my way."

As Mona started rattling off acronyms (or was it initialisms?) Luke pulled out his smartphone and began searching the Internet. He hated the lazy-brains who couldn't get facts straight. Then he found Dissociative Identity Disorder. As he stared at his smartphone screen he heard her say, "Some dummies confuse it with schizophrenia. They're not the same. You hear me? They are not the same. MPD is a major problem nowadays. I know. I get them blackouts sometimes and can't remember what I did the day before, and my doctor, she says it's cause I got this brain disorder and she's going to help me. And she wants to help Jane too."

Before he had a chance to respond to her crazy statement his mother bellowed, "Quincella! Hurry up. I don't have all damned day." He turned in his seat and realized she'd been sitting on the barstool by the door and had been a witness to his interrogation of her best customer. As his mother gave him the stink-eye she said, "Luke. I need to talk to you. Now." Then she turned to Mona and addressed the woman in her professional bartender voice, "Sorry, Mrs. Lawson, I just want to borrow my son for a second."

Luke stood up and slipped his smartphone back in his pocket, "I'll get you something to munch on Mrs. Lawson. How about some popcorn or maybe a bag of potato chips?"

"Thanks kiddo, I'll take a bag of pork rinds if you don't mind," Mona Lawson said smiling for the first time.

By the time he'd traversed the short walk from the booth to the bar, his mother beating him to the snack display managed to threaten him with bodily harm if he dared to drive away her best customer. The speedy exchange took place in heated whispers. At the same time as he was being chastised in one ear, he could hear Quincella stomping down the stairs from her bedroom with the other. Both he and his mother turned to watch Quinn walk into the bar with her suitcase in one hand, her makeup case in the other and her huge heavy purse slapping her hip as it dangled from her shoulder.

"I'm ready Mom. Let's go," Quinn said moving toward the door oblivious to the charged atmosphere in the room. His mother gave him a warning lift of her brow and followed her daughter out the door. A few seconds later, she returned to flip the sign on the door to closed, kick the door stopper away and say before locking up, "Don't let anyone else in. You can let Mrs. Lawson out the side door when she's finished. We're closed for the rest of the day. You hearing me Luke?"

"Sure Mom," he said absently as he handed the bag of pork rinds to Mona.

With the main door shut, the inside of the Woolly Man was dark and airless. Luke switched on the overhead fan. The four globes in the center with their halogen bulbs cast a forgiving light on Mona Lawson's face and helped dispel some of the gloom while the large wooden blades managed to cool the air only a few degrees.

As if they hadn't been interrupted by Quinn's dramatic leave taking, Mona got to the crux of her answer, "Dr. Bishop asked me to keep an eye on Jane. They don't know her real name. No one has come forward to claim her. She was found somewhere between Canada and Minnesota. In the Boundary Waters area, I think."

"What was a little girl doing all by herself miles from civilization?"

Mrs. Lawson leaned closer and whispered, "Don't know. There were rumors about an angel carrying her away from a fire and setting her down smack in the middle of the Boundary Waters. I don't believe in all that nonsense. More likely there'd been sexual abuse. You know what I mean? Poor thing. The monster tried to set her on fire. Yeah. Yeah. Nasty huh? Poor child. Years of skin grafts and surgeries."

Luke leaned back unable to hold his breath any longer. Damned. The woman needed a breath mint bad. He wasn't too keen on her testimony either. He doubted a real doctor would reveal so much about a patient to another patient, "Were you Dr. Bishop's patient at one-time Mrs. Lawson? I'm not sure why he recommended you," he added quickly, "other than that you both have similar symptoms."

"I guess he hoped that perhaps her true self would emerge if she came back to where she used to live."

"If no one claimed her, how did he know she use to live in Idaho?"

"Oh, I see what you mean," her deprecating laugh didn't fool him. "That is odd isn't it? Well, you know, now that I think on it, he did tell me to keep her away from water, that she was deathly afraid of water."

"How does a fear of water fit in with knowing she comes from Idaho?" Luke asked smelling more than just bad breath in her wildly irrational disjointed story.

"Don't get all snotty with me boy. I'm just telling you what I heard. All I'm doing is helping out a fellow sufferer and I was told by Bishop she may have come from around here. Don't ask me how he knows. Don't ask me why she's afraid of water. Maybe she nearly drowned once. Who knows?" she finished with a shrug of her painfully thin knobby shoulder. Mona looked like she was made of weathered rawhide held together with sticks.

"Want another drink?" Luke asked.

It was nearly midnight before the real story came flooding, bubbling, and burping out of Mrs. Lawson. After a bottle of scotch and a couple of beers she was sharing more than he wanted to know. And then through the morose pity-party came a bit of truth, "She's my old ant on my Dad's side of the family you see." With a finger to her cracked dry lips she continued, "Don't tell. Promise. They were friends in college, Dr. Bishop, and my Ant. I mean Aunt. She's the doctor in the family. She does a special kind of research."

Mrs. Lawson paused with her lips pursed trying to remember what sort of research her aunt conducted. She dug in her nearly empty memory box and after coming up with nothing frowned and swatted at the forgetfulness with an irritated air, as if forgetfulness was a real person bent on making her look stupid. Eventually, she got around to finishing her thought. "It was some sort of research anyway. Dr. Bishop talked to my Aunt and she told him Jane Smith should come to me for help."

"What's your Aunt's name?"

Mrs. Lawson's vacuous expression turned sly, "Oh no, you don't. Can't tell you that. Big secret."

"Why mention your Aunt at all if it's such a big secret? You know it's easy enough to find out who she is. I could ask around town. Mom might even know. Or wait, how about the Internet? You're old enough to be included in ancestry databases. I bet they even have your high school yearbook photos."

"I went to a small school in Oregon, really small. Doubt there are any pictures of us left. As I recall there was only one of me and none of my Ant. She graduated the year before me."

"How can she be your aunt if you and she are only a year apart?"

"Don't you know anything?" Mona asked with a sneer.

"Yes. I know a lot of things. And I admit that was a stupid question. Which is it? Your aunt is your mother's younger or older sister?" he said ignoring her smug smile. Wow, he thought, stupid goes a long way with this one. So now he knew Mona Lawson's aunt was about the same age and had gone to the same school in Oregon as her niece. All he had to do was find out her mother's name or search the Internet.

And then he remembered the phone call earlier in the day before Navan Keys entered the Woolly Man. The snooty old bat on the other end of the line had called him an Oxford Man. She'd said, "Tell Mona, Violet called." His mother had told him about Mona's relative. She was some sort of plastic surgeon, a surgeon who worked on celebrities. No problem. He could find out her name easily enough. How many plastic surgeons were called Violet? But why bother? Knowing the name and address of Mad Mona's relative wouldn't help him figure out where Leona was headed driving his stolen truck.

"Does Jane Smith have any connection with Professor Wade?" he asked her not expecting an answer.

"Who?" Mona Lawson asked leaning forward with a slack face and bleary eyes.

She'll be comatose soon, Luke thought and asked her urgently, "The woman who disappeared back in 2001. She worked at Boise State and disappeared one day. They say she'd been abducted."

"Oh, I don't keep track of the goings-on in Boise," Mrs. Lawson said sending the capital city of Idaho to perdition with a dismissive toss of her arm. "Those mucky mucks and their fancy houses and their snooty kids don't concern me."

"But Dr. Bishop or your aunt must have told you more? They wouldn't invite some stranger to your home without telling you her history," Luke insisted.

"Oh, they reassured me that Jane Smith is a perfectly well-behaved young lady and would be no trouble at all," Mrs. Lawson said.

"We know THAT isn't true."

"What?" Mrs. Lawson asked and a second later caught the joke in midair and carried it beyond the boundary of good taste exhilarating the joke to a shrill prolonged cackling that hurt his eardrums. As if the unaccustomed laughter finally shut down her brain, she collapsed head first onto the table nearly colliding with her glass of beer.

If Mrs. Lawson wouldn't give him the name of her ant/aunt, Luke would find out another way. He had plenty of resources. There was something fishy about Mad Mona's story. In his excitement at the way events were beginning to move in his favor, he jumped up from his chair. While Mrs. Lawson slept off her drunk, he'd do some sleuthing.

Then his great-grandmother's rotary phone rang. When he answered on the third ring, he looked back hoping the jangling sound had disturbed Mona enough she might wake up and answer some more questions. Maybe he could get some real answers this time. The man on the other end of the line identified himself as an Owyhee County Sheriff and asked if he knew a woman calling herself Acacia Pierce. He answered in the affirmative. The officer told him his missing truck was at the ION just outside of Marsing, Idaho. When he described Leona to the officer's satisfaction, Luke dropped the phone back in its cradle and turned to look at Mona Lawson.

Maybe Mad Mona might be of some use after all.

He called his brother. Zak answered on the first ring.

14

The lovely specimen of awesome maleness took the keys out of the stolen pickup and locked the driver's side door. Standing between the truck and the Camaro Eve waited patiently for him to finish fooling around. She wasn't surprised when he said, "I'm making a citizen's arrest." When he pulled his cellphone out of his pocket and began dialing, she grew alarmed. Had she lost her magic?

Anticipating his next move, Eve threw up her arms, "Don't. Don't do it. Please don't get the cops involved. Just let me explain."

When he shut off his cellphone, she smiled inside. He stepped closer scrutinizing her face. She would have loved to know what he was thinking now. The others shoved, and she obeyed taking a step closer to him. He spoke first, "Go ahead. I'm waiting."

"Why don't we go somewhere quiet," she suggested. "Maybe have a bite to eat. I'm starved."

A tense moment passed as they waited for him to make up his mind. When he opened the driver's side door for her, everyone cheered. Then Eve took over and slipped inside the Camaro making herself comfortable. She looked in the backseat and grinned. He apologized for the mess which confirmed her first impression of him and made her even more infatuated with him. He bent down to look in her face and said, "I just need to leave a note for my brother. You won't go anywhere, will you?"

"Where would I go?" she asked gesturing toward the empty fields all around them.

By the time he returned she'd bound her ankles with old strips of cloth and was in the processes of doing the same for her wrists. He tried to stop her saying, "Are you nuts? What do you think you're doing?"

A faint odor of car wax and cleaning polish entered her nose. She couldn't help but giggle. Zak's face was so close she could smell his sweat and something salty maybe chips or peanuts on his breath.

"What's so damned funny?" he asked, scowling at her.

"If anyone were to come along and stop and see what you were up to, you'd be the one bound and hauled off to jail, not me," Eve said with a hiccup. "Let's get going, shall we?"

Zak's stony expression dissolved. There was something different about the woman, different than the weird transformation outside of the Woolly Man. This time the woman seemed to be flirting with him. Even her lips looked fuller and her eyelids sort of sleepy as if she'd just woken from a sweet dream. Trying to ignore this new personality and the feelings she provoked, he strapped her into her seat then tried to untie the smelly rags from her wrists. She pulled away. He did the next best thing and covered her bound wrists with his old windbreaker. When she didn't toss the windbreaker aside, he relaxed.

A new energy entered the space between them. The air grew dense. Zak couldn't explain what happened next. All he remembered was that his knuckles had brushed up against her arm as he tried to get the stubborn strap to unlock from the floor. By the time he'd locked her securely into the seatbelt, he felt an overwhelming urge to look into her eyes; and after their eyes met, all he wanted to do was kiss her. A car alarm brought him back to reality. His lips were bruised, and he tasted blood in his mouth. He couldn't look at her for fear he'd lose himself again.

By the time he'd shut her door, took a couple of deep breaths of fresh air, and walked around the front of the Camaro he felt composed enough to get back in the car and face her.

"What's going on?" he asked her. "Are you screwing with me? Are you using some sort of hypnosis on me? Well, it won't work; shut it down. You hear me. I'm not playing games anymore."

Her eyes were dilated. Was she on speed? Maybe. Maybe not. Who knew? He took a quick peek at her. Her lips were slightly parted, and she was breathing heavily. Then Zak's eyes traveled down her throat to her breasts. Her nipples were showing through her blouse and in response to her excitement Zak's penis began to throb. With shaking hands, he started the car, made an illegal U-Turn, and drove straight to the nearest roadside motel.

By the time he'd paid for the room and returned to his vehicle, his penis was once again its normal size, no longer obeying the capricious whims of his overcharged libido. He considered going back to the office and asking for his money back. After glancing at his watch, he figured he might as well get a good night's sleep. In the morning, he would find someone to tow his brother's vehicle to the nearest gas station.

Be honest Zak, he told himself, spending the night in a motel is just an excuse to get her to bed. He stood in the lobby staring out the window at his Camaro. Well, not exactly. The only object of any interest to him for miles around was the woman sitting inside his car. Sure there were people. But if he were called upon to describe them, he wouldn't be able to. All he could see was the woman sitting inside his car. Sure, he was tired, and it was also true birth control pills prevented HIV.

Idiot. You're going to regret this tomorrow.

There were times when he wanted to wrap his hands around his brother's neck and choke him. Luke was a pain in the ass sometimes, especially when he got an idea in his head that nobody could shake. This woman was trouble. Why were they wasting their time with trouble when they could be doing some real field work making a name for themselves in a legitimate way?

When Zak opened the passenger door and bent down to release the woman from the seatbelt, the sensation which had overpowered him earlier returned, only this time with the intensity of a supersonic jet. Within five minutes, he'd bundled her into the motel room. She was laughing softly under her breath. His forehead was soaked with sweat as he unwound the strips of cloth she'd tied around her wrists while his penis continued to throb and push against the confines of his jeans. With real relief he stepped out of his jeans and underwear and threw off his shirt.

The woman lay back on the bed and watched him with interest, her pupils still dilated, her lips slightly parted. The only time she protested was when he tried to tear off her blouse. He had to wait several precious minutes as she slowly slipped off the blouse, bra, then the skirt. Finally, finally, she stepped out of her panties.

Only afterward was he ashamed of his performance. He'd never been one of those guys, not even his first time. He'd always been the one prepared to take all night if necessary. Eve sensed his embarrassment and ran her fingers through his dark spiky hair and with a smile in her voice said, "We've got all night honey. That was just foreplay. Now turn over. Go on, turn over, I'm not going to hurt you silly."

Eve watched as he obediently turned over. When a man wanted something bad enough he could be trained. Eve ran into the bathroom and as expected found the three little bottles resting on the tub rim. She returned to the main room holding the bottle of motel lotion in her hand. As she stood over the bed examining the beautiful man lying prone before her, blood seemed to rush through every pore of her body making her hot and horny all over again. She began applying the lotion to his back, rubbing the liquid into his strong tanned shoulders, feeling his muscles relaxing at her touch.

The male, whether lean or chubby, tall or stocky, smooth or hairy, rough or tender, all had something in common, well, especially if they were heterosexual – a divine sense of their own importance. It amused her how much the world worshiped the male. When did it begin? Were mothers at fault for worshipping their sons over their daughters or were males born with a predilection for grabbing all the attention, adoration, and love in the world?

She didn't know. All she knew for sure was that she got a thrill just watching her lover breathe. She didn't give a damn whether he had broad shoulders and a tight butt. What mattered to her was a man's honesty, courage, and kindness. She loathed bullies and blowhards.

The soul was what mattered to her.

Oh yes indeed. She had an animal instinct about true malefactors. It had to do with smell. She could pick out a pestilent soul from a crowded, sweat-soaked, stinky men's locker room. She must have been a bloodhound in a former life, because she had an incredible sense of smell. The nastiest ones tended to use way too much soap and cologne. Yep, she could smell even the faintest odor of spiritual deformity. If she had to describe it, she would have to say that a deformed spirit smelled of urine, not the colorless kind of urine or a baby's wet nappy; no, this urine was usually thick and yellow and rank reminding her of an outhouse on a hot summer day.

Oh yeah, she had a nose for trouble. She giggled at the thought, nose for news, nose for trouble. How cliché. Ana would have a fit if she heard Eve repeating a bunch of clichés. Poor Ana, too cerebral to relax and have some fun. Like the fun Eve anticipated with this beautiful man with the kind soul. His lean muscular body smelled of lemon grass and sage. Here he was before her, sweaty with a good kind of musky smell, none of that dead vegetation turning to stinking goo for this guy; oh no, this guy smelled of newly mown grass, fresh turned earth, and hot sidewalks. What a weird combination. Yet oddly reassuring.

He smelled perfect. This man made sure to eat the right foods, just the perfect combination of fruits and vegetables with only a little white meat and a few carbohydrates. She could also tell that he avoided milk. What a relief. Milk breath made her gag. He must be in training. His body was firm yet there was nothing narcissistic about him, none of that tanning-booth crap and exfoliation for him. Men who pampered themselves like an insecure woman made her nauseous. She wanted to press against a man, a person confident in their hairiness, their all-over maleness.

Although, she did detect a whiff of stale beer a few days old. Um, well, that would eventually fade. She detected something else even sweeter beneath the surface. The smell intoxicated her, reminding her of a similar experience when she consumed chocolate cake. Her whole body would light up with pleasure, every cell moaning and wanting more. This man made her mouth water. He would not get away until she was fully satiated. That might take all night or perhaps more than one night.

Making a detour, Eve climbed off the bed and grabbed the other two small bottles of lotion. She poured some of the lotion into her palm and climbed back on the bed straddling Zak's buttocks. The muscles in Zak's back tensed. Eve moved slowly so as not to frighten the beautiful man. She finished off his back than moved down to his hips, massaging, and squeezing the tense muscles until she felt them begin to loosen up beneath her finger tips. Once the skin felt hot under her fingertips, she moved on to the buttocks, rubbing the heel of her palms over the softer skin and hard muscles. Um hum, so nice and smooth and firm, she thought. Her scalp began to tingle.

She forced her thoughts elsewhere concentrating her attention on the landscape painting above the bed. The scene reminded her of the time she and that boy kissed on the shores of the Columbia River. She remembered how shy she'd been back then just waiting for something wonderful to happen. He bent down and. She stopped herself in time. She turned away from the painting and stared at the lamp. The folds of the lamp shade reminded her of. She turned her attention to the telephone. That seemed to work.

When Zak felt her warm hands rubbing the lotion into his shoulder blades, then her firm but soft fingers moving slowly up and down his spine, he began to relax.

"Nice," he murmured. "Yeah, right there. That's great."

"You like that huh?" Eve said with that perpetually sensual smile in her voice. The bed bounced several times before Zak realized that Eve had turned herself around and was now facing his feet. He stopped thinking. Other parts of him perked up in anticipation of something marvelous to come. He felt her warm fingers begin to massage his buttocks and move down across his thighs all the way to the soles of his feet.

He woke to her voice urging him to turn over. Obedient to her every whim, he turned over. The massage only got as far as his abdominal oblique otherwise known as his love handles before the sensation of having a naked woman with healthy bouncing breasts massaging him made him crazy. With his right hand behind her neck he forced her head down and opened his mouth to taste her lips and tongue. The second time was intensely pleasurable and lasted nearly an hour, what with Eve's gentle instructions on what to do with his fingers and tongue to please her. He learned more about the relationship between a man and a woman in that hour than he had in his entire twenty-seven years. She was a good teacher, one of the best he thought, as he laid back exhausted with droplets of sweat sliding down his temple into his right ear. She lay beside him and they both stared up at the ceiling with twin expressions of contentment.

Zak woke when the bed moved, but kept his eyes closed pretending to sleep. He heard the faint sounds of Eve moving about the room then entering the bathroom. Now tense, the pleasure of an hour ago gone, he remembered she'd stolen his brother's truck. He also remembered the conversation with his brother on the cellphone as he searched Woolstone and Twin Falls for any sign of Leona. Luke told him the Owyhee County sheriff had called the Woolly Man to check if Luke's friend, Acacia Pierce had permission to drive his vehicle.

Acacia Pierce? That was a new one.

Luke claimed Mad Mona knew her real name and it was Jane Smith. The day couldn't get any more surreal, could it? What were the odds of two crazy women living a thousand miles apart convinced they were sworn enemies. How many fake names did Leona have? Who was she really? He was pretty sure her real name wasn't Jane Smith. And why in the hell did his brother need to talk to her anyway? She was a con artist who'd dreamed up a bunch of lies to impress his brother. She sold worthless snake oil. Her supernatural powers were embarrassingly mediocre. And her trances wouldn't fool a five-year-old. Although. The honest part of him conceded her portrayal of Multiple Personality Disorder deserved an Oscar.

Still there were benefits for being the first one on the scene. He'd convince himself he was protecting her from self-harm. He'd even convinced himself he was keeping an eye on her for his family's sake. Yeah. Right. He was keeping an eye on her, ALL OF HER, until reinforcements arrived.

Then what?

When Luke and Mad Mona do arrive, what if Eve panics and does that weird metamorphosis again? And if she just shifts gears and becomes someone else will she even remember their time together? The image of waking up in the morning and finding someone else in the bed beside him was bad, sure. The thought of Eve treating him like a stranger, even a monster was far worse. And what if Eve screams bloody murder, wakes up the neighbors, then tells the police he'd abducted and raped her? Shouldn't he be slipping on his clothes and sneaking out the door instead of waiting impatiently for her return?

Because the libido was more powerful than a speeding bullet, no better yet, more powerful than a rocket launching into space. Wow. Even his metaphors were full of sexual innuendo.

He remembered the way Leona had looked and behaved when meeting Mad Mona for the first time, the way she eyed her like she was something nasty that had stuck itself to the bottom of her shoe and wouldn't let go. The way she'd stood with her feet apart poised to rip the old lady a third eye.

Everything about her had changed. In a nanosecond, she looked and acted alien and worst of all felt alien, as if a strong El Nino had blown threw the open door burning their skin with its heat. The person they'd spent hours talking to and watching and thought they understood had disappeared. It had been some serious creepy shit. The eyes – one dreamily incurious as if she'd already met you in a past life and the other filled with hate eager to hurt you in this one. Even Acacia's walk had been foreign completely unlike Leona's stumbling, bumbling shuffle. It made you wonder who was the crazy one – her or you.

If Luke showed up, would Acacia Pierce take over and try to kill his brother? Could they keep her in this room without hurting her or getting themselves hurt? The weirdest part of the entire mess was that he preferred Eve over Leona and Acacia – yet – they were the same damned woman!

He so wanted Eve right now. Thinking about Eve made him horny. He waited impatiently for her to finish up in the bathroom and come back to bed.

Eve peed into the toilet as quietly as possible wincing at the tinkling sound which seemed to echo and get louder and louder with each stream of liquid. Perhaps she was inordinately worried about waking Zak but really, she wasn't to blame, these cheap bathrooms had paper thin walls. Why couldn't they be sound proof? And why couldn't she sleep? So maybe she didn't feel like sleeping, maybe she could wake him up with her tinkling and they could go for another round? What was so wrong with that idea? They were consenting adults after all.

At that precise moment, unfortunately, Acacia chose to butt in, her voice dripping with annoyance, "We don't have time for your bullshit Eve. Get yourself dressed and loose the ditzy hunk with his finger up his ass. We've got more important things to do than participate in your sex-feast."

"Leave her alone, Acacia. The girl knows what she's doing," Leona chimed in.

"Shut up, Leona. I know you've got the hots for him too. Do you want to find yourself back at Deliverance with those idiots prodding and poking you?" Acacia asked.

Leona retaliated, "Don't you dare compare the Woolly Man with Deliverance. You don't know anything. And quit calling Idahoans dumb-asses. You don't know what you're talking about."

"At least Eve is enjoying herself. I'm impressed with her skill and enthusiasm. I hated the job. Did you know I'd never had an orgasm with any of my johns? Never. Honest...to...God!" Frankie declared in amazement, self-aware for the first time in her life. "I just felt it would have been a betrayal to Denzel."

"Oh, you poor thing," Ana said. "Why would you continue to abuse your body and your soul in a profession you despise without the fringe benefits of orgasms? I'm at a loss to understand why women punish themselves. Might as well kill yourself, I say."

"Holy shit woman," Acacia said. "You can't be that stupid. Don't you know Frankie's playing with your head? Don't you watch movies?"

"I have better things to do than watch the boob-tube."

"That's right, go ahead be judgmental. At least Eve isn't judgmental. She loves everybody, even women. And yes, it is true, in all the time I was working the streets, I never got hot for any of my Johns. And here I am today really appreciating a true connoisseur of men. Johns were just work to me, a way to make a buck but Eve, she sees men as little morsels of chocolate. She's a hell of lot better at it than I ever was," Frankie said with a shallow laugh.

"Well they're not the same thing – I mean your former profession and Eve's lifestyle choices. That's the key word – choice. Eve chooses her men," Ana said. "She can say no anytime. When you were in the business you didn't have the luxury of turning them down."

"Ladies we're digressing," Tessa warned them. "Make up your minds. What shall we do? Let Eve stay with the young man or sneak out? Eve, just remember, we've got more important things to do. We must finish what we started. Remember?"

At the thought of what she needed to do next, a rush of fear followed swiftly by lightheadedness washed over her. She had to drop her head between her legs to stop herself from fainting and falling off the pot and maybe breaking her damned neck. She waited for the dread to subside. Once her head cleared, she realized that there would be plenty of time for fun later. If she didn't do something by morning, everyone would be disappointed in her and she would hate herself forever.

"You're right Tessa as usual. I've had my fun. But now, it's time to move on," Eve stated with determination, even though part of her regretted her altruism and wanted desperately to go back into that room and ravish that beautiful man again. Afraid to flush the toilet, Eve wiped herself, rose to her full height, and reluctantly left the seat up. She couldn't afford to make a sound, not even a peep. She pressed her hands to her mouth holding back a desire to break out in hysterical laughter. What a sight she must be right now. A mouse couldn't get out of this tin can without being noticed. She would try anyway.

Pleased with herself, she began to slip on her bra and underwear. By way of an apology Frankie joked, "Forget Denzel. Frank F. Smith is my true love. He just doesn't know it yet."

Zak had fallen into a partial doze but woke when he heard voices. At first, he thought they were coming from next door. Then he realized with a chill the voices were much closer, in fact coming from the bathroom. He had to sit up and strain his ears to be sure. He tiptoed over to the bathroom door and held his breath listening in disbelief. Yes, it sounded as if a crowd of women were in the bathroom arguing with each other.

Each voice had its own distinctive intonation, inflection, dialect, brogue, burr, and grammatical habits, all the parts of speech that made it possible for people to pick out unique signifiers and distinguish friend from foe. Oh yeah, that linguist class had been a bitch, but at least he'd remembered something from it. He heard someone from the southern states, someone who sounded like a cowboy, oops cowgirl, a tight-ass who could have been his least favorite professor in college, and of all things a senior citizen. Why was she pretending to be all these people? Or was there something else going on?

All those women couldn't possibly, not in a hot-hades minute, fit into that tiny bathroom. He had only seen one person go in. Eve. Only Eve went in. Yes, admittedly she was the same woman who introduced herself as Navan Leona Keys. And according to his brother she had a driver's license which identified her as Acacia T. Pierce. What the freaking hell was going on? His first response had been to freeze like a puddle of urine in the Arctic. Then his brain warmed up and he thought his safest move would be to dress and take off in his car before she came out of the bathroom.

A few seconds ticked by giving the executive part of his brain time to take control. The hairs on his scalp relaxed, the sweat on his body evaporated, and his heart stopped pumping madly. It would have been prudent to leave right there and then. He didn't. His treacherous memory recalled the last three hours and several unforgettable moments. The suicidal part of him asked: why not risk the possibility of death if the outcome meant experiencing once again the best sex of his life?

So instead of fleeing or fighting, he just stood by the bathroom door and listened and waited for some sign that the conference was over. He rationalized his decision to stay in the motel room with the thought that Luke would be pissed if he let her get away. But Luke wasn't present or creeped out by what Zak was hearing. Maybe because of the stakes involved, Luke wouldn't care if she had three heads and a long tail? Logic suggested if only one woman had entered the bathroom and he heard five or six different voices, something wasn't right. Occam's Razor then – the simplest explanation was the most likely to be true.

Either Zak was dreaming or Eve was listening to the radio, or she was on her cellphone having decided in the middle of the night to take a conference call. Anybody with a good pair of ears knows the difference between a radio talk show, a cellphone conversation and a group of women in a heated debate. The voices were coming from the bathroom not a radio or a cellphone.

Did he care? He thought about that for a minute. Did he really care that she was bat-shit-crazy? Well…

Three people might be able to stand in the bathroom, if they didn't move around much, but would six or seven be able to stand in there comfortably? And where had they come from? How had they slipped into the hotel room unnoticed? He'd woken as soon as Eve slipped out of bed. There was no backdoor to this room. There was no window in the bathroom. The fact was that the woman he'd just had incredible sex with suffered from some sort of psychosis, most likely Multiple Personality Disorder.

Did he believe in that psychobabble shit? Not really. Yet, as Leona she'd mentioned a doctor. She called him Dr. B. He threw up his arms. Maybe only a crazy woman would be so eager to do the things they had done? Would the average female perform some of the acrobatic feats they had performed tonight? With a stranger? Or maybe, the two of them just fit, the way two puzzle pieces were meant to fit. Maybe he'd finally found his perfect mate?

The sound of his hands smacking against his bare thighs alerted the person inside to his location near the door. No sense in jumping back now. The door opened a crack and an eye much reddened by crying looked out at him. Did she think he was a stalker, so consumed by her beauty, he couldn't wait for her to get out of the bathroom? What had made her cry? His performance? Then he remembered the conversation between the women. He realized with dawning joy that part of her struggled with ambivalent feelings too. She must like him. He would find a way to reassure her, convince her he was one of the good guys.

"Are you okay? You need anything?" he asked in what he hoped was his most agreeable voice. "Come on back to bed, Eve." He wandered over to the nightstand and picked up his watch. It was ten o'clock in the evening. Plenty of time. He returned to the bathroom door. He saw her standing in her bra and underwear inside the room. Her abundant breasts flowed over the top of the lacy bra. The bra had been made for someone smaller. Her small waist and hips made her breasts appear huge. He liked her legs. They were slim and firm. Just perfect. He remembered how those legs had wrapped around his back and held on tight.

He shut off the rational part of his brain and ignored everything but his desire to get her back into bed. She watched him with her head tilted to one side and her big green eyes reflecting delight and desire for him. Most women pretended not to care or pretended they weren't interested. Not her. Her face reflected every thought and emotion. She had honest eyes.

He knew people. He'd been figuring out people for twenty-seven years. At this moment, he was convinced she was someone he could trust. It was madness he knew. Madness to trust someone so completely, someone he'd just met. Yet even though he had the suspicion she might be certifiably psychotic, deep down inside he knew she wouldn't hurt him. She was incapable of hurting a living soul.

His body responded to the sight of her in a particular fashion. The sight made her smile.

"Have you ever played the Love Boat Game?" she asked sweetly.

He laughed, "Say again?"

She stepped out of the bathroom and pushed him toward the bed, her palm flat on his chest. Her hand felt warm and soft and sent fire through him. He reached for her and tried to throw her on the bed, she pulled away with a soft laugh and said, "Now hold on. You're not the winner yet."

"Winner of what?"

"By the way, when the game's over, the winner gets to choose the position and the event," she said unable to hold back a squeal of delight that sent Zak's heart racing.

He watched in perplexity as she wandered around the room. The bathroom incident still nagged at him and he knew he had to ask her about it. "You got one of those little radios on you?"

Eve paused in her search and glanced over her shoulder. "Why?"

"Well, I thought I heard voices in the bathroom. I figured you were listening to the radio, maybe NPR or some female talk show," he said wondering if he were just trying to convince himself.

"No. I didn't bring a radio with me. All my stuff is back at your place. Your brother has probably gone through my stuff. He won't find much, just the keys to the rental and," she paused and bent down to retrieve something off the floor. She examined his boot curiously and wheeled around still dangling the boot in front of her. "Aren't these hot and uncomfortable? I mean they're biker boots. You don't look like a biker."

"Forget about my boots honey," he said trying with difficulty to contain his impatience. "What's really going on here?"

"Call me Eve. Calling me honey or sweet cheeks sounds so sexist and impersonal. And I know you're not a sexist pig. You're just too eager to learn how to please a woman to be a sexist. Most of those guys don't think about us as human beings. We're just objects to them. All they're interested in is their own pleasure. But you, oh boy, you are so fine, so very, very fine. I haven't had so much fun since, oh I don't know."

"I thought your name was Leona?"

"No, you've got me confused with one of your other girlfriends. My name is Eve. I'd appreciate it if you called me Eve instead of honey," she said with an inflection of annoyance in her sultry voice.

The weirdness seeped back into the room. All of a sudden, he wasn't interested in sex games. "Please answer my question Eve," he said stressing the name. "I asked you about the voices."

Eve dropped his boot and started wandering around the room again with her head down and her backside his only view. The sight of her nakedness, those long gorgeous legs, those firm rounded buttocks, and the beautiful back that narrowed to that small waist, all that and more just wandering about the hotel room bending here, straightening there, and the stretching, oh man, the stretching to see if there was anything on the closet shelf made him confused and crazy and he had an urge to jump up and throw her on the bed even if she was shy a couple of spark plugs.

Her searching ended when she pounced on his shirt lying on the floor. She used his shirt to cover her nakedness. Instead of putting the shirt on like any other woman would do, she tied the shirt sleeves around her waist leaving her breasts exposed. He found himself sitting on the edge of the hotel bed wondering what she would do next. He'd never played a sex game before.

Zak's experience with sex began when he encountered an attractive female, took her to bed, performed the requisite foreplay which resulted in copulation and for him orgasm and hopefully for her multiple orgasms. Most of the time, he simply fell asleep for an hour or two then found some lame excuse to leave. But after considering the last few hours, he realized that sex could be relaxing and playful and downright fun. The massage had been fantastic. He couldn't wait to find out what she planned to do next.

"Ok. Here we go," Eve said with a sly grin, "First you have to name the part of the body I'm concealing then what you think I have hidden under the shirt."

"That's easy honey, sorry, I mean Eve, your love tunnel, of course. Come here."

"No. It's not what you think. I picked up something while you weren't looking and I'm holding it in the folds of, well. Oh, and I forgot you need to use the medical term for the part of my body. Now I'll give you three clues and you figure out what I'm holding. Okay?"

"I was watching you the entire time," he said with a laugh. "You didn't pick up anything but the boot. And you can't possible hold onto my boot with your vagina."

A secretive smile played across her lips then vanished, "Are you sure you were watching my hands? I've got a feeling you were watching something else."

Zak shoved aside the disturbing moment in the bathroom and gave into his baser instincts. Why not? Instead of spending the remaining hours just staring at each other, they could be doing something far more pleasant. Why waste this precious time probing her about her mental state. Why would he want to subject himself to arguing or crying? He hated when women cried. Convinced he was doing the right thing, Zak moved down toward the foot of the bed in order to be closer to her and sat crossed-legged watching the rise and fall of her breasts with real pleasure.

Skin. He loved her skin, the way her arms and legs were slightly darker than the belly and breasts, the few freckles that seemed more like beauty marks than ordinary freckles between her breasts and along her right hip. But if he was going to get her into this bed, he'd better concentrate on what she might have picked up in the room. It had to be small enough to pick up without him noticing.

"Clues," he demanded with a lift of his brow. "You said something about clues."

Eve blushed and looked away. But not for long. He was so handsome. His blue eyes beneath those black sweeping brows and those long lashes just made her shiver with anticipation. This was the best yet. The others were nothing. This man was her Mr. Right. Yet her heart dropped at the idea of having to be true to one man only, one man for the rest of her life, one body she would eventually know better than her own.

"Eve. Having trouble thinking of a clue? Let's forget the game. Come here," Zak said in his most seductive voice. His baritone rang true and real and sent vibrations down her ear, through her chest, into her stomach, and straight to her pelvis making her all warm and wet. He had it all: the body, the face, the voice, even the eagerness to learn. She shook herself and got back into the game.

"OK, the first clue is this: This object if used improperly can cause serious damage to other vehicles."

Zak jumped up, "Easy. You've got my keys. OK so I win, and I get to choose the position and the event. Now by event. I'm assuming you mean—"

Eve interrupted him, "Hold on Speedy. You've got it wrong. I don't have your car keys."

Zak stood before her with his arms resting on his hips completely naked and delectable and Eve had to force herself to keep her eyes glued to the telephone on the nightstand. She used her left arm to push him toward the bed. "I'll give you the second clue."

"Come on. What else causes serious damage to other vehicles?" Zak demanded.

"Do you want to hear the second clue?" Eve asked.

Zak threw up his hands, "Sure. If it gets this game over with and you and me on here," he said padding the bed invitingly. "I'm all ears."

Eve wanted to blurt out, "What a coincidence!" But she forced herself not to reveal the object too soon. She had a bad habit of finding coincidences enchanting.

To her they were confirmation of a higher power acting on her behalf. Acacia, an atheist and Ana, an existentialist had no patience for spiritual matters or references to a higher power. Eve disliked conflict. She believed in the hidden energy all around her, the energy of pleasure, kindness, and love. If only the energy of the world sent out kindness and love to all the people on the planet. If only people would stop fighting and killing each other. Someday. Maybe someday. She wasn't sure if the man with her now was confirmation of a higher power acting on her behalf or a sign of trouble to come.

Her nose was itching. An itchy nose meant trouble.

While wandering around the room pretending to look for the object she'd chosen, she thought about the second clue and knew the game wasn't a game anymore. So, she would now have to rethink her present situation. Her throat tightened threating to ruin everything. No crying now. It was with real regret she turned and looked at the beautiful man sitting on the bed. When he noticed her looking at him, she looked away afraid he could read her thoughts.

Zak got a kick out of watching her lift her chin and stare at the ceiling with that frown of concentration on her face. She was adorable. From his brain, a rational thought intruded. What was happening to him? Was she playing some sort of mind game? His behavior so far was embarrassing. What had happened to his indifference? His usual routine was getting the woman to bed, taking her to a cheap diner for supper and/or breakfast, drop her off at home and promise to call her. This situation he was in now was unique because he had to keep an eye on Eve for Luke. Or was he fooling himself and he just wanted more time alone with her?

Eve noticed Zak fidgeting and desperately tried to think of another clue. "OK," she said. "Sorry. The clue I had earlier just seemed too easy, but now I think I've got it. Wait, here it comes. Yeah, this one should do. OK. The object I hold in my hand used to be much larger."

"What!" Zak remonstrated. "Come on Eve. How does that help me?"

"You're right, you're right. I'll give you the third clue. The object I hold in my hand has been around only in the last twenty years."

"Are you kidding? That's not enough information to make an informed decision?" Zak protested. An urgent need to pee gave him the excuse to leave the room. He shut the bathroom door unnecessarily hard. Her attempts to seem clever were annoying him. He had too many unpleasant memories of secretive women, especially the secretive ones in his family.

From the other side of the door he heard her say, "I guess my clues are too ambiguous. I'll give you another. How's that?"

He threw up the toilet seat and peed. There was silence on the other side of the door. He flushed the toilet, washed his hands, and exited the bathroom. She stood in the same spot in front of the dresser blocking the television screen still staring at the carpet. Her look of apology made him feel like a jerk. She was still sweet, well, and crazy, no doubt of that. Grudgingly he said, "I'd appreciate a little more information that's all."

Eve smiled, and her smile made him feel good. Weird this need between them to make each other happy. How long would that last? Until the fifth or sixth orgasm?

"OK. I thought of something that would really help. Here goes. It is possible that the television show Star Trek was the inspiration for this device. Everyone on Star Trek had one," she announced, jumping up and down in her delight at thinking of a better clue. He had to laugh.

He threw himself on the bed and lay back with his arms crossed behind his head, "Star Trek huh? Hum. Let me think." He watched her sway back and forth with a big smile on her face hoping he would figure out the object she held beneath the shirt.

Just before he gave his answer, he noticed Eve jumping up and down and laughing with triumph as if she knew that he knew, as if she'd read his mind a split second before he knew the answer. Could she have read his body language when he finally figured out the clue? He would rather believe she had psychic abilities than she had a gift for reading people. Why did it feel so good to think of her as psychic? He let her wait another minute realizing with a shock how much he didn't want his brother Luke to get his hands on her.

"I know," he said pretending to just think of it and straightened. "You've got my cellphone. Am I right?"

For a split second she looked sad. It was gone so quick he thought maybe he'd imagined her disappointment.

He swung his legs off the bed and said, "Now what?"

"Now you have to find an object and give me three clues. You see for there to be perfection, no, not just perfection but nirvana, yes that's the word, nirvana between the two of us, we both have to be winners to go to the next level," she explained with an unexpectedly serious expression on her face. The seriousness dissolved into anticipation as she handed him his cellphone and jumped onto the bed.

He looked at his cellphone dubiously wondering if she'd really held it between her legs. Impossible! She threw back her head and laughed. "You are a virgin. Don't you know any magic tricks?"

Zak waited for Eve to scramble into a sitting position with her legs crossed and his eye full of her love triangle. Desperately he searched for something else to look at in the room. The only way to avoid looking at her and the entrance to her secrets was to wander about the room and search for a likely object to use in the game. He would have to be as tricky as her.

How had she managed to lift his cellphone from out of the pocket of his jeans without him noticing? His eye had been on her the entire time. He would have to be as clever as her. When he glanced at the bed, he noticed that the skin on either side of her impressive nose was bright red. She turned away from him and stared at the telephone as if she were urging the thing to ring.

He went back to his search. Since her eyes were occupied elsewhere, he took the opportunity to retrieve the motel matchbook from the small table in the corner of the room near the window. He looked over his shoulder to see if she'd noticed. At that precise moment, something alien crossed her face, an expression that didn't belong to

Eve. It was fleeting, so fleeting he began to wonder if he'd misread the look. So far, Eve had never expressed despair or sorrow. It made her look even younger, if that was possible, like a child lost in a department store convinced that no one would come to rescue her.

But he must have misread her. While he surveyed her face, she began to smile, the smile he associated with her, anticipatory and seductive, as if she were imagining the two of them romping in bed. Zak made a big production out of his search and then grabbed her silk skirt off the floor and made his way toward the foot of the bed. Eve looked into his eyes. Her eyes glittered. She waited patiently for him to begin.

He turned his back on her for a moment and wadded the skirt up a bit to give the impression that the object was much bigger than it really was. He turned around and smiled down at her.

"Are you ready for the first clue?" he asked in mock seriousness.

She wiggled a bit on the bed and giggled, "Yes."

"Here goes. The first clue is: this object sleeps in a bed with nineteen other brothers and sisters."

Eve sat back. He watched her as she thought about his clue. She appeared to be deep in thought. But less than thirty seconds passed before she opened her mouth; and when she opened her mouth to speak, just before she voiced her thoughts, he knew she knew exactly what he was hiding in the folds of the skirt. She gave no sign, no sign at all, not even with a knowing look in her eye, or facial grimace or even a telltale body twitch that she'd figured out the clue so fast; yet, he knew the precise moment when she knew. Cold liquid slid through his intestines. The cold sensation gradually dissipated. It was uncanny. It was disturbing. It wasn't fair.

Absently, he heard her shout, "A matchbook."

He must have looked the way he felt because she jumped off the bed and ran into his arms. She squeezed him tight, so tight he grunted and when she stared up into his eyes, her expression was suddenly serious. "We're both winners and since you're new at this game you get to choose the position and the event," she said hurriedly searching his face with hope in her eyes.

By now he should be used to the uncanny, the weird, the unexplainable. Why should such things ruin his fun? He squeezed her waist and leaned down to whisper in her ear, "Vertical. In the tub. And the event will be Jacque Cousteau searching for the beautiful mermaid princess of Atlantis."

While holding her in his arms, he wasn't sure where he began, and she started. His goose bumps had become hers. When she shivered, he lifted her up into his arms and made a big production out of carrying her into the bathroom. Her deep throaty laughter filled with anticipatory excitement made him lose his balance and he nearly toppled them both onto the bathroom floor. His cellphone began to ring just as Eve's foot touched the bottom of the tub. Eve looked up at him in alarm and he smiled reassuringly, "Bad timing on someone's part. Now, where were we?"

15

Zak woke to the sound of pounding on his motel door. When he tried to get up he nearly tore his arms out of their sockets. He gazed up at his wrists tied to the bedpost. Zak recognized his brother's voice bellowing his name from the other side of the door. The pounding and shouting stopped. Zak waited about ten minutes before he heard a key turn in the lock. He forced himself to watch as the door opened, and the motel clerk entered the room followed closely by his brother. Behind Luke, Zak saw Mrs. Lawson entering the room.

He shut his eyes and groaned. Too much. Just too frigging much. "Get her out of here," he shouted. He waited patiently (what else could he do but wait?) until Luke persuaded Mad Mona to go back to the car and wait for him.

Five minutes later with the clerk's wicked laughter still ringing in his ears and Luke outside dropping money into the clerk's open palm, Zak saw Mad Mona backing out of the parking lot and heading east down the road. She was driving Leona's Ford Taurus. Who had given her the keys? As he hid behind the small table by the window peeking through the crack in the curtains, Zak covered his nakedness, pulling on his jeans first then his cotton t-shirt. He was sitting at the foot of the bed pulling on his socks when he saw Mad Mona drive away. Before Luke had a chance to enter the room, Zak asked him, "Why is Mona driving Leona's car?"

Luke stepped into the room and sniffed the air then glanced at his brother with an angry glint in his eye. He dropped into a nearby chair with a stony expression, "All this time you been fornicating with some female in this shit hole of a town? I thought you were going to get my vehicle back. We might have never crossed paths again what with you joy riding down to Nevada."

"How'd you find me?" Zak asked curiously.

"I got your message, stupid. Don't you remember? Or were you too drunk to remember texting me. See you in Paris. Funny. What is this all about anyway?"

"I sent you a text message?"

Luke rolled his eyes and shook his head, "It was a damned good thing Lawson was with me. She spotted your Camaro straight away.

What the hell have you been doing? Screwing some old girlfriend instead of tracking down the thief that stole my truck? All I asked you to do was go to the ION truck stop, find out what direction Leona was headed, follow her, then call me. Instead you lost her and found one of your cheapy girlfriends and didn't even bother to text me until four in the morning. Why bother to text me that you were at this dump, if Leona was already long gone? Don't you give a damned about our family? Well say something."

Zak thought about telling him the truth and decided against exposing himself even more to his brother's ridicule. He was pretty sure he hadn't text Luke, so that left only Eve. Before Eve left, she text his brother mentioning the Paris, Nevada motel. It was the perfect joke on him. Tie him to the bed naked and let his family find him. The conflicting emotions running through his head made him crazy. "Something like that," Zak muttered as he grabbed a towel and headed to the bathroom. "And stop your bitching. I found your damn tin can. It's across the road. I planned on filling the tank with gas today."

Luke leaned forward resting his elbows on his knees, "That's a relief. She ran out of gas again huh?"

"Yes, looks that way. I found the truck and she was long gone," he said looking anywhere but at his brother in case Luke could tell he was lying. "She must have got a ride from someone. No telling where she is now," he finished as he slipped inside the bathroom, shut the door, and sat on the toilet seat to collect his thoughts. He remembered the weird scene yesterday afternoon – Leona in the bathroom and all those strange voices talking to each other, damned if he understood how she had done it.

Had she been having a conference call with a bunch of women? No. It hadn't sounded the way a conference call would sound with interference from multiple cellphones, feedback, and people talking over each other. Instead the voices sounded as if they were coming from inside the bathroom.

Was she in some sort of gang? Or had she slipped a hallucinogenic into his beer? He pulled out his cellphone from the pocket of his jeans and looked at his latest texts. The one from his brother was interesting. He jumped up and opened the bathroom door and stuck his head out to call to his brother. Luke was standing at the dresser counting change in his pocket, "What?" he asked impatiently. "I was going to get myself a coke from the machine."

"Is Mad Mona coming back?" Zak asked.

"You got balls little brother. If some old lady had seen me lying butt naked tied to a bed with smelly old rags, I'd hope never to see her again."

"Come on. Is she coming back or not? If not, we need to meet her somewhere pronto. I got some questions for her."

"About what?"

"Why is Mona so damned concerned about Leona? Huh? And why would Leona's doctor recommend his patient stay with another patient with the same mental illness? It makes no sense. It makes more sense that he'd recommend a halfway house, or she stop in and see a social worker."

Luke walked toward him with his thinking face on. When Luke got that look Zak knew he had his brother's full attention and he was probably already two steps ahead of him. Luke studied his face intensely which made Zak nervous. He wasn't so good at thinking out loud.

"Yeah, well. I think ah, Leona, or Jane Smith, whatever the hell her real name is might not be so crazy. Maybe someone else is orchestrating this whole grotesque show?" he finished lamely.

"You think huh?" Luke asked.

"Shut your face Luke. I don't need your bullshit today," Zak started out, tired of Luke's superior attitude. He continued, "I've been thinking about what happened at The Woolly Man yesterday. Navan Keys walks in and she starts babbling about private stuff. She convinces us she's some sort of clairvoyant and you run for the Navaho blanket thinking she's going to help us find Amara. Either she played us or someone else is playing us and she's just a pawn. Well, I think Mad Mona might know something, maybe a lot. The old biddy practically lives at the Woolly Man. I bet she's been spying and listening in on our family secrets for years. I bet she set Leona up to con us, told Leona all sorts of garbage about Nate and me and our family history."

Luke pulled his cellphone out of his pocket and started dialing a number, "That doesn't explain what happened on the butte. That woman nearly killed me. She wasn't anything like Navan Keys. She was one mean, nasty viper." When he heard someone pick up on the other end, Luke spoke into the phone, "Hi Mrs. Lawson. I didn't have time to thank you for giving me a lift here. Where are you right now? Yeah. That's perfect. Can you stick around a little longer? Please. We'd like to treat you to breakfast. OK? See you in twenty." Luke closed his cellphone and dropped it into his pocket. He and Zak exchanged looks.

Just as Luke opened his mouth to make the statement they both knew he would make, Zak quickly closed the bathroom door, "I'll shower and be ready in ten," he said in a rush, avoiding recriminations. Luke must have just figured out the woman he'd slept with and the woman who had tied him to the bed was the same woman they were pursuing. Zak suspected Luke had another reason for wanting to find this woman, not just that she might know something about Professor Wade.

As the hot water poured down his back, Zak remembered the night Luke came home and found him holding the Navaho blanket. He had demanded to know where Zak had gotten it. Later Zak wondered about their conversation. Luke had a talent for keeping secrets, but Zak had known him long enough to sense when he was holding something back. Now Zak could connect Luke's interest in the Navaho blanket with his obsessive quest for Amara. Of course, there was a connection. He wasn't interested in finding Wade. Luke was more interested in finding Amara and proving the family legend. Maybe he even believed all the crap about prosperity and immortality for the Nerin descendants.

He looked at himself in the mirror. He needed a shave. He shrugged at his image and then threw up his hands and said, "Good luck shaving without a razor, buddy." At least there was a tiny bottle of shampoo and conditioner in the shower.

On the other side of the bathroom door his brother asked, "What'd you say?"

Leaning against the door and still looking at himself in the mirror, the bathroom was that big, he said, "I don't have a razor but at least there's shampoo, the super great kind, you know, motel shampoo. Whoop-tea-do-da-day."

There was no response from the other side of the door. Zak dumped his clothes on the floor and stepped inside the shower, closing the door behind him, annoyed about his lack of toiletries and doubly annoyed with his brother. Why had Luke bothered to ask a question, if he planned to ignore the answer? But that was the way the Nerin family worked – they weren't really interested in other people. They were primarily focused on their own immediate problems.

It was no surprise when he asked his mother why nobody had bothered to do any real, authentic historical research on their family's immigration to America and she said they didn't need to because they had the word of Hera Katsaros and her story of the legend. Perhaps the family feared what they might find if they really did research the origin story of their direct descendent?

When he pressed her, Jule Nerin shrugged and looked at him blankly as if she couldn't care less. He had his answer.

Several years ago, after having spent the entire summer researching the Nerin family history in New York, Zak had a new appreciation for record keeping, libraries, and archivists. The persistence of the family legend in a time of 21st century science and technology seemed insane and counterproductive.

During his research at the New York Public Library, he found a folder of old clippings from the Lower East Side's Greek community newsletter. In the folder was a pamphlet he later discovered had been created by his ancestor Hera Katsaros which she distributed on the streets of New York and in her neighborhood. The pamphlet had no date. Yet, he could imagine the Greek community's uneasiness, perhaps even revulsion, toward the writer of the pamphlet.

No one liked a braggart, especially someone with the nerve to claim she was a descendant of a demi-god. Would a guy claiming to be the grandson of Hercules be believed? No. He would have been run out of town.

When Zak first arrived in the archival room, he'd glanced at the table set up for him with real pleasure. Here was history, his family history. He felt awed by the documents on the table. The first thing he saw was a legal sized paper yellowed from age. There was a postcard stabled to the pamphlet. At first, he thought the library had defaced the document and felt a rush of anger. But on closer examination, he realized the postcard was as aged with time as the pamphlet. There was no name on the postcard, so he assumed it had been stabled to the pamphlet by a family member or maybe a historian from the same time period as Hera.

For the moment, he ignored the postcard. A rush of excitement surged through him at the thought he held something in his gloved hands that had been created by his ancestor. He hadn't even read the pamphlet, yet he was already proud of her. Weird. It was written in English which was amazing since the date 1851 indicated she had only been in the country for a few years. It began:

Dear Neighbors,

I am new to America and English. Forgive me my mistakes. My friend and neighbor Christophoros writes down my words. Some of you call me witch. I am not a witch. I cannot enter your church for good reasons. It would be blasphemy. I would be punished. I wish to explain why. I wish to tell you about my family and to warn you if you continue to turn your back on the ancient ones all Greek people are in danger. Yes. You are in danger. We are all in danger. Zeus is not happy with the Greek people. If we continue to ignore him, he will bring such wrath and fury upon us we may all perish. Let me tell you my family story and how I know this to be true.

What followed was the bedtime story he had heard every night for years – word for word. He had to conclude that some of the family must have kept copies of Hera's pamphlet. Unfortunately, his side of the family, the restless wanderers, had long since lost their original copy. The signature at the bottom transfixed him. If he could not find a picture of her, at least he had her signature. He flipped the postcard up away from the pamphlet and took out his cellphone. He wanted to record his 4th great grandmother's words and signature. After taking the photo, he debated whether to send a copy to his mother. He decided to wait until he got home.

Maybe someday he would take the photocopy, have the reproduction enlarged, framed, and hung up in his trailer. When he was satisfied with the pictures he took of the pamphlet and the other historical items on the table spread out before him, he returned the postcard to its original position and took a picture of it as well. Obviously, the writer had not been a member of the family but perhaps some historian, probably a student of Freud's psychoanalysis. Zak could barely read the scribbled note on the postcard – something about the "cure for lunacy continues" and "her neighbors call her poutána of the harpies" with a euphemism "French disease" printed in the right-hand corner.

Zak thought about that euphemism and the question mark long after. He felt sick inside – yes, he'd read somewhere how asylums practically emptied overnight when penicillin cured many ills of the Bedlamites. But penicillin as a cure for syphilis didn't happen until the late 1930s, too late for many unfortunate sufferers. Hera Katsaros had been born in 1833. Yet, he doubted the accuracy of the postcard writer's diagnosis since sufferers of the "French disease" were mostly male, often heavy drinkers and died young.

In the 1850s, a woman without family or wealth had few choices; she either worked in a sweatshop or on the streets as a lady of the night. Hera had no family in New York. Unfortunately, her eccentricities further isolated her from the Greek community. She refused to step inside a Greek Orthodox church claiming she would be punished. And when she met people in the neighborhood, she encouraged Greeks to come with her to the sea and pray to Zeus and Poseidon as a charm against storms and other natural disasters.

Her insistence there must be an animal sacrifice branded her as a crackpot. She had everything going against her – her beauty brought jealousy, her profession brought condemnation, and her delusional talk of demi-gods and harpies brought derision.

The postcard writer had been wrong. If Hera Katsaros had had advanced syphilis she would have died very soon after exhibiting symptoms. But she did not die young. She lived a long and interesting life. After delving into the library's collection more thoroughly, he uncovered a rather romantic ending to poor Hera's sad story. It began badly though when she was sent to the notorious Blackwell Island's Asylum. One of her neighbors must have contacted the authorities (probably a jealous wife) and shown them Hera's pamphlets claiming to be the descendant of a demi-god and a harpy. Initially, the authorities arrested her for prostitution and then after her "story" sent her to Blackwell's Island Asylum.

With the help of a friendly archivist at the library, he uncovered the horrifying facts about Blackwell Island's Asylum. Hera Katsaros had been admitted in 1851 at the age of eighteen. The police and the asylum staff misspelled her name so many times, it took the archivist weeks to find her in any of the records. After a year at Blackwell's Island, an alienist studying the moral treatments used to cure the insane rescued her from her life of hell. He may have been from a middle-class family of doctors, but he had many wealthy and prominent friends. He undertook her cure, pronounced her sane, then claiming her as his ward, released her from Blackwell.

Until his death, he supported Hera and provided her with the finest of accommodations. It was only after his death that his legal wife discovered her husband's three children by Hera Katsaros. He left Hera and her children nothing in his will. Yet Zak's ancestress had been resilient and found a new benefactor and had a child with him; and after her second "husband" died finally met the man of her dreams, a wealthy

Greek industrialist who eventually married her. She had three children with him. All her children were indoctrinated into the pamphlet's mythos, and per her strict instructions, the legend was passed down to each succeeding generation.

If she'd been born a hundred years later, doctors would have put her in an insulin coma, or given her electroshock, or perhaps performed a lobotomy on her. Another cure had been the drug Thorazine which would have calmed her down but maimed her children for life. The medical professionals of Hera's time believed in a combination of cures such as isolation, hard labor, and/or punishment. The punishments raised the hairs on Zak's arms. Could people have been so criminally stupid back then? Of course, they could. As even today, there are criminally stupid people who believe the poor are morally defective and deserve their punishment, maybe not with ice baths, hard labor, beatings, and meager food but in subtler ways.

Even though Hera's incarceration had been forgotten, the emotional terror of being found out by authorities had endured for her offspring. No wonder the family legend became the family secret. No one wanted to endure Hera's fate. He now understood why his mother had been so furious with him when he bragged about the family legend to outsiders.

It was Zak's opinion Hera Katsaros had been a perfectly sane young woman, just an unfortunate product of her crazy family's belief system. When every other Greek had moved on from worshipping the Hellenic religion to accepting the new Christian religion, Hera's family clung to the old ways but with a twist. It was the twist in the Hellenic tradition that probably pissed Greeks off the most. Hera had made three big mistakes: attempting the fruitless conversion of immigrants desperate to assimilate into American society, ignoring the ancient traditions of the Twelve Gods of Olympus, and above all claiming to be the descendant of a demi-god.

He blamed Hera's ancestors for her eccentricities. In fact, he felt sorry for poor Hera. She had been duped. Like her, he had been raised on the legend of Amara and duped into believing all the bullshit until his awakening. And now as an adult, he had finally set aside his family's indoctrination. What if public records in Greece couldn't discover any documents about Hera or her grandmother Adoni? What if there weren't any records of a family called Katsaros living in Crete or a woman called Adoni fighting for Greek Independence? And even though ship manifests in 1849 showed no record of Hera (Katsaros) landing in New York, she had to have come from somewhere.

Hera had been a flesh-and-blood creature. She'd existed. There was a record of her. She'd existed in 1849 and in 1851. She'd been eighteen when they trotted her off to Blackwell Island's Asylum. And there was a death certificate for her on microfilm with the name Hera Katsaros Papapole. It should have been Papadopoulos, but what the hell. Clerks were notorious for misspelling or deliberately anglicizing immigrant names especially the census takers. He found all sorts of variations on Katsaros from census records. Even now, clerks are probably unwittingly or deliberately burying family histories as they speed through their daily tasks oblivious to their part in the interment of another's ancestry.

She died in 1917. His cousin said, "We didn't bother to fix the death certificate since she introduced herself as Katsaros to everyone anyway." She died in 1917. If she'd really had the powers of a demi-god, she would have vanquished all her enemies and lived for eternity. But she died, she died in 1917, died like any other mortal.

There was no legend, no fantastical Amara, a beautiful woman with wings and claws, flying through the sky like an avenging angel, impossibly dressed all in white, swooping down on her prey and scooping them up in her claws. No such thing could happen now, not in these crowded skies, not with so many airplanes, helicopters, and drones shoving aside birds and bats and other small winged creatures. And the idea a human female with huge white wings would be flying around New York without being noticed boggled the mind.

Before he left for home that summer, his cousins invited him to see her grave. They told him that every year the family set a wreath on her grave, a wreath decorated with oak leaves and white feathers. The feathers symbolized the feathers of a dove. He sincerely hoped they were just symbols, not the real feathers of a dead dove. As he and his cousins stood before Hera Katsaros' grave, several of them insisted he leave an offering to her. He had nothing to give, so they handed him sweet bread freshly baked, a dozen in a woven basket. It had been the most uncomfortable hour of his life. He didn't want to appear rude, so he played along and sat on the blanket provided for him, ate the bread and cheese, drank the wine, and listened to the same story he had heard a hundred times before – the legend of Amara.

His cousins' playfulness at the cemetery made him even more resistant to the myth. It had become a stupid family tradition just like any other man-made celebration in modern society – an excuse to eat like a pig, drink like a fish and spend money like a greedy capitalist. As his cousins got up from the ground and began to fold their blankets and collect their empty wine bottles, he tried to pick up the offering of bread with the intention of throwing the pastries into the nearest garbage bin. His cousins were outraged.

"Don't!

"Don't do that!"

"Are you tempting the fates?"

"Leave it be, Zak. It's alright. The caretakers don't mind."

"Don't worry about it. You'll see. Someday you'll understand."

One of the cousins took his hand and insisted he leave the food on the grave inside the wreath with the other offerings. He pretended to go along with them. Outside the cemetery they were supposed to part company. His cousin, the tallest and Greekest looking of them all with his thick black curls and large brown eyes walked with him back to his motel room.

By the time he got rid of his cousin and returned to the cemetery, it was nearly ten o'clock and dark with only a sliver of moon to light his way. He stood at the foot of the grave and looked down at the wreath and the offerings. Then he heard a sound from above. There were several old oaks in the cemetery. The imposing oaks were even more impressive at night. A large bird erupted from one of the branches and circled the sky above him. He tried to identify the bird from its wingspan. It was too dark to see more. Did turkey vultures live in New York? Maybe. The bird lazily circled the sky above the cemetery and then after a few sweeps disappeared.

When he bent his head to examine the tombstone, he noticed his pastries looked odd. He knelt and touched the other offerings, one by one, feeling the surfaces searching for signs of wetness. Then he examined the basket of sweet breads. His first thought was that perhaps the sprinklers had soaked the grave. All the other offerings except for his were dry. The pastries crusty brown outer layers were all soaked and when he touched the bread he could smell mold. He pulled his hand away wiping the slime onto the dry blades of grass beside his knee.

There must be a logical explanation.

He blamed his cousins. Someone had sprinkled the pastries with a chemical. He wasn't a chemist, but he suspected with the right ingredients the trick could be accomplished. "Good joke guys," he called out wondering if they were watching him. After standing up and looking around the cemetery he sensed a presence nearby. When the trickster remained hidden, he walked away. By the time he got to the street he was practically running.

The legend of Amara Katsaros had been created by the Katsaros family. He assumed the legend started in Greece over some stupid feud with a neighbor and each generation chose to pass down the feud to keep the hate alive. Only Hera went against family protocol and by diverting from the original story decorated up the petty squabble of a scorned woman with a glorified version, a fantastical adventure which included betrayal and ended with triumph over adversity.

Therefore, Hera, her overworked imagination adding fuel to the grudge created a new twist to the story, turning Adoni and Amara from average victims of male cruelty into struggling heroes, no, better than heroes, turning the two women and their descendants into superhumans revolting against a family curse.

Clever.

Yet?

What about the turkey vulture? How had the pastries decayed so quickly, and the pears remain the same? Why was there no link to Greece? Hadn't anyone gone over to the old country and searched for the truth? One day, he would find out. There was one way to know for sure, one way which none of his family could ignore. He could spit into a tube and uncover his family's secrets. If he could verify his origins on the isle of Crete, he'd be content. If the test revealed some sort of mutant human/harpy/demi-god DNA, he would go to his mother and beg her forgiveness.

Seriously? He'd yet to spit into a tube and he was already apologizing to his mother?

His bark of laughter startled a couple walking ahead of him. The young men were holding hands. They turned as one and waited for him to pass as if prepared for an attack. "Sorry, folks. I'm not laughing at you, just thinking about something my cousin said. He's a riot. Have a good night," he told them reassuringly and ran across the street before the light changed.

Yep, he'd do it. He didn't care if his entire family shunned him. After the cost of DNA tests dropped to an amount most people could afford, family members reminded everyone of the horrors Hera endured at Blackwell Island's Asylum and insinuated the same thing would happen to anyone who revealed the family's true nature. It became a continuous loop, warning members not to repeat the mistakes of the past, emphasizing the dangers of discovery and the possibility of incarceration. But all that fear depended on the accuracy of the legend.

If some lab tech found an anomaly in his DNA, what would they do – send him to a secret underground prison? Asylums were a thing of the past. No one could be kept in an asylum today against their will. And the most time he would spend in a psych ward would be thirty days.

Zak emerged from the bathroom in a fog of steam and bumped into Luke standing by the door scowling at him. "I thought I'd have to call the fire department. What the hell were you doing in there? You couldn't have been shaving, you told me you don't have a razor." Zak ignored him and began to dress. Luke sat back down at the little table by the window, drumming his fingers on the top and drinking his coffee. Zak looked at his brother with disgust. Luke jumped up, "What's that look for?"

"You remember the night you burst into my room and demanded to see the stuff I stole from Ansel's store?"

"Yeah, so what?"

"How did you know the blanket belonged to Constance Wade? And why didn't you tell me?"

"You need some coffee Zak. You're talking crazy. Why would I lie to you?"

"Because you don't trust me with the truth and I'm sick of being treated like a kid. What's so important about the blanket that you'd lie to me about it? I want the truth. Now, Luke."

Luke studied Zak suspiciously, the lines in his forehead deepening, "I told you the truth Zak. Dr. Krutcher said that Constance—"

"Professor Wade to you."

"So, what? Her first name is Constance, her surname is Wade, w. a. d. e., Wade and she earned a Ph.D. which makes her a professor. I don't have to keep calling her Professor Wade. She wouldn't care. And she's not here to correct me, anyway. Do you see her anywhere in the room? What does it matter? Do you think she'd honestly be offended if she was in the room and I called her Constance? I doubt it," Luke said looking around the room as if she might be hiding under the bed. "Anyway, as I was saying before I was rudely interrupted; she owned an authentic Navaho blanket. It was some sort of family heirloom."

"You're not telling me everything. What are you hiding? I want to know. Now."

Luke looked at his watch, "Mrs. Lawson's waiting."

"Then tell me on the way."

Zak slipped on his jeans and shirt from the day before while Luke talked.

"There's nothing to tell. Chill. Come on, hurry up. We don't have all day," Luke said growing impatient and pissed by Zak's belligerent attitude. "We've got to convince Mad Mona to go home. I don't want her tagging along and getting in our way."

"Bullshit. You know something. Eve might be crazy but this whole setup stinks of conspiracy. I bet Mona's involved. I've always thought Mona was a psycho at heart," he said as he shoved his cellphone into his pocket and searched for his keys. That's when he realized she must have taken his keys. "Holy Harpies and all that's fucked!"

"Hey, that's blasphemy. If Mom heard you, she'd wash your mouth out with soap," Luke said as he watched Zak search the room. Luke's face registered his dawning disgust. "She stole your keys, right? The nut-job stole your keys."

Zak brushed past Luke impatiently and opened the door stepping out to look at the cars in the parking lot, "But not my car. Weird, huh?"

Luke followed Zak out to the Camaro. The car door was unlocked and with relief Zak began to search inside. He found the keys in the ash tray, an ash tray that had never been used other than to store coins. He also found a note. It read: *Thanks for a spectacular night Zak. Hope to see you again soon. Love Eve.* On the back of the note, Eve had drawn him a little map. When Luke tried to snatch the note out of Zak's hands, Zak stepped back and shoved the note in his pants pocket. "No. I'm not saying nothing until you to tell me what is going on. There's more. I want to hear it."

Luke climbed into the passenger seat and waited for Zak to get in, "After I talked to Dr. Krutcher about Constance–"

"It's Professor Wade to you."

"No! It's not, dumb-ass. What is it with you and names? So what if I call her Constance? Anyway, it was common knowledge on campus that Wade had a major fight with Krutcher. Nobody knows what the fight was about, but I think they found Amara and Wade wanted the world to know. Krutcher must have hidden the evidence and without the evidence she knew nobody would believe her. If she really intended to tell the world that they had found a ..."

Zak started the Camaro and glared at him, "A harpy, right? Is that what you're trying not to say? Where are we going?"

"Big Joe's Diner. She's eating breakfast at Joe's and if we don't book it, she'll be gone and on her way home. Yes, that's what I'm trying not to say. Keep your voice down. You want people to think we're crazy?"

Zak reversed without respect for the Camaro or any pedestrian foolish enough to walk behind him. He left rubber on the parking lot asphalt as they tore out onto Main Street. "I don't have time for your mind games, Luke. Just tell me what Krutcher said. Go on. Finish your story," he urged in a voice Luke had never heard before. Luke blamed the nut-job for turning his brother into a stranger.

"Krutcher wouldn't tell me anything. When he left his office, I broke in and searched for his notes. I found pictures. I made copies of his notes and the pictures and put everything back where I found them. And the pictures didn't look anything like the drawings in our Family Genealogy. She had long dark wavy hair, thick bushy black brows, green eyes, gorgeous big breasts, a small waist, luscious long legs and – oh yeah – here it comes – wings, huge wings at least six feet long. She wasn't lying in some coffin or a hole in the ground nothing but petrified bones and a few stubborn hairs sticking to her scalp.

No.

She looked as if she'd just woken from a deep sleep. Sleeping Beauty awakened by a kiss, perfectly preserved with long luscious hair and creamy skin. Her cheeks were flushed for god's sake! And this is the creepiest part of all – she had creamy brown skin. Are you following me Zak?"

"You're saying that Krutcher took a picture of one of his lovers dressed as a harpy?" Zak said absently his mind concentrating on avoiding a daredevil cyclist.

"You know better than that Zak. No self-respecting archeologist would waste precious time taking pictures of a woman dressed up like a harpy. If anything, his photographs would have depicted people dressed up as homo sapiens which would have proved his theory Europeans were the first to discover America."

Zak broke in, "I know about his theory, Luke. It was as nutty as he was. Is. North America was already inhabited – by Native Americans. They'd been here long before Columbus. We all."

Luke interrupted him, "Yes, yes. Long before Columbus, long before ancient Native Americans crossed the Barren Straits. Blah, Blah, Blah. That's not my point. My point is why would he keep those pictures around? If those pictures had been discovered by any of his graduate students or his colleagues, he'd have been laughed right out of the university and branded a nut for the rest of his life.

Remember Krutcher and Wade had only a few graduate students to help them with their dig. Do you really think Krutcher would have spent his precious time and money dressing up one of his female students in wings and talons just to fulfill his erotic desires? No. What about the woman? You think she'd keep quiet about something so crazy?

See, I knew this was going to happen. I knew you'd freak out. You're looking at me as if you think I'm making this up. I'm not. Holy Hell. I've got the copies at home. I'll show you. Amara is alive. Do you get it? She was alive in 2001. If she was alive in 2001, then she must be alive now. Remember she's immortal. She can't die unless someone kills her. Well…the pictures prove that in 2001, she was still alive. It also proves Professor Wade knew about Amara."

Zak pulled into the parking lot of Big Joe's Diner. He saw Navan Keys' rental, the Ford Taurus parked near the restaurant door and Mrs. Lawson sitting at a booth drinking a cup of coffee. He bet she'd have preferred a nice cold beer instead.

"How'd you get ahold of the Taurus?" he asked his brother.

Luke had been staring at a text on his cellphone. He glanced through the Camaro windshield toward the Taurus, "Nate found Leona's satchel and the keys to the Taurus were inside. He and Mom took off after my truck. They drove around Twin Falls searching for her, then drove the Taurus back to the Woolly Man. When I got the call from the sheriff about my truck, I decided to deliver the Taurus to Leona personally."

"Why is Lawson with you?"

His brother shrugged, "I thought she could persuade Leona to tell us about Wade."

Zak left the Camaro idling and turned to his brother, "Get out."

"What?"

"I said get out. Now."

"Zak. Come on. Don't be this way."

"Get out now or you'll regret it. I'm this far away from beating the piss out of you," Zak warned.

Something in Zak's face made Luke nervous. For the first time in his life, he had no authority over Zak. He knew Zak was tough. He'd fought him before. They'd always been evenly matched, never able to pin the other down when wrestling. But today Luke suspected Zak would follow through with his threat. He'd never seen him so icy calm.

Luke climbed out of the Camaro and leaned forward to peer in at Zak, "You used to be a believer. What happened to you? Is it Leona? Has she turned you against us?"

"Are you still looking for Wade? Do you think she's still alive?" Zak asked through tight lips staring at his hands throttling the steering wheel.

Goosebumps broke out along Luke's arms. Zak was too furious to even look at him. "Yes. I think she's still alive."

"How do you know?"

"Because she walked into Mom's place yesterday morning," Luke said.

Luke saw the look of shocked disbelief cross Zak's face, "What?"

"Brent Wade had photos of his mother all over his house. Well, actually Leona's house now. When his mother went missing, he paid the mortgage. Seven years after she was pronounced legally dead, he petitioned to buy the house. I stopped by after the memorial service at the Lookout. I saw the photos. I didn't recognize Wade when she first walked into the Woolly Man. I didn't put it all together until after she took off. It was when I was looking through my notebook and came across the photo of his mother, that's when I realized the woman in the Woolly Man calling herself Navan Leona Keys must be Dr. Constance Ann Wade."

"You fuck," Zak said looking at him through new eyes, eyes of hate. "You lying-fuck. Eve, I mean Leona can't be Wade, because Wade if she's even alive would be nearly sixty by now. Eve's younger than me. And I know that for a fact, douche bag."

"She's calling herself Eve now? I know who she really is. She can call herself Acacia T. Pierce or Navan Leona Keys, or Bilbo Baggins for all I care, but she's really a fifty-seven-year-old mother of two and former professor at Boise State. She's a Sagittarius and her birthdays coming up soon."

"You can't count birthdays if you're dead, moron," Zak said.

"She's not dead. Yeah. I know it all sounds crazy. But if you'd been more attentive when Mom talked about our heritage, you'd know that Eve at twenty and Wade in her late fifties could be the same person. Wade found it Zak. She's found Amara. That's got to be the only explanation for her youthful appearance. She's never returned home, because she can't go back to her sons looking younger than them. It all makes perfect sense."

"You're as crazy as Mom," Zak said preparing to back out of the parking space. He saw Lawson sitting at a table inside the restaurant watching them through the window glass.

Paris, Nevada was a small town but even in small towns people generally migrated to the main part of town. An elderly man was sitting on a bench next to the hardware store and a young couple were pulling into the parking lot. Luke glanced around as if searching for spies, then stuck his head inside the Camaro to whisper urgently, "Don't you get it? Wade has tapped into the fountain of youth, maybe even immortality. She must know where Amara is buried. Someone has Amara sealed away. If she were free, she'd have found us by now. If we let Wade get away, she's going to destroy the evidence. We're the descendants of the Gods. You hear me, Zak?"

"Get away from the car. I swear Luke if you don't move, I'll be dragging you down Main Street behind my bumper," Zak threatened. "Her name is Eve Endicott. It's not Constance Wade, no matter how much you want her to be. I know you don't give a shit about people, not really, they're just a means to an end. You don't even realize how crazy you sound. All this harpy garbage is just the family's way of making us feel important, when we all know deep down inside that we're just ordinary immortal redneck poor white trash.

Guess what? I don't care that we're just like everyone else. I don't even care that we're poor. I'm proud we come from a long line of hardworking people. I'm proud we've never shafted other poor people or conned anyone out of their life savings. I'd rather be poor than a greedy rich predator trying to figure out how to take money away from sick kids and old people or to be the offspring of some insane Greek God who rapes mortal women and unleashes his vicious hell hounds on an old blind man.

Some dim bulb in our family wants her kids to feel special, so she makes up a story and the story is crazy enough to appeal to their kids and soon the story is passed down from generation to generation. Well, it's a load of crap. There is no such legend in Greek mythology. In all my research, I never found any mention of Zeus' harpy Ocypete or King Aiolos ever meeting, much less falling in love and having a love child together.

I can't believe in evolution and then turn around the next minute and believe in the supernatural. I tried to make myself believe, for your sake, because I just wanted to fit in with you and Mom. But why would I want to fit in with people like you, when I don't even respect or like you very much? It just came to me. It just came to me this very moment. You're sick. You need help, Luke. Go get help."

The entire time he'd been talking, he hadn't looked at Luke once. Zak shoved the Camaro into reverse. Luke fished something out of his wallet and tossed Wade's picture inside the car. The picture landed in his lap, "You'll see. Look at the picture. Look real good. You'll see what I mean. Come on Zak. Don't do this."

He no longer trusted Luke, because Luke had proven he would go to any lengths to find Amara, even using his brother to trap an innocent woman. With a final glance in his rear view mirror, he saw his brother running for the restaurant. Zak left Paris, Nevada in a cloud of blue burning rubber smoke and headed for the highway. He wanted to be long gone before Luke figured out which direction he was headed. Ignoring the twinge of guilt in his gut, Zak turned the radio on full blast.

A memory surfaced tickling his senses reminding him of a long-ago betrayal of the family trust. At least back then, he'd had a good excuse for his blunder. He'd been nine years old. Maybe he should sit back and let Luke go ahead with his crazy schemes and expose himself to the world as a crackpot? Maybe then the family might forgive him his childish indiscretions and add Luke's name to the list of black sheep?

Zak's betrayal of the family secret happened the first week of school. At the time, he wasn't even thinking of his family's obsession, he was just excited to be able to talk about his heroes. Yet, once he spoke the words aloud, he wished them unspoken. The humiliation had been absolute. It happened on Friday, the first week of second grade. He exposed a hundred and forty-nine-year-old family secret to a bunch of kids who had no idea of the enormity of his betrayal.

He stood before his classmates during Show & Tell and showed them the notebook his mother had given him for his birthday, the leather one with the female harpy embossed on the cover. Zak remembered his childish words, the older version of himself now embarrassed for that long-ago Zak, the child he'd once been, who had been so damned trusting and innocent. "My mother gave me this notebook. She gave it to me because she knew I wanted to be an archeologist someday. I plan to discover where my ancestors once lived and find their ancient city and learn more about my people.

On the cover of the notebook is a map of the world and the words are written in Spanish. But my family isn't Spanish. We're Greek. Nerin in Greek means – from the sea. My people are from the sea but we're also other things."

Danny Ferris sitting in front raised his hand, then asked, "You mean fishermen? Your people are fishermen?"

"No. We're like Jaeger, you know from the comic books. Jaeger's real name is Branken Swift. He used to be a villain. He used to hunt and kill other people. Then he fell in love and changed his ways. He joined Hawkman and helped him fight evil," little Zak said. "We have a mutant like Jaeger in our family. She's my ancestor. She was born in ancient times in Greece. She was immortal, which means she can live forever and hundreds of years ago she came to America with the man she loved.

She could fly just like Jaeger. Like Jaeger, she could hunt for her prey in the sky and kill them in the sky. She could swoop down and grab her prey in her mighty claws and kill them instantly. Sometimes she fought bad men and killed them too. All living creatures fear her. Her husband abandoned her and left her to die. She was rescued by some Native Americans who lived near the Columbia River. They took her in and fed her and saved her life. Later when the white man's sickness made the Indian's sick, she saved them from dying."

What followed remained only a remembered ache. The teacher had been a shadow in the background, as were the students, minus one. In Zak's memory only Danny's face remained clear, his expression of disbelief slowly changing to pity which over the years became an insurmountable humiliation for Zak. Danny, like every other kid in school, knew about the comic book character Jaeger known as Branken Swift, most often referred to as Ken by his family and friends. When the kids all spoke at once eager to explain comic book heroes and villains to the teacher, Zak ran from the room.

For two days, he convinced his mother he was sick. His teacher never told his mother about his humiliating day and Zak was relieved to find that most of the kids had already forgotten about his embarrassing moment at Show & Tell. Only Danny avoided him, acting as if Zak had cooties. But his teacher couldn't ignore the problem when Anderson raised holy hell the following week. He'd never cared about Anderson's opinion of him, but Danny's attitude hurt. And from that day forward, pity had become his enemy. He would rather have people fear him than pity him. Even now, as an adult, he blushed remembering his stupid boast.

And worse was to come.

On the day Anderson had his hysterics, Zak walked home instead of riding the bus. His mother had been anxious and all through dinner she tried to find out what had happened at school. That night Luke had his maps spread out on Zak's bottom bunk. Zak had swept the maps off the coverlet and laid down with his head facing the wall. Then Luke returned with his arms laden with books and saw the maps on the floor.

"Hey. Why didn't you put them on the desk?" Luke asked perplexed.

Zak heard the books fall to the floor and Luke dropping to the ground to collect his maps. Zak kept his face to the wall. Then Luke's hand touched his shoulder trying to turn him over. Zak shrugged off the hand and told him, "Leave me alone."

"Not until you tell me what's wrong."

Angry at his family and himself, Zak turned over and jumped off his bed standing with his fists clenched, "It's all a joke. You hear me. She's been lying to us all along, telling us stupid stories. There's no such thing as Amara. It's just a made-up story."

The first punch shocked Zak. And the next nearly paralyzed him. Luke's face twisted into a mask of hate which scared him, "You liar. You dirty liar. Shut up. You hear me. Shut up."

At first Zak put up his hands to protect his face, but when Luke had him against the door, Zak thought he would die and he knew he didn't want to die. He began to fight back. He had to use his elbows to push Luke away. The thing before him had become a sweaty, red faced fury unrecognizable as his older brother. Luke was bigger and stronger, and Zak would never have dared to fight back under normal circumstances, but something inside wanted to live, and so he started hitting back using his fists and his feet and his teeth.

A pounding of feet running up the stairs signaled that the adults were on their way. Zak and Luke were beyond caring still punching and kicking each other. Their parents burst into the room and took in the situation. His father grabbed Luke and dragged him kicking and screaming from the room. His mother stood before Zak with her arms crossed and a look of disappointment on her face. The memory of her disappointment reaffirmed his new understanding.

The following morning, when his father packed his clothes in a suitcase, Zak ran outside and held onto his father's hand begging him, "Take me with you." But his father shook him off, "No son. You stay here. I'll be back. I promise. I'll be back." Like his mother, his father was a liar.

Zak had heard the stories about their family history so often he'd absorbed them into his core identity. It had always been kind of cool to think of one's self as a descendant of a demi-god and a mythical creature that could fly. But in grade school, he discovered the shame of living such a lie. Not only had he been reprimanded for telling wild fibs but his mother had been equally furious with him for revealing the family secret to outsiders.

What was the big deal? The second time he betrayed the family trust, he'd told only two people, people he believed were his closest friends, Anderson and Jankowski. Anderson had proven himself to be the biggest butthead in the school by running off to tell the teacher all about Zak's "lie" and how Zak would go to hell for claiming to be God.

Andrew Jankowski, his best friend to this day, instead of mocking Zak or laughing at him, had been curious about the legend and wanted to know more. Fortunately for his family's future reputation, Zak didn't have a chance to explain the history behind the legend, because his teacher pulled him off the playground, just at that critical moment. The principal wanted Zak to visit the nurse and then the school counselor.

He never understood why the principal ordered him to visit the nurse. He hadn't been sick. It was only years later he figured out why.

Later he heard his mother had been called to the principal's office. And when she arrived, she assumed she would be speaking only to the principal. Instead, she found herself facing a circular firing squad of school staff: his counselor, his speech therapist, his loudmouthed nasty smelling PE teacher, and finally his classroom teacher who, at the time, he had had a secret crush on.

After that day, he lost all respect for his classroom teacher and most of his future teachers and the school system, until the day he walked into his first college classroom at Boise State University and came face to face with Professor Constance Wade who introduced herself and her subject – Introduction to Anthropology. From that day forward, he had nothing but admiration for the discipline of anthropology.

At every family gathering, he is reminded of his blunder. His mother loves to relive his infamous betrayal and tells any family member willing to listen the details of that infuriating and humiliating moment, "It was like facing the firing squad or inquisition," she would begin. "I tell you they were determined to lock my son up in a loony bin or make him take drugs to keep him pacified. They claimed he was always telling lies and needed counseling. I told them to back off and leave my family alone. And if they didn't treat my son with respect, I warned them, I would take my grievances to the highest authorities making sure they all lost their jobs."

Quinn's father coined the term "circular firing squad" which his mother appropriated as her own when retelling the tale. Years later he told Zak, "Boy, if they weren't such idiots, I'd feel sorry for those teachers. They didn't have the smarts to realize what was in store for them. Your mother is an old-time Greek, an eye-for-an-eye kind of Greek. It took her a few years, but she got them good. Whenever she tells that story, I see a circular firing squad. They didn't know it, but they'd shot each other in the face that day."

As a kid, Zak didn't pay much attention to school politics or the personal lives of his teachers. When he got older though, he discovered some interesting facts. When Zak had nearly finished 4th grade and Luke, two grades ahead, was preparing for graduation and middle school, the P.E. teacher lost his job. He made the mistake of confronting Harrison as Harrison was changing out of his football uniform. When the argument heated up, Hoops slammed the locker door on the kid's arm fracturing his wrist in two places. When Harrison returned to school with his arm in a cast, Hoops was gone for good, never to be seen in their town again.

As adults, many years later in Boise, he and his friends entered their favorite bar and were surprised to see Hoops bar tending. Where was the raging bull now? He looked like a lamebrain. The whole time they were in the bar, Hoops ignored them. Jankowski must have noticed the surprise on Zak's face as Zak stared open mouthed at his old gym teacher. As was his habit, Jankowski needed to analyze the situation by discussing the issue openly in front of everyone, even people Zak barely knew.

Jankowski addressed Zak first and said, "You didn't know Hoops worked here, huh? He's been bar tending for about a year. No school will touch him. And what happened years ago follows him everywhere he applies for a job. I bet you didn't know why he was screaming into Harrison's face that day. It turned out Hoops thought Harrison had loaded dirty pictures on his computer and that's what got him in trouble with the school board.

Hoops still swears someone pulled a nasty joke on him. I've heard him talking to some of the regulars about the crime committed against him by the school board and the person or persons who ruined his life. He doesn't remember me, so he just keeps flapping his lips thinking he's talking to a bunch of strangers. Hoops may be a jerk, but he isn't stupid. Why would he keep dirty pictures on a school computer, huh? That's just asking for trouble. Hoops tried to prove his innocence, but it was too late. The school board and the principal had no choice but to fire him. Whoever thought that one up is a scary mother. They've never come forward, but I think I know who might have had access and opportunity. You see, to get into the teacher's computers, you would have to know their passwords and —"

The tension in Zak's gut disappeared when Stanley interrupted Jankowski's ruminations, "Yeah, well, it wasn't just Hoops who got his comeuppance. Although he deserved it more than anyone else. The principal thought she'd gotten a job in Boise and quit before school started. The letter claimed the school needed someone right away, that it was an emergency and there might be a chance to relocate to a different school in Boise permanently. The letter claimed the current principal had been diagnosed with cancer and needed to leave the state for treatment. Well, she called the school to confirm the principal's condition and learned from someone who answered the phone the facts were true and indeed the school was looking for a replacement.

Our principal sent a letter accepting the position and received an answer back within a few days. On the first day of school, after quitting her job, selling her house, and moving to Boise, she discovers the placement offer had been a fake and the confirmation letter acknowledging her acceptance had been a fake. Somehow, someone had intercepted her acceptance letter. No one knows how it all had been done. It might have been an inside job but none of the staff were ever implicated. Since our school had already hired a new principal, she had to find a job quick. She ended up moving to Arizona because she couldn't find anything in Idaho. Weird huh?"

"I would love to see those letters," Jankowski said. "You would need the proper letterhead paper and have a working knowledge of the professional jargon used in the education field, all such skills would be necessary to fool the reader into believing the letter was genuine. Then the forger would have to figure out a way to intercept the principal's acceptance letter. Wow. I am impressed with this guy. What a genius. Once the principal realized she'd been conned, I wonder if the police got involved?"

Stanley shrugged, "How the hell should I know? I got this information third-hand from my older cousin who worked as a part-time special education aid. And she only found out when she overheard two teachers gossiping in the teacher's lounge. My cousin told me the teachers were laughing themselves sick. I guess her reputation as a butthead was known far and wide throughout the lands."

Stephen Beckett laughed.

"What about what's-her-name the school speech therapist and Mrs. Gardiner, the counselor?" Zak asked afraid to hear the answer. Each one at the table looked blankly at the person sitting next to him or her. In unison, they shrugged. Zak decided at the first opportunity he would search for their names on the Internet and find out what had happened to them.

The only woman in their group, Maisy Dale spoke up for the first time, "I felt really sorry for Miss Simon. I had so much fun in second grade with her as my teacher. She was so sweet."

A sense of dread churned around in Zak's stomach and he couldn't help but ask, "What happened to her?"

"The new principal insisted she go back to school and get more training, but she couldn't afford to travel to Boise and back every week, so she quit. She's teaching in Vegas now. She must be really old, at least fifty, and you know how people treat new teachers. And if they're old? It's not pretty. And I hear they don't pay much more than we do." He relaxed. His mother wasn't savvy enough to know the ins and outs of teaching. But she could have asked someone who might have known? And then he remembered Quinn had been assigned to Miss Simon's class and his mother had made a big fuss to get her moved to a different teacher.

It was all adding up to something so Machiavellian it boggled his mind. But then again, his mother was nothing if not persistent. And he'd never talked to anyone about his school boy crush, not even to Luke. His mother might have gone easy on Miss Simon if she'd known how much the teacher was liked by him and everyone else. But he was beginning to suspect his mother had had an accomplice and he thought he knew who it had been.

Luke had been two grades ahead and even though he hated contact sports, tried out for the team. Inwardly, Zak had trouble reconciling such a diabolical scheme with what he knew about his brother. The idea that Luke would risk his own skin to get educators fired seemed crazy. The idea that his mother would spend so much time hatching a plot so intricate was even crazier. Keying cars, making anonymous calls, and dumping ants and mice in an empty house were more her style.

Would Luke have taken time out of his busy social life as a member of the Twin Falls Chess Club, the secretary of the Magic Valley Young Lapidarians, a junior member of the Idaho Outdoor Club, and a member of the Young Archeologists Club to execute the villainous tasks dreamed up by his diabolical mother? Zak couldn't even wrap his head around the idea. His mind kept rebelling unwilling to believe his brother could be so ruthless.

Instead, his unconscious mind substituted Luke and imagined a shadowy figure as the conspirator. It wasn't Luke, it was some faceless person who planted porn on Hoop's computer and wrote the fake letter. And it had to have been some faceless person who stole the principal's acceptance letter from her out basket. Try as he might, stupid thoughts squeezed past his defenses. The crimes required the conspirator to be familiar with the school and in a position of trust. Had Jule Nerin slept with the vice-principal just to seduce him into committing acts of sabotage against his co-workers?

Luke might be a bully sometimes and even vindictive sometimes, but hardly the kind of person who would spend, even an hour, much less months plotting, planning, and executing revenge. And would Luke risk his future dreams of being the next Donald Johanson? Would he sneak around school planting porn, stealing letterhead paper, and intercepting letters for the family honor? Jule Nerin was vindictive enough to do it, but not smart enough to pull it off so brilliantly. He refused to believe Luke would spend even a second doing his mother's dirty work.

What bugged Zak the most was the rolling log of disasters which had befallen so many because of a stupid story he'd told to impress his classmates. If he'd kept his big mouth shut, no one would have been hurt. Wait. Why was he blaming himself? He'd been a kid. It had been up to the adults to resolve the problem. As an adult, his mother should have ignored the whole thing. Instead, like other family members before her, she'd chosen revenge.

Revenge was never the answer. He loved his mother, but hated her vengeful nature. Not only had Hera Katsaros passed down the lie of Amara, she'd passed down a culture of family conceit. And when the conceit didn't fit with reality, then other people were to blame for the misfortunes of the Katsaros family. He was so sick and tired of hearing about how the enemies of the Katsaros' family must be destroyed. Such poisonous conceits were ruining them all.

His guilty thoughts were interrupted by Maisy. She asked no one in particular, "Why do you call Mr. Whitcomb – Hoops – if you hate him so much? Isn't that supposed to be used only for really good basketball players?"

With a straight face Zak turned and addressed Maisy, "I'll show you how it works." He turned to Stanley and asked, "Are you chewing gum again Stanley?"

Stanley saluted him and said, "No, sir. I swear I'm not sir."

"Open-up, Stanley. Come on now; let me see."

Stanley opened his mouth and the guys grinned.

"What's that Stanley?"

Stanley closed his mouth and shook his head, "Nothing sir. I swear."

"Spit it out, Stanley. Go on spit it out."

Stanley leaned forward and pretended to spit the imaginary gum on the floor. Zak bent over to look at his shoe and all the guys imitated the sound of a loud revolting fart. And Zak pretending to be Mr. Whitcomb said in the sham voice of a marine drill sergeant, "A week's detention for you, Stanley. You hear me, Stanley, that's a week's detention. Pick up that filthy piece of gum and march straight to the principal's office. Pronto, mister. I say pronto. And the rest of you open-up. If anyone else is chewing gum, you'll go straight to detention along with Stanley. Open-up now."

Magically, for one moment, as if their thoughts were synchronized and their bodies transported back in time, history repeated itself. Jankowski leaned forward and whispered in Zak's ear. Zak, instead of whispering in Stanley's ear, chose to address the group aloud his words muffled by the ruckus in the bar, "Oh no. It's a Mutant Rear. Help! Open-up Oscar's Poop-hole Stinks." Only their table and the table nearby heard the childish joke.

There was a long silence as the adults around the table remembered a moment in their childhood in which they had won a small victory against petty tyranny. Then Maisy giggled and pointed over Stanley's head, "Guess who finally gets the joke." Everyone at the table looked up in time to see Oscar Whitcomb watching the group from behind the bar. His face was as red as a freshly picked tomato and his scowl was filled with murderous intent. Stanley nearly fell off his chair he was laughing so hard. They sobered up when Stephen Beckett said, "Hey folks, pipe-down, remember, the bartender has the right to refuse service if he thinks we've had too much to drink."

The whole situation had turned ugly. Zak knew he'd had enough to drink. He stood up and the others followed suit. He was the last one to leave. Maisy glanced back at him and he waved her on, "I'll be there in a sec." Instead of following the guys outside, Zak moved toward the bar and Oscar Whitcomb. Like usual Whitcomb was hopping mad, his face still flushed with rage. It was difficult to ignore the old man's anger coming at him in waves of injured hate. Zak ignored his body's flight or fight response.

He had something to say and it needed to be said quickly before he lost his courage. "Mr. Whitcomb, I know you hate my guts and I don't really care. I know you're pissed off and I still don't care. I'm not ten years old anymore and you don't scare me. Maybe later when you've had time to think, you'll call this number and give me the names of the people who had access to your office computer. What you did was wrong but there was somebody else at fault too. I want to find the person who put those dirty pictures on your computer." He handed Whitcomb a folded piece of paper with a phone number written on the inside.

Whitcomb glanced at the paper on his bar counter and looked up with a sneer and said, "Get out of my bar, Nerin or I'll throw you out."

"Yeah right. You and who else. Don't worry. I'm going. And I won't be back," he said as he looked around the place with a shake of his head.

There is a cure for conceit. And his confrontation with Whitcomb had been the first step. He couldn't do anything about his family's grandiosity, but at least he'd done something about his own. He would be different. He would break the cycle of misappropriated greatness. Yes, they were poor. And what of it? According to his family, in due time, when they found Amara, Zeus would forgive her and as a consequence all of Amara's descendants would be forgiven. Once powerful again, the Nerin family would enjoy all the entitlements of the Twelve Gods of Olympus.

For now, our destiny is on hold, he jeered. *Soon. Soon we'll be rich and powerful and terrible to behold.* He couldn't even cough up a chuckle. The mindset of such a belief system was so dishonest and insanely ludicrous, it bordered on perversion.

16

Acacia fought and kicked her way back to the front lines and found herself in a pathetic excuse for a bar, no more than a counter in one corner with a couple of barstools beneath it. The floor was disgusting. It smelled of urine and beer. But the most disgusting thing of all in the place was the asshole nuzzling her neck. The kid couldn't have been more than twenty. She shoved him away and he fell off his barstool and landed on the dirty floor. Acacia yanked her blouse and bra back into place, stood up, stepped over the boy, and headed for the front door. The boy struggled to his feet swaying in the breeze of her passing. The floorboards were so old she could feel them move up and down as he came running after her.

As he leaned down to grab her arm, she smelled a whiff of his beer-soaked breath and something even more rancid, something wrapped in garlic and onions. She nearly spewed the little food left in her stomach out her nose. Then his breath stirred the hair near her right ear. It was too much, too much to take in all at once. As if in a nightmare, Acacia's senses were assaulted from all sides and with all the bent-up frustration of the last few days boiling inside her stomach, she swung her elbow back with a savage jab into the horny kid's belly. Her elbow met tight muscle and the bones in her arm protested sending a shutter of pain up her arm and into her neck.

Her jab worked; the boy was caught off guard. She heard the whoosh of air leave his lungs and his groan followed by the thud as his six-foot frame hit the floorboards. The bartender's applause and admiring whistles followed in her wake.

It was a relief to step out into the bright sunshine. From the position of the sun she figured it must be around three or four in the afternoon. She had no idea where she was, and she wasn't about to ask the scuzzy skank lurking in the depths. It made Acacia nauseous just imagining what dirt Eve had been rolling in for the last twenty-four hours. The first thing she would do would be to take a hot shower and use plenty of soap; maybe, she should stop by a clinic and get tested too? Acacia blamed Dr. Bishop for the appearance of Eve Endicott. He'd been playing around in the body's head desperate to find a way inside and learn all the body's secrets. Asshole. His incompetence had generated another personality, one who thought about sex 24/7.

That male nurse had been the catalyst, most significantly, the second bath and rub down by Josh Pascula's gentle hands finalized the transition. Those hands with their tapered fingers and soft skin. Those confident and sure hands, glistening with lotion and gliding over her body. Yeah! Those hands that had never touched a greasy engine or a hammer. Hands which might have been the hands of a musician or an artist, potentially the hands of a surgeon, of which she discovered later, Pascula aspired to be one day.

A stirring inside warned Acacia before Eve broke free. Acacia quickly replaced the college freshman's six foot three inches two hundred and ten pound muscled and bronzed body with the image of a toilet bowl full of excrement. The stirrings subsided. A poster glued to a street pole on the corner informed her that rock-hounds were welcome at the annual Nyssa Gemstone Convention in May. Yet as she looked up and down the street, Acacia realized with profound misgivings that Main Street was the only street in town.

In fact, she suspected that this town wasn't even Nyssa. As she continued walking west, her suspicions were confirmed when a sign announced to motorists that Adrian had approximately 351 residents. Adrian . . . where is Adrian?

Acacia had been walking for nearly an hour and received several offers from motorists for a ride when a metallic green 1978 Mustang loaded with two obnoxious males stopped and the driver leaned out his window and offered her more than a ride. Acacia lost her temper and marched across the hot asphalt with car exhaust burning her eyes and the smell of the onion fields nearly choking her throat. She was in the process of reaching inside the Mustang to grab the driver's ear and twist it real hard when some instinct urged her to look up and to her right.

A patrol car appeared over the rise, just in time to save the driver from a beating he would not soon forget. Acacia realized with a sinking in her stomach that she had left her satchel back in the bar. She had no identification on her, nothing that would assuage the cop's suspicions. Eve would only have made matters worse, but Ana, now Ana had the intelligence people admired and an odd juxtaposing of innocence which people found especially charming. Acacia was loath to give up the opportunity to bloody someone's nose, but she knew Ana would manage somehow to persuade the cop they were law abiding citizens and victims of fate.

The patrol vehicle pulled up behind the Mustang and the police officer climbed out. He approached the Mustang warily standing behind the driver's door rather than in front of it. With cars whizzing only inches from her, Acacia moved to a safer location. She stood on the edge of the onion field and tried to hear what the cop and the creep were saying to each other. She nearly tripped over a bunch of onions rotting on the ground and kicked them away as she surreptitiously watched the patrol officer question the driver.

When the patrol officer finished questioning the driver (which from the familiarity of their discourse she figured was a regular event) the cop turned and addressed her, "Are you aware that hitchhiking is illegal in this state and dangerous too, ma'am?"

Acacia crossed her arms to hold in her gathering annoyance, "I wasn't hitchhiking. That man," she pointed at the driver. "He asked me a question. I couldn't hear him over the tractor, so I walked up to his car and that's when you showed up."

The police officer looked up and down the road then back to her, "What tractor?"

Acacia realized her mistake too late. It was time to let go. If only she'd had the chance to pull one of those bastards out of the Mustang and beat him senseless. It was her last conscious thought before Ana Evans took charge of the situation.

Mary Ana Evans woke to sunlight beating down on her head and the chrome from a car blinding her for a moment. She put a hand up to shield her eyes and through tears noticed a police officer staring at her as if waiting for an answer. Answer to what? Ana didn't care for the way the driver's friend in the passenger seat kept grinning at her, so she decided to move around the Mustang and closer to the nice officer. She had a feeling the officer would be a safer target than the creep with hair and teeth which needed a brisk cleaning and brushing.

The officer stood six feet two inches in his stocking feet, so what with his uniform and gear and boots and blonde crew cut he was an impressive sight, although she preferred them tall, dark, and intelligent herself. She did admire his thoughtful brown eyes though. He couldn't have been more than twenty-five and probably hadn't been in the police force for long. Any authority figure whether that figure be of the police or a judge or a government interfering in the freedom of the proletariat annoyed Ana on principal alone. Ana did her best to appear cooperative and was indeed relieved to see someone who might be able to help her. Yet, she had the distinct feeling this man already knew she wasn't a big fan of his profession.

The driver in the Mustang equally as unwashed as his friend with his leering eyes made Ana uncomfortable. Something of what she was feeling must have registered with the police officer. He took her arm and guided her behind his patrol vehicle, so they would be out of the driver's hearing. Ana looked up at him and tried to figure out how much he would accept if she told him she had no idea what had happened in the last few days. Here she was on some strange road with a pair of lecherous jerks and a police officer was waiting to hear her story.

What story? What had she been doing for the last few days, no, make that months? The last memory she had was of herself and her friends' makeshift picnic by the banks of a creek. And before that she remembered staring out her hospital window trying to find a better word to use than "maintained." The laptop computer Dr. B had given her had been staring accusingly at her, daring her to type something on its screen, further insulting her intelligence with a blinking cursor which demanded her attention. Well, that had been months ago. She had to deal with this moment. Something inside began to protest, a voice began to bellow in concerned outrage and Ana was nearly no more. She fought back.

Someone a long time ago had accused Ana of the bad habit of wanting to tell everyone, even strangers the whole truth and nothing but the truth. But today what could she honestly tell this man? She didn't even know the month or the day. She had no clue where she was, nor did she particularly care for the strong smell of onions in the air. She looked about and realized that she was on a road between onion fields and nothing else, not even a house. In the distance she could see mountains. They looked familiar. She'd been here before.

While Ana desperately tried to place those mountains, the policeman spoke to the men in the Mustang. Together Ana and the policeman watched the Mustang pull out onto the road and head east. Then everything clicked into place. She was in Oregon, only a few miles from the Oregon/Idaho border. To the east she knew she would find

Succor Creek National Park. To the west she would be heading toward Vale or Homedale depending on which road she took.

The Mustang took the road to Homedale. The mountains to the south she recognized as part of the Owyhee Mountains. Nestled among the Owyhee Mountains would be the Owyhee Reservoir and Leslie Gulch. Her memories of hikes through Leslie Gulch brought tears to her eyes. Someone had been with her during those hikes. Wait, not just someone, but two very important people who had meant a great deal to her back then. She wanted to remember them but someone she trusted cautioned her to hold off for the present and revisit the memory later.

"I don't see any tractor, ma'am. You want to revise your story?"

"I didn't say tractor. I said traffic. There were a couple of cars that went by earlier, you see, and I couldn't hear what the man was asking me. I thought he might be trying to offer me a lift to the nearest telephone, so I could get in touch with my friend."

"May I see some identification ma'am," Officer Andrews asked.

Ana had been dreading this moment. She considered several options, "Well, that's the problem you see. I left the house in a hurry and didn't bother to take my purse."

"Why?"

"It's really stupid I know but my sister said she needed me, so I just jumped in the truck with her and took off down the highway. I regretted it immediately because she kept talking about her stupid boyfriend. After a couple of hours, I finally got sick of hearing her complain about him and demanded she take me home and she said no she had a deadline and then we started to fight for real. I decided I didn't want to stay another second watching her get drunk and act stupid, so I walked out of the bar and down the road. You see I was looking for a payphone. I was planning on calling a friend to come and pick me up."

His frown made her realize how lame her story sounded. "Let me get this straight. You and your sister were drinking. Where were you drinking?"

She knew details were always helpful. When the officer asked her where she'd been drinking a name immediately came to mind, "The Slipper."

"You were drinking at the Golden Slipper in Vale, Oregon?" he asked in surprise.

259

Ana hesitated then decided that particular detail would add verisimilitude to her story, "Yes, we were. We were at that bar back there somewhere." She pointed west toward Vale, Oregon.

"Are you serious, ma'am?"

"Of course. She and I used to drink there a lot back in the day. I mean we still sometimes drink there."

"Where? In the rubble?"

"I don't understand?"

"The Golden Slipper's been empty for a long time. Just this winter the roof caved in. Come on now. It's time to tell me the truth."

Ana threw up her hands, simultaneously grief-stricken at the news and embarrassed she'd been caught in a lie, "Yes, I lied. I haven't been in this part of the world in decades. I've been living in Chicago and figured The Golden Slipper would always be there. My grandfather used to drink in the Slipper when I was a kid. The last time he was there, he fell off his barstool and the doctors discovered he had cancer. Ah, ghee, I don't remember what year that was. But so what? So what if I lied?"

"Your name and address ma'am."

"My name is Mary Evans and I'm on my way to the Oregon coast. I've been invited to stay with friends. At the moment, I have no current address." She refused to give out her last address. Instinct told her she'd end up straight back at the Recovery Center. Once again, Dr. B would make her his pet project and she would be forever a prisoner of the 8-Ball Ward.

"You said you and your sister were drinking and had a fight. What is your sister's name and which bar were the two of you at?"

"Her name is Luann Freshman. She's a truck driver. She took me to some cheap bar between here and Homedale. I can't remember the name."

The highway patrolman blinked and said, "That's a long way to go for a drink, ma'am."

"I know. When I called my sister and told her I was headed to the coast, she told me she was on the road and would meet me in Homedale. She did, and we ended up drinking in some dive and she got in a fight with some guy and I left disgusted with my sister and the guy and the place," Ana continued doing her best to imitate the fake Luann Freshman's voice and lexicon.

As she conjured up the image of the fake Luann she gave her a clown face full of makeup, a pierced nose and pierced eyebrow, tattoos, and the voice of a two pack-a-day cigarette smoker, "I'm sure you've met her on the road. She drives this route all the time. She has reddish blonde hair, brown eyes, pierced nose and eyebrow, tattoos on her right hand. Oh, and she wears lots of makeup."

"Your sister's name and address please, ma'am," the officer asked.

"I can't, officer. Sorry. She's on the road a lot and we'd just met the other day after three years apart. It was hard to get her to tell me any news, much less her address," Ana said and gave the officer the name of a trucking outfit she remembered from long ago, hoping by the time he reached the company and discovered there was no Luann Freshman working for them, she'd be long gone.

The last memory Ana had, the one at the computer when she couldn't think of a better word than "maintained" returned and she remembered a nurse telling her it was the year 2017. The nurse's name had been Shirley. Ana knew another Shirley. Even if Shirley had moved on to husband number four, Shirley would never give up her married name and go back to her last name of Shrinker. Shirley had been a classmate of hers at Evergreen College in Washington. When they were both bombed out of their mind from a night of drinking and smoking pot, Shirley confessed to Ana that when she was a child the kids used to call her stinky Shrink. Ana gave the officer Shirley's name and last known address.

Once the Malheur Sheriff's Department verified the identity of Shirley Butterworth who amazingly enough still lived in Ontario and still taught at Treasure Valley Community College, the officer gave her a ride back to Vale. She promised the officer she would get help for her drinking problem. His odd behavior and even odder remark as they drove the winding back road to Vale still irked her though. She'd been sitting in the front passenger seat with her knee touching a rifle mounted near the glove compartment and wondering why it was necessary for a huge gun like that to be placed in such an awkward location when the officer glanced over at her and asked, "You had one of those major makeovers or something. Right?"

"I'm sorry. I don't understand. What do you mean makeover?"

"You know, the television show, the one where people go under the knife and get a whole new face or body. Did you get one of those?"

Ana had no idea what he was talking about. Even before her memory loss she hadn't been one to watch television much. Evidently, television catered to the masses obsession over looks and the superficiality of what constituted beauty. By her second year as an undergrad, Ana had thrown away her makeup, hot itchy nylons, and tight skirts for more comfortable jeans and sandals. Who had time to fix one's face after pulling an all-nighter to get a research paper finished by the next morning? Besides the oddballs on campus were the ones who wore too much makeup and dressed as if they were on the cat walk.

By the time Ana was a graduate student, the competition was for grades not looks. Sure pretty women got special treatment, well at least, lots of smiles and smirks, but in the long run sleeping with one's professor didn't guarantee a diploma. No woman is willing to sleep with every damn professor, not unless she's a bisexual nymphomaniac who just happens to be drop dead gorgeous and appealing to all intellectual types.

When the officer frowned at her, Ana realized she'd taken too long to answer. She blurted out the first thing that popped into her head, "I still don't understand what you mean. I've never watched the show you're talking about, but I'm assuming you think I've had major surgery. That doesn't make sense. I look the way I look because I was born looking this way. And to tell you the truth I think people who get plastic surgery are terribly, terribly insecure.

They need healthier strategies to improve their lives. It's ludicrous to imagine that you'll be loved if you're just ten pounds lighter or have a different nose. Even gorgeous people get dumped you know. Even gorgeous people live miserable lives, so beauty may help you get a job, but that doesn't guarantee you're going to keep the job or even want the job in the long run. So, I guess, no, I don't understand what you mean."

Ana stopped talking when the officer began to chuckle and said, "Well, I guess you've answered my question. If I understand you correctly, you haven't had an extreme makeover. That must mean you are one of those lucky people who never looks her age, huh?"

During her tirade, she hadn't noticed they'd arrived at the Malheur County Corrections Building right across the street from the Malheur County Courthouse on 151 B Street West. Ana had a new appreciation for the smoothness and comfort of these newer patrol vehicles. Since Ana had never owned a new vehicle in her entire life, other than the new vehicle her first husband bought himself and allowed her to drive on special occasions, Ana admired the way the patrol vehicle seemed to glide across the ground in its beautiful well sprung cocoon.

Before the officer had a chance to ask her another searching question, Ana leaped out of the car and waved briskly at him while walking backwards as if she fully intended to enter the building. The officer waved back and made a sweeping circle in the parking lot then merged with traffic. She waited until Officer Andrews and his Cloud 9 patrol vehicle disappeared from view.

Without hesitation she walked in the direction she believed would bring her to A Street and Main. Instead of making a call to her imaginary sister or real but long-lost friend from college, she decided to return to the Slipper and persuade someone to give her a lift as far as Ontario. She was also thinking about having herself some Rocky Mountain Oysters and maybe a cold beer.

As she hurried toward Main street, she remembered fondly how she and her Grandpa used to sit on the barstools, she with a soda and he with his beer and bowl of nuts waiting for their order. There was no television playing in the background, only a few customers having a quiet drink. Years later someone told her "oysters" was a euphemism for something else. The truth didn't make them any less tasty. What had mattered more to her about being in the bar with her grandfather was the company not the cuisine.

Every so often she looked back to be sure the policeman hadn't changed his mind.

What amazed her was his total lack of interest in verifying her story. One phone call to the trucking company would have proven there was no such person employed with them by the name of Luann Freshman. And a visit to Shirley Butterworth would have proven Ana was a big fat liar. One phone call to the little bar in that little Idaho town would have confirmed she was a consummate liar extraordinaire, because no one in the place would have been able to identify her from the officer's description.

Knowing the way Eve and Acacia worked, she wouldn't have been surprised if there had been some bar somewhere and some guy somewhere either beaten up or ravished with sloppy drunken kisses.

She stopped in her tracks remembering what Officer Andrews had told her about the Slipper. Well he said the roof collapsed in the winter. It was summer now. They'd probably fixed the place up as good as new, maybe even newer. She bet that if she walked inside, she wouldn't recognize the place at all. Would they still have the old beer hall counter with decades of cigarette burns and water spot rings embedded in the polished wood? Would the counter still stretch from the door to the restrooms in the back? How many barstools had there been in her grandpa's day? Fifteen? Twenty? She remembered the interior as dark and cool with a blue haze of cigarette smoke just above her head.

Her last visit to the Slipper had been after her miserable talk with Krutcher the toad and her determination to find Constance Wade. Wade had been upset when she discovered Krutcher took all the credit for the Smithers' excavation and left her completely out of his paper which was published in the Journal of the Pacific Northwest Archeological Society. Even in his report to the director of the anthropology department he barely mentioned Professor Constance Wade's contribution to the discovery.

Connie had shown her the copy of the letter and how she'd figured out the clue. The first clue had been in the last paragraph of Ezekiel Underwood's letter. The second clue led to the discovery of Underwood's personal relationship with one of the women who had been a member of the indigenous people of the Columbia. Putting the clues together, Constance figured out where the two men - Smithers and Underwood met for their final showdown. Ana remembered her last conversation with the snake in his office. She remembered saying, "It's amazing how you pieced together the clues which led to the Smithers discovery. So tell me again, which part of the letter led you to the spot where Smithers and Underwood met?"

Ignoring her question, Krutcher opened his briefcase and showed her the original letters sent to Smithers by Ezekiel Underwood, the minister assigned to the spiritual needs of the Columbia indigenous people. When she kept pushing for an answer, he refused to explain how he had come up with the location of Smithers and Underwood's final meeting place. It dawned upon her quickly enough that Krutcher was clueless, ignorant of even the most basic findings of a major expedition. Sickened by the man, Ana couldn't wait to get out of the room and get drunk.

On autopilot she managed to reach Vale, Oregon without killing herself or anyone else stupid enough to be on the road at the time. Sitting on a familiar barstool in a familiar place helped her to think about what she must do. Everyone knew Krutcher was a vindictive asshole. She couldn't tell anyone just yet, not even her closest friends about Connie's complaints or he and the university would counterattack and spread rumors about her, perhaps finishing her career for good.

Yet if she accepted the position at the university and didn't speak up about Connie's grievances and her own suspicions that Krutcher was doing something shady, something which had nothing to do with the university and everything to do with some rich anonymous backer, she might be tainted with the same reputation as Smithers, forever ridiculed as a crackpot.

The letters had been written by the missionary Ezekiel Underwood and were difficult to read due to the age of the paper and the flowery script. Her first reaction to the letter's significance was distaste. How a man of God could be so thoroughly duped baffled her. She understood that as a Greek scholar, he might be entranced by the idea; yet, as a minister he should have been dismissive of the story as just another attempt to undermine Christianity's message. Or did he think the people of the Columbia saw an angel? Unfortunately, no one would ever know because true to his education, he left his own private thoughts out of the letter and faithfully recorded his "flocks" story to Smithers.

As she read the final paragraph and the significant passage which Connie had mentioned to her, Ana set down the letter on Krutcher's desk and looked him in the eye and asked again, "So which part led to your discovery? In your abstract and your report, you never mention the clue. Some of your own colleagues and Connie's students are beginning to wonder if perhaps Connie, after all, was the real detective who discovered Smithers' artifacts in Nevada."

Instead of answering her question, he gathered up all the documents including the Underwood letter then stuffed them in his briefcase and put the briefcase in his safe. "I must go. I have a meeting to attend. Good day to you, Professor Evans." In retrospect, it had been a colossal mistake to have threatened him. Her words still rang as clear as a bell ringing the death knell for herself and so many other innocent people, "I'm not finished with you, Krutcher. This whole situation stinks. Connie is missing, and I believe you know what's happened to her. When your part in this comes out, your reputation will be ruined."

As she walked toward The Golden Slipper and Thunderegg Dining Room, she realized belatedly that her last teaching job had been many, many years ago and she had not taught Introduction to Anthropology for a very long time. Catching sight of a magnificent mural painted on a two-story brick façade, she paused in delight to appreciate the artist's attempts to capture the spirit of the period. The sheer stubbornness and fortitude of mankind was exemplified in the mural. Many scholars had written about the hardships of the early pioneers of the west.

Whenever she thought of those courageous people, she could not help but compare society's current pampered existence with the pioneers harsher and much deadlier every day experiences. Instead of taking months to journey from St. Louis to the Pacific Ocean, today's mode of transportation took hours or days. What attracted her the most was the artist's rendition of the Conestoga wagons drawn by oxen and the pioneers as they crossed the river. The river looked so inviting. Its appeal reminded her of her epiphany many years ago.

Although the mural before her was of a river winding through a mountain range, she remembered her first sight of a river winding through a range of skyscrapers. She had been in the dark one moment and then suddenly in a room flooded with light. Her epiphany occurred at the Recovery Center while on the 8-Ball Ward in her hospital room. That had been two years ago. As she recalled, the explosive awakening was ignited by the view from her room which had been spectacular. She remembered gazing in wonder at the sight of the magnificent river running by the hospital. When she asked a passing orderly for the name of the river she was looking at, he kindly informed her she was looking at the Chicago River.

Like a person awakening from a coma, she saw everything as she imagined a newborn would see the world – with wonder and awe. The sight of the river inspired her to write a novel; and many months later, the view continued to inspire her, and she wrote two more novels, which she was delighted to know were selling better than anyone had expected. With the help of the orderly and her favorite nurse, she managed to smuggle her novels out of the hospital right under Dr. Caleb Bishop's long nose. Once the royalties started coming in, she recompensed her helpers based on the risks they had taken on her behalf. They were as delighted with her success as she.

When she finally reached The Golden Slipper on A Street and Main and found a pile of rubble nearly fifteen feet tall, she pivoted on the curb opposite the site staring in disbelief. Where was the neon golden slipper sign? Where was the two-story red brick building nearly one hundred years old? In a daze, she crossed the road and heard the blaring of a horn warning her to wake up. She stepped back onto the curb and waited until the cavalcade of cars made their way out of town and onto Ontario and parts unknown. She knew this was the scenic artery to the Pacific Northwest for those travelers who enjoyed the back roads rather than the smelly crowded Interstate.

Once Main Street was clear of traffic, she walked slowly toward the chain-length fence and the rubble contained inside the fence. The sight of the devastation made her furious. Who had been so criminal as to destroy such a landmark? All she had now of her grandfather were dim memories. She needed a drink bad. No. That would be a mistake. It was important she remain sober and alert.

She didn't know how long she'd been standing on the sliver of sidewalk, a sidewalk barely safe for one person to walk, much less pedestrians marching two abreast. She stared in disbelief at the destruction, oblivious to the traffic and a group of people across the street just coming out of the restaurant. She woke to her surroundings when a series of odd noises broke her concentration. She tried to ignore the attempts to get her attention.

The annoying sounds persisted. They were not coming from occasional vehicles or townspeople passing by instead - the wheezes, sniffles, and grunts – she discovered, when she turned her head were coming from a body standing so close she could have rubbed elbows with him without moving. It seemed the old man was sharing her sorrow at the sight of old beams and tar paper dumped in a fifteen-foot mound of funeral pyre in what used to be The Golden Slipper.

Along Main Street part of the wall was still standing, a crazy quilt of stucco on one side and local sandstone slabs artfully arranged on the other side. There was an old door still with its glass intact inset into the standing wall. Piled up against the standing wall as if holding the wall up with its weight were what remained of the red bricks used for the top floors. As she moved around to A Street she could see piles of two-by-four boards, studs, and trimming.

At the foot of what formally had been magnificent trees were large sandstone blocks. And as they walked a few steps down A Street they could see another standing wall which she recalled had been the entrance to The Thunderegg Dining Room. It was so sad to see the door still intact inviting one inside for a great meal and just as disheartening to see the empty marquee clinging to the top. The sight of the devastation and the No Trespassing Signs made her want to cry.

She was startled when the old man moved closer and glanced up at her and said, "You just passing through? If you want I can tell you the history of the place. I've lived in Vale my entire life."

"No, thanks. I'm just looking," she told him stepping back and getting a good look at him. He looked relatively normal, maybe a tad over eighty years old. He might even have known her grandfather. Any other time, she would have been fascinated to hear the history of the place, but not today. Today, she needed something to eat.

Her stomach began to protest. The old man chuckled good-naturedly. She took a good look at him from his stained cowboy hat sitting cockeyed on his sweat-soaked head, to his baggy jeans needing a hitch-up every so often so as not to fall around his ankles, and finished the examination by studying with curiosity a pair of cracked and dusty leather boots. She should have felt pity for the old geezer. She didn't. He reminded her a lot of her grandpa.

"The place to go is the Wagon Wheel. They have the best barbecue in town. Just walk down there. It's not far. You can't miss it," he said nodding his head in her direction before walking down A Street toward what appeared to be a municipal park and baseball field.

She watched him make his way across the road and onto a sidewalk passing what used to be the Vale Hotel down to a still intact two-story dwelling called The Stone House which had been converted into a museum. Maybe she should have allowed him to regale her with the history of the Slipper. Her stomach reminded her why the old man had recommended the Wagon Wheel. Forced to walk in the designated parking area until she passed the rubble which was once The Golden Slipper, she arrived at the eatery recommended by the old man.

The dim interior of the Wagon Wheel reminded her of countless times in the past when she would enter the Slipper with her grandfather when she was a kid. Back then children were allowed in bars. The old floorboards sagged alarmingly. She made her way to the bar and waited for the bartender to acknowledge her. People were so rude. She stared straight back at the stranger sitting on a barstool who was ogling her and thought about telling him off, but then the bartender noticed her for the first time and gave a low whistle, "Well hello there, sweet thing. What can I do for you?" and Ana began to wonder if everyone had gone bat shit crazy during her sabbatical.

She assumed the bartender was drunk from the odd way he was staring at her. "I don't suppose I could borrow a quarter to make a phone call?"

"No problem sweet cheeks," he said with a wink handing her four quarters. "It's gone up to a dollar. The payphone's in the back near the restrooms."

Ana worried about that wink all the way to the payphone which happened to be between the restrooms marked Cowboy and Cowgirl. Realistically, she had no one she could call without sending the others into fits of rage or tears of betrayal. Even if she could track her family and former colleagues down, they would be hurt by her abandonment and wonder why she'd taken so long to break her silence. Anything she said thereafter would be tainted and might even result in a trip back to Chicago. Dr. B appeared to believe her stories.

Although based on his lack of interest in her former profession and boredom with her observations about his profession, she often doubted his honesty. Maybe his boredom had something to do with his misogyny? He was from a generation which considered women empty headed and ornamental. Or maybe his boredom had to do with his secret resentment of his wife's many successes? Another explanation for his glassy eyed stare and frequent yawns might be simple – he knew exactly what had really happened to her. From the little clues and hints he dropped, she'd often wondered if perhaps he'd been given an incentive to keep her in custody longer than the law allowed.

The incentive wouldn't be money. He had plenty of money. It would have to be something else. Respect. Yes. Respect rang true. Like other mediocre people, he craved respect from his peers. Mystery solved. She hoped she could remember all this later. It might help one day.

Everything will work out for the best. Soon she'll be able to go back to her old life and see her family and teach again. It will happen. It must happen. Her friends had a plan and the plan would unroll without a hitch, in all its intricate glory. Everyone had agreed the plan was full proof. It was only at moments like this, when Ana stared into the smudgy mirror above the dirty sink in a bathroom for Cowgirls, in a place called the Wagon Wheel, when she had doubts, doubts about the plan and doubts about her sanity.

It was difficult to reconcile the lived experiences she remembered with the young woman in the mirror. It just didn't make sense to her how all of them could live in this puny excuse of a body.

There wasn't enough room for a child much less five others. As the one with the most education, she should be able to figure out how all this mess began and how to fix it. She left the bathroom determined to find a solution and found herself in a dim hallway lit by a single bare lightbulb dangling from the ceiling. She searched the dimness and discovered the pay phone with a groan of disbelief.

As she picked up the heavy receiver between her thumb and finger, she wondered how many germs she would encounter by touching the sticky surface, dialing the numbers on the pad, and speaking into the mouthpiece. Probably thousands, she decided, thousands of nasty cold and flu germs for sure because . . .

A – everybody had cellphones nowadays, so the only people in need of a pay phone would be snotty-nosed children, the poor or the very drunk.

B – nobody paid attention to ordinary household equipment.

C – nobody gave a damned about the unseen critters populating the world.

While in the bathroom, she had thought of one person who might help, and that person happened to live only thirty minutes away. She would try his old number and hope and pray he would pick up on the first few rings. Like the old Ana, he'd been hostile toward commitment but sexually faithful. The absence of mad passion kept them friends long after the sex faded. Yes, Bobby would be the one to contact in an emergency.

Whatever his faults, Bobby's redeeming quality was his instinctual desire to help others. And if she asked him, he would keep her existence secret as well. She wasn't ready to reveal herself to the other significant people in her life. And even if she did, she had the panicky feeling they wouldn't recognize her, much less believe her story. But Bobby, she knew private things about Bobby, things he wouldn't want anyone to know. He would keep her secret. And if he was still selling pot on the side, she'd have additional leverage.

Primed and ready to be cheerful and sweet, she was disappointed when she only got his voice messaging service. She changed her mind about the kind of message to leave and chose instead to leave an urgent message signifying an unspecified distress. She was confident Sir Galahad would answer her distress call. Reluctant to leave the anonymity of the hall, Ana had to mentally chastise herself to feel shamed enough to move. She tripped over a loose rug. No one noticed.

There were only two men sitting at the end of the counter, as far away from the door and the late afternoon light as possible, while positioning themselves close to the tiny stage with an uninterrupted view of the whole floor. Their hands were busy lifting glasses, cracking nuts, and waving wild conjectures in the air, so deep into their conversation, they could have been alone in the room. When the bartender saw her, and began to pour her a beer, she shook her head and said, "No thanks. I'm just waiting for a friend."

"The guys bought you this one," he said winking at her.

"I don't drink alcohol."

"How about a soda?"

She accepted the drink and smiled at the middle-aged men then sighed when they took her gesture as an invitation to move closer. Beggars couldn't be choosers; some old duffer had told her. Or had that been her mother? Her mother used a dictionary full of clichés, old adages, and pithy words of wisdom for every occasion, even non-occasions.

Introductions were painlessly brief. First names only. Hugo wore the black cowboy hat and matching boots. Calvin wore the tight-fitting jeans and checkered shirt. He looked as if someone had had to pour him into his clothes. From the cologne wafting her way, she guessed him to be on a serious mission to find himself a woman tonight. There was no clock in the place and no rational reason why she wouldn't know the day of the week and the time of the day. But she could find out the time at least.

Calvin provided her with the time, eager to show her his expensive Rolex as proof that he could buy dinner and a movie without going Dutch. His, "It's seven thirty-five, sugar britches" made her want to retch. Ana made a mental note to complain to the others about her wardrobe. How could she possible be respected wearing such a ridiculous skirt with a pair of army boots?

Sipping her soda, she pretended to listen to the argument between the two men. The argument concerned Iraq and what was going on in the Middle East. Puzzled and alarmed, she listened attentively as they discussed a war that America happened to be in. No, correction there, not present tense, but past tense. Wait, maybe, she was wrong, maybe we were still in this current war? She stored the information away for later. She would find a way of learning more about something called

9/11, not 911. It seemed 9/11 had been the instigator that got them involved in a war.

Knowing nothing about a major war scared her. Why hadn't anyone told her about this war? Dr. B must have known. The staff must have known. Why hadn't they told her? Equally crazy was the reference to the Twin Towers. Did they mean the Two Towers by Tolkien? She peered at them closely, frightened and intrigued. These men didn't look like readers of fantasy fiction. How could she tell for sure? Honestly? And then Calvin noticed her watching him and licked his lower lip suggestively. No. Not Tolkien fans. Maybe the 9/11 War started over something else? Communism? Nah. The Cold War had been over for decades. The 9/11 War wouldn't be the last. This 9/11 had something to do with laundry.

Someone shook her arm. Some of the liquid from her soda slopped over the side of the glass and a few droplets fell on the back of her hand. She stared Calvin down. The vacant look in his eye reminded her of her ex-husband's equally opaque thought processes. It was just easier spewing familiar rhetoric and clichés than doing the demanding work necessary for critical thinking.

"So, what do you think about all this?" Calvin asked.

"You got the time?" she answered with a question, letting him know from her expression that she could care less what he'd been discussing with his idiot drinking buddy. She refused to waste her time or her breath on these morons.

"It's been fifteen minutes since you asked the last time," he said with a wicked smile and followed up with his best repartee. "What's the rush honey? If you need a ride somewheres, I'll be happy to give you a lift," and with a knowing wink continued, "if you know what I mean."

The idea of sitting beside this man in a tight cubicle masquerading as an automobile made her nauseous. She gritted her teeth waiting for the exasperation to pass. His errors in judgement and occasional lapses in grammar bothered her more than the obvious lechery. When his friend stood up and sauntered toward the buffet table, for the first time, she noticed his t-shirt. On the 100% cotton surface of his big belly was emblazoned a face. She knew that face. Then she remembered the recent tragedy. Oh, did everything change because of the 9/11 war?

Hugo noticed her perusal of his shirt and puffed up his chest. She felt as much compassion and sadness for Hugo as she did for the nation. The shirt symbolized something profoundly broken in American politics and in the world. Hugo dished up his empty plate and returned to the bar. Calvin padded his friend's shoulder, "What do you think? Looks good on him, doesn't it?"

"For Sure. Guaranteed to get you a date with a trucker, no doubt about it," Ana found herself saying, not bothering to mention she'd been thinking of her sister when she mentioned truckers. Seconds later, she discovered her words had created an international incident.

Calvin's friend pushed him aside, so he could get a good look at her and said, "Are you saying I'm a . . .?"

"A what?" she shrugged. "I don't understand."

"You saying I'm playing on the other team?"

"You mean that you're a Democrat?"

The old geezer who had recommended the Wagon Wheel to her earlier started laughing and slapping the table. The bartender joined in the laughter. Ana thought she should clarify her remark, "I'm sorry if I gave offense, but when I mentioned a date with a trucker, I was thinking of my sister. My sister is a long-haul trucker. You do know there are women truckers?"

Hugo looked around the room at the curious people watching him. The planes of existence in a small town versus a big city were a different breed of cat. In a big city, a person can disappear into the multitudes and find other likeminded people, but in a small town if you stand out too much you'll be branded an oddball.

"So, you're one of those bleeding-heart liberals, huh?"

"Just because I'm not interested in joining the discussion doesn't mean I'm automatically against you. How about if I agree with you, will you leave me alone then?" she asked.

The bartender's attempts to get her attention were appreciated, but unnecessary. She could take care of herself. Both Hugo and Calvin leaned back and gave her identical astonished looks as if a mouse had suddenly roared.

"We got us a towel-head lover here," Calvin said.

"A what?" she asked impatiently.

All three men looked at her as if she'd lost her senses. Ana was beginning to think she might have because she had no idea what they were talking about. Her ignorance about the epithet exorcized the demons gathering in the room. Any chance to educate an ignorant woman was a treat for these guys. Once they believed her to be a naïve female, the threat to their manhood evaporated. Relieved, the two men resumed their conversation, talking cheerfully about their favorite subject – foreigners in America and foreigners in foreign places.

All Calvin had to say was "You know those towels the Arabs wrap around their heads, that's why we call them towel heads," for her to know what he meant. Instinctively Ana knew Hugo enjoyed provoking her.

Before he had a chance to start a new fight and because she didn't want to hear any more of his crap, she said, "I take it you fellows aren't from around here. I can't imagine anyone local wearing that man's face on his body, especially with the American flag in the background and an American bald eagle flying in the sky. From the barbecue sauce dribbling down the front, it looks like the eagle is crapping on the guy's head. Why would you insult the Stars and Stripes or the American Bald Eagle that way?"

While Hugo bent his head to peer at his t-shirt, Ana turned to Calvin and said, "I suggest you get rid of your wing-man. He isn't giving you the lift off you need. In fact, he is doing just the opposite; he's sabotaging your mission. No. Hold on there. I'm not flirting with you. Far from it. I'm just giving you some advice. I bet if you got rid of Hugo and his infomercial, some fine lady might just come along and snatch you up. It might not hurt to try."

"What's my mission, little lady?" Calvin asked with a smirk.

"I think you're looking for a good woman, someone who'll love you for yourself and keep you company in your old age," she told him.

Hugo chimed in, "She talks weird, doesn't she? Most kids her age don't talk like that. She reminds me of a teacher I used to have, and not in a good way. What's her problem with my shirt?"

"Why don't you go back to Boise, Hugo. I'll hitch a ride home. There's plenty of libtards to piss off in the big city," Calvin threw over his shoulder, smiling at Ana in a disturbing way.

"I haven't finished my dinner yet," he said and walked to a table near the window with his plate. After a moment or two of silence, everyone heard Hugo say, "I thought you were about bros-before-hoes, Man, but you're just a traitor like all the rest."

Soon Ana could go back to thinking her own private thoughts.

"Earth to Bernice," Ana heard from her right. She turned in time to see Calvin inching closer. Well, slithering would be closer to the truth. Yuck.

"Hey, sugar britches where you been? You look to be a million miles away, darling."

"What time is it?" she asked glancing at the front door which the bartender had left partially open. It must be summer because there was still sunlight streaming through the crack in the door.

"Eight-thirty," the bartender said. She glanced down at her soda. Her soda had been replaced with a new glass and the new glass had ice chips floating on the top.

Bobby wasn't coming.

She looked Calvin in the eye, "So that's the worst epithet you can call them huh? Towel-heads," she said with a sneer.

"Epa what?"

"A derogatory label."

"Derogatory? Is that bad?"

"We've got all sorts of nasty-mean epithets for other nationalities and races and religions, but the worst one you can come up with for these guys, who you claim have killed civilians in public places is towel-heads. Why do you think that is? Hum? You think maybe deep down inside you sort of admire them, that maybe their brutality answers your own instinctual pleasure in brutality? Or are you attempting to demean an entire culture? I don't know what your motivation may be, but if someone were to call me a towel head or cap head or dyed head, I would just laugh in their faces and think they were a bunch of dumb-ass idiots."

The bellowing from within began before Ana finished her speech and though Ana did her best to fight off the assault, Acacia broke free. Leona warned them all that their immediate goals were fast vanishing, so Frankie made an executive decision. Acacia was chosen as clean-up crew. Damned if Frankie and the others would let Ana sidetrack them by upsetting the locals and creating an incident. They didn't want trouble. They didn't want the police delaying their mission and messing with their timetable. Ana thought she could get out of any situation with clever words. Sometimes words only made the situation worse. Not everyone dealt with the world intellectually.

When Acacia jumped off the barstool and surveyed the room with a sneer, the men sitting next to her and the bartender watching in bemusement were unable to reconcile the sudden change in the young woman with their own gut reactions to her. They'd gone from being mildly entertained by the stranger's behavior, the way one is tickled by the cleverness of a toddler to being terrified. Years later, they would ruminate over what had happened that day convinced they'd been a witness to something supernatural.

The poor posture and intellectual snootiness vanished. In their place stood a tall athletic woman with feet slightly apart and a back as straight as a 2 by 4 block of cedar. The posture wasn't the only giveaway that something was truly out of kilter though. It was the foreign expression in the eyes and something menacing about the mouth. Because this new woman stood taller and appeared meaner than the one they'd been talking to just a few seconds ago, some in the room with better sense, looked away and pretended a new found interest in their dinners. The little lady wearing the scarf skirt and army boots surveyed the room with the cold disgust of a marine sergeant surveying his troops. "Where the fried-shit am I now?" she asked staring pointedly at the bartender.

"You're where you've been for the last hour or so ma'am, in the Wagon Wheel," the bartender said with an uneasy smile.

"I meant what town?"

"Vale, Oregon. You're in Vale, Oregon ma'am."

The man sitting closest to her tried to grab her arm, "Come on honey. Come back and I'll educate you about your epa-whats-evers. There's a damned good reason we call them towel-heads."

By the time Calvin Dale found himself on the floor staring up at the bartender, Acacia had left. The bartender was staring at something near the entrance. Calvin turned his head to see what was so fascinating. Someone had flung open the big double doors and left them open. Late afternoon light transformed the dull beige hallway, its ceiling, walls, and floor a stormy violet. On the threshold of the bar in the pool of violet light stood an elderly couple. They peeked into the room with their eyes wide. Calvin heard the woman say to her companion, "I wished I'd had my camera. Nobody's going to believe us, Georgie."

"How'd she do that Calvin?" the bartender asked in a muffled voice.

Debating for a moment whether or not to assist his bros-before-hos fair-weather friend, Hugo Frank left his drink on the table and reached down to clasp his friend's hand, "You alright buddy? Did she sucker punch you? That's the only way she could have done it."

Calvin struggled to his feet until all of his six feet three inches were vertical. Wearing his size thirteen boots, weighing in at a stringy but tough one hundred-and-eighty-five pounds, he debated within himself on his next move. Then planted his butt back on the barstool and tried to ignore his friend. He sneaked a peek at the bartender and shook his bottle of beer. They could hear the liquid slosh around in the bottom. He said to him, "Give me two more for the road, Bob."

As he rubbed his right arm remembering how she'd yanked him effortlessly to the floor, the occupants of the room resumed their places and the newly arrived customers found an empty table near the window. The old man turned to Bob, "I'll have a scotch and soda. How's the food here? Pretty good?"

His wife chimed in, "If you're going to drink, I'm driving the rest of the way to Burns."

Calvin refused to meet anyone's eyes. He figured he'd have bruises by morning, nasty ones too. After a moment's reflection, he suspected he'd dodged something far worse than an STD.

17

Once outside the Wagon Wheel squinting at the street signs to get her bearings, Frankie asserted herself completely. At this critical moment, muscle was the last skill they needed. What they needed was her talent for creative economics and acquisition of critical assets. She sneered at the others. All of them assumed one had to have cash in hand to do anything. Amateurs. She'd been on the streets most of her adult life. She knew how to sell, and she knew how to find the ideal customer.

Well, that one time, she'd been duped. Of course, she'd made the most rooky of mistakes feeling sorry for the upset white woman with the MOP mentality; yet in retrospect, Frankie had survived the experience and even made a profit from her pain.

The moment of panic subsided once Frankie took charge. She pushed her way to the front of the line concerned their foolish mistakes would get them noticed and arrested. She heard a desperate voice calling out to her reminding her of their plan and their destination. As if she could forget. Wasn't she the bread winner of this group?

Wasn't it a fact the sales of her books had grossed over six figures last year; while Ana's literary fiction barely made the finish line at four figures? So what if a few reviews by some stuffy academics brought her respect in the literary world? You couldn't keep yourself warm and fed on a good review, now could you? The irony of it all was how much more time Ana's stuffy books took to get published compared to the speed of Frankie's little paperbacks moving from her computer monitor into her bank account.

There was nothing more real than writing a piece of fiction based on one's own experiences while ignoring the tawdry parts and embellishing the lifestyle. The world loved sin, especially if they could live vicariously in a sinful world but know themselves to be safe, superior, and distant from its consequences.

Rich sinners were so much more fun to read about because they were above moral and civil laws and capable of doing outrageous things with impunity. She supposed her writing attracted voyeurs. So what? The average reader, after a day fighting traffic, clueless bosses and/or cranky kids just wants to relax at the end of the day and read something that doesn't require a dictionary, preferably something simple with a familiar beginning that excludes taboo subjects like poverty, immigrants, and politics. It must have an exciting nail-biting plot and a satisfying conclusion. And if some of it includes sex, torture, and the occult, they love it even more.

Standing in the hot sun, Frankie finally realized her briefcase was missing. It was a habit of hers to jot down a to-do-list. At the moment she wanted to remind herself to contact her agent about her book sales for last month. But when she looked down she realized Leona had dressed them today in a ridiculous purple and pink swirling skirt and what appeared to be army boots. How could she attract a buyer wearing army boots? She needed her laptop and her cellphone and her scheduler right away. For a nanosecond, a wave of uncertainty assaulted her. She felt naked and exposed without her stuff. Where was the Taurus with her luggage, laptop, briefcase and cellphone?

On her side of the street there were several red brick buildings and a rubble of brick and fallen beams on the corner. Next to the rubble above a shop were curtained windows which suggested apartments. Across the street, she noticed a store catering to farmers and ranchers. On the opposite side, next to Winkle's Five & Dime, a middle aged woman wearing slacks and a conservative blouse entered the door of Lucy's Beauty Salon while down the block three teens were huddled together watching the screen on a friend's cellphone. The town was so small it didn't even have a stop light or neon signs. Nor did she see a means of transportation such as a cab or a bus stop.

She frowned in concentration. Without money or a car, her only option would be to do what she'd done in the past. But unfortunately, this town wasn't exactly a hotbed of sin. She would stand out like a magpie among doves if she tried to attract a customer. The last thing she wanted to do was to call attention to herself and find the police cruising by and asking her uncomfortable questions. Evidently, she'd been standing too long on this particular corner because a farmer in a truck full of dogs waved at her. Someone tapped her on the shoulder and she spun around wondering if she'd attracted the police already.

But the man standing behind her looked harmless enough. She could usually size up a guy. This one's smile reached his eyes. "Hi. I saw what you did in there," he said pointing back to the Wagon Wheel Bar and Grill, its sign offering the best barbecue in town. "I was impressed. Nice job. What was that, judo or something?"

"I have no idea," she said and surveyed him with interest. He looked to be over twenty-one and under thirty. His hair had been cut close to his ears in front and left to grow an inch or two longer in the back. He'd shaved this morning too. All good signs. He also had clear brown eyes and a sweet smile. The ubiquitous baseball cap, a green felt one with orange stitching, sat tight on his shapely head. She also noticed he wore loose blue jeans and expensive hiking boots. His polo shirt accentuated his broad chest and muscled arms. Altogether he looked clean and presentable.

From what she could tell as he glanced back at the Wagon Wheel, he had clean, well-groomed hair. Then he took off his cap to wipe the sweat from his brow and she realized that he was prematurely balding. How sad. No wonder he seemed so shy. Some Johns equated balding with impotency which was completely ridiculous. Impotency had more to do with the inside than the outside of a man's head. She'd discovered long ago that some men who were impotent also happened to be cruel, nasty creatures that should have been aborted before they were ever allowed to leave the womb.

Straight away Frankie realized her good fortune and made a point of being extra nice to her prospective customer. She didn't want to alarm him so she used her lack of knowledge about the town in the hopes her stranded condition would appeal to his chivalry. It was a relief to discover he possessed a sense of chivalry. Some males were born without it, or most likely, they had never been properly trained.

After smiling up at him, he invited her to dinner implying he would pay. At her look of consternation, wondering if she dare go back inside the Wagon Wheel and confront Acacia's mess, her customer quickly assured her there was another restaurant in town. She agreed to go with him. They walked to the restaurant. She soon discovered the restaurant was only six blocks away on the outskirts of town. Brian chose a booth near the window and sat facing the door. Frankie sat on the opposite side and looked around while Brian joked with the waitress. She must have been someone's great, great, grandmother but still spry and susceptible to flattery.

"I'll have my usual aperitif Lucy, my sweet angel," he said with a grin.

Lucy glanced down at Frankie and said, "He's one strange fella ain't he, young lady? He always orders dessert first. How's that for putting the cart before the horse?"

The waitress handed Frankie a sticky menu and trotted away to serve coffee to another customer.

Frankie leaned over the table, "Is she your mother?"

Brian laughed, "No. But she thinks she is. I've known Lucy forever."

A few minutes later, Lucy returned carrying two vanilla ice cream cones. She handed one to Brian and the other to her. Frankie hadn't asked for one but mentally shrugged and decided when in Rome do what the Romans do.

"I thought you ordered an aperitif?" she asked.

"I did."

"But."

"But what?" he asked taking a huge bite out of the ice cream on top of his cone.

She hesitated wondering if she should correct him. It wasn't all that important in any case. So what if he thought an aperitif was a dessert.

"Nothing. Just wondered if you'd been to France."

"Oh you're thinking of the word I used: aperitif. It's nothing. Just an inside joke. How about you? Have you been to France?"

"No. But I met a bunch of Frenchmen in Vegas once. Their reputation is exaggerated, believe me."

"Reputation as what?"

"You know – great lovers."

Brian broke out in a fit of coughing and covered his mouth with his napkin. When he recovered enough to speak, something had changed between them. His joking mood had been replaced with a new reserve she found uncomfortable. She could have kicked herself for mentioning Vegas and the Frenchmen. That had been stupid.

Brian licked the last of the ice cream off the top of his cone and finally asked, "What happened to him?" before popping the rest into his mouth.

Frankie's head hurt so bad she thought she might throw up. She closed her eyes.

Ana looked around the room. She was in a diner, a small town diner sitting across from a handsome man in his thirties who happened to be eating an ice cream cone and smiling at her. He asked her a question, "What happened to him?" She got the impression this hadn't been the first time he'd asked her that question.

"To whom, ah, who?" Ana asked remembering she was supposed to be linguistically challenged. She had to wait a moment or two until he'd swallowed the cone.

"Your boyfriend. I'm assuming you two had a fight back in the Wagon Wheel."

The food arrived on hot steaming plates and Ana waited until they'd been served before answering. While Brian cut his steak and chewed, she told the stranger she'd had a fight with her friend, a friend who ditched her. She did her best not to stare as Brian chomped away on his steak. She'd always had a good sense of people. But lately? The napkin in her hand occupied her attention long enough for him to finish swallowing.

"You're from?" he asked with interest.

At some time in her life, she'd been told if you're going to lie, stick as close to the truth as possible. The thought of lying though made her physically ill. The headache returned. Frankie had no such qualms about lying. She'd thought of dozens of them while impatiently awaiting her chance to reassert herself and without hesitation told the puritan sitting across from her, "The Midwest. Can't you tell from my Canadian twang?"

"I have a few friends there."

"All of the Midwest? That's a lot of territory," she said trying with difficulty to hide her mistrust.

"Oh yeah," he said with a half-hearted laugh. "I guess my attempt at a joke didn't go over so well, huh?"

Not really," Frankie said realizing too late she'd probably offended him once again and tried to make amends in a rush of words. "I don't feel comfortable telling people I barely know, my life story. TMI, you know."

"What's that?" he asked.

"You know," she said throwing up her hands and smiling. "Too much information."

"Where's home?"

"Ah, you wouldn't know it."

"I know most every place in the Midwest. I used to drive truck for a living."

Frankie searched desperately in her memory for a town and settled on one she'd known briefly a long time ago. "St. Cloud. I live in St. Cloud. Well, actually I'm homeless right now. I decided I wanted to see the world and find a place to settle down where the temperature remains a constant 70 degrees."

"Really? St. Cloud? That's a tough place to live. Winters are nasty."

"Yeah, well that's true."

"So you're stranded?"

"Yes. It's complicated. My friends wanted to go on a road trip. We rented a minivan and took off. It didn't work out. When it got claustrophobic traveling in the van with six women, four of them decided to return home. Then there were only the two of us left and we didn't need the minivan, so we turned in the minivan for a compact. The last thing I remember is having a few drinks somewhere between Idaho and Oregon. We must have had a fight because when I sobered up, my friend was gone and so was the rental. A nice police officer in Adrian drove me here. I thought for sure my friend would be waiting for me. We'd made plans to travel the back roads to California. She has everything, my luggage and my purse."

"Alcohol," he said nodding his head knowingly. "Sometimes drinking can turn friend into foe. You know what I mean?"

"So true," Frankie said with relief. She kept her eyes on her plate and cut her steak carefully.

"I noticed you hardly touched your beer in the Wagon Wheel," he said. Their eyes met for a moment. A twinge of unease settled on her shoulders. He'd been watching her too closely and that made her uncomfortable. All sorts of reasons chased themselves around in her head until she realized with relief – of course – she'd been the only female under forty in the place. And she wasn't all that bad looking. It would only be natural that he would have noticed how much she drank.

A voice in her head said, "You need cash. Find a way to get yourself some cash. Money isn't the root of all evil. Money makes the world go round. Come on. You can do it."

Since he was such an excellent observer of human nature, Frankie would take the opportunity later to capitalize on his interest in her but for now she needed cash. A conversation about money might elicit the kind of arrangement beneficial to her and him. "Does this town have a Western Union or a place where money could be wired to the local bank?"

He shook his head sadly from side to side and for a moment he looked embarrassed as if the town's lack of business acumen was a personal reflection on him. "No. Not here in Vale; but there are several banks in Ontario and Ontario is only a hop, skip, and a jump away."

"A hop, skip and a jump," she said with a genuine smile. She hadn't heard that idiom used in a long time.

He shrugged and grinned, "You know. It means not far."

"Oh yes. I'm familiar with the phrase. I just haven't heard it in a long time."

"So you have folks willing to send you money huh?" he asked absently as he bit into his steak.

"My accountant can send me the necessary money, maybe, even arrange for me to rent a car. If there is a place to rent a car around here," Frankie said. "Ontario. Right?"

"Yeah. It's Ontario but Ontario has only one rent-a-car business and I wouldn't recommend him. The closest town that might be able to help you would be Boise and Boise is only forty-five minutes to an hour by car."

"Boise is east of here isn't it?" she asked pretending complete ignorance.

"Yes. But as I said, it's the closest big city around. Boise will have your bank where you can cancel your credit cards or debit cards and get travelers checks too."

"Well, I'd rather not travel backward. It's best I keep going west."

"So what were your plans? I mean where did you and your friend decide to end your trip?"

"The ocean," she said off the top of her head.

"That's a lot of territory to search."

"I don't think so. I got a feeling I'll be meeting her soon."

"I'm sure you will," he said with a smile and padded her hand. "We'll figure out how to get you on your way. Don't you worry."

Frankie struggling to keep up the charade that she found his conversation interesting, tried to push away a gathering hot flash. She so hated those damned hot flashes. Had she eaten too much sugar? Sugar always made her body temperature soar. Frankie wiped her sweating upper lip with her napkin and between the seconds this motion took to the moment she opened her mouth to speak she found herself once more in charge of the situation.

By the time they'd finished eating dinner and gotten through the preliminary getting-to-know-you phase of the unspoken contract (which happened more often than most people realized) Brian got down to business. Surprised by his savvy, she responded cautiously having been taken in once by an undercover cop posing as a john. "Well that's kind of you to offer me money, but all I need is access to a phone in order to call my accountant. I'll get to Ontario by taxi, I guess, and rent a car, then find my way to the ocean. Once I've found my friend, I'll be able to return the rental car and fly home. No problem."

He leaned forward with an earnest look in his eye, "But even if you get to Ontario, you need identification to rent a car and drive. Since your friend has all your identification cards, what will you do?"

Frankie slashed the air dismissively, "No problem. Eve will cool down eventually. I've known her a long time. At first, she'll be angry, then feeling guilty. She'll find me."

"How will she get in touch with you if you don't have a phone?" he asked softly.

"Well, I can call her boyfriend, I guess, and leave a message with him," she said looking around the restaurant at the three customers and the one waitress.

"Wait, that won't work because I don't know where I'll be," she shrugged, pretending indifference. "I can't stay here. Oh well. Something will turn up. It always does. She might be looking for me right now, as-we-speak."

Frankie read friendly concern in the man's eyes and when he asked, "What will you do in the meantime?" she wondered if he was leading up to something, maybe offering her his couch for the night or access to a spare bedroom.

Instinct told her there was something off about him. He asked a lot of questions for someone who seemed disinterested in her situation. It was frustrating that he hadn't offered to drive her to Ontario. Time was running out. Had she lost her touch? The crust from the apple pie melted on her tongue. Her taste buds went ballistic. She'd have to remember this place.

Eve especially liked the look of farmer Brian, friendly but reserved.

Acacia couldn't stand him. He was a nosey middle-aged fart.

Leona thought he might have been in the military.

Ana found him a total bore without an ounce of social and political curiosity.

Frankie was pretty sure he was another SOP. It was time to switch gears and find a way to safely remove herself from this gluey guy. An older man she figured to be twenty years Brian's senior, tall and lean with the walk of a competent horseman entered the restaurant and spotted Brian. He approached Brian and slapped him on the back, "Well, I see you've taken my advice sheriff," he said glancing down at her. "Having fun on the first summer of your early retirement?"

Brian ignored the dig and introduced them, "Scott this is Frankie Stewart. She came into town just this afternoon. It seems she was left stranded by a friend."

"Wouldn't call that guy a friend little lady," Scott said with a condescending chuckle she found especially irritating. But Frankie kept a tight smile plastered to her lips as the two of them exchanged insults disguised as jokes. She'd met guys like Scott before. They swaggered and told stories but had little more to offer than the next guy. He was a small irritant compared to the new knowledge farmer Brian used to be a sheriff.

Had he been sheriff of this town? What did Scott mean by retired? He wasn't old enough to retire. She worried about why he'd chosen to pick her up and rescue her. All this time, had he been checking her out, doing his good cop routine? Maybe he could tell she was lying or he had some sort of instinct she might be in the trade.

Her brain shut down for a moment and then something Brian said to Scott caught her attention, "Hey Scott. You still heading down to Klamath Falls tomorrow? Ms. Stewart's stranded here and she needs to get to a bank. Maybe she could hitch a ride with you?"

Scott glanced at her speculatively and said, "You know I can't take passengers Brian. Monroe would spit bricks."

Frankie decided she'd had enough of Brian's game. She pushed her chair back and stood up. Brian followed suit with a smile of curiosity. He waited for her to speak. She forced a smile, "Thank you so much for lunch, Mr. Butler. I wish I could return the favor. If you'll give me your address, I'll be sure to reimburse you."

Brian looked shocked, "No way. It was my treat. It's been a pleasure getting to know you Ms. Stewart."

As she moved toward the door, he stopped her, "Hold on there, Frankie. Where are you off to? You gonna walk all the way to the ocean?"

"Well, no, of course not, but maybe someone might be heading to Ontario and I can get a lift from them?"

Scott stepped back indicating his lack of interest and smiled perfunctorily in her general direction then wandered toward a table near the counter where several old men were sitting at a booth playing chess. Brian dropped his napkin on the table and said, "I wish I could help you Frankie, but I'm not allowed to drive."

Frankie surveyed him carefully hoping her face registered only mild interest, "Really, but didn't that man call you sheriff?"

"I was until I got my second DUI," he said shrugging as if every policeman had similar problems. "Now I'm taking it a day at a time."

"I see. So, you used to be the sheriff here in Vale?"

"Oh no. My grandfather owned a ranch in Vale before I was born. My Dad talked about the ranch all the time. I joined the air force after graduation. After being deployed, I wanted to see the country. I've been all over North and South America. Finally, I settled down when I ran for sheriff. It's a small town like this one called Mintlaw. In Idaho. Have you heard of it, Mintlaw, Idaho?"

"No. I'm not familiar with Idaho. Well, thanks again for the meal. Good-bye," she said moving surreptitiously toward the door.

A pained look crossed his face, as if he regretted divulging so much personal information to a stranger. She empathized with him having gone through the same experiences. Those AA meetings where your counselor warns you constantly that 'lying makes you sick' and 'admitting to yourself and others you have no control over your drinking" affects every facet of your life. Soon the urge to confess spreads like an oil spill across the waters of everyday lived experience and you find yourself telling complete strangers that you're a recovering alcoholic, and no, you'd rather drink lighter fluid than a cold beer.

At least she'd managed to get a meal out of the brief partnership; and as a bonus without laying on her backside to pay for it. They left the diner together and stood awkwardly in the parking lot unable to think of anything else to say. Frankie noticed a couple of teenagers filling up at the gas station next door to the diner. They seemed to belong to the expensive yellow Hummer. Behind the Hummer, a trailer hedged in by fancy wrought iron rails contained two jet skis and what appeared to be a catamaran. She estimated the total cost to be around $50,000.00 for the vehicle and the toys.

One of the boys circling the vehicle and fancy trailer protectively was making sure the ropes, hooks, and chains were secure. The other one walked inside the gas station.

She pointed at the kids and Brian glanced over his shoulder, "Maybe they might give me a lift to Ontario? Do you know them?"

"No," he said scrutinizing them carefully. "Don't know them. They're definitely not local."

She made motions to leave, "Well thanks again Mr. Butler for everything."

"Call me Brian."

"Brian," she said and started walking backward. "It's been nice meeting you."

"Hold on there," he said as if he had an idea. "I think I might be able to help you. If you'd like I could give my friend a call. He is a deputy sheriff here and he might be able to find someone to give you a lift."

"You've been so much help, I don't want to impose any further. I'll just ask those kids over there for a lift."

"Kids?" he said with a puzzled expression.

She turned to look at the boys and pointed helpfully, "Well yeah. Those guys, the ones with the jet skis."

Brian took off his cap and ran his hand over his bald spot then put his cap back on, "Ok. I'm totally confused. I'm going to try to keep an open mind Frankie," he said, then hesitated as if wondering how to proceed. Something about him had changed, a reversal in perception. He looked angry. What had she said that had made him so angry?

"I mean I told Bob if he ever served a minor again in his bar, I'd personally drag him down to the county jail. He admitted he hadn't asked you for identification which worked out because you didn't drink anything but a coke. At first," he said with a raised finger. "Then those guys bought you a beer and you took a sip. Maybe a sip isn't a federal crime, but it doesn't look good for our town. Even though I'm retired, I still consider myself an officer of the law.

I should have dragged you out of the bar, but I didn't. Then you did that martial arts stuff on Calvin and I got a kick out of the surprise on his face. It showed you can take care of yourself. At the diner," he said pointing at the restaurant, "you told me all this crazy stuff about having an accountant and wanting to wire money to the nearest bank. Well, if you're so rich, why not call your parents and have them hire a rental for you in Ontario? And what about those fancy words you used to impress those goons back at the Wagon? Are you a child prodigy? You sure sounded like one. I've seen kids on television as young as five who talk like Einstein, so yeah, it's possible. Yet, in the next breath your propositioning me like you're ah, well, a hooker."

When she opened her mouth to defend herself, he raised his hand for silence and then pointed at the Hummer, "But when I hear you refer to those guys over there as kids, I'm wondering what sort of crazy you really are?"

As he outlined his concerns about her mental stability, Frankie took cautious steps backwards trying to put as much space as possible between them, in the event he tried to grab her with the intention of making a citizen's arrest. With each bullet point, the volume of Brian's voice climbed into the higher decibels and she fleetingly considered running. He was so wrapped up in his emotions, he seemed oblivious to her cautious attempts to separate herself from him. One step backward, then another, and another and the distance between them widened.

Then his policeman's instinct took over and he moved in trying to establish his authority again. And all the while she thought: What was his point? What did he mean by minor? A minor was someone under age. Good God. Most of her life had been spent in and around bars with her Dad and Mom and then her husband. The good times all went to shit when he died in Iraq. Don't go there Frankie. Yes, nicotine and alcohol were in her blood, most certainly in her DNA by now.

The truth dawned and the truth made her dizzy. Her mental image of herself and her life experiences were foreign to the body she inhabited. She accepted the situation in this moment, in the here and now. This multitude of being made sense to her. But how to explain such an epiphany to him? What would pacify him? Her most recent awareness of the multiverse of existences within one psyche would only confuse him? Someone had once told her about a philosopher named Nietzsche and how Nietzsche had said there was no such thing as truth.

Frankie thought perhaps Nietzsche meant a person created his or her own truth and truth depended on what a person's experiences and beliefs had created over his or her lifetime. And the only truth real to her, as real as the army boots on her feet and the swirling dervish skirt on her hips were her friends: those women who had proven repeatedly their honorable intentions, their strength of purpose, and their trustworthiness. They were her truth and everything else was a lie.

"I'm a geek. Big deal. I like being around older people. I like being around smart people, people who challenge me intellectually. Get over it mister," she said with a shrug. "I refuse to apologize for being me. I have a baby face. That's not my fault. It's just genetics, you know. And if I had my driver's license on me, I could prove I am of legal age to drink. But my friend has my stuff, so here we are again – in a state of inertia."

"I want to believe you," Brian admitted and stood with his hands on his hips. His eyes tracked something behind her. She turned in time to see the kids climbing into the Hummer preparing to leave. This was her only opportunity. She glanced back at Brian, "I've got to go. Thanks, and good-bye." She ran toward the Hummer.

As she stepped onto the sidewalk, she heard Brian shout, "What exactly does inertia mean anyway?"

The driver of the Hummer dumped his package inside the vehicle and was just climbing inside. The other guy finished tightening a loose rope which held the catamaran tight to the rails. He landed on the asphalt with the ease of youth and was walking toward the passenger side of the Hummer. Frankie reached the window of the driver's side door and forced what she hoped was a sweet smile onto her unwilling lips. The man inside glanced down at her with an appreciative smile. His response was disconcerting. Rarely did young men look so eager and happy to see her. Most of the time, they were all business wanting a quickie before going home to their wives, girlfriends or lonely beds.

"Hey, I was wondering if you could give me a lift. I'm stranded and need a ride. Would you be willing to take me to—"?

"Don't say Boise," he groaned with his eyes alight raking her from head to toe. "We've just come from there. It would be mad if you wanted to go to say, Cali, maybe see the ocean, maybe ride a few waves?" he asked with a hopeful grin.

Frankie wondered if she had the patience necessary to sit in a vehicle with two young males for hours on end. She debated whether to find a phone at the diner and beg a few quarters off the old waitress instead. Someone else thought otherwise and pushed her ambiguity aside with ruthless enthusiasm.

Relieved beyond measure and taking this moment as a sign that luck was finally on her side, Eve jumped up and down and squealed with delight, "Oh my God! That's so wonderful. That's where I'm going. Isn't it amazing? All along I've been trying to find somebody in this place that's going to Cali and here you are. Honestly, you're going to Cali? And you'll take me?"

"Hey dude, move your ass in the back and let the hottie sit here," the driver said padding the passenger seat. He was still young enough to be anxious about the possibility this 'hottie' would change her mind.

And then they were off. Eve sat in the front and looked out the window at the beauty of the countryside as the canary yellow Hummer drove out of Vale, Oregon. It wasn't long before the young men grew impatient with her silence and her continued obsession with the view. According to their thinking, she should be concentrating all her attention upon them. It was only fair since they were doing her a big favor.

In Klamath Falls on the corner of 5th and Main, the "dudes" eagerly let Acacia out of the Hummer. No one had any energy or enthusiasm left to fake their real desire – the urgent need to separate themselves from each other without involving the cops. Enduring five hours of banal conversations about surfing, drinking, and dirty jokes had given Acacia a major headache. She must have slept most of the trip. If not, she suspected she would have done them an injury.

The smaller one who had been forced to sit in the backseat the entire trip eagerly climbed out of the Hummer, saying, "I'm shotgun again," and opened the passenger door making himself comfortable next to the driver. He had a nick on his forehead, just a small curved indention where someone's nail had left a mark. On the right side of the driver's face, she noticed a black eye and an ugly bruise on his cheek.

Ah, oh, had she done that? She supposed she should apologize. Fuck that noise, she thought, I'm too hungry and they probably deserved it. The driver had enough energy to grimace and give her the thumbs up sign. He looked like one of those frightened horses, his pupils dilated with his eyeballs wide open. He watched her from the whites of his eyeballs sort of pretending not to look but too tense not to be vigilant, as if at any moment, she might lunge at him and bite his head off. His frightened expression made her want to laugh. The vehicle tore away from the curb leaving rubber behind.

After walking a bit, she found a place that might accommodate her. The creepy motel had one redeeming factor; there was a restaurant across the street selling pizza and beer. She crossed the street ignoring the pedestrians waiting patiently for the light to change. The motorists honked angrily at her threatening to run her over. As if they would. When Acacia's body met the cool air conditioning inside, she smiled. Nice. The man and woman exiting the place glanced nervously in her direction. In a moment of clarity, Acacia realized she had no freaking fucking money on her. Shit a brick. Fuck a duck.

"Where's your bathroom?" she asked the clerk at the counter who had just set a large cheese pizza on the pick-up counter and rung the bell. Acacia breathed in the delicious aroma and her mouth began to water.

He pointed toward a hallway to his left. She walked down the hallway furiously thinking about how she could miraculously get some cash and book a room in the shitty motel across the street. The women's bathroom was all her own. She entered the stall furthest from the door and a voice inside her head told her to take off her right boot. She shook the boot and a thin wad of cash fell to the floor along with a couple of credit cards. Now why hadn't she used them in Vale? Frankie could be such a cheap bitch sometimes.

As she looked at herself in the bathroom mirror, Frankie cursed her stupidity. Her regular voice sounded as if she'd been smoking two packs a day for twenty years. Well, she had smoked two packs a day for twenty years. Her street vocabulary also must have seemed odd to the people in the restaurant. She thought about going away, sinking back into the abyss of her dark thoughts. But nothing happened. The continued silence frightened her. The others remained stubbornly mute. They were pissed off at her.

She remembered walking out of the bathroom earlier and into the pizza parlor. She remembered ordering a pizza and several bottles of beer. A couple of guys came up to her table and asked if they could join her. One of them had a deck of cards. She remembered having the time of her life eating pizza, drinking beer, and screwing the SOPs out of their daddies' money.

A void swallowed her up and she hid in the stall waiting for the trembling to go away. Eventually, Leona's butt got sore and she stood up, flushed the toilet, and made herself leave the stall. The woman washing her hands at the bathroom sink ignored Leona. Leona washed her hands repeatedly searching for the courage to walk out of the bathroom and confront the pizza employees and the customers, all strangers to her, all she suspected shocked by her behavior. She was sure she had done something wrong; she just couldn't remember what she had done.

When she made herself leave the bathroom and step into the room decorated like a cabin in the woods with a fake fire lit by electric logs as a centerpiece and dead antelope hanging from the wall, she paused wondering if she had walked into the wrong room. She backtracked toward the bathrooms and glanced into another room where she remembered she had been sitting. She returned to an empty table littered with used napkins, dirty glasses, and bits of pizza still clinging to the tray. Part of her mind acknowledged alarm while another part sagged in relief as if she'd been given a reprieve from an unpleasant root canal. Leona realized she would have to do some damage control.

A woman with a black apron tied around her tiny waist walked into the room in a cautious manner as if she thought she might be thrown out at any moment. God had Frankie threatened to hit her? While the waitress talked, Leona studied the name tag pasted to the white blouse. She must be a new employee. Or maybe they gave convention style temporary name tags to every employee due to high turnover? The name on the paper tag was written in black permanent marker and Leona couldn't help but wonder why a grown woman would make her y look like a shrimp tail.

The waitress paused with her hands close to her belly as if preparing to recite a poem, "The guys at the table by the window said they were impressed. They said that they'd never seen someone so honest before. Yeah," she said as if convincing herself she had got the message right. "They said something that sounded French – bushwah something. That the bushwah needed to be shook up, that money was just paper after all. And they were wrong, and you were right; a flush beats a straight. I hope I got the message right. They gave me a nice tip too," she acknowledged with a self-congratulatory smile. She thrust an envelope into Leona's hand and told her, "They asked me to give this to you."

Leona peeked inside and discovered ten twenty-dollar bills. She nodded politely to the woman and left the restaurant. The sight and smell of the money brought a tingling through Leona's entire body and a voice began to scream in her head. She let the triumphant Frankie out. "Ten Jacksons," she said kissing the envelope. "Oh, my sweet poke. You did it again."

As Frankie squeezed the envelope full of money, she hurried across the street anticipating a lovely warm shower and lovely night's sleep alone in a big king-sized bed. Wow, she thought, this time she didn't have to lie down in some smelly motel room and fake an orgasm; instead, all she had to do to make a few bucks was to impress some strangers who did not like bushwahs. Acacia had wanted to mess-up those dudes for acting ignorant. Good thing she hadn't. Once Frankie was clean and rested, she'd find a ride out of town.

The best plan would be to find a likely looking John preferably married, middle aged, and from out of town on his way to California. As she crossed the one-way street and headed toward the AAA Motel, she looked around in the hopes of finding a likely looking prospect. At this time of day, the streets should have been filled back to back with people. Instead the town looked dead. Was it Sunday? She didn't think so.

It was nearly dusk, and Frankie realized with a throbbing between her eyes she didn't even know the day or month or the year. The last date she remembered had been March 5th, the day she left the hospital. Today the intensity of the heat outside and relentless rays of the sun indicated a much later time of season, perhaps July or August. For the most part, the people she passed or watched as they drove by in their cars were wearing shorts, light dresses or skirts, sandals, and sneakers. Their pale washed-out look of winter was long since gone. Most had healthy tans or nasty sunburns.

Then she saw a banner across the street. The banner was attached to the top of a chain linked fence in front of a dealership selling all sorts of boats and water apparatus: *4th of July Sale Extended, Prices Reduced 20%.* It must be sometime after Independence Day. Why had it taken three months to travel fifteen hundred miles? What had happened between March 5th and now? A voice had been screaming at her for days, "Get to Crescent City, California. Don't forget Crescent City, California."

Another voice said, "Look in your right boot next time, cheapskate."

Frankie marched toward the AAA Motel. She would find a way to rent a room for the night and then trawl for potential customers. First, she would need to take a shower and change into some more suitable clothes. Then she remembered she didn't have any identification. She entered the motel office with different possibilities swirling around in her head. The AAA Motel looked familiar and just one night's lodging would cost her seventy of her two hundred dollars. She would pay with cash and give them a false name and address.

It was best to stay close to the truth, well as close as she dared. The clerk behind the counter might have been any age between forty and sixty and looked as if she'd seen all types come through those doors. The wrinkles between her eyes and around her nose and mouth indicated someone who hadn't bothered to smile in years. Frankie remembered to use a young sweet voice and the appropriate vocabulary. "Hi there, ma'am. I was wondering if I could rent a room for the night."

"Are you over eighteen?" she asked suspiciously.

"Yes. Of course. My boyfriend and I had a fight. He took off. I don't know where he went."

"Do you have any identification?" she asked, opening a drawer, and pulling out a card for Frankie to fill out.

"That's the trouble. He's got everything: my suitcase, my purse, everything."

"Ah huh," she said without blinking.

"I can pay though," Frankie said hurriedly sensing the woman was going to throw her out. She pointed to the pizza place and turned to look into the woman's eyes hoping she exuded just the right amount of sincerity. Opening the envelope and pulling out the twenties seemed to help. "He left me some money and I know he'll be back soon. My Dad's going to be furious."

The woman's lack of interest in her plight made Frankie nervous. Then the woman said, "Where are you from?"

"Boise, Idaho, ma'am," she said watching the woman closely, nearly holding her breath wondering if the clerk would give her a chance. She should have known instinctively that the clerk would accept her story. It was unfair but true that under the circumstances, the body she was in allowed her far more privileges than Frankie had ever known growing up in Vegas. As a middle-class female, clerks and cashiers seemed to readily accept that the body must be innocent and free of corruption because the body was young, pretty, and white.

"Any long-distance phone calls will have to be paid ahead of time," the old bat said and pushed the registration card toward Frankie.

Fifteen minutes later, Frankie found herself outside. To get to the second-floor rooms, Frankie had to climb the concrete stairs and walk around the outside balcony which in her state of mind appeared flimsy and potentially dangerous. She made her way quickly around the building toward the back. The wooden planks substituting as a rail about four feet high running completely around the second floor supposedly kept patrons from plunging down to the asphalt parking lot. But Frankie suspected more than one patron had slipped over the side at some point. She practically clung to the wall as she made her way toward her room.

As Frankie stepped onto the next landing, she saw a middle-aged man approaching and her heart leaped. Here she might find her john. Then she noticed the child behind him and dismissed him. When he passed her with a cold look, Frankie did everything she could not to brush up against him or feel his eyes upon her a moment longer than necessary. She forced herself to look down at the child and record every tiny detail for the police: three feet tall, five or six years old, dark brown curly hair, brown eyes.

The child's expression bothered her the most. She looked resigned practically catatonic. Then she threw Frankie a big excited smile and announced with shivering delight, "I'm going to Disneyland." The transformation from blandness to joy triggered an old memory. It made her sick.

Even though her mind refused to process any new thoughts but the one uppermost – getting to her room, instinct had taken over and her legs climbed the metal steps one after the other without faltering. From far away she heard the man say to the child, "Don't be talking to strangers, Casey." She recognized the voice with a shiver as if a cold blast of winter air had swept through her. His perpetual expression had always reminded her of a catatonic. He and the child seemed to have something in common.

Once on the landing and free of him the stink of him, Frankie clenched the rail and watched as he marched toward a red and white suburban. It was an old suburban neglected with rust like chicken pox all over its poor body. Frankie read the license plate number and repeated the number in her head terrified she'd forget. She hurried to her room, unlocked the door, and frantically searched for writing tools. She found a pencil in a dresser drawer next to a black bible. She wrote down the number and then walked back outside wondering which direction he had gone. But the suburban remained parked in the AAA parking lot close to the stairs. She peered over the rail and saw the two of them, the man and child walking up the street toward Joe's Pizza.

In the last ten years, Leland Ansel had aged dramatically. He looked grayer and shorter than she remembered. He'd even developed a pot belly. With real satisfaction she thought about the cut above his eye and his swollen jaw. These signs indicated he had been in a fight recently. Maybe he'd met someone savvy enough to pick up on his predatory lifestyle and that someone managed to get away and cracked him a good one too. Or maybe the child had put up a fight. He had to have lied to the little girl though, told her some bull story about taking her to Disneyland to get her into his suburban.

Frankie fought off the rising nausea and sat down on the edge of the motel bed trying to think what to do. My God, what could she do? She had to put her head between her legs so as not to faint. She had to stay focused. He and the child were staying at the hotel. She had some time. Not much, but some. She paced the room.

When Frankie looked at her dripping face in the mirror, she replayed that moment when she recognized him on the stairs. He hadn't recognized her. They had been so close, too close, only a foot had separated them; yet, when he'd looked into her eyes, he looked at her with disinterest as if looking at a stranger he would never see again. She prayed that she had been as impersonal when she glanced his way. But he wasn't interested in young attractive women or little girls or much that had to do with intimacy between people. Leland's sexual high came from buying and selling things; he could didn't give damned about the goods just so long as he made a profit.

The only reason he was in Klamath Falls was because of the child. The child must be his next piece of merchandize. Then she realized who his buyer must be. Her resolve to call the police trickled away. Leland Ansel could be the means of leading her straight to the Butcher Queen. But what about the kid? Could she live with herself if she endangered the kid? She spoke to the image in the mirror in a soothing voice which helped restore a feeling of safety and security. It was a voice she knew and trusted, "Listen Frankie. Leland is expendable. We know what to do. We know where to go. Don't be afraid of him. He's a nobody."

Of course, she was right. They no longer needed him.

An hour later, after making her phone calls and talking to Thomas, her life realigned itself once again. Thomas would notify her bank about the loss of her personal belongings. He also assured her he would contact the motel and pay for an additional day, just long enough for him to send new bankcards and cash and find someone to drive her to her next destination. Unfortunately, she'd have to wait until she was back in Chicago to replace her lost driver's license.

Once her life had stabilized, Frankie felt confident enough to leave her motel room and check out the surrounding neighborhood. She wanted to find a place far from the motel in case Leland's memory returned. As she walked down the busy street, she noticed a line of arborvitae behind the motel. Some of the arborvitaes were big enough to hide behind.

When the sun sank behind the mountains, the few streetlights were no help and made her task more difficult. After an hour of searching up and down the boulevard, she realized with rising irritation there were no phone booths near the motel. She couldn't use the phone in her room. The police would be able to track her down and they would insist on talking to her. There could be no more delays. She and her friends had wasted enough time traipsing around the damned countryside. After passing the same bar twice, Frankie thought about sneaking in and asking to use their phone. Bars always had phones. She remembered in time how she might look to the bartender and how her lack of identification would bring too much unwanted attention.

Yet. She paused. Disposable cellphones were cheap and easy to use. She turned and smacked into a woman about her height and size. Frankie apologized in her own voice and hoped the people wouldn't notice, then tried to brush past the couple but the young woman stopped her, "Hey, it's you? Bill, it's the girl I was telling you about. Are you ok sweetie? He had no right dumping you in a strange town. That was real cruel."

Frankie turned to look at the woman. A man standing next to her looked resigned to his wife's accosting of strangers. He waited patiently and politely. His expression told her he was a long-suffering bystander. Frankie recognized the waitress from Joe's Pizza.

As Emily moved closer, Frankie stepped back, "I'm fine, thank you. I got a room," she said pointing over the waitress' shoulder. "But now I need to call my folks to tell them where I am, but I can't find a phone booth."

Her man said, "Why don't you use the phone in your room."

"It's a long-distance phone call and they won't pay for it."

"Call collect."

"I tried and nobody's answering."

"Try until you get someone," he said in a gentle way as if he were talking to a mentally challenged person.

Emily hushed him, "Leave her be Bill. She's all alone in a strange town." Then she turned back to face Frankie, "What can I do honey?"

"Where's the nearest grocery store? I've been thinking I can buy one of those disposable cellphones and won't have to mess with the front desk anymore."

"Sure, there's a Super Mart about five blocks down that way," she said pointing behind Frankie. Frankie glanced over her shoulder and noticed a mini mall in the distance.

"Thanks," she said and turned to leave.

"You shouldn't walk alone at this time of night, sweetie. We'll give you a lift," Emily offered. Emily's friendliness was getting on Frankie's nerves.

Frankie stepped back practically up against the bar's brick wall, "No. You don't need to go to so much trouble. I'll be ok. Honest. But thanks for the offer," then she turned and walked purposely away, hoping the two would go on with their business and leave her be.

Faintly Frankie heard Bill say, "It's only five blocks. She'll be fine."

With the setting of the sun, the air grew cooler. And in the shade of the arborvitae the air was practically Nordic. Frankie hid behind the tall old bushes and alternately plugged her nose and held her breath against the odor of urine. She stopped breathing through her mouth altogether. Swallowing the odor was worse. There was no other place to hide. She waited and waited, shifting from one foot to the other, sometimes sitting down or pacing and when she heard voices or a car, she would peek through the foliage and see just beyond the flood lights if Leland and the child were returning to their room.

He had to come back to his room sometime. She fingered the disposable cellphone in her skirt pocket and watched the second floor imagining she might have missed him and he was already inside. There had been a bad moment when she imagined Leland having disposed of the child somewhere before returning to his room. That couldn't happen. No. He needed that child. She was his asset, something he could bargain with to get something he wanted. But what did he want from Ray? There might be another explanation for Leland's bruised face.

Another hour passed before Leland showed up. Her heart pounded in her ear and her vision blurred for a moment. She shook her head and peered at him watching as he led the child toward the motel room. The child tripped along behind him with a huge bag clutched to her chest. Then she began to hop, and wiggle and whine and Frankie heard her say in a shrill penetrating voice of a spoiled child, "I gotta pee now."

Leland opened the motel door and shoved the child inside, "Then pee, damn it."

Frankie took note of the room number and pulled her cellphone out of her pocket. Twenty minutes later, Frankie saw the blue flashing lights from her window and popped out to watch as Leland Ansel was escorted down the stairs to a patrol vehicle. A female police officer was consoling the little girl and Frankie heard her say, "He may be your uncle, but we need to talk to your mom honey. Where do you live little lady? What's your momma's name? Do you know your phone number?"

"Sure. Momma made me rememberize it," the little girl answered helpfully.

Approximately twenty minutes later, the five patrol vehicles left the parking lot of the motel. Several people had come out of their motel rooms to watch but the rest of the neighborhood remained behind closed doors. Evidently, five patrol vehicles were a familiar sight in this area. As Frankie took the long way around the block back to the motel, she wondered if that had really been Leland's niece. Irony indeed. It was disgusting but typical for someone as sick as him. Leland was a cold calculating monster, scum of the earth, having perverted capitalism into a fetish.

There was no longer any doubt that he would use whatever was available to hook himself a bigger fish, even his niece was expendable. People were objects to him, objects to be manipulate for his own gratification. His niece was no more important than a tool in his garage or the objects in his pawn shop. She was a means to a future profit and the profit would be to lure Ray Millhouse out into the open. He wanted Ray's help for something, something nasty, she was as sure of his intentions as she was of the winged creature circling the sky above the motel.

On shaky legs, Frankie made her way back to her hotel room pushing aside the dark silhouette threatening to overshadow her triumph.

18

Only after leaving Paris, Nevada long behind him and heading north on I-95 did Zak lean back in his seat and let go his death grip on the steering wheel. When he glanced in his rear view mirror, he saw Mrs. Lawson driving Leona's Ford Taurus. She was driving recklessly, weaving in and out of traffic in a futile attempt to catch up to him. At any other time, he might have found the whole situation amusing, but not today. A room that had once been dark was now flooded with blinding light, a light that made his head ache and eyes tear up.

His recent outburst played forward and backward in his head. He had no regrets. It had felt good to finally call bullshit on his brother and the crazy family legend. Amara was Santa Claus, the Easter Bunny, and every comic book hero created since Stan Lee. What if the legend of Amara had been around for a century and a half? The longevity of a legend didn't make the legend true.

Shaking his head to clear his thoughts, he shut out the memory of his summer in New York and concentrated on the moment. He was in his car driving down the road chasing after a woman he had met only yesterday. And the why no longer mattered. An instinct stronger than himself set him on this path. It was the same compulsion he'd had when he set his sights on a college education. No amount of teasing by his family or roadblocks from his teachers changed his mind. According to his mother, Luke was a suitable candidate for college, but not Zak. "College is tough sweetie. It takes a lot of patience and money. Do you really want to be in debt and still have nothing to show for it?" he remembered her saying. Well, he showed her. And he proved something to himself as well.

Today, the feeling in his gut set him on a westerly course. He trusted her. She had left the map. She wanted him to find her. And if he was going to meet up with Eve soon, he needed a clear head and a steady hand on the wheel. The questions bumping around in his head just generated more questions which led him further down the rabbit hole. He had to stop thinking about Eve and his brother and his eccentric family for a while.

He looked out the window and soaked in the valley floor and the blue mountain range on either side of the valley until he felt his entire body relax. The sight was a reminder of the complexity of nature, seemingly constant and unchanging, yet decades of rain and wind were eroding their peaks and sending rocks and boulders tumbling down their sides. The dichotomy of the mountains reminded him of the nature of his family, the way his mother's family appeared rational on the surface and unchanging, yet, the harpy myth had begun to unravel their unity.

Everybody in the family blamed him for his youthful indiscretions. He had exposed the family's secret fantasy to the world. Yet, it had been perfectly alright for Aunt Esther to blab to everyone she met that their famous ancestors were the Greek Gods Zeus and Poseidon, while he was forbidden to say anything about Amara to anyone. And why had he become the only traitor in the Nerin family dynasty? The family's overreaction to his innocent remark made him more determined than ever to have his name legally changed to his father's surname. (He hadn't done so yet, but he would do it. One of these days).

His mother's response to his childish remark about Aunt Esther's loose lips had been to say, "Nobody believes Aunt Esther. Everybody thinks she's dealing with dementia. You think the average citizen is going to listen to the likes of someone who walks into a grocery store in her pajamas? You think walking around in public in your pajamas is rational?"

"Yes," he said to the mother of his past, still arguing with her in the present day. "Because all kinds of people run around in public in their pajamas these days. And if they could, they'd run around outside in their underwear too." Reluctantly, he had to admit there was another reason people might wonder whether Aunt Esther was crazy. Upon every encounter, she expected people to bow to her or make a curtsey and when they didn't, she did, upon occasion, go into a fit of royal rage or ignore them or whack them with her cane.

Because the family never spoke about Amara to anyone outside their circle, they had never been exposed to incredulous looks of disbelief and mocking laughter like he had been. When you bring your thoughts out into the light of day, sometimes, the light can burn away your illusions. But his mother and brother and little sister never had to face reality. Even as a fourth grader, Luke had been cunning enough to sidestep questions and ignore the whispers and innuendos. Zak's humiliation bounced off Luke's colossal ego and never penetrated his bottomless belief in their family's greatness.

But Zak was tired of pretending, pretending to believe in the myth. His real desire was to be a reputable archeologist, to work on important digs and contribute his knowledge to the field of archeology. He had yet to be a part of an important dig. His only goal now was to find a dig worthy enough to include on a resume and build a reputation as someone willing to get dirty, work long hours, learn, and never give up.

If anyone in the archeological community ever learned the truth about their family legend and Luke's scheme to find Amara, Zak's career would be over before it ever began. What if they found something resembling the legend and Luke went psycho and reported his findings to his peers? It would ruin them. Every legitimate archeologist in the world would have good reason to call them crackpots. They would never be able to cover up the stink.

Zak wouldn't let that happen.

He'd worry about his career later. His pressing concern was Eve. Where did Eve fit in? When he was apart from her, intellectually he knew she had to be bat shit crazy, but his body didn't give a damned about logic. It craved her more than beer or his mother's mosaic cake. Or was she pretending to be crazy to hide her real reasons for coming to their town? He didn't believe for one nanosecond Eve and Wade were the same person.

A more logical connection would be if Eve knew Constance Wade somehow. But how? His mind played around with different scenarios as one might gently examine a sore tooth with the tongue. Eve and Wade. Dr. Wade and her disappearance. Eve might have been Wade's student? It was one explanation for how they knew each other. Would a student know private things about a teacher?

They'd been lovers at one time?

No. Dr. Wade wasn't like that. She wouldn't fool around with one of her students.

Eve was Dr. Wade's secret love child?

Hell, he was playing poker with mittens.

Eve's doctor in Chicago recommended Mad Mona. Eve shows up at the Woolly Man asking about her. Why would an old lady like Mad Mona chase after a young woman she'd only met once? No sane person would take off at a moment's notice to track down a stranger, not even a Good Samaritan would go to such lengths to return a rented car. In fact, back at the bar, Eve threatened Mad Mona. And what about the prayer? Wow, that had been surreal.

Why an exorcism? Come on. Even Mad Mona couldn't possibly believe Eve was possessed by the devil. If so, then by that logic Mad Mona must be possessed by the devil too. Well – Mad Mona's thought processes were skewed on so many levels, she could be. Maybe if she believed Eve was possessed, she might want to hunt her down and finish the exorcism?

There it was – a pattern he couldn't see. There were too many coincidences, too many odd reactions to the bizarre events that had happened so far. First, Navan Keys shows up at the Woolly Man. Then Mad Mona arrives. And what ensues is a crazy feminist version of two primates displaying dominance behavior. Mad Mona is the silverback and the younger woman is the interloper. The silverback loses to the more aggressive younger woman. Oddly, the younger woman leaves instead of taking possession of her territory. It is only when Luke pursues her that she becomes dangerous. Soon after, Leland Ansel's shop is robbed. Mad Mona agrees to help Luke find Leona. Why? Mad Mona lost the fight. What does she have to gain?

It looked as if he needed more information about Wade's disappearance.

So far, the behavior of everyone involved, including himself, made no sense. According to Mrs. Lawson, she had been instructed to meet the young woman and help her adjust to life outside the hospital. Who was this Dr. Bishop dude anyway? And what had Leona/Eve done that was so bad she had to be kept in a psychiatric ward most of her life? He didn't trust Mrs. Lawson's story or Luke's version of things. The liars were stacking up: his mother, his brother, Mrs. Lawson, Leland Ansel, maybe even the unknown Dr. Bishop. And what about Eve? Would she really be in Crescent City waiting for him? The worse liar of them all had been his father. He remembered his last words, "I'll be back."

The memory of his father's promise blinded him for a moment. His father never came back to see them, not even once. Zak took his foot off the accelerator and pulled over onto the shoulder of the road. He could feel the rage surging through his body, beginning in the center with his stomach cramping, then spreading out to his limbs, his arms and legs, every part of him was shaking. He grabbed hold of the steering wheel feeling the thrum of the engine beneath his palms. He longed to hit something, someone. When he saw the Ford Taurus in his rear-view mirror, he spun back onto the road merging with traffic and managing to get at least three car lengths ahead of the Taurus.

The conjuring of Eve laying naked on the bed looking up at him with her amused sexy eyes dampened his rage. The way her body told him how much she appreciated his efforts made him feel warm all over. She was the best thing to happen to him in years. She understood him, and he understood, on another level, the overwhelming pain she hid inside herself. Last night, with her, the heaviness in his head and heart had lifted. It wasn't just his libido. For the first time, he'd seen the woman beside him in his bed and he realized he liked her. He liked her goofy laugh and the way her eyes narrowed when she was thinking.

When she thought he was occupied elsewhere, her face would register grief, pain, and yearning. Was her yearning love? Love for someone else? He should have been jealous. Why hadn't he been jealous? Unlike other women he had known, his body and mind responded instinctively to her mixed emotions. And when he realized that he could accept her, even her weirdness, he knew he had gone beyond lust.

For the first time in his life, he revisited that old shame without flinching. Suddenly he knew. The shame belonged to Leland and the scummy clerk he'd hired. Zak had nothing to be ashamed of and if he hoped to heal, he would have to forgive the man who made him feel that shame. Could he?

All he'd ever wanted to do was find the man and beat the shit out of him, beat him until he begged for mercy. Leland Ansel might know where he's hiding. Did he really want to get involved with those two smarmy, stink-heads? The clerk tried with him but failed. Maybe getting beat up by Luke served him a good turn in the long run? He'd learned to defend himself at an early age. It was too bad he'd had to defend himself against an adult.

He had to set aside the past. All that was important now was finding Eve.

If Eve could be so joyful even in her pain, maybe he could meet people half way? But it would take time, a lot of time before Zak could trust again. The dead were much easier to deal with. They just lay there quietly allowing the living to examine them and dig them up and display them. The living, on the other hand, the living were unpredictable. Some attacked without provocation. Others tried to manipulate you for their own ends. While the passive - aggressive ones liked to humiliate you and pretend innocence. Yep, Sartre was right – hell **is** other people. The living were the real monsters and the dead were the ones to forgive. It made no sense to hate the dead.

His musings almost made him miss the exit. Luke, right behind him, turned on his signal indicating his intentions. At least he wasn't tailgating. Zak, sensing a whisper of his old sense of humor returning, welcomed the feeling. But once he was off I-95, Zak pulled onto the shoulder of the road leaving a trail of dust in his wake. He hoped Luke would choke on the dust. Shutting off the engine, Zak leaned forward and stared at a hill on the other side of the two-lane black-top road. He'd been on this road before and recalled paved and unpaved portions of the highway. It would be one hundred and fifty-two miles. What would he find at the end? Did he really think he could persuade her to stay with him? Did he even want her that much? He could just as easily return home and forget her. Or could he?

His conscience nagged him. Professor Wade deserved better. Better than the way she'd been forgotten by her students and colleagues. Whoever had kidnapped her, hurt her, or killed her needed to be punished. Sure, there were lots of people who had gone missing over the years, the most tragic were the missing children, yet, there were organizations searching for those children. Nobody was looking for Wade any more. She'd been pronounced "dead" by a judge and was no longer officially missing. Wade had been such an important part of his growing up. If he did nothing, he would never rid himself of the ghosts of his past. He wanted to achieve something in his lifetime. He was sure Eve Endicott would lead him to Wade's killer and unmask the lie behind the Amara legend.

On her last excavation before her kidnapping, Professor Wade had discovered something extraordinary, something Krutcher had been determined would be kept secret. It seemed crazy, but his instincts were telling him if he found Eve, she would be the key to unlocking a multitude of secrets. He was afraid for her. Something dangerous was coming her way. A rational part told him she could probably take care of herself; he ignored it.

"Hey Zak. What's going on?"

In his surprise, Zak jumped bashing his hand on the roof of the Camaro. He leaned back in his bucket seat and glared up at his brother. Luke was agitated which delighted Zak. Luke, usually so reserved, such a cold fish most of the time looked less menacing when he was agitated.

Zak no longer feared the maniac. He had fought that dragon years ago and won.

"Zak, you got to let me ride shotgun," Luke said, a desperate note in his voice. "She's crazy. I mean catching bugs and eating them crazy."

From inside the Ford Taurus, Zak heard a high-pitched giggle. He had to shove Luke aside to see what was going on. Mad Mona had stepped out of the Taurus. She scurried across the road and under the highway bridge zig-zagging as if desperately searching for a lost item. Then belatedly he realized she was searching for a place to pee. The way she moved creeped him out. Her legs were spread wide, as if walking on the deck of a ship in a storm. She reminded him of a crab, the way she swayed from side to side using her skinny hips to move herself forward.

What made the episode so much worse were the high-heels on her big feet. No woman should walk like a crab and wear high-heels. It was blasphemy. Equally as awful was the straggly white hair and wrinkled skin accompanied by coquettish tosses of the head and seductive swishes of a bony bottom. "You see what I mean," Luke said in a desperate voice as he began to run around the Camaro preparing to climb into the passenger seat.

Before Luke touched the door handle, Zak peeled out. He heard his brother screaming after him, "You bloody shithead! You bloody wanker! Come back here!"

Luke's misery made Zak's sudden decision worthwhile. He thought about Eve's note and the carefully drawn map on the back of it. He didn't have to rush. She'd be waiting for him in Crescent City, California. And he would finally get some answers, answers to Wade's kidnapping and how Eve was mixed up in his old professor's disappearance. He might even learn, finally, whether there was any truth to the legend of Amara. With his intentions uppermost in his mind, all his doubts receded. Like the dust behind him, the doubts flew out the window and merged with the desert.

Even the view outside his window brought a sense of purpose and comfort. By the time, Zak descended into the valley near Lakeview, his butt was numb. He'd made a few stops along the way to stretch and visit the restrooms and talk to fellow travelers, but for the most part he'd driven straight through in the hopes he might catch up to Eve. Once in Lakeview (which boasted two gas stations, each at opposite ends of the town) Zak choose the one which would lead him west toward Klamath Falls. He managed to fill up his tank in peace.

With renewed optimism, Zak believed he'd outrun his brother at last. Either Luke had gotten lost or he decided to put Mad Mona on a bus and send her home. Even better yet, Zak hoped Luke had given up and turned back for home.

Hunger ate at Zak's belly. He would take the chance and stop at the nearest grocery store. He needed supplies for the remainder of the trip: bottled water, chips, sandwich fixings, maybe some cheese sticks. He entered the convenience store and searched the room. The designer of the establishment had chosen early warehouse and bachelor mess. The metal shelves held mostly junk food and the one ancient cooler held beer and a few name brand sodas. Otherwise, the mint green walls were bare of posters. Zak was so hungry he didn't care. He bought four hot dogs, a bag of chips, a six pack of Cherry Cola, four candy bars, and a bag of beef jerky.

It wasn't until Zak was a few feet from his Camaro that he noticed his brother leaning on the trunk. He stopped with his arms loaded thinking he could shove Luke aside and jump in his Camaro and take off. Luke had parked the Ford Taurus so close to the Camaro's driver's side door, Zak would have had to climb in through the passenger door and over the pearl handled stick shift. Preparing for a fight Zak set his bags down on the hood of the Camaro.

Warily Luke watched Zak approach, his body alert as if anticipating a blow. Mad Mona passed Zak with a grunt and a curt nod. Evidently, she was old Mrs. Lawson again. A momentary pity rekindled as Zak became aware of Luke's state of dishevelment. At any other time, Luke's frazzled expression, messy hair, and twitchy skin would have been hilarious but not now. He felt rather sorry for his brother. Maybe his trip, a therapeutic ride through beautiful country reminiscing about his summer in New York had made him more observant and less judgmental. His thoughts crystallized. He had an epiphany. No more hating. No more humiliation. The past would stay in the past. At last he had a goal, a plan, a potential future.

Luke unfolded his arms and followed as Zak opened the passenger door and threw his purchases in the backseat. When Zak turned to face his brother, Luke asked, "Well?"

"It's not enough that you keep things from me, but the worst part is that you keep thinking I'm interested in what you're interested in," Zak said having thought about his grievances for over one hundred and fifty-two miles. "From now on, check with me first before you go and plan some stupid-ass scheme, because maybe I'm not interested in achieving immortality and infinite power." The last part he said with a sneer because, of course, it was all bullshit anyway. He tried to get back on the path to positive energy and failed.

"Absolutely," Luke said his entire being transformed which Zak figured wouldn't last long once Luke got his way. "I'll be sure to check with you. I'm sorry man. I keep thinking I've got to be the big brother, you know, always protecting my little brother from the painful truth. I realize now that you're a grown man and don't need me telling you what to think and what to do all the time."

"Cut the crap," Zak said. "You're giving me a sugar rush."

The familiar cold calculation never surfaced. Instead Luke's face twitched for a moment as if he couldn't decide how to approach the problem. When he finally spoke, Zak was creeped out enough to feel kind of sorry for him, "Don't fuck with me Zak. I'm on the edge. I'm this close. I swear. She's driving me nuts. All the damned way here she's flirting with me and giggling and acting like she's sixteen. I tell you I can't take much more of this. I'm gonna end up killing her or myself. Please, Zak. Just let me ride with you. Take pity on me, I'm begging you."

"I'm still standing here, aren't I?" Zak said, not bothering to hide his own exasperation. Mrs. Lawson's voice startled them both. They turned around. She looked serene and thoroughly sane. Zak wondered if it had all been an act on Luke's part, a way of manipulating him again to get a ride. After all, Luke was Svengali, the master manipulator and Zak was the proverbial mark, a sucker for any hard luck story.

In a voice they knew well, Mrs. Lawson demanded, "Why am I in Lakeview, Oregon? I'm supposed to be at the rock show in Ontario tomorrow."

Luke answered her quickly, "You offered to give me a lift, Mrs. Lawson, remember? Your vehicle wasn't working so we took that girl's car? I think you called her Jane, Jane Smith. Remember? She ran out of the Woolly Man and disappeared, and we went after her hoping we could rescue her from her troubles? Don't worry. Once we find her and you return her car to her, I'm sure she'll be very grateful. And if you offer her your home along with some handy tips for dealing with, ah, your mutual disorders, you'd be assisting in her recovery," he said with an innocent air, demonstrating his gift for manipulation.

310

The last part of Luke's speech horrified Zak. Over-his-dead-body would he let Mad Mona imprison Eve in that smelly old house or brainwash her into believing any of Mona's wild theories.

Everybody knew about Mrs. Lawson's (MPD) multiple personality disorder, but he'd always assumed she was faking it to get attention and free stuff. After seeing the way she'd been at the highway bridge, he hoped she'd forgotten all about seeing him bound to the bed and naked. Since she'd been someone else, maybe that someone else didn't come out so much. No such luck, he realized, when he saw her watching him with a smirk in her eye.

Her disorder was an act. The old battle axe. She was putting Luke on. If she had MPD for real, she wouldn't remember what her other personality had seen or done, would she? With the beginnings of a headache pinching his forehead, Zak looked over Mrs. Lawson's shoulder at the road curving to the west and leading away from Lakeview.

Mrs. Lawson, equally embarrassed, avoided looking at Zak. He had no doubt Mrs. Lawson would keep quiet. She wasn't stupid enough to piss off Jule Nerin. His mom had been out of town when Leland's pretty boy had tried one on Zak; and later, when she learned the facts, she didn't talk to anyone for days. When she finally did talk, she ordered everyone to keep their mouths shut. The pretty boy was long gone by the time Leland experienced a string of bad luck: three flat tires, a long ugly gash down the length of his new truck, followed by a series of raids at his pawn shop by agents of the DEA and Immigration.

No one came out to the bar to question his mother. Why would they? Leland didn't want anyone knowing about his clerk's sick habits.

Her response to the circular firing squad should have been a warning to Leland and his clerk. Since she couldn't find the clerk, Leland became her chief target. God help the clerk. If his mother found him, he would be in a world of hurt. What followed was a dry spell, a trick his mother employed to lull her victims into a false sense of security.

A year after Leland built his new home on the same spot where the old house had been before the fire, he came home one day to find an invasion of sugar ants, hundreds of them, all over his kitchen and in the dining room. Someone had left a trail of honey in the sink, on the counters, on the floor, all leading to the dining room. There were even pools of honey on each of his expensive upholstered dining room chairs. When Leland stormed into the Woolly Man shouting at his mother, she laughed in his face, "Oh that's a good one. I wish I'd thought of that. Who else have you pissed off lately, Leland the Louse?" He left. No one came to arrest her.

The resurrection of his high school nickname must have driven him crazy. Zak shrugged, why was he feeling sorry for the asshole? The guy had knowingly hired a pedophile to work in his shop right next to a candy store. Instead of working hard to improve his image and forge a new future, Leland just kept on being the same old louse, stocking his shop with junk and overcharging his customers.

For about a year, peace reigned in Leland's world. He got rid of the ants and went about his business. Then he came home one day to find mice in his walls, mice in his furniture, mice everywhere. That broke the dam. He called the cops and lodged a complaint. The deputy sheriff came out to the Woolly Man and questioned his mother and she asked him, "Now why does Leland think I've got a grudge against him? Answer me that. He's welcome in my bar anytime. I've told him that before. But he's too hoity- toity to step foot in my place."

Evidently, Leland's bad luck was never ending. While Zak had been waiting in line to pay for his gas in Marsing, Idaho, the television screen above the clerk's head showed the local news. They were reporting a burglary at Leland's place *Around the World Pawn*. They showed a clip of the front of his shop, then a view of the back alley concentrating their attention on the door and the dumpster. The reporter stood between the dumpster and a cheap door made of particle board. The sound was off but the text streaming at the bottom of the screen claimed a burglar had nearly killed the guard dog, kicked through the door, and stolen some petty cash.

Zak was glad he was hundreds of miles away and no one could pin the burglary on him.

After texting his mother to tell her about the burglary, she text him back using the Nerin form of communication, a combination of numbers and symbols only the immediate family understood, swearing she'd had nothing to do with the burglary. She finished with, **Do you really think I'm that stupid?**

No. He did not. Impulsive? Yeah. Vengeful? Definitely. If she thought she could get away with it, she just might break into Leland's shop for a laugh. As he looked at Mad Mona tottering under the bridge, he knew she knew, if she ever spread the story of Zak in a motel room bound to the bed and naked, Jule Nerin would either beat her skinny ass black and blue or worse lull the woman into a false sense of security and then executed the perfect revenge.

"I need gas money to get home," Mrs. Lawson said to no one in particular, thrusting her hand out with the palm facing up between the two of them. She waited patiently with her eyes directed at the ground.

Zak kept his hands in his pockets. He would be damned if he would pay her; she was Luke's problem. Luke reluctantly fished out two twenty-dollar bills and put them in the palm of her hand. She saluted them with a snarl and walked toward the Taurus, "Cheap aren't you. You keep your promise to me, Luke Nerin, or I'll fetch Itty Bit on you." And just as she reached the door of the Taurus, she stopped and went to the back of the Taurus and opened the trunk. "What should I do with all this stuff? It looks like Jane Smith had a convention of women riding in her car. There's all sorts of suitcases and briefcases and makeup cases and god-knows-what cases."

"The car doesn't belong to you Mrs. Lawson," Zak reminded her. "You'd better just park the Taurus in front of the Woolly Man the way Eve, I mean Jane left it. Your vehicle is probably still at the bar. I'll check with Mom to be sure you arrive safely," he said and looked at Luke with a smile. "Oh, and be sure to give the keys to my mom. I'll text her now and let her know you're on your way."

They watched her slam the lid of the trunk unnecessarily hard and stomp toward the driver's side door. She scowled at Zak. "You got a lot of nerve, kiddo, accusing me of theft. Your brother's the one who stole her car. Not me. I'm just doing your mom a favor. I got to go. I got things to do." She gunned the engine and peeled out of the parking space reckless in her rage.

Luke grabbed hold of Zak's arm before he could run after her. Her showboating ended when she pulled over to the gas pumps and docilely waited for the attendant to pump her gas and wash her windshield. Luke got bored and went inside to get himself a coffee and a newspaper. Mad Mona stuck her arm out of the window, gave Zak the finger, and headed east toward Idaho. Yeah, she was back to her old self, her nasty old bat self.

"Who's Itty Bit?" Luke asked sourly.

Zak waited until he could no longer see the Taurus and then climbed into the driver's side bucket seat, "I think Itty Bit is her dog. You know, her Great Dane. Who cares? Come on we're wasting time." He saw relief wash over Luke's face when Mrs. Lawson headed out of town traveling north on Highway 395 and he couldn't help but grin at his brother's terror over a little old lady who barely weighed ninety pounds who had once nearly fallen off War Eagle Mountain as she stood on the edge of the summit and a gust of wind nearly swept her off her feet and down the mountain.

When Luke leaned back in the passenger seat and sighed, Zak let out a whoop and a holler, "Your sorry ass. You're not clear of trouble yet. Mom has to deal with Mad Mona when she returns to the Woolly Man and she'll take it out on you."

The migraine miraculously disappeared the further Zak traveled west. With a peculiar mixture of hope and dread, Zak imagined his reunion with Eve. Physically he thought he might be coming down with the flu, yet, his body hummed at the memory of her soft curves spooning with him. Mentally, he imagined them playing sex games and it was all he could do to act normal in front of his brother. Another side of him though, the rational side knew there was a twister of ugliness coming his way, maybe spirit crushing rejection or much worse bored indifference.

The next time he and Eve met she might be Leona and not remember a damned thing to do with him or Paris, Nevada. On the other hand, he might meet up with Eve and Eve might have found herself some other guy to play hide-the-matchbook with. He blinked away the rush of jealousy and rage. Belatedly, he realized that his fingers were cramped and sore. He loosened his death grip on the steering wheel. Well, he thought, I guess I've covered all the bases.

Or maybe not. He'd forgotten about the scary one, the one with predatory eyes and electric reflexes. Fear hiked his blood pressure up a couple of notches. He took a deep breath and tried to relax. He remembered his shock when she overpowered Luke. Within seconds she'd had him on the ground. Equally awe inspiring had been the fluidness of her reaction a second later. She'd kept on moving, moving straight to Luke's truck like a prairie falcon hunting its prey, single-minded in its purpose.

The Acacia side of Eve had run with such ease and grace he couldn't help but feel awed by the sight. Her agility reminded him of the falcon he'd been privileged to see years ago as it flew inches above the desert floor, so effortless in its motion, avoiding rock and sage as if one with the earth. And a second later, when he was sure the falcon would make its final kill only to miss the target, like the falcon, Acacia didn't give up. She exhilarated, moving forward so fast his eye couldn't track her until she'd opened the truck door and jumped inside.

He remembered hearing the engine roar into life and seeing his brother reach the driver's side door. At that point, his brother's body blocked his view of what happened next. He turned in his seat to ask Luke what had happened, how Acacia had got away with the truck and then saw the results of Luke's encounter with her. In the motel room back in Paris, Nevada, Zak had been too embarrassed and preoccupied with his own humiliation to take stock of Luke. Now he saw what she'd done. Like a weird tattoo, one side of his neck was a flowering bruise of green-and-yellow. An outline of white suggested the side of someone's hand had dropped him a second time to the ground with one strategically placed blow. The fact the bruises were green and yellow meant they were healing and had been black and blue the day before.

Then he noticed the blood on Luke's collar. Just a few drops the size of dimes. The spots of blood were on the same side as the bruising. At one point he must have washed the blood from his head wound. And now after a night and nearly a day, he had a lump the size of a walnut just above his ear. Zak had to readjust the image in his head of the attack. She'd struck Luke first in the throat and when that didn't stop him, she struck him a second time only harder in the head. The fear disappeared. The marks on his brother helped him understand her better. If he didn't pose a threat to her then she wouldn't try to kill him and might even give him a chance to redeem himself. It was a risk worth taking.

Unlike Mrs. Lawson's kind of crazy, Zak was beginning to appreciate Eve's kind of crazy. Feminists would say that he was superficial, objectifying the female in his relentless thoughts about sex and his lust to fulfill his baser needs. Maybe in the beginning he'd been superficial. Not anymore. He'd been thinking about his reaction to Eve back there on the roadside and concluded that there had been more than simple lust, especially once the night progressed. He smiled, remembering some of the highlights of the evening.

An odd calm came over him when he finally accepted the fact that he and she were meant for each other. If one considered the lengths to which their mismatched lives managed to connect, one could only conclude something divine had been operating behind the scenes. He headed toward Klamath Falls switching out CDs from his player removing the heavy metal and choosing a medley of Stevie Ray Vaughn, JJ Calle, and a little Toni Lawson.

Even though Luke pestered him to talk about his night with Eve, Zak remained stubbornly quiet. He knew Luke wasn't interested in his love life. Luke wanted information about Amara, as if Eve, in the throes of passion would give him coordinates to Professor Wade's whereabouts. Luke just didn't get it. He didn't get Zak and most definitely didn't get Eve. When Zak turned to look at his brother, he saw Luke lick his pen with a deep air of concentration and scribble something down on the crisp, lined, beige paper inside his journal.

Unlike Zak's leather-bound notebook, Luke preferred permanency and neatness, another clue to the difference between them. The cover pieces protecting Luke's pages were unique, one of a kind and precious to him. It was approximately seven inches wide and nine and a quarter inches long made of two thin pieces of petrified wood cut precisely by an amateur but gifted rock hound. It had a red patina polished to the smoothness of glass having been designed by Luke and cut by Quinn's father. Each piece lay in an ebony cradle made of thin metal and the hinges which kept the front and back pieces together were of silver.

Parker Youngblood, Quinn's father had been and probably still was the best rock hound and gemologist of his age. When Luke discovered the slab of petrified wood on one of their hunts, Parker offered to cut and polish it. Luke's design impressed Parker so much, he decided to make a business out of constructing useful and unique gifts for consumers. Not only had Luke made the biggest discovery of his life at fourteen, he'd unknowingly provided Parker with a means of support other than their mother. Armed with his fantastic designs and disgusted with his wife's vengeful nature, Parker Youngblood ran off never to return. He sent postcards once a year, and if he remembered, they would get birthday cards but nothing else, not even a phone call on Christmas Day.

Christmas Day didn't mean much to the Nerins anyway. They worshipped the old religion and one of the perks of believing in Zeus were the trips to Hawaii or Tahiti with feasting and drinking near the sea. Since Luke was the eldest he was in charge of planning the vacations. The evidence of Luke's anal obsession with detail proved once again how different Luke was from the rest of the family. His brother's thought processes might be similar to Sherlock Holmes, especially his intensity over the smallest of observations, but only when the observation came to objects. People were secondary.

Zak recalled with a grin how Luke had been the most anal Boy Scout in his troop, always prepared, neat, organized, driven to outperform everyone with more merit badges than any of the other boys. During Zak's second year in the Boy Scouts of America, he dropped out hating the whole thing, the orderliness and regimentation, the nitpicky rules and brainwashing. He also despised taking orders from kids his own age especially his brother.

Luke's satchel and duffel bag were evidence of his complete lack of concern for the welfare of people. Instead of rushing in hot pursuit of his missing truck, Luke chose to interrogate Mad Mona for information about Eve then pack carefully for a long trip. Typical. Luke's overconfidence drove him crazy.

But something about Luke's possessions bothered Zak. He glanced over at Luke and then down at the floorboards noticing the black nylon duffel bag resting at Luke's feet, noticing with interest how the bag bulged at the seams, a piece of luggage which more than likely included several pairs of underwear, an extra pair of jeans, maybe a couple of polo shirts, his razor, his shaving cream, and his cologne. Oh, and of course, his comb and hairdryer. The man was a neat freak.

"Back at the motel, how come you didn't lend me your comb and razor Luke?" Zak asked.

Luke lifted his ballpoint pen in the air holding it over the page he had been writing on in the expectation of continuing to jot down his thoughts once Zak's question had been answered. He frowned then focused on Zak's face, "What? Oh that. My stuff was still in Mrs. Lawson's, no I mean, Jane Smith's Ford Taurus."

"Well?"

"Well what Zak?" Luke frowned glancing down at his page eager to record his thoughts.

"What about now? Help me out here Luke. I don't have cooties."

For several seconds nothing happened, then with deliberate slowness Luke carefully capped his ballpoint pen, slipped the pen in his shirt pocket, closed his journal, and set the journal on the backseat. He took his own sweet time searching in his duffel bag for his comb and razor. "You can't shave while you're driving," Luke reminded him with an edge to his voice setting the comb and razor on his lap.

"I do it all the time."

"Not with my stuff you don't. Find a place to pull over."

K McVere

"No. I've got a better idea. I'm going to find us a place to spend the rest of the day. I need a shower and some sleep."

"That's not necessary. I can drive the rest of the way to Klamath Falls."

"No. You're not touching my car. I've seen the way you drive. We'll stop at the nearest diner or truck stop. I've got an idea."

From the corner of his eye, he saw Luke sitting as still as a statue his face expressionless. Luke was pissed, and Zak didn't care. Zak could see the effort it took his brother to turn in his seat and look at him. "OK. What's going on?"

"We don't need to rush, bro. I know where she'll be. We've got time to stop and make a phone call. I hope you brought your computer. We need to find a place that offers free WIFI and showers."

"What's up with you Zak? This is stupid. If you know where she's going then let's beat her there."

"Don't worry. She'll be there. You keep asking about Professor Wade. We'll talk to the people who know her best. OK? You got time for that?"

"I have no choice. Do what you want."

"Good because I see an exit up ahead and there's a sign. See. A knife and a fork. We can expect food soon. I hope it's good, I'm starving."

Luke turned to look at the empty bags and soda bottles littering the backseat. Zak shrugged. "I'm a growing boy."

Forty minutes later, in the one and only truck-stop diner, Zak sat down on the red vinyl bench opposite Luke avoiding the long tear bleeding yellow foam which ran down the center as if someone had taken a knife and stabbed the poor bench to death. Hope it wasn't because of the food. With his thick black hair still wet, he leaned his elbows on the Formica table top and smiled. He hadn't bothered to comb his hair just toweled it dry letting the hair stick up in short spikes all around his head. At least the black stubbles on his face had been removed. "Did you find the number?"

Ignoring his brother as Zak dripped water from his head onto his place mat, Luke patiently watched the computer screen. An eager waitress watched with disbelieving eyes as Zak entered the room, her body fairly vibrating with delight. She successfully maneuvered through the crowded room managing to overlook a number of customers trying to get her attention and stood before the two gorgeous men with her notepad ready, a huge smile on her face. Luke sighed. Zak decided he would be the adult and smile at the waitress.

He felt great! There was nothing better than a long hot shower. He felt clean all over. Even his teeth zinged. Zak ordered the buffalo burger and a plate of fries, a large cola, and apple pie for desert. After the waitress left, Luke, still staring at the screen said, "How are you going to explain the Navaho blanket?"

"It's time the truth came out. I'm going to start by telling the Wade brothers about Leona."

"Are you nuts? The fewer people who know about her the better. I sent an invitation to Chris Wade. He's a full-time lecturer at BSU now. He sent me a text message instead and his response was lukewarm. I suspect former students of hers have been kissing up to him for years. On a hunch, I left a text message on Brent's phone with a link requesting a video chat. I mentioned his mother in the hopes he wouldn't brush us off like his brother did. I believe we'll have better luck with him. It looks like he's a building contractor in Portland and doing very well. Hold on, I think he's answering our call."

Excited Zak jumped up and ran over to Luke's side of the table elbowing him to make room. Not happy but not willing to make a scene, Luke scooted over to make room for his brother. Zak looked eagerly at the computer and smiled when he saw Professor Wade's son appear on the screen. Brent Wade was sitting at a desk in what appeared to be his office. To Brent's left there was a large picture window showcasing the view of Portland's skyline in the distance. His office must have been outside the city limits. To his right was a wall covered in pictures and awards.

Brent Wade had sandy brown hair and green eyes. He looked like an easy-going guy. Zak was relieved. Chris Wade sounded like a pontificating nincompoop, a lot like Krutcher, but this guy was different. Brent looked wary, yet, curious.

Luke spoke first, "Hello Mr. Wade. I'm Luke Nerin and this is my brother Zak. Zak and I were students of your mother and we just recently discovered something interesting and thought we'd better get in touch with your family. I'm sorry for the imposition. I know you are a very busy man, but I hope you can take a few minutes to talk to us."

Brent shrugged and said, "I have some time. What's up?"

Before Luke could answer, Zak leaned forward, "Hi Brent. I just want to say, it was an honor knowing your mother. Professor Wade was the coolest professor I ever had. She's the reason I stayed in college.

The reason we wanted to talk to you is because we believe there is some potentially new information about her disappearance. You see there's this guy we know, he owns a pawn shop in Twin Falls and he claims that you gave him a bunch of your mother's possessions back in 2003.

Now this was years ago, I know, and you probably don't remember all the details. It was shortly after the memorial in the Lookout Room," Zak pointed at his brother and looked back at the screen. "We were there. I'm sure you don't remember us. The room was packed with people that day. We heard you give the eulogy and we shook your hand. I hate to rehash old pain, but I think this is really important."

Luke broke in, "Yes well we'd been on enough digs with your mother to wonder if the blanket might be hers. If the blanket really is your mother's, we think you should have it. We haven't any proof the blanket belonged to your mother - no provenance or valuation by an expert but even so the questionable nature of Leland Ansel's stock and how he acquired this object has been nagging at our conscience for a long time. You can always pay an appraiser to determine its value. We're just concerned the blanket might have been stolen and sold to Leland illegally."

Zak started talking before Brent had a chance to respond, "I'm going to come clean with you about this blanket Brent."

Luke jabbed him in the side.

Zak ignoring the pain finished his confession without a hitch, "I stole the Navaho blanket about five years ago. It was a stupid thing to do but I knew the blanket didn't belong to Leland. If you want to tell the police what happened, I'm okay with that. I'll do my time if necessary."

"Don't get the wrong impression about us Mr. Wade. We're not crackpots," Luke said glaring at his brother. "It's true Zak stole the blanket from *Around the World Pawn*. We've all done stupid things when we were young. But now we want to make amends and do what's right. Zak and I respected your mother a lot and just want to see justice done for her."

Pushing his brother aside, Zak said, "Also, a few months ago Luke bought a geological map from Ansel's pawnshop which may have belonged to your mother. It looks as if it might have been used during the Smithers' excavation when your mother and Professor Krutcher discovered the remains of the carriage. The map really should be included in the Smithers' collection at Boise State." As Zak talked to Brent, he felt Luke stiffen in shock as his brother gave away an important piece of information that might lead to the discovery of Amara's grave.

Determined to lay out the facts before his brother interrupted, Zak ignored the furious trembling going on in the body seated next to him and finished his speech in a rush, "As you can tell, we are concerned that these items might have been stolen? Also, a young woman showed up at our bar, the Woolly Man Bar & Grill in Woolstone and she said some curious things which led us to believe she may have known something about your mother's disappearance. We plan to meet up with her in Crescent City and hope to learn more about her relationship with Professor Wade." The unspoken rage radiating off his brother were hard to ignore. Zak managed not to laugh and continued to smile and nod and be agreeable for Brent's sake.

They waited for Brent to say something. It was a lot of information to absorb all at once, information which could potentially resurrected a painful time in his life. Yet his face remained composed. Reassured, the Nerin brothers recognized in his expressive eyes the same sharp intelligence and quiet strength of his mother, "I thought the Vegas police still had the Navaho blanket?"

Before Zak had a chance to further incriminate himself, Luke answered Brent's question, "Ansel claimed he bought the blanket at a garage sale in Stanley. It seems the wife of a former Vegas police detective thought the blanket was a contribution to the garage sale because it was stored in a simple brown paper bag in her husband's foot locker. An easy mistake to make really. Most people know important evidence is always carefully sealed, stored, and labelled. Somehow, he ended up with the blanket. Maybe at his retirement party someone thought it would be a good joke to give him the blanket as a parting gift." Luke shrugged. "It's anyone's guess."

Brent shifted in his chair, "Hold on a minute." He stood up and moved to the wall on his right. He removed a picture from the wall and returned to his desk. "Is this the blanket you have?" As he set the picture upright on his desk close to his computer, they could hear the suppressed fury in his voice. Someone was going to get an earful right after this conference.

Both Luke and Zak leaned forward to peer at the picture. Professor Wade was sitting on the brick stoop before a large fireplace. On each side of the fireplace stoop rested pots of poinsettias. Above her head, holly had been draped on the brick mantel piece. To her left stood her sons holding up the Navaho blanket between them. Zak recognized a younger version of Brent, his hair cropped in the mullet style. Compared to other pictures he'd seen of the mullet, Brent didn't look like a complete idiot. The blanket looked a lot like the one Zak had in the trunk of his Camaro.

"Yes," Luke confirmed. "It looks exactly like the one we have."

The view changed. They saw Brent at his desk with his arms crossed and an unhappy look on his face, "I'll meet you in Crescent City in two days' time," he said as he glanced at something to his left beyond their view. They assumed it was his desk calendar. "I just need to wrap up some unfinished business here. I'll call you when I arrive in Crescent City. Wait for me."

They hadn't expected so swift a response and as Luke tried to figure out a polite way to postpone the meeting, Zak spoke up, "Sounds good to me. See you in two days."

They saw Brent nod curtly acknowledging Zak's remark and the screen went blank.

For the next hour the only sound in the Camaro was Zak's music. Ordinarily, Luke would have been complaining about the noise but not today. Somehow the strain between them had finally penetrated Luke's self-absorption. It wasn't until they reached the tiny town of Dairy outside of Klamath Falls that Zak unbent enough to talk to Luke. "We'll be in Klamath Falls shortly. I'm starved. I'm thinking either pizza or Chinese, what about you?"

Luke had been rereading his notes and glanced suspiciously at Zak as if he didn't quite trust his brother's cheerful mood. Reading his brother's thoughts correctly, Zak said with a smile, "Don't worry. I'm not going to dump you in Klamath Falls."

Expressionless, Luke looked out the window at the spectacular landscape and said, "You've been acting weirder and weirder ever since that woman entered the bar. And then you go and confess everything, even stuff you don't have to. What's wrong with you? If I didn't know better, I'd say Jane Smith put a spell on you."

"Don't go there," Zak warned. "The less said the better."

"And why not? We have to agree on this one Zak. It's vital. If we're at odds, Amara will slip through our fingers. You took away our chance to find her. Why did you tell Brent about the map? Jane Smith may know where Amara is buried. She might even be heading toward Amara's grave right now? But if we can't find Jane Smith at least we have the map as backup."

"Would you stop with the Amara shit," Zak said. "Your theory is full of holes."

"How so?" Luke demanded turning to face Zak eager to debate him. "I saw the photo. So, did you. She couldn't have been more than thirty something. Her kids were barely preteens when that picture was taken. It was her right down to the color of her eyes."

"Everybody has a double. Do you remember the time someone kept saying they knew Mom and it turned out Mom had a doppelganger in Caldwell?" Zak argued. "Remember when the woman stopped by the Woolly Man?"

"They didn't look anything alike. It was all smoke and mirrors, all a collective hallucination. One guy sees a resemblance and suddenly everybody is seeing the same thing. Well, maybe from far away there might have been a resemblance, but when Mom walked up to her, you could tell the difference. They were nothing alike up close. And this double theory. There is no such thing. It's a literary device. Besides the face is as unique as a fingerprint. Even identical twins don't have identical faces. Has there ever been any real data on doppelgangers? Huh?"

Until they stopped at a nearby gas station to refuel and Zak could stretch and buy himself something to tide him over until dinner, the two of them argued about whether there was such a thing as a double for every human being born on the planet. The last thing Zak said before climbing out of the Camaro was, "There are a finite number of physical features to the human form and face. You must admit that Luke. So more than likely, there is someone with similar features like yours and mine on this planet."

"You are so wrong," Luke said as he moved to follow Zak. "A human being is born with the potential of an infinite variety of features with variables dependent upon the complexities of DNA, gestation, the mother's prenatal care, etc. Just look at large families with the same parents. None of the kids look exactly alike. They may have similar family characteristics and mannerisms, but for the most part they appear different from one another. Your theory has an *infinite* number of holes in it."

"How can you prove *infinite* anyway? It means no end. So how can you proof there is no end to facial features?" Zak asked with a disparaging laugh. Luke hated when Zak had the last word, so he followed him into the store to argue with him further but came up short when Zak spun around and said in an unexpectedly curt tone, "Hey man, don't forget to lock up. This is a strange town."

Zak watched as Luke obligingly returned to the Camaro and locked the passenger door. An inexplicable depression came over Zak at the sight of his brother eagerly doing Zak's bidding. There was nothing victorious about turning someone into a slave. Part of Zak wanted his bossy, know-it-all brother back; the other part wanted Luke's respect. Why did he and his brother have to constantly compete?

As he wandered down the aisles trying to figure out what he wanted, he thought about the way his mind was going and sought to divert it by looking around the store at the people. Most of them appeared socially savvy and willing to cooperate. But people were complex. They might appear docile but dark emotions boiled beneath the surface. Any one of the people in this place might have the potential to strike out and hurt someone.

What would he do if someone put a gun to his head and threatened to kill him? Would he be willing to give up something precious for the sake of someone else? The first thought he had was the Camaro. The idea of losing his Camaro, his baby, made Zak's upper lip moist and his heart lurch. Embarrassed, Zak looked around the store. As if people could read his mind? Why had he thought about the Camaro anyway? Why hadn't he thought of his family first?

On his way to the cooler for a couple of bottles of soda, Zak grabbed several bags of trail-mix and freeze-dried fruit. Maybe he'd thought about the Camaro first because the idea of losing his brother was inconceivable to him. He just couldn't imagine not having his brother around. Even if Luke was a pain in the ass, he'd always been a part of Zak's life.

After Zak chose a liter bottle of sweet soda, he regretted the decision when he realized he would be contributing to the pollution of the planet. Where had that idea come from? Then he remembered Eve and the moment he returned from the motel lobby vending machine with their dinner and her tirade about plastic bottles ruining the land and how she avoided convenience stores because customers were forced to buy products encased in inappropriate packaging. After a second or two of fierce inner debate, Zak threw the plastic bottle back in the cooler and chose a cup of coffee and hot dog before paying for his gas. He'd read somewhere Styrofoam decomposed.

As he stood in line waiting to be served, he glanced outside and saw someone admiring the Camaro. He didn't mind if they looked; he just didn't like it when they put their grubby hands on his beautiful finish. The man had a woman with him and she seemed to be intensely interested in something in the backseat. She used her hand to shield her eyes from the sun's glare in order to see inside. Zak whistled to get Luke's attention. People turned, and a woman stared at Zak as if he'd farted in public. Annoyed Zak hissed his brother's name then jerked his head toward the couple circling the Camaro like vultures. Luke glanced in the direction Zak pointed and shrugged as if he didn't see anything peculiar about their behavior.

By the time Zak had paid for the gas and purchased the food, the couple had disappeared. Even though they may have been simply admiring his baby, he double checked the Camaro's blue finish running his hand over the roof and down the sides, even the white decals along either side of the RS-style nose. He wanted to be sure those two hadn't tampered with his car. Jealous bastards were known to key the finish of nice rides like his or take a hammer and pound holes in the hood, maybe even puncture a tire or two. Who could comprehend the crazy vicious things people do out of envy and ignorance?

With a once over, he was relieved to find no new scratches, just the one during his pursuit of the crazy Leona on Fox Ridge Road, a thin scratch barely discernable to most people. He hadn't noticed the spiny horse-brush until it was too late. A bit of detailing and no one would ever know the difference.

"Are you quite finished fondling your beloved Zak?" Luke asked as he climbed into the passenger seat with a bag of snacks in his arms.

Zak ignored him and climbed into the driver's seat, "I want to stop at the parts store near here."

"Spare me," Luke said. "Just drop me off at that diner across the street. I'll order for you."

"Spanish Omelet and hash browns," Zak began.

Luke climbed out of the Camaro clutching a bag of chips. "Yeah, yeah, whatever. Go ahead and turn your stomach into an acid bath," he answered dismissively and waved Zak off without turning back to look at him. A surge of irritation rose up from his belly. Zak shoved the Camaro into reverse and with tires smoking nearly ran Luke down. Luke jumped aside before the Camaro's eighteen-inch tires crushed his toes. Through the open passenger window, Zak said in an icy tone belied by his performance, "Don't assume anything with me anymore. I'm sick of your patronizing attitude. You listening? I said don't be disrespecting me."

Luke threw up his hands, "How many times have I ordered a meal for you Zak? Huh? I know what foods you like and don't like. I've been doing it forever. Man, that woman has really screwed with your brains."

"Leave her out of this Luke. Just remember. Don't assume anything anymore."

"I got you. Don't worry. I won't disrespect you anymore. I swear."

After exiting the parking lot with less smoke and more sense, followed by a quick forty down the block and to the right, he pulled into the auto parts store in less than two minutes. Somehow Zak wasn't surprised when he spied a patrol vehicle following. At first, he thought the cop had witnessed his temper tantrum in the diner parking lot; then he began to wonder if he'd gone over the speed limit between the diner and the auto store. More likely the Camaro had attracted the cop's suspicions. Muscle cars had a reputation for trouble after all.

Not until the cop got out of his patrol vehicle did another possibility dawn upon Zak. He twisted his body around to look in the backseat and noticed the box full of bones. The woman peeking into the back had noticed the bones and probably called the cops thinking he was some sort of grisly murderer. Zak waited for the cop to approach his side of the Camaro then noticed the cop had unbuckled his gun from his holster. That's when Zak knew he was in big trouble.

Within five minutes, two more patrol vehicles pulled in behind the Camaro and Zak watched from the backseat of one of them as the police began to search his car. Handcuffed and humiliated, Zak turned to look through the back window. Luke had to have noticed all the commotion. But he didn't see his brother anywhere. He saw lots of rubberneckers watching with avid curiosity as the cops peered inside the box. The female cop glanced down at him with searching eyes as if she couldn't believe someone who looked like Zak could be a psycho.

When he tried to explain nobody would listen. When they opened the trunk, and found his collection of shovels and digging tools, there was a great deal of excitement and confirmation between the dozen or so police surrounding him.

"I'm a student studying archeology," he said to the female cop. "Those are my tools. I keep them in the trunk just in case I find something interesting in the desert. Honest, like I said before, just contact my brother Luke, he'll explain everything. He's an archeologist too. You can check with Dr. Baleiff, he'll confirm what I'm saying. He's a professor at the University of New Mexico. He used to teach at Boise State. He knows me."

He might as well have been talking to the wind. Resigned to his fate for the moment, Zak stared down at his feet and waited. When the driver's side door opened, and the cop sat down, the vehicle rocked from his weight. Zak with his hands cuffed behind his back leaned forward to speak. His partner, the female police officer, climbed into the adjoining seat. Before Zak could speak, the man twisted around to get a good look at him.

"Not now. You'll have your chance to speak to a judge. We've read you your rights and its time to sit back and relax. You hear me?"

Zak sat back and stared blindly out the window wishing he'd had the forethought to leave the damned box at home. An encouraging thought popped into his head. Once they realized the bones belonged to a jackrabbit, they'd have to release him. Zak relaxed. He wasn't alone. Luke would figure out what happened. Zak would get his obligatory phone call and he'd be back on the road again. Then he remembered the burglary charge ten years earlier. Shit. Wait. He'd been a juvenile. Those records were sealed. Stay calm, he told himself, just stay calm.

19

Luke waited for Zak at the diner for nearly an hour. When another fifteen minutes passed, he considered marching across the street and yanking Zak out of the auto store. He changed his mind when he considered his brother's new attitude. It might be dangerous confronting him now when he was all hyped up over Constance Wade. After two hours, he decided to call the Napa auto store. It took all his charm to get the waitress to bring him the local phone book.

"Were you aware you can make directory assistance calls on your cellphone sir?"

He made himself smile at her, "I know that ma'am. But why should I have to pay a dollar and forty cents just to find out a number when there is a perfectly good and free phonebook right there?"

Unbeknownst to him the waitress strolled into the kitchen with all the appearance of someone who had nothing on her mind and promptly confessed to the cook she would never see a tip from the tight-wad in the corner. If anyone were to ask Luke what had happened in the last few minutes, he would have said that a brief but informative conversation between himself and the clerk ensued and when apprised of the details, Luke got his way once again.

Luke closed his cellphone with a snap and waved frantically for the waitress. She managed to ignore him for a good two minutes more. Her directions to the Klamath Falls Police Station were simple – walk out the door, turn right, and walk three blocks, then turn right again and walk two blocks. Unlike police stations on television or in movies that want to insinuate a picture of frantic chaos and brutal authority, the Klamath Falls Police Station, like the Boise Police Station, reminded Luke of a museum foyer.

Standing in the foyer without anyone to greet him Luke searched for a door or a hole in the wall where he might be able to talk to a human being. In the distance, he could hear footsteps moving smartly away on a tiled floor and phones ringing and whispered conversations, so he knew the police were in the building somewhere. Evidently, criminals were ushered through a backdoor and visitors must be a rare occurrence. Then he noticed a phone on the wall. He lifted the receiver to his ear and saw the note instructing visitors to dial zero for the operator.

He dialed zero. A woman answered on the third ring. "Hello, I'm looking for my brother Zak Nerin. I was told he'd been picked up by the police at the auto store in town. I want to post bail for him."

"Please find a seat sir and an officer will be with you shortly. Thank you for your patience." the woman said in a neutral, polite voice which for a split-second Luke confused with a prerecorded message.

"How long is shortly, ma'am?" Luke asked struggling to hide his impatience. "We're on a tight schedule and it's imperative that we continue our journey without delay."

"As I said sir, an officer will be with you shortly," she responded in the same neutral tone which irritated Luke more than if she'd snapped at him. Shortly, for the officer, turned out to be twenty minutes for Luke.

Two hours later, Luke sat himself down on the king-size motel bed and stared at his cellphone wondering how he would break the news to his mother. She'd be furious. He couldn't think of anyone else who might be able to help them, unless that someone happened to be Andy. Andy would be his last resort. Andy had no money. The man was poorer than Luke.

Luke left a message with his mother and decided to call Andy anyway. When he had no desire to communicate with others that was the time when everyone wanted to talk to him and interrupt his work, but not today, today when he really needed to speak to someone urgently, he found himself confronted with recorded messages or beeps or bits of techno sound which passed for conversation nowadays.

His mother received a cryptic message: "Hi Mom. Luke and I are in Klamath Falls and there's been a slight misunderstanding. I'll explain everything when you call me back. Please, call me back. It's urgent."

Andy received the following recorded message which he had to string over two calls: "Andy, it's Luke. I need your expertise urgently. You remember those bones you were examining yesterday? Well, Zak is in jail because the police are under the misapprehension Zak might have done away with some kid. Ludicrous huh?

Of course, you know as well as I do that there is some debate about whether those bones are human in the first place, and couldn't possibly be. . .Well, anyway, it's just idiotic. The whole idea is crazy. I just need you to give me a call. I have this plan and I think you might be able to help us. Don't forgot to jot down the time and day I called, Andy. Call me pronto, alright? This is important Andy."

By nine o'clock that evening Luke had seriously considered returning to Woolstone and convincing his mother to wire Zak bail money. He couldn't though. Only Zak knew the mystery-woman's destination. It was frustrating: this waiting and not knowing. When he heard the first few strains of Beethoven's Symphony No. 9 in D minor, Luke nearly dropped his cellphone in his excitement to answer the call. He saw his mother's name with relief. "Where have you been? I've been trying to get you for hours. We've got a situation here—" he began and wasn't able to finish.

"Enough. I already know everything, Luke. I called the Klamath Falls' Police Station and spoke to an Officer Gale. What is going on? I left you to keep an eye on the place. I don't care if Nate is a friend; I still expected one of you boys to be there for me. But what do I find when I come home from Boise? I find Nate drunk on the floor and strangers making themselves at home with my best liquor. So? How are you going to pay for this mess Luke?"

"Mom, you've got to pay close attention. What I'm going to tell you is critical."

"If it's about Mona, don't worry. She arrived safely, dropped off that crazy female's rented car and took her Pinto. Although Nate says she was talking about hunting down the bitch herself. Don't know which bitch that might be and don't give a rat's ass. What'd she do? Mess up Zak's Camaro?"

"I'm. What? Mad Mona's going after Constance? She can't do that."

"Who is Constance?"

"You know who. The woman who showed up in our bar yesterday, the one asking for Mrs. Lawson. She gave Zak a map and told him she'd meet him," he stopped himself from finishing that sentence. He'd rather his mother didn't know where they were headed. It was going to be complicated enough dealing with Brent Wade much less their infuriated mother.

"What is going on Luke? Are you lying to me? I can always tell when you're lying."

"In a way," Luke said and followed this suggestive remark by raising his voice and firing off the most important part before she interrupted him again. "But it's for your own good. If you know where we're heading, you might tell Mad Mona. And we don't want her anywhere near Constance."

"Who is this Constance you keep talking about? I have no idea what's going on with the two of you. Zak is in jail and you need to get him out of there right this minute."

"I already told you, the woman who came into our bar and claimed to be Navan Keys is really Professor Constance Wade. She used to be our teacher at Boise State. She'd be about fifty-seven now, but she doesn't look any older than Quinn. Do you get it, Mom? She knows where to find Amara's grave. She's going to lead us straight to Amara."

"Don't be an idiot Luke," his mother said with a snort. "She can't be your old teacher; she's younger than you."

"She is, and she will. I swear. Her pictures were all over the Wade house. You remember when Zak and I drove to Boise to the memorial service? I didn't make the connection until Constance took off with my truck. I've got her photo in my cellphone. Her son Brent let me take the picture when we were invited to a private gathering at his mother's house. I'll send you a copy. You'll see that I'm right. It's the same woman, only younger. And you know what that means?"

"It means she has a daughter or she is just someone who looks like her."

"When Constance Wade disappeared, she had two sons. No daughters. Just two sons. Mom, think. Dr. Wade found the stage coach. She's got a nose like a bloodhound. Obviously, she and Krutcher moved on from the Smithers' excavation and found Amara. Krutcher disappeared shortly after Professor Wade disappeared. And what about those pictures in his office of the harpy? I bet Krutcher disappeared because no one would believe him if came back to the university and said he was Krutcher and hadn't aged one day since his disappearance. They would think he was nuts. You know what happens to people when they get too close to Amara."

He heard a gasp and paused letting the idea sink in for a second, "That's right. Both Krutcher and Wade can't come forward, because they would have to prove they are still Professor Krutcher and Professor Wade. It would be impossible to be believed the way they look now. Krutcher would be around eighty or so by now; Wade close to sixty. It has to be the only explanation for why they're missing. We've got to get Zak out of prison. He knows where she's going next. She gave him a map. She wants Zak to find her."

"How is it that Zak managed to seduce her and not you? If you would just smile occasionally, honey, and maybe crack a joke or two. Women love men who have a sense of humor."

"I don't have time for a lesson in courtship, Mom. I need bail money to get Zak out of jail. We need to get out of Mayberry and back on the trail."

"You're jumping the gun, Luke. I talked to Officer Gale and he said Zak hasn't been officially charged yet, but they can hold him for twenty-four hours pending an investigation."

"But once they examine the bones they're going to freak out. Andy was sure the skull was human. He couldn't explain the jaw, but what if Zak found some sort of genetic mutant or some crazy damned thing that came from outer space and can't be explained by ordinary means? Then what do we do? We've got to find a way to get him out by tonight or tomorrow at least."

"They haven't set the bail yet," his mother said in a voice he didn't recognize.

"Well when they do, I need to pay it and get him out pronto," Luke said not bothering to hide his exasperation. He was getting tired of people hemming and hawing, unable to make up their minds. He wanted action. Sitting in a motel, stuck in a strange town, and unable to move either forward or backward was unproductive and a waste of his precious time. Luke then realized that his duffel bag full of clothes was still in the Camaro. Truly pissed now, Luke swore.

"What's wrong now?" his mother asked, responding to his exasperation with her own.

"My clothes are in the Camaro. They impounded the Camaro. Damned. I can't even change."

"That's the least of your worries, Luke," his mother said in a tone Luke recognized as acerbic. Her lack of sympathy annoyed him the more. Why couldn't she be more like other mothers?

"You'd be pissed too if you had to wear the same damned underwear for days on end."

"Be a man for god's sakes," she said with a sigh.

"Oh, and wearing dirty smelly clothes for days on end makes you a man, huh?"

"Deal with what you can deal with right now Luke. Life tends to work itself out eventually."

"Tell that to the victims of the Holocaust or 9/11 or the people dying all over the fucking world!"

"Are you on something Luke? I've never seen you like this before."

"You can't see me Mom. We're communicating via the satellite through fancy unnecessarily expensive walkie-talkies. And no, I am not on drugs or drinking. She's getting away damned it. What if she doesn't wait around for Zak, huh? Then we've lost her for good. Do you know how hard it is to track down a person if they don't want to be found? In a country with billions of people in it?"

"You're thinking of China, honey. America doesn't have nearly that many people."

Luke threw up his hands and stared at the ceiling for guidance. It was an effort not to scream into the phone and tell his mother to go to bloody hell.

Somehow his mother seemed to sense the bent-up fury waiting to explode and spoke in a more conciliatory tone, "Okay, I'll wire you the money in the morning, five hundred should be more than enough. If it's not, let me know. Where shall I wire it?"

"I saw a Western Union in town along the main strip."

"What's the name of the street?"

"How should I know? Wait. I'll go out and check."

Ten minutes later, Luke found himself on the street corner with the cellphone up to his ear as if the cellphone could save him from the unfamiliar streets, the elderly couples smiling in his direction, or the giggling teenagers congregating on the doorstep of what might have been a Community Teen Center. After walking the three blocks to find the Western Union and finishing his phone call with his mother, Luke held the phone to his ear for a few more minutes afraid to let go of his tenuous hold on the comfortable known.

He had this odd feeling that life would never be the same again. Certain events were now invariably set in motion. A guy who might or might not have been a cowboy driving an old beat up rusted green Chevy truck pulled into the lot of the Western Union and shot him a fiery glance as if he anticipated a victim in need of rescue and wasn't in the mood to rescue anyone that day.

Luke shoved his cellphone in his jean pocket and started back to the motel. Occasionally, he would look up to see where he was going. An unfamiliar ticking had been going on inside his head for the last thirty-six hours. The ticking grew louder and more insistent. He stopped in his tracks and held onto his head fearing a major migraine. When he woke to reality, the traffic noise had receded, the exhaust smoke, the hot burning sun on his head and down his spine, all the normal sensations of being alive, vanished.

He couldn't remember where he'd gone or how long he'd been gone. He checked the time on his cellphone then the amount of time he'd spoken to his mother. He'd lost ten minutes. He looked around. A ruler thin old man with shoulders growing forward into his chest cavity puffing away at his zillionth cigarette stood under the eaves of a convenience store. He looked away as if embarrassed for Luke. What had Luke done during his black out? God, he hadn't even had a drink.

While the traffic rushed by and exhaust fumes rose up from the asphalt, Luke hurried back to his hotel room. Stress was the only explanation. As he struggled to unlock the hotel room door, his cellphone rang. With relief he saw an old picture of Andy with wild red/yellow hair and a cherub face. He heard him say, "I heard the news. Too bad about Zak. I don't know what I can do to help but I'll do whatever I can, man."

"Who do you think they'll find to examine the bones?" Luke asked.

"Well, I seriously doubt if they've got a forensic anthropologist on call. Probably the coroner."

"Is there some way you could get in touch with the police and explain who you are and your findings?"

"You sure you want me to tell them the truth?"

"No. Yes. Well. Forget it. Your testimony would only make things worse for Zak."

"Not really. I mean I would be telling them that after a cursory examination my findings are that the anterior fontanelle strongly suggests the bones belong to a human infant between nine months and nineteen months as do the scapula, clavicle, humerus, and ulna, although, the secondary incisors are more in keeping with a mammal, perhaps a jackrabbit. I might also say, it's my opinion that the rate of deterioration suggests a time period approximately five thousand years in the past.

And one explanation for the oddity of the bones might have to do with burial rites than any theory of malevolence; perhaps the infant died, and the parents included the infant's pet in the grave or perhaps the grave site might be the result of foraging animals dragging away bones to be consumed later. Nonetheless, further testing would have to be done to determine if the bones are separate entities. In my opinion they are separate entities."

"But you just implied the skull belongs to a human child and the jaw to a hare and they were fused together. How can they be separate entities?"

"I don't know. All I know for sure is that at this present time in our history, the two species are incompatible; after all, a human female can't copulate with a male hare and give birth to a hare/human. Of course, some scientists are experimenting with the DNA of unlikely hosts."

"You mean that story about combining the DNA from a tomato and pig?"

"Yes. I remember hearing about that. I can't remember the other host DNA, I'm certain it wasn't a pig, but I'll look it up for you if you really want to know?"

"Let's stick to our problem, Andy. My brother's freedom is important right now. In any case, I appreciate your efforts. If you can be sure the bones are five thousand years old, there may be a chance Zak won't need bail. But can you be sure? I mean you only examined them for about five or ten minutes. I know you didn't have the necessary equipment to confirm carbon dating but—"

"If the bones had been recent, there would have been flesh and muscle attached. And even if the flesh and muscle had been stripped away from the bones, no one could disguise the fact that they are old. Luke, even you know that. The soil deposits, the pinholes, even the discoloration all indicate the bones are older than say a hundred, even a thousand years at the very least. They're practically fossilized for Leakey's sake."

"Shit. You're right. What was I thinking? Of course. Of course. Okay," Luke said as he paced the floor of his hotel room, his heart beginning to beat at its regular speed once again. "Then by all means, if you should get in touch with the Klamath Falls' coroner for me and confirm your findings. That should save Zak's sorry ass for sure."

"No problem. What's his number?"

"I don't know. But I know the number to the Klamath Falls Police Department."

"That'll do."

"I really appreciate this Andy. Zak will be grateful too."

"Ah, Luke, your brotherly love is heartwarming to hear," Andrew Jankowski said. "Yep, you're are real hoot, my man. See you later. Have a safe trip home."

Luke woke still exhausted having tossed and turned most of the night alternately worried and angry with Zak. If Zak had had the presence of mind to hide the frigging box or just leave it back at the Woolly Man none of this would have happened. They'd be on their way most assuredly. At this very moment they might have been waking up in a motel room not far from Wade. As soon as he decently could, Luke called the police department to find out if they'd charged Zak. The officer who answered had little information and told him to call back in an hour. The rumbling in his stomach indicated a need for sustenance. He was stuck in limbo for the moment, so why not eat?

Luke walked the seven or so blocks back to the Little Turtle Diner. He could have stopped at the convenience store and bought a burrito but the idea of eating a burrito on an upset stomach was less appealing than eating live grasshoppers. Besides the waitress had been friendly and he could sit at a booth and make a few phone calls without being interrupted. He entered the diner and waited for the waitress to notice him. As he examined the other morning patrons cursorily, he noticed a woman sitting in a booth near the window. He experienced the wave, a moment like a ride at the fair, one of those rides that hurls a person up and down and around and the body winces in anticipation of cracking its head on the ground.

She hadn't seen Luke. Then she looked up and stared straight at him as if she didn't recognize him and then away again. A normal person would have reacted, would have either flinched or smiled in acknowledgement of someone they knew. The woman simply returned to her examination of the menu with a thoughtful air. She had looked at him as if he had been a stranger. Luke then noticed a subtle difference in her demeanor. She seemed more confident and worldly than yesterday. In fact, her sharp green eyes and air of superiority reminded Luke of those corporate executives with their fancy suits and briefcases and money deals.

Just as the waitress walked toward him, Luke pointed to the woman and said, "I'll sit with my friend. Thanks." He strode over to her booth and slipped into the seat facing her.

She dropped her menu on the table and stared at him speculatively, "May I help you?"

He noted her confident amusement. "You don't remember me, do you?" he began.

An annoyed expression passed across her face and vanished as quickly, "I see. Well, you've obviously mistaken me for someone else."

"Maybe. But I get the feeling we'll be of use to each other soon enough."

"Can you afford my fee, Mr. ah?"

"Nerin," he said extending his arm to shake her hand. "It's Luke Nerin." As he shook her hand, he speculated whether the proximity to Amara might have caused her lapses in memory. And then his brain finally registered her odd question. He asked in surprise, "What fee would that be?"

"Stewart, as in Frankie Stewart. How de do to you too. Fee? Well, a fee is a payment for services. I charge an upfront fee of one hundred dollars for a consultation," she said lifting her menu once again and examining the contents with interest.

"Consultation?" he asked annoyed when the waitress approached and handed him a menu. Couldn't she tell they were having an important conversation?

"Yes. I'm a consultant for FAS Limited. We match people with appropriate businesses, corporations, organizations, and research groups. Most often we work with corporate executives and on occasion professionals such as physicians, attorneys, athletes, etc."

"How about historical archaeologists or cultural anthropologists?" he asked jestingly.

"Yes. As I said, we connect people with other professionals in their chosen field."

"No kidding?" Luke said his interest aroused despite the other part of him, the practical part of him which tried to bring his thought processes back to reality.

Luke pretended to read the menu while his mind chased around the oddness of this new transformation. As his eyes wandered over the page, he wondered what game she was playing. Did she want to put him off his guard? Did she fear he might hurt her or kidnap her again? Well, he and his brother hadn't really kidnapped her per se. They'd just detained her for her own good. Did she really think her new act would fool him?

He had to admit she was much better at this personality shifting than even Mad Mona and her personalities were heads above Mona's choices. While trapped in the Taurus with Mrs. Lawson, Luke had sensed something anomalous just under the surface, a wisp of a signal, as if Mrs. Lawson were amused, as if her adolescent personality were a deliberate attempt to annoy him. The Taurus? How should he bring up the Taurus with this woman who continued to pretend they had never met?

After Frankie ordered and Luke decided on what he wanted to eat, he began to question his earlier assessment of the woman. It seemed like a complete transformation. Each personality was characterized by a complete set of mannerisms, even voice range, and something in the eye. Leona rarely looked anyone directly in the eye and when she did the look behind the eye reminded him of a lost child's. While the female warrior moved with an economy of energy storing all her vindictive moves for the moments when she had to maim or cripple someone. And only Zak had seen Leona who from the condition of Zak and the motel room must be the nymphomaniac.

This woman across from him looked like she belonged on Wall Street. Or was she just an accomplished actress? Yet the eyes and the way she moved, everything she did and said appeared completely different from the others. Leona's shoulders had been slumped as if she wanted to crawl inside the cushions and hide. This woman stuck her chest out so that everyone could admire her ample breasts. Her back remained marine parade stiff and head high. And this Frankie Stewart not only looked him directly in the eye but had a certain calculation in her demeanor as if she were assessing his credit worthiness.

He preferred Leona's surreptitious peeks about the room, even if she appeared afraid of what she might inadvertently witness. At least Leona seemed more like a woman than this suit before him. He had a hunch Zak would be turned off by Frankie's brisk efficiency and knowing smile. When Luke realized he missed Leona, he began to wonder about his own sanity. How could he miss someone who was sitting right in front of him?

"Is your interest personal or professional Mr. Nerin?" Frankie Stewart asked as she lifted her coffee cup to her lips.

"Ah well, to be honest you looked like someone I knew so I came over thinking I might be able to hitch a ride with a friend."

"I'm sorry. What did you say?" she asked, her expression indicating her confusion. Evidently, she had been expecting something different. She seemed all business, so he suspected her mind had been concentrating on how she could connect him with the right people in the field of archeology. For a fleeting moment, he seriously considered asking her to help him find the right people. Then he realized who she was and mentally kicked himself.

"You see I'm stranded. I got a ride from my, ah, brother, and he ditched me. We had a difference of opinion."

"Really? And what makes you assume I'm from out of town?"

"Well that's obvious. You look more like a sophisticated urban type than someone who belongs here. You said yourself you're a consultant for FAS Limited. And from your accent I would say you're from one of the Midwest cities like Chicago or Minneapolis."

"Which one are you: the archeologist or the cultural anthropologist?" her question indicating a relaxation in her former defensiveness.

"I'm both actually. Can't decide between the two."

"And you expect me to pick up a stranger in a strange town and take him—?"

"I'm heading west. Just drop me off at your final destination and I'll hitch a ride from there. How's that? Oh sure, I'm definitely planning to pay my share of the expenses."

Evidently, his offer of money pleased her, as if her earlier reserve had something to do with the absence of commerce in their dialogue. Luke had forgotten about the thousands of people in the world that considered money the only worthwhile reason to communicate with each other. In his world, people tended to talk about dead cultures and mummies.

He mentally examined his wallet and realized he had only enough to pay for the meal he ordered. He would have to decide quickly. This was his chance. He didn't have time to bail Zak out of jail and still be able to leave town with the most important person in the history of the Nerin Family. Which was more important: finding Amara or bailing Zak out of jail?

"When were you planning to leave?" he asked, hoping he sounded only mildly curious.

"My driver should be here in an hour."

"Driver?"

"Yes, I've hired someone to drive me. I hate to drive. Such a waste of time."

"Would you do me a favor and tell them to hold my breakfast? I'll be right back. It shouldn't take me but ten or fifteen minutes. Here's a twenty. That will pay for both our meals I should think."

Frankie glanced at the twenty on the table between them and up at him with a smile he had trouble understanding. Something passed between them, something electric and rather erotic. He had no time to examine the moment because as she smiled up at him, he was in the process of getting up and heading out the door. Her smile held a promise of some kind. Luke hurried past the waitress and saw his food on the plate with a momentary regret. By the time he returned from his errand his omelet would probably be cold. He sprinted for the Western Union ignoring the rumbling in his stomach.

When he returned to the diner, he forced himself to finish the cold omelet. Just as he dropped his fork on his empty plate, he was privy to the sight of a white stretch limo pulling regally into the parking lot. Frankie looked up from her second cup of coffee and frowned, "Good Lord, Stefan," then turned to face Luke. "My accountant tends to be overzealous sometimes. Well, I guess we should go. Do you need a carryout?"

Luke shook his head in the negative and managed to wolf down the last few bites of his cold breakfast. It was only when they left the diner and headed for the limousine that he discovered, he could have finished his breakfast with plenty of time to spare and even ordered dessert to go, as well. The driver had already gotten out of the limo. He was young and fit and wore a pair of tight blue jeans and an expensive jacket. And he also happened to be carrying several packages with the names of expensive department stores emblazoned across the bags and boxes. Frankie accepted the packages without question and turned to Luke, "I won't be but a minute. Go ahead and make yourself comfortable inside." She followed this extraordinary request by wheeling about and heading back to the diner.

Luke and the driver exchanged looks. He didn't care for the driver's smirk, so he climbed inside the limo and waited for Frankie to make her next move. He absorbed at a deeper level, the rich tan leather and smell of newness and look of luxury inside the limo while thinking abstractly about this new phase of the Leona matrix and what her real intentions might be. He was damned if he would walk away from this opportunity to learn more from her. She had to be Constance albeit a loony Constance Wade.

As the minutes ticked by, he began to worry that perhaps she had been planning all along to ditch him and leave him with the cost of the rented limo. It was with profound relief that he watched her stride out of the diner with a swish of her backside that did something to his stomach. She walked with her head high and eyes bright. Her arrogance unnerved him a bit. It rather reminded him of someone else. But when the driver opened the door for her and Luke scooted over to the other side, she said, "Stefan outdid himself this time. I've got to give that man a raise, don't you think?"

Only when they were down the road sitting in the backseat cocooned in the luxurious leather and mahogany interior, which could have seated at least eight more people comfortably, did Luke consider Zak's plight. He winced at the image that came to mind, the image of Zak sitting on the bottom bunk of some Spartan jail cell surrounded by drunks and criminals who might be tormenting him at that very moment. He brushed the thought aside. He had no time to feel sorry of his brother.

Mom would find a way to get Zak out of prison. Or Zak would convince someone to release him. On the other hand, Andy had probably already contacted the Klamath Falls Police Department and spoken to the coroner. The coroner would surely realize the bones were too old to be of any use as evidence. Maybe a night in jail would remind Zak to be more careful about his artifacts. And when Luke found Amara, the Nerins would have the future they were destined for – a future of prosperity and power. Luke couldn't turn back now. This lucky turn of events meant he was on the right track. He leaned back in his seat and relaxed for the first time since he'd left Woolstone.

He heard Frankie chuckle and glanced her way. She had just crossed her legs and he noticed for the first time what she was wearing. How many business professionals of the female persuasion wore tight dress suits with plunging necklines and hooker heels? Her open toed black heels looked sort of dangerous too. But what did he know about the corporate world? Nothing really. Her sharp burgundy nails with the diamond points matched the burgundy stripes in her gun metal gray dress suit. Somehow the whole ensemble from her glossy blue-black hair, jade colored eyes, cream colored satin and lace undergarment, tailored and expensive dress suit, and eye-popping heels looked just right on her.

Absently, he wondered when she'd had time to shop and where in this town she could have found that assortment of garments and accessories.

As if she'd read his mind, she said, "Stefan is a genius. Who would have thought one could Fed Ex Rodeo Drive anywhere in the world, especially here?" Luke opened his mouth to say something banal, but she forestalled him. "I know. You're thinking I must be the shallowest creature alive. Well, I am."

"A shallow person would have left me back at the diner fending for myself. No. You're hardly shallow."

"It's early days dear," she said with a speculative look. For a second, Luke's initial reaction was fear. Sanity prevailed. For one thing, he was bigger and taller than her and must outweigh her by at least fifty or sixty pounds. And his years of digging and climbing had improved his agility and strength. Besides the day Zak grilled his ass on summer break from college, he had decided to take a few martial art's classes. No way would he let anyone, much less his little brother throw him to the ground again. Now that he was prepared, he could defend himself against her assault too. Uncertainly, he touched the lump on the side of his head, now hidden by his hair.

Just before the limo reached the outskirts of town, Luke realized the driver might become an encumbrance at some point. It would serve Luke's purpose to drive. He just wished he had known about the limo and offered to drive her himself. The driver would be a witness that Luke had accepted a ride from Frankie Stewart. Well, there wasn't much he could do about it now. Better to leave well enough alone.

"You know I feel like a sycophant here. Why don't you let me drive for you? Then I'd feel useful," he said tentatively.

"Don't worry Mr. Nerin. I'll find a use for you somehow, some way," Frankie said cryptically which made Luke more nervous than he'd been a moment ago. What had he gotten himself into anyway? The only way he could relax was to remember that Leona and Eve were inside this woman and those two personalities were more tractable. His nervousness returned when he remembered the fierce one with a gift for garroting people. She seemed to have gotten real pleasure out of chopping him in the throat with the side of her hand. He hadn't expected that move, especially from someone dressed in purple scarves.

20

The holding tank where Zak sat on a hard bench consisted of a public toilet open to everyone's view, several narrow windows seven feet above the south facing brick wall, and four men in various positions about the room. The largest of them slept precariously on the narrow bench directly opposite Zak. He lay full length on the bench taking up all the available space. The views were limited to a sliver of sunshine barely penetrating the room from the tiny windows above his head, the large window in the hall leading to freedom and opposite his holding cell another holding cell with windows just as small as their cage.

Compared to the guys in the cell across the hall and the guys inside his cell, the sleeping giant only two feet from him was the scariest of the lot. He had a shaved head with tattoos on his arms, as well as, tattoos on his back and chest. He wore a muscle shirt that revealed huge rippling biceps. Incongruously though, the lower half of him might have been from a different man. He had a pot belly and spindly legs. What appeared to be pieces of metal were looped like knitting between the folds of his flesh along his forearm. The ornaments had been set inside his skin next to the tattoo of a big breasted female. The ornament's symbolism eluded Zak. What did a bird's wing signify? He would have expected a swastika from someone called Oxley.

Occasionally the bald guy's snoring would be interrupted by sputtering and coughing. Then the man would turn over on his side and resume his dreaming. The thin short man sitting in the far corner reminded Zak of a geek, one of those incredibly smart geniuses that knew nothing about hygiene or girls. He watched everyone with terrified eyes, his body constantly moving: crossing and uncrossing his legs, holding his arms tight to his chest and then reaching out to hold onto the walls, as if he thought he was on a roller coaster.

Coming down from a bad trip? He had the look of someone familiar with prisons. Zak sensed an underlying nastiness. He seemed like the type of guy who could do some real damage to anyone stupid enough to test his manhood. Just as a nervous dog might turn into a vicious beast when threatened, this guy would probably snap and bite, kick, and claw anyone that threatened him.

As soon as Zak spotted the last remaining member of their group, he knew he would be in for a long humiliating and painful twenty-four hours. Leland Ansel recognized him at the same time he recognized the owner of *Around the World Pawn*. The man had changed a lot in ten years, at least physically. He used to be a rotund butter ball of a douche bag. He must have lost at least sixty pounds. He still wore dark slacks which made his stick legs look even skinner than normal and penny loafers which made his big feet appear bigger.

Leland's signature greasy gray hair was still parted too far over on one side as if his comb knew more about Leland than Leland, as if the comb knew Leland was unbalanced. Leland did his habitually annoying toss of the head which swept his stringy hair out of his eyes and sideways. Zak recalled the moment Leland confronted him about the missing Navaho blanket and peace-pipe.

After ten minutes of silence between them, Zak counted fifteen head tosses. Why didn't he just cut the shit off? And the huge black horn-rimmed glasses accentuated unflatteringly Leland's oblong face and enormous black eyes. He'd gone from looking like a malevolent turtle to looking like a bug. Not an attractive bug either. More like what a praying mantis would look like with glasses. The lack of color in Leland's pupils confirmed Zak's suspicions that the man was an alien from another planet. It was impossible to read the man's thoughts because his face and especially his eyes registered little emotion. Psychopath. According to experts, psychopaths were glib, charming, and manipulative.

As far as Zak could tell, Leland rarely if ever demonstrated glibness or charm, only a lucky ability to manipulate the naïve or bone deep dumb. In fact, Leland had few social graces. Well, glibness and manipulation were hardly social graces, but some people less comfortable in their own skins tended to equate glibness and manipulation with strength. Other people even found such traits sexy.

When Leland stood up as if to wander toward the bars of the holding tank, Zak watched him warily anticipating a confrontation. Leland spent exactly thirty seconds surveying the empty hallway. The view consisted of a narrow corridor with pastel brown walls and several thin windows facing the alley. The windows were designed specifically for prisons with their heavy wire construction interlaced between the panes of glass. At the end of the corridor stood a steel door from whence officers of the law and other personnel from the Klamath Falls Police

Department entered and departed. And these comings and goings were so rare, most likely Leland would have nothing of interest to see beyond an occasional fly on the wall or a spider swinging from the ceiling.

Beyond the steel door, Zak knew freedom waited. All he had to do was to wait for the police to come to their senses or his brother bail him out. Surely, Luke must have figured out by now what had happened to him and was at that very moment in the process of getting him out. He could count on Luke. He'd never known Luke to let him down before. Well, there had been the time at the Gorge during a rock concert when Luke had been drunk and left him behind. But Zak had managed to hitch a ride home with a couple of sweet ladies who made the trip worthwhile. Then there was the time...

Zak heard someone speak. "I'm not surprised to see you," Leland said. Zak looked up and saw Leland. Leland stood two feet away with his arms crossed and his black eyes probing. His stare unnerved Zak. It seemed to go on forever. Emotionless. Empty. A void of coldness that gave him the shivers.

"Well, good for you," Zak said. In the back of his mind he knew he couldn't back down from Leland's attempts to intimidate him. Not in this place. Zak jumped up and stepped inside Leland's comfort zone, in the hopes Leland would back down and leave him alone. "You got a problem with me?"

"Got an itch, don't you? Can't control that itch to take what don't belong to you. Yeah, I know your kind," Leland said, fairly spitting the words out with venom uncalled for under the circumstances.

"And you're a model citizen huh? You live off the misery and debt of others and you think that makes you better than me?" Zak said wanting to get out of this place so bad he could taste the staleness of the air in his throat.

"I don't need to justify myself to you. You're just a small-time thief and a whore living off old ladies," Leland said with a smug smile.

Zak forgot everything but the desire to wring Leland's scrawny neck but when he heard someone say, "Hold off there. Let go now, son. You want to spend more time in this shithole?" Zak discovered he was on the floor with Leland beneath him and his hands were wrapped around Leland's skinny throat. He was in the process of choking him to death.

Or at least that's what he wanted to do. The man who pulled Zak off Leland happened to be the big guy with the bald head who'd been sleeping off his drunk. The man was so strong he only had to use one arm to yank Zak to his feet and shove him back onto his bench. Then the drunk returned to his sleeping quarters, the hard-wooden bench next to Zak's. He spread himself out on the bench as before and turned onto his side facing the wall.

Demoralized by his violent reaction, Zak leaned back until his head touched the cold tile and stared at the ceiling. He could hear Leland shouting for an officer. Zak heard the steel door squeal in protest from rusty hinges and hit the opposite wall with a clatter of metal on brick. Footsteps approached. The officer stood with his hand resting lightly on the holster of his gun belt and listened politely to Leland's gasping narration of the events that had just transpired, "Get me out of here. That guys crazy. He tried to choke me to death."

Zak didn't have to look to know Leland's finger must be jabbing the air and pointing accusingly in his direction.

The officer addressed everyone in the holding cell, "Anyone witness the assault?"

The drunk continued to snore. The other guy, the thin nervous one, shrugged and looked at the floor. His response surprised Zak, "I didn't see anything."

The inexplicable silence alarmed Zak. The charged atmosphere in the cell made him jumpy and alert. He surveyed the holding tank and the police officer in the same manner he used to survey a chaparral where a cougar or a wolf might hide. In only a few hours, he'd come to the realization that this place held more danger than any landscape he'd ever hunted in. Even as a kid he hadn't been all that enthusiastic about hunting or holding a weapon; yet, now in his present situation he longed for a gun to hold in his hand, a gun which would keep the crazies and the violent at bay. From where had this paranoia come?

When Leland's probing eyes moved past Zak and onto the police officer, Zak had an opportunity to watch Leland closely. Leland stood stiff and erect on the bench and surveyed the officer with those opaque eyes. The intensity of his stare, Zak realized with amusement, bothered the officer as much as it bothered Zak. Then Leland smiled, and the smile radiated such charm, Zak nearly fell off his bench. The transformation was astonishing. For a moment, Leland looked younger and happier. He even sort of looked handsome. The tone of his voice had changed as well. Instead of a consistent blandness, Leland had managed to include a sort of southern inflection and a soothing rhythm which was appealing at first until the words penetrated Zak's conscious thoughts.

"This must all seem bizarre to you, Officer. I understand. I may have provoked Mr. Nerin, but I assure you it was unintentionally. You see so much has happened lately. I mean my pawn shop was robbed just a few days ago. And this young man, officer, ten years ago, he was lurking around my place when I was robbed the first time. So naturally, I wondered if he had tried to rob it again. I can't believe anyone would be stupid enough to do so. But then again, the crime would be rather clever if perpetrated by the same criminal. Who would suspect the same person would rob the store twice?

And I still have Indian artifacts. Artifacts this young man covets, by the way. Those missing artifacts were legitimately acquired by me. This man seems to think they belong to him. So, of course, I'm thinking there must be some sort of connection between the robbery and this man sitting over there. Is he following me, perhaps planning to rob me when I get out of here? Your guess is as good as mine. But I don't believe in coincidences. This man is up to something, officer. And it's no good I assure you."

The police officer stood facing them with the bars of the cell separating them from him and he seemed extra special relaxed and thoughtful as if he were listening to his grandmother recite a familiar bedtime story. Yet Zak noticed with interest how the officer's eyes were attentive elsewhere. Actually, he seemed more curious about the tattooed man whose snores reverberated off the walls than Leland and Leland's accusations. After Leland had finished, there was a long, punctuated silence. Strange how a minute can drag until a minute feels like an hour. When the officer spoke, Zak noticed Leland begin to toss his hair which signaled his uneasiness.

"Oxley," the officer shouted. "Hey Oxley. Knock it off. We can hear you clear in the lobby." The tattooed man turned onto his other side and the snoring stopped yet Oxley's eyes remained firmly closed.

"Thanks," the officer said cheerfully. "And Gail says she'll have breakfast for you in the morning." Then the officer made a sweeping survey of the holding tank behind him and left with a squeal of rusty hinges and a firm clank of the heavy door.

Leland who had his elbows on his knees, bent his head and held his head in his hands for several minutes as they all heard the guys in the holding tank across from them break out into ruckus mocking laughter.

347

The laughter continued for some time, signaling their disgust with snitches like Leland. Everyone sobered up after someone said something Zak couldn't quite catch. Leland who was closer to the hall heard what the guy said. It was Leland's response to the words which drained the blood from his face. Zak thought he heard the word mole or something to that effect.

Silence reigned supreme for nearly an hour until the drunk woke in a sputter of snorts and gasps and walked over to the toilet to pee. It took Oxley nearly two minutes to empty his bladder, two full minutes. There must have been a shit load of drinking going on for that man to pee gallons of liquid into a toilet bowl.

Trying to shut out Oxley's urinating marathon accompanied by farts and hawking of spitballs into the toilet, Zak stared at Leland who had his hands still covering his face in shame. Then he remembered, Leland hated crowds. This must be the most excruciating time in his life, Zak thought, and the realization gave him a great deal of pleasure. It was about damned time the bastard got his comeuppance.

Even when Zak was younger, he remembered stepping toward Leland and Leland flinching. His mother had told him that the one-time Leland had come into the bar, Leland had gotten nervous when a couple of guys stood too close to him as they questioned him about the authenticity of a Stratocaster he had for sale. Evidently, the guys had unwittingly invaded his invisible personal space. Leland's boundary line was different from every other person's in that he felt uncomfortable if people stood even two feet away. That's why he liked to be behind a bullet-proof plexiglass counter while dealing with customers. Zak remembered the sweat on Leland's forehead and how he bolted for the door before they had a chance to finish asking their questions about his merchandize. He remembered laughing along with his brother as they watched the turd run out of the bar.

So why had Leland, moments ago, stood so close to Zak? Could his sudden courage have had something to do with his precious pawn shop? And what about that remark of his – "living off old ladies?" How had Leland heard about Patricia Steel and Amanda Williams? It had been years ago. He'd just turned twenty-one, and was in Jackpot, Nevada celebrating with a few friends. The friends took off wanting to get home before dark. He refused to leave. No matter how drunk he might be, he never jeopardized his Camaro.

When he couldn't find a room, he decided he'd just sleep in his car. By the time he recognized the women, he was plastered. With his inhibitions long since gone, he must have told them about the lack of available rooms and they must have offered him the couch in their room. Amanda and Patricia had been coming into the Woolly Man since he was a kid. He'd never thought much about them until that weekend. The two older women, gorgeous older women who looked half their age had offered to buy him dinner. And before he knew it, he'd woken up in a luxurious hotel room finding himself sleeping between two naked women close to his mother's age.

After that night he cut back on his consumption of alcohol. Yet he remembered bits and pieces of what took place with real pleasure. It had been awesome for sure, a never to be forgotten time in his life but nothing he ever wanted to repeat. Lucky for him, they were nice women who once they realized what had happened were equally as embarrassed. Instead of rushing off in shame, they all went down to the dining room and had a nice meal and a good talk. Amanda made a joke about getting together on his twenty-second birthday, but Patricia shook her head, "Honey, this beautiful man has better things to do then run around with a couple of old broads. Leave him be."

Or had it all been an act? His stomach heaved at the idea Leland had had something to do with his encounter with those women. No. Not possible. Patricia and Amanda were seasonal regulars in the Woolly Man. The two friends and their husbands wintered in Sun Valley, had homes in San Diego and New York, and spent part of their summers in southern Idaho. Every year the couples flew to Boise, rented cars, and spent a few weeks fishing and gambling.

They would have no reason to help Leland with his nefarious schemes. They were rich and beautiful and smart. They probably had lovers in other states anyway. Besides, they wouldn't have dared mess with Jule Nerin's sons. They knew her reputation. His mother would have found a way to ruin their cushy pampered lives somehow. Although, the idea of Leland spying on him made Zak feel violated. The scummy bastard.

And how had Leona known? Did she know Patricia and Amanda? Hell no. How could she? He was getting paranoid. Or. It was possible she knew about Patricia and Amanda because Mad Mona knew. Mad Mona always knew shit about everybody in town. Maybe Mad Mona had spent some time back east in the same hospital as Jane Smith and maybe she'd said something to Jane/Leona? Why? Leona had never met him until the day she stepped into the Woolly Man. Why would anything Mad Mona had to say about the people back home matter to Leona?

Suddenly, the walls seemed closer than they had been before. The room smelled like an outhouse. And up in the corners he swore he saw molt where the damp had eaten through the ceiling. That moment of looking about the room eased the intensity of Leland's stare, so when Zak looked back at him fleetingly, he noticed for the first time the tremors in Leland's legs as Leland made his way to the bench along the wall directly opposite. Leland sank down on the bench and clutched his knees as if to force them to stay still.

The tension in the room was overwhelming. Zak had been uncomfortable earlier but now he sensed something dangerous oozing through the cracks in the brick. Even though there were no physical signs from Leland, well, maybe one, Zak sensed the man's intense hatred just beneath the surface. Leland no longer tossed his head which made Zak even more cautious. Instead, Leland stared around the room through his camouflage of greasy locks, unfocused and emotionless.

A new ugliness had entered the room. The big guy, Oxley, with the tattoos on his arms and neck sensed the change as well. After his waterfall, Oxley returned to his bench and flopped down and looked around the room with peevish annoyance. The big guy wasn't exactly happy to be there, but Zak realized his first impressions of the tattooed giant had been completely wrong. His upper body bigness was deceiving. Oxley was probably an easy going and good-natured guy and the tattoos were just decoration. If Zak were wrong, those muscular arms could do some real damage to his puny body.

Aikido had nothing to do with fighting per se, mostly balance and defense. In a tight spot like this holding tank, Zak would have only one opportunity to throw the big guy down. But just one punch from Oxley could knock Zak out or potentially kill him. He would rather not have to test his skills against those fists. The guy had to be nearly seven feet tall and about two hundred fifty or so pounds. Zak might as well be fighting two people instead of the one. That's almost an extra person per pound. There was very little fat on Oxley. All muscle. No. Zak wouldn't stand a change without some means of escape. He was grateful the big guy appeared to be amiable.

Leland's voice rang out hysterically, "I know it was you Nerin. You broke into my shop again. That's why you're here. You're trying to sell the stuff you stole from me."

"I don't know what you're talking about Ansel," Zak said glancing nervously at Oxley wishing Leland would give it a rest. The tattooed giant rubbed his eyes and shook his head as if to clear his thoughts.

"Shut up," Oxley said cutting Leland off. "Your squeaky voice is giving me a fucking headache. Screech. Screech."

The thin dark-haired guy now chewing his gum so rapidly the snaps were in synch made a sound which might or might not have been a giggle. Evidently, the sound amused Oxley. Couldn't Leland sense the abnormality of the situation? Those two knew each other. They were probably drinking buddies. Instead of paying attention to the change in the atmosphere, Leland leaned forward to stare at Zak with blank black eyes. When Leland, now more restless than ever, decided to get up, alarm bells went off in Zak's head, especially after Leland chose to sit close to Zak, ignoring his own boundaries, so close he was near enough for Zak to be able to smell Leland's rank sweat.

Leland's nearness gave Zak the willies. The creep went so far as to twist his torso around as if by using his eyes, he could cause Zak bodily harm. I can kill you with my eyes, Zak thought and struggled not to laugh. He felt betrayed. Beyond his prison, he sensed something had gone seriously wrong. An unexpected numbness swept over him, a sense of fatality. He imagined himself encased in gauze, gauze which would insulate him against the trouble to come. Leland seemed oblivious to the danger and addressed Zak in a whisper with enough venom that his mouth showered spit on Zak's shirt.

While Leland's scary eyes darted nervously about the room, Zak avoided looking directly at him, not wanting to see the void up close. The absence of emotion in the man was unnerving enough from far away. Leland had predatory eyes, eyes of some ravenous animal, one of those nocturnal creatures that preferred to hunt at night. Only now, the creature had a baboon to content with in the same cage. If Oxley hadn't been in the holding tank, Zak imagined Leland would have found some way to slip a knife or something sharp into Zak's ribs. Whoever said the weak were meek had never had one caged inside a ten-foot by twelve-foot room with them.

"Two days ago, I came home from my vacation and I found that someone had broken down my door, the bottom half of my door," Leland whispered in an unsteady intense voice. "My shop door, mind you. And only someone with martial arts training could do such a thing, could break through a thick wooden door like that with their boot. The police claim whoever broke the door couldn't have used a hatchet. It had to have been someone's foot. What about my dog huh? He'll never be the same again.

I'd never have figured you for a poisoner, Zak Nerin. Yeah. That's right. They found the poisoned T.V. dinner in the alley. But he was smart. He didn't eat it. But I got no use for him anymore. He's a whimpering mess peeing all over my floors and whining all day long now. And my office. That was pure spite rummaging through my personal papers. You had no right to mess with my private stuff. I know it was you Nerin. There could be no one else. What'd you come back for anyway? You forgot something the last time you broke in?"

Zak knew that to maintain some sort of authority he had to stand up to Leland. Moving away would only signal weakness. So, he sat there and listened to the guy's nutty thoughts spoken aloud and heard the hate vibrating beneath the surface. He'd heard about the break in on the news. Zak knew he hadn't broken in, but he began to wonder who might have and what he or she might have been looking for. The blanket and pipe had been the most valuable items in the shop. What else could there be worth stealing: old television sets, phonograph records, toasters, maybe a microwave? Hardly.

When Leland in his excitement leaned forward and Zak smelled his stale breath, Zak discovered his comfort zone and shoved Leland forcefully away, so forcefully Leland fell onto the floor at his feet. Instead of returning to his original place across the room, Leland returned to Zak's bench. He made a big production out of brushing imaginary dirt off his pants. Zak did his best to ignore him but the hairs on the nape of his neck were telling him something was seriously wrong with this guy, something nasty seemed to be bubbling up from the ashes of an old resentment.

A momentary glance in Oxley's direction revealed something equally disturbing. Oxley happened to be looking at Leland at that moment, looking at him with a sort of respect mixed with distaste. Evidently, Zak's fury had been outmatched by Leland's creepiness. Zak's uncomfortable memory reminded him of a study done on hierarchies in the criminal world. Criminals respected power. No one had as much power as the guy who feared nothing, not even death. But even Dahmer had met his match. Zak sensed a seriously disturbed childhood in Leland's past. Zak imagined himself surrounded by these three like a fawn surrounded by hungry wolves.

He had to get a grip on his fear. Sure, the three of them might be wolves but this was a holding cell and the police were just beyond the door. Oxley might be a Hell's Angel, maybe even one of those enforcers he'd heard about, capable of unspeakable brutality. And then again maybe not. His expression had been so benign earlier. Zak shook the fear off him. No. He was being paranoid.

Oxley's current behavior indicated a familiarity with prisons and criminals and police officers only. If he had really been a Hell's Angel, the police would have treated him differently. For one thing, he would have been isolated in his own cell. Instead, he was among the general population and the police knew him well enough to joke around with him. Oxley was just a drunk. And the other guy, just Oxley's drinking buddy, a guy who would only knife someone in the dark if his life were threatened. And Leland. Leland was the creepiest of them all. Zak hoped he could last the night without getting knifed or beaten up or worse.

An odd voice penetrated Zak's musings. The deep bass edged with a slight southern drawl began with an amusing anecdote. Zak missed the first part of the anecdote so mesmerized by the sound and rhythm of the voice. The voice belonged inside an actor, one of those Shakespearian actors, not Oxley's drinking buddy, not the skinny geek tucked in the corner of the room. The geek ignored Zak and Leland and spoke directly to Oxley. As he spoke, Oxley nodded his head in acknowledgement, occasionally grinning wickedly at the man's play on words. Then Oxley's amusement changed dramatically, and an expression of distaste played about his moon shaped face. His big brown eyes grew smaller. The wicked grin disappeared.

Zak listened carefully this time and heard the guy say, "Never met one quite like this guy though. According to Gail someone called the cops anonymously. Someone must have recognized him from American's Most Wanted maybe. Sure enough the cops found him in the motel room, you know the one, just down the road close to the exit. He was in the room with that little girl. He claimed she was his niece. They say the first victims are usually family members. I heard that on Oprah once. Cute kid too. Hey Bug Eyes, what is it about kids that gets you off anyway? I don't see it myself. My momma used to say it were better for everyone if your kind got your peckers wacked off. The world would be a better place. Oh yeah."

All the while the man was addressing Oxley, Leland remained still as a mouse. As the voice droned on, Zak inched his way toward the end of the bench. He didn't want to be associated with the creep at all, not even by proximity. Spellbound by the man's voice he listened and waited, waited for the inevitable shit storm. The difference between Zak and Leland's response to the anecdote was the difference between the sun and the moon. The sun was a living fiery furnace. The moon was a cold dead planet. While Zak was simultaneously nauseated and enraged by the images conjured up by the Shakespearean voice, Leland seemed bored by the whole thing. From the corner of his eye, he was shocked to see Leland blink himself awake as if he'd nodded off for a second.

Wow. What a scum bag. It was like sitting next to a piece of furniture. There was a sense of something solid to his left but nothing living. They all seemed to hold their breath in anticipation. Was Oxley's friend some sort of sadomasochist? He seemed to be setting up the room for war, eager to see blood and carnage. The geek was happy as he pumped up the fires spreading the outrage from their cell to the one across the hall. "His niece, can you believe it? She looks like a cute kid, sweet with her big blue eyes and blond curls. A little angel. She reminds me a lot of your youngest kid Ox. I heard her telling the cop how she was promised a trip to a real princess' palace and wanted to know when were they leaving. She kept saying she wanted to see the princess. Who the hell is Petal Run? The princess or a ride?"

The analytical part of Zak questioned the intentions of the geek, wondering why he chose to bring up the subject at this time? Then Zak began to wonder about the dynamics of space. Would the four of them have reacted to each other differently, if they had had more space between them or been able to move about freely? Was the nastiness he had noticed earlier a separate energy generated by the anger inside them all, an anger made possible by the confines of this small space?

In any case, Zak had his doubts about Leland Ansel's predilection for children. He'd been going to the pawn shop off and on for years with his friends and his brother. Leland didn't strike him as particularly interested in kids. In fact, Leland seemed to hate kids more than he hated women. They annoyed and irritated him. Actually, he disliked everybody. Zak was pretty sure Leland was more of a misanthrope than a pedophile. Now his clerk, yeah, his clerk, on the other hand, was definitely a pedophile.

All these thoughts and questions ricocheting off the walls of Zak's mind. They took a minute or two to come and go and in last second of that last-minute Oxley had had time to get up from his seat and charge toward Leland. Zak's first instinct was to get out of the way and duck in anticipation of a blow. He heard Leland make an animal sound, a sort of high pitched shriek of pain. The sound stopped. All Zak could hear was the pounding of flesh against flesh and a crack as bones broke.

He couldn't stand by and do nothing. Even though he hated the guy with all his being, he made himself stand on shaky legs and move toward Oxley. A quick glance at the scrawny geek who'd incited the riot confirmed what Zak had previously guessed. The guy was in heaven, his eyes filled with glee. Both Leland and the geek made Zak sick. He was sickened even more by the sight of the geek shadow-boxing the air imitating Oxley's punches.

It took all of Zak's willpower to jump on Oxley's back and pull his shoulders with all his strength, futilely trying to get him off Leland. He had to beat on Oxley's head and shoulders and the weak part of his arm where the forearm met the biceps to even manage to get Oxley's attention. The big guy tried to shrug him off, but Zak clung to the man's broad back in abject terror knowing if Oxley turned his anger onto Zak, Zak would look like the thing writhing on the floor beneath them both. Adrenaline surged through his bloodstream, clouding his vision for those few moments, giving him a euphoric sense of invincibility, as if he could fly if he so desired. He was Jaeger fighting off the Night Stalker with his wits and his speed.

He used his adrenaline high to try to incapacitate the enraged beast beneath him. It wasn't until later, until the officers poured into the holding tank and pried them all apart, until he'd been taken to the nearest hospital and his wounds examined that Zak realized the knuckles on his right hand looked as if they'd gone through a grinder. Soon enough they began to swell up and he couldn't make a fist.

All his training in Aikido had deserted him. He'd reacted on pure instinct without using his skills or considering the consequences of his actions. He could have sat by and watched the beating like the cockroach did who started the fight, but Zak had always considered himself a champion for the underdog. Even if the underdog happened to be a sick fuck like Leland Ansel, Zak liked to think of himself as a civilized human being.

Today he'd seen the other side of man, the side he hoped he'd never see again. The adrenaline had dissipated somewhat but he noticed with detached interest that every nerve in his body still trembled in reaction to what had happened. From what he could tell from the angry worried expressions of the police officers and their superiors, someone would have to pay for what had happened. Oxley, Zak discovered, happened to be in the hospital as well, somewhere on a different floor. Zak had no idea what had happened to Leland. The bloody thing on the floor suggested Leland would be spending considerable time in the hospital hereafter.

A plain clothes detective threw open the sliding door and entered the examination room where Zak had been left in peace to rest and recover. Earlier, Zak had been congratulating himself on finally having some privacy. There was nothing better than to be treated with a little bit of dignity, nothing better than to be lying in a soft bed with clean sheets and a comfortable cushy pillow, and especially after having to fight for your dear life just for a little bit of space like a rat in an overcrowded cage.

When the detective entered his room, he started worrying again. Just as the detective opened the sliding door, Zak heard screaming followed by muffled moaning. He suspected the sounds were coming from Leland Ansel's throat. He winced and was relieved when the detective shut the door and cut off the sounds of an animal in pain. The detective was middle aged with an impressive belly. As the detective stared at Zak with curiosity mixed with amazement, Zak's fear meter went way up. What fresh disaster was he in for now?

"Mr. Nerin, I'm Detective Murphy. I won't keep you long sir. We've got your testimony and now we just need your signature at the bottom here and then you're free to go."

"I'm what?" Zak asked in surprise.

"You're free to go sir. According to our coroner, the bones have been authenticated by a forensic specialist and the coroner agrees with the expert that the bones are too old to be from a recent crime. You've got yourself something pretty fantastic Bill says. A five-thousand-year-old mystery. Anyway. Before you go, we just need to clear up this other matter."

Zak accepted the clipboard from the detective and glanced down at the typed piece of paper. He read the summary of events which had taken place the day before, nearly eighteen hours ago which would have been around five in the afternoon yesterday. His words had been accurately recorded on the page. With the hope of release, Zak signed the paper and wrote the date then handed the clipboard back to the detective.

"How's?" Zak, under the circumstances had trouble wrapping his tongue around Leland's name.

The detective seemed to understand and said, "There was a lot of blood and it looked worse than it really was Mr. Nerin. I hope you'll keep that in mind."

"This Oxley guy. What's going to happen to him?" Zak asked, self-preservation uppermost in his mind now.

"That's not your problem Mr. Nerin," he said in a haughty officious tone, then leaned forward in a more conciliatory manner and said the most extraordinary thing. "Oxley wanted me to tell you, he was impressed by your guts, kid. He says hardly anybody's ever stood up to him when he's in a rage."

"I'm relieved to know Oxley's not thinking about revenge," Zak said. "But I'm wondering what's going to happen next?"

"As I said, you're free to go."

"What about my car?"

"You can pick it up at the yard."

"Where's the yard?"

"Behind the police station. An officer will give you a lift back to the station."

"So, I can go now?"

The detective opened the door and called to someone. Another police officer appeared at the door and peered in and one look at the expression on his face told Zak that the whole Klamath Falls Police Department would have either hired him on the spot if he'd chosen the profession or voted him as mayor of the city.

All Zak wanted to do was to be long gone from Klamath Falls and Oxley. He'd had enough of testosterone and paranoia for one twenty-four-hour period. It took another two hours before he could retrieve his personal belongings. With his wallet and keys in his pocket and the retrieval of his Camaro from the impound yard, then and only then, could he call himself well and truly free of Klamath Falls' authority.

Still there had been no word from his brother and he was beginning to suspect a typical scenario of abandonment. Zak decided to go to the diner where they had originally planned to meet and find out what had happened to his brother. He was also starving for some real food, something without a plethora of carbohydrates and processed sugars.

After having thoroughly checked his baby for any scratches or indications of misuse, Zak climbed into the Camaro and paused to watch a young blonde with a nice pair of shapely legs climb out of a much-abused minivan parked too close to the curb. He soon lost interest when he noticed the child's safety chair in the backseat. Too bad, he thought, aware from a cursory glance at her license plate that she was from Idaho too.

Nevertheless, he took a moment to appreciate the fluidness of all her parts, especially those magnificent legs as she climbed the steps and entered the police station. Just as he started the engine and listened to his baby greet him with a throaty hello, another car zipped into the empty space beside him.

He heard the wailing long before he spotted the perpetrator. Zak had to wait impatiently for this new person to squeeze her fat ass out of the driver's side door. He winced at the hysteria going on in the backseat of her blue sedan, a cacophony of sounds which pierced the eardrum. The child of five or six continued to scream and kick the back of the passenger chair in front of her, her face dripping with angry sweat and her cheeks green and sticky with snot. There in that backseat was another excellent reason why he preferred the single life.

In annoyance he realized the woman planned to walk around her vehicle to open the back door and assist the child out. Unable to move without running the lady down, Zak waited impatiently, effectively pinned in until the woman released the miniature harpy from her restraints. Harpy. Funny that. No. Maybe not so funny. He watched in relief as the creature stopped crying. It was a miracle, almost like the shutting off of a tap. The miniature harpy stood upon the ground and surveyed her domain with a familiar expression. The familiar look in her eyes electrified his scalp, every hair jumping to attention as if on high alert.

Leland Ansel came to mind. Those eyes were just as blank and black as Leland the Louse's bug eyes. Zak watched her carefully, filled with misgivings, wondering who would be her first victim. Or maybe she already had a plethora of victims traumatized by her psychopathic behavior.

The elderly woman in the blue sedan seemed oblivious to the ruckus the child made which Zak found unfathomable. How could anyone not hear that cacophony? His only consolation was when "legs" reappeared at the glass door of the police station and came running down the paved steps. The situation crystallized for him. Of course! The child must be Leland's niece and the magnificent legs must belong to his sister. Zak surveyed "legs" dispassionately. She didn't look anything like her older brother. Leland had to be at least twenty years her senior. Unashamedly, he rolled down his car window and pretended to be searching for some music as he listened to the conversation between the elderly woman and the young mother interspersed with sobs and angry recriminations from the little girl.

"I'll take her now," legs said holding out her arms for her child.

"I'll release your daughter Ms. Avery in the station in front of witnesses. Please follow me," the social worker said still holding tightly to the little girl's hand. "There will be paperwork to sign."

"She made me eat spinach. Tell her I hate spinach," the little girl cried.

"Never mind that now Celia. We're going home."

There was an ominous silence. As Zak anticipated, the hysterical screeching began anew only this time mixed with words which he translated as, "I will too go. He promised. I will go. Uncle Lee said."

"Yes," Celia's mother interjected suddenly aware of her mistake in mentioning their destination. "Of course, we're going to go. We have to talk to the nice policemen first and then we can go. How's that?" Lying to a child is never a good idea, Zak thought shaking his head. The mother would be better off taking the harpy by the talon and just holding on for dear life until the little girl's earsplitting disappointment was over. But she didn't and with a shrug Zak watched as Celia's tears dried up and a smile transformed the ugly vestige of flushed cheeks sprinkled with dried snot. The social worker allowed the mother to take hold of her child and escort her up the stairs to the glass door. All three entered the police station together.

Zak left the parking lot with a renewed sense of relief at his own status as a bachelor. He would never get himself in such a situation. No pint-sized little demon would ever rule over him. It took him ten minutes to reach the diner. He entered the building and looked around. What had he expected - to see his brother waiting at a booth? The waitress pouring a customer coffee paused to stare at him in awe and admiration. He blinked. Still carrying the coffee pot, she walked up to him and smiled tentatively, "Hi. May I help you sir?"

Her body language told him she would be willing to help him with more than just a meal. The smile came naturally and over the years had lost its sincere quality, but most women failed to notice. "Yeah, I'm looking for my brother. We missed each other yesterday and I was just wondering if you saw him. He's my height with dark hair, sort of looks like a reject from the '60s with his tie-dyed shirt, moccasins, and long hair. He usually wears his hair back in a queue."

"A what?"

"You know, like a pony-tail."

"Oh my God. Yeah," she said and was promptly interrupted by the annoyed customer still waiting for his coffee to be refilled.

"Sure, I remember him," she said as she started walking backwards. "Hold on a sec. I'll find you a booth. OK?"

Zak shrugged, "Sure. I might as well have some breakfast before I go." He waited patiently for the waitress to refill the elderly man's coffee cup and fetch some pads of butter for the woman sitting next to him at the counter before she returned to show him to a booth in a far corner away from the main door and close to the swinging kitchen door. "The man you described sat here yesterday for a good two hours," she said as Zak settled into the booth and accepted the menu from her.

When he looked up from the menu, she was still standing in the same spot. She turned to point at a booth near the front window and said, "And he was sitting there facing Main Street just this morning with a woman who came in earlier by herself."

Zak dropped the menu, "What did she look like?"

"Oh, ah, I don't know, about my height with dark brown hair and green eyes. She was wearing purple scarves, or I thought they were purple scarves, but it turned out to be a skirt or something. And she had on army boots if you can imagine. But then she got some packages and went into the restroom and when she came out she looked totally different. There was a white limo waiting for her. I mean she looked like a totally different woman, more professional, like some sort of high powered business woman, you know. She was wearing this awesome dark gray pinstriped dress suit and the cutest shoes. They were black silk

I think. I mean I hardly recognized her when she came out of the bathroom."

"A white limo?" Zak asked totally unprepared for this unexpected news. The woman the waitress described must have been Eve. But how had Eve gotten the money to buy new clothes? Where had the white limo come from? The thought that she'd met someone else and the guy was paying for everything upset Zak more than his brother's desertion. No. She wasn't callous. Not Eve. There would be some logical explanation for it all. He couldn't wait to meet up with her in Crescent City. And he wouldn't jump to conclusions, just yet. Until he talked to her, he'd remind himself about Paris, Nevada and how much fun they'd had together.

"Yes, and your brother got into the limo with her."

"What?" he said nearly spilling his water.

Evidently, the waitress tried to get his attention several times before he woke from his stupor. In a voice he didn't recognize, he ordered the Super Deluxe Fried Steak and Potatoes meal, instead of his usual oatmeal, fruit, and egg whites. By the time he'd finished breakfast, he'd also ordered a Boston Cream Pie to go.

21

He didn't even own an umbrella. It was just the green, the green overwhelmed him and the fact he couldn't see for long distances made him feel claustrophobic. He wanted to know what was ahead of him. He wanted to be able to prepare for any possible eventuality. This countryside was a place where a person could hide out and be secretive. The woman sitting next to him had *secret* written all over her.

She called herself Frankie Stewart. And for the last hour and thirty minutes, she'd been on her cellphone chatting away with her accountant followed by her investment broker and finally her editor. Luke gathered from the one-sided dialogue that she wrote books and her books were popular. Currently, she and her editor were arguing over a scene. The editor (from what he could tell) wanted the scene eliminated, a scene (Luke gathered) which contained too much gratuitous sex, very little meaning, and did nothing to move the plot forward.

Frankie, adamant the scene stay in the book, chose repetition and browbeating as means of persuasion, "Titillation my dear. Titillation is what my readers want," she repeated into the phone. "Like I said before, titillation is the reason my readers pick my books, Edward. Who cares about plot development? Sex runs the world and Janelle is the epitome of desire, beauty, and sexual prowess."

At the mention of Janelle's heightened libido and her power over men, he gathered that Frankie's fictional character Janelle must represent those soft porn novels women loved so much. Janelle was the archetype of Helen of Troy, a fantastical female of impossible beauty and charisma, which of course, drove all men to the heights of insane desire. Typically, in these novels there was one man she couldn't entrap with her beauty because he was her equal and kept himself tantalizingly at a distance.

Janelle, of course, as an innocent pawn attracted the attentions of other men. It wasn't her fault these men were beasts. She had to fight them off and sometimes unwillingly succumb to them depending on the historical period in which the fictional world was placed. If it was a bodice ripper from the Gothic period, she would be trapped in some powerful man's snare fighting for her virginity. If she was a modern woman, the difference between her and a whore was her inner purity and goodness.

Why not profit from sex? Readers rarely bothered with nitpicky distinctions between purity and promiscuity. All a writer needed to do was titillate readers with sex whether subtle or obvious to keep their attention riveted to the page. Sex sold. Everyone accepted this fact without question. But in what form? There were all sorts of sexual encounters and reasons for sex: young love exploring unknown territory, illicit love between married people, lust, propagation, gratification, sex as a means of staving off loneliness, sex as reward for finishing the honey-do list, or sex as a means of reaching nirvana. Whatever the underlying motivations, sex sold books.

For the last hour or so, Luke had been surreptitiously admiring Frankie's magnificent breasts and shapely legs. The woman sitting beside him exuded sexual power. Unlike the banker he banged in Arizona who for some weird reason thought he was into mermaids, Frankie Stewart's honesty about her own needs and wants was a refreshing change. Like his brother, he had no trouble attracting women. Unlike his brother, Luke was more discriminating. His women had to be strong, aggressive, and driven. He overlooked the irrationality of preferring Frankie over Leona. So what if they were the same woman? There was no doubt he was sitting next to Leona, only Leona dressed up as a powerful, intelligent, sexy capitalist.

Earlier, back at the Woolly Man, he'd been rather miffed at Leona's lack of interest in him. After all he knew his worth. Even as a child, females exclaimed over his beauty and he accepted their adulation. Now, as a grown man, he had come to expect the backward glances, the widening of a female's pupils in delight at seeing him. He was no stranger to admiration. So, what was up with Leona? Maybe she preferred women? No. He'd seen how she reacted to Zak.

But Frankie, Frankie was a different woman altogether. The signals Frankie gave off encouraged him to think she found him as sexy as he found her. The uncrossing and crossing of her long beautiful legs, the tapping of her high heeled shoe attracting his eye to her slender foot and perfect ankle, the leaning forward to look out his side of the window exposing her cleavage to his appreciative view, and a dozen other mannerisms which signaled she found him equally as attractive, provided him with enough evidence to make his move. He brushed aside caution.

From the corner of his eye, he heard her end her conversation with her editor and saw her throw her cellphone in her little black purse. Now he had her full attention. In order to persuade her to open up and be herself, he would have to give up a bit of his dignity for the greater good, advancing archeology to its next inevitable evolutionary phase.

He blinked away the residue of anger still seething in the pit of his stomach when he remembered the way Leona's eyes used to track Zak's every move as if his brother were some sort of delicious sweet she was forbidden to touch. It was time for a bit of acting. He'd had two semesters of theater in college, so there was a good chance he could fool her into believing he was attracted to her. He forced himself to pretend embarrassment at being caught openly admiring her legs. Then he looked into her eyes to check her reaction.

A hot wave of shame moved up from the pit of his stomach and exploded through his body. The crinkling of her forehead signified dismay. She was dismayed that he found her interesting! As if a man's sexual interest in her was repugnant? What about all her provocative cues? Had she been playing a game, after all? Or was she a lesbian? Fighting his doubt, he leaned toward her at the same time she leaned toward Thomas, the chauffeur. Luke reversed course and leaned back against the padded seat, pressed his lips together to hold back what he wanted to say and watched the woman and the chauffeur interact.

"Mr. Bambrey, let's stop in Medford and find a place to grab a bite to eat."

The chauffeur's inscrutable dark eyes met hers in the rear view mirror as he replied in an accent and tone Luke laughingly thought of as phony New York City tough, "You can call me Tom, ma'am."

In his head, Luke parodied the chauffeur's voice only instead of sounding like Tom, the voice sounded like Tony from the Sopranos. Luke stifled a laugh, but too late, and tried to hide his amusement by staring out the window. But the glass reflected Frankie's fleeting irritation as she leaned back against the leather cushion. Her expression reminded him all too vividly of his mother's frowning disapproval when he said something or did something to embarrass her in public.

When Frankie turned to look out her window and pointedly ignored him, Luke turned to watch her unobserved. He watched as she said, "Alright then Tom, you can call me Frankie." Luke recognized her smile as the one most people reserved for trusted friends, babies, and favorite pets.

For the first time in nearly fifty miles traveling in the backseat of the limousine, Luke paid closer attention to the driver wondering what was so attractive about him. Before their departure from Klamath Falls, he'd been vaguely annoyed when Frankie insisted Tom keep the glass partition open because he'd been planning on learning how much she knew about Professor Wade. And he couldn't interrogate the woman if some stranger was a witness to their private conversation.

In the movies, the rich preferred privacy and always kept the partition closed especially if conducting business. And her business had been more than just about boring spreadsheets and future sales projections, she'd been arguing about the amount of sex in her soft porn novels for Zeus' sake. What was so special about this guy? She'd just met him. She had no idea who he was or what he would say after he dropped them off. And he didn't look all that trustworthy. He looked as if he'd just stepped out of boot camp with his sandy hair cut above the ears and the way he seemed to be standing at attention even when he was sitting down.

Maybe it was his dark brown eyes and thick lashes. Women went loopy over that kind of macho crap. The Jean-Claude Van Damme look was so yesterday. He looked like the kind of guy who thought everybody was a commie and guns should be in every home. Maybe what attracted her to him was the scent of danger mixed with choir boy good looks. He was messing with her mind, making her relax her guard and trust him. Don't do it, Frankie. Don't be a fool. He's just using you.

Defeated for the moment, Luke sank back in his seat and considered his next move. Frankie seemed too smart to fall for someone like Tom. No. She must be playing Tom against him. She must be trying to make them both jealous. It was the only explanation. The limo exited the freeway and headed for downtown Medford. Luke, amazed at the luxurious interior, the luxury creating a sensation of floating in midair, watched as others less fortunate in their dull, dusty, dubious vehicles tried to keep pace.

He even felt a bit sorry for all those idiots driving their cramped uncomfortable foreign cars just to save a few bucks on gas. Sitting in the limo made his dreams seem so much closer to being realized. Yes. Anything was possible. This luxurious ride was a taste of what was to come. Never again would he go hungry or humiliate himself by begging money off his mother. Soon, very soon, he would be free to travel and plan his own expeditions to faraway places.

It wasn't long before the limo turned into a mini mall filled with retail stores. The art deco style was one long unimaginative beige and brown stucco, the roofline a cheap Italian knock-off. Thomas had to park the limo in two parking spots. When he climbed out of the limo and sauntered off, Luke realized this might be his only opportunity to do an intervention and get the woman back on track. If he just blurted out what he wanted, Frankie would think him insane. But if he approached her in another way, a subtler way, perhaps she might be more receptive.

The sensation inside the limo was like being at home in his bed, well, someone else's bed, one of those beds from outer space that cradled every part of one's body with gentle firmness. He liked the juxtaposition of those sensations: gentle and firm. The words brought other idea to mind. He glanced surreptitiously at Frankie wondering if she sensed his mood and discovered to his chagrin that she was busy reading her emails.

He had to bring out the real person hiding in Frankie's body. He searched his pockets until he found his grandfather's watch. His mother had given him the watch shortly after his grandparents returned from their final expedition into the furthest corners of the Amazon. They had been following the rumors of a white woman living among the indigenous people. This small group of people among hundreds of Amazonian tribes called her "the beautiful one" and according to surveyors the eyewitnesses believed she was their protector. Even with the incredible survival skills of the indigenous people along the Amazon River, they could not withstand the encroachment of developers, tourists, ranchers, farmers, and foreign interlopers and were forced to flee further and further away from their ancestral homes.

Luke's grandparents believed Amara was the group's "protector" disguising herself as a Harpia Harpyja, a Harpy Eagle. Under normal circumstances, female Harpy Eagles are a third larger than the males. Yet his grandparents were hearing claims of "the beautiful one" being not quite as big as Quetzalcoatlus or a pterosaur but far bigger than the average Harpy Eagle. Eyewitnesses claimed the harpy they saw soaring above the canopy was two meters tall with a wingspan of four meters. That meant she was a little over six feet tall with a wingspan of thirteen or fourteen feet.

As a kid, he often imagined how she might have looked in flight. He drew different versions of her in his notebook determined to think like a scientist and imagine the practicalities of a homo sapien with wings. They would have to be impressive. Even though family renditions showed her with long reddish gold hair, he drew her with short curly black hair. Tradition claimed she was large breasted, but he drew her with small firm breasts, slim hips, and long legs. The thought of Amara, so beautiful and kind, forced to hide from humans as if she were some sort of freak sickened him.

His grandparents had felt the same way. They had spent their entire adult lives searching for Amara. From 1946 to 1959 and from 1962 to 1995, Grandfather Foraché and Grandmother Nerin traveled to South America searching the Amazonian River from one end to the other in the hopes of finding Amara. They had spent nearly fifty years searching for her. Luke had no doubt if his grandfather were alive, he would appreciate Luke's efforts to fulfill the family mission and he would shrug his shoulders at the lengths he must go to reclaim the family honor. It would take ingenuity and all the charisma he had to discover the secrets buried inside Frankie Stewart.

Luke swung the gold watch with its intricate fleur-de-lis design in front of him. Frankie paused in her reading to look up. He smiled at her. "This was my grandfather's. I inherited the watch after he died. He was a great man. He was more like a father to me than my own father. He was the one who got me interested in archeology. You see, he'd never had formal training but read everything he could get his hands on and learned from the best. Leaky told him he had real talent."

Luke extended the watch toward Frankie and swung it slowly from side to side. Frankie watched the gold orb swing back and forth, back and forth. After a breathless thirty seconds, he saw her lift her brows in puzzlement then calmly bend her head and return to reading her emails. Luke dropped his arm and stared at the watch holding back the urge to grab the woman and shake her awake. He slipped the watch into his pocket and tried to think of another tactic to get her tongue to loosened up. Then he noticed the liquor store next to the pizza place. He opened the limo door and responded to her questioning look with the inane words, "I'll be back soon."

Luke chose a cheap whiskey and hurried back to the limo. The limo driver hadn't returned yet. There might still be time to get her to talk. Luke slipped inside with his bag of goodies and said, "Thought we might indulge in a drink before lunch. What do you say? Whiskey and coke sound good?" Frankie stared at him until he grew uncomfortable.

367

Damned her, why couldn't she just unbend a bit, after all, he was doing his best to show he liked her? Who did she think she was fooling anyway? The tight fit of the business suit and the stiletto heels screamed do-me, baby.

At a loss, Luke decided he needed a drink. He placed the bag on the floor between his feet and poured himself a scotch. He'd managed to finish one plastic cup before Tom the Trojan Tank returned. The smell of hot cheese, garlic, pepper, and herbs filled the interior of the limo making Luke's stomach rumble in response. Tom placed the two large pizza boxes on the seat beside him and began to slice the pizza into equal triangles.

He'd even had the forethought to purchase paper plates. What a guy. He turned to the opening between the front and back compartments of the limo and handed Frankie a plate filled with pizza. Luke did not expect Tom to offer him a plate. When he did, Luke accepted the plate with its delicious contents, several cheesy triangles of carbohydrates and artery clogging fats, both trans and saturated, along with a high sodium content as graciously as he could. He murmured the usual words of appreciation, yet, he had to force himself to be gracious.

If only he'd had the courage to decline Tom's offer. If only his stomach hadn't betrayed him with hunger pangs. It was after he accepted the plate, he realized he hadn't offered to pay his share. Since both of his hands were occupied, one with a plate of pizza, the other with a cup of scotch, he couldn't reach into his pocket for his wallet. An idea came to him.

"Hey this is great. I'd like to pay my share. How much was it Tom?"

"It's been taken care of Mr. Nerin," Tom said as he handed Frankie a napkin.

"No. No. I insist. If my hands weren't full, I'd pay you now."

"You do seem to have your hands full most of the time, don't you Mr. Nerin?"

"Call me Luke."

"I have an idea how we might fix your problem," Frankie said as she set her plate on her knee. "Tom would you drive round to the back of the mall please." Luke watched as Frankie took a big bite of her pizza. Of course, the cheese had a mind of its own and refused to tear itself away from the crust. She ended up gently persuading the trailing cheese to come off the crust and with its surrender dropped the yellow threads into her mouth.

Luke sipped his scotch and watched with what he hoped was an enigmatic smile. What was she up to? Was she offering herself as dessert? Effortlessly, Tom managed to drive around the mall and eat his pizza without mishap, so that by the time the limo maneuvered through the crowds and the cars, the man was on his second slice. Show off.

"Pull up here Tom," Frankie requested. "Yes. That's good."

Obligingly, Tom pulled up to a nearby dumpster. Luke assumed Frankie planned to throw the pizza boxes away. Luke finished his scotch and just as he bit into his first piece of pizza, Frankie scooted over next to him until her hip touched his thigh. Her hand descended toward his lap and reached down between his legs. Cold sweat broke out on his forehead. Did she really think he could perform in front of witnesses? But when she straightened up, he realized with a rush of relieve she had his brown paper bag with the bottle of scotch inside. She whisked Luke's plastic cup from between his nerveless fingers, dumped the cup into the bag, leaned forward until she was practically sprawled across Luke's lap, then pressed the button to lower Luke's window.

With her face just inches from his, Luke could smell the perfume in her hair. It smelled of raspberries and almonds. He liked the scent. He liked the other view from the other end as well. Without warning, something brown flew past him. Luke turned his head in time to see his bag with the bottle of whiskey fly through the air and land in the dumpster. He heard the sound of glass breaking.

Still holding his half eaten pizza, he watched as she pressed the button to close the window, then with her hand on his leg used his weight to propel herself back to her seat and resume her customary position near the window. He was so mad he couldn't speak. It was difficult to process all the emotions churning around in his head: rage was at the top of the list and in second place, a feeling he couldn't quite pin down. Disappointment? Sadness? Humiliation?

What had just happened?

From far away he heard her say, "There will be no alcohol around me gentlemen. It is something I just won't tolerate. You may drive on Tom."

Luke was too upset to notice Tom's thoughtful expression as he drove the limo back toward the front of the mall. As he stared out the window, he tried to collect his thoughts and compose himself. He'd never been treated so shabbily in all his life, not by anyone. Never, ever. The heat washed over him as he replayed the scene in his head. No one had ever deliberately tried to shame him. Minutes after the event, he realized he would do anything, anything at all to make sure this bitch suffered for the humiliation she had caused him.

He made himself look at her. He expected her to be smirking with self-satisfaction. Instead she appeared sad and maybe even regretful as if she had been forced to humiliate him. Her regret was meaningless. He had no other choice but to pretend indifference. One way or another she would lead him to Amara. That was all he had left; all he cared about now. And if along the way, he could humiliate her as she had humiliated him, he would do so without a second's hesitation.

With a supreme effort of will, even though his throat felt tight and dry, he forced himself to finish off the rest of the pizza. When next he looked at Frankie, she was offering him bottled water. He accepted the water and drank the eight ounces down in one gulp washing away the tightness and the dryness and the stain of the previous moment. As he looked around the interior of the limo, he realized that Frankie had put away her play things and had been staring out her window with a thoughtful frown between her brows.

Without thinking, he said, "I'm confused by something. Just the other day, you told me your name was Navan Keys. Yet today, you say you're Frankie Stewart. Why is that?"

Frankie scrutinizing his face with her electric vamp eyes then looked away as if she had seen all she wanted to see, "I don't know what you're talking about. I don't know anyone named Navan Keys."

"It was at the Woolly Man. You came in wearing a skirt made of scarves and army boots on your feet. You said you were looking for Mrs. Lawson. You acted real strange. You remember. You remember how you made Nate mad, my mom's friend Nate? Remember what you said to my brother Zak? How about the fact that you and Zak did the nasty in the Paris Motel? You forget that too? You were calling yourself Eve. Yeah. That's what Zak told me. Don't look at me as if you don't know what I'm talking about. It's true. So, what's going on huh? And who's the other one, the warrior princess. What's her name?"

"I think I've heard enough Mr. Nerin."

"Leave the lady alone," Tom said, as Luke looked up in time to see Tom's penetrating eyes watching him through the rear view mirror.

"Our business is none of yours Tom," Luke said, emphasizing his first name. "This matter is between me and the lady." He turned back to look into Frankie's eyes. Frankie smothered a yawn. Stunned, Luke sat back and thought about what had just happened. He gave up. Nothing he said seemed to penetrate the shield of nuttiness that encapsulated her smug shell. Just as he thought he had lost, he saw a silver Camaro with black racing strips sweep past them. The Camaro swung into their lane and unexpectedly slowed down forcing Tom to a crawl.

Tom honked and tried to pass the Camaro. The limo swung back into the slow lane when an old truck hauling a makeshift house made of pressed wood appeared on the horizon speeding toward them at a generous thirty-five miles an hour. When the limo tried to pass the Camaro again, Zak effectively boxed them in narrowly missing an oncoming car in the process. Tom seemed to think he was dealing with a crazy person. "What's that buggin' doing? What's his beef with us?" There was no one ahead of them now, no one in the fast lane either, just the Camaro and the limo, neck and neck traveling eight-five miles an hour.

When Luke looked ahead he saw a semi hauling two flat beds loaded with steel beams. It was gaining speed close enough for everyone to see the driver and his attempts to slow down the behemoth. The Camaro would either have to pick up speed and pull ahead of the limo or back up and pull in behind. Tom chose to speed up, leaving the Camaro no choice but to back down. Zak waited two seconds too long before he swung in behind the limo. The semi's weight and the speed with which it was moving made both the limo and the Camaro shutter as it passed them.

Both Frankie and Luke turned to stare out the rear window. They saw the driver of the semi give Zak the middle finger. Luke made a mental note to kick Zak's butt. Then Luke began to wonder if Zak had simply wanted to unnerve the limo driver enough to pull over at the next stop. Before Tom could pick up speed, the Camaro shot forward and pulled in ahead of them.

Luke leaned forward and shouted, "You can't beat him, Tom. The Z28 is turbo charged, twin turbo charged, and this limo is too damned long and too damned heavy." Tom ignored him, muttering obscenities under his breath. When Tom tried to pass again, Zak swept into the fast lane effectively cutting the limo off. Tom over corrected and nearly rolled the limo. He slowed down. Zak slowed down. They were running at sixty-five mph on a two lane highway with a hill up ahead. Zak rolled down his window. Tom rolled down his window. Before he could curse Zak out or threaten him with bodily harm, Frankie leaned forward and said, "The man wants to talk. Pull off at the next exit and we'll see what he wants."

No one could mistake Tom's aversion to that idea. There was no doubt in Luke's mind Zak would have won the contest. He was the better driver. Luke had seen his brother play chicken with lots of guys. Zak's gift or curse, whichever, was that he didn't fear death. Yet Tom didn't try to change Frankie's mind or talk her out of a confrontation. Instead, he slowed the limo and flipped on his right turn signal. Luke began to get nervous. Tom looked as if he could probably pulverize Zak into a bloody mess and still have energy enough to stomp on Luke's head and hold him pinned to the ground. The idea was revolting. A confrontation would ruin his chances of getting Frankie to help him.

Still showboating, Zak slowed down to practically a crawl and ignored the car behind him, then executed an insane maneuver by squeezing the Camaro between the limo and a Dodge Dart with inches to spare between bumpers. Instead of blowing his horn and sticking his middle finger in the air to demonstrate his annoyance with Zak, the driver of the Dodge Dart with long curly hair tied back in a ponytail cheerfully waved his brother on. Evidently, people were still churning out flower children in Oregon.

Luke smoothed back his own queue neatly braided in the style he preferred feeling the strong straight strands slip through his fingers. The two of them had nothing in common. The Dodge Dart guy would be a loser all his life. People would step over him and get ahead of him and try to squeeze him off the road and he'd just smile and wave thinking he was doing the world a favor with his positive energy. Shit head. That wasn't living, that was just getting by. And then Luke belatedly remembered the guy who gave his life on the Portland Max train and felt ashamed of himself. Why was he such a jerk sometimes?

Tom took the Rogue River exit and Zak followed the limo around the curve to the designated rest stop. It all looked so civilized, the neatly marked parking spots in yellow chalk, the red brick public restrooms, and the groomed plants and magnificent trees all around them. Tom parked next to the bathrooms. At first, Luke thought Tom intended to rush around the front of the limo and jump on Zak and start punching him in the face. But no, instead, like the gentlemen he pretended to be, Tom walked around the back end of the limo and opened Frankie's door. She accepted Tom's arm and stepped out of the limo as if she were the Queen paying a visit to a commoner.

Meanwhile Zak pulled up beside them, threw his car into park, hopped out of the Camaro as if it were on fire, his body language suggesting he expected a fight and was prepared to defend himself. Luke tried to step between his brother and Frankie, "No. Zak. Don't. Just cool down. I can explain everything." Luke's intervention was unnecessary. Tom had already anticipated Zak's move and placed himself boldly between Zak and Frankie holding Zak off with his hands pressed against Zak's chest. Zak tried to look beyond Tom's broad shoulder at Frankie.

"Eve. Tell this guy to back off. What's going on? Why are you dressed like that?"

Frankie eyed Zak as if he were a bum begging on the streets.

Luke spoke in the charged silence, "Frankie Stewart this is my brother Zak Nerin. Zak this is Ms. Stewart's driver, Tom Bambrey. I'm sorry folks. Let's just calm down. Disregard my brother's rudeness. He gets kind of crazy sometimes. He seems to think he knows you."

Frankie took a step closer to the limo separating herself from the three men. When she shook her head, her look reminded Luke of the one he'd seen on his mother's face quite frequently when he was young, a look of annoyed disbelief in the folly of men. "Your brother is mistaken. I've never met him before."

Zak and Tom squared off, occasionally grunting like primates as one pushed, and the other pushed back. It was all very silly and embarrassing, and Luke seriously considered stepping in. A few seconds more of forces pulling and pushing and grunting and Zak managed to yank himself free of Tom's grasp. When Tom glanced at Frankie to get his cue from her, Zak sucker punched him in the head. Tom fell backwards into Luke's arms. Luke held him up for a moment and felt the muscles in Tom's back tense ready to spring.

For a few seconds, Luke debated on whether to put a choke hold on Bambrey. He stopped himself, knowing Frankie would only see this maneuver as further proof of his duplicity.   Zak had already pissed Frankie off. Luke relaxed his hold and Tom broke free going for Zak. There was a brief struggle. Tom hit Zak in the face and blood spurted from Zak's nose. Zak grabbed Tom's fingers and twisted them backwards sending Tom to his knees. Tom moaned. The pain must have been excruciating.

"Leave him alone. Stop it! Stop it!" a woman screamed. The scream bounced off the trees in the park and the bridge beyond them. And the pitch grew louder and higher. Zak loosened his hold and stepped back using his shirt to stem the blood from his nose. Luke's ears were ringing from the volume of her screams. He wouldn't have been surprised if motorists passing by had heard her. The men watched as she stumbled toward the park restrooms clutching her purse to her breasts. Without a backward look, she disappeared inside. Luke helped Tom to his feet. Tom followed Frankie like a magnet and stood outside the restroom door.

"Ms. Stewart, are you alright?" he said holding his hand as if his fingers might be broken. "Ms. Stewart, don't worry about me. I'll be fine. Are you alright?"

There was silence.

Luke could appreciate Tom's pain. Zak had performed the same move on Luke years ago and Luke shivered with remembered agony. Impressed with Tom's stoicism, Luke looked down at his hands trying to control his sudden resentment and envy. The guy was too fucking perfect to be real. Then Luke remembered Zak. The look on Zak's face made Luke forget his petty jealousy. Several emotions were rippling across Zak's face: despair at Frankie's reaction and disgust with himself. The appearance of furrows on his forehead and around his nose and mouth made him look years older. The hurt Zak was experiencing made Luke uncomfortable.

How odd? He hadn't expected to feel empathy for his little brother, but he did. In fact, he felt rage that anyone dared hurt his little brother. Luke looked away out of respect for Zak's feelings.

Twenty minutes passed before the woman stepped out of the restroom. Luke thought there was something odd about the way she was moving, and as she got closer he scrutinized her face searching for a clue to the reason. Before she reached them, he knew her. How odd to recognize Leona, only Leona in Frankie Stewart's business suit and stiletto heels. The haunted expression in her green eyes and horror peeking out from behind the dreamer's face were familiar.

Unaware of the sudden tension emanating from the Nerin brothers, Tom matched steps with her. He had noticed the change, yet he did not have the experience to understand what was going on. For a moment he looked scared. A frightened Tom seemed impossible. Even when Zak pinned his fingers back, Tom had been in pain but never scared. Now he was frightened. The wilding could do that to a person. And the bizarre nature of the situation made everything unpredictable.

Leona dug in her purse and extracted a roll of bills the size of her fist. She turned to Tom and handed the money to him with a slight frown and tentative smile saying in her Leona way, "She says I'm supposed to give this to you. It's your fee. Please. Take it. I'm sorry for the mess." Three shades whiter and barely holding it together, Tom accepted the cash and watched warily as Leona turned to face Luke, "I guess you want to know where she's buried. I'll take you to her. And then you can go home and leave me alone. I won't show you the place until you promise to go home once you've seen her."

With the natural world all around him, the gentle breeze cooling his face, a modern blacktop highway behind him, the sound of cars wheezing past the rest stop, all the things which convinced him he was still anchored in the 21st century, the worst possible sight was the sight of Zak staring at Leona with hope and desire and dread all fighting for supremacy. Luke stepped forward, his stomach dropping, and made himself say, "We promise."

"No. Not you. He has to promise," Leona said with a toss of her head.

Zak wiped the blood from his nose with his shirt sleeve and stared at her with glittering eyes. Luke, not sure whether or not Zak was going to break out in tears or punch someone, spoke up, urging him to answer her, "Come on Zak. Give her your word. Come on. We've gone too far to back down now. You turd, do the right thing."

It seemed like an hour but must have only been minutes before Zak looked up into Leona's eyes. His nose had stopped bleeding. He looked so damned stupid standing there with his shirt torn and blood spattered on the front of it and his nose beginning to swell. Yet incongruously with bated breath Luke waited for him to speak.

"If you want me to say that I'll go straight home after Luke gets his prize, then we'll be here for eternity. Nobody tells me what to do. I come and go as I please. I'm not stalking you. If you think I'm stalking you, you're wrong. I just want an explanation. I want to know why you lied to me and tricked me. I've got the right to know, don't I?"

Leona looked confused, "I don't know what you're talking about. I never lied to you. I told you what I knew about the blanket and I've already explained about the other stuff."

"I'm not talking about the damned blanket. I don't give a shit about the blanket. I want to know why you left me naked in a motel tied to a bed. I also want to know why you dumped me but still left a note telling me where to find you?" he demanded pulling a wrinkled note out of his jean pocket and handing it to her.

The note lay in Leona's hand as she stared blankly up into Zak's face. She didn't have a clue. Anyone could tell she didn't have a clue what Zak was talking about. She read the note. Her cheeks turned red then ghostly white. She stepped toward Zak and handed the note back to him without a word, shaking her head sadly. When Luke moved to follow Leona to the limo, Leona glanced over her shoulder. He saw the sadness in her eyes and wondered belatedly why she felt sorry for him, "No. You go with your brother. I'm taking the limo."

If he had to choose between the women, he would have chosen Leona above all the rest. When Leona looked at him, he thought he saw regret as if perhaps she might share his feelings. Luke turned away. Zak ignorant as usual wanted to stay and pick a fight. Luke climbed into the Camaro and watched as Zak walked up to Leona. He also noticed Tom saunter away from the three of them as if he were just stretching his legs after a long journey, enjoying the smell of pine trees and the magnificent view.

You shit.

Deep down inside, he grudgingly admired the guy. Tom had something. Something Luke believed would be his one day. Once he got his hands on Amara, he'd have the same unbreakable confidence.

As Tom paused to admire the center piece of the park: a green circular grove surrounded by asphalt with a colorful boulder artfully arranged on one side of a baby blue spruce, the rest were separating like negative particles. Tom sat down on the boulder and watched as Leona and Zak continue to quarrel. Luke looked at his brother and the mad lady of Shallot. Well, arguing was a tad bit inaccurate. Zak talked, and Leona bent her neck and crossed her arms looking anywhere but at him. It was nay impossible to argue with this woman, Tom believed. Finally,

Zak gave up and marched to the Camaro and climbed inside with a hard look in his eye.

Inwardly Tom shook off the strangeness of the events so far. He really didn't want to delve too deeply into the woman's problems. Obviously, she had some really big problems. But after being paid for his services, he no longer had to deal with her problems. Luke, on the other hand, had a new set of problems, chiefly his brother's sulking. He'd just about had enough of testosterone and machismo today.

It was time to consider the reality of the situation and appreciate what had happened. He hadn't been the instigator of change this time. Zak had the one to drive Frankie away and bring Leona out into the open. It was all good. It would turn out good, one way or another. Luke had faith. In his relief at being once again with family, Luke wanted to slap his brother on the shoulder and buy him a drink. He thought better of the idea. In Zak's present mood, he might just get a bloody nose of his own. When the powers manifest themselves, he would buy Zak a fleet of fast cars to ease his heartache.

Thomas Bambrey watched the limo circle around him while the woman inside waved merrily and blew him kisses. For a moment, he thought Ms. Stewart might be the one blowing him kisses, letting him know she was thinking of him fondly but no, it couldn't be Frankie. Ms. Stewart wasn't the type of woman who blew men air-kisses. Ms. Stewart would more likely take him out behind the trees and do some kinky stuff with him. No, Ms. Stewart was gone and the woman blowing him kisses seemed to be doing so at the urgings of someone else. For a moment, he thought there were two women in the limo. The idea made the hairs on his back and butt stand up in supernatural fear.

He thought back to the moment he knew something was odd about Ms. Stewart. When he realized she'd become someone else, the knowledge had been quite a game changer. He was relieved to be on his own and out of that muddled bit of mess. Here he sat on a rock stuck in a park near the Rogue River with just about a thousand dollars in his pocket, thanks to Ms. Stewart, the easiest thousand he'd ever made. The idea of getting it on with Frankie Stewart was a distant memory. She had turned out to be more than just too sexy and too cool for him, she was too damned bat shit buggin' for his peace of mind.

22

In a blind stupor, Zak followed the limousine while on autopilot, only aware of the size and shape and color of the vehicle ahead of him, none of the more minute details of his surroundings such as the cars behind him and the ones passing him. All the while the blood pounded inside his head and chest, the rage ebbing and flowing like the tide. Enough of the trembling had subsided for him to hold onto the steering wheel and press down on the accelerator. *What have I done?* That was the second time he had used the sucker punch. His brother had been the first. And as a result of his actions, his father left them and was never seen again. For the first second or two, the elation had been like a heady shot of tequila warming his stomach. The drunken euphoria died when Eve screamed.

The sound of her scream shot through him like a knife. It traveled through his ears, hit his eardrums, and kept on going, right down into his groin. The primeval sound of anguish and terror startled him so much that for a second he lost sensation in his body. Novocain. Just like Novocain. Once the screaming seized, the place where he stood snapped into focus again. No longer the master, he'd become the thing he'd always hated, a bully, a slave of his jealousy and resentment, a tool of humiliation and pain.

He could smell his own sweat and the other man's, the baking asphalt, some crushed pine nettles beneath him, even a bit of damp earth, and something else, something he couldn't quite place. The stench weaved around his head, nauseatingly elusive. And then he knew. It had been food, spoiled food. He remembered how he'd turned his head and seen, just a foot away, a familiar fast food wrapper. Long after he'd let go of the man's fingers, long after he'd stepped back from the scene and watched Leona running to the restroom, he found himself still swallowing the scent.

After a while he couldn't stand the taste in his throat and tried to breathe through his nose. It smelled of old blood and tasted like the bottom of a skillet. He still couldn't get the sight of her reaction out of his head, the way she made sure not to look at him, as if the sight of him was too repugnant, and the way she searched blindly for him, not so much to see him, but because in her terror she wanted to be sure she knew where he was. That image was sealed in his memory forever. He couldn't help but rehash the moment, over and over, wishing he could have done it all differently, wishing he could go back and fix it. But it was too late; he had become a monster. In her eyes, he was a monster.

The Eve he wanted to see smiling back at him, running toward him with her mischievous sexy eyes, no longer existed. His Eve was buried somewhere inside a body, a body both familiar and an enemy. The soul inside the head that moved the limbs had become the soul of a stranger, someone he was beginning to fear. How could he imagine them together after this? The idea of resurrecting their night with the stranger who had invaded her body appalled him. In his disgust, he lashed out wanting only to protect what had once been his. He'd seen the chauffeur as an obstacle, a threat to getting Eve back. He hated the way she looked at the chauffeur as if he was dessert. He wanted to wipe the self-satisfaction off that man's stupid face.

So fine. Now that he had examined the events from all angles and determined he was a fool, how did any of it help him? It didn't. Leona feared and loathed him. Maybe Eve felt differently. But what the hell? Was he really thinking about killing off Leona and the others and making sure only Eve remained? Holy shit! Just listening to himself think, scared the madness away and brought back a bit of sanity.

Gradually, with his heart beating at a steady pace and his breathing back to normal, the cacophony of thoughts shrieking inside his head subsided long enough for him to pay attention to what was going on inside the car. He became aware of his brother sitting quietly beside him. Whoa, what was up with that? He also became aware of the other cars whooshing past him or braking fast up ahead. With only a foot to spare, he managed to stop the Camaro before colliding with a blue Prius just ahead of him. The elderly couple in the front seats never once turned to look back. Such trusting souls.

Five minutes passed. The silence stretched on and on. The occupant sitting in the passenger seat beside him remained unmoved by their near collision staring straight ahead as if in a daydream. What disturbed Zak the most was the length of time Luke must have remained perfectly still and sphinx like in his muteness. Zak glanced nervously at his brother and then back toward the road. Under ordinary circumstances, Luke should have been preoccupied with his all-consuming goal. He should have been busy reading his notes or checking his maps. Or more likely he should have been screaming in Zak's ear and calling him every dirty epithet in his arsenal. But he didn't.

Instead he sat with his hands in his lap and his eyes immersed in the intricacies of the crack in the passenger side window, a hair line crack that started at the left-hand corner near the frame and traveled midway across the window and abruptly stopped in the center where it widened to the size of a pea resembling most clearly a finger, a finger directing the viewer to look outside at the beautiful view just beyond the glass.

Instead of appreciating the view, Luke followed the fissure again and again with his eyes then used his own finger to trace the path of the cut. Disturbed by Luke's behavior, Zak grabbed his brother's shoulder and shook him roughly. "What's up with you? Huh? You're better than this, man. Get a grip."

Luke turned a wan face toward Zak, "A grip on what?"

"What are you smoking, man? You've got what you wanted and now you're sulking? How is that possible?"

"I've been thinking," Luke said as he tried to rub the furrows from his brow. "I've been thinking about this craziness and wondering if it's all a ruse, a ruse to get us away somewhere deserted so she can stab us or do something really demented."

When a middle-aged guy in a sporty new foreign car tried to pass Zak, Zak accelerated just enough to keep him from slipping between the Camaro and the limo.

"Who was that woman back there?" Zak asked.

"She calls herself Frankie Stewart," Luke said with a disheartened shrug. "Or she was Frankie Stewart. Now she's Leona. I think. I don't know. Who gives a shit? She's certifiably neurotic; no, make that psychotic, yeah, she's definitely psychotic. That's all I know."

"She's pulling off," Zak said unnecessarily. He followed her off the exit and into a nearby truck stop. They were on the outskirts of the city of Grants Pass, Oregon.

Luke looked down at his hands in his lap, "You're the one with the interest in loonies. What do you think her problem is? Is she MPD or schizophrenic? What do you say, Herr Doctor?"

"She isn't suffering from schizophrenia," Zak reminded his brother. "We've talked about this before, Luke. You said she was faking mental illness to be interesting. You think that's true now?"

"No."

"Bad huh?" Zak asked.

"Absurdly bad," Luke said. "Oh yeah. This is really bad. Nobody would believe it. If I can't believe it, how? Um. Well, let's see. In her mind everything is straightforward and clear, but for me, having seen her as Leona Keys, then the Spartan warrior, and most recently Corporate Barbie, I am fast becoming a believer in possession. No really. I'm beginning to realize why everybody was so damned scared of people like her. No wonder preliterate people thought her kind were possessed by demons."

"Or gods? Depending on the culture, people might have thought she was another Joan of Arc," Zak reminded him.

Luke sat up straighter and looked around with more interest than he'd displayed the last twenty miles. As Zak knew from experience, a rational analysis of the situation usually brought Luke out of his depression. Analyzing events comforted him because intellectual familiarity kept the bogeyman away. Pre-Eve, Zak had enjoyed the mysterious and the weird. Not any longer. Those days were as done as burned toast. Even though Luke entertained crazy theories about their family obsession with Amara, deep down inside, the weird made him uncomfortable too. He craved the tested, the practical, the scientific method.

When Luke shot him a questioning look, Zak shook his head wearily. Instead of trying to explain, Zak followed the limo. Luckily, he managed to pull the Camaro up to an empty pump just behind the limo. He climbed out of the driver's seat and stretched. Before talking to the gas attendant and filling the tank, he leaned inside the car to get his brother's attention, "Keep an eye on her."

"Are you kidding? You have to ask?"

With an economy of movement and a fluid yet muscled grace, a grace Luke secretly envied, Zak talked to the gas attendant who nodded his head giving Zak permission to pump his own gas. The woman inside the limousine, the woman calling herself Leona now, seemed oblivious to the conversation between the two men. She sat in the driver's seat looking down at something in her hand. Luke assumed she had her cellphone and was reading or watching something on the screen, a modern-day way of ignoring others without appearing rude.

Zak pulled the hose out of the pump, stuck the hose in his gas tank, chose his octane level, and moved away from the car. No fumbling, no hesitating, just one fluid movement followed by another. For the first time, Luke watched his brother with a sense of awe as he strode toward the Food Mart with his unique loping stride. Zak had this habit of looking from side to side and all around him as if his senses were alert to prey as well as predators.

The science of Zak's dexterity reminded Luke of the wolf he'd encountered one hot summer day. It was near dusk, in the Owyhee Canyonlands. Once the sun went down in the canyonlands and if there were no moon to light your way, you could barely see a few feet ahead you. You might see a few lights winking in the distance from farm house's miles away, but unlike towns and cities, the Owyhee night belonged to the nocturnal hunters there: cougars, coyotes, and badgers. In all his years trekking up and down and all over the Owyhee Canyonlands, he'd never been lucky enough to see a wolf. That had been his first sighting and had left a deep impression on him.

He'd been on his way home taking the shortcut on McBride road. There were farms and ranches on either side of the road and plenty of cows and calves dotting the landscape. He hadn't yet had to worry about his headlights. Stupid truck. He was reaching for his bottle of water when the bottle slipped out of his hand and spilled all over his lap. He had to pull over onto the side of the road near a barbed-wire fence. He shut off the engine and searched for a paper napkin or a rag to soak up the water. Something made him look up. He saw an animal moving in the distance. He thought it might be a lost calf that had managed to slip under the barbed wire. Then he thought it might be a rancher's dog, although it was bigger than any collie he'd ever seen before.

The animal's proximity to his car had been the most frightening thing about that night. No more than a few feet from his vehicle, he saw it: one hundred and fifty pounds or so, gray, and white with a magnificent head and long lean torso. Only a few feet separated them as the animal passed Luke and trotted carelessly across the road, as if he feared no one, not even Luke.

Once the wolf crossed the road, the ground dipped into the numerous dry creeks and Luke thought he'd lost sight of him forever. He forgot all about his wet jeans. A few seconds later, he saw the wolf making its way up a ridge, occasionally glancing back as if feeling Luke's eyes on him, all the while seemingly aware but unimpressed with Luke's presence. Perhaps, the wolf even smelled Luke's scent on the wind?

Equating the wolf's powerful grace with Zak's movements didn't diminish Luke's ego. He wasn't envious of his brother's strengths because even though Luke may lack agility, he had other strengths and he knew one day everything would balance out. Maybe because he had temporarily lost his pride back in Medford, he no longer wanted to compare himself to anyone or feel humiliation, envy, or anger ever again. He knew his strengths and accepted his weaknesses. Unlike his brother, Luke didn't have the need or the desire to fight injustice. There was just the one driving force in his life and sometimes even that force scared him.

A tiny part of him acknowledged that if the legend was a lie, he would rather not know. But his gut told him there had to be some truth to the story. So, in Luke's mind, it was alright to be proud of his brother's agility while simultaneously accepting his own clumsiness, because in the end, Amara would give him the power of the Gods. Whoever found her first would benefit from her gratitude. As a reward, she would surely give her descendants the gift of immortality and so much more. It had long been told in his family that Amara had other amazing talents. Not only was she a demi-god and the best huntress in the sky, she had the ability to destroy or reanimate life.

The possibilities were endless.

The longer he thought about her powers, the more he was convinced when he found her, he and his family would sit at Zeus' table and rule the world.

Luke listened to the sound of the gas flowing into the tank and as always wondered if he should step outside and maybe do something manly like wash the windshield. Spurred on by his sudden discomfort at the disparity in their natures, Luke reluctantly got out of the car and began to squeegee the windshield while scrupulously keeping his eye on the woman sitting in her limousine as the gas attendant pumped gas into her tank and washed her windshield. He grappled with the idea of calling her "the woman."

Names were important to him, a way of identifying the world, and sometimes a clue to a person's identity. An archeologist could call an object by the names handed down from previous archeologists. A piece of clay was usually a pot shard. But just giving an object a name wasn't enough. Other archeologists, as a means of identification, would want to know where the pot had been found and what had been the purpose behind the pot shard. Giving the pot shard a name provided other archeologists a clue to its origin and purpose.

When they conquered England, King William and the Norman Lords insisted on surnames. Some people used them and others dropped them. It was a mess. It's still a mess. Gradually surnames spread to other countries. But what about the first community of homo sapiens? Most communities were around two-hundred and fifty strong. Some claim the oldest languages are Sumerian, an older form of Egyptian, and Mycenaean. Today the Greek suffixes -ides or -ades mean son of, but Mycenaeans didn't use the suffixes.

Critics claim the San of the Kalahari Desert speak the oldest language because of the clicks in their language. Critics of the critics claim no one knows for sure. It's impossible to say which language is the oldest because languages evolve over time. No one speaks Old English anymore. Few speak Latin in every day speech either. Even today language is changing so rapidly that maybe by 2117, the language we speak today will sound as funny as Old English.

Where was I going with all this? Luke asked himself with a frown. *Oh yes, the origin and purpose of naming objects which led to the naming of people.* Forget about today, what about ancient history. Some of the villagers must have had the same name. Did they distinguish between the two, a shorthand using origins, status, and occupation? And what did that mean for him?

His family came from Greece and called themselves Katsaros, but his mother chose Nerin to signal their origins from the sea. The sea was a big place. My home is the ocean. Oh, yeah? Where? Don't know, somewhere out there in the big blue ocean. And his status? One of the educated poor who claim middle-class status, but realistically are nothing more than dirt poor red-necks. What's your occupation? Unemployed archeologist who tends his mother's bar. My Mycenaean neighbors would have called me: Luke-the-bartender by-way-of-the- ocean.

Wow. Now he felt really miserable. Hold on. He was a descendant of a demi-god. How many people in the world could claim that honor?

Luke watched in amusement as the woman he'd first met, who back at the Woolly Man called herself Navan Leona Keys struggled in Frankie Stewart's tight charcoal gray pin-striped business suit to get out of the driver's seat and make her way to the gas pump. The gas attendant was busy checking her oil and did not see her stare at the meter with a bemused expression which did not fit with her power-suit.

As he watched her struggling to figure out the intricacies of the pump meter, he wondered which personality would pop out next. Frankie was gone. But for how long? Frankie would never have pulled and yanked at her skirt or wiped her dirty hands on her expensive jacket. Luke noticed a guy moving in as if to help and decided it was time for him to intervene. Frankie would never have acted so clueless and helpless.

When he stood close enough to see the freckles on her face, he recognized Leona looking back at him through those big green eyes with those impossibly long lashes.

"You need some help, ma'am?"

Leona looked relieved, "Oh, it's you. I know you. This thing won't stay on," she told him clicking the pin under the nozzle.

Luke bent down and as gently as possible released her fingers from their death grip around the nozzle. "Let me see what I can do. You see here. This is Oregon, ma'am. In Oregon, drivers don't pump their own gas. They have gas attendants who do the pumping and servicing of the vehicles. It looks as if the tank is full now. You see here. It shows you how much money you've charged to your credit card," he said as if he were talking to a child.

He remembered too late how Leona shied away from contact with others. He couldn't see her face because she was staring in disgust at the pointed tips of her shoes, but when he reached out to escort her into the store, she brushed his hand off and started back to the limo making a pretense of looking for something inside. Eventually she found what she was looking for – a sleek black leather purse. With an air of determination, she slung the purse over her shoulder, all the while making sure not to look at him as she walked toward the building. Since she had used a credit card to pay for the gas, he assumed she planned to use the restroom or buy some snacks inside.

Rather trusting of her to leave the limo to him, he thought as he stepped over to the driver's side door and peered through the glass. She was forgetful for sure. He saw the keys dangling from the ignition. Flaky? A pint short? A screw loose? Air head perhaps? None of those descriptions exactly fit Leona. Otherworldly? Maybe. Damned, what was the word he was looking for? Practical Dreamer? A blissful Guru? No. Definitely not. A Haunted Hottie? Yeah. He liked that one. Luke amused himself for several more minutes with other descriptors before she returned. It looked as if she'd bought some maps and a guide book in the store but no snacks for the trip. Then he thought about her driving the limo in her present mental state and found himself asking her aloud, "You want me to drive the rest of the way?"

She avoided his eyes and nodded ascent, "Um? Well? Yeah. Good idea, I guess. Wait. No. Maybe not. Well…alright. Here. Take these." She handed him her purchases and continued, "Sure. That would be nice," then climbed inside where Frankie had been sitting only a few hours ago. Frankie had taken up the entire backseat with her personality. In contrast, Leona seemed to shrink squeezing her already small frame into an even smaller space.

Zak appeared at Luke's side and glanced at Leona in the backseat. "What's up with her?"

"I offered to drive her. She's in no condition to drive."

"I'll follow you then. And don't ditch me like you did the last time," Zak said remembering his other grievance against his brother.

Luke had forgotten, "I was afraid she would disappear again."

"What are you holding there?" Zak asked noticing the maps, the guide book, and an envelope in his hand.

"She gave them to me," he said shrugging his shoulder in Leona's direction.

Luke tossed the maps and the guide book inside the limo. They landed on the passenger seat. He proceeded to open the envelope while his brother looked on with a frown. He found numerous sticky notes inside. He read the first one: *Every twenty minutes or so be sure to ask me who I am.* Luke handed the note to Zak. Zak held the note between his fingers for a second, frowned, then handed it back without a word.

As Luke watched Zak return to the Camaro, he knew he would be happier sitting beside his brother talking archeology and philosophy than sitting in a limo asking a woman who she was every twenty minutes. Even a root canal might be preferable to the mental discomfort of wondering when "the woman" in the backseat might decide he was a giant cockroach and squash him with a single blow to the back of his head.

Once the gas attendant had finished checking the oil, Luke climbed into the driver's seat and proceeded to pull carefully out of the gas station. The Camaro practically rode his ass all the way to the freeway and Luke suspected Zak would ride his ass all the way to their final destination. No wonder people glared at Zak and on occasion flipped him off. Zak's car was an extension of his personality: aggressive and frequently impulsive.

Luke paused before pulling out into traffic and asked the woman in the backseat, "Which direction?"

"Toward Winnemucca," she said.

"Winnemucca is in Nevada," Luke said. "We're in Oregon."

The silence dragged on and in the rear view mirror Luke studied the two objects which concerned him the most: the Camaro with the engine throbbing noisily even with the limo's sound proofing features and Leona's face in profile, the dark hair resting on her cheek as she stared out the window and bit her lower lip to shreds. For the first time in his life, Luke realized he had to go easy with this woman, so he said, "Did I hear you right? You said Winnemucca, Nevada? You want me to go to Winnemucca, Nevada?"

He thought he saw terror in her eyes as she glanced in his direction and then quickly away, "Yes. The first stop will be Winnemucca. Yes. Oh. And you forgot to ask me the question."

"It hasn't been twenty minutes yet."

"Well, just go ahead and ask me."

Luke swallowed his irritation and asked, "Who are you now?"

"My name is Navan Keys, but I prefer to be called Leona."

"Yeah. I know."

"Now you're supposed to look through the sticky notes for my name."

Luke had to pull the limo into a fast food parking lot and turn off the engine. He searched the envelope mindful of Zak who had pulled up beside him throwing his hands in the air as if to say, "What the hell?"

Luke ignored his brother's impatience and turned to the backseat, "I can't find your name on any of these notes."

"That's right."

"Well if you knew it, why did you ask me to look?"

"I want you to do that every time you ask the question. This is a practice run."

"Can we go now?"

Leona looked down at her hands, "Yes."

"Hold on. I have to let my brother know our change of plans," Luke told her, shutting the partition, and lowering the driver's side window. Before Luke had a chance to rest his arm on the limo door, Zak had jumped out of his car and ran around the hood to stand in front of Luke. Zak's expressionless face and relaxed pose alarmed Luke more than a furious tirade. Slowly Luke climbed out of the car and moved toward the trunk of the limo pretending to look at the rear tire. Imitating Luke, Zak knelt near the tire with his elbows resting on his knees and stared into his brother's eyes. Luke looked away.

"She asked for help," he explained, shrugging his shoulders. "What could I do? Frankie's gone, and Leona is back. She hates to drive. So, I offered to drive her wherever she wants to go, and she says she wants to go to Winnemucca."

"Are you forgetting Brent Wade? We promised to meet Brent in Crescent City, two days from now. Winnemucca is in the opposite direction. Driving hundreds of miles out of our way to appease the flower child is stupid."

"I know. I know. I'll think of something. Just let me gain her trust and I'll keep you updated. Texting only. Okay?"

The limo door opened, and a pair of silk stiletto heels landed on the ground. Both men's eyes traveled from the heels to the gorgeous legs to the tight skirt. Luke jumped up and moved toward her anticipating trouble. Very slowly Zak rose to his full height and waited for Leona to speak. "Is something wrong?" she asked directing her question to Luke and ignoring Zak as if he weren't even there.

"No, ma'am. I just asked my brother to check the tire. It looked like it needed air. He says it's just fine. Did you need anything? There's bottled water in the trunk."

A sick expression crossed Leona's face and Zak leaped forward concerned for her, then in less than a nanosecond he skidded to a stop when he heard her say, "How could someone add to the destruction of the planet? It makes me sick to think someone could be so thoughtless. What is wrong with the world? Did you know there's a mini fridge in the backseat with ice and sandwiches and all sorts of fancy chocolates," she said pointing to the interior of the limo. "It's consumerism at its most obscene. Who ordered all this junk? What's wrong with an apple? Or an orange?

The only sensible thing in this entire gas guzzling polluting monstrosity is the stainless-steel water bottle. It will last forever. It can be cleaned and reused. It can be used for hot drinks or cold drinks. The only thing that would make it even better would be if it decomposed. Now if they can create the Internet and get us to the moon, why can't they create containers that are biodegradable? Huh? Honestly. And the sentiment on the lid, what's that all about? The fancy calligraphy is the most tasteless piece of celeb-caca-poo-poo I've ever read, *I am a Goddess*. Give me a break."

When the Nerin brothers looked blankly at her, trying to wrap their heads around the fact that the person who hired the limo and chose the case of bottled water and chose the chocolates in the mini fridge and bought the fancy stainless steel water bottle with the celeb-caca-poo-poo calligraphy on the lid was now upset with those choices, they were speechless. As the silence dragged on, Leona sighed in resignation, "If you're finished testing the tires can we get moving? Please?"

Five minutes later, Luke pulled roughly out into traffic hearing the faint sound of pissed-off honking in his wake. He ignored them all and fumed inwardly wondering how he'd managed to be such a fool. Just as he pulled off the exit and onto the freeway, he noted the time to be sure to ask Her Highness her name again. He understood the rationale at work, the so-called method-in-her-madness, but since her reasoning appeared flawed, he could only follow blindly trusting in his brother's help when she finally plunged into the abyss at the bottom of crazy town tower.

It amazed him that after all the excitement in the last twenty-four hours, it was only four o'clock in the afternoon. It should have been dusk. Instead they still had six hours of daylight left. With their present speed, he estimated they would arrive in Winnemucca around . . . they had about four hundred and six miles to go before reaching Winnemucca...at an average speed of sixty-five or seventy miles per hour they would reach Winnemucca in six and a half hours. If his calculations were correct, they should arrive around ten thirty or eleven o'clock in the evening? No problem.

Luke drove sedately along Interstate 5 South and occasionally glanced in his rear view mirror and side mirrors to check up on the state of Leona and the Camaro. He was pretty sure Zak was grinding his teeth to nubs and wishing the limo and its occupants in purgatory. At this point in the journey, Luke didn't give a damn about Zak's impatient nature and sense of honor and he really didn't care if people thought he drove like a senior citizen.

Better to drive like an old man than attract the attention of cops. He would get his charge safely to Winnemucca without incident and she would come to trust him and soon, soon, he would know everything she knew.

Nothing would ever again block his path toward finding Amara.

No more delays, no more cops, and no more fights.

All smooth sailing.

He smiled.

The cliché fit with his current situation inside the limo with its heavy-duty shock absorbers and thick cushioned leather seats, so soft and smooth, a cocoon of luxury. He felt as if he was in a yacht on the water drifting steadily out to sea.

With a supreme effort, Zak held onto his temper as he stayed glued to the limo's behind. It felt like they were a part of a funeral procession as they traveled toward Klamath Falls creeping slowly around curves and barely touching fifty on the straight-away. They headed south on Interstate 5 then took Oregon Highway 140 and U.S. 95 South heading towards Klamath Falls and Zak noticed with a shake of his head that the limo's turn signals were blinking on and off. The turn signals had been used purposely in town but on the highway, had become a reflection of Luke's state of mind. He watched the green arrows blink left, right, left, right, over and over, repeating the process again and again, for miles and miles.

It was a standing joke in their family. Zak had long ago given up trying to break Luke of his annoying tic. Friends and family would tease him hoping to change his behavior through humiliation. The jokes didn't seem to bother him. Even a few citations by local cops wasn't enough incentive for his brother to stop. His mother used to sit beside him and when she noticed him playing with the turn signals would pinch his hand. He learned to suppress his tic when his mother was in the car, but anyone else who dared pinch him got a slap or a smack.

His sister tried to curb Luke's tic with New Age music and meditative mantras. Zak, once wrestled Luke's right arm behind his back which forced Luke to drive using only his left hand; yet, Luke managed to flip the blinkers on and off and steer the vehicle as best he could on the back roads around home, even drive one-handed down washboard roads and hairpin turns. Eventually, everyone gave up curing Luke of his bad habit.

The turn-signal castanets were a manifestation of Luke's chaotic thoughts. Luke used the turn signal indicator like a Catholic used a rosary, to give himself some comfort and remember his prayers. Luke's litany happened to be the Pacific Northwest discoveries in American archeological history. On the back roads near Woolstone the neighbors rarely complained. But here on the freeway amongst so many unknown drivers, Zak realized Luke's turn signal addiction could get him into trouble.

It was lucky then Zak drove so close he was practically French-kissing the limo's bummer, close enough to keep bemused or annoyed motorists from noticing the turn signals continuous uncertainty. Why was the limo signaling a left turn when there wasn't a left turn anywhere for miles? And now it was signaling a right turn, why?

By the time they reached Klamath Falls, Zak's legs were cramping, and his ass was numb. Gratefully, he pulled up to a pump next to the limo and climbed out of the Camaro and stretched. Eve Endicott or Navan Keys or whatever she was calling herself now made her way toward the convenience store. When she tripped over an air hose, he figured she must be Leona because only Leona ignored the physical world until the physical world collided with her. While gas pumped into his tank, Zak wandered over to his brother who happened to be scrupulously washing the windshield. Luke's uncharacteristic sense of vehicle-grooming was beginning to annoy Zak. There was enough weird going on already.

"How's it going?" Zak asked, watching his brother carefully rub out the smears left by a suicidal bug.

Luke ignored him still absorbed in cleaning the glass. His attitude unnerved Zak. Zak chose to walk away, "Never mind. I'm going inside to get something."

"Hey," Zak heard his brother say. He stopped and turned examining his brother's face closely. Luke's steady regard confused Zak even more. Lately, it was as if Luke had difficulty choosing the right words. Another first. Since the day he'd been born, Luke took control of language the way Michael Jordan took control of the basketball court.

"Every twenty minutes I'm supposed to ask, who are you now? And then if she says she's somebody other than Keys, I'm supposed to give that person one of the sticky notes she created this morning. I suspect Frankie was the one who created the sticky notes. I miss Frankie. Now there is a woman with skills. She's organized, ambitious, a problem-solver, and sexy as hell. Why can't Leona be more like Frankie? OMG, do you hear what I'm saying? I had to deal with Mad Mona all those long frigging miles in the Taurus; now, I'm trapped in a limo with Leona, and pretty soon, I bet you, I'll be handing people sticky notes and telling them to ask me my name."

For the longest time Luke just stared at the spot he'd been cleaning. Zak nodded impatiently waiting for him to continue, then Luke threw the wad of brown paper he'd been using to rub the squashed bug off the windshield into the trash bin and said, "I can live with the games she's playing. What I'm having trouble with is the silence. There's a sort of black hole of silence that seems to suck all sound and light and happiness out the window. It's not so much malevolent as it is uncanny. We've driven nearly two hundred miles and she has yet to say a word, a word. She has yet to do much of anything a normal person would do.

It doesn't matter, she's so damned sexy. I can't figure out which part of her I like best: the eyes, the hair, the breasts, or the legs. And she's not conventionally pretty, she's striking, you know what I mean. I find myself sneaking peeks at her and wondering what it would be like to—"

The words burst from Zak's lips without hesitation, "Shut up. Just shut the hell up."

Luke ignored Zak and talked over him, "I mean she doesn't move, Zak. She just stares out the window or down at her hands in her lap. Normal people wiggle around a bit, you know. And when I try to ask her a question or make a comment about the view, she avoids looking directly at me and politely nods her head or says, 'Oh.' That's all she says and nothing else. If she read a book or slept or did yoga I could deal with the silence. But not when I sense—"

"What?"

"I can't quite put it into words."

"Well try."

"Terror. I guess I sense terror. She's terrified about something, maybe where we're going or something that happened to her a long time ago. I don't know. It may even have something to do with Amara. If she's been anywhere near Amara, her essence is incredibly powerful, so powerful that she may be able to twist the mind, make the average person insane. Maybe that's why she's a basket case? She's been close enough to Amara she's now traumatized beyond all hope."

Annoyed by Luke's interest in Leona, Zak started backing away. He was remembering back home how Luke's hands encircled Leona's waist as he hoisted her onto the barstool. He remembered the sight of Luke hitting the ground and clutching his throat as Acacia knocked him away and stole his truck. And uncomfortably, Zak recognized with misgivings the intensity and obsession in Luke's eyes whenever he talked about Leona and Amara. Did he think Leona was the reincarnation of Amara? He'd better not share that thought with his brother, it might give him ideas.

Did his fussy behavior over the limo indicate he'd already arrived at the same conclusion about Leona? All Zak had to do was consider Luke's treatment of the limo compared to his truck back home. The truck hadn't been showy enough for pampering. It didn't represent money and power. Just like the Woolly Man had been a shack and an embarrassment to Luke all his life, he never concerned himself with the broken pipes or rough floorboards.

But now, now Luke was rubbing out suicidal bugs and imaginary specks of dust off a limo that didn't even belong to him. Now he was willing to risk his own sanity for a crazy female, alternately complaining and then complimenting her. And it all had to do with the limo a symbol of power. Was Leona also a symbol of power? Did he really think she might be channeling Amara and by keeping close to her, he might just channel some power his way?

Zak looked around and realized Leona had been gone a long time. "What's she doing in there?" he asked.

"What people usually do when they make stops on the road – stuff their faces and drain it out the other end. By the way, she's Leona right now. At least for the last ten minutes she's been Leona. I'll let you know in another ten if she becomes someone else," Luke said with a frowning shrug.

Zak strode toward the convenience store and just as he threw open the door, Leona came out. They collided. He held her shoulders for a second until she regained her balance. While he tried to get her attention, she kept her eyes stubbornly focused on the ground. "Eve. We've got to talk. I know you were scared the other night. I know we don't know each other well enough yet. But I want to—"

Gradually, he became conscious of her response to him. At first, he was stunned. Women rarely shudder when he touched them. Yet he could feel her shudder through his fingertips, a shudder that ran from the top of her head to her toes, as if she were standing out in an Arctic wind or had just woken from a terrifying nightmare. He dropped his arms to his sides and stepped back.

How had he become her nightmare? As he watched her walk away, he witnessed the metamorphosis take shape. She seemed to grow taller with every step. The former meandering, the zigging and zagging and tripping over objects in her path had now become a purposeful march to the limo. With an economy of movement, the woman strode up to Luke and with her hands on her hips stared into his startled face.

"I need a beverage, preferably alcoholic with a dash of ice. Where might one procure such a libation in this uh, this backwoods hamlet?" she asked waiting patiently for him to respond. The way she stood and her commanding, but friendly voice reminded Zak uncomfortably of his high school English teacher Mrs. Farmington.

Reminded unhappily of the way Leona had become the kick-ass warrior witch in a matter of seconds, Zak watched in fascinated horror as the transformation happened in real time. As an added treat, he had a perfect view of the expressions chasing after each other across her face: intense concentration, followed by bewilderment, overshadowed by annoyance, and then a moment of confusion mixed with fear and disbelief, and finally the final expression, resignation to the inevitable. After all, she had warned them of what was to come. After what seemed like an eon, Zak heard Luke asked this new personality, "And who are you?"

"Of course. How stupid of me. How do you do, you must be my driver. My name is Evans, Professor Ana Evans. And your name?"

"Luke Nerin."

They shook hands. Luke was careful not to look at Zak who stood behind her with a frown, nor did he indicate in any way that the situation was abnormal. A peeved expression crossed her face, "Well, Luke. Do you have an answer to my original question?"

"No. ma'am. At least not in this town. I'm not familiar with Klamath Falls. I come from Idaho. Oh, and I nearly forgot. I'm to give you a note from a friend."

"Really. How extraordinary. In these backwoods?"

"I have been instructed to give you a posted note from a friend of yours. Hold on and I'll get it," he said while moving toward the limo and opening the door. His head and torso disappeared inside as he searched for the envelope he'd shown Zak earlier. Then the woman glanced over her shoulder sensing a presence and Zak got the shock of his life when he looked into the woman's eyes. If he overlooked the familiar bone structure and coloring, she could have been mistaken for an older woman. What was the most disconcerting of all was the quick intelligence and brutal assessment in her eyes as she examined him from head to toe. She looked as if she'd seen everything, done everything, and had no illusions about mankind or life in general.

What upset Zak just as much was Luke's attitude. He didn't recognize his familiar pontificating brother. Now he behaved as if he had just bumped into royalty, practically genuflecting when he handed the sticky note to her. Ana Evans read the note, crumbled the paper into a tight ball, and threw the wad in a nearby trash can. Her movements were economical to the point of curtness as she strode toward the limo's front passenger door and briskly opened the heavy door and disappeared inside. Luke looked at Zak in desperation. Barely able to hold back a desire to laugh, Zak waved him away, "Go on. I'll catch up."

Once the limo was on Oregon 140 East towards Winnemucca, Luke tried his best to lean back and get comfortable, even with the woman sitting in the seat beside him. She hadn't stopped talking since he'd climbed into the limo. Memories of his days as an undergraduate resurfaced, those interminable hours of listening to the professor lecture on and on and on, only understanding one word out of three. The old panic and bewilderment compounded by insecurities rose up to haunt him.

Nobody used terms like "hamlet" or "libation" these days unless they wanted to be ridiculed. Only someone familiar with, no, marinated in the language of their profession for decades could come across as rude and insular. Like himself, Ana Evans had difficulty shutting down the teeming thoughts inside her head which were begging to be shared and critiqued by an audience of her peers.

Although her continual monologue made him nod off a couple of times, he forced himself to pay attention for two very important reasons. First, she might disclose a critical clue about Professor Wade's past excavations. Second, he recalled excruciatingly embarrassing moments as a student when former professors stopped to ask him penetrating questions which he was clueless to answer. There was nothing worse than to be professionally mocked by a wordsmith. His vigilance paid off when he heard her mention a familiar name. He tried to hide his triumph.

"When she matriculated into my classroom, oh, back in 2001. Was it? Yes. It was 2001. I soon realized how exceptional she was. What a shame she chose anthropology as her field of study. I urged her to try out for the MFA program. Believe me; it was singular to find an undergraduate with such an exceptional grasp of language. But alas she was adamant about her future plans. Adamant about becoming a grave robber. You know the type."

"You mean an archeologist?"

"Well, it's all a matter of perception wouldn't you say? More so, I would say, if one looked at the situation dispassionately. Say for instance, I told you that I saw a man digging in one of the local graveyards and I accosted him and demanded to know what he thought he was doing and his response was, 'But I'm an archeologist. It is my right to uncover the past.' And my response to him might be, 'But that's my Grandma Maud you're digging up.' Now would the word archeologist and all its implicit semantics both historical and cultural, as understood by western minds, be forever changed?

You see it's not just a matter of perception but a matter of timing. We think nothing of an archeologist digging up hundred-year-old bones; but, when the bones belong to Grandma Maud who died just last year, then what? I don't know. Sounds more like grave robbery to me. What would the cutoff date be – a decade, maybe, or a century, certainly? In other words, where would the line be drawn, what would be a tasteful period of internment before the archeologists could exhumed Grandma Maud?"

"But archeologists don't dig up local graveyards unless they receive permission."

"Ah."

Between gritted teeth, Luke said, "I know where you're going with this. But it's not the same thing."

"How so?"

"Once a grave is discovered, there are many steps an archeologist must take to ensure the integrity of the site and the integrity of the bones. And today even more stringent laws must be followed, and permissions be granted. Also, if I might add, there is still considerable debate as to which New World bones belong to which group of people."

It took another fifty miles before Luke could get Evans back on the subject of Professor Wade. "We could argue this point for hours and still not agree, Dr. Evans. Now what were we talking about before?" Luke asked.

"We have only discussed one topic thus far."

"Oh no. I clearly recall another topic. It was about a woman. You were telling me about Constance Wade and her genius at finding artifacts."

Ana shot him a considering look which warned him his disinterest had been exposed as counterfeit. "Professor Wade only worked as my assistant for a semester and then chose to pursue a career in archeology with the Great Jerk."

"Dr. Krutcher?"

"Yes. How clever of you to figure out my sobriquet."

"The word archeology was my clue."

"Um," she said with a thoughtful look in his direction. "The crude epithet came to me at one of those interminable faculty meetings when once again Krutcher disregarded civilized behavior and regaled us with his imitation of a Kaguru or Trobriand, I can't remember which, who after the yam harvest dances with his imaginary kula partner in order to get her valuables. His antics on the dance floor were his way of annoying and embarrassing the female faculty."

Luke spoke before Evans could continue, aware he was being rude, but unable to stop himself because she had her information all twisted around and totally misunderstood Dr. Krutcher's intentions. He wanted to be sure to set the story straight, so that she would no longer look upon cultural anthropology or archeology as a white man's attempt to ignore and invalidate other cultures or women. At first, breathless with his urgency to make her understand, his words tumbled out making little sense even to his ears. Then he paused. He took a deep breath and opened his mouth to speak. He appreciated her silence. She hadn't tried to jump in during the void and speak over him or interrupt him. She appeared to genuinely want to understand. He spoke carefully enunciating every word.

"Kula has to do with the Trobriand's ideas about the sea and about the male/female relationship. The Trobriand believe the sea to be female and potentially dangerous but fruitful, a way of being able to act out the undeniable power of procreation. The female after all has the ability to bear children, to bear ancestral spirits through her womb. The male wishing to have such power uses the sea as a source of creation. You see, the baloma, the spirits of the dead live underground, well, below, where humans used to live. The Trobriand believes balomas are immortal. Their distant ancestors, when old, were able to shed their skins and grow new ones. That is why the Trobriand equate snakes, crabs, and lizards with the underworld and believe these animals are immortal and as immortal beings mediators with the baloma.

So, when Dr. Krutcher acted out the Trobriand belief system, he only did so to show you all how much he appreciated the power of procreation and as a man who isn't capable of giving birth, he wanted to demonstrate other ways to symbolically give birth. At least, I believe that must have been his intentions. I mean I'm not that crazy about the guy. Actually, I agree, he is a jerk, but, I believe, in this case only, his intentions were good."

"Well, we've digressed so far off the map, we're in no man's land," she said glancing at him thoughtfully. "I can see that we have. You've completely forgotten our original topic. Remember? You wanted to know about Professor Wade, didn't you?"

"Of course," Luke assured her.

"Well, I'll tell you then. At least the little I know. Connie came to me the week after she'd catalogued and shipped the Smithers' artifacts. That was about fifteen years ago. Yes. It must have been fifteen. Dr. Krutcher had asked her to stay on at the site and search for more artifacts but she had other obligations. Her children. At the time, her sons were adolescents, hardly capable of taking care of themselves. Dr. Krutcher had been disappointed by her refusal.

Evidently, he had hoped that G. K. Smithers had found the mythical harpy sighted by the people of the Columbia. There were rumors that Connie's disappearance coincided uncomfortably with the time of the Smithers' excavation. Some people hinted Krutcher may have had something to do with her disappearance. I found the idea ludicrous. Krutcher, as a mastermind? So sad.

Some people wondered if while Dr. Krutcher was occupied in placating and schmoozing the big wigs in Ely, Nevada, Connie had found other treasures and hid them from Krutcher. What horseshit! Connie was incapable of subterfuge or for that matter, larceny. She was the type who when handed too much change went out of her way to return the money, no matter the inconvenience to herself. In fact, she was nauseatingly honest. Too honest in my opinion.

Her candid personality made Dr. Krutcher nervous, that's why he dealt personally with the local ranchers and townspeople. Ironically, it wasn't Connie who outed him when the university discovered he too had caught the Smithers' obsession. He outed himself when a student discovered a glossy photo of a naked woman wearing fake wings in his office. No one was able to identify the woman, so he wasn't fired for inappropriate behavior with a female student, but the university did encourage him to take a year's sabbatical. And then he never returned. Many believe he chose to retire early, so as not to lose face with his peers. What a silly man."

On high alert, he waited for Evans to tell him the name of the student who outed Krutcher. It couldn't be him. He'd only told Zak recently about breaking into his advisor's office all those years ago. Well, actuality, he hadn't stolen anything from Krutcher's office. He'd made copies of secret documents, but that wasn't stealing, not exactly. Semantics were his defense mechanism. When the silence dragged on, he got nervous and stole a look at her face to try to read her mind. She had Leona's face, yet, she looked twenty years older. He shut his eyes and opened them and looked at her again. The illusion had to be because of the furrows around her eyes and forehead when she was thinking; and since she frowned when she was thinking, her habitual expression was a sort of concentrated perpetual bowel movement.

After some time, Evans continued, "Anyway, I met with Connie shortly after she returned from Smithers' dig and then one terrible day, she disappeared." The woman did something which scared the living bejesus out of him. She looked down at her hands and said as if she were talking to herself, "Professor Evans, you forgot to mention that you've been missing almost as many years."

Maybe it was the surreal moment which led Luke toward his epiphany. He'd gotten so caught up with the whole unpleasantness and confusion of multiple personalities that he'd forgotten the most important fact – he had a picture of the real Constance Wade in his shirt pocket. He could take out the picture, right now, right this moment, and he could present the picture to this woman, and then ask her to look in the sun visor mirror and compare the woman in the picture with the woman in the mirror. And what might that do to her? He was no psychiatrist. Perhaps he might do irreparable harm?

Luke stared in amazement at the woman speaking, hearing the echo of her words in his head, spoken from the lips of Professor Wade.

It was the same voice, the voice of his old teacher at the university. He was positive, for just that brief moment, when he turned to face the woman, the words still ringing in his ears, he saw Professor Wade sitting there, as real as the steering wheel in his hands. There could be no other. The features were so similar there could be no doubt. Yet she spoke about herself in the third person and more profoundly poignantly, in the past tense. He had little time to assimilate the juxtaposition before he was forced to listen closely to the rest of her speech, so as not to miss a single word.

"As I recall, she seemed preoccupied and anxious. She wouldn't tell me what was bothering her, but she did mention having been invited to see the old ovens the Italians built in the mid-nineteenth century just outside the town of Ely. She said an "old geezer" as she described him showed her around the town and the ovens and had plenty of wild stories to tell her. One in particular intrigued her. It was an old legend about an ancient race of people traveling from Asia to the Americas and making their home in Nevada.

Connie assured me he hadn't been referring to the Eskimos or what we know today as the migration of the preliterate Native Americans. No. He said these people were unlike the people that had come before them and there were never such a people heard of again. The legend goes that they had no pigment in their hair or skin and they had dark brown eyes, eyes as big and gentle as a baby seal's eyes. He said they were forced to travel at night and hide under cover of the sun during the day, because the sun could kill them. He told her where the legend had begun, and Connie thought she might investigate the legend during summer break, when her sons would be spending time with their father. That was the last time I talked to her."

"Did she mention where the old man had told her the legend originated?" Luke asked leaning toward her intently.

He heard a shout, "Mind the road," and realized he'd drifted into the other lane and had just enough time to turn the wheel sharply to the right to avoid colliding with an oncoming truck. The owner of the truck honked and stuck his middle finger in the air. Luke pretended not to notice and cheerfully waved back.

Luke turned to Evans, "Sorry about that."

"Have trouble multitasking, do you?"

"Of course not. I was just entranced with your story."

Her laughter rang as false as his flattery. He knew that she knew he was only after information about Professor Wade. Yet they both remained polite out of professional courtesy. Luke's difficulty had more to do with making sense with what his ears heard, and his eyes saw. When he was busy driving and only paying attention to the words, he could imagine a much older woman, a professional woman, a professor of English at a good university sitting beside him.

When he glanced at the person sitting in the seat next to him, the mental image jarred with the visual image of an extremely young, sexy, striking woman wearing a tight-fitting Armani suit speaking with careful diction. He heard a hint of a midwestern accent and tried to remember where Professor Wade had been born.

"We'll be in Winnemucca in another hour or so. Good. We'll stop there for supplies before moving on," she said.

"It'll be dark soon," Luke said. "Stores will be closed. What supplies will we need?"

"A shovel for sure. A couple of flashlights, I suppose, since it'll be dark. Or we could wait until morning to start digging."

"You don't need to buy shovels. Zak has plenty of them in his trunk."

"Who's Zak?"

"You know. My brother Zak. He's driving the Camaro that's been following us for the last one hundred miles," he said and thought without speaking. "You know. The one you probably broke ten lascivious laws with in Paris, Nevada."

Evans glanced behind her beyond the rich earthly interior of leather and wood and soft beige carpet through the window at the racy 1969 Camaro following close behind them. Luke had a difficult time discerning whether Evans was acting out a genuine curiosity or she really believed she'd never met Zak before. "I hadn't noticed. How odd," she said softly as she turned back to face the front. "Sometimes, when I'm thinking about something that interests me, I get lost in the complexity of my thoughts. My student evaluations often include comments, well complaints, about my hyper-focus. I remember the time we were discussing *Time's Arrow*. Have you read it? Fascinating piece of literature. I'll try to summarize it for you. Unless of course, you plan to read it someday?"

"I don't think so. At least not in the recent future," he said and that was the last word he was allowed to speak for nearly an hour. Of course, he could have interrupted her at any time and he did figuratively speak once or twice, he made grunting sounds to let her know he was still listening. Meanwhile, as Evans discussed the book's themes and the critics' theories and her own, Luke nodded his head in ascent agreeing wholeheartedly with her former students about her hyper-focus. As he drove, he listened as closely as he could, because even though she happened to be hyper-focused, her ideas were fascinating. At any other time, he would have been mesmerized by all the new knowledge he was accumulating.

He drove on autopilot with half is mind on the lecture and the other half wondering if Evans really existed? He should have someone research public records and see if there really was an Ana Evans teaching at a university or community college. First, he had to interrupt her at some point and find out where she taught. But his questions could wait. Best to let her finish her lecture on the circularity of time or the absence of linearity in time, well, he was pretty sure, her subject had to do with time.

Once they arrived in Winnemucca and Luke had a chance to stretch and listen to his own thoughts in the sudden blissful silence, he wondered if he had the patience to deal with more of Evans' lectures without wanting to scream or stuff her mouth with napkins. It was a relief to see Zak striding toward him. Zak had run over to the diner across the street and bought sandwiches and snacks for them. Evans was taking a potty break or as she would say "powdering her nose."

Luke wanted Leona back so badly, the feeling was more like a physical ache than just wishful thinking. Zak handed Luke two brown bags and held onto the third with his left hand, "A Reuben for the lady and a roast beef with bacon for you. Nasty, man. Don't you think you're going overboard with this carnivore fantasy? After all, we've evolved Luke. We're no longer hunter gatherers."

"Yeah, right, like you eat wholesome foods. Hey, Zak, do me a favor and see if you can find out if there really is an Ana Evans somewhere in the world. I had this idea on the way here that maybe Professor Wade is imitating real people, not just figments of her imagination. Could you do that for me? Obviously, I can't."

Zak's face expressed exactly what he was thinking. No wonder the guy is a terrible poker player, Luke thought. He was simultaneously annoyed and worried. Annoyed that Luke would bring up the subject again and worried that Luke might be right. Zak snapped, "I've told you before. She's not Wade. She can't be Wade."

"Okay. How does Jane Smith sound? Any better? You can keep on calling her Eve…um? What's her full name? We know Leona's; it's Navan Keys. What about Eve?"

"Her last name is Endicott. Her full name is Eve Endicott, no middle name."

If looks could vaporize a person on the spot, Luke's body would be nothing but particles of DNA floating in the air or something similar as in – died as a door nail, six feet under, anti-Luke Nuke. Whatever the outcome, he didn't like the idea, or the menacing way Zak moved toward him. He held his temper as best he could and said, "Just humor me. Please? Watch out. Here she comes. Shit."

"Shit what?"

"I forgot to ask her who she was. For the last hour, she's been talking nonstop."

"Talking like who?"

"Yeah. I see what you mean. No need to ask her who she is, she's been the lecturing professor since Lakeview."

When the woman walked under the lights above the gas pumps, Luke could tell Evans was still with them. He groaned inside and forced a smile as she drew closer. Zak handed her the brown bag and she smiled graciously up into his face like a queen bestowing a gift upon a favored courtier. Zak's wary look deepened. He walked off with his face blank and a ring of white around his lips. Evans hadn't noticed his reaction because she was busy peeking inside the bag and smelling her sandwich.

"Dr. Evans," Luke said a bit too loudly, loud enough for Zak to hear. Zak paused in the act of opening the Camaro door. Luke continued, "So which university do you teach at?"

As the young woman walked around the limo to once again ride shot-gun, she said absently, "At the moment, I'm on sabbatical. I've taught at Boise State University as an associate professor and at the University of Berkley and Brown as a full professor. I plan to co-teach at the University of Minnesota in the fall." Confident Zak had overheard the woman's academic credentials, Luke ran to the other side of the limo and made a point of holding open the back door. She hesitated a moment, eyeing the front seat with regret, then taking the hint she slipped inside the back remarking, "It seems so autocratic to be riding back here. I disapprove of such obvious class distinctions."

"I completely agree. Might I suggest we take turns at the wheel? You rest now and relieve me later. What do you say?"

"I say, onward young man."

"Oh, and Professor Evans, I forgot to ask. Where are we going next?"

Evans looked up at him thoughtfully and Luke wondered with a cold sensation trickling down his spine whether she could read people as well as Leona. "Our next destination is Ely, Nevada. Do you know how to get there?"

"I'll consult with my brother. He has the maps."

"Excellent."

Luke skipped over to the Camaro and rested his elbow on the roof of the car then leaned forward to look at his brother's face, "What are you doing?"

With one hand holding his cellphone to his ear and waving Luke to be silent with the other, Zak mumbled, "I've been trying Andy's number. Shut up. I've got his voicemail. Hey Andy. Give me a call, bro. Thanks again. I owe you, man." Instead of dumping his phone on the seat beside him, Zak started calling another number.

A sensation close to dread washed over Luke. He heard Zak say, "Hey, Mom. How're you doing? Yeah, I'm out of jail. How'd you know?" Zak glanced at Luke with a furrow between his brows then away as if the sight of his brother made him sick. While Jule talked, Luke stared pointedly out the car windshield. "Is that right? Hum. That's interesting. The bail money? Oh yeah. It came in handy. Let me check with Luke and if there's any left, I'll send it back to you. Yeah. No problem."

For a minute all Zak did was listen to Jule. No doubt she was demanding they both return home immediately. Zak had to interrupt her to say, "Hey, Mom. Yeah, okay. Also. Yeah, right. Hey. I'm going to have to take off here soon. I'm calling about Andy. I left a message for him, but I guess he lost his cellphone again."

There was another long silence and Luke began to twitch wondering what the hell was taking so long. "He's there? Great. Could you put him on? Thanks. I love you too. Sure, I'll send Luke your love." Luke refused to move from his spot even though Zak vibrated with righteous anger. If Zak wanted to punch him in the face, Luke would accept the challenge. In fact, he longed to show Zak his new moves.

As Luke waited, he remembered Tom Bambrey (the poor sucker) and the condition Zak had left him in. Replaying the sucker punch, he prudently took a few steps back on the pretense of giving Zak some privacy. To pretend indifference and calm his nerves, Luke began stretching exercises. He bent forward and backward several times. He leaned to the right and then to the left as far as he could go. He lifted his right leg then the left as high as it would go. Anyone watching would have assumed he was preparing for a long drive rather than warming up for a major beating. While he stretched, Luke listened to the one-sided conversation.

"Hey there Professor. I owe you big time man. Big time. You are the man. You are the greatest. You are the Ali of Greatness." There was a pause as Andy responded to Zak's fulsome praises. Luke thought he might gag. "Yeah. I owe you a beer, maybe two if I can afford it. But hey, my big brother's come into some money and he's offered to buy us drink's all night. When I'm back in town, I'll look you up, bro. Hold on. Don't go yet. I got another favor to ask. I met this lady and I think she might be playing us. She claims to be ..." Zak looked up at his brother, the glittering anger in his eyes a reminder Luke wasn't out of the lion's den just yet. "She's telling us she taught at BSU and Berkley."

Luke, in one bound, reached the Camaro and interjected quickly, "And she's claiming she has a gig coming up at Brown." Sweat from his stretching exercises dripped into one eye and down his neck. Something else was making him sweat too, a sudden sense of danger. He resumed his perched position by the driver's door in what he hoped appeared nonchalant. "Yeah, she said Brown. And she said something about the University of Minnesota too. It's Ana with one n and her last name is Evans. Ana Evans."

"You hear that?" Zak asked into the phone. "Great. You think you could check it out? See if she's for real. She calls herself Ana with one n, last name Evans. Yeah. Funny? No. Sounds okay to me. No, I've never heard of her. Hold on a sec," Zak glanced up at Luke and asked, "Is her first name Mary?"

"Yes, No, I don't know. I think she was pulling my leg," Luke said unhelpfully. "It sounded familiar, but like a joke, you know what I mean? She calls herself Ana Evans. Oh, and ask him to check out the other names: Navan Keys and um, Frankie, yeah, Frances Margaret Stewart. And a business called FAS Limited. Their headhunters for the academic world. Let me see, oh yes, how could I forget Acacia T. Pierce? Anyone else I might have missed from the menagerie?"

Still addressing Luke, Zak said, "He's checking his personal database and there's about sixteen current and former higher education professionals called Evans. Wait. He found an Evans that might fit. This Evans goes back to the 1990s. Her name is Mary Ana Evans. There's nothing more after 2002. She'd be about eighty years old by now. That can't be her."

Luke leaned forward, "Wait. I know that name. I got it. Mary Ann Evans. Holy shit, of course. George Eliot's real name was Mary Ann Evans. It's possible her parents were clueless about the George Eliot connection. Or its possible they twisted the name a bit in the hopes maybe their daughter might become a literary genius one day. You can't fake a CV. Not for long anyway. Was this Mary Ana with one n, a real person?"

Pushing Luke away from the window, Zak said, "Occam's Razor, you idiot. It's far more likely she's playing us." Zak turned his attention back to his cellphone and his friend Andy, "Check Navan Leona Keys and Frances Margaret Stewart. Also, a company called FAS Limited? It's some sort of headhunter business for the Ivory Tower set. What do you mean? Oh, that. Yeah, she's got a couple of friends with her," Zak said and raised an eyebrow signifying an attempt at humor which he wasn't feeling. "Well, you know Luke. He's as greedy as an old man with a million bucks. Thinks he's gonna be robbed, the Scrooge."

"Damned right I am," Luke said, hearing his own hearty laughter with a wince. Pretty soon he'd end up acting like an obsequious jerk unable to lead because he was too busy kissing Zak's ass. Angry with himself Luke strode over to the limo and opened the back door and peeked inside. The young woman inside still appeared to be Evans. Of course, she was. She had a spiral notebook on her lap and a pen in her hand. At the moment, she happened to be busily jotting down her thoughts, probably a recap of her monologue on *Time's Arrow*. She glanced up at him with an absent frown. "We won't be long. We're still figuring out the best route," he told her with what he hoped was a facsimile of an honest smile.

"So be it," she said and resumed her writing.

Luke returned to the Camaro and climbed inside the passenger seat. Zak was still on the phone and evidently someone had told him a funny joke because he slapped his thigh and laughed with his head back and his mouth open. Andy must have handed the phone to someone else because Luke was pretty sure Andy didn't know any jokes, funny or otherwise. It was getting late and they didn't have time to be visiting with people long distance. Already the street lights had begun to illuminate the town and with the sun setting the air had turned cooler.

With mounting urgency Luke tried to get Zak's attention. His brother with equal determination was ignoring him. Zak was still pissed. So what? There were more urgent matters to take care of than a petty family squabble. Well, he still had around three hundred dollars left, out of the five hundred Jule had wired. He fished the money out of his pocket and began to count the bills. He couldn't be sure the woman claiming to be Mary Ana Evans would continue to pay for the gas. He had no doubt Frankie would have paid and taken care of everything else besides.

Evans seemed like a penny-pincher. She hadn't offered to pay once or even to pay for his meals or drinks. And would she still be Dr. Evans once they got to Ely? Realizing he needed the money to get Motor Mouth to Ely, Luke kept one hundred and fifty dollars and stuffed it back into his wallet. Zak was so busy bullshitting with his drinking buddies, he hadn't noticed Luke counting out the money.

When he offered the money to Zak, Zak continued to ignore him. Luke threw the money into the Camaro's glove compartment and grabbed the Idaho, Oregon, and Nevada maps from the backseat. When he jumped out of the vehicle, he slammed the door. Camaro doors are heavy suckers and the end result was satisfying. He smiled knowing he'd finally got his brother's attention. Once he was safely inside the limo, he locked all the doors.

As he searched through the maps for the best route to their next destination, the force of his unfolding nearly tore the map in two. It took a couple of deep breaths and a lift of the brow from Dr. Evans in the backseat before he could calm down enough to perceive the lines and squiggles on the map as having some sort of meaning. Luke searched for a place called Ely, Nevada; and then realized he'd been through Ely a hundred times. Ely was the shortcut to Vegas. Of course. They could take I-80 all the way to Wells, Nevada then down U.S. 93 South. Too long? Or they could take U.S. 305 to U.S. 50? But if 305 or 50 were anything like 140, he would rather walk. He wished Zak would get off the phone.

The incessant honking from the Camaro got Luke's attention. He dropped the map on the seat beside him and turned the ignition. Instead of driving off, he decided to park alongside the gas station in an empty space. He would wait and consult with his brother and this way he could assess the damage. Zak had the cellphone to his ear as he moved away from the pump and pulled up alongside the limo. Zak's window was still down all the way and his arm was resting on his door.

Cautiously, Luke pressed the button allowing the window to drop an inch and then another inch. Zak was still talking on his phone, "Hey, Fred I got to go. Luke looks as if he's constipated. Yeah man. Talk to you later. Great to hear from you. Oh, you want to say hi to Luke? No. I'll tell him." With a snap, Zak closed his cellphone and stuffed the black metal inside his jean pocket, "Fred says you still owe him a hundred bucks and he's going to take it out of your hide the next time he sees you."

"Never mind that. It's getting late Zak. We've got another three hundred miles to go."

"Say what? I thought we were here. Didn't she say Winnemucca?"

"Now, she wants to go to Ely."

Zak glanced at his watch, "It's late. Let's find a motel here."

Luke glanced in the rear view mirror. Evans had stopped writing long enough to look up and address Luke's eyes in the rear view mirror, "He's probably right. How far is Ely from here anyway?"

"About two hundred and seventy-one miles."

"Four hours. Yes. I agree with your friend. Find two rooms or three if you don't want to share a room with your brother," she said and then returned to her notebook.

About ten minutes later, Luke pulled into the brick arch of a posh hotel. At least from the opulent appearance of the façade facing the street side, the hotel looked comfortable, clean, and genuinely expensive. He figured Frankie Stewart would have insisted on a place like this to stay the night. He wasn't sure about the present occupant of the backseat though.

Maybe Evans would think the hotel was too ostentatious. Well, he was tired of second guessing which personality would pop up next. After spending hours with Mad Mona yesterday and today trying to survive Jane Smith's entourage, he was mentally and physically exhausted. Even worse was the state of his clothes and the rumbling in his stomach. They would stay here because he had a feeling the other motels in town were probably full up.

As he climbed out of the limo and jumped to open the back door for Evans (just to piss her off) Zak tore through the brick arch, the Camaro engine throbbing, a blue exhaust trail behind him with tires leaving rubber on the pristine asphalt. Luke pretended not to know him and followed Evans into the hotel lobby. At the counter while filling out the hotel card, she glanced at Luke and frowned, "I don't know the license number of the limo. Would you go out and check for me please?"

Luke bent down near her ear and asked, "Leona told me to ask every twenty minutes the following question: Who are you now?" He straightened and looked down at her curious to see her reaction.

Her eyes looked away from his first, "What an impertinent question. You know very well who I am," then she lifted up the card and thrust it under his nose. She'd written Dr. Mary Ana Evans on the card. It was the first time he'd been introduced to someone who had really existed, someone verifiable. Ana must be a nickname. She really did think she was Dr. Evans who had disappeared in 2002, Dr. Evans who would be in her late sixties by now? How could she reconcile the contradictions? If he could find a picture of the real Dr. Mary Ana Evans maybe she would snap out of her delusion?

When she handed the card to the desk clerk, she looked up at Luke to be sure there was no confusion and said, "My friends call me Ana; you can call me Dr. Evans." The name Mary Ann Evans brought back unhappy memories of his freshman semester in a literature class filled with English majors. On the midterm final, he'd gotten that question and several others wrong. It had been his first B and he'd been furious.

"I'll get that license number for you," he told the fake Evans as he passed Zak on the way out the revolving door. He told his brother, "You're free to get your own room if you don't want to share one with me."

"I'm free to do any damned thing I want big brother," Zak said with a grin. "But I'll let you pay for the room. Right now, I want to talk to the lady."

Luke stopped in his tracks and wheeled around, "Hey. Zak. Hold on."

Zak ignored him.

In the end, Luke paid for a room with two king-size beds while "Evans" slept in a plush suite on the top floor of the Mahogany Tree Hotel. The only reason Luke knew about her fancy accommodation was because he carried her heavy suitcases up to the room. It was only after she moved toward her purse as if to tip him, changed her mind, and dismissed him with a brief nod that he began to question his own sanity. He'd gone from being an Harvard graduate to a chauffeur and sometime bell hop.

In the last two days, he'd become a stranger to himself. Instead of a professional archeologist on the scent of a new exciting find, he might just end up an orderly at a loony bin. In alarm, he wheeled to face her hotel door concerned he'd shut it a little too hard, perhaps annoying, or even alienating its occupant. Was he morphing into Igor to her Dr. Frankenstein?

When Luke entered the room he shared with his brother, he heard Zak in the shower and decided he was sick of them both. He shut the door behind him with a firm click, walked down the beige carpeted hall, descended to the first-floor rooms in a mirrored elevator and wandered into a richly furnished bar where the clientele expected nothing but the best: thick carpets, mahogany furniture, real brass fixtures, cut glass goblets, and piped in classical music. His scotch and soda cost as much as a dinner at a fast food restaurant. He had three.

Before he left the bar, he made a phone call to Brent Wade. He got Wade's voice mail. Uncomfortable with the turn of events, he spoke curtly into the phone, "Hi Brent. It's Luke Nerin. I know we promised to meet you in Crescent City, but it looks as if we'll be delayed. I'll call you when I know more."

Zak stepped out of the shower and rubbed himself dry. When he pulled his jeans back on and started to pull his shirt over his head, he smelled day old sweat and tossed the shirt he had been wearing for the last two days on the floor. He noticed Luke's bags were sitting on the bed closest to the window. Zak took one of Luke's clean shirts. After using Luke's razor, cologne, and hairdryer, he tucked in his shirt and smoothed down some unruly hairs on his right eyebrow, then examined the finished product in the mirror. He grinned at the handsome devil smiling back at him. It was time Eve woke up.

Ten minutes later, Zak returned to his hotel room and dropped onto the bed he would sleep in alone. The woman in Room 410 had been amused and flattered, but unlike Eve Endicott not willing to jump into bed with a stranger. All the way from Lakeview, Oregon, Zak had been scheming and planning and hoping he could persuade Eve to snap out of her foolishness. An odd thought bubbled up from his disappointment. Perhaps Eve was hiding from him deliberately? Hold on. Maybe Eve no longer existed? Of course, she existed, he'd been with her for twenty-four hours in a motel room. Eve was sleeping in Room 410. Someday she would wake up and remember him and this whole nightmare would end.

Unable to relax after his crushing defeat, Zak wandered around the room. The second time he passed the phone on the fancy table, he remembered the Wade brothers. He dialed Brent's number. Brent answered on the first ring surprising Zak. "Hi, who's this?"

"It's Zak, Zak Nerin. We talked the other day about your mother."

"I got a message from your brother. He says something's come up and you can't make it to Crescent City. I've already booked a room and I still want to see the blanket. When and where can we meet?"

Remembering Eve's map and the inscription on the back, Zak said, "I got a feeling Crescent City is still on. Sometime this week, I'll be there. I don't know about my brother. I will definitely be there. I'll call when I know more."

"That's what your brother said. Are you sure, you guys know what you're doing?"

"Absolutely not. We don't know what the hell we're doing. We're winging it every damned minute. And I mean that sincerely. Don't worry. Unlike my absent-minded brother, I keep my promises. Hey, instead of Crescent City, why don't you drive east and check out Woolstone? There's a motel in town. It's not fancy but its cheap. My family owns a restaurant just outside of town called the Woolly Man. Anyone can give you directions. I'll let my mom know you'll be stopping by this week."

"I plan on checking out Crescent City first. It might mean something. I don't know, it's worth a try. But yeah, I'll guess I'll have time to take a trip to Spudville."

"Ha, ha. Haven't heard that one before. Bye."

"Keep in touch."

And when Zak set his cellphone on the table and looked out the window he saw his brother searching the limo's trunk. All Eve's belongings were in her room. What was Luke up to now?

23

Ana Evans, born Mary Ana Evans, awoke feeling safe and secure. She sensed a presence in the room with her, someone watching over her and making sure she slept peacefully. What a joy, she thought, as she stretched her arms and legs in a slow ballet of delight. The feeling lasted only as long as the time it took to open her eyes. The foreign bed, the space between her and the walls, the shape of the furniture, they were all wrong. She spent several anxious minutes trying to orient herself to her strange surroundings. She was lying in a bed, she knew that much. In the gloom, she sensed she lay in a big bed. Gigantic in fact, because unlike her bed at the hospital, even when she stretched her arms above her head and pointed her toes, she still couldn't feel the headboard. She figured she must be in a bed much too big for her and therefore not in her hospital room in the 8-Ball Ward.

The sheets felt different too. She rubbed her thumb and forefinger between a fold of the top sheet and realized with delight that the sheets were made of real cotton, cotton from India maybe. Sublime. No. Not so much sublime, that was too over-the-top. Not sublime but rather nice. Yes. The sheets were nice. Sublime would have been if she'd allowed that gorgeous man to come into her room and do what his eyes wanted to do. But she knew better. As a teacher she'd been tempted before. She'd stopped herself in time knowing how foolish she'd have felt in the morning if she had succumbed to her passing fancy.

Embossed upon her psyche were her frantic years to complete her undergraduate courses while working full-time and raising two children. Children? Where had they come from? She didn't have any children. Silly me, she thought. I'm confusing my life with Professor Constance Wade's life. Ana's thoughts drifted back to the young man last night. What a waste. Last night she thought she had been fighting her libido. Maybe not. The longer he stood on the threshold, the faster an unknown fear crept into her mind. Its origin suspect, she had chosen to follow her instincts and tell him no. Although, today with the bright sun outside and a good night's sleep, she was thinking what a shame, what a waste.

When Ana flipped over onto her side and rubbed her cheek against the soft cotton pillowcase, she could see the dark imprint of the room's furnishings. For a moment, she thought she imagined someone sitting in the cushioned chair near the window. Forced to lift her head, she decided it was time to get up anyway. She swung her legs off the bed and walked past the chair to the curtains, swept them open, and spun around to make sure no one was sitting in the chair.

Of course she was alone in the room. How silly.

She showered, slapped makeup on her face, brushed on a bit of mascara, dressed quickly and finally covered her dry lips in a clear gloss, all the while, feeling a prickling at her neck as if someone was watching her. While moving about the room, she'd been careful to avoid looking in the direction of the chair. She told herself she didn't believe in ghosts.

An hour later with Luke walking behind her dragging her three-piece olive green rolling luggage set down the emergency stairs, thump, thump, bang, thump, without concern for the contents or the other occupants sleeping in the hotel, Ana leading the way carried Eve's ivory and gold makeup case in one hand, Leona's napkin-sized black leather clutch purse under her other arm and her red leather satchel over her shoulder ignoring Luke's tirade about elevator phobias, as if by the sheer volume of his argument and his voice he might convince her that elevators were safe.

Instead of listening to him go on and on comparing elevators to automobile accidents, Ana thought about all the silly stuff she had draped over her shoulders and under her arms and in her hands. Even now she couldn't remember how she'd managed to accumulate so much junk: the laptop, the cellphone, the organizer, the computer notebook, the spiral notebook, the pens and pencils and erasers and rulers and flow charts, they all seemed excessive while the portable calculator and a doohickey which calculated Euros into American money, now that made sense, only if you happened to be traveling through Europe. What did they need with a bowie knife or nunchucks?

Ridiculous for her to stand here and wait like this. She could just as easily have followed Luke out to the parking lot and climbed into the limo on her own. But Luke seemed to be carrying this charade a bit far, so here she stood waiting for him to pull up to the door and usher her out as if she were royalty. While she waited, she thought about that moment when she awoke and believed someone was sitting in the armchair near the window watching her sleep, someone elderly, perhaps a family member. She got the impression he'd been in the room as a guardian, someone watching over her, protecting her from harm. It had been eerie yet comforting. A movement caught her eye and she stopped thinking about the guardian ghost.

It was lucky for her she had managed to avoid a confrontation with Zak. It looked as if he'd been up and out of his room for some time. She watched as he checked his tires while sipping his hot coffee and eating his morning donut. Without volition or any conscious thought of her own, elation ran up and down her body at the sight of him. The elation melted down around her stomach and into her groin which made her cheeks hot and sweat break out on her upper lip. She dabbed at the sweat with a wadded-up napkin from breakfast and tried to find something else to look at in order to stop her treacherous body from completing a public orgasm, right there in the lobby with people coming and going and phones ringing in the background.

Like a spigot shutting off, the pulsating below stopped. Relieved, she realized how close she had been to total humiliation, even if she and her vagina were the only participants aware of what had taken place. What a nasty experience, she thought, panic replacing elation and desire. She'd always prided herself on her self-control.

Lately, she didn't seem to have any self-control at all. And the gloom that had been hers the moment she knew she was alone in the hotel room returned, just as the gloom had made eating her breakfast impossible, and the gloom now congealed into dread. They were on their way. It had never been far from her thoughts. It had become part of her and distance and space really didn't matter in the scheme of things. To be three thousand miles away or three feet away made no difference in her mind and her memories. Her body knew. The messages had been written on her body long ago and though most people couldn't see the messages, she knew they were there, written in large welting scars that bled and bled and refused to scab over.

Once in the back of the limo with the paraphernalia sorted around her, the woman leaned back and waited for Luke to finish his limo driver duties. Once behind the wheel, Luke glanced in the rear view mirror and froze. Acacia recognized his fear and grinned, anticipating some good times ahead. He recognized her too but asked the question anyway.

"Who are you now?" he asked sounding like a petulant child.

Acacia told him, and he handed her a note written in Leona's handwriting. She read the sticky note and then crumbled it up and threw it out the window.

"Take the fastest route. Four hours. That's all we'll need."

"Ely, right?"

"Fuck no. Give me the map."

Since Acacia refused to move from her spot, Luke decided instead of tossing the map through the partition, he would climb out of the driver's seat, open the back door, and offer her the map like a gentleman. She snatched the map from him with a stony expression which made him uneasy and proceeded to unfold the map with a precision he rather admired. She noticed him and frowned, "Well?"

Once they were on the road, he heard her bark out, "Take 80 east. Near Battle Mountain watch for 305."

"Which way onto 305?"

"It's an artery between 80 and 50 and only goes south. Once 305 merges into 50 go east again and stop in Eureka, Nevada. Got that?"

"Yeah."

"Don't just say, yeah, like a fucking hick. Recite back what I said."

The silence lasted longer than a minute. He watched the clock on the console and realized that he had sat like an idiot for nearly two minutes and Acacia Pierce had remained still and quiet as moss. Luke had used the same technique on his mother with good effect. Unfortunately, the silent treatment only seemed to work on his mother.

"This is ridiculous. Since you insist I'll agree," he began.

"Why not just say *I'll submit to your demands*," Acacia asked curiously.

Luke ignored her attempt to be funny and said, "So I take 80 East and around Battle Mountain I look for 305. I can only go south on 305 because it's an artery. Then once I'm off 305," he paused for a second, "I'm assuming I'll be off 305, then I take mile marker 50, ah, wait, yeah, okay, I take 50 east. I stop in Eureka. Not California, but Nevada. Eureka, Nevada? Right?

"Correct."

"I see. Are we good now?"

"Smart ass."

And that was the last conversation Luke shared with Acacia Pierce until they reached Eureka, Nevada. Now he knew her name. Now he knew that the woman who had nearly broken his windpipe called herself Acacia after a prickly tree. A perfect Christian name for her. And to compound the nastiness of her personality, she'd given herself the surname Pierce as in sharp, pointy, and/or painful.

So, Simon renames himself Peter after the Greek word Petros meaning rock because he is "steadfast in [his] faith" and Jane Smith renames herself Acacia Pierce, not because she's a devote Christian, but because she is "steadfast in [her] prickliness." Whatever the reason for her fake names, the Christian name Acacia and the surname Pierce made perfect sense.

In fact, all the names were beginning to make perfect sense. There was method to this crazy lady's madness. The names were of significant because the names implied the real person buried inside had initially chosen those names to differentiate between her different personas; therefore, the real person, most likely Professor Wade had to be reachable. But now, whether she was Wade or not no longer mattered. The woman in the backseat of the limo would take him to Amara and he would have no further use for her.

He closed the glass partition between the front seat and the back then called his brother. When all he got was his voice mail, he left a message noticing how Acacia seemed to be following the conversation with interest. How could she hear him? Did she have bionic ears? He threw the phone on the dashboard and kept his eyes straight ahead. At this point, he could care less if she overheard his conversation. His life was on the line. He didn't trust Acacia T. Pierce. He didn't trust any of her other personalities either.

And at this point, he damned well didn't want to know what the letter T stood for. It would just be his luck if the T stood for terminator or terrorist.

Once again, an urgent need to reach out to a sane person overwhelmed him and he thought about texting Zak instead. He reached for his cellphone and began pressing keys. Forced to drive and text, he wasn't sure if he was making sense, but just in case his brother slipped behind and lost track of the limo, he wanted Zak to know where he was headed. And if he disappeared forever, he wanted someone from his family to know where to begin searching for his body. He had no doubt Acacia would dispose of him if he proved an obstacle. Yes. And he had no doubt of her ability to inflict incredible pain and suffering upon anyone who threatened her.

Absently, he rubbed his neck. The bruising was nearly gone. Like Acacia, Zak seemed to get a kick out of pain, as if pain made him feel more alive. Once upon a time, Luke enjoyed the science of pugilism and all those manly activities and sports like football, hunting, fishing, and drinking beer. And then he ended up at Harvard and discovered people like himself and realized fighting was for primitives. And why was he worried anyway? She could only hear his side of the conversation.

His text must have alarmed Zak; his cellphone began ringing and he recognized the tone. He grabbed it and put the phone on speaker. "Hey. Listen up bro. It's important. We're heading for Eureka, Nevada. That's right. We're going to take 80 east and drive to Battle Mountain, then look for the 305 which will take us south to 50. On 50 we'll go east until we reach Eureka. Yeah. You got it.

Oh, and in case you're wondering who you were chasing in my stolen truck the other day, I can tell you her name. She calls herself Acacia T. Pierce. I found out later what the T stands for. Before I got up the courage to ask, I figured it must be terminator or terrorist. It's not. It's much worse. It's Tomoe pronounced Toe Moy. I had to look the name up and an English speaker pronounced the name as Two Me, another one as Two Mo, and a translation site with a Japanese speaker pronounced the name Toe Moy. Acacia pronounced the name as Toe Moy, so I'm pronouncing her full name as Acacia Toe Moy Pierce.

According to the Internet, Tomoe had been a 12th century Japanese samurai. A woman. And if the stories are true, she killed a shit load of people. That's right. I'm not screwing with your head, man. When I handed her Leona's note and as per Leona's instructions asked who she was, she told me her name. And about fifty miles later, I just couldn't stand it anymore and asked her what the abbreviation in her middle name stood for. She told me. No...shit...Sherlock."

At this point, Acacia lost interest. Luke and his imaginary victories made her want to laugh. What a clown. So now he knew her real name – Acacia Tomoe Pierce, as if knowing her name gave him some sort of power over her. Not true. In her opinion, people believed in way too many idiotic superstitions: a rabbit's foot meant good luck, walking under a ladder – bad luck, a black cat crossing your path – bad luck, and the dumbest one of all, knowing your enemy's name means you can cast a spell on him and curse him and consequently he'll get sick or die.

So stupid.

Knowing the name of someone or something does not give you power over the person or the thing. Was a war ever won by throwing insults at your enemy until he cried? Did the caveman survive the Ice Age by insulting the snow? Did bestowing the name "ice" on an iceberg make it go away? How about two cavemen insulting each other's mamas? How would that play out?

Too excited to give a rat's ass, Acacia leaned over and examined the custom-built cabinet made of real mahogany wood which stretched the length of the backseat of the limo from door to door. Beneath the counter the craftsperson inset a stainless steel mini-fridge behind the limo driver. Equally clever were the small black boxes placed like dinner plates at each end of the custom-built bar. They were speakers. The speakers belonged to the entertainment system: the stereo, the gaming unit, and a television set. The knobs for the stereo system and television set were near her elbow. The gamepad for the gaming system was lying on the floor of the limo where someone had thrown it.

Probably Leona. Leona had a better understanding of the spirit world than the material world. A video game would be boring compared to the games she got up to in the spirit world. Acacia debated whether to refresh her skills with a quick game. It wasn't even worth the effort. Playing a stupid video game no longer had the same thrill for her. She bent down and picked up the gamepad, the head phones, and the controller then tossed them on the seat next to her.

A twenty-five-inch LCD television monitor sprouted from the expensive credenza. The whole setup looked very showy, decadent, and boring as hell. It might as well be hell since she was steaming in the hot interior of this pampered world. Give her a real live flesh-and-blood thinking adversary to throw herself at and pummel to death any day. Her thoughts were rudely interrupted by the yahoo in the driver's seat.

It was rather hilarious hearing him chattering away. Everything he was saying was coming out of several speakers in the backseat, the closest speaker was the tiny one on the armrest only inches from her elbow. The tiny speaker broadcast Luke's terrified babble into her luxurious bubble. She turned the laugh into a cough. Now that his normal baritone had deserted him, he sounded like a squawking man-baby. The words were flying in the air running for their lives as if the hounds of hell were on their heels.

Acacia could hear everything. It took all her self-control to keep her expression neutral and her mouth shut. Luke thought he was having a private conversation with his brother. Should she inform him otherwise? No. Not yet. When she felt a tickling at the back of her throat, she ducked her head and pretended to search for something to drink in the mini-fridge. The rattling of bottles and her soft sniggering nearly gave her away. She quickly switched off the speaker and looked up to check if he had noticed. She could see the back of his head. He was still sporting a queue, his glossy black hair swept sternly back from his face, the braid intertwined with the soft leather, not so much as one hair out of place.

Judging from his clueless posture and obsession with whatever his brother was saying, Luke didn't seem to have noticed anything out of the ordinary. She'd already overheard enough to know Luke Nerin had every intention of taking her to Dr. Victor Ingolstadt's cabin. The fact they had a mutual interest in reaching the cabin helped her immensely and meant she could relax in the meantime. The Nerin brothers were only of interest to her as a means to an end. The others were welcome to ooh-and-ah over the brothers' gorgeous bodies and piercing intellects, but she found the men too high-maintenance for her liking.

Although, it was kind of funny how Frankie played with Luke like a cat playing with a mouse, driving him to distraction with her silly mind games; yet, even a mouse can be a dangerous adversary when cornered. Just ask evolutionary biologists who know a great deal more than the average citizen about the Black Death, just ask them if they think rats and mice are cute and cuddly playthings.

Returning to her inspection of the mini-fridge, Acacia crossed off the alcoholic beverages knowing she had to be sharp and alert for what was to come. Instead, she chose to drink the bottled water. Hydration was critical especially in the summer in the high desert. And where they were going hydration meant life or death. Life or death – why had she gone there? You dumb-ass.

An unwelcome memory popped into her head. She experienced once again a thirst so powerful not even saliva could ease her suffering. Smoke burned her eyes. Every time she opened her mouth to breathe, she swallowed smoke and the smoke made her gag. Unable to escape the searing heat and the smoke, she ran with the others. She stumbled into trees and brush and boulders. Branches hit her face. Then she saw a spring.

On her knees beside the spring, she scooped up handfuls of water, her body screaming for more. It must have been a record – a week without water. That body had responded with a ferocity she would never forget. That body never forgot. It demanded she pay attention. It demanded ever afterward that she listen. Plenty know thirst and hunger. But do they know the fierce kind, the kind willing to kill anything in its path to appease? Thirst, hunger, and searing pain were written on her body, flowing through her molecules, stamped in her DNA.

An hour later at Acacia's request, Luke pulled off into a rest area just outside Eureka, Nevada. Impatient to be free, Acacia stepped out of the limo just before Luke had a chance to jump out and run around the limo and open her door. How ridiculous he was. What a waste of good energy. Acacia still annoyed with the idiot headed straight for the woods. She passed the restrooms and moved into the shelter of the pine trees. When she leaned against a young sapling no wider than her waist and looked up into the canopy of leaves and saw bits of the blue sky, she tried to remember that the others depended upon her. She brushed the tears away, angry at herself and her moment of weakness. She could do this. She must do this.

When she returned to the clearing and the place where Luke and Zak were waiting, she stood in the shelter of the trees and watched the brothers. They were in a heated debate. The one she knew to be her driver Luke leaned against the Camaro with his arms tucked in close to his chest. He looked as if he needed reassurance. The other brother stood comfortable in his own skin with his hands on his hips and his eyes watchful, moving from his brother to the restrooms to the trees. She couldn't hear what they were discussing, but she was pretty sure they were arguing about what to do with her. She would make the decision for them soon enough.

Acacia walked into the pool of sunlight between the surrounding trees and the limo and lifted her head toward the light letting the sun warm her face. Like the touch of a mother to a child, just as a mother might brush back a strand of hair from a child's eyes, a breeze swept through the clearing and cooled Acacia's forehead. Her friends drank in the light and the beauty all around them.

Enough sentimental crap.

Acacia dropped her head and did what she habitually did when in a strange place, she surveyed the terrain and assessed the danger. They would be ascending the range of mountains called Ruby Lake National Wildlife Refuge soon and although the highest peak was only six thousand feet above sea level, for some of them, the prospect was as daunting as imagining themselves walking on hands and knees across America. The best way to get across rough country meant attention to detail, an overwhelming curiosity about what might be over the next ridge, and a reward at the end of the journey. Acacia's reward would be to see these two idiots riding off into the sunset albeit in their Camaro, while she rode off in the opposite direction albeit in the limo.

For one fleeting moment, she considered drawing Luke a map and leaving the guys to find the place themselves. She imagined taking off in the limo and heading back toward the Pacific. No. Her map would be sketchy at best. The only way to resolve this problem would be to stand upon the ground and search the area herself. As she remembered, before reaching the cabin they would have to travel through a narrow canyon with a creek running along the left side of the dirt road and a cliff face on the right, a cliff which had been hone out of the rock by men and cut diagonally to prevent rock slides.

But before she could reach that narrow canyon, she first had to find a familiar landscape that led to the cabin. There was a road, of that she was certain. More a track than a legitimate road, a rough dirt track riddled with rocks and sage and hairpin turns that could topple a vehicle onto its side. She had her doubts about the limo. Even though well sprung, could the limo make it through the narrow gap and rough terrain? Nor did she believe the Camaro would make the journey successfully without some damage to the undercarriage. Both vehicles would end up high-plaining somewhere, maybe even tearing off their exhaust pipes or tumbling down a ravine.

Not a bad idea.

With that cheerful thought, Acacia moved toward the men. They met her half way. "We've got about fifty miles of highway to go, then about ten or fifteen miles of rough, sometimes, dangerous road ahead. We would be better off with a four-wheel drive vehicle, a vehicle meant for such terrain," she said tensing when she noticed the look in Zak's eyes. What reason did he have to be angry with her? If he wanted a fight, she would be more than willing to break a few of his bones. Then she noticed Luke vibrating like an excited puppy with an eager sentimental expression on his face. What a greedy little bastard. The thought of Luke and the limo bouncing along the rough road with his head smacking the ceiling brought a smile to her lips.

Luke mistook her smile as a sign of a truce between them. Idiot. "Fantastic. And it's not even nine o'clock yet," he said as he rubbed his hands together. "Well, what are we waiting for? Let's be on our way. We can celebrate in Ely with a big scrumptious lunch afterward."

Acacia and Zak faced each other. Their posture suggested fighting mode. Acacia waited for Zak to make the first move. Luke had walked toward the limo in anticipation of leaving, but turned when he realized no one was following. He stood beside the limo and watched them. Everything around her in a five-yard radius was illuminated. Her senses came alive as she waited with the blood coursing through her veins and her scalp tingling. She knew what he was capable of doing. Yet a part of her sensed his weakness. Back at the Rogue River Exit he had come face-to-face with his primal side. He hadn't liked what he'd discovered about himself. The savagery had disturbed him. Maybe he was questioning himself, second guessing his responses to his adversary? If so, she might just win.

People made choices every day. Acacia had learned to listen to the body and wait for the blow. On this occasion, her body and mind were at peace, prepared for anything. Not her opponent, his body and mind were at odds with each other. His muscles were tense, his legs apart in preparation for combat and the biggest clue were his hands; his hands were clenched into fists. Yet, his eyes were sad and there was something else – regret. Then Zak relaxed and stepped backward mocking her with a salute to the brow. Acacia simply stared in surprise, noticing the wistful light in his eye. She pitied him. Women were his weakness. Poor man. Now there was a fool. Never let lust get in the way of a good fight.

Luke opened the limo door with a flourish and Acacia climbed in and tried not to gag at the avarice vibrating in every muscle and tendon and pore of Luke's body. She heard Zak shout out, "Luke, did you hear what she said? About the road? I'm leaving my Camaro behind. You hear me? I'm not risking the Camaro for your stupid wet dream."

Luke ignored his brother and climbed into the limo.

Fifty miles were nothing compared to the journey for Acacia and her friends to be back in this spot – sixteen years, two months, and three days later. And here they all were, three people standing under an open sky with the sun beating down on their heads and the others watching from a safe place. While she surveyed the area, and watched the Nerin brothers as they busily dug test holes a couple of yards away from her, in what used to be Victor Ingolstadt's cabin. She and the others remembered how the place had looked before the fire.

Currently, all that was left of the two-story A-frame cabin with an attached root cellar and mudroom were the granite foundation stones poking up from the dirt. Beyond the cabin used to be a two-car garage made of cheap metal roofing placed up against a rock wall. Someone had cut through the hillside probably mining for rock and someone else came along years later and thought the rock wall would make a good buttress against the harsh winds and heavy snows. More recently someone had removed the posts and the metal canopy of the garage. Near the back porch, she could still pick out the rusty hand water pump surrounded by thirsty blue-bunch wheatgrass and onion-grass. Beyond the cabin, she could see acres of mountain sagebrush, antelope bitterbrush, and rocks.

If she turned and looked behind her she would see the limo and the Camaro parked down below the cabin and the dirt road winding its way down the mountainside to the highway. Only hunters or the lost would bother to risk their vehicles on this washboard, switch-backed road. If she turned her head to the left she would see the creek bone dry and pathetic and the chaparral of mahogany sagebrush, wheatgrass, and bottlebrush squirrel-tail desperately trying to stay alive.

She wasn't ready to look toward the creek just yet.

The Nerin brothers were standing in what used to be the crawl space, a dirt floor stretching from one end of the cabin to the other minus the rickety old porch. The crawl space had been big enough for a grown man to crawl through on his belly and a child to stand up in if they were no more than three feet tall. She ignored the others clamoring to get out. Luke was concentrating his attention on the kitchen area. She had to concede he had skills. Most people would have tested the part of the cabin near the porch first. But that's not where the bodies were buried. As she remembered, oh so well, the trap door to the crawl space used to be in the pantry. When Acacia escaped the first time, Mad Mona ordered the security guards to buy a heavy-duty bolt with a lock effectively eliminating any chance for the others to get out.

If she'd just stayed in her room...

If she'd kept away from the nursery...

If mother-fucking Mad Mona hadn't been such a high-strung paranoid Nazi-bitch...

Maybe they'd all have remained in the spare bedrooms resting in their comfortable beds with sunlight streaming through the windows, heat hissing from the old radiators, clean sheets beneath their broken and bleeding bodies, and blankets keeping their poor souls alive for just a few more weeks.

There it was – the victim taking responsibility for her imprisonment and torture, a masochistic reaction to explain the horror of crimes against humanity. Fuck that noise. Fuck them all. She'd just been doing what any creature would do – gnaw its foot off to get out of the trap, bite and claw its way to freedom, anything to save herself. Acacia had done what she did, and she couldn't undo it. She'd slipped out the backdoor and the security guard sitting on a chair next to the kitchen window never noticed her, he was too busy sleeping and snoring. He never heard her running down the cedar steps and up the hillside behind the cabin.

And the next morning, she'd made it as far as the highway. The bottoms of her feet were bleeding from a dozen cuts, her legs slashed from the bitterbrush and hardwood sage. Her throat had been as dry as sandpaper. In the hopes a car would show up, she'd hidden herself behind a tree confident some tourist would rescue her and take her to a hospital. And nothing happened.

Then she heard a familiar engine as the truck tore down the mountain in pursuit. As the guard was dragging her toward the truck, finally, a car came around the bend and the occupants saw her and the guard. She waved and shouted for help and waved some more, but it was too late. They'd been going so fast down Little Antelope Summit, they never saw her. And that was what the guard told Mad Mother-Fucking Mona. And still the bitch freaked out.

Even if the occupants hadn't really understood what they'd seen, maybe later, they might have wondered how a young woman wearing nothing but a dirty hospital gown got herself lost in the middle of nowhere. And that was why the Nazi-bitch ordered the security guards to take her and the others down to the crawl space. She was terrified the local police would discover people strapped to beds, wrapped in bandages, and drugged to keep them quiet in a cabin miles away from the nearest hospital. But more than being found out, the Nazi-bitch was terrified "they" would learn about her stupid mistake and never let her into their inner circle ever again.

The Nerin brothers had no clue what lay beneath their feet. And she wasn't going to tell them a damned thing. What did they think they were digging up anyway? For the first time in a long time, she got out of her own tormented thoughts and wondered what these two yahoos were really looking for at the Ingolstadt cabin. Victor Ingolstadt had been dead for nearly twenty years.

Maybe they were Nazi hunters? Did they know about Victor's nefarious doings in Poland during the war? Did they know his daughter had inherited not only his medical practice but the results of his experiments on victims of the war, both innocent and guilty: Jew, Christian, Gypsy, German, Pole, Frenchman, any healthy body he could get his filthy hands on? Did they know his daughter had inherited the Nevada cabin, his practice in Crescent City, and his obsession with immortality? Did they also know, she'd nearly forgotten about the cabin until she needed more space for her laboratory?

Acacia watched them closely and shook her head. They didn't know shit. If they'd known, especially the feisty one, he would have called all the news stations in the country and told anyone who would listen about his suspicions; and there would have been camera crews, reporters, gawkers, and police combing the area searching for gruesome crimes against humanity.

A few days ago, she remembered Leona had said the Nerin brothers kept asking about Connie. Well, they just might find some pretty gruesome shit, if they kept digging where they were digging. Acacia was disgusted with the whole sick scene. They looked like lowlife grave robbers. If she'd had a gun, she would have shot them both dead. She hated them with a fury that shook her body, the nosey pieces of shit. How dare they disturb the dead? They had no right. Keep your focus on the prize, Acacia told herself. This wasn't the prize. This was the yahoos' obsession. She had bigger things to worry about than the past. The past was no more. She had places to be and things to do.

It had been too easy getting up here. It was a bad sign. She'd hoped the road would have been impassable with boulders or fallen trees blocking the way. For several miles the road remained level and paved with superheated tar and bits of gravel, then it began to climb up into the higher elevations and curl around a mountain ridge where the evidence of man's intervention had almost disappeared.

Even with the occasional sapling and sage growing in the middle of the rutted road and the wood's attempt to gather the road into itself again, there were no deep ruts to cut off access or stretches of rocky ground to tear at their tires. And just as odd were the familiar landmarks along the way. She'd thought she'd forgotten the way, convinced she wouldn't remember which fork in the road to take. But everything had snapped together: she knew exactly which road to take and where to turn and what they would find up ahead.

There was evidence several heavy trucks had come this way recently. Maybe two or three years ago this road to the ridge top had been popular. But there was evidence of neglect too, years of neglect in which plants were reassuming their dominance over the road. Trucks had come and gone, before and after the fire, she figured. She noticed in the crevices and washouts nearly two feet deep how the rain water from periodic storms must have rushed down the road cutting its own path through the dirt and gravel. But along the shoulder of the road where the strong grasses held the soil tight, their tires were able to avoid the worst ravines and washouts.

It took more time to navigate the curves and vertical stretches, but all told the journey had been easier than expected. Zak, with noticeably loud bellowing and lots of cursing stubbornly continued to follow the limo. He refused to leave his beloved vehicle where any stranger might come along and accidentally run into it or steal it from him. They drove on, moving at first at a decent pace, between thirty and forty miles an hour, then in the higher elevations, near their goal, at a slug's pace with frequent stops to cool the engines and hot tempers.

Acacia had ignored the men and their complaints. What sissies. What a lot of whining over a bunch of metal and rubber and chrome bits and pieces. When the limo had traversed the worst part of the road and entered a clearing, Acacia spotted the chaparral of mahogany sage and wild blackberry bushes to her left and the butte of rock beyond, mesmerized by the butte with the granite boulder poised on the edge of the table jutting out like an accusing finger twenty feet above their heads. Yet when her eye traveled down to the clearing below and with a wince found emptiness instead of what she'd expected, she was alarmed.

Were they lost? Had she mistaken the way?

It wasn't until she climbed out of the limo and ran down the slope toward where she thought the cabin should be that she tripped over a corner of the foundation. She reeled back nearly falling on her behind in her haste to avoid stepping inside the stones. Her eye traced the outline of the foundation. There it was, the limestone eating away at the good earth, disintegrating, and depositing its poison into the ground, contaminating the future. She stood back a bit and followed the line of stones, her eye traveling from one corner to the next a way of keeping her mind in the present rather than the past.

In a faraway place she heard the chink of metal on metal and turned in time to see Zak pulling several shovels out of the trunk of his Camaro. Luke grabbed one of them and marched toward her with an eager eye. Had he been crying? Acacia struggled with an unexpected fury. It seemed so long between breaths. The fury spun around inside her with its heat and light cramping her intestines. Something of what she was feeling finally registered with Luke and Luke prudently stepped back. She turned away from him unable to stomach his excitement and pointed to the southeast corner of the cellar. "She's there." Then with a sense of fulfilling an unpleasant duty, Acacia turned and walked away from the remains of the Ingolstadt cabin.

An hour had passed, and she was still standing a few feet away on what used to be the graveled driveway which had, once upon a time, led the visitor to the front door of the cabin. The drive continued around the side of the cabin to the rock house and garage in the back. She watched the brothers dig and was damned if she'd give these ghouls anymore help. Let them work for their prize. Let them curse and sweat and find nothing.

Every so often she would stretch her legs and walk casually near where the rock house and garage used to be. There was still evidence of the brush fire which had swept along the top of the ridge in the remains of a few blackened mahogany sagebrush on the outer edges of the property. If you knew what you were looking for, you could see where the fire had blazed and the point when the fire had been contained. Some of the burned sage had been crushed under the tires of vehicles taking shortcuts up onto the mesa.

For the longest time, she stayed at the other end of the foundation as far away from the brothers as she could get pretending to sift through the rocks scattered about the property, her eyes going back to where the rock shed used to be, again and again. The brothers were concentrating their attention at the other end of the property near the kitchen.

Memories were beginning to stir. The rocks fascinated her the most. She could tell by their coloring, shape, and size that they were no ordinary rocks, these rocks had been collected for years by a rock-hound

428

and had come from all over the Pacific Northwest. Some of them were even cut. She found a few pieces of picture jasper, some quartz, some agate, a bunch of sandstone, a few small thundereggs, all sorts of specimens a longtime rock-hound would recognize as part of a collection.

The big pieces had been carted away, pieces someone knew had been valuable. Acacia didn't think the owners had cared about the little stuff. They were just rocks to the Ingolstadt family. The shed had been no bigger than a closet added to the cabin at a later date by a previous owner. At one time it had had its own door. She stood looking down at the bits and pieces of old wood which she identified as a part of a window frame. She also found a rusted doorknob in the dirt and a couple of rusty hinges.

Right here had been the shed and inside had been boxes filled with rocks, some boxes piled to the ceiling, waiting to be cut and cleaned with diamond wired drills, a bull wheel, a grinder, a wet polisher, and a rock tumbler. A counter top had been specially built along the wall opposite the cabin and there had been a single-paned dirty old window facing the gravel drive. The rock-hound had made sure to have a panoramic view of the chaparral down below the property where the mahogany sage grew near the creek.

As she walked back toward the front of the cabin, she stood beside a mound of freshly turned earth. And here had been the old root cellar. With the toe of her army boot she kicked a foundation stone. The root cellar had been much deeper than the cabin. The root cellar had gone down nearly five feet below the cabin. She knelt by the limestone block and brushed her hand over the fresh earth covering the deep hole.

Her stomach began to heave. Instinctively, she chose to move toward the shade of the chaparral. In the protection of the chaparral, Acacia crouched down by a small creek between mahogany sage and a big boulder. She remembered following the creek up to the mesa, up to a spot where a cave had been honed out of the rock by water. Water seemed so innocent, insubstantial when one's fingers tried to hold onto it; yet, water could be incredibly destructive when carving out a path of its own. Water's contradictions were extraordinary, such fluidness could destroy rock, carve out canyons and yet be tender enough to quench a person's thirst.

The voices like filthy flies swarmed above her head, around her face, inside her body.

"He looks so young and strong, ouch, that lean body, that firm back and buttocks, why not give me the night? Please. He likes me better than Frankie. Let me have one night with him, just one night," Leona begged.

"Shut it down, you idiot woman," Acacia demanded.

"She must have dismantled the cabin piece by piece and carted it away in dumpsters and flatbed trucks. See the tracks. Something huge has gone through here, something as big as a lumber truck," Tessa observed.

"It must have cost a small fortune to pull the cabin down and cart all evidence away. But resources are no obstacle for that Butcher Queen. She probably has millions to blow, maybe trillions. She probably overheard all my great ideas and stole them. The pet gym. At least the pet gym is still mine. I've been talking to Stefan and he's lining up investors. It's just a matter of time now," Frankie assured them.

"Anyone might have come this way at any time during the dismantling process and wondered what was going on, maybe asked some uncomfortable questions. But no. All the luck went to her. How is it possible to have such god-damned good fortune? Surely, she has the devil on her side," Acacia growled.

"Now that the walls are down, and evidence removed, no one will ever ascertain the truth. Although, someone might trip along one day, a hiker or hunter perhaps, admiring the vista and pause in contemplation of the beauty and espy by chance the foundation stones and say to themselves, hum, what mischief is this perchance?

They might even wonder at the incongruity of such a sight, of man's invasion into the wilderness and then after sifting through the property, like those smart young men over there, they might dig deeper and find the real treasure. If it's still in the root cellar which I regret to say knowing the Butcher Queen as I do would have been incredibly stupid of her to leave behind," Ana speculated.

"What a crock. I could have said it simpler. Some chuckle head has probably already snooped around this place and found nothing to steal and went on his merry way," Frankie said with a snort.

"Think about it girls. The root cellar has been excavated and the crawl space ignored. Someone came to this property with a backhoe and dug a trench into the root cellar, a trench five feet deep or more. And did you notice where they dug, only in one corner of the root cellar? And why? Because the owner had to get the thing away before nosey people found it.

And why would she need a backhoe or truck? Because it is heavy, very, very heavy. It's gone, girls. She took it with her. Now, where might she take it? Maybe someplace close to home, someplace nearby where she could periodically check on it. No. I'd think she'd want to get rid of it for good. How do you get rid of a leaded coffin? Hum? How?" Tessa asked them.

"Why do we give a shit about her? What did she really do for us, huh? We helped her. No. Connie helped her. And all she did was grab the kid and take off. She left the rest of us behind. She didn't give a damned about us. And why are we coddling these yahoos? Haven't we learned anything by now? Will we continue to be victims the rest of our frigging lives, walking up to strangers and saying, yes sir, kidnap me please sir, yes sir, use me as your guinea pig, ma'am, oh thank-you ma'am for bleeding me dry," Acacia hissed, hoping to build some backbone in the chicken-shits all around her.

Without warning, everyone saw a bird's eye view of the cabin, the last image of the fire as it inched its way up the wooden posts of the porch, along the old cedar boards of the porch, boards which had been left to bleach in the sun and turn into combustible fuel for the fire, a fire which found another source of fuel in the shed's siding made of cedar-shingles which had been left to decay on its cheap skeleton, but finding nothing to spark a flame on the ribbed-steel panels of the roof.

They'd looked for the marks of scorching and found none on the outside walls, the walls made of sandstone. But inside, inside there was wood everywhere from the beams to the frames to the hardwood floors to the furniture. It was a perfect backyard grilling machine, twenty feet tall, allowing air to come in through the gaps in the walls, the windows, especially the old floorboards and stoke the fire to a red-hot fury inside a chimney of sandstone walls and ribbed-steel roofing.

They'd heard the fire had started with a cigarette, no, it had been careless campers, no, it had been an engine's heat which set the dry grass and brush ablaze. Firefighters were on their way. But the road up to the cabin was already choked with cars and trucks fleeing down the mountain. Instead of rescuing them, they saw the guards running back and forth from the well to the cabin throwing buckets of water on the walls. And the very, very last thing they saw was Mad Mona rushing out of the burning cabin toward her Pinto station wagon. Without a backward look, she jumped inside and took off like a shot down the mountain driving like the crazy-ass-bitch they'd grown to hate.

The sound of twigs snapping alarmed them. As one they moved. A man screamed. Another set of arms with more determination and muscle yanked us off the man. A sharp jab to the belly made the other man grunt in surprise. While the two brothers were preoccupied sorting out their pain, we ran to the limo and climbed into the driver's seat noticing with relief the keys were still in the ignition. The dangerous one erupted from the chaparral and we knew what must be done.

We put the limo in drive and pressed down on the gas. The big white monster bucked a bit but eventually moved forward. With our left hand we searched blindly for the buttons that would lock all the doors. We ignored the banging on the windows and the man's curses. The other one came out of the brush holding his nose while blood trickled down his shirt like a crimson spit-bath. He stopped and watched impassively as his brother tried to smash the driver's side window.

In our side mirror, we saw the cursing-one still holding onto the door handle as he ran alongside the limo. His luck ran out when we reached the narrow passage between the ravine and the rock face. There was no room for him and the limo to squeeze through the opening at the same time. He was forced to let go.

It seemed like hours before the road became more docile. And when the limo's tires touched gravel, the others conceded to the stronger personality. Another thirty minutes and tires were on asphalt and the limo moving down the road at fifty-five miles per hour, then sixty-five, and finally seventy-five, and once again Acacia was at the wheel in control of their destination. Yet even Acacia was not immune to the body and its memories.

When the shaking started, she found a spot where she could pull off the highway and remain hidden in the shadows of the trees. She unclenched her fingers from the steering wheel and looked at her hands and willed them to obey her. She had no energy left to scream, not even to cry, not one single tear. The darkness descended. She remembered crawling through the hole and seeing sunlight above her head. She heard Tessa on the other side calling her, urging her to come forward into the sunshine, "Come on, honey. I'm here. We're all here. You're safe now."

With the sudden quiet, Zak thought about the insanity of the last ten minutes replaying the scenario over and over, wondering what they could have done differently. He remembered being on edge the entire time they plotted the site and decided where to dig. He and Luke were so busy discussing their strategy, only in hindsight did he recall how Acacia circled the property like a caged lioness, watchful, angry, and too damned quiet. Even with the playback reel in his head, he had to admit he'd chosen to ignore the warning signs.

Because they were trespassing, because they might be interrupted at any moment by a rancher, or a hunter, or some kids on dirt bikes, he figured his growing alarm had to do with getting caught and going to jail again. Yet, part of him knew his alarm had more to do with the woman than being caught trespassing on private property. That was why he would occasionally pause in his digging to track her whereabouts. For the first hour, he was pretty sure she'd remained Acacia, annoyingly restless, striding back and forth, stopping, playing with the rocks near the shed, kicking rocks, throwing rocks, and generally behaving like a bored petulant child.

At least that's what he thought he saw. He even found himself resenting her for not offering to help dig. But after his grisly discovery, he felt a gut-wrenching shame for thinking of her as just another high-maintenance pampered female.

He should have questioned why she avoided the spot where they were digging as if there was a high-voltage wire surrounding the foundation. He assumed Acacia hated his brother so much she wanted to be as far away from him as she could get. And when she made her way toward the chaparral, he let her, reminded of the moment when she ran into the bathroom and shut the door and he heard the voices. But Luke, so wrapped up in his delight, believing erroneously that everyone in the vicinity was as excited as he over the discovery of Amara, completely forgot about Acacia.

Even as Zak forced himself to relax and stood with his hands on his hips and tried to get his breath back, his eyes were alive with the beauty all around him. Whoever had built the cabin had chosen the perfect spot, with a clearing between the chaparral to the right and a gentle curving road hidden by a hillside to the left. And beyond the clearing, there was another set of mountain peaks in the distance. But his appreciation of the beauty around him could not stop his mind from replaying that moment shortly before she disappeared, before Luke entered the woods to find out what she was doing.

Zak saw her again, circling the foundation stones like a cat circling water, always keeping at least two, sometimes, three feet from the stones' perimeter. And then without a word, she marched toward the little wood below the cabin as if she knew the place well. At one point, he considered following her but thought better of it. Then Luke had called to him impatiently and he decided to attend to his brother's needs first.

Walking back to the dig with sweat dampening the back of his shirt and trickles of it pouring into his ears, he thought about his part in the recent mess and wished he could undo his attempts to stop her. Now she would equate him with all the other people in her life – as a savage. If only Luke knew how to read people. If he had seen her face, he would have left her alone. Would any rational person burst upon a lioness in her lair? Of course not. Luke had gotten what he deserved, and Zak had no sympathy for his hurts. With that final thought, Zak passed Luke and picked up the shovel and began to dig.

Luke wiped at the blood still trickling from his nose with the end of his shirt and stopped in his tracks when he noticed where Zak was digging. He said, "What the hell are you doing Zak? She said to dig over here."

"You dig over there. I want to know what's here, what she thought was so interesting over here," he paused in his digging and pointed at the ground. "You see those hinges. I bet she saw them too. She was right in this area for a long time. Maybe she's been playing us all along."

Luke grabbed a shovel and ignoring the blood still dripping from what he thought might be a broken nose began to dig further down into his test hole. He was pretty sure the spot he was excavating had either been a bedroom or a kitchen, more likely a kitchen because the well and the hand-held pump outside would have meant the woman of the house would have had only seven or eight steps to take to fill a bucket for washing or fill a pan for cooking. Artifacts were more likely to be discovered where people congregated, where they cooked and cleaned, and sat in the evening by a fire or a warm wood stove.

After another hour of intense digging, he managed to dig out three more feet of dirt all around the corner and uncovered two sides of a concrete block approximately five feet from the south facing wall and three feet off the east facing wall. Each shovelful of earth had been set aside carefully for later examination, just in case he might have inadvertently scooped up bits of bone. But for the most part, all he found was the loose dark earth on the top layer and about a foot below what appeared to be soil which had never been nurtured by sun or moisture. The soil reminded Luke of a crypt: dry, gray, crumbly. He got real excited then.

He scooped up the dirt and crushed the bigger pieces in his palm and let the particles fall onto the mound at his feet. It would have taken years for the soil to reach this condition. The cabin must have been really old one, probably built before this land became public property. It must have been grandfathered in as private property when Ruby Mountain became a National Park. If he checked public records, he would probably find a prospector's claim and nothing else.

While his brother dug at the other end of the crawl space, Zak bent down to examine the foundation stones along what must have been a root cellar noticing that one of the blocks had been chipped away with a sharp implement and there were bits and pieces lying nearby as if someone had been working the limestone block. The outline of the limestone blocks protruding from the dirt reminded him of an old man's mouth, the teeth chewed down to bits with a few teeth still bravely standing erect.

When Zak directed his flashlight inside the cavity, he discovered what appeared to be a hole made by a burrowing animal, maybe a gopher or a prairie dog. A prairie dog would be the best guess from the burrow's size, a family of prairie dogs had probably used this gap to enter and exit the cellar. Perhaps the burrow was big enough for a small woman or a child to crawl through too? He was still trying to figure out how the bones had ended up under the foundation of what had once been a root cellar.

He got down on his belly and reached inside the hole touching the walls and the roof of the burrow searching for any evidence that Amara might be resting inside. He considered widening the opening then changed his mind. He might set off an avalanche of dirt and bury the hole for good. He would need timbers to hold up the stones. Then as he pulled himself up, he noticed something by the toe of his shoe, something white protruding out of the soil near the bottom of what had once been the cellar's dirt floor.

With his brush, Luke swept away the loose soil around his trench. The hairs on his scalp began to tingle with excitement. His eyes recognized the shape of a knuckle then a finger. He began to brush more vigorously ignoring his training in his excitement. In the back of his mind, his senses were aware of the time, of the fading light and the need to find the artifact and get out before someone came along and asked questions.

He glanced over his shoulder and in the distance noticed the sun setting along the edge of mountain peaks. It wasn't until total darkness fell, that he managed to uncover a hand. The bones were beneath him. He backed up and backed right into somebody. When he wheeled around he saw Zak. The moon's light helped him see, at least recognize a series of test holes where Zak had spent most of his time digging. He counted three small test holes and one large hole.

"What in bedlamite are you doing? She told us to dig here. Here. Where I've been digging. And guess what Sherlock? I found the bones right where she said they'd be."

Zak turned a dirty sweaty face toward him and said, "If I'm right about this. God, I don't know though. The impressions suggest I'm right. I found a few personal articles of clothing, some pieces of jewelry, and even a sort of alter made of stones and what looks like a figure made of dried up plant roots. There are roots running all along this cellar and I think someone had had the time to pull them up and dry them and twist them and make them into this." He pulled the object out of his shirt pocket, but it was too dark for Luke to see clearly what his brother held between his thumb and forefinger. "I can't see a damned thing. It's too dark."

The light from Zak's key chain illuminated the object he held. Luke glanced at the thing warily. "Yeah, I guess it could be a figure made of dried roots. But that's not important right now, Zak. This isn't an ordinary excavation. I need your help uncovering Amara's bones and we're going to have to do it dirty rather than clean. But we need more light. I'll stay here, and you go find us something to eat and buy some supplies, especially plenty of equipment for lighting, and a tent for sure, and, ah, I don't know, maybe a couple of kerosene lamps, a table, and plastic storage containers for the bones."

"A coffin," Zak asked with a sneer.

"Funny. Come on Zak. This is important. It's important to our family. For God's sake, how many generations does it take to make this important for you?"

"What I've found is equally important. These mounds suggest something weird was going on in this cabin, maybe, they were practicing witches or wannabe Satanic worshipers? Do you understand? I've uncovered an alter and the tiny bones of birds, squirrels, gophers, even a cat. See over there at the furthest end near the root cellar? I found a skull right there. I don't dare dig any further. I might contaminate the crime scene—"

Luke squinted in the general area where Zak's finger pointed. "I can't see a damned thing in this light. So what? We don't have time for your forensic wet dreams. If the former owners worshipped Satan, I don't care. If they sacrificed bunny rabbits, I don't care. We do not have permission to dig on this property. We are trespassing. They will arrest us and put us away as grave robbers. Do you get it? We've got what we came for – we've found Amara. Come on. Help me here."

Without a word Zak climbed out of the cellar and threw down his shovel then strode toward his Camaro and got behind the steering wheel. When he started the engine, Luke ran after him shouting, "Hold on. I'll go with you. I've got money."

It took them several hours to find all the supplies they needed which irked Luke no end because all he could think about were Amara's fingers laying exposed to the elements. And if someone were to walk by, a hiker or hunter, or some lost vacationer, then everything would end. But when they returned to the site, the place looked exactly the way they'd left it with both shovels still in place, one lying on the ground where Zak had thrown his and Luke's resting alongside the length of the woman's body.

Luke and Zak set up the folding table and lamps first and then arranged the two-man tent close to Amara's bones. It had to be a cheap used-tent because between them they only had two hundred dollars. Zak always kept an extra sleeping bag inside his trunk rolled up and ready for use at any time. Luke bought a cheap blanket instead of a sleeping bag knowing he would be off Antelope Summit by the next afternoon. In fact, if they worked all night, they could be finished before dawn. He mentioned this time table to Zak.

"You go right ahead, I'm getting some sleep. I would rather wake up free of guilt knowing I hadn't meaninglessly destroyed something important because I was too eager to dig."

"We'll have the lamps."

"Natural light is best, and you know it."

At dawn, Zak crawled out of the tent and stood up and stretched and watched the amber light like liquid fire squeeze between the mountain peaks, as if the light struggled to escape the confines of the earth. He stood and watched until he spotted the tip of the sun just above the tallest peak. When he turned to face the cabin, he saw Luke already down inside his test hole madly brushing away the top soil from the skeleton. They had no permit. They had no right to be here. Obviously, someone still had grandfather rights to this property. Records might show who owned it which might lead him to Eve. But why bother? He knew where she would be.

It took Luke five more hours to uncover the rest of the skeleton. Both men stood looking down at the bones staring in shocked disgust. Luke groaned and threw his brush away. "All this work! For what? For what? Bloody hell. Bloody damned hell. All this time wasted for this abomination? That bitch. She knew. Remember when she pointed to this spot, right here, this spot, and she said, she's here. Do you remember? I'm gonna kill her. I swear I'm gonna kill her."

Even Zak was dumbfounded. His eye traveled again from the top of the skull down to the neck to the shoulders and arms and fingers and then the torso and finally what should have been the legs but were not. The sight of the hip bones melting into the vertebrae of what appeared to be a large mammal approximately the size of a dolphin horrified him. It was unnatural, against all the laws of nature and evolutionary progress. His eyes kept going back to where the legs should have been, his brain unable to process such an anomaly. There must be some logical explanation. He squatted down and studied the bones considering the possibility that someone had fused the spine of a woman to the vertebrae of a dolphin. But how and why?

She lay in the dirt, her right arm thrown up as if pleading with her captors just beyond the foundation stones. Even her skull had been set in such a position as to suggest she had been looking at something above her. What appeared to be a bracelet or manacle encircled her left wrist. Its surface was rusted beyond recognition. The bracelet appeared to be iron or an equally porous metal, its substance now fused to wrist and post by time and the elements. Luke had been silent too long. Zak looked up at him and saw Luke examining the skeleton closely chewing on his lower lip in feverish thought.

While Luke knelt to run his fingers lightly along what appeared to be the fish vertebrae, Zak turned and looked at his night's work. The largest hole was at the furthest corner of the root cellar near the front entrance of the cabin. Digging five feet down and three feet across he found the stone alter and the bones of the small animals. He'd also found a child's jewelry box covered in dirty faded blue silk and inside the jewelry box, the root doll shaped like a tiny harpy. When he had shown the doll to Luke last night excited by his discovery, Luke had been preoccupied and dismissive which pissed Zak off.

But this morning before he ever climbed out of his sleeping bag, he'd examined the doll in the morning's light and realized what he'd thought had been a cape had been a crude rendition of wings on the doll's back. He didn't examine too closely his reasons for keeping the discovery to himself. It just felt good to have something in his possession his brother couldn't commandeer. Fearing he would damage the rest of the root cellar he turned his attention to his earlier test holes at the other end of the crawl space.

Even with his knowledge of what the holes meant, Zak made sure to examine each hole again in case he'd missed something. But he'd been right the first time. He'd only had to dig a foot down before finding them. The indentations in the ground indicated three different people of various sizes and ages had lain in the crawl space, resting here long enough to leave their imprint upon the soil, long enough for pieces of bone to be forgotten in an obvious hasty attempt to gather up the evidence and dispose of the crime. For what he saw before him had to be evidence of a crime. Even prospectors and pioneers would hardly bury their dead in a cabin's crawl space. With all this land surrounding the cabin, pioneers would have had plenty of places to bury their dead.

"Could she be from the Pleistocene, do you think Zak?" Luke asked with wonder.

Zak heard his brother's words, but didn't have the heart to speak. The idea that Luke could ignore this much more recent tragedy disheartened him. He stood where a horrendous crime had been committed and knew he had inadvertently tampered with potential evidence which might have linked the murderer with the crime. The guilt washed over him in waves and he had to get out of the place before he did more damage. Had Acacia known? She must have. After all, she had led them to the cabin. How had she been involved? Had she known the murderer? Had she been one of his victims, but managed to escape?

"No," Luke answered his own question. "That can't be. That was before the Iron Age. It's a shame."

"What is?" Zak asked, turning to glare down at Luke's bent head.

"What? Oh. That. We won't be able to carbon date these bones."

"Why not?"

Luke straightened and turned to face Zak, "Are you joking? Need you ask?"

Zak noticed Luke's black and blue eyes and the way his nose had swollen to twice its size. Luke was lucky; the nose didn't appear to be broken. He must have moved an inch or so beyond the thrust of her palm; otherwise, Zak wouldn't be talking to him now. The degree of skill used to create such carnage suggested Acacia had martial arts training. With enough force and momentum, she could have shoved the bones of his nose right into his skull. But Luke had been lucky, lucky enough that an inch had saved his stupid life. Evidently, Luke's amazing find had superseded any pain he might have normally felt by now. Anyone else would be on his or her way to the hospital begging for pain killers.

"Well, you'd better get your prize out of here quick because I plan to contact the authorities and tell them what I found so far."

"Are you nuts? If you do that everything will come out."

"Anonymously. I'll tell them anonymously, stupid. Don't you even care? I count three graves here. Three people were murdered, and the murderer tried to cover up the fact. But you can never really cover up murder. These bodies had lain here long enough to make an impression in the soil. They probably left DNA behind. I haven't touched the shards of bone or bits of fiber and hairs. I'm leaving those clues for the forensic team to find," he said sweeping his arm out to encompass the area he had excavated including the root cellar where he'd found the alter and animal bones. "All this area around us suggests a killing field and he's probably still killing people. There may be more graves. He's got to be stopped."

Luke grabbed his forehead as if he finally felt the pain of his injured nose. His eyes were wild as he took in Zak's discovery, "You idiot. They'll know. You've probably left your bloody damned DNA all over this place too."

Zak had already been thinking the same thing. The fact that maybe a strand of his hair or a bit of his skin or spit might be uncovered hardly seemed important. Nothing mattered now, nothing other than the authorities be notified and the crime recorded. Because the dead who had been left to die in this hole mattered. There may be numerous people anxious to know what had happened to their family member or friend. He wouldn't be able to live with himself if he just walked away and did nothing.

Luke sensed the direction of Zak's thoughts, "Fine. Okay. Then help me get this one out of here first. She may not be Amara, but she's bizarre enough to create an international incident. We can't leave her here."

All of Zak's training and instincts protested at the desecration of the site, the hasty way Luke dug around the skeleton, the way they had to create a trench a foot down and a foot wide all the way around her remains and scoop her out like so much manure. There might be valuable artifacts buried beneath her; and yet, Luke was so afraid of getting caught he refused to take his time.

If anyone in the field of archeology discovered Zak's part in the discretion, he would never work again. And any future finds would be put under a microscope or dismissed summarily. And the same would be true for Luke. Yet Luke wasn't concerned as far as Zak could tell, Luke seemed oblivious to the potential erasure of his career. This whole mermaid hybrid could be a hoax. She could even be an elaborate joke set up by the murderer.

Luke saw the hesitation in Zak's eyes and said, "She could be Amara. We don't know for sure. They could have found her and thought, hey, wouldn't it be cool to remove her wings, cut her in half, and stick a dolphin's tail on her? Did you ever think of that? The only way we'll know for sure, is if we take her home and examine her closely."

At most, the skeleton probably weighed no more than five or ten pounds but the two inches of hardpan soil beneath her weighed probably as much as he did. Luke had been thinking ahead and brought along a surf board. Before making the trip up the mountain, they'd stepped into the sportsman's store and noticed with delighted surprise the yellow surfboard mounted like a trophy above a glass cabinet full of hunting rifles.

The clerk, immune to the absurdity of a surfboard in the desert, helpfully explained, "It was a joke. Some guy came through and pawned it and my uncle bought it for ten bucks. He keeps it up there on the wall as a joke. Sort of saying to folks: a surfboard in Ely, Nevada, yeah, right, a surfboard in the desert, in a place surrounded by mountains and rock — real useful huh? The only water we got here is Ruby Lake further north and don't even bother with Newark; it's dry, so that's not really a lake anymore, so a surfboard won't do you much good around here, now will it?"

"It'll do me fine. How much?" Luke asked with his brightest and falsest smile.

When Zak caught sight of the surfboard on the wall, his first thought had been — Luke will take this surfboard as a sign from Zeus. Before Luke bought the board, Zak tried to talk him out of buying it. The surfboard was a bad sign. Buying it would be noticed and discussed. When they returned to the Ingolstadt cabin, Zak knew Luke had finally lost what little common sense he'd had.

The hardened soil remained intact under the skeletal remains while the looser soil fell off in chunks. Zak refused to sacrifice his sleeping bag, instead, he offered an old green tarp he kept in the backseat. With some rope and a primitive wench, they managed to extract the poor woman from her resting place. When Luke tried to persuade Zak to put the skeleton in the backseat of the Camaro, Zak seriously considered driving off and leaving his brother to fend for himself.

"I'm not risking another night in jail."

"We've come too far. Look around you. Everything we've touched, every place we've walked is tainted with our presence. Even a second grader could figure out what happened here and who to blame. Let's get something out of this mess that might help our family. Do you want to wonder for the rest of your life if we left an ancestor behind? Do you want to think of her stuck in some body bag in a lab's deep freezer?"

They had to pull everything out of the trunk to make room for the poor thing which had to include her bed of earth. The spare tire, jack, jumper cables, toolbox, containers of motor oil, window washing fluid, and spray paint were deposited in the backseat of the Camaro. The

442

green tarp was laid down on the bottom of the trunk and the skeleton placed on top of it. Zak winced as bits of grave dirt crumbled off the woman's earthen bed and rolled under the tarp. She was small enough to fit inside – close to four feet. The sight of her lying there looking so fragile and tiny terrified him. He would go to jail for life. There was no doubt he would go to jail if anyone found her in his trunk.

Even though the digging and the lifting had left his muscles sore, even though the sweat dripped down his neck and into his ears with bits of debris irritated the crevices of his eyes, his state of mind had nothing to do with any physical reality, but with the idea that such a creature, such a chimera would be transported in his vehicle. The juxtaposition of these two dissimilar objects boggled his mind. What a cosmic joke, the idea that a combustion engine contained such a sad little creature. Luke obsessed with hightailing it down the road hurriedly stuffed everything into the backseat: the shovels went on the floor along with the brushes and scrapers, the folded tent and card table on the bench seat, the kerosene lamps on the floor, the sleeping bag and blankets thrown over the spare tire and boxes. Soon the junk was piled so high, Zak could barely see out his back window.

Zak glanced at his watch and noted the time. It was nearly two o'clock in the afternoon. They were leaving just around the same time they had arrived. As he watched Luke search the area for the fifth time, Zak thought about Eve and wondered if she had reached her destination. Depending on her speed and if she had driven all night, she could be in Crescent City by now. At this very moment, she might be pulling into town. As who? Would she still be Acacia? Or would Leona decide to take over?

"Ouch, sweet gee sauce that hurts," Luke cursed and paused to hold his nose. "Golly god free, damned-it-all and holy frigging hell, that hurts. Bitch. If she were standing here right now, right this minute, I'd wring her damned neck."

Why couldn't Luke empathize with Eve's trauma instead of bitching about the damage to his face? "Everybody pays a price for the things they want badly enough," Zak told him. "And I guess your price is a pair of black eyes and a swollen nose. It could be worse, Luke. You could be dead."

When Luke retraced their steps back to the cabin for a final check, searching the ground carefully, peeping over the edge of the root cellar for the hundredth time, he finally decided they could leave the miserable haunted place. Zak had already taken his last look at the root cellar. His test holes had been covered up where he'd found the alter and bones of sacrificed animals. He left the test holes exposed to the elements; he left them open and insisted Luke leave them open for a very good reason. He did not want the dirt or any other covering to contaminate the evidence. By the time he made his phone call and they were back home in Woolstone, the police or sheriff or someone in authority would have come up for a look-see. He sincerely hoped they didn't send an idiot up Ruby National Wildlife Refuge to investigate the crime scene.

The last thing he did was go back to the hole where the creature had been found only because he wanted another look at the post which lay on top of Luke's pile of dirt. It was obvious the post had been cut. One could see where the blade had sliced through the timber. The post measured two feet by two feet now, but when it had been new it could have been as tall as four feet. It had been right by the little creature's head leaning against the limestone foundation. There had been just one wooden post in the crawl space. No others. If the post had been used to support the upper floor, there should have been more of them in every corner of the cellar. But there was just the one post.

Luke had found the skeleton buried two feet below the post.

Why had the murderers removed three bodies yet left the poor creature behind? Wouldn't she have been just as incriminating? A thought came to him and he turned to his brother, "How far down did you dig before you found her?"

Absently, not even bothering to look up from his journal, Luke said, "I had to go down five feet." While his brother grabbed his notebook out of his bag and searched for a pen, Zak drove away from the cellar with his thoughts circling like a vulture, wondering at the purpose of the post. They managed to squeeze through the narrow crevice between the cliff face and the ravine and at several points along the way had to stop to let the engine cool. Part of him acknowledged his colossal relief at leaving that place of horror. But soon he would have to figure out how to inform the authorities. Until he reached the valley floor, his concentration remained fixed on keeping his vehicle on the road and his paint finish from being damaged by blackberry bushes. Once they had descended into the valley, he relaxed.

In the distance he could see a faint outline of black highway. Along this stretch, the road was level, so he pressed down on the accelerator until he was going twenty-five miles an hour. He surveyed the terrain drawing a mental picture in his head to be used later when he called the authorities to report the crime. Unbidden an image flickered across his mind, the image of a woman with her arm outstretched and her wrist chained to the post. Then everything solidified: old gray crumbling subsoil on top and fresh rich dark soil underneath. That made no sense.

Someone had placed old subsoil on top of fresh dirt, in a crawl space which no one would ever see or ever care about. Why? Then he thought of his mother, he remembered numerous occasions when Jule would dig a hole for her plant, keeping the old soil nearby, until she had placed her root ball containing the rose cane tenderly inside the new cavity. If she didn't have enough fresh dirt from her compost to ensure a secure bed for her rose, she would use some of the old gray crumbling subsoil, trying to revive the old soil with plenty of water and mulch, doing her best to ensure all parts, old and new were compact and free of air holes.

In his imagination he saw floorboards running from foundation wall to foundation wall, two or three feet above where the original soil had lain. Then he saw the others, the dead covering the cellar floor from the northwest corner to the other end where the little mermaid's skeleton had lain. There had been a child's body buried in the cellar too, its body still making an impression in the soil as it curled up next to the adult for warmth and comfort. And all alone in the far corner, the little mermaid had been deliberately separated from the rest, separated as one would separate the clean from the unclean.

Someone had dug up the little mermaid and then reburied her. Why? What would be the sense in doing that? And why would a murderer go to all the extra effort and annoyance of crawling around under his floor digging graves for his victims? Wouldn't it be more sensible to just go out into the wilderness and dig a deep hole and dump them all in it? One theory might be that those test holes weren't graves at all; instead, they were indentations of where bodies had been lying for a very long time. The fact they were so uniform reminding him of graves which meant those people had probably been drugged and unable to move.

Even though those poor creatures had probably been drugged and left to die in the crawl space, one of them had had enough presence of mind to be curious about what lay beneath her body. He might be wrong, but he didn't think so. It seemed as if Professor Wade and Amara Katsaros were tortuously linked. He and his brother couldn't separate one without losing the other. Zak had never believed for a second Eve was his old professor resurrected into a new body.

If he was right, the real reason the little mermaid had been found with old gray crumbling soil as the first layer and then fresh new soil underneath was because someone had recognized an anomaly and was curious enough to investigate. Well, all the facts lead to someone digging up the little mermaid and then hurriedly reburying her. Why? In order to hide the skeleton from the other poor buggers trapped in the crawl space? Why would they give a shit? Or was she reburied because the little mermaid was an abomination? No. He thought he knew the real reason – to protect the little mermaid for future generations? And why would a person under such horrific conditions go to so much trouble for the benefit of future generations?

Zak stomped on the brake pedal and the car skidded to a sudden stop nearly sending Luke's much abused face into the windshield. Zak put the Camaro in park.

"Man. What was that? Did you run over something?" Luke asked.

Unable to speak, Zak threw open the door and tumbled out. They were only a few feet from a hillside. He made a run for the brush.

Luke returned to his notes busily drawing from memory the site they had just cleared. Zak disappeared among the mahogany sage. It wasn't until Luke glanced at his watch and realized the engine had been idling for nearly ten minutes that he became alarmed. Just as he moved to get out of the car, he saw his brother heading toward him. The look on his face shocked Luke. Zak climbed back into the driver's seat and drove toward home. The entire two hundred or more miles, he didn't speak or even look at Luke.

The only time he saw Zak open his mouth was at a pay phone in Wells, Nevada when he was talking to someone on the other end of the line. Luke had a pretty good idea who his brother was calling and considered for just a second rushing up and grabbing the phone away from him. He didn't. The police would record the phone call, of course, and the police would discover where the call had been placed, of course, and then they would question the store clerk in Ely and get a copy of the video recording of them buying the surfboard and soon there'd be a knock on the Woolly Man door.

The woman at her shoulder held the tray steady and waited to be noticed. Dr. Winter finished her newest entry in her journal and set her reading glasses on the open page, then looked up into Farrah's eyes. Farrah's smile was tentative as the familiar assessment of her facial bones and scars began anew. Farrah had grown used to Dr. Winter's clinical gaze. In fact, Farrah had come to anticipate the look with real pleasure. She waited for the eyes to drop to the tray of food.

"Is it lunch already?" Dr. Winter declared glancing at her gold wrist watch as if questioning the validity of the time. "Well, yes, it is. Just put the tray over there. Thank you, Myrtle."

"Dr. Winter?"

Violet Winter barely glanced at her assistant, "Hum?" she murmured absently going back to the report on her newest patient.

"It's Farrah now, not Myrtle. I had my name legally changed to Farrah Zee Foster-Koodark, Farrah as in Farrah Fawcett, because increasingly people are now mistaking me for her while my last name is more in keeping with my heritage. I come from a long line of Fosters, so I went back to my maiden name. And then there's Koodark which is my mother's family name. And-"

"Yes, yes, I remember now. It's Farrah. I will do my best to remember. But you must forgive me since I've been calling you Myrtle for nearly twenty years. Habits are hard to break after all."

"Dr. Winter? You said perhaps in another week or two after the old scars heal you might consider liposuction on my arms and the fat around my waist. Have you? I mean have you considered my next surgery?" Farrah began and hesitated unsure how to continue without sounding like she was begging. Dr. Winter hated it when Farrah begged. With surgically chiseled nose and large dark eyes free of wrinkles, Dr. Winter reminded Farrah of one of those magnificent birds of prey, a hawk or peregrine falcon as she turned to examine Farrah.

"You know I'm going to be extremely busy for the next few weeks. There's the conference in San Francisco and of course my newest research. I've been contemplating the possibility of another major experiment. I've been thinking about marine worms. Extraordinary results. When denied food and light, they shrink and paradoxically regress into their originating state of existence. What I'm thinking is that the rate of regression would be easier to observe with someone much younger, say eighteen months. I believe I've been going about this experiment wrong. I need to change my perspective. It would be beneficial if —"

"Dr. Winter," Farrah threw out in alarm, hearing a voice shouting outside the door of the Winter laboratory. "I'm so sorry to interrupt you again, but there's something I forgot to mention earlier."

"Myrtle, have you seen to Anderson? He needs your attention now. Then. Yes, what is it?" Dr. Winter asked with a crease between her brows. She hated to be interrupted when she was on the verge of a new idea.

"It's Farrah. And what I've got to say is important. He came unannounced. The landscaper left the gate open while he was mowing the front lawn and he just walked right through the gates," Farrah began.

Winter interrupted her, "Who? Come on Farrah. Spit it out. Can't you see I'm busy?"

"That man, the one who used to be so gorgeous, the one you examined last year? He's back and he won't leave. He's changed so much. He used to have such beautiful hair. His eyes haven't changed, they're still as blue as the sky. Anyway, sorry. He insists on seeing you and says he won't leave until he's talked to you face to face," Farrah said.

Dr. Winter climbed off her stool and stood in her surgery contemplating the far wall. Farrah waited to be told what to do. The wail of a child waking from a nightmare galvanized Dr. Winter into action. "I'll deal with him. You deal with the child."

But when Farrah grabbed the tray and started down the hall to the door, Dr. Winter's commanding voice stopped her in her tracks. "Stop. What are you doing, Myrtle? You aren't listening to me. Listen carefully. I want you to deal with the child first. I'll deal with our visitor. He knows full well there's nothing more I can do for him. I'll send him packing and then we'll get started on my new strategy."

As Farrah set the tray down on the surgical table and walked toward the steps that led underground, she muttered under her breath, "It's Farrah, not Myrtle. Farrah, Farrah. Farrah." Over her shoulder, she watched as Dr. Winter on her sturdy legs marched down the hall toward the Botticelli Door. Light from outdoors spilled down the hall and into the surgery and Farrah could smell fresh air mixed with the staler air of the surgical chamber. She hesitated. Just as Violet grabbed the handle of the Botticelli Door, someone on the other side shoved hard throwing the door open. He stepped inside. The brilliant sunlight cast a halo around his bald glistening head. As his eyes tracked her progress, a pair of sleepy eyes snapped with irritation, "I've been waiting forever. Where is she?"

"Get out of my laboratory this instant," Dr. Winter ordered. "You've had your chance and you blew it. Go find yourself another kiddy to molest, you poor excuse for a man."

"Me," he said pointing at his chest, "you're saying I'm worthless? How about you, you friggin mad scientist."

Ray Millhouse pushed her aside and hurried toward the surgical chamber. Farrah skipped down the stairs and ran to the bunk closest to the stairs. She perched on the edge of the bed and put her hand over the child's mouth. "Shush now," she said placing her finger to her lips. Farrah felt the hot moist skin of the child beneath her fingers. She wanted to rub away the sensation, rub the sticky filthy germs off her hand and onto her surgical gown. She dared not, not until Ray Millhouse went away. She noted with relief that the restraints were still in place. And then a shadow extinguished the light from above and the man ran down the stairs calling "Pumpkin, hey, Pumpkin, where are you sweetie?"

When the man saw Farrah, he ignored the child laying on the bed and instead his sleepy blue eyes bore down upon Farrah mesmerizing her with their heat. No one had seen her the way he saw her. And when he drew close, nearly touching her, she shivered in anticipation. Then he stepped behind her and tossed his arms around her shoulders. She thought he was going to bestow some magnificent jeweled necklace around her supple neck. The last person she saw was Dr. Winter staring down at her with angry astonishment. The outrage on Dr. Winter's face should have terrified Farrah but it didn't. She didn't care what the old battle axe thought. Ray had finally declared his love for her.

When Dr. Winter stepped forward as if to descend the stairs, she seemed to fly like some predatory hawk, her body blocking out the light. Ray Millhouse watched Mindless Myrtle frantically flailing her arms as she tried to fight off his choke hold. Her sharp nails dug into his arms. He punched her in the head several times. She let go and landed on the cold concrete floor. Her eyes stared blankly up at the ceiling of the chamber. Without warning something dark and huge swooped down from above hurtling like a missile straight at him.

Instinct propelled him backward, just in time to avoid all seven feet and one hundred and eighty-five pounds of Dr. Violet Winter. A few more inches to the right and she would have landed on top of the scarred freak dead on the floor beside her. If Dr. Winter had landed on Myrtle, Myrtle's skinny body would hardly have cushioned her fall at all. Even he knew if you landed on a concrete floor on top of a thin mattress, you'd still end up breaking bones. Unfortunately for Dr. Winter, her velocity and mass landed the old woman on the floor of what had once been an air raid shelter beneath which lay a ten-inch-thick solid concrete foundation. Nasty.

"You've had more than enough time with this one. It's my turn," Ray said to the old woman sprawled like a broken toy on the floor staring in shock up at him. When Ray moved his hand instinctively to brush back his long glossy brown hair from his eyes, he remembered with real anguish that it was all gone, all gone, the looks that had helped him in the past, the stamina and vigor of his youth, all gone now. The sight of the living pincushion sprawled beside Dr. Winter made him sick with revulsion. One was dead and the other. Hum? She might not be dead yet, but it wouldn't be long from the look of her. He examined her briefly flinching at the sight of her skirt riding up her hips. The sight made him want to barf. He held back the urge.

With her eyes registering bewilderment, she opened her mouth to speak. Ray heard Dr. Winter's moan but ignored her in his urgent need to remove his pumpkin from the mad scientist's lair. He carried her up into the light, into the fresh beautiful light of day. When his pumpkin started scratching at his face and wriggling like a slippery eel (a final betrayal amongst many) one of her fists hit him right in the throat. He let go. She dropped to the ground like a rock. Unlike a rock, she scrambled up onto her feet. My God, the little monsters were quick these days.

He ran up the steps clutching his throat. Before he'd managed a few steps, he heard the kid's black patent leather shoes slapping against the tiled floor as she ran out of the surgery and down the hall. A few seconds later, he heard a series of grunts and gasps as if she were dragging or pushing something heavy. When the vaulted door closed, effectively cutting out all the natural light from outdoors, he chuckled.

Like that would save her, he thought with a shake of his head. He had to admire his little pumpkin's ingenuity. Still clutching his throat, he burst into the surgery and ran down the hall. In the dark, he groped for the handle. Eventually he found it and twisted and turned the damned thing. The door refused to open. When he realized she had locked him in, he got mad, really mad. He pounded on the door and shouted her name.

When shouting her name didn't work, he screamed, "Open this damned door. You hear me? Get back here and open this damned door or you're going to get a spanking you'll never forget." When nothing happened, he leaned against the door rubbing his throat and said in a more consoling voice, "Pumpkin, are you out there? Open the door sweetie. I've got some ice cream and chocolate bars for you. You want to see the pony now?" Nothing happened. He was astonished. "Open the fucking door. Right now," he screamed. When he stopped pounding on the door, the side of his hand began to throb.

A voice from the bunker below the surgical chamber called out weakly. Ray strode down the hall with one arm holding his aching throat and stood at the top of the steps, "What do you want, you stupid bitch?" he asked.

"Help me, "she said weakly. "Please help me."

"Why should I help you?"

"You consummate ass," he heard her say and then she groaned and said in a more conciliatory voice. "Oh, Sweet Jeezus, the pain. The pain. My leg. Please help me. Money. I'll give you money. Just get the emergency kit. It's in the top left-hand drawer of my desk. The kit includes a syringe and morphine, everything I need. Please hurry."

"I don't need your money Dr. Frankenstein. I just want my Pumpkin."

"Oh God, oh God," Dr. Winter gasped. "Help me. Someone please help me."

"I can't. I can't do a damned thing because the door won't open."

"The code," Dr. Winter said.

Ray moved to stand on the top step, "What did you say?"

There was silence for so long he thought she might have died. Then he heard her mumble, "Help me. . . the code . . . I know . . . going into shock . . . help."

Ray bit his lip and said, "I don't know. Can I trust you? Leland says you never forget a betrayal and carry grudges like the homeless carry head lice."

"I promise," he barely heard her say. "I . . . oath."

"I will. Just give me the code and I'll call the police," he said both aware that as soon as he was free he would search for the kid and leave her to rot.

"God, no," she said. "Just you, me now. You can take her. Promise. Don't need her. Plan. I need younger test subjects. Yes. Younger. You can get me more?"

He sat at the foot of the stairs and grabbed his head wondering what he should do. The old bat didn't trust him. What should he do? He lifted his head, "Okay. I'm sorry about Mindless Myrtle. She had it coming, she stole my pumpkin. She had no right. Okay. I've got an idea. I'll carry you to the door. Right? And then you give me the code and we'll get out of here. What do you say?"

"Leg broken. Idiot. You want to kill me?"

"We'll both die if you don't tell me the code."

"One."

"Yes."

"Nine."

"Yes. Come on hurry up."

"Five."

"How many more for Christ's sake?"

"One."

"One more number or the last code number is one?"

He waited several minutes before it dawned on him that she had passed out again. It took five or ten minutes for him to find a pencil and paper and copy down the numbers he had so far. In the surgical room he searched for a landline. There was none. Standing on the threshold of the cavern below which in its day had been someone's idea of safety in a time of nuclear Armageddon, he forced himself to sprint down the stairs, step over the bodies and search quickly for any sign of a landline or pager or alarm system.

There was none. Of course not. Why would the old fart keep a landline inside her super-secret sick laboratory? He went back up the stairs and searched the upper floor for a means of communicating with the world outside the hellhole of his prison. There was none. He returned to the Botticelli Door and stared at the keypad willing the damned thing to open. It did no such thing. Fucking machines. He punched in the numbers. And waited. He punched in the numbers again. Still nothing. He decided to start with zero for the last number. By the time he got to nine, he realized the code must require five numbers.

The next day he was still punching numbers.

"You're going to leave me here to die, aren't you Ray?" he heard her call up to him from below, her voice barely registering.

He walked back to the shelter door and sat himself down on the top step, "Now why in the fuck would I kill the money machine? Are you seriously that paranoid?"

"Your pumpkin. Leland said you were no longer on our side. He warned me, said you'd found Jesus since the cancer."

"Would a good Christian abandon a woman to such a cruel death?"

Ray moved down a step to peer into the woman's face. Her mouth opened as if she were searching desperately for the right words. She closed her eyes and then opened them. The woman had always been a cold fish. Now she seemed almost human. Ray leaned forward. He heard her whisper, "Water, please."

"I'll get you all the fucking water you need AFTER you give me the rest of the code. No. Don't pass out again. Come on. It's been twenty-four hours now. We've been in here twenty-four hours. No one is going to come for us. Alright, sorry for the profanity. I know you hate profanity. I promise, I'll get you your … water. Sorry. Forgot," he managed to say between clenched teeth. And on the way to the tiny kitchenette, he shouted his frustration to the four walls.

When he reached the bottom of the shelter he discovered she'd passed out again. He left the water within reach and returned to the door. The paper he'd been using to keep track of the sequences so far had become stained with his sweat and filthy from the dirty floor, altogether the paper was barely legible. Unable to stop the trembling of his lower lip and barely able to hold it together, he tried another sequence of numbers.

On the second day, he heard a sound which reminded him of the mulling of a kitten. He rolled off the surgical table and made his way to the shelter, prudently stopping at the door to peer down into the gloom below. Gradually, over time, it dawned upon him that she was trying to say water. "Okay. I'll get you another glass of water. Hold on."

By the time he returned from the little kitchenette, a sound outside the Botticelli Door rooted him to the spot midway between the shelter and the surgery. In the time it took to fill the glass with water, Dr. Winter had managed to claw and crawl her way closer to the second landing. Now she lay on the landing with only five more steps left to reach. The glass he held in his hand sloshed as he moved toward the locked security door. "I hear someone. Hold on. I'll bring the water in just a tick. It might be pumpkin."

Ray opened the peephole and peered out. "Is there anyone out there?" And from the shelter below like an annoying mosquito buzzing in his ears, he heard the bane of his life say, "They can't come in. Don't let them in. I'll be ruined. Give them Leland's number. Leland will come. He'll take care of this mess."

Ray's eye didn't have time to blink. At first, the pain was so overwhelming he could only gasp. Then the screaming commenced and he didn't stop until he'd passed out.

24

Acacia stared at her hands in disbelief. They refused to do her bidding. It was only later that she realized she must have looked like an idiot with her hands suspended in the air. It took nearly an hour to stop the trembling and another twenty minutes to wash her face in the park restroom and another few minutes to find the courage to get back into the limo and drive to the nearest gas station. She made herself drive back to Winnemucca with the radio off and the silence profound. There was no thinking or talking to one's selves. There were no recriminations or regrets or silly playbacks of what might have been. All she need do now is think in the moment, no, not think, but be. To be in the moment.

If she were to stay in the moment, all would be well. If only she could find a way to get her mind off the past which would never come again and stop ruminating over an unpredictable future, she would find power in the present, power in concentration, and a reward at the end, a huge reward in the possibility of true serenity. There had been a child once. Acacia recognized the shape of her, knobby arms, and coltish legs. She remembered mud cakes, home-made ice cream and fireflies. That child had been in the moment every day until...

In Winnemucca, Acacia bought bananas, peaches, apples, avocados, almonds, tomatoes, olive oil, oven baked potato chips, several bars of dark chocolate, and four gallons of bottled water. While in the grocery store, she scared off several teenagers who followed her around the aisles with large smiles and appreciative stares. At one point, she made herself look down at her clothes. Blood would ruin this expensive suit. She decided to ignore them. She arrived in Winnemucca on fumes, grateful that her luck still held. She filled up the greedy gas tank. By midnight she reached Medford. In Medford, she booked a hotel room near the highway. It seemed like a waste of money since her body refused to rest and continued to vibrate and twitch all damned night. People had gone without sleep before and still managed to drive.

By six o'clock the next morning she was on the road and on her way to Grants Pass. If circumstances had been different she supposed she would have enjoyed the beautiful scenery along the way, especially along the winding road with a forest of evergreens and lush vegetation below her. At a few locations where she could pull off, she paused to stretch and smell the pine and the earth beneath her feet. Her eyes registered the beauty around her, but her mind kept leaping ahead to the moment she encountered the past and rectified the future. The warmth of the sun on her head and shoulders contributed to a false sense of peace. At least her skin appreciated the clean cool air, but her other senses continued to catalogue the potential danger.

She saw a suburban sweep around the curve of the road, reduce its speed, and coast toward her. The leprous red and white striped vehicle looked as if someone had used it for target practice. She had noticed it before, outside Medford. He'd been following her for the last fifty miles. But he did not pull onto the shoulder of the road as expected, rather he slowed down which was foolhardy on this winding road. He leaned forward with his baseball cap touching the glass of the driver side window, a glass she noticed with disgust was smeared with a yellow film of nicotine stains. He stared at her. Did he really imagine a woman would find his lecherous look attractive?

Acacia stared at him disappointed when he drove on. He had no choice. A Mazda swept around the curve. But before he disappeared from view, he rolled down his window and shouted, "See you in Crescent City, baby." Maybe she'd still have an opportunity to wipe-the-lech off his face.

For now, Acacia had better things to do. She returned to the limo and followed the lush Eden path along 199 with the tail lights of the champagne colored Mazda ahead of her riding the nauseous ass of the moron in the suburban. Eventually the Mazda turned off onto a side road and the suburban disappeared somewhere down a hole. Before Acacia reached the ocean, she stopped at a roadside cafe for a cup of fancy coffee and a bagel.

When she thought she'd had just about enough of all this glorious beauty and greenery, she broke out into a clearing and saw the ocean. It was gorgeous. The ocean met the gray sky and in a sexy maneuver brushed its back up against the darker clouds. The signs of a storm brewing on the horizon fit perfectly with her mood. She found a parking lot near one of many piers and on this particular pier, she noticed a restaurant with old bleached timbered walls and rusted ornaments hanging artfully here and there, as if tourists needed further proof they were enjoying the sea air. Several freighters and a few sailboats were anchored on the docks as an added atmospheric bonus.

When Acacia climbed out of the limo, the wind hit her in the face and simultaneously her senses were assaulted by the bellow of a foghorn, the chorus of a herd of walrus on a floating dock and the shrieking of gulls overhead. While the cacophony washed over her with the wind blowing her hair into her eyes and ears and mouth, and the air cooling her blood, she battled the elements with a sense of exhilaration. Soon. Very soon. It would all be decided, soon. The end was so close. Adrenaline surged through her body. She needed a phone and then remembered all the junk in the limo. Thanks to Frankie and Ana, she could have her pick of a multitude of communication devices.

Twenty minutes later, after riffling through the baggage inside, Acacia stood with the trunk open and stared down at all the modern paraphernalia people thought they needed in order to survive, well not all people, but people like Frankie. A cellphone needed to be recharged periodically. It also needed a tower for reception. And an iPod in a thunderstorm would just be asking for the Grim Reaper to come visit you before your time. And all those damned pens and fancy notebooks were useless as a means of finding shelter and food. And how might a calculator help you if you were stranded in the woods or in the desert? She imagined what Frankie might say, something cocky like – well, let's see, a calculator might help you pass the time; you could count trees or maybe rocks, or better yet, all the planes flying over your head.

In addition to Frankie's junk, Acacia found a man's black nylon duffel bag which she assumed must be Luke Nerin's personal possession. Too bad, chump. She imagined him still digging frantically to find his lost treasure. The thought of him with his crisp neat clothes all soaked with sweat and dirt and his ponytail askew made Acacia want to laugh. She saw him in her mind's eye diligently sifting through the dirt careful not to damage his artifacts. Artifacts? Where had that word come from? A surge of anger washed over her. She bent down and waited for the sensation to pass griping metal between her palms thinking about the grotesqueness of modern man, how they could be in such fawning awe of something five thousand years old and dismissive of someone who had died just the other day. Why weren't the recently dead seen as treasures too?

Eventually after dumping the contents of Frankie's purse onto the floor of the limo trunk, Acacia found a cellphone. In this place of modern conveniences with its stores and gas stations and restaurants and banks, a cellphone was a necessity. After examining the numbers faithfully recorded in the address book, Acacia came across the number she needed. She called the number and listened to the ringing on the other end of the line. No, it wasn't a so-called "line" any more. It was now airwaves. Or was it? Modern technology now interfered with the air itself. Air was for breathing not sending signals. She waited for the mechanical voice to apologize for not being ready and waiting to answer the caller's call that very second.

Then the familiar voice reciting the proscribed apologizes sent a bolt of paralyzing fear through her entire body, starting with a lightning bolt into her eardrum, traveling down her throat, through her chest, all the way to her spine. She never really took in the words because the words had become mixed up with an assault of similar sounding words from the past. Intermixed with the gulls' screams and the bellowing of the walrus, she heard the familiar voice. She tried to brush the voice away too terrified to listen.

Fighting her way back to the present, back to consciousness and clarity and the need for some protective anger, she threw back her head and screamed as loud as her vocal cords would allow, "You fools. Shut the fuck up," and after calming down a bit with her head on straight and in a more composed voice, she listened to voicemail asking whether she wanted to review her message. She chose to delete her screaming tirade and turned off Frankie's cellphone.

She told the others, "We are so close. Don't chicken out now. She's human, just like us. She bleeds, just like us. And she will one-day experience pain and blood and all the indignities of death. I promise you."

Feeling eyes on the back of her neck, Acacia glanced over her shoulder seeing an elderly couple walking arm and arm toward the fancy restaurant on the peer. They stared at her in shocked surprise, appalled at her uncivilized behavior. The wife took off, but the old man paused and glanced at the walruses. With a stern reprimand in his voice, he said, "They're just animals, young lady. They don't understand you. Go somewhere else if you can't stand the noise." When Acacia turned to face him fully, something in her expression frightened him. He scurried after his wife.

It took an hour of phone calls to finally get the information she needed. On the fifth ring, the receptionist answered the hospital phone. Sick people must be a rare event in this town. "Peninsula Hospital. How may I direct your call?"

"I'm looking for V. E. Winter. Is she there?"

"Are you trying to reach Dr. Violet Winter?"

"Yes, I am. Her full name is Violet Euphemia Winter."

"Interesting. I'd always wondered what the middle initial stood for. No, ma'am. Dr. Winter is no longer associated with Danvers County Hospital. You can reach her at her private number. It is." Before the receptionist hung up, Acacia could hear her say, "You're not going to believe," and then the connection between them went dead. Another fan of Dr. Violet Effin Winter. Acacia grabbed a pen and one of the notebooks and jotted down the number. She quickly dialed Winter's private line only to get the same answering service as before.

Acacia called the hospital back. She recognized the receptionist's voice. This time the receptionist sounded as if she regretted her earlier easygoing attitude. Maybe someone had warned her not to give out the doctor's personal number to a stranger? "I really need to reach Dr. Winter. It's a matter of life and death," Acacia said and used her free hand to cover her mouth, stifling a hysterical giggle tickling the back of her throat.

"We are equipped to deal with emergencies here at the hospital, ma'am. Feel free to come in. Or should I send an ambulance to you?"

"No. It's not a medical emergency for me. It's a personal matter."

"Are you a relative?"

"Yes. I'm the . .. her niece," Acacia said.

"Oh hello, Mrs. Lawson. I didn't recognize your voice. You sound so, ah, different."

"You mean happy?"

"Sure, happy."

"No, you didn't mean happy, not really. I know what you're thinking. You meant young, didn't you? I sound young. Yes. I know. I know. It's fantastic. Even Effie doesn't recognize my voice any more. I've found the most divine voice coach."

"Well, you sound great Mrs. Lawson."

"I've just auditioned for a new play at the Morrison Center. Wish me luck."

"Well sure. Good luck. Oh, wait, no, it's break a leg. Isn't that what they say? Break a leg? In our business that would be rude," the receptionist said with a nervous laugh. "Any who, you just be safe, okay? I wish you all the best Mrs. Lawson."

Attempting her best imitation of Mad Mona, Acacia said, "I've got places to go and people to see, so let's wrap this up, hon. I really need to get in touch with Effie. Where is she?"

"Dr. Winter had a medical conference to go to in San Francisco this week," the receptionist said. "It's my guess that she stayed over for another day. Have you tried her cellphone?"

"Of course, I have and her home phone and just now her private medical number. She's not answering any of them. Do you think she's avoiding me?"

"Well, I don't think so, Mrs. Lawson. She always speaks very highly of you. I'm sure she'll return your call when she can."

"When is she due back?"

"Any day now I suppose. Her liposuction tomorrow at three canceled, so, maybe she's sightseeing."

"In San Francisco? You must be joking," Acacia said remaining in character with an effort, aware of Mona Lawson's opinion of San Francisco.

"There's lots to see in San Francisco," the receptionist said sounding mildly offended. "I'm sorry I can't be of more help, Mrs. Lawson."

The long pause was significant. Acacia waited her out. The silence dragged on suggesting to Acacia that the receptionist might be debating within herself as to how much she could safely reveal without getting into trouble with Dr. Winter or her own bosses at the hospital. "I must tell you Mrs. Lawson that Dr. Winter is no longer associated with Peninsula Hospital. She's sent all her patients to other plastic surgeons."

"Lawsuits huh? I knew it. It was bound to happen."

"How'd you? Ah. Wait, no ma'am, there are no lawsuits. You see, she told us she wants to dedicate her life to those who can't afford her services. She's planning to travel to South America and work with the poor who need her more than we do. I guess she decided instead of returning to Crescent City, she'd fly down to wherever she's most needed. You know those places down south, the ones where they don't have clean water or electricity or sanitation? That's where she's going. She's just amazing. I wouldn't have the courage to just up and leave my home like that. She really is a hardworking, dedicated, doctor. We're all real proud of her here."

"I see. Yes. That sounds like her. Well, maybe you're right. Maybe I should just send her an email and tell her she's made the right decision finally. Effie and I have often wondered when she would pursue her original dream of helping those less fortunate. I know this is a terrible inconvenience for you honey, but could you give me her address? I've lost it again."

"Just a moment Mona, I mean Mrs. Lawson, I have to answer this other line and when I'm finished I'll get that address for you."

Once Acacia had concluded her conversation with the helpful receptionist, it took some time to find a phone booth with a phone book still intact. Where had all the phone booths gone? Those words sounded familiar. Then she remembered the song and began to sing under her breath– where had all the flowers gone? Long time pa ... ass ... sing ... She couldn't remember the rest of the words, so she just hummed under her breath.

So where had all the phone booths gone? The phone booth cemetery? Maybe? She hoped not. Then she spotted a phone booth on the corner near a drug store. Acacia flipped through the pages of the phone book and found a map of the town. She tore the page out of the book and started off toward the peninsula where the map told her she would find Dr. Violet Winter's residence. Then she belatedly remembered the conspicuous limo.

Backtracking to the pier, she found a receipt for the rent of the limo in the glove compartment and spent the remaining afternoon driving to Brookings searching for a way to rid herself of the limo. Once in Brookings destiny took over. The manager of the dealership insisted on serving her himself. The rumor of money had its benefits. The manager accepted without question her request for a more economical vehicle and sent round for a cream-colored Toyota Corolla for her to use while in town.

As she walked out with the manager carrying papers and the keys to the car, she passed a tall young man with curly brown hair and hazel eyes. He wore a red and white checkered shirt, loose fitting jeans, and brown hiking boots. He held the door open for her and smiled down at her. Normally she would have kept on walking. Instead, she looked up at him and smiled back. She didn't know why. He had kind eyes, familiar eyes, where had she seen him before? Then he disappeared inside, and she never saw him again.

Soon she found herself back on the highway driving the cream-colored Toyota. By dusk, she reached Crescent City and exited the highway onto Viewpoint Drive. There was only one property on the entire point which by her mileage was three miles long. She followed the one-way road which circled the outer edge of the point and ended right back on the highway. She reentered Viewpoint Drive and made another circuit of the property, this time driving as slowly as she could without calling attention to herself. When she passed the black wrought-iron gates, she tried to get an impression of the property.

All she could see was a driveway cutting through a green landscape of manicured lawn and lush vegetation. She wanted to stop and get out and take a good look around, but knew the sight of a strange vehicle and a nosey driver would be noticed by the occupants of the house. Frustrated, she continued at a sedate ten miles an hour searching both sides of the road for some way she might be able to access the property. There was no place for drivers to park and look at the view or even much room to turn around without ending up in the ocean. On the left-hand side of the road was a ten-foot wall which completely surrounded the property and on the right-hand side was a sheer drop down about half a mile to the ocean below.

At a lookout point further up the highway, she found another cape, this one public where sightseers could park and walk down to the beach. She ate her dinner and scrutinized the peninsula, an exact duplicate of the one she was on, in the hopes she would find a weakness in the property's security. Now that she could see the entire cape and the property in detail through her brand-new binoculars, she realized 2323 Viewpoint Road was set on a fake peninsula. The clerk at the sporting goods store recommended a general-purpose pair of binoculars, since any extra magnification would require a steady hand and she knew setting up a tripod in public might look fishy.

Fishy, what an appropriate description! Even with the window down a few inches, a fishy smell outside the car and a fishy smell inside the car competed for her attention. With the binocular's support, she discovered the owner had spent a small fortune dumping rocks and boulders and dirt on what used to be a little lump of rock in the ocean.

As she searched for a gap or way inside the fortress, she dipped a piece of fried fish into some tartar sauce and popped it into her mouth. The fish and chips were delicious. The sight was not. Disguised as a lighthouse, the mansion's facade which faced the ocean lacked the old-world charm of a real lighthouse. It was a modern-day facsimile, as false as a facelift, as unblemished and shiny as a skin peel. Someone had made it worse by covering the white stucco in layers of glossy paint. And bizarrely enough, the architect or owner, more likely the owner, set atop the toy lighthouse a fussy cupola; its surface and window trim lavish with Victorian molding.

A flash of light alarmed her. For a few anxious seconds, she imaged someone shooting at her from across the beach, then she wondered if the owner or one of the staff might have stumbled upon the glint of her lenses as she canvassed the house. She moved her binoculars up a quarter of an inch and adjusted the scope. Then she saw the ornament swiveling in the wind at the very tippy-top of the cupola. It was a weather vane. A huge shiny metal thing. It might have been a bird, maybe an eagle or a gull; it was hard to tell. When she thought of the owner, she instantly thought of a vulture. Yeah. If it was a vulture, the "good" doctor would be flying her true colors.

Dropping her binoculars, she saw the grounds surrounding the lighthouse, the great beige wall, the gardens inside the wall, and the black tarred private road shaped like a demented horseshoe. When she swept the binoculars left, she could see a series of structures attached to the back end of the monstrosity. Someone had replaced good design with a design bordering on the obscene. The buildings attached to the lighthouse reminded Acacia of an ugly bustle, a lumpy cancerous protrusion stuck on a woman's rear end. She tried to ignore the bustle and concentrate on the grounds. The property was at least five miles outside of town and half a mile above sea level nestled securely in the embrace of pine trees and expensive flora.

To add to the opulence, a ten-foot fence made of concrete blocks covered in sandstone veneer encircled the grounds providing security and exclusiveness. A lush array of local plants was artistically arranged on either side of the brick driveway, a driveway which led up to a series of stone steps and a set of massive red cedar doors. Everything was so grotesquely tasteless, Acacia smiled with wicked glee. Then she frowned remembering Tessa's observation years ago, "Of course appearance is an obsession with Violet, but in her frantic attempt to capture beauty, she invariably ends up perverting beauty, destroying beauty, and redeeming nothing."

Once she was finished with her dinner, Acacia threw on a windbreaker and sturdy hiking boots, locked the rental and proceeded to run down the steps leading to the beach below. The beach was between the public cape and Dr. Winter's property. She passed several beachcombers who had a fire lit and were busily drinking wine and celebrating the good weather. On the other side of the beach, she found stairs leading up to Dr. Winter's private property. Acacia had passed several signs warning her she was trespassing. She ignored the signs, jumping over the flimsy rope, and running up the stairs. The beachcombers were too busy enjoying themselves to notice her.

It took Acacia all of twenty minutes to get from her rental to Dr. Winter's private road. She stood near a metal call box and looked through the gate. She was so close now. She would let nothing get in her way, not a gate or a wall or an ocean. Debating whether to press the call button, she studied the driveway, the wall on either side of the gate and the gate itself. She had several options: wait for the owner to show up, climb over the gate, lure a staff member outside with a fake story about car trouble, or find an easier way inside the property.

In addition to the other skills she'd acquired over the years, she'd also been practicing with some success at calling forth the emotions trapped in her body's memory and using that memory to stoke her anger and built up the will to act. The final step would be calling forth her imagination, the use of which she had managed to corral into quite an effective tool. The first time she used her new skill had been shortly after leaving the hospital. It had taken her two nights of wandering the streets before she found someone willing to fight her.

She'd acquired a quilt of different colored bruises and a lump on her jaw, but the end result proved her theory. If she pictured the outcome precisely, right down to the positioning of her legs and arms while also considering her opponents possible responses, then rehearsing the scenarios mentally and physically, she discovered her body automatically performed the steps without hesitation.

As she stood on the other side of the gate wondering how she might get inside, her thoughts automatically analyzed the facts. So, the Butcher Queen would be changing careers soon. Why? Research had been her whole purpose in life. She would never give it up. But if she were planning to leave, her leaving meant a) someone was blackmailing her or b) she was under investigation. Nothing else would drag her away from her research.

On the other side of the fancy gate, something large crashed through the brush. And within seconds, she saw them, two well fed, muscled Doberman Pinschers galloping toward the gate. They pranced before her with tongues hanging out and black eyes waiting. In unison like thoroughbred horses, they paced in front of her probably hoping she'd be stupid enough to jump over the gate, so they could toy with her for a while and then eat her. The presence of the dogs meant someone still lived in the house, someone who fed them and set them out at night to guard the property. Would the Butcher Queen leave her beloved animals behind? Never.

Acacia returned to the rental and fished in the trunk for her Sai case. Most of the beachcombers were gone and the fire had been extinguished. On her way back to Dr. Winter's property, she averted her eyes from the couple, not even bothering to hide her case because the couple were too busy moaning and thrashing about inside a sleeping bag to notice her. She circled Dr. Winter's wall searching for a way inside the property.

The wall covered in an attractive sandstone facade rose high above her. About twenty yards beyond the gate, she found a trumpet vine growing along the inner wall. It must have been thirty or forty years old, in some places, the vine's shoots were thicker than her thighs, winding in the crevices of the wall and spreading its limbs along the top and then down the other side.

The gardener must be lazy or security stupid, she thought. Maybe security thought the dogs would keep most people away? She used the vine to climb the wall. After a cursory examination of the other side where the brush and trees grew thickest, she got on her belly and swung her legs over the top and dropped down to the earth feeling the rich humus beneath her feet. The Doberman Pinschers burst out of the underbrush. Acacia got down on her hands and knees. She gathered up all her anger and tenderness and wove herself a shield preparing for battle.

Puzzled by her odd behavior, they paused for just a second or two in surprise. Most prey will run. Acacia held the Shirasaya swords in either hand her fingers wrapped around the cherry wood handles. As she waited for the Dobermans to advance, the jolt of electricity started at the base of her skull and traveled down her spine like fire. The rush of blood and adrenaline through her veins warmed her body.

She was ready. When the dogs stopped baring their fangs and growling, she tensed in anticipation. Five years of practice with carving knives stolen from the hospital cafeteria, graduating to Shirasaya swords she'd bought online had prepared her for this moment. A calm certainty took charge. As easily as manipulating a knife and fork, she would harness her weapons as tools of destruction.

The smarter Doberman took a few steps back colliding with the trunk of a pine tree and sat down on his haunches to watch developments. The impulsive one leaped at her, fangs bared. She kicked him away. He tumbled into a flowerbed head over haunch. Even before he ceased tumbling, he leapt up and fled toward the house as if his paws were on fire. From her left a large dark shape burst into view heading straight for her in long loping strides reminding her of the movements of a big cat on some distant savannah as it chased after prey. When it lifted its head, and stared straight into her eyes, she fell back in disgust, pity, and alarm. She had only half a minute for the truth to sink in, for her brain to catch up with the sight before her eyes.

It was male, as big as a fully-grown jaguar with the sleek muscled body of a Doberman, black as midnight from head to paws. The sleek body, short hair coat of black fur, cropped ears and cropped tail were true to the Doberman breed, while its composure and curiosity reminded her of something completely different. He stood watching her from a distance, assessing her as she was assessing him. She kept trying to rationalize what she was seeing. Doberman Pinchers were bred to protect the family and the home. Doberman Pinchers were intelligent and loving family dogs. It was rare for Dobermans to attack humans.

But this creature wasn't all Dobie. The body and the head looked like a Dobie, but it was far bigger than any Doberman she'd ever seen. Most stood less than three feet at the withers. This animal stood twice as tall and twice as long, the head nearly on a level with her own. The eyes, oh god the eyes, she made herself look into those eyes without flinching and had to accept the reality.

There was no time to do otherwise. Like a trapped animal, she knew in a matter of seconds one of them would be dead. By looking directly into its eyes, she was challenging his territory. She nourished a slim hope that there was still a bit of humanity in him. She kept her eyes on him watching for signs of attack. She kept going back to his eyes: the irises a brilliant green, the pupils large and dark. Her temperature dropped. An icy prickling began at the top of her head and plunged down her spine. She forced the name from her throat, her muscles tensing prepared for the savagery of his assault. At first all that came out of her throat was a croak. She tried again and managed to say his name, "Travis."

He cocked his noble head and took a step backward appraising her thoughtfully. Just for a second, she looked away flinching at the sight of him, unnatural, wrong, so wrong. And as if he read her thoughts, she saw in his eyes shame and fury. He lunged, his teeth only inches from her head. The blood from his slashed throat sprayed out in an arc and lay in droplets upon the ground. A drop of his blood landed in her eye. She blinked the spreading darkness away waiting for the other two to attack. She resisted the urge to wipe the blood away. They would charge. Yes, they would charge, because these dogs had been bred to attack and the smell of blood would encourage them.

The cautious one backed up and up and up and finally turned and ran. The other one, the one she'd kicked earlier, watching from a safe distance with his hind quarters quivering looked at Travis where he lay, the dogs demeanor dismissive. The Doberman fled around the corner of the house. It wasn't until the next day, she found the Dobermans hiding in their kennel.

Sickened by what she'd done, she tried to find excuses for herself. She had none. Then her treacherous memory tried to make sense of it all. Had she really seen Travis close his eyes before he lunged. In a split second, his fury changed to exaltation as if he were throwing himself off a cliff. Had he wanted to die? Instead of throwing all his mighty weight onto her body pinning her to the ground, his jaws missed her head by an inch. She felt his hot breath on her face. She felt the heat of his body as he passed. There had been no tearing of her flesh or clawing of her shoulders. And he'd closed his eyes at the end. Had he closed his eyes at the end?

Acacia with her own limbs quivering managed to stand on her feet. For the longest time, her eyes refused to see. She waited for peace to return. She closed her eyes and whispered the prayer, at first under her breath, then after several repetitions in a normal voice feeling her muscles relax and her breathing slow, "As the earth nurtures us. As the sun shines down upon us. As you sleep beside us. We are safe. We are warm. As you show us the way. We are at peace. We are brave. Dear one. Brave one. We take the next step. And when our job is done, we will rest beside you. We will feel your warmth. And peace will come to us all."

Feeling her muscles relax and peace return, Acacia stood up, shook the dirt from her pants, and began walking around the periphery of the grounds keeping to the groomed trees until she was confident there was no one about, her legs and arms still quivering from the threat. Parts of her were revolted by what she had done. She had had no choice. She had made a promise to Tessa to go on living and never give in or give up. Her neck and forehead were dripping with sweat. She used the hem of her shirt to wipe the sweat off her forehead and out of her eyes. She tasted tears and realized she'd been crying.

A memory broke upon her like a sparkler, vivid and blinding. It had been a beautiful autumn day. Her mother and father were there, sitting across the picnic table from their guests. Everyone had a drink, bottles of beer or glasses of wine. The dogs were circling the picnic table in the hopes of getting the scraps of food left on the plates. Travis Wendall Hunter had a beautiful Rottweiler and his brother Terence had two mixed breed collies. Their Golden Retriever had recently passed away. And she was in her tree house lying on her stomach, quietly listening, and watching the adults, mourning her dog and afraid her mother would notice her and send her to bed.

The twins, Travis and Terence Hunter, were sitting on the other side of the picnic table. Between them sat Terence's wife Sally. The sun was setting behind the ridge. She heard her father say in his irreverent way, "You look like a gigantic cream filled cookie, beautiful and delicious." Everyone laughed, Travis laughing the loudest. There they sat, the Hunter brothers, two gorgeous beautiful black men, gentle and kind, loving and just. It had been a long time ago, a long, long time ago. The brothers looked enormous towering above everyone. They were even taller than her father. Instinctively, the brothers reached around Sally and hugged her close and smiled. Everyone joined in the laughter.

Then Acacia saw a different Terence. It had been so dark and cold. She heard Tessa's wise sweet voice echoing in her head, "Color has no meaning in the dark." Once she thought of one of them, all the voices began to clamor for her attention:

"No. Don't go there. I see others like us, thousands."

"Tread carefully."

"Hell no. Save yourself."

"Memory adjourned. Go with Plan B."

"What about the little ones?"

The softest voice overrode them all, "Let her decide."

468

Keeping an eye out for the other dog, Acacia looked up at the monstrosity. It wasn't a home. It wasn't warm and cozy and tasteful. Instead the mansion reminded her of an overweight lumpy lighthouse with a cupola at the top and a vulture for a weather vane. Then she realized the wings of the bird represented the capital letter V for Violet. What kind of architect would put his name to such a laughable piece of folly? As she circled the mansion searching for a way inside, she could hear waves breaking against the shore down below and in this wilderness of green marveled at man's ingenuity.

How did she keep such rare plants alive in such an inhospitable place? The wall must shelter the plants from the constant wind. But what about in the winter? Did she uproot the plants and trees in the winter? Winter. Violet Winter and her vulture house. We used to call her, Violet Winter. We used to get a kick out of calling her Violent instead of Violet.

Until the day Tessa told us to stop with our childish name calling and explained why, "I know the likes of them folks. I've known them all my life. I was born in Mississippi and the Ingolstadt family has owned me since I was born."

Only Ana had the nerve to interrupt Tessa, "That can't be. Slavery was abolished in 1865."

"Do I interrupt you when you're talking? You want to hear my story or not?" Tessa asked. Everyone told Ana to hush up, she apologized, and Tessa continued with her story, "My first owner was Conrad Huber. He was a liar, a cheat, and a very stupid cruel man. He made enemies wherever he went. He'd already pissed off his father, enough so his father Kasper disinherited him and gave the shop in Ingolstadt to Conrad's sister Anke. In a tiff, Conrad immigrated to America, set himself up in Mississippi as a nobleman and called himself Ingolstadt. Most of the plantation owners bought his lies about being a nobleman, gave him credit, and sold him slaves with the promise of a huge return at the end of the season. A year went by and he still hadn't paid a dime to anyone.

When they came for their money and their property, he's already sniffed the wind and knew he was in trouble, so he hightailed it back home to Ingolstadt taking his sorry-ass- lazy-no-good wife and his son with him and kidnapped me and my mama too. My mama told me I was a year old when we arrived in Ingolstadt. I don't remember anything about Ingolstadt, because I was five when we returned to Mississippi.

My mama told me Anke Huber was one fine smart woman and she and her husband sent Conrad packing. He tried to get work in Ingolstadt, but everybody knew he was a liar and a cheat. He died in prison and his sorry-ass-lazy-no-good widow, and only son Berthold, a year younger than me, returned to America taking us back with them. Conrad didn't own us anymore, because of the emancipation of the slaves, but we might as well have been slaves, for all the good our freedom did for me and my mama. My mama didn't know how to read, and I wasn't permitted to read.

Conrad and his sorry-ass-lazy-no-good wife told us the north lost the war and we were still his slaves. We only learned about the Reconstruction Act of 1872 and our right to vote during our passage home on the ship. After some words between my mama and the widow, the widow agreed to pay my mama twice a week. The widow's parents preferred to hire a cook and a maid when they needed to impress someone and didn't want anything to do with us or her. Even though we were poor, we especially enjoyed the come-down of the sorry-ass-lazy-no-good widow. Her cabin was just as mean as ours and we didn't feel a lick of sympathy for her.

She was so lazy, she didn't even care that there were dirty nappies all over the cabin and outside the house reeking in the noonday sun, for anyone to see. You had to hold your nose just to go inside. We knew that was the reason the widow's penny-pinching family let her live in the old cabin in the backwoods, because even though they were as mean as her, they had aspirations to one day move up the ladder.

So, we stayed in the old slave quarters and twice a week walked down the lane to the filthy Ingolstadt cabin. When we arrived, the widow would leave and take Berthold to town. Once they were good and gone, my mother would put on her old dress, tie a rag around the lower half of her face to protect her nose and mouth from the stench, slip a pair of old gloves on her hands and work from sunrise to sunset clearing away rotten food, the widow's bloody napkins, and all the other filth a human being is capable of accumulating. And when I was six years old, I insisted on helping my mother.

Conrad's widow was a mean-spirited stupid woman and so was everybody in her family except for Berthold. Me and Berthold got along fine until the widow and her family pointed out he was white, and I was black, well mulatto. Then Berthold met a rich widow from Maryland in 1884 and moved us all up to her fine house. It was in Maryland I learned to read and write. There was a teacher who lived in a small cottage on the rich widow's property and she secretly taught me to read.

My mama died in 1887 when I was twenty-three years old. As soon as she was buried, I took off for Chicago. I heard Conrad's sorry-ass-lazy-no-good mother died a few weeks later. When Berthold's son Victor needed a nanny, Berthold hired a Pinkerton detective to find me. I told the Ingolstadt family to go to hell.

A year later, Victor came to my house and asked politely if he could come in. I was flabbergasted. He sat on my living room couch with his hat in his lap and told me two amazing things. The first amazing thing, which I'd already figured out for myself, was that Conrad was my father. Berthold and I had already come to that conclusion by the time we were ten years old. We kept our knowledge of the family secret to ourselves. Of course, his sorry-ass-lazy-no-good mother had no clue. Well, she didn't have a clue about much of anything. She was as dumb as a box of rocks.

The second amazing thing Victor told me was that my weasel of a father, Conrad Huber accepted money from an apothecary in Ingolstadt and the apothecary would offer me little cups of his new elixirs then test my reaction to the drugs. It did not surprise me that an old white man would test his poisons on a two-year-old black child. No surprise at all. Then he told me, the apothecary happened to be his wife's grandfather. No surprise there either – like meets like. And those creatures find each other, wed, and have more like themselves.

And I said to him, so what? And he said to me, you are my aunt and as my aunt you are entitled to half the Huber inheritance. Anke Huber, the smart woman she was, had already figured out I was Conrad's child. When Anke died, she left a trust fund for me. Because the lawyers couldn't find me, they located Victor and asked him to search for me. He handed over the will and the information about my trust fund, then had the nerve to insist I come with him to Ingolstadt and be his daughter's nanny. It was 1936. I told him to go to hell. Then he asked if he could take some of my blood and I told him to get on the express elevator and go straight to hell or I'd kick his ass all the way to the curb.

When I woke up the next morning and went outside to collect my newspaper, there was a basket on my stoop and a little baby girl wrapped in blankets inside. There was a note from Victor Ingolstadt and in it he begged me to take care of his daughter while he was away, that his wife had died in childbirth, that he must return to Bavaria and take over the shop, and he had no one else to care for his daughter. So, instead of taking the child to the authorities and giving them Victor's note, I made the biggest mistake of my life and kept her with me. For ten years, I treated her like my own child. I changed her diapers. I rocked her to sleep. I read to her and I learned to love her as my own. Then out of the blue, Victor returned shortly after the war and took her from me.

In 1947, some men in suits came to my door and started interrogating me about Victor Ingolstadt. I figured from their questions, Victor had probably done something very, very bad. After all, he was the grandson of a sorry-ass-lazy-no-good grandmother and a liar-and-cheat grandfather. I was lucky. I may have had that liar-and-cheat as a father, but my mother's family were all hardworking, upright, good Christian people. I bless my mother and her family every day, giving thanks that I am nothing like the Huber/Ingolstadt people. A year later, I read in the paper that Victor Ingolstadt had been accused of war crimes by a victim of the Holocaust who recognized him on the streets of Portland in the state of Oregon.

Victor's daughter was born an Ingolstadt and told me many times over the years, even at a very young age, she would never be someone's slave or beholding to any man. Then she marries Walter Mason Winter and even if she loves her father fiercely, she gives up his name and calls herself Violet Winter, not Violet Euphemia Winter or Effie Winter or Euphemia Winter, but Violet Winter. Why? Think about it for a moment. Why would a woman want to be associated with something cold and cruel?

Well, why not?

Women's names throughout the ages have been a way to keep women docile and manageable. Think about women's names – most of their names end in an a or an e. The names sound soft and sexy, just the way men want women to be. Also, women are named for flowers which are fragile and pretty. So, calling her Violent Winter only reinforces her belief that she is unique, gifted, and destined for greatness. In her mind, every human on earth would do anything to remain young and beautiful, and most of all, to never fear death again. She believes the world of medicine will recognize her greatness, canonize her, and future generations will worship her as a scientific genius. What she doesn't realize is that if she were to achieve her wishes, Earth would not be able to sustain the burden of all the immortals polluting and raping the planet."

Acacia stopped in her tracks and held her head. She tried humming to keep herself from remembering any more. The images kept coming anyway and she shouted at them, "No more. Go away. Leave me alone." One voice refused to obey. That voice belonged to the dead. She'd been dead a long time. Yet Acacia couldn't stop the next memory from playing out in her head. For the first time in many days as we – Violet Winter's test subjects – lay waiting for the orderlies to rescue us from the crawl space and return us to our hospital beds, Tessa in her quiet assured way spoke her thoughts aloud giving us the courage and strength to carry on.

Most of us knew her stories were about distracting us and keeping our spirits up. This time though, she was much more open about her past. It was as if she sensed a change in the air, that perhaps time was no longer on her side. Her explanation for Violet's delight in being thought of as cold and cruel were just a prelude for a more ambitious plan. As a quiet assured woman, Tessa rarely spoke. Yet on that day she kept on talking, warning, encouraging us with an urgency we could no longer ignore. She revealed secrets about herself, not because she sought our pity, but because she wanted to remind us that in the world today there were all types of slavery going on right under people's noses and people had to push back against this new brand of tyranny.

And then the voice Acacia dreaded to hear asked the question on all of their minds, her voice carrying all the way from the far end of that dark and damp place asking. "Ms. Mourning Dove, if your story is true, which I have no doubt it is true, because you are a woman of integrity and wisdom, then that means you are one hundred and forty years old. How can that be?"

"Yes. I am one hundred and forty years old. And I do not know how it can be. At the age of one hundred, I had to conclude I wasn't like other people. My neighbors assumed I was in my early sixties. I've seen black people like myself who appear much younger than their actual age and assumed I was also gifted in that way. But then I got to talking to my neighbors and learned they suffered from diabetes, arthritis, all sorts of age related illnesses. At the age of sixty, I felt the same inside as I did when I was ten years old.

One day I was in the classroom and a student dropped off some computers. They were the big old heavy ones from back in the 1980s. I picked one up and carried it over to the other side of the classroom just as I would have at home. Too me it weighed no more than a napkin.

When I turned around the students looked at me as if I had sprouted wings. After that day, I was more careful to hide my strength and agility from people. Sadly, for I did love to teach, I eventually concluded I would be safer retiring and living quietly alone.

When I turned one hundred, I knew I couldn't continue to live in the same neighborhood. Renters come and go, but some of them stick around living their whole lives in the same apartment. I was starting to get funny looks from the woman across the hall and knew I had to do something soon. Violet came up with the idea. I know now it was the biggest mistake of my life to trust her. She helped me set fire to my bedroom. We left a body behind, a body Violet chose, the right age and race and height. As a scientist, she has the means of finding someone suitable for my age and genetics.

No one was the wiser. Since I never married or wished to marry and have no children, there is no one alive to question my death or demand answers about my disappearance. It is Violet's belief I am her greatest asset. Well, that might have been so when I was in Violet's care, but no longer. Now there is a woman just as stupid and lazy as my former mistress in possession of me and in charge of us all and I wouldn't bet on our chances of getting out of this situation alive. I may be one hundred and forty years old, but I'm not invincible. I will die someday. And unlike the rest of you, I am looking forward to that day."

"Now I understand what you meant earlier about being a slave all your life," the voice whispered. "You are a remarkable woman and if I had just an ounce of your courage and wisdom, I would think myself lucky."

"You do. We all do," Tessa said. "And it's time for us to go. Little one, I know you can do this, you figured out the handcuffs and leg irons. It was very clever of you to come up with the codes. And then you amazed us even more when you and Terence found the weak spot in the foundation and removed what you could. The gap is too small for Terence to squeeze through, but not for you or me and not for some of the others.

So, now it's time for us to crawl through the hole and see what's on the other side. I know you don't want to leave Terence, but Terence wants you to go and find help. He's too big to fit through the gap. We can help him by getting out and finding a way to open the trapdoor. I know you're scared, but you can do this. Come now little one. You can do it. Watch me. I'll go first."

And Acacia heard the voice of the dead woman say, "I'll be right behind you Minty Breath. Come on, we can do this together. The three musketeers. All for one and one for all." The voice brought back the face. And the face brought back the memories of her parents, of her home, and the last time she and her Aunt had been in the sunlight together. Aunt Connie had recognized her in the backseat of Leland's car and had refused to leave her side. Aunt Connie had fought them all: Leland Ansel, Ray Millhouse, and Violet Winter.

And that last terrible memory came to her without warning, the memory of Tessa in the lead crawling through the gap in the foundation and her following Tessa with her Aunt Connie in the rear rubbing her leg and encouraging her to move forward. And then the fall into the root cellar and the light and looking up and seeing an old door and a dirty window in the door. Then she saw thick roots growing on the walls, water dripping between the cracks in the stones, the altar, and finally the lead coffin. And her Aunt Connie delighted with the lead coffin insists we all help push the lid off the coffin. And we do. Then she sees the dead bunny lying on the alter near the coffin and at the same time hears a rustling noise and suddenly something is coming out of the coffin.

A rush of panic surged through her body and feeling the blood rush from her head to her toes, she dropped to the ground on all fours. Slowly the memory faded. In the background she could hear the ocean waves breaking on the distant shore and the gentle wind rustling the leaves of the trees in the Lighthouse Garden. She rose to her feet and looked around the grounds. The Doberman Pinchers were nowhere to be seen. She resumed her investigation of the property, determined to stay on task and get the job done.

Two hours later after searching the house which had eight bedrooms, five bathrooms, tiled floors and cedar wooden hallways, antique glass doorknobs, copper faucets and gleaming kitchen equipment, Acacia climbed the circular stairs all the way to the cupola and stood in the center of the room to admire the view. Later that evening, she found a study with an impressive desk that would have taken four men to lift. The desk had been placed in the corner of the room facing a series of paneled windows along the west and north facing walls. The windows stretched from the vaulted ceiling to the cedar floorboards. They also provided a breathtaking vista of the promontory and the ocean beyond.

Acacia crossed to the fireplace near the desk and on the mantel, she looked up at the oil painting of a man who obviously believed himself to be the "picture" of respectability. She giggled at her pun. His eyes were stern, yet his lips made a pretense at smiling. It astonished Acacia to think that anyone would choose to look that ridiculous for eternity. "Make up your mind old man," she shouted up at him. "You don't fool me. You're a low-life-snake-in-the-grass not an Ingolstadt."

As she passed the coffee table, she saw a familiar face and grabbed the silver framed picture and walked over to the French doors and threw the picture on the hardwood floor stomping on the face repeatedly. With the glossy photograph free of the glass, she tore the picture into tiny pieces and threw them in the air like confetti. Then she carefully unlocked the French doors and walked outside.

At the far end of the property near the sandstone wall, she discovered a separate garden with Greek statues in several spots surrounded by benches. She jumped on one of the benches and looked to her right seeing the twin promontory where her Toyota was still parked. Then she turned to the left and noticed how the ten-foot wall seemed to undulate rather than run parallel with the hillside. It was too regimented, too linear to be a natural contour of the promontory.

Obviously, a human mind bent on perfection had created and constructed the wall; yet, that mind purposely messed up the left-hand side. She stepped back to get a good look at the top of the wall, her eye traveling along its surface realizing that the left-hand side of the wall was fatter than the right-hand side. Instead of being four feet wide, the left-hand side was twice the size. The wall as far as the eye could see ran around the entire property and shut out the spectacular view of the sea as if the concrete blocks and sandstone façade as well as the black obsidian at the base held the sea at bay, preventing the ocean waves from bursting through the wall and taking back the garden, the Greek statues, and the pond.

Acacia paused by the pond to watch the sturgeon swim by. There were at least five in the pond gliding past each other silently. She knelt on the artfully placed slap of granite jutting out over the water and watched them swim in circles. That's all sturgeon can do in this prison – swim in circles, eating, sleeping, defecating, and when lucky screwing each other. Eighty years, or maybe, as much as a century of circling the edges of their world, in the same water, with the same sky above them, endlessly circling.

476

Here in this haven with the trees as shelter from the cold biting wind off the ocean, Acacia thought she heard a cry for help. She wandered toward the bulging wall. The stone was cold and smooth reminding her of the memorial. Only this memorial was a sterile copy without the names that would have given it purpose.

In the cavity where an artist had hung an embossed metal piece of art taller than herself, she discovered when she rapped on the artwork something heavy was on the other side and realized the artwork hid a heavy steel vaulted door. Embossed on the door was the figure of a woman riding a seashell. The woman's naked body, her hair cascading down her left shoulder, the ends modestly covering her pubic area reminded Acacia of a painting she had seen a long time ago. The woman riding the seashell had peepholes for eyes. Why?

As Acacia leaned in closer she realized the mouth was just an indentation, not a real hole. Then an impatient voice inside her head said, "Oh, for god sakes people, it's a copy of the painting by Sandro Botticelli called the Birth of Venus."

When Acacia put her ear to the door, she thought she heard noises coming from inside the wall. That was impossible. The door was just decoration. How could someone fit inside the wall? Yet she took a deep breath as if she planned to dive inside as she would dive into a cold ocean. She searched for a doorknob or way to open it. Then she heard the sound again and the sound was indeed coming from inside the wall. She pushed on the door and jiggled the artwork. Nothing happened. Then she noticed another cavity to her right, a small cavity not very deep. Inside was a keypad and beneath it on the bottom of the keypad was a place to insert a key.

On the other side of the door, she heard several heavy thuds as if someone were using a battering ram to break down the door. She searched for a key. There must be some sort of key. She heard metal grating on metal and realized the eyes of the face embossed on the front piece of the door were opening. She stepped back with the hairs on her neck stiffening in disbelief. A wild eye with a sapphire iris looked out at her from the left eye hole. Then lips appeared at the nose hole.

A man's voice sounding desperate asked her, "Is there anyone out there?"

She heard another voice shouting from somewhere beyond the sapphire iris and his response as he said, "Shut up you old bat," then turning his attention back to her, he said. "I see you there. I see your shape. Are you one of the maids? Do you speak English? Habla Anglais? Help me. The damned door's shut, and I'm locked inside. You've got to go fetch help. My baby has the key. Go find my baby."

"Your baby?" Acacia asked pressing herself closer to the Botticelli Door.

"Yes. My little girl. She must be there somewhere. She can't have gone far. Doggies scare her. She wouldn't go out the door not with the doggies patrolling the yard. She must be inside the house. Go get her. She'll have the key. If you find her tell her to come back to Uncle Ray, tell her Uncle Ray isn't mad."

"Uncle Ray?" Acacia asked in disbelief and moved closer to the door. "You mean you're Ray Millhouse?"

"How did you?"

Without a moment's hesitation Acacia struck. She heard his savage screaming, a screaming that included rage as well as unbelievable pain. The eye was a very tender area. And to have a knife jabbed into the eye can be excruciating she imagined. She returned to her seat by the pond and listened to the screams subside becoming mere sobs. A momentary pity overwhelmed her. Poor creature. Poor, poor, creature. No. Stop it. That's what we females always do – strike back in defense and then feel sorry later.

"Please let me out," she heard him beg. "I've made a mess of my life and I'm sorry. You won't leave me here? You aren't made that way. Don't forget me? Don't leave me here to die alone."

Acacia walked back to the door and leaned against the cold metal feeling the coldness seeping into her shoulder. The cold felt good. And then she said, "We all die alone, you fucking-idiot. Even conjoined twins die alone. Never mind the pity party dumb-ass. I thought I heard another voice. Is Dr. Winter in there with you?"

There was a moment of silence and then his voice less robust answered her, "Yes. She's here. She's hurt. We're both hurt. There's so much blood. I feel so cold."

"Don't you worry, Uncle Ray, I'll never forget you."

"Say again?"

"Don't you remember me Uncle Ray? I remember you. I'm sad you've forgotten me already."

"I'm not an uncle."

"I know. But that's what you do; you pervert an honorable family position into something sick and twisted. We all know you're not an uncle or a brother or a son. You're not even a man, you're a sick perverted scum sucking cockroach that needs to be exterminated from the face of the earth. Isn't that right Uncle Ray?"

"I don't know you. I'm trying to think. God. It hurts."

"Why do people ask for God's help all the time? You should be crying out my name. If you remember my name, I might think about letting you out."

Acacia returned to the pond to contemplate the moon rising above the ocean's horizon. What a magnificent sight. She heard a faint moan that rose to a crescendo, "Oh my God! You're killing me. Stop, stop. Let me rest."

Ray Millhouse screamed, "Listen you fat old cow, we don't have time for your blubbering. She says if we can remember her name, she'll let us out."

"Help me up, damned you," she said, gone were the clipped patrician tones of earlier, now she sounded like a screeching whiny brat. "Oh, god, oh, god, just a few more steps. Hold on, we're almost there. Oh god, oh god. Set me down, you moron. Set me down, now! I can give you the code, but you must promise to help me out of here. You must press the buttons on the keypad and then turn the key to the left. Are you listening?"

"There isn't any fucking key. What the hell are you talking about you old smelly bat? Did you hear me? There is no key."

"It must be on the other side. Myrtle, oh no, she calls herself Farrah now, Farrah must have left the key in the outside lock."

In the peaceful silence, Acacia sat down by the pond to watch the sturgeon and wait for someone to say her name. A song popped into her head, the one back in Brookings, "Where have all the phone booths gone? Long time passing…" She tried to stifle the shout of laughter and was unsuccessfully. It bubbled up from her stomach and burst out of her throat like a fog horn, then returned to her from the sandstone wall.

She heard Ray with his lips pressed against the nose hole say, "It's Lindsey, right? My pretty Lindsey. Yes?"

"Nope," Acacia said. "You'd better hurry up. It's getting cold out here and I'm thinking of going home."

The woman screamed and said in disbelief. "Kallan? Is that you Kallan?" When the woman realized the rendition of the name would not produce the desired results, she tried another tactic, "Oh Kallan honey. Where have you been? I've been looking everywhere for you. I've been sick with worry. Mona said masked men came into the cabin and killed the orderlies than hit her on the head. She said she woke up and found the cabin on fire and you were gone."

Overriding the woman's voice, Ray shouted out, "It's Dilly! You see. I remember! Oh, sweet dill. Kallan Dilys Fremantle. Yes. Yes. That's your name."

They had her name wrong, all wrong. Freaks. Unnatural freaks. The impossible had happened and they still had no idea. Acacia watched the whiteness spread across the ocean floor. It wasn't sinking. No. The whiteness rose up out of the water. She waited and watched in wonder. What a sight. No one could take away the beauty. There before her was real beauty. No one could doubt its grandeur. She watched the moon and the moon showed her the way. She could see the path taking shape on the water and above it the sky drawn by a magician's hand. The moon a perfect circle. A moon watching over her.

In one fluid motion she rose to her feet and walked toward the door. It was then she saw the key lying on the ground. She picked up the key and slipped it in her pocket. As she stood near the door, she said, "You're not fit to lick Tessa's boots, not fit to walk the earth, not fit to even be in hell. You're an abomination. Tell me Huber the goober, how much food and water do you have inside there? Hum? Gandhi survived twenty-one days without food. The body can survive one hundred hours without water, but no more than that. Let's test the experts and see what happens. I have all the time in the world, all the time in the world."

"How dare you walk away from me, you ungrateful child," Dr. Violet Winter said ending her complaint with an earsplitting scream, the sound hurting even Acacia's ears and she was on the other side of the door. As Acacia wandered down the path admiring the flowers, she heard Violet say, "Come back. Don't you dare leave me like this. I've broken my leg. I'm in pain. Kallan! I'm begging you. Kallan, come back."

The voice faded into the background of other noises: the ocean crashing against the waves, the sound of traffic on the scenic highway, and seagulls calling to each other. Acacia lifted her head toward the sky and smiled. It was going to be a very good day.

The kitchen was pristine, not a cup or plate out of order. The equipment gleamed and hummed. Everything in its place just the way the Huber goober liked it. She could pretend to be Mona. She knew enough about the Butcher Queen to carry it off. How long would she have to pretend to be Mona? It might take a month or maybe a year, well, a month for sure. Violet was tough. The truly nasty ones usually are – as tough as beef jerky and just as gross. Acacia stepped outside and looked around. Then she remembered Travis. She'd have to do something about Travis. She didn't want anyone looking at him like he was a freak, freeze drying his body and studying him until the end of time. He deserved a dignified memorial, some peaceful place to rest.

And what about the Dobermans? She'd have to feed and water them and make sure they were safely in their kennel. It took her most of the night to finish her chores. She found a huge furnace in the basement, just like the ones undertakers use in funeral homes for disposing of the dead. She could fit a horse inside this one. Didn't any one question Dr. Winter's choice in household appliances? It took her nearly an hour to lift and drag Travis down to the furnace. In the closet marked supplies, she found a gurney. It took her another age to figure out how to lift him onto the gurney and a rat's ass time to figure out how the hell to work the motherfucking damn controls.

By the time Acacia was finished her face was a sloppy mess of tears and snot. Every thirty minutes she would run downstairs to see if the furnace was off. When it finally shut down, she had to wait for the inside to cool before opening the glass door and scooping Travis Wendall Hunter's ashes into a big zip lock bag. She found the perfect container – a huge cherry wood box filled with Cuban cigars. She threw the cigars in the trash and put Travis in the box. The remains which were too big to burn – his skull and larger bones – she placed in a medium sized steamer trunk. The trunk had been kept in the study as a decorative piece. Then after a nap, she carried the steamer trunk filled with Travis down to the public beach.

The moon guided her steps as she picked her way down the rocky staircase while the crashing waves hitting the shoreline muffled the thumping of the trunk as it hit the stone steps. By the time she was on the sandy beach, she was so tired she had only enough energy to drag the steamer trunk a few feet, rest a bit, then do it all over again. Her luck held when she discovered a boat on the dock. It wasn't fancy. It lacked the flash of Violet Winter's lifestyle but looked seaworthy. Hot wiring boats couldn't be much more difficult than hot wiring cars. She stayed close to the coastline and picked her spot carefully. It took all her strength to throw the trunk over the side of the boat. Since she'd never been particularly religious, she gave Travis Wendall Hunter a mental kiss, said a quick good-bye, and sent him on hopefully to a better place.

After her chores were done, she ran up the stone staircase, down the road, up the drive and into the house. She took the longest and the hottest shower of her life. Wearing one of the bathrobes hanging on the door, Acacia poured herself a tall glass of wine and stepped outside. As she paused to sneer at the fake Lighthouse, a great battle was going on inside her head. It felt as if she wore an iron crown and the iron crown was getting smaller and smaller digging into the flesh of her forehead, into her ears, squeezing the back of her head. She fell to the ground and blissful darkness descended.

25

My body drained, I lifted myself off the floor and looked around the room. I was in Violet Winter's study. The room was a mess, as if a hurricane had blown through and laid waste to everything. The expensive Persian carpet was covered in debris. Every book which had been carefully set upon the mahogany shelves had been yanked out one by one and either dumped on the ground nearby or thrown across the room. Some of the tomes were oversized coffee table books, others heavy medical books, and still others a series of encyclopedias. I noticed how the rolling ladder attached to the last remaining set of books on the top shelf hung precariously like a drunken uncle on Thanksgiving Day barely attached to the structure, as if someone had tried unsuccessfully to pull the ladder out of its sockets.

But that someone had had the necessary strength born of an all-consuming rage to toss each and every book around the room no matter how heavy or clumsy the material. There were piles of books littering the study, smaller ones thrown clear across the room, like missiles aimed at their targets. Small knick-knacks had been toppled like bowling pins, vases made of crystal had been smashed into shards of dangerous glass, rare clay pots were cracked lying on their sides like wounded soldiers, while pictures lay askew on the wall or in defeat had fallen to the floor with their protective armor of glass wounded with a savage horde of cuts. Even the chandelier dangling from the high ceiling had not escaped the fury of the vandal. The vandal had tossed enough books at the teardrop crystals to leave only a few still hanging from their delicate golden chains.

Between the twin book shelves stood a window which provided a view of the left side of the property, the side few guests saw where I could see beyond the manicured green lawn a series of magnificent pine trees, blue spruce, and maples. The trees cut out the noise from the constant traffic on the ocean highway and provided enough privacy to fool the residents into thinking they were miles away from civilization. As a typical curious human who wanted to see more, I walked up to the window, hearing the crunching sound of broken glass underfoot and leaned out the empty space where glass had once been to get a better look.

I saw a driveway made of crushed seashells which circled back to the front of the house. It must be where the vendors and guests parked to unload packages, groceries, or heavy merchandize. The window had been smashed to smithereens. All the glass in the center of the window littered the floor at my feet. The cool breeze blew past me and into the room.

I turned back to face the room and examined the destruction in awe and wonder.

The velvet couches facing the fireplace were torn to shreds and the culprits, a set of stainless steel butcher knifes were lying on the coffee table between them. The pillows which had been decoratively arranged on the velvet couches were torn to ribbons, their cotton stuffing dumped on the floor. Containers filled with rare plants had been overturned and the soil ground into the Persian carpet. A smell of burning led me to a grotesque sight behind the desk where someone had carefully arranged a stack of papers and what looked like hair from several combs and brushes making the whole a funeral pyre. That person had attempted to set the pyre alight, but from the evidence the vandal had given up in frustration. The room still reeked even with the cleansing breeze from the smashed window.

As I moved toward the French doors which allowed the viewer to admire the beautiful garden with its Greek statues and pond swimming with fish and beyond the garden the sight of the Pacific Ocean in all its glory, something unusual caught my eye. I paused with my hand reaching out to open the door and looked up at what had caught my eye feeling stunned surprise and disgust. I wasn't disgusted with the trespasser, but with the image created by the painter. The name Victor Ingolstadt popped into my head. But why? I'd never personally met the man, yet, the trespasser had known him and hated him enough to tear at his face with what looked like bare claws.

Impossible. I looked down at my hands. My fingernails looked alien to me. They were perfection. Not so much as a hang nail marred their perfection. Someone had manicured my long-tapered nails and polished them with a glossy red paint. Obviously, my fingernails couldn't have been the weapons which had destroyed the face of Victor Ingolstadt. Instead of being upset with the mess, I admired my nails recognizing Frankie's handiwork. She must have taken me with her on a girls' outing and insisted I have my nails done. I stepped closer to the painting and squinted up at the slash marks which had ripped through the face and along the body trying to wrap my head around the idea of stainless steel knifes doing so much damage.

Unable to stand the smell or the sight of the room, I stumbled out and shut the door behind me. My headache gone, I wandered through the dark house and listened to the sound of the sea beyond the walls. I thought I heard someone calling to me from outside and, so I went out to investigate. On the clipped green lawn, I stood and stared up at the gigantic moon resting briefly on the horizon. To my left I noticed a wall of sandstone veneer and a steel door. Trumpet Vine and Virginia Creeper grew along one end. I saw the door. It had an image embossed in the metal. I walked over to the object and traced with my forefinger the outline of the face.

Things were crawling out of her hair, little black bugs. As I traced the image, my fingers knew them. They represented her long flowing hair, Venus, the birth of Venus. Why did people equate beauty with goodness and deformity with evil? It had to a man's fault. And just as interesting, why had women allowed men to treat them so unfairly? For centuries men maligned women and made up stories about Eve seducing Adam with an apple and witches eating babies. Why had we accepted such obvious lies? More importantly, why had men felt it necessary to malign us in the first place? Were we that scary? No. It must be jealousy. They envy us our ability to give birth. According to them, we're the furies, emotionally insatiable and untrustworthy.

I heard a child crying. Since the door was just for decoration, a piece of art in a topiary, I knew the crying must be a trick of the night. I returned to the house and the crying grew louder as I climbed the staircase to the third floor. I searched the upstairs and finally found her in the bedroom closet of one of the smaller guest bedrooms. How typical. She had curled herself up into the folds of a silk gown fingering the softness as if the touch could shield her against monsters. Her face was dirty, her legs scratched and bleeding.

I got down on my hands and knees and crawled toward her.

The only way to stop the terrified screaming was to arrange the gown over my shoulder and urge the child out of the closet. She clutched the gown under her arm, sucked her thumb furiously with her left hand and fingered the silk with her right. Once I let her loose, whenever I tried to touch her, she would flinch and draw back. In the days to come, I had to find ingenious ways to coax her out of her hiding places and then the crying would begin anew. Eventually she began to trust me enough to seek out my company. And when she followed me down the stairs dragging the gown behind her, I felt triumphant and a little bit smug. I was a child whisperer.

I took her down to the kitchen and pulled out a chair for her at the massive oak table. We chose to seat ourselves near the refrigerator and stove. She climbed up onto the chair as I poured her a glass of milk. She stopped crying. I set the milk in front of her. The sensitive membranes of my inner ears still vibrated from her shrill screams. Children had the most penetrating of voices. She couldn't drink the milk for her body still shuttered with an old terror. That terror had memories of its own. The memories infected me which I didn't care for at all. My legs grew too weak to stand. I was forced to sit down beside her.

The only activity possible when one's legs are trembling and one's hands refuse to obey the mind is to look around. I didn't want to look too closely at the house. I really didn't want to be here. If I'd had my way, I would have walked down the drive and never looked back. But the others demanded I stay and finish the job. Not yet. We're not quite finished yet, they told me. I looked around the room and noticed the copper pans hanging artfully above the stainless-steel stove. I noticed the stainless-steel refrigerator beside it. I had opened that refrigerator and found a carton of 2% milk inside which astonished me. Even though the refrigerator looked as if it could contain all the fresh produce and calcium and meats to feed a family of twelve, there had been just that pathetic carton of eggs and 2% milk.

Evidently the doctor had been serious about leaving Crescent City. Had she really intended to live in South America and work with the deformed poor? Her compensation, of course, would have been the look of dogged devotion on the faces of the patients and their mistaken belief in her as an angel sent from God. And the doctor would have had her pick of patients, people no one would miss. I dismissed the Butcher Queen. She was no longer on the agenda. Instead I studied the little girl curiously as she began to hiccup through her tears with a milk moustache above her trembling lip.

She was so pale I could see the blue veins popping out on her forehead and running amuck all over her skull. It looked as if someone had taken an electric razor to her tiny head and cut off all her hair. Her blonde eyebrows and even paler eyelashes suggested Nordic ancestry, the sort of female who would grow up with thin whitish blonde hair and blazing blue eyes. Or was I wrong, and she was really sick? Maybe the poor kid had cancer?

No. If she'd been sickly, Millhouse wouldn't have wanted her. But in order to attract the Butcher Queen's attention the child had had to have a deformity of some kind. As far as I could see, the little girl seemed normal: two good arms and legs, ten fingers and. I looked under the table. Her feet were bare. Yes. She had ten normal toes on each foot. Had Leland gone soft in his old age? What, no disfigurement? Had Winter complained? Or had Winter moved on to the average looking?

When I at last found my voice, I asked the little girl, "What's your name?"

She continued to rub the ball gown's silk skirt furiously and stare vacantly into space. I jumped when the grandfather clock in the hall chimed the hour and couldn't calm my galloping heart until the last chime. It rang loud enough to be heard on practically every floor of the house. It rang ten times, yet, the child remained in her seat, now sucking her thumb, and rocking gently back and forth. Perhaps she was in shock? She would need help. Ironic to think that my mind would instantly leap to a physician, a practitioner of medicine, someone like Winter who would want to check the pulse and the dilation of the eyes and perhaps take blood and maybe poke a few holes in the patient, in order to release the phlegm or bile or whatever they called it these days: bodily fluids, bile, pus, blood. Barbaric.

If I had my way, I'd take her straight down to the local police station and tell them I found her in the woods. No, bad idea, cops are nosey. I didn't have time to be a good citizen, I still had much more to do, many more places to go. She had to have a family somewhere. She had to belong to someone. If she had a family? She might just be an orphan. Well, that wasn't my problem. Speculating was getting me nowhere. In order to take her to her people, I needed more information, her name would be helpful.

I had a suspicion the task would be impossible. She feared me. It might take days, maybe weeks before she trusted me enough to talk. Or was I wrong about her problem having to do with trauma? Could there be another reason she wouldn't talk to me? When my legs became my own again, I struggled to my feet. Since I was in her line of sight, the child lifted her head and followed me with her eyes. I stood behind her and pretended to open the cupboard doors. I waited until she was looking elsewhere then grabbed two pots hanging from a ceiling mounted rack above my head walked behind her and began banged them together like cymbals. They clanked and clonked and clinked making such a racked the Dobermans began to whine and left the room.

The little girl remained seated still sucking her thumb and rubbing the silk gown. Not so much as a muscle twitched, not so much as a flinch or a flutter. I rehung the pots and stood with my hands on my hips and stared out the kitchen window at the beautiful Trumpet Vine growing over and down the wall. I had illegally entered the Winter property from that vine. I was trespassing. Well, I was planning on doing far worse. The child delayed my plans. Should I be mad? Why? It wasn't her fault. Ansel and Winter had kidnapped her and used her as a fucking test subject. She was the real victim here.

So. What was I to do with her now? There were services. The police would probably have an Amber Alert on her. But if I call the police, they will come and take the little girl away and ask me a bunch of impertinent questions, and they might even stumble upon the Butcher Queen's secret laboratory. Not a good idea. A few weeks wouldn't matter, just a blink in a child's life. Hunger is a powerful force. Even when insanity reigns and the desire to die are all consuming, people still have a more primitive need for the basics: shelter, food, and water. Nature is so unrelenting. How many days had passed? At this point in my life, I should have been celebrating. All I had to do was wait for a week maybe two. We, me, and the little girl, we'll wait for Leland. No. There are no more we. I am the only person in this room, in this body.

On the first day, I discovered the little girl. On the second day, I discovered incongruities in the mostly bland cream and white decorating scheme. There were these small pictures hanging from several rooms in the house, some hanging crookedly on the walls and others which clashed with the colors and décor of the room. I peeked behind one of them and discovered an intercom or the mangled remains of what used to be an intercom behind the picture. Each weirdly placed picture hid an intercom which had been ripped from the walls and bashed in with some sort of hammer or mallet. Someone, a neat freak I suppose had carefully swept and cleaned the floors and carpets hiding the evidence of their crimes against 21st century innovation, even going so far in the hall near the front door to patch over the gashes left behind and repaint the entire wall a lovely shade of Aztec Dawn.

On the third day of our stay at the Winter Resort, I called a local grocery store, Shop Mart and asked if they delivered. The man who answered was surprised by my question, "Yes of course we deliver, and Dr. Winter has been our best customer for years. We have an arrangement to deliver groceries for her once a week every Monday morning. All she does is go to our website and choose the produce she needs and any other necessities."

"Well, I'm Dr. Winter's new personal secretary. While she's in South America, she asked me to take charge of the house and pay the bills."

"Oh, that is good news. We were under the impression she planned to shut up the house and would no longer need our services."

"She decided it made more sense to have a house sitter and dog sitter all in one. The Dobie twins hate traveling."

"No problem. Ms.?"

"Miss Lawson."

"Dr. Winter didn't cancel her account, so, I don't see any problem with the delivery. All I need is confirmation. Do you have her password, Miss Lawson?"

"Her password? Where might that be? I'm sitting at her desk at this very moment."

"Didn't she tell you?"

"No. She seemed to think I could figure everything out for myself. She had an emergency surgery in LA and didn't have time to go over the household accounts, just threw the keys at me and told me to kiss the boys for her. You know her, always rushing here and there, so many irons in the fire."

"Well, I don't know where she would have left the password, but if it's any help the password is a combination of five letters and five numbers."

I was prepared. I was sitting in front of her laptop with the accounting software running. On every surface of the huge mahogany desk, I had the necessary tools I would need to fool the outside world. I had her bank statements and grocery receipts spread out in front of me. I had all her accounting books stacked up nearby. I even had her address book and the local phone book at my fingertips.

First, I tried the software searching for a ten-digit code with five numbers and five letters. It wasn't in there. I then glanced at the receipts from the grocery store. They would do me no good. Desperate, I tried the monthly statements sent out by the grocery store. Peppering the most recent statement was a shitload of numbers and letters: Universal

Product Code numbers, prices for the merchandize, and even purchase discounts for being a rich fuck. Then I found a set of digits which included five numbers and five letters. I read the numbers carefully into the receiver.

"That's it. Great. What do you need?"

With a sense of destiny at work and the hairs along my arms and my neck tingling, I read from the grocery list I'd made earlier that morning.

There was a pause, and then the man said, "I'll need your full legal name ma'am."

"Mona S. Lawson."

"And the letter S stands for?"

Suddenly my hand holding the phone began to tremble. Damned what was the bag-of-bone's middle name? A name popped into my head. Before I had a chance to speak, the manager sounding suspicious said, "Miss Lawson, perhaps I should contact Dr. Winter and get her permission for you to use her grocery account."

"Oh, don't bother her. She's so busy. And she has this fabulous new research project coming up. I would hate for her to be sidetracked by something so minor as this little household problem. My hesitation has to do with embarrassment. It's just I've always hated my middle name and don't really like to give it out to strangers. It's Silke. S. I. L. K. E. It's a Bavarian name. My mother thought it sounded so beautiful. Too bad she'd never asked what Silke meant. I've been meaning to legally change the name one day."

As I talked into the phone, I found myself shrugging helplessly as if the stupid shit was in the room and could see me acting the part of Miss Mona Silke Lawson, "You know how it is. One day turns into two and then, whoops, its three decades later. I didn't want to hurt Mom and Dad's feelings, so I waited until they passed away and then it seemed silly to go to all the trouble of sending out notices in the newspapers and paying for an attorney."

He interrupted me and said, "I hate to do this, but I must."

A coldness settled over me, "What?"

"My clerk refuses to go beyond the gates anymore. The last time he delivered groceries to the lighthouse, your dogs' nearly took a chunk out of his thigh."

"No problem. Just ring the bell and leave the groceries by the gate. I'll come get them."

"Good. We should be able to fill this order before five o'clock."

"Thank you and goodbye."

"It's been a pleasure Mrs. Lawson?"

"No. Not Mrs. It's Miss."

"Yes. My mistake, Miss Lawson."

That first week waiting and waiting in the ugly lighthouse was as boring as watching someone mow the lawn or fiddle with a vacuum cleaner. And what was worse was that the child refused to leave my side. When the scaredy-cat Doberman appeared in the kitchen one morning and on shivering legs sidled up to me, she marched over and began to pet him. We named the scaredy-cat, Stanley and the shy one, Harry. Even when I went out to fetch the Toyota and planned on being gone just ten minutes, the three of them insisted on following me out to the driveway and into the garage. I hid the Toyota because I didn't want nosey people remembering details about the rental, then telling the cops the color of the vehicle and/or the license plate number.

Obviously, the Mercedes belonged in the garage. It was typical of Violet Winter, what had been a gorgeous symbol of affluence, she had transformed into a glaring neon monstrosity choosing orchid-violet and fuchsia as the vehicle's primary colors. Was fuchsia really a color? What did it matter, the rich were different. Since most rich people call a cab when leaving town thus spending hundreds of dollars on chauffeurs or rentals, no one would question why the monster was in the garage. The shocker was walking around the side of the house and finding a crappy piece of rust and metal parked near the mudroom.

Another jolt to my heart was when I recognized the Buick. So, Ansel had given his crappy leftovers to Millhouse. I bet he dickered over the price and made Millhouse pay more than the car was worth. Then I realized the Buick was going to be a real headache. I forced myself to check the doors. The driver's side door was unlocked. Of course, there were no keys dangling from the ignition. I checked the glove compartment and the floors and the seats. No keys. Then I remembered Josh Pascula's story about locking his keys in his car five times in one year and the magnetic key box fiasco.

I spent the rest of the daylight hours with Harry close on my heels and the kid holding onto the tail of my shirt, both getting in my way as I searched the filthy rust-bucket from top to bottom in the hopes Millhouse had hidden an emergency key somewhere. The next day I looked again, this time waiting until the kid was sleeping, and the Dobie twins were locked in the kennel. With a flash light and hands covered in grease and dirt, I finally found the emergency key. I was so overjoyed I flooded the damned shitty car and had to wait an hour before trying to turn over the engine once more. In a cloud of black smoke, I got the Buick inside the garage and parked the obscenity next to the Mercedes. Beside the Mercedes, the Buick looked comical. I couldn't help but laugh and laugh. The Buick would have looked better in a crusher than in a fancy garage.

A brilliant idea came to me. Before returning to the garage, I slipped into the spare bedroom to check on the kid. She was still sleeping. I tiptoed down to the first floor and back into the garage. In the storage closet I found several cans of paint stripper and poured them over the Mercedes. And after every meal I took our leftovers out to the garage and dumped them inside the vehicles. One day the leftovers would go in the Mercedes, the next day the Buick. The kid held her noise each time we went out to the garage and watched me with blank expression.

It was on the day the groceries were delivered that I remembered the rental car parked on the public promontory a half a mile away. After doing the necessary chores, the kid and I walked across the beach and up the stairs to fetch the Toyota. Once I had parked the Toyota near the mudroom where the curious could not see it, I remembered the dealership. Of course, the dealership continued to accept the money I wired to them from Frances Margaret Stewart's personal account. Another week passed, and I had the brilliant idea to call them and make a deal to buy the car outright with cash. They accepted my offer and mailed the documents to my new post office box in Brookings.

The child and I never went near the Botticelli Door or the pond again. Instead we chose to play in the shelter of the house near the drive and the gate. The gown disappeared. She seemed to have accepted me as someone she could trust. The beauty of children. Their innocence and trusting natures. She was rather needy, but that was understandable. I tried to give her what I could, but that part of me had atrophied a long time ago. Logically, I knew she couldn't flourish with someone like me. And besides I didn't have the energy or will to learn her language. The day she started doing her finger thing at me made me realize we were not meant to be together.

26

It was nearly dark by the time Zak pulled up to the Woolly Man Bar & Grill. There were still a few vehicles in the lot: a familiar Volkswagen owned by Andy and Luke's ugly truck beside his mother's old Bronco. On their way home, they stopped in Paris, Nevada to pick up Luke's truck. While waiting impatiently, Zak watched in ever mounding fury as Luke fussed over the ugly monster. Luke didn't trust the dinosaur to turn over, so Zak was forced to park his Camaro behind the truck, wait for the truck to come to life, and then follow Luke home at a boring fifty-five miles per hour, since that was the fastest the truck could go without falling apart.

Obviously, even after a couple of days sunning itself on the side of a busy highway, no one had bothered to tow or steal the piece of crap; and why would they anyway, since it was too old and ugly to risk prison for? By the time his brother had given the monster just enough gas to get him to the next station, Zak was ready to go. Luke had wasted enough time running back to Zak to inform him in a delighted voice that he'd seen his satchel dangling from the passenger seat headrest. But his delight over the return of his satchel was short lived, for when he jumped in the truck to start the engine, Zak heard a piercing scream, so loud and long Zak could hear him over the noisy traffic whizzing by.

Alarmed Zak rushed to the truck, all sorts of scenarios racing through his head, the worst one being that Eve was lying dead inside. The cab looked as if some insane troll had sniffed each possession, and when she realized she couldn't eat it, she tossed it away. The compass, trowel, and tape measure were flung here and there on the passenger side floor, the contents of the medical kit had been dumped on the seat, Luke's sunglasses, bandana, and gloves had been tossed over the headrest, while one glove looked as if it had been stabbed. It looked as if the troll had wiped her mouth on the glove, smearing the soft leather with lipstick and ketchup residue. And worst of all, the thing that made Luke howl the most was the marking flags poking out of his upholstery, every one of them stabbed into the cushions from door to door. The backseat looked like a convention of yellow porcupines.

All the way back home, Zak got an earful of Luke's plans to get even with Acacia T. Pierce. Did he really think he had a chance to overpower Acacia? His bruises were beginning to fade around his throat, but now he looked like a boxer who'd spent most of the fight on the floor being beaten to a pulp. The woman didn't know her own strength. The woman wasn't normal.

The last remaining vehicle in the Woolly Man parking lot was Navan' Ford Taurus. It was parked in the same spot where she'd left it only a week ago. His eyes refused to see it. It was just on the periphery of his vision, a foreign object which made his heart race one moment and plunged him into despair the next. The damned thing symbolized twenty-four hours of bliss with Eve Endicott which might never come again.

When Zak climbed out of the Camaro and stretched his cramped muscles, he turned automatically to face the west and watch the sun drop behind the butte. He'd seen the gray clouds to the south of him and smelled the coming rain in the air, but to the west he saw only the melting of colors, the orange spreading across the blue, the black merging with the orange. In anticipation of what would come, he waited. The fire's light turned the tip of the butte honey as if the color itself might hold at bay the icy blue sky. From the west, dark clouds crept closer threatening to extinguish the light.

Instead of regretting the coming darkness, Zak welcomed the night. In the dark they could pull around to the back of the Woolly Man and deposit Luke's grisly treasure somewhere safe, until the family could decide what to do with her bones. The threat of rain, he hoped, would keep the patrons inside drinking and sharing stories. The stories were all shit, but at least talking about the crappy world and complaining and cracking jokes kept all the shit in prospective.

Absently, Zak heard the crunch of someone's boots on the gravel drive and without moving his head continued to observe the setting of the sun and waited patiently for his brother. When Luke's head blocked his view of the butte, he kept his mouth shut. He didn't want to spoil the moment by complaining. As soon as Luke stood in front of him, Zak pushed him aside. Perplexed, Luke frowned at him; Luke was all business, all of the time. The guy might as well be a calculator, because he sure wasn't an appreciator of sunsets.

When Luke turned to see what had caught Zak's attention, he shook his head and snorted in disgust, then walked away. Ignoring his brother's juvenile behavior, Zak continued to watch the setting sun until he found himself standing alone in the dark. All the while, he'd been listening to the nonstop squeal of the screen door as customers went in and out of the bar, the slap of wood on wood when it shut behind them and the stomp of feet as they moved about inside shaking the loose floorboards in their passage from the pool table to the bar.

All day, his mother had been waiting and watching for them. She'd left the main door wide open, so she would have an uninterrupted view of every passing car and the screen door shut to keep the bugs out. It was also a cheap way to cool the interior as the outside air circulated in and out of the building. Summer was almost over. He could sense fall moving forward to take its place. An unbidden image of the root cellar at Antelope Summit flashed before him. He tried to brush the picture away. He didn't want anything to disturb this peaceful almost Zen moment. The sight of so much death renewed his vow to live each day as if it were his last. What was the matter with him? What sentimental crap. Just to stand here and watch the sun set. That would be enough for now.

When the colors along the butte's back was washed away by the night and the massive pile of rock and dirt could only be sensed rather than seen and the willow at its feet receded into the shadows, Zak turned toward the Taurus. It was somewhere to his left, parked off to one side close to the dirt road, set apart from the other vehicles. He knew Mad Mona had driven the Taurus back to Idaho from Oregon and suspected his mother had insisted Mad Mona park the Taurus in the same spot Leona had parked a few days before. So even the way Leona parked fit her personality; someone who was finnicky enough not to want her rental car to touch other cars, someone who avoided crowds and spent most of her time in her head.

Three days ago, Leona had been a stranger, now the way she parked seemed to make sense. It dawned upon him she might just return to the Woolly Man to collect the rental. The idea brought his heart rate up. Fool. It wasn't Leona he wanted. Besides, it was much more likely she'd call the rental agency and tell them where to pick up the car. He turned his back on the night and headed toward the Woolly Man seeking its modern conveniences of electricity and bottled beer. Ah yes, electricity, bottled beer, and the bones of an unknown female who may or may not be the legendary Amara were all a man needed to be happy these days.

Just as he touched the handle of the screen door an idea came to him. He turned back to stare at the Taurus. Mad Mona had mentioned all the stuff Leona had left behind. He would get the key from his mother and comb through the car for anything that might help him figure out her identity.

He entered the bar in time to hear his mother announce to her customers, "The boys are here, and they've offered to help me install a new wood stove, so we will be closed for the next few days. Sorry about the inconvenience, but by winter your cold asses will be thanking me." Andy deep in conversation with Luke forgot to laugh. Harold Applegate laughed a little too long and Zak looked away from the wet pleading look in the poor man's eyes, embarrassed by the guy's undying devotion to his mother. "Don't be a fool," he wanted to warn him. "She'll just break your heart."

The next morning Luke's bellow could be heard clear across the lot and inside Zak's trailer. With his head throbbing and his mouth tasting like rancid meat he rolled over in bed and tried to muffle the sound of the fight taking place just outside the bar. From the gist of the argument, he figured his mother really intended to replace the old wood stove with a new modern pellet stove.

"Listen to me Mom," Luke shouted. "Will you just listen one damned minute?"

Zak couldn't hear his mother's response.

"Let's think about this for a minute," Luke said in a normal voice and when her answer didn't please he bellowed, "You're not seeing the big picture. We don't have time for these side jobs. We've got the discovery of the century in our garage. It will take all our expertise and all our time to prepare for tomorrow night."

God, Zak thought holding his pounding head, his brother had a big mouth. And he knew why Luke was so pissed off. Luke's ranting wasn't just about his precious cargo, but about avoiding manual labor. As Zak strained to hear the rest of the argument, Luke came to his senses. You just didn't argue with Mom. Blissful silence reigned. With his head still pounding, Zak stumbled down the tiny hall hitting the wall every so often on his journey to the bathroom and entered just in time to throw the toilet seat up and pee a waterfall of last night's beer into the bowl. As he stood before the bowl weaving from side to side attempting to focus his eyes on the picture of the double-decker outhouse hanging above the toilet, he swore he would quit drinking for good. It was time. Tomorrow. Yes. Tomorrow. The buzz was great, but the hangover blew great big chunks.

For the next two hours, Zak lay on the sofa with his fourth cup of coffee cooling on the floor beside him while his eyes followed Esmeralda's progress. The spider had been busy in the last few days extending her web as far as the cupboard door on the west wall and the trailer door on the south wall. He hadn't always liked spiders, but lately he'd grown to appreciate their good qualities. He rarely needed the fly swatter and didn't have to go to the effort of chasing the little bastards all over the trailer. No. All he had to do was patiently wait for the fly to stumble into the web and the spider took care of the rest.

He'd forbidden his mother and sister from ever entering his home and attempting to clean the trailer specifically because he feared they would wipe away all evidence of his pet's existence. She'd become his spider. She was about the size of a quarter and had a white circle which reminded him of a tiny opal on her black hairy body and the most awesome web constructed in the corner of his front room directly above his feet. If a fly happened to sneak inside the trailer, he could anticipate a quick and efficient death. Why did he need insect spray when he had Esmeralda to take care of his pest problems?

The sound of someone approaching the trailer alerted Zak before the idiot pounded rudely on his door. Since his home had the structural integrity of a soda can, noises were automatically magnified. There was no need to pound. A tap or two would have sufficed. "I swear I'll break your arm if you touch my door one more time," Zak yelled, then grabbed his aching head.

The pounding stopped.

With a groan of inevitability, Zak made himself get off the couch and walk the two steps to the door. The throbbing between his temples had begun to dissipate. He opened the door and went back to his sofa. When he turned and noticed the fastidious puckering of his brother's lips and the way his brother's eyes darted from the pile of dirty dishes in the sink to the dirty clothes draped over every available surface, Zak knew he wouldn't have to worry about Luke overstaying his welcome. Without the preliminary greetings familiar in most polite cultures, Luke stood with his hands on his hips and announced, "You've got to drive to Boise and pick up Quinn."

"Why?"

Luke stared at the ceiling and when he saw the size of the spider web backed up and nearly collided with Esmeralda who now was in the process of swinging herself toward the sink. She, more prudent and efficient than his brother vaulted over his head with only inches to spare and landed on the refrigerator. Luke hadn't noticed Esmeralda. A good thing. "Because we can't do this without Quinn. According to Mom, Quinn is the all-important key. She has to be here, or it won't work."

"Because she's a virgin," Zak said in a snide tone. "And only virgins can perform the animal sacrifices necessary to appease the Gods of Olympus?"

"Don't be an ass. I've got enough problems today without having to explain the obvious to you too."

"I know all about Quinn's importance. No. My concern is why I have to go and get her? You go. This is your deal not mine."

"Mom wants me to take Harry's truck and pick up the pellet stove in town."

"Well, you can pick Quinn up on the way back."

"No, that'd take me all day. I can't anyway because there won't be any room in the truck. She'd have to ride in the back with the stove."

"Why?"

"Because my truck is still sitting on a road somewhere in Nevada and the only transportation we could get was Harry. So, Harry graciously offered his truck and he's coming with me. I'm not Superman. I can't lift the stove by myself."

They stared at each other for a few minutes in silence. Luke had prudently shut up. In the past, he would have simply ordered Zak to fetch Quinn and Zak would have gotten to his feet reluctantly with only a few mumbled curses. But their relationship had changed since Leona. Luke coughed and made a production of holding his nose. Evidently, even with all their adventures lately, Zak's home still made his brother gag. He probably envisioned all sorts of bacteria running amok in the place, E. coli for one, probably anthrax for another.

No, not anthrax. The Black Plague. Luke probably thought Zak had rats running around the trailer with infected flees on their backs and those flees were spreading disease over everything even the very air he was breathing. Forget the fact Zak was in perfect health and spent more time in the trailer than anyone in the family. That fact didn't matter. Luke would claim Zak had an immunity to infection because he lived in a gigantic petri dish.

Zak's amused smile made Luke's shoulders twitch.   "Fine. I'll get Quinn. But you have to promise me you won't do anything stupid while I'm gone."

"You will? Excellent. Believe me, you'll thank me later."

"Don't think I'm doing this for you."

"I'm sure you have your reasons. As long as both parties are satisfied, why should I quibble? Huh?"

"Go away. Wait. Hold on a sec. What about the lady in the trunk? I can't be driving around the damned country with her bones in the back of my car."

"All taken care of. You are lady free," Luke said, unaware his joke had inadvertently dug the knife deeper in Zak's psyche.

After using his handkerchief to open the door, Luke left Zak's trailer, turned around on the stoop, grateful at last to be out of the stink. He sucked in a lungful of fresh clean desert air. The idea of any sentient creature content to live in such filth mystified him. If Zak took out the garbage just once a week and maybe washed a few clothes, the place would still be a dump, but not a stinky dump.

Strange really, the way Zak could live in such filth, but always look as if he bathed three times a day and shaved even more. Luke often wondered how Zak did it. Even with no change of clothes, Zak's three-day old blue jeans which should have been wrinkled with a few food or dirt stains on them still appeared as if they'd come straight out of the dryer. Even his sweat smelled better than a high-priced men's cologne.

Luke hadn't been paying much attention in the past, but lately he'd noticed the differences between them, not physical differences because they both had dark hair and the Nerin good looks, but there was a subtler difference, a difference in body chemistry he figured. Deep in thought, he wasn't paying attention to where his feet were landing. When he tripped over something on the ground, his arms shot out like pinwheels.

Once he'd righted himself, he noticed a pool of black liquid on the ground and spots of it on the toe of his right shoe. He turned around and noticed a pan which had been full of used motor oil lying face down in the dirt. He swore, "Zak. Damned it. I don't care if you want to live in a petri dish oozing with bacteria, but I do care about the integrity of this property."

The trailer door swung open and Zak poked his head out, "What are you going on about?"

"This," Luke said pointing at the pan of oil and the droplets of oil on his best pair of shoes. "You've got a biohazard here, clean it up."

His brother's lack of concern made Luke even more furious. Under other circumstances, he would have pretended an indifference he didn't feel, just so Zak didn't get the impression he could push anymore of his buttons. Oh yes. He knew Zak thought he was a clean freak. So, what.

He liked everything organized, tidy and smelling fresh. But now life seemed sadder, uglier, dumber, more gray, and worthless. The truth of the last three days had crystallized. His pissed-off mood had to do with Frankie/Leona and the way she responded to Zak. All Zak had to do was walk into the room and she'd act weirder than usual, if that was possible, eyes tracking his every movement, eyes either adoring him, fearing him, or hating him.

What hurt the most was Frankie's change of attitude toward him. All those hours in the backseat next to her, only inches away, and she barely acknowledged his existence. Instead, she was on her cellphone or her laptop or flirting with the limo driver. He might as well have been a mannequin. It still made Luke sick to his stomach to think Frankie preferred that Neanderthal limo driver over him.

For some inexplicable reason, Zak had the power to terrify her no end or drive her insane with desire. Both were strong emotions. Yes. Note that. Although polar – both were equally strong emotions. Whereas with him, she was lukewarm as if he were some ordinary guy and not particularly interesting or mysterious either. Zak could have smelled like an old jock strap and she would still have wanted to tear his clothes off and make love to him. And he, Luke Nerin, might as well be invisible for all the attention she paid him. He sniffed his armpit to make sure that, yes, he smelled of the great outdoors, pine trees and freshly mown grass. And he washed his hair every day and kept it neat and was considerate enough to pull his hair off his shoulders with a piece of sweet smelling hemp. And he kept his trailer clean and tidy and smelling fresh. So why did she perk up whenever he was in the room?

He tried to shake the whole ugly comparison out of his head, but he couldn't. His throbbing nose and black eyes fairly shouted the truth. There was no way he could go back and be that other person, that cocky guy who thought he was so damned clever and good looking. Today, he knew himself to be short, stupid, and ugly. But the offering would change everything. The offering would bring back the glory of the old days. He would be like a King ruling over his subjects. Women would beg for his kisses. Men would bow down before him. Eager to get started, Luke crossed the vacant lot and headed toward the garage to get one last look at the "lady." He couldn't quite believe his luck. The thought that her bones were probably ten thousand years old excited him as much as the idea that she would soon bring his family prosperity and power.

She was in a sense truly a part of their "family."

Forcing himself to get dressed, Zak, a witness to his brother's inexplicable behavior wondered what was riding up his butt. While peeking between the curtains, Zak watched Luke cross the courtyard and head toward the garage. Most of the evening had been spent searching for the right container for her bones. Eventually, Luke found their father's old army footlocker. Zak laughed softly to himself, the air from his lungs making the curtains shiver. This was better than a movie, he thought, as he watched his brother moving back and forth like some demented ant with a heavy burden.

From this distance, a person might wonder why a grown man was feverishly sweeping dirt off a solid chunk of dirt. It truly did look odd, the way Luke was bent double as if he were some old fart industrially brushing, sweeping, chipping, blowing, watering that chunk of earth. Real creepy. Zak wouldn't have dared. He wasn't an archeological conservator. He didn't have the training and neither did Luke.

After a night of deliberation, his brother decided the footlocker would be a perfect fit for the poor creature and had spent countless hours removing the dirt around her bones, then once the bones were exposed and free of their grave, just as freakily, he laid them on top of his mother's picnic table on a clean blanket to soak in the sunshine. And once they were "soaked" to his liking, his brother set them carefully inside the footlocker on top of a dense white foam mattress arranging the bones like a bizarre jigsaw puzzle. Zak had grown bored just watching the fool work and sweat for hours. He decided it was time to get dressed, wash down his breakfast with a beer, and slowly make his way across the lot to the garage to get a closer look.

Standing on the threshold of the garage, Zak stuffed his hands in his jean pockets and watched his brother work. Even though Luke was supposed to be some sort of genius, he still had to get out his old anatomy textbooks and check to make sure he was placing the bones correctly. Back when he was a kid, Luke wanted to be a forensic anthropologist. While watching the skeleton take shape and listening to Luke mumble and complain and at one point stomp his foot like a petulant child, Zak realized Luke had made the right decision, not to become a forensic anthropologist.

When Luke placed the last bone in the footlocker as ceremoniously as if he were bestowing the crown upon a monarch's head, a ring of applause echoed through the garage, his mother's applause not Zak's. Disgusted by their gloating, Zak left the garage and opened the cooler. He chose a soda instead of the beer he really wanted and sat on the cooler to watch the two of them. The two buzzed around the artifact like bees around a flower. It was painful to watch.

There was no science involved. He heard Luke throw out words, but they weren't words a forensic scientist would use; they were words a magician might use to fool his audience into believing the trick was real. In disbelief he heard Luke say, "It's impossible to tell exactly how tall she'd been. But if we factor in her torso, we can guess she might have been between four feet three inches and a few inches below five feet tall. She's the right age, in her mid-twenties. You see the teeth. These are the wisdom teeth of a young woman around twenty-two or maybe a few years older. But no older. They're healthy and strong. If she were older, they would show signs of aging. And her skull. She has a perfectly developed skull.

Also, there are signs someone has cut into her shoulder blades. Of course, there's the lower half of her body too. Someone removed her legs and attempted to attach this foreign matter to her spinal cord. Assuredly, her body would have rejected the vertebrae. It appears to be from a dolphin. She might have lived a few days at the most. I don't know. It's the cuts along her shoulder blades that interest me the most. Could the surgeon have removed her wings? I'm not quite convinced. Yet, there is something here.

If we had more artifacts such as beads from jewelry she wore, or personal belongings buried with her, we could pinpoint her time in history more accurately. There were hundreds of pieces of material around the body which from their disintegration might be very old. It's hard to tell at this point though. I've placed them in a box and plan to examine them under a microscope.

If I had the proper tools, I could find out more, much more. I could find out if she were a woman of the 18th century or more recent. During the 18th century, in that era most people wore clothing made of gingham, calico cotton, linsey-woolsey and leather. If she lived among the indigenous people of the Columbia Gorge, she would have worn leather-hide. But if the bits of cloth I find are rayon or polyester, then she is a product of the 20th century. From the evidence we have here, I am optimistic this female is from the 18th century."

His family had come unraveled, Zak decided. That poor female in the footlocker wasn't the famous Amara Katsaros. There was no such creature as Amara Katsaros. She was probably some hapless young woman who had been lured into the clutches of a psychopath's monstrous delusion. Obviously, his brother was right about the murderer's profession. He had to have been a surgeon or had some medical training. Barbers used to have medical training, maybe he'd been a barber. Cut your hair for a penny and saw off your leg for a nickel.

As his brother drooled over the poor thing, he wondered why he continued to ignore the evidence in the cellar? The markers of where people had lain, likely dying a horrible death suggested there had been more poor souls like the female in the footlocker. Who had he been, this Dr. Frankenstein wannabe? Jane Smith must know, after all she'd led them to the cabin. No, Acacia Pierce had led them to the cabin. She'd already known something grisly had happened there. Maybe just being near the foundation stones stirred up forgotten memories? And her explosive reaction to the place had nearly killed Luke.

Old newspaper clippings from Ely, Nevada might tell him the names of the present and past owners of the cabin. And he could probably find the owner through the office of the City Clerk or through Archived Land and Deed Records. The cabin must have been built before Teddy Roosevelt created the United States Forest Service and designated over 200 million acres to 150 national parks. So the cabin could only have been built before 1906, legally anyway.

Today a person can't just plop a cabin anywhere he pleases. He has to get a permit and find an inspector and make sure the building is up to code. At least in today's world these things are necessary. A hundred years ago, maybe not. Even though the cabin is long gone, carted off and stored in some warehouse, parts of the foundation were left behind. And what is the purpose of the wooden post buried three feet below the crawl space? The old foundation stones, the rusty pump, the root cellar all suggest age. It was more than likely pioneers settled on Ruby Mountain, built their cabin, raised their children, and bequeathed the cabin to their heirs.

So, no he didn't think it a stretch to assume the cabin was a hundred years old and the owner kept it in good working order up until the fire. The fact that the female had been buried far deeper than the other graves indicated someone had been doing these grisly perverted experiments for a long time. He hated to dowse his brother's enthusiasm, but even if Luke can prove when she died, she still might not be Amara.

Whoever the kidnapper had been, he'd been one sick piece of garbage. If he had been a doctor, he'd not only betrayed his Hippocratic Oath, but committed numerous crimes against humanity. Nauseated by his brother's palpable eagerness, Zak headed for the bar and had a few beers. Only when his mother came in and he heard her say "sacrifice" did Zak jump up from his stool and return to the scene of his brother's crime. Luke ceremoniously laid the last bone, the right thumb in its proper place and with a flourish of his arm announced the obvious, "Viola, she's finished."

What an ass, Zak thought privately.

Today with the pounding in his head lessening as the aspirin took charge and with his sunglasses on, he set up a folding chair on the stoop near his trailer. Holding a cup of coffee, he watched his big brother stumble toward the garage as if he were a devote worshipper rushing to the alter of a saint.

Luke wasn't the same person anymore. Maybe Luke was the same and Zak had changed? He didn't know for sure. All he knew was that he didn't care for Luke's air of vulnerability and his recent indecisiveness. The legend of Amara had dug her claws deep into Luke's psyche. Luke's former skepticism had vanished. Now he acted as if the bones really belonged to Amara. Instead of processing the evidence without prejudice, he was going through the steps ass-backward. He began the process prejudiced and used the evidence to prove his case rather than find out the truth.

A momentary pity for his brother washed over him. He must have been up all night to get so much accomplished. Zak admired his brother's energy and passion, yet, he feared his brother was in for some real pain very soon. He wished his family would wake up and realize it was all nonsense. It was clear the poor female wasn't the right age. Soon his brother would come down to earth and realize the same. And then what would Luke do? Once they'd performed the ritual and nothing happened, what would his mother do? Would they go their separate ways and live with the knowledge of their failure? Or would one of them do something really nuts?

He hoped not. No police please. No media frenzy. No padded cells. Let our family insanity remain a secret and sink into the dust of history never to be resurrected again.

An hour later, Zak found a clean shirt tucked away in his closet and slipped it on. He shaved and combed his hair. Now he was ready to run to Boise and get his sister. Before driving to Boise, he stopped inside the bar and found his mother piling the chairs up against the back wall with an air of suppressed hysteria. She spun around at the sound of the screen door whacking the flimsy frame as he entered the room.

"Zak. You scared me."

"Sorry Mom. Need some cash for gas."

"Damned. You should have left an hour ago. Quinn's probably anxious by now."

"Well, cars don't move on prayers alone."

His mother strode to the cash register, pressed a few keys and when the box sprung open with the cash carefully laid in increments of ones, fives, tens, and twenties, with the fifties and hundreds lying under the box supposedly, a wave of pity washed over him. Just a quick count made the point: there could no more than a hundred bucks in the cash register. He reviewed the night before. The Woolly Man had maybe five customers at the most at any one time, a total of fifteen the entire night. And most of the customers were cheap shits anyway. How had his mother paid his bail? And Luke lying about where the money had gone?

The thought of Luke's duplicity made him furious, a fury so deep he had to pace the floor to rid himself of the pain. He did his best to hide his thoughts accepting the two twenty-dollar bills his mother handed him while simultaneously feeling sick and guilty for being a drain on his mother's resources. Before leaving, he squeezed her tight and kissed the top of her head.

Jule pushed him away and stared at him suspiciously, "Still hungover hon?"

"No. I'm good. Thanks Mom. I'll pay you back. I promise," he told her, looking at her with new eyes. She was still gorgeous yet, he did detect a few extra wrinkles around her eyes and mouth he hadn't noticed before. The way her eyes suddenly lit up with barely contained delirium indicated she'd switched from worrying about Quinn to thinking about the poor creature in the footlocker and what would take place tomorrow evening.

He stood at the door and watched her. She was so engrossed she thought she was alone in the room. He wasn't surprised. When she got worked up about something, she turned into a whirling dervish. With agitation broadcast in every line of her body, she picked up the nearest chair and carried it to the back wall near the bathrooms. Without ceremony she dumped it on the stack near the backdoor effectively cutting off the exit. Then she dragged a café table toward the corner. He turned away thinking if it had been his event, he would have simply stuck the footlocker on top of the pool table, chanted a blessing in Greek, and drank himself into oblivion.

Why go to all this trouble to rearrange the furniture and decorate the room for some made-up ritual by an insecure ancestor?

On his way out of the Woolly Man, Zak quickly stuffed the money in his back pocket before Nate could see them then nodded in the cook's direction. Nate entered the room with his usual exuberant flourish. And indeed, his entrance was as exuberant and colorful as usual. Zak took in Nate's outfit and postponed his departure hoping for an opportunity to say something funny.

He didn't have time to listen to Nate's long winded explanation for the costume, but he couldn't just leave without knowing what the hell was going on. Nate dressed in sandals, Bermuda shorts, and his six-pack barely covered in an eye-catching Hawaiian shirt threw his straw hat on the bar and pulled off his cheap sunglasses to smile at everyone. At the moment, everyone in the room happened to be Jule and Zak. The size of the audience didn't matter, just as long as one particular pair of eyes were on him when he made his grand entrance. Zak noticed Nate's sunglasses were embossed with black snakes along the arms and the matching earpieces.

"Hay," Zak said. "Nice glasses. Dollar store special?"

Nate responded in kind with a cheerful, "Hay brother," and a smile that showed his gleaming white teeth and healthy pink gums, then he slip-slapped his way into the middle of the room and looked around in surprise. Not wanting to be around for the soon-to-be shouting match, Zak hurried to the Camaro hoping he'd be out of earshot when Nate heard the real reason for the closing of the Woolly Man. Jule and Nate were both passionate people and the coming fracas would probably last the entire time Zak was on the road. It would take him two and a half hours each way, five hours total, maybe more if Quinn still had packing to do.

Luke, in the process of climbing into Harry's truck saw him and said, "He won a Caribbean cruise. Can you believe that guy's luck?" Luck meant a lot to Luke. An odd belief system for a calculator, well, maybe not, when there were numbers involved. Between the grating of Harry's pistons, the chugging of the old truck's exhaust pipe, and the rattle of the rest of the old bucket, Zak seriously wondered if those two would make it even to Twin Falls. As Zak lifted the trunk of his Camaro, he heard his brother call out, "See you tonight Zak," as if Luke's words were some sort of incantation which when spoken aloud bound Zak to Luke and further bound him to the Woolly Man and tomorrow night's event.

Relieved, Zak surveyed his clean trunk. Someone, most likely his mother had vacuumed out the trunk. There were no longer any incriminating leftover chunks of grave dirt, grave dirt which had cradled the mermaid in its embrace for nearly a century. It still wasn't much of an improvement. His trunk was a mess. After vacuuming out his trunk, she'd thrown all his stuff back in without regard to the importance of the object. His tool chest should have been closer to the front. Hell, what difference did it make now?

His mother had vacuumed and wiped away all evidence of their crime. A clean trunk was little compensation for the misery to come for the Nerin family. Yes. He would obey his mother's command and fetch Quinn. And that would be the last task he would do for his mother or any of them. He'd wasted enough time believing in an idiot lie. Before he'd ever gotten shitfaced drunk, he'd ripped away the pretty packaging and seen the ugliness of his family's insecurity. Nothing seemed to work. Nothing he had done so far had been of any benefit to him or his family. Even when he applied himself seriously to the task at hand, the fruits of his labor ended up benefiting strangers and landing him in jail.

As he navigated the winding washboard road, he made a mental list of what he'd accomplished so far. He'd hunted down a woman who'd stolen his brother's shitty truck. And once he apprehended the thief, he'd made a citizen's arrest and managed to seduce her into his bed, then while he's sleeping, she handcuffs him to the bed and runs away. He gives chase – again – with his brother in tow, is arrested for having a suspicious box in his vehicle which turns out not to be the remains of a child, but a four thousand year old jackass rabbit.

When he's released from jail, instead of going home like any sensible man should have done, he chases her across Nevada and into Oregon and back to Nevada where she delivers them to a cabin in the wilderness and manages to run away a third time. Instead of chasing after her, he and his brother dig a dozen test holes in the crawl space and discover where a bunch of people have been murdered. Instead of calling the cops, they scoop up the poor pathetic creature from its grave and take her back to their home because she is a demi-god and the only way of bringing back their family's honor is to sacrifice her in a sick ritual created by an insecure woman. And all this trouble is supposed to make them immortal Gods. Holy shit. He was in big trouble.

Wait a minute, he seduced her? Oh no. He couldn't take credit for seducing her. Hell no. He'd been seduced, mightily and happily seduced. Now, unlike his insane brother, he had placed his cards on the table and realized he'd lost, lost the best thing to come his way. What should he do next? How could he convince the authorities a crime had taken place on Ruby Mountain without revealing his family's part in it?

If anyone discovered the truth, anyone outside the family, everyone, even Quinn might end up in jail. The cops would see them as stalkers and say they'd pursued an innocent female through three states because they were white slavers. That meant the FBI would get involved. And where would that leave him? He'd be forever known as a kidnapper, maybe a rapist, definitely a grave robber and a Satanist once the ceremony was over

The picture of himself stuck in a small cell wearing an orange jumpsuit shook him up, so badly, he had to pull over. His chest began to hurt. He felt a million years old. He struggled to suck air into his lungs. Panic Attack. Jesus. He was in so much shit. How could any rational person believe he wasn't complicit? If Eve told the police anything at all about her night with Zak, there would be no way he or Luke could ever convince the police of their innocence.

There were too many witnesses: Mad Mona Lawson, those two fishermen dudes, Nate Cooper, Harold Applegate, and Andrew Jankowski. Had he forgotten anyone? What about all the cashiers and clerks and gas station attendants they'd met along the way? Oh hell, he'd even forgotten Brent Wade and the video chat when he told Dr. Wade's son about the Navaho blanket.

That reminded him Brent expected Zak to deliver the blanket to Crescent City, California any day now. And what about Nate? Nate had met Leona first, but he wasn't a witness to the transformation of Leona into Acacia. There had been a few other patrons in the bar too, people he remembered vaguely. They had seen her enter the bar. They had heard her asking about Mona Lawson. They also were witnesses to her muttering and mumbling about a long-ago kidnapping.

If Zak were to call the police with an anonymous tip about the graves, the police would ask a shit load of uncomfortable questions. Every question would lead to a new question which would lead to more questions and soon someone would step into a store in Ely, Nevada and that friendly clerk behind the counter would be more than delighted to rehash the funny story about those weird guys who came in one day to buy sleeping bags, shovels, and trail mix. Oh, yeah and they bought something really interesting. Who could forget two guys buying a surfboard while camping in the desert? Well, Zak could claim they used the surfboard as a table. But how would they explain beating up the limo driver? Because Luke really wanted the job?

Their tracks would lead the cops to the cabin on Ruby Mountain and to the crawl space and the root cellar. The tread of the Camaro would put both his brother and himself in jail for life. There was no going back. All the evidence led to the same conclusion: that he and his brother were freaks who had abducted a stranger, subjected her to psychological trauma, and robbed a grave. They would never work in archeology again. Of course not, you moron, Zak shouted at himself, because you'll be behind bars.

Zak searched his pants pocket. Lucky for him all his clothes had been dirty, and he was still wearing the same jeans from his night with Eve. The map was gone. He searched all four pockets again. The map had been in his right pocket. He remembered watching her take off in the limo after blooding Luke's face. He'd slipped his hand in his pocket to make sure he still had the map. He planned to chase after her, but Luke persuaded him to stay and finish the job. And he thought he had plenty of time. Then last night nothing seemed worth pursuing.

Eve's map signified something else just as crucial. The map proved what had happened in Paris, Nevada had been consensual. His mood brightened. Yes. She'd wanted him as much as he'd wanted her. What had he done with the map? While he replayed the night in his mind, his cellphone rang. He pulled it out and checked the caller. He saw the old photo of Luke standing outside the Woolly Man with a smug smile. Zak answered the call.

"Yeah."

"Where are you? Quinn says you're late."

"I'm on my way. What difference does it make if I'm an hour late or two hours late? She can study or watch television."

"We've got a lot to do tonight Zak. Remember?"

"I told you. I'll be there," Zak said and cut him off then stuffed his cellphone in his pocket. That motion reminded him of something. He remembered looking at the map in the bar. He'd go back to the bar and check every inch of the floor especially near where he'd been sitting. He'd probably dropped the map last night. Or the map could be in his trailer? He'd check the trailer too.

He turned around and headed home.

When he ran into the bar, he noticed how big the room appeared without the chairs and tables. Good thing his mother couldn't move the counter and for that he was grateful because the counter had been where he'd parked his butt for the whole night. He checked the floor near the stool where he'd been sitting and when his fingers found only the usual peanut shells and dirt, he searched the rest of the floor. He even checked under the pile of chairs and tables at the far end of the room, then under the pool tables thinking maybe he'd played some pool and hadn't remembered. He tried the bathrooms next.

His mother stepped out of the kitchen wiping her hands on her apron with a frown of surprise and annoyance at the sight of him.

"Zak, what are you doing?"

"Was this where I sat last night?" He asked pointing at the stool then padding the seat.

"Yes. So what?"

"Are you sure? Did I sit anywhere else?"

"No. Quinn is waiting for you. It's nearly six."

"This is important Mom. Just try to remember. Was this where I sat last night?

"Yes. All night. Well, until Luke carried you back to your trailer," she said, and then followed up with, "where are you going?"

"I've got to check the trailer and then I'm gone. No problem."

The map wasn't in the trailer. Only when he left the trailer and headed across the vacant lot did he think of Luke. Could Luke have searched his pockets and found Eve's note? Zak knew logically that he didn't need the note. He already knew where she would be, but she might not be there anymore and there had been a phone number on the note. It had been a California area code, the rest he couldn't remember. Fuck a duck. Most importantly, it was evidence, evidence their night together had been consensual.

Faintly, he heard his mother's screech when he shoved the Camaro into reverse and tore out of the parking lot kicking up pebbles and rocks and dust in his wake. If Luke had taken the note, then Eve could be in danger. He would beat the truth out of Luke tonight. His ruminations about the trouble they would be in if Eve spoke to the cops had probably already gone through Luke's mind. Luke was the analysts, the plotter, and planner.

What would he do? What was he capable of doing? Zak relaxed remembering Luke would hardly jeopardize tomorrow night's ceremony. He'd been dreaming about this day since he was a kid. He wouldn't do anything to postpone the ceremony, not even to shut Eve up. Not yet anyway. All Zak had to do was keep an eye on his brother and follow him.

When Zak pulled up in front of his sister's place, he understood why she'd chosen to live away from home, but not why she'd chosen this roommate. Even though Zak was an hour and a half late, Quinn still wasn't ready to go. Before Zak could knock on the screen door, Quinn's roommate Breanna opened the door with an unnecessary flourish and one of her toothy smiles which worried him a great deal. Her eyes devoured him. An instinct for self-preservation made Zak step back. He nearly tumbled down the stoop, but caught himself in time.

"Come on in Zak. Quinn's fixing her hair. It'll be a few minutes. You want some cookies? I've been baking cookies all morning. We've got this assessment test to take in math next week and we've been going over and over math problems like you wouldn't believe. What a drag huh? Don't just stand there by the door. Come on in. Sit yourself down. Here. It's your favorite chair. I'll get you a cookie. Smell those. Um. Good huh?"

A walk across a plank on a pirate ship would have been preferable, but Zak knew his sister would take her own sweet time getting ready. Everybody in an all fired hurry to get him out of the door and now he had to wait. He could smell the chocolate chip cookies wafting toward him from the kitchen and decided if he had to endure Breanna at least he could enjoy a treat in the meantime. But just to make sure, he called out to his sister, "Quinn. Luke's waiting on us. He's in a toot. Hurry up."

He heard a muffled, "I know. I know. Hold on," and at the same time accepted a plate of cookies and a brimming glass of cold milk from Breanna who plopped herself down on the couch next to him to watch him eat. Breanna talked while Zak bit into the hot soft chocolate chip cookie. His tongue tasted the chocolate and sugar and demanded more. They were so good. Damned they were good. Even with the onslaught of pleasure signaled by his taste buds, his mind refused to stay in the moment and appreciate the treat.

Zak barely heard what Breanna said through his own confused thoughts. He was thinking about tonight's preparations and then tomorrow night's ceremony. Maybe he could slip away without being noticed? But they would hear the Camaro's engine fire up and know he'd taken off. Maybe he should park the Camaro down by the willow tonight? Once the ceremony was over, Luke would figure out what had happened. He might even chase after him. If he had stolen the map, he might even find Eve. And then what could Zak do?

"You haven't heard a word I've said, have you?" Breanna said with one of her little giggles he found so annoying. When Eve laughed, she laughed with her whole body especially her eyes. Breanna laughed with her lips while her eyes pleaded. Eve had been about the moment, appreciating the moment, and living for the sheer joy of living. No sexual hang ups either. In her opinion, the body was meant to be explored, touched, caressed, and kissed. Damned. Zak jumped up from the chair and realized he still held the plate of cookies. He put the cookies on the coffee table and walked toward the door, "I'll wait for Quinn in the car. Tell her to hurry, huh."

"You've changed Zak," Breanna said, her face odd looking without its perpetual smile. "What's going on? Are you in trouble? Can I help?"

He touched her shoulder absently and made himself pause and look down at her. His cues had flown over her head. He would have to be blunt. "I know you think you and I might have something someday Breanna. I'm sorry. It's not going to happen. I think of you as a friend. I hope we can stay friends." He thought about telling her the rest that he'd met a woman and he was now seriously considering settling down for the first time in his life.

The look on Breanna's face stopped him from saying any more. She hadn't heard a word he'd said. In her face he saw worry, concern for him, love of him, and the worst possible emotion – hope. Even if he married someone else, it might not be enough. Damn. Her single-minded devotion terrified him more than her giggling.

The girl was Quinn's antithesis: a bubbly obedient girl who had been trained from infancy to please the men around her. The idea of having such a woman occupy his trailer for any length of time made Zak shutter in horror. She would get rid of Esmeralda first off, then she'd pick up all his clothes and wash them and probably fold his underwear. And he could expect a future of nourishing tasty meals and lots of kids. In his imagination that would be a slice of hell. He'd end up in a predicable marriage with seven or eight kids and a cheerful, energetic, talk-you-to-until-your-deaf wife.

He managed to get out of the apartment without incident and was grateful she didn't decide to follow him to the Camaro and pressure him into eating more sugar-coated treats. When Quinn appeared, and ran down to the car with her small overnight bag, he knew he probably had an idiot smile on his face. He was so relieved that he would no longer have to pretend to be reading while Breanna pressed her nose to the living room window. Her hands propped on her chin and misty eyes following his every move were so creepy, he thought about driving to the end of the street to wait for his sister.

Instead of being mad at Quinn, he was mad at Luke. Luke could easily have picked Quinn up in town after purchasing the wood stove. This favor had eat-shit-brother-dear all over it.

"I'm not coming back here again," Zak told his sister as she climbed into the car. "You feeling me? You ever need a ride somewhere, we'll meet at the stadium or better yet at a bar. She won't go in one of those."

"Who? Breanna?" Quinn asked, glancing at the twitching curtains. "Oh, come on Zak. She's harmless. You should be used to women slobbering all over your pretty face."

"I mean it, Quinn. She gives me the willies."

"Like I give a damned about your willies. So fine. I'll walk all the way over to the Student Union Building just so you don't have to be bothered by poor old Breanna and her crush on you."

"It's more than a crush. It's an obsession. I can just see her coming at me with a knife because she's mad with jealousy."

"You're still thinking about what happened with Danika. Well Danika finally faced the fact that you were no good for her. She's going to be married soon. Yeah. That's right;" Quinn said with a shake of her braids. "So don't be thinking you are God's Gift to Women and every woman in the world is gonna die if she can't have some Zak."

"You think I'm that shallow? And would you quit talking that way. What's up with that?"

"It's good huh? I sound hip, don't I? I've been practicing. People expect it. Look at me," Quinn said, and Zak looked at her braids and her skin and remembered that she was going to Boise State University where the ratio of white to black was about 10 to 1. "Some kids come up to me and start talking as if I grew up in the hood, so now I'm practicing how to talk hood."

"Come on. Stop it. It's not you."

"It would have been if I'd been raised with my own people."

"Where is all this coming from? Raised with your own people? You were raised with your people. Remember: Parker, Jule, Me, and Luke. We're your people. I'm sorry Mom and Parker divorced, and Parker had to move to Arizona to get away from Mom, but you see your dad every school break. I miss him too, he was more of a father to me than David the creature from the Gassy Guy Lagoon. Even Nate is your people."

"You just don't get it."

"Try me."

"Forget it. This conversation started with you. You always do that, don't you?"

"Do what?"

"Do that thing. You know. Bait and switch. Confuse people. Steer them away from sensitive subjects. Now I didn't say you were shallow. You implied you thought you were shallow by asking," and in a bad imitation of Zak's voice continued, "Hey, Quinn. Am I shallow?"

Zak tried to turn the radio on and Quinn snapped it off, "Come on Zak. Can't we be real for once?"

"You're nervous, aren't you?"

Quinn shook her head in the negative and sighed, "There you go. A bait and switch move. Once again."

"That's it, isn't it?" Zak said with a laugh. "You're nervous about tomorrow night. I knew it."

"Even though you're trying to change the subject and turn this on me, I'm going to answer your question, big brother. No. I don't think your shallow. I think your spoiled and conceited. Mom's spoiled you. And your conceited because you're so used to women falling all over themselves to get in your pants. You know you can get any woman you want."

"Well you're wrong. I can't get any woman I want."

"Oh yeah? What's up with that?"

"Would you stop talking that way?"

"You want me to talk like Luke. Like I should say: Did I hear you correctly, brother dear? Are you suggesting perchance you might be mortal or even, shall I say – flawed? Quelle surprise! Or as we say at jolly old Oxford, how extraordinary, my dear boy. Some female is immune to your charms, you say? Oh, my. Tut-tut and all that rot. No need to cry in your soup. Chin up now. Let's soldier on. Right. Left. Right. Left."

"Holy Saints Preserve Us! Can I have my sister back? Please?" Zak asked as they drove over the bridge into Twin Falls.

The eight hours of preparation for the coming ceremony left Zak exhausted. Alternately, he found himself driven to crazy boredom for hours then frenzied activity the next. His mother had them all moving stuff and doing her bidding. Somewhere she'd gotten her hands on several old books. The books were the size of car manuals and weighed even more. Unlike car manuals which could be greasy with motor oil, Jule's books smelled musty. The books were too heavy for her to carry, so she left them open on the counter and studied them when she needed more advice about the lighting or the space or the arrangement of the furniture.

The first important piece of equipment they needed was a stone alter. Both his mother and Luke insisted on having a real stone alter built inside the bar. They argued about whether to have the altar built in the center of the Woolly Man floor. Quinn suggested they build a sort of stone hearth and have another piece of stone laid on top for the altar. Mom liked the idea, but Luke wanted the ceremony to take place outside under the stars preferably on the butte above the bar, because tradition demanded we do so to appease the Gods.

Zak didn't realize he'd spoke the words he was thinking aloud until he looked around and everyone in the room frowned, "Of course we should because the Gods of Olympus will be pleased and if they are smiling down upon us, we know we're not crazy."

His mother rejected Luke's idea citing her worry the candles might be seen from town and people in town would think she was having a witches' Sabbath. If anyone were to find out what they were really doing, she was sure the townspeople would petition for the closure of her bar and run her out of town as a dangerous cultist. Zak assured her the few Mormons and Catholics in town had more important things to think about than whether she was a witch. In fact, he seriously doubted whether anyone would care what they were doing in the middle of the night. Luke accused Zak of disrespecting the Gods and if he was going to keep up with his negativity and his perpetual grumpiness then he should just get the hell out.

Fitting the suggestion to the action, he was almost out the door when his mother called him back. Quinn broke up the fight by observing, "It'll be midnight before we make up our minds and I'm not coming back, not until Thanksgiving Break. I've got to finish Moby Dick, folks. I haven't any time to waste with bickering bros. So, come on. We'll throw the dice; that's worked before. Whoever gets the highest score chooses one of the three rituals set out in Hera Katsaros' book," she said pointing toward the book closet to them on the bar where Jule had left five books open with markers in each one. "Are we all in agreement?"

They all agreed. Of course, Jule won the toss. She chose the third ritual, the most pernicious of the rituals which would require an altar, an animal sacrifice, and the drinking of the blood of Amara. Since the substitute of Amara was the poor creature discovered buried under the cabin on Ruby Mountain and judging by its condition had long ago exsanguinated, the "blood" would have to be some sort of proxy for real blood.

Each of them threw the dice a second time to decide where to hold the ceremony and a third time to choose the animal which would be offered to the Gods of Olympus. Quinn won the second toss. Zak won the third toss. Quinn chose the place – it would be her Dad's rock house. Zak made a suggestion and even Luke seemed thrilled by the new location. Desperate times and all that rot, Zak thought. He was forced to forsakes his secret place to save the family from a lifetime of bad press and public humiliation.

27

After two months, I decided Leland had made other plans and we had to leave the house. It had become our prison, a sort of dusty tomb of someone else's artifacts and mementos and that had never been the plan. She and I would take the Toyota and drive somewhere safe. But where? Back to Dr. B? No. Definitely not to him.

And then the idea came to me. Of course. Of course. At the end of the second month, I phoned Mr. Adams and explained to him that Dr. Winter no longer needed my services and she would be discontinuing the weekly grocery delivery. I also cancelled all the other services which made Dr. Winter's life so carefree: her cellphone service, lawn maintenance service, internet, heating, electricity, and water. I had everything shut off.

Each representative I spoke to never questioned my authority. It was a valuable lesson. Evidently people were – just too damned trusting – just as trusting as the child I carried down to the Toyota and covered in blankets. It was cold by the sea and colder still outside. The little girl accepted me totally. I had let down my friends by my decision to leave. But what could I do? Leland should have arrived weeks ago. No one was answering his phone at the pawn shop. What the Sam-Hell was he doing? It looked as if I would have to find him myself.

The dog sitter service arrived to take Stanley and Harry to the Doggy Hotel. The payments to board two big dogs were automatically taken out of Dr. Winter's bank, so I need do nothing else. That was when I learned she'd named the dogs – Rommel and Wagner. Typical.

When I opened the gate from my warm and cozy place inside the study, I was forced to communicate through Dr. Winter's laptop instead of being able to use the anonymity of the intercom. Some lamebrain had destroyed all the intercoms in the house. While leaning back in Violet Winter's comfortable chair wearing a blonde wig I'd found in a guest bedroom and my nose and mouth covered with a ball of tissues, I explained to the dog sitter I had a terrible head cold. "Would you be a dear and take care of the dogs without me?"

I could see she was a no nonsense type of woman, athletic and confident. She nodded up at the monitor and said, "Sure Ms. Winter. Are Rommel and Wagner in the kennel or inside the house?"

"Dr. Winter is in South America. I'm her cousin Mona Lawson. She asked me to housesit while she's away. No, they're not in the house. I've been too sick to play with them today. They're in the kennel, all ready for you."

"No problem, ma'am."

The morning before I decided to leave the estate and take the child with me, I had an overwhelming curiosity to see what was behind the Botticelli Door. When I opened the door, even with the surgical mask covering my face, the sweet stench of rotting bodies assaulted my nostrils. Two months without food, hum? There'd been water available. The tap gushed cold water. But without food? I stepped over Winter's legs and circled around Millhouse's body in order to walk down the hall to an open arena where a surgical table stood in the center of the room and the tools of Dr. Winter's trade remained ready on the cart to do its magic. I looked up at the ceiling and saw the familiar lamps watching the proceedings like some grotesque alien with multiple eyes.

I followed a rawer stench, something even worse than Millhouse and Winter's decaying bodies and found an opening to the far left of the room where a series of steps descended into another chamber below the surgery. The opening looked primitive compared to the newness of the surgical ward with its sterile metal walls and florescent lights running from north to south. These lights crackled and hummed raising the hairs on my body and even for a few minutes made me sweat profusely. The old lights alone with their hundred-watt bulbs would have kept the airless room warm even in bitter cold weather. Evidently the lights had contributed to the rapid decay of the bodies below.

I peered down the stairs. The steep iron stairs and the limestone walls reminded me of something. Then it came to me. An air raid shelter. Of course. Dr. Winter had built her laboratory above an air raid shelter. Rather than climb down the stairs, I got down on my belly and stuck my head inside. On an army cot closest to the door, I saw something that resembled a human; its top half was a man, the bottom half wrapped in bandages was one solid mass. I looked away in horror. Whatever they had done to him, he was out of his misery now.

Then I saw something on the floor, the hem of a skirt and the tail end of a white surgical coat and then the leg, a muscled leg of a woman who enjoyed her ten mile runs and her toning exercises. But this leg included a piece of protruding bone from the thigh. That was enough for me. I already knew who she was. There was no need to investigate any further. She wasn't worth it. The smell coming from her decomposing body made me want to retch.

It must have been all those bananas and beans Myrtle Foster-Koodark enjoyed eating. I couldn't allow my bile to end up inside this room. I fled the place covering my nose and my mouth with my hand. But even after I stepped out into the cool clean air, I could still smell the place on my clothes. I ran back to the lighthouse and up the stairs and stepped inside the shower fully clothed. I turned on the tap. I stood under the warm water for at least twenty minutes trying to wash away the smell.

On the day we left, the girl with no voice clung to my hand. Since I had left the remote for the gate inside Violet Winter's Mercedes inside a locked garage, I was forced to get out of the car and open the gate manually. It took me a few minutes to figure out the security box and which buttons to press and then I noticed something curious – the right-hand post included two shoots drilled completely through, so that when the mail carrier dropped off the mail and the daily newspaper, the materials would land on the property side in a fancy receptacle. Which meant, the mail carrier never had to enter the property, all he or she had to do was drop the mail and newspapers into the bin. The receptacles fit the overall décor of the gates. They were both painted black to match the wrought iron gates.

My first impression was that the larger receptacle must have about a weeks-worth of newspapers. But I was wrong. When I lifted the lid, I discovered two major daily newspapers inside the receptacle and the date on both was the same. Had I really been here for two months and one day? I confiscated both newspapers to read later. I had been right. Violet Winter had stopped delivery of her newspapers, because she had planned to be gone for a long time.

What interested me the most was the smaller receptacle. What was its purpose? When I opened the lid, I found three cellphones inside. The inner lining of the receptacle was made of a soft rubbery substance, I suppose to protect the phones from getting banged up on their way down the shoot. I fished the cellphones out of the receptacle. The gaudiest one, a pink and white one, I assumed by the glittery protective cover had to belong to Myrtle, while the cheap flip phone must belong to Ray. The larger and more expensive cellphone had to be Violet Winter's. Now why would her cellphone be inside this box when she was the owner of the property and had no reason to suspect herself of recording her private conversations or of causing a security breach?

The realization brought a smile to my lips. She didn't trust anyone or anything, not even her own phone. Everyone and their baby knew cellphones could be infiltrated by hackers and how hackers could listen in and record private conversations without the owner ever knowing. Ah ha, so this was why no one had shown up to break Violet Winter out of her laboratory. I started laughing and couldn't stop.

By the time I stopped laughing, exhausted, as if I'd run a marathon and unable to hold myself upright, I leaned forward holding onto my knees and waited until I could regain my composure. Once I was calm, I straightened and wiped the tears from my cheeks. It was at that moment the idea came to me. I knew exactly what I had to do with these ridiculous pieces of 21st century surveillance, vanity, and paranoia.

Once I sped away from Violet Winter's house of horrors, I began to relax. I still had the three incriminating cellphones in my luggage, but I wasn't worried. Soon they would be put to good use. I could hardly wait for the outcome. Anyone with a brain could tell how eager the child was to be gone. Her abrupt change in attitude was contagious. Like her, I found myself leaning forward in my seat, as if by such an act, I could propel myself faster and further away from the house than the speed allowed. By the time we were in Brookings, I was grinning, and she was grinning and soon we were laughing for no good reason at all. The day was sunny, the world was gorgeous.

Some primitive insight recommended Klamath Falls to me. I remembered how efficient those women had been when they reported a child-molestation. Therefore, I decided to return to Klamath Falls. I found a perfect receptacle to place the child in so as not to call attention to myself or have people remember they had seen me with her. These days it was best to be cautious. The place I found was perfect for her. I chose the most expensive hotel in Klamath Falls with room service and delivery of meals charged to the suite and even a pool, sauna, and gym in the basement.

Once settled in our room, I ordered my usual medication from Frankie's account. Dr. Bishop's office received the order and Nurse Phillips promptly phoned Frankie's cell number and wanted to know if I was still having trouble sleeping. For the greater good and the promise of fulfilling my plan, I accepted her impertinent questions about my state of mind and physical health and when she was satisfied with my answers, she agreed to Fed Ex the necessary prescription to my hotel.

By the end of the week, the little girl had accepted her glass of milk as a routine part of her day. On our last morning together, she fell asleep curled in my arms. The crushed half of a sleeping pill with a few drops of chocolate powder to hide the taste worked wonders. She'd been so good and quiet the whole week and had accepted the oddness of hiding in the trunk during those times when the cleaning staff found it necessary to change the sheets, vacuum, and wash the tub. I'd poked holes in the trunk where the holes wouldn't be seen by any casual observer.

No one questioned my need for privacy or my lack of interest in the town. I had my computer set up on the desk by the window and whenever room service arrived, I pretended to be busy typing. Of course, no one asked what I was writing. They didn't seem to care what I did for a living which was all to the good. It was all good really.

The tricky part would be getting her out of the hotel room without anyone noticing. On Sunday morning after her bath and breakfast, I dressed her in her new clothes – a silk baby doll dress with pink and white flowers, white socks, and shiny black patent-leather shoes. With a soft brush, I combed her thin blonde curls. Her hair had grown a few inches. One of the curls wanted to wrap itself around my finger; I wouldn't let it. And when she stepped away from me with her eyes bright and full of anticipation, I noticed a cluster of reddish gold curls growing just above her pale and impossibly slim neck and had to turn away to hide my betraying emotions.

She was such a trusting, sweet little thing. I knew I would miss her terribly. Shame washed over me. It was nature's tricky way of seducing adults into caring for the young. Something in our makeup made us gravitate toward the small and helpless and cute. A mistake. To love another is a mistake. I'd seen enough of the ugly side of love. I must remember what Dr. A used to tell me, "That's not love. That's a twisted perverted lie."

The knock startled us both. She ran back to me and clung to my legs. "Just a minute," I shouted to the person on the other side of the door while attempting to peel the child's clinging hands off me. I ran to the steamer trunk and opened the lid. She jumped inside and lay on top of Winter's silk ball gown and curled up into a ball with her thumb in her mouth and her fingers rubbing the silk skirt. I closed and locked the trunk and opened my hotel door. The man who stood on the threshold frowned in annoyance at the delay.

At first, I mistook him for an off-duty police officer in his blue jeans and blue blazer then he spoke, "Ms. Stewart?"

"Yes," I said and stepped away from the door.

He stepped into the room and glanced around sniffing the air like a cat sensing trouble, "I'm here to collect your luggage and escort you to your taxi."

"My luggage is over there," I said pointing at my luggage resting on the floor near the table which beside my steamer trunk included someone else's set of matching blue suitcases. The rude man dragged my steamer trunk out the door. I followed carrying the briefcase and other accoutrements bought by my former predecessors. In old movies the actors would call such a man in front of me, a bell-hop or bell-boy which implied someone who did another's bidding at the ringing of a bell. Of course, back then they had bells rather than telephones. But this man looked to be in his middle years and reminded me more of a retired cop or marine than a bell-hop. Nor did the man appear to do much hopping either. He seemed rather disgruntled, especially annoyed at the weight of my steamer trunk.

"Be careful there," I snapped at him unable to hide my anxiety. "I have some precious artifacts in there; and if you so much as break any of the crystal, it will come out of your salary." The man's cursory glance at the steamer trunk made me realize that the usual person who performed this service must be sick. It wasn't until the steamer trunk was safely in the taxi that I relaxed enough to dig in Acacia's purse for some spare money. I offered him two limp dollar bills and like two strangers passing on the street, his eyes flicked over the money with a smirk, as he pretended to ignore my offer and brushed past me without a word. I wasn't surprised.

The taxi driver dropped me off at the train station. He accepted a tip at least and offered to drag the steamer trunk into the lobby. I dissuaded him and watched him leave. It was pure luck that no one was a witness to my arrival. I found my Toyota in the parking lot and pulled around to the front of the train station. A man came out and noticed my struggles to get the steamer trunk inside the back of the Toyota. Together we managed to set it inside and he even went to the trouble of locating some rope so that I could secure the lid.

Needless to say, I drove like a granny until I'd reached the outskirts of Klamath Falls. When I opened the steamer trunk, the child looked up at me with her eyes puffy and red. I used the hem of the silk gown to wipe away her tears and tried my best to remove the dried mucous from her cheeks. I wanted her to look her best, not grotesque but adorable, definitely adorable.

As I carried her in my arms toward the front seat, I told her, "It's bad now. I won't lie to you. I've been cold and unfriendly. That's because I don't know you. I'm not your mother and you're old enough to know I'm not. It's sad really; sad you've lost your innocent trust in people. You'll probably never get it back. I haven't. But eventually you'll find your parents. In this day and age with a television in practically every home, someone will see your face and recognize you. Yes. You'll find your parents." I spoke in a voice that started out falsely sentimental and ended up feeling like the truth which rather surprised me.

I deposited her in the front seat next to me and strapped her in and handed her a chocolate kiss. She held the kiss in her hand all the way to our destination. I drove down the alley and parked two blocks from the church then turned to the child.

"I know you understand me. You're capable of reading lips, aren't you? I think you can even hear a little bit? You are resilient and smart. I've figured that much out about you. You'll do fine with these new people. They will find your real momma and poppa," I said watching her closely for a reaction. No reaction to momma and poppa, so I tried mother and father. No reaction. Then I tried the word Mommy. She moved in close and peered intently at my lips knowing I was trying to communicate something important to her. When I said Mommy, her lips widened, and her hand grabbed for my arm, then she looked around anxiously as if the person she longed for were only inches away.

I tapped her shoulder. She looked up at me again. I said, "You believe me, don't you? The people in the church will find your Mommy." Even though the child was deaf, I knew she could read lips. She nodded her head in ascent and smiled for the first time. Children were so trusting. It nearly breaks one's heart. "Now eat your candy. I have some more goodies for you. Eat up, baby." She opened her mouth as if to speak. Words came out, but I couldn't quite understand them. Her lips and tongue were unable to wrap themselves around the words, but she tried, she tried really hard. I waited patiently until she was finished.

"Ana ll ack ere," she said and pointed toward the backseat.
"What?"

Then she did a curious thing. She touched her shoulders with two fingers of each hand, then turned her hands outwards and began to flap them in imitation of a bird flying and said again. "Ana ll ack ere." Then she stopped flapping her hands in that weird way and took her right hand and pressed her fingers and a thumb together then raised this shape to her face and proceeded to circle her face with her fingers several times and say, "Poohe. Poohe."

I had no idea what she was trying to communicate; yet, I pretended to understand. It was essential that she eat the candy, so I nodded and smiled and said, "That's wonderful. Poohe to you to. Now eat your candy."

What a relief to finally be able to hand the child over to a reliable source. I walked away from the church knowing she would be in good hands and continued to walk for several miles before deciding I could safely turn around to begin the walk back to where I'd stashed the Toyota. Free as a bird. I flapped my wings and laughed. An elderly couple walking toward me paused and the woman approached me and smiled. Then she began to do the finger thing like the child had done. Annoyed, I tried to pass her. Her companion appeared embarrassed and said, "Hailey. Don't practice your sign language on strangers. She might be foreign for all you know and not understand anything you're trying to communicate."

I stopped and turned, "You know sign language?" I asked the woman. She reminded me of a teacher with her clear gray eyes watching me with studied assessment; always assessing people those teachers, a lifetime of judging and figuring out how to pour knowledge into little minds, yes, teaching, a necessary evil.

"A little," she said with an eager expression as if learning was fun. Weird.

"What does this and this mean?" I asked doing the signs I'd seen the little girl do shortly before she fell asleep.

"Ah wait. Yes," she looked at the man as if he could tell her. He threw up his hands in defeat and she looked away concentrating, "Not bird. This is bird," and she proceeded to show me the sign for bird. As if I really gave a damned. I waited patiently. She snapped her fingers, "Ah yes. Angel. That is the sign for angel. And the other one is pretty.

A deaf person must have signed pretty angel to you. How sweet. He must have been flirting with you."

"No. I'm sure he meant something else, because he did this after angel," and I demonstrated by throwing my hand over my shoulder and pointing my index finger. "Then he did the sign for pretty."

"That sign might mean back, as in your physical back or the hand over the shoulder probably has to do with time, as in yesterday or in the distant past. If he was pointing, he might have been trying to sign the word for location as in over there. He must have seen a pretty angel in the recent past? Not a long time ago though because he would have tapped several times to indicate a longer period of time. No. I'm wrong. When one taps the back that means something like: I'll be back, or I'll return, unless the signer is inexperienced in sign language. Show me the sign again."

Concerned I was calling attention to myself and might be remembered, I stepped back, "That's okay. I was just curious. I've got to go. Thanks though."

I started walking briskly down the street sincerely hoping the couple never heard about the deaf child discovered at the church. If they heard about her from the news, they might remember my odd question. I couldn't have that happen. No one was supposed to have seen me. I had chosen to deposit her on the steps leading to the alter during the lull between services, just after the last person left the parking lot and just before the others arrived for the second service.

I'd waited for the priest to enter the rectory before carrying her inside the church. The marquee included the times of each service. There were two on Sundays, one at 9:00 a.m. and the last one at 11:00 a.m. Each service was an hour long with a thirty-minute break between. I'd figured she would lie on the carpeted step near the alter for only about ten or fifteen minutes. And there was also a good chance some early bird would show up and discover her.

And I wasn't worried about getting caught by some clever detectives. Everyone, even people as far away as New Guinea probably knew about fingerprinting and DNA identification. So I had been careful, very careful from the moment we entered the hotel room to constantly wipe down every surface she and I touched and while waiting for our taxi checked the room to be sure we hadn't left anything behind. When she climbed into the trunk at the hotel and the bellhop carried her down to the taxi, I wiped the doorknob for good measure. While dressing her in the hotel room, I covered my hair in a shower cap and wore disposable gloves. After I dressed in my Sunday clothes, I wore my matching gloves and covered my head in an attractive silk scarf.

Yes, I had been careful with the details. And even if I'd left some of myself behind, in other words, my DNA, forensics would learn only that I had spent my childhood at Canal Critical Care and Recovery Hospital and went by the name Jane Smith. Surely by this time, if my parents had been alive, they would have come forward and claimed me as their child. No one had come forward, so people knew me only as Jane Smith. I was no longer Jane Smith. I had many identities now. I could easily slip in and out of my many disguises.

But what about those other two yahoos? They wouldn't stop looking for me, at least the older brother would press on, once he discovered he'd been cheated out of his prize. Even just to think of him brought a spike of searing pain into my eye. I pressed my fingers into my forehead, desperately conjuring other faces and other images. A good thing I still wore my costume on my long walk around Klamath Falls. I was covered from head to foot: a scarf covered my hair, sunglasses hid my eyes, and I was dressed in a ridiculously flowered cotton one piece with a long skirt nearly brushing my ankles.

Everything had been accomplished without a snag. Other than missing the opportunity to teach Leland a lesson he would never forget. Thinking of Leland had reminded me I had a phone call to make. I called the number I'd been given, and a man answered, "Yeah? Well, do you have him?"

"Hi again, it's me, Mona Lawson. Well, I received the money, but there's a hitch. The guy never showed up. I'm so sorry. I don't know what else to do. And he would have been perfect. Never smoked in his life, never drank alcohol. And a vegan too. I can't give back the money. Sorry. I've already spent it. I'll keep looking for him and when I find him, I'll give you a call."

"We'll be in touch," he said and hung up. From his tone she suspected "in touch" might be a quite painful experience.

She laughed and thought – sure, like I'm going to be stupid enough to stick around so you can use me for spare parts?

That evening I lay on the thin coverlet on my new rough bed in a new town and watched the local news. Without fail, the news reported the discovery of the abandoned child discovered in the church of Our Lady of Peace during services. The news showed a picture of the child being carried in the arms of a female police officer. The anchor woman mentioned a possible witness, a woman who might have seen the perpetrator carry the child into the church. The witness described a young woman barely out of her teens wearing an old-fashioned dress, gloves, and a paisley scarf. She might have been a brunette, then again, she might have been a redhead, but most definitely, she had been young.

I looked in the mirror and grinned at the face looking back at me and relaxed. Everyone appeared young to the elderly. The anchorwoman pleaded with her audience to report any news to the local police regarding the child's identity or the kidnapper's identity. I suppose I could have left her at a church in Idaho, since I had a sneaky suspicion she belonged to someone in Idaho, most likely someone who lived near Leland's pawn shop or Ray Millhouse's old apartment. After all, the addresses of registered sex offenders were posted on the internet. Yet Ray Millhouse may not be registered because as far as I knew he'd never been caught. I wondered if I should send an anonymous note to the Klamath Falls' Police Department. I changed my mind, choosing not to get involved. I had done what I could. I would wait and watch.

It wasn't until Friday of the next week I learned that the little girl had been identified based on the news broadcast which evidently had reached a viewer in California who happened to be a friend of the child's parents and recognized the child. The news channel showed the three now reunited, well, five, since the little girl had two siblings, an older brother and a younger sister. She looked content sitting on her mother's lap. The Pennington family looked nice. The newswoman called her Skeeter, born Christina Pennington, but known as Skeeter. That name sounded so familiar.

It began with an ache in my throat I couldn't swallow away. The fit left me weak, so weak I had to lie down on the floor like a dog and rest my cheek against the smelly carpet to keep my dinner down. I knew it wasn't over. My eyes were swollen. I could feel their puffiness. I could barely see as I stumbled toward the bathroom. Throwing water on my face didn't help. The aspirin in Frankie's purse didn't help. Laying on my back and staring at the ceiling while a car chase ensued on television with its ubiquitous guns blazing and screaming tires and metal crashing masked my crying, but did not stop the flow.

No more tears. No more pity. No more sentimental bullshit. What a sight? What a pathetic hysterical fury? How dare she ruin this face with her useless emotions? An hour later, ice wrapped in a hand

527

towel brought the swelling down around the eyes and a quick hot shower rejuvenated her body. It was a flaming circus locating a pair of decent jeans and a comfortable top. But eventually she found something comfortable to wear sans lace, silk, or beads. But someone had thrown out the boots which really pissed her off. She had to settle for a pair of sneakers and hoped the jeans covered the ridiculous pink embroidery along the tops of the socks.

Once on the street, she found a nearby bar where they served alcohol and even though she could barely see her way through the maze of tables and chairs and people with her sunglasses on, she managed to reach the bar without tripping or stepping on anyone's feet. The bartender swept past a guy with his mouth open who had been in the act of ordering. The bartender walked toward her as if he could read her mind.

"A scotch neat."

"Ice?"

"Did I say ice?"

"Here you go, baby."

He poured the scotch into a shot glass and handed it to her. When he ignored the money she slapped on the table, she knew she would have to pay for the drink some other way. No good deed goes unpunished, she thought with a grin. He interpreted her grin as acceptance. Let him think what he liked. She sipped the scotch and looked around ignoring the needy ones. They do try to hide their inadequacies, but she could usually pick them out. They were the ones that laughed a little bit louder than most and had a trunk full of bad jokes.

Hours later, I woke up having forgotten the night before.

By the time the fit had passed, I had become a dried bag of bones, a skeleton of rough skin and wet sticky hair. A strong wind would have toppled me over. Easily. I had only enough energy to crawl to the bathroom and puke up the contents of my stomach which happened to be mostly liquid, rest my hot cheek on the cool bathroom tiles, and hope never to remember the night before. For the first time, when I closed my eyes, I saw only darkness. No faces mouthing inexplicable words at me. No faces growing bigger and bigger then receding into the abyss. Just dark. Blissful dark.

I woke with a trickling sensation in my chest as if I could feel the blood pumping through my veins. My head still throbbed, and my eyes were sore; yet, I was hungry, so hungry my belly growled at me. The sticky stuff in my hair turned out to be blood. I tried to remember what had happened. The night remained a blur of faces. Smells came back to me though, alcohol and cigarette smoke, and then the musky scent of a man's armpit. Then I knew.

It took two hours to shower and dress and try to look normal. Makeup hid most of the swelling and the sunglasses protected my eyes from the curious. I managed to leave the room minutes before the maid entered to make the bed and take out the trash. I walked away from the hotel briskly with the sun on my shoulders and the smell of melting tar and a hot afternoon in my nose. Even the tar and car exhaust smelled of his sweat.

I passed a familiar white stucco wall and entered the alley. I saw blood on the wall and walked up to its stucco surface to examine the stain more closely. The alley was wide enough for two trucks to drive comfortably side by side through it to the end. The alley led nowhere. At the end of it was a factory with its chimneys bellowing black smoke into the air. The alley must have been the store house for old couches, mattresses, and used pallets. Someone had even dumped a toilet among the rubbish. On the other side of the alley, she saw a semi. He might or might not be inside the cab sleeping off a drunk.

At this point I didn't care who saw me. I wanted to remember. I feared the worst. I stared at the blood on the wall and the ground and tried to remember. Half of me noticed the sun begin to push back the shadows. When the sun's refection off the white wall made my view of the blood spatters blurry, I looked around and realized time had slipped by me once again. The door flew open. I jumped back behind a pile of old pallets.

A man stumbled down the concrete steps carrying two heavy garbage bags. He set the bags down and I watched as he lifted his bandaged hand to cover his eyes. I managed to sneak behind the semi and kneel to peer under its belly, so I could watch the man throw the bags of garbage into the dumpster. With relief I assessed the damage. He had a cut above his eyebrow, bruises on his neck, and scratches on his cheek. But he was alive. Yes. Alive. Evidently, the head wound must have bled a lot. He did not linger. Nor did I.

Problem solved. Leland the only problem left. Maybe he had become despondent in his old age? Maybe he had already fled the country? He would never leave his business. The pawn shop was his lair.

But maybe he has other webs? I had been scrupulous in waiting for him in that soiled tomb. He had a gift for survival. A cunning predator. I hate mysteries. I hate loose ends.

Then I realized what the child had been trying to tell me.

Angel. Angel back there. Pretty. Pretty.

Violet Winter? Would a child have mistaken her for an angel? Maybe. Surely not. Popular culture depicted angels as blonde, blued eyed, pretty ladies wearing white gowns with enormous white wings. Never the Butcher Queen, not with her white hair, numerous facelifts, dermal fillers, laser treatments, Botox, and chemical peeled skin. Images of angels danced in her head: pretty blondes with porcelain skin and big blue eyes. And the only blonde—

Myrtle?

How odd.

So critical in the past, yet, so easy to forget.

Maybe Myrtle had been right all along.

No one paid her any attention.

28

The site for the ceremony would be just a few yards away from the old Morrison farmhouse on the banks of Willow Creek. The Nerin family were in the process of preparing the site for the coming ceremony. In the hollow near the creek, there was a place just right for them. Everything would be perfect. Tonight, there was a full moon. As they prepared for the ceremony, the moonlight glittered on the waters of Willow Creek transforming the ordinary into a place of serene beauty.

To their right was a chaparral of blackberry bushes and a magnificent Scarlet Oak nearly eighty feet tall and fifty feet wide planted by one of the original Morrisons in 1907. The oak blazed; all its leaves were a gorgeous scarlet. Zak had been privileged to see the tree just before the sun set. While everyone else was still at the Woolly Man dressing and preparing for the ceremony, he had been tasked with finding a suitable sacrifice. "The bigger the better," his mother had said. His mother was bloodthirsty enough to want the real thing. He wasn't about to oblige her.

In his personal cooler he had several bags of ice surrounding a syringe filled with the blood of his neighbor's prize bull. Since the personal cooler which until the first year of the 21st century had been the normal means of delivery for donor organs, he felt secure in the knowledge he was still in line with the spirit of the ritual without actually having to lead a bull to the walrus rock and cut its throat. He glanced at his watch nervously. The bull's blood would remain fresh for another three hours and ten minutes. What the hell was going on with his family?

It wasn't until he saw the three of them walking toward him he realized why they had been delayed. They came into the sacred place single file. First to appear was his sister Quinn who disturbingly refused to look into his eyes, instead making her way to the walrus rock with her armload of gifts to the Gods of Olympus. His mother followed closely behind Quinn carrying a basket which clinked whenever she moved. He figured she'd brought the food and wine.

Luke entered last pulling a red utility all-terrain wagon, a wagon big enough for three grown men to sit in. Luke's smile was so smug, Zak grew nervous. Intuition made him jerk forward to take a quick look inside the wagon. Whatever was inside looked big. He couldn't tell much because a sheet had been thrown over it. Then the truth dawned upon him and with a sickening feeling, he knew. Luke recoiled at the expression on Zak's face.

In front of the Nerin family stood the mound his friend Jankowski liked to call Little Serpent Mound which was a reference to a much larger mound called Great Serpent Mound in Adams County, Ohio. Whereas the Great Serpent Mound had been created by indigenous people long ago, Willow Creek's mound had been created by local farmers and ranchers who for decades dumped their dirt and rocks along this area to make way for fields of wheat and corn.

Even though the mound was man made, the significance of the structure so close to the creek, along with the magnificent oak and the walrus rock made this place unique. As a kid, he believed, the combination of natural and unnatural objects made the place sacred. Now his sacred place would become the Nerin temple to the Gods of Olympus. The irony was not lost on him. He would rather give up his sanctuary than see his family humiliated or in jail.

After watching his brother Luke drop the utility wagon handle, he stepped forward recognizing the yellow surfboard inside. There was something large wrapped in several old sheets tied together with rope. Zak feared the worst. "Hey you ignoramus, are you trying to get us all put away for life? If that's the hybrid than you've made a huge mistake; the hybrid won't work. And... if that's a live human being possibly kidnapped and drugged just for this special moment, I'm going to beat you into a bloody pulp," he whispered fiercely, the seriousness in Zak's voice startling all of them, even his mother who instinctively moved in front of Luke, as if her body could protect his big brother from Zak's desire to punch the grin right off his face.

"Don't you dare touch him," his mother began. "He had nothing to do with this. I found this predator sleeping under my porch. Do you want your sister and me to end up dead because you're too soft to kill it?"

"What are you talking about Mom?"

"This," she said throwing the sheet off the body which had been strapped to the surfboard with bungee cords. It was about the same size as the hybrid they'd found on Ruby Mountain, but this was a hybrid of a different kind. He recognized the big black cat he'd seen before. In the light from the candles placed strategically about the area, he recognized the creature he had come to think of as an imaginary product of his trauma, trauma brought about by Leona's accurate mining of his past life. In some circles, people called her ability – retrocognition. He didn't believe in precognition or clairvoyance or retrocognition. In the last 12,000 years of modern civilization no one had been able to prove without a doubt that people had such abilities.

Why would he digress from the horror right in front of him to think about Leona and debate with himself about what is fake science and what is real science? Maybe because he was staring down at a jaguar with human ears and the executive part of his brain refused to believe his eyes? He paid special attention to the jaguar's ears and nearly threw up at the sight. The ears weren't fake. The ears were real human ears. His brother noticed where he was looking and leaned forward, "Awesome isn't it?"

"It!" Zak hissed. "You piece of shit, this is a sentient creature. A living breathing part of our earth with just as much right to live as you and me. And you plan to-"

His mother cut him short and said, "Luke doesn't plan on doing anything. Now calm down, Zak. Give us some credit. Let's get started. We don't have much time. Come over here boys and stand beside me." In his eagerness to get the show on the road, Luke jumped to attention, his feet bounding over the ground like a basketball star leading his team to victory. Before Luke had had time to settle in beside his mother, Zak had thought of and discarded several plans to rescue the jaguar. Maybe he could carry the jaguar in his arms without breaking his back? Maybe he could reach the car before Luke jumped on him? Or maybe he should call the cops and rat out his family?

Instead of doing the rational thing, still feeling uneasy, he moved toward the altar hoping he could intervene or his family would come to their senses. In amazement he shook his head. Maybe one of them was bloodthirsty enough to do it, but not all of them. He knew his sister Quinn wasn't capable of killing anyone much less this magnificent creature. Even his brother as a scientist would hesitate to kill such a rare specimen. His mother though, well, he wasn't so sure about her. In the past, she'd had no trouble wringing a chicken's neck or setting traps for mice, but would she really kill something so noble? And then he remembered Y2K and all the hysteria going on at the time.

The back of the walrus rock had been covered in a silk altar cloth of white. On the cloth lay a crystal bowl filled with flowers and seeds. On the other side of the bowl lay a familiar kopis sword with its smooth bone handle which had been in Jule's family for generations. Jule claimed her ancestors, including Hera Katsaros herself, had wielded this same kopis sword in all their celebrations. Maybe. What he didn't know until he turned thirteen and officially joined the Amara Fan Club was that his own mother following in her mother's footsteps really did sacrifice live goats and lambs with that exact same sword.

Having already ruined Christmas for Zak by telling him there was no such thing as Santa Claus, Luke proceeded to ruin the Greek Holy days for him as well by recording the Easter celebration when Zak officially became a member. Parker Youngblood and his mother must have had some sort of arrangement, because he was never around during the celebration of the Greek holy days. Most Sundays, he would be off before sunrise taking his shovel and his buckets and wouldn't return until late in the evening, long after sunset.

When Zak was thirteen, the venue for the ceremony changed. Instead of setting up the altar in the barn where Parker kept his most famous find, a huge square piece of travertine weighing a hundred pounds, his mother decided to have the ceremony inside the Woolly Man. From that day forward all celebrations took place in the bar. No one was surprised since last year their celebrations had been interrupted by a couple of hunters wandering onto the property looking for a beer.

It took all four of them to carry the heavy chunk of travertine from the barn into the bar. While they rested, Jule prepared the room for the celebration. The white travertine looked spectacular in the middle of room especially against the soft brown of the polished oak floor. But their mother insisted the travertine altar had to be near running water. All of them had to figure out how to get the heavy stone near water. Quinn came up with the brilliant idea of setting the stone on Parker's dolly, the one he used to unload his rocks.

They put the bars back on the dolly and Jule draped a clean white sheet over the bars to hide the stone until the ceremony. Several locations were tested. Everyone agreed the corner between the bathrooms was a really bad choice. In the end they chose to put the stone beneath the serving window. On the other side of the window was the kitchen prep area with a full counter and a stainless-steel sink.

That year, the year he lost all his innocence was the year everything seemed to work to Luke's advantage, so that instead of Jule disappearing into the dark recesses of the barn to do her dirty work which would have been difficult to record on Luke's cellphone, they had a clear video of Jule at the prep counter slashing the lamb's throat as it lay on the cutting board. So instead of presenting as an offering to the Gods a symbolic facsimile of blood, their mother was handing them real blood from a freshly killed sacrifice.

Not only had his family ruined Christmas and the Greek Holy days for him, they had made the owning of a pet seem like a cruel monstrous act of betrayal. Maybe his mother didn't really cut the throat of the family cat one winter, maybe the cat really did run away from home, and maybe the gerbil really did get eaten by the cat. Yet, after seeing the video of his mother slashing the throat of a drugged lamb, he refused his mother's repeated offerings to buy him a pet. In fact, he made it his business to free any animal that dared to come into the Nerin home on its own or by adoption.

So he supposed that was why they had kept him out of the loop when they drugged the jaguar, tied it up, and carted the magnificent animal into what had once been a sanctuary and would now forever be a filthy reminder of his family's insanity.

"Please Quinn," Jule said waving her hand toward the altar. "Let's begin."

Quinn extracted a silk robe from her packages and slipped the robe over her slender arms. As she covered her head with the robe, Zak noticed for the first time that she had shaved her head completely. All her beautiful curly hair and those colorful beads were now in some damned garbage bag, he thought in disgust. He glared at his mother and then his brother. They were too busy eagerly awaiting Quinn's words of wisdom. Why did they demand she do such a thing? How would having a cue ball for a head make her more worthy?

"Oh, Mighty Gods of Olympus," his sister began raising her arms toward the sky, the silk of her sleeves whispering. "We are gathered here to welcome you to our sacred place. Mothers and fathers, sons and daughters, brothers and sisters of Zeus, we welcome you all to our most holy shrine."

Looking up at the starry sky, Zak thought about thousands of years of evolution and scientists today capable of so many extraordinary things and yet here they were like pagans of old begging capricious Gods of Olympus for favors. While he looked up at the stars using the beauty of the night to calm his gathering disgust, he heard his sister say, "Welcome noble Zeus. We are gathered here to welcome you to our sacred place. Join us at our table. Most holy one, join us in this sacred place. We would be honored by your presence."

Quinn lit the thick stubby candles on the altar stone one by one and said, "Come share our wine and food, noble ones. Come join us at our banquet. We are ready for your wisdom and generosity. Show us the way back to the beginning." When she finished lighting the candles, she turned to face them with her arms spread wide, the long sleeves of her robe nearly touching the ground. Jule bowed her head and closed her eyes. Luke bowed his head and closed his eyes. Quinn looked into Zak's eyes, cocked her head slightly and smiled. He thought about what to do and decided he would go along with the farce for a little bit longer. He bowed his head but did not close his eyes. When his brother jabbed him in the side, he closed his eyes.

As one the family spoke the words he'd heard a thousand times before, on Holy Days marked by the three-major religious, on birthdays or any time the family gathered to celebrate an event: an A on a quiz, Luke's acceptance at Harvard and Oxford, Quinn reaching puberty, and Zak hitting a home run. And so, as he recited the prayer, he looked around his former sanctuary where he and his friends used to play. He no longer recognized the place. On the walrus rock stood a bunch of candles, a bowl filled with seeds, and a short sword used to kill. He found by the end of the prayer, he was barely able to form the words for the loss he felt for this special place.

"Come share our wine and food, spirits of our ancestors. Come join us Ocypete, Adoni, and Amara, wise and noble ladies. Come join us Aiolos and all your kin. We welcome you all to our hearth and home. Peace to you all, dear ancestors. We bless you. We love you. Welcome." And as Zak recited the prayer half-heartedly, all the while aware of the utility wagon behind him and the offering inside, he had an overwhelming urge to spin around, grab the handle and run for his life.

Just as he finished his thought, the leaves in the oak tree rustled. The wind, he assumed, relaxing. The rustling intensified. He froze as terrified as one of his pagan ancestors, for one frightening moment believing the dead had really come back to join them in this place by Little Serpent Mound and Willow Creek. He wasn't alone in his terror. His brother's shoulder twitched, so he knew Luke had heard the same sounds. When his sister Quinn faltered and dropped her arms, Jule hissed, "Go on. Don't be afraid Quinn. Say-"

Taking a step back and lifting her arms once again, Quinn spoke the words exactly as they had been written down one hundred and sixty years ago in the Hera Book of Prayers, "We are ready to receive you here in this sacred place, Gods of Olympus. Show us the way back to the beginning." Was it really happening? Had he been wrong all along? Then his mother curtly said to Quinn, "Now is the time for the blessing. Read the blessing onto Zeus, Quinn."

His sister nodded her understanding and turned to face the altar. She lifted the bowl filled with seeds over her head saying, "We bless you mighty Zeus for all you have given us. As your children, we bless you mighty Zeus for your love of us. As your equals, we bless you mighty Zeus for your power and strength to vanquish our enemies. A thousand blessings onto you, most powerful one." We heard the screeching first and then a bird flew out of the oak tree and took off into the night sky. Later, Luke swore the creature had been a bat, not a bird. Nobody argued with him. Everyone had been frightened, even Jule. It took Zak several precious minutes for his heart to start beating at its normal rhythm – too long a time recovering to save the magnificent jaguar.

With the breaking of the spell, the youngest members of the Nerin family had left their assigned places and were congregated near the altar close to the light. The light might have been feeble, but it was better than standing in the dark, not knowing who was behind you. In the short time, Zak, Luke, and Quinn had huddled close together by the altar, Jule had had time to pull the utility wagon the few feet into the light cast by the candles. She threw back the sheet covering the jaguar's body and shouted, "Quinn, hand me the kopis. Hurry. We don't have much time now. He's waking up."

Quinn turned slowly to do as she was bid, but Luke got to the kopis first and rushed to Jule's side before Zak had had enough presence of mind to stop him. Just as Jule lifted the jaguar's head to slit his throat, there was a struggle going on in the oak tree. All of them froze. They all heard the high piercing screams of a dying animal fighting for its life followed by a sudden bone-chilling silence, then the sound as a body fell from a great height crashing through the foliage, and landing with a loud thump on the ground near Jule's feet.

Zak got to Jule and took the kopis out of her hand and in two strides had retrieved the dead animal on the ground near the altar. He picked the squirrel up by its tail and threw it on the altar. The squirrel's stomach had been torn open by a predator's claws. Blood and intestines were spilling out onto the altar cloth.

Zak lifted his head to the stars and shouted, "Oh, mighty Zeus, we are gathered here in this sacred place to offer you this our small gift, a tribute to your greatness, your generosity and your goodness. We thank you for allowing Ocypete and her daughter Adoni Katsaros to live and die as freeborn. We thank you for permitting Aiolos his freedom. We beg you now noble one to forgive Amara Katsaros her sins and allow her and her descendants their due as immortals of the Gods of Olympus. With this sacrifice, we do pledge to obey you to the ends of our days and we pledge to worship the Gods of Olympus to the ends of our days and we pledge eternal loyalty to you and the Gods."

Not to be outdone, Quinn stepped forward and put her hand on the dead squirrel and repeated the Offering Prayer word-for-word exactly as Zak had spoken them.

Everyone heard the scrambling of claws as the big cat woke from his sleep and sprang out of the utility wagon in one lithe motion. It was one of the few wonders of the world. Zak would never forget the sight of the beautiful creature, so long and lean, moving so fluidly as if he had all the time in the world and wasn't afraid of anyone. For one incredible moment, the jaguar turned to look at the family as they huddled together by the altar, every one of them sure they would be maimed or killed or eaten.

Instead of feeling threatened by them and charging, his yellow eyes studied them curiously and Zak swore his head moved slightly to the left reminding Zak of a domesticated cat watching the antics of a silly mouse, wondering why the mouse wasn't running away in terror so he could chase it. Then the jaguar turned his head toward the oak and demonstrated another monumental achievement orchestrated by evolution. In one bound, he launched himself up into the tree clawing his way to the heaviest branch and there he rested among the scarlet leaves watching and waiting for their next move.

Barely above a whisper, everyone heard Jule say, "We still have the Healing Prayer and the Invitation to Zeus before we can wrap this up and go home. Come on now everyone; we're so close. Don't worry about the cat. He's not stupid. He won't hurt us." Zak wasn't so sure about his mother's reading of the situation. He wanted to get the hell out before the jaguar felt threatened enough to attack. Evidently his brother and sister didn't agree with his assessment of the situation;

instead of gathering up their belongings and getting the hell out, they relaxed and moved back into their respective positions: Quinn to stand facing the altar stone, Luke to stand beside the utility wagon facing Quinn and Jule to stand a few feet from Luke.

Since Jule was closer to the oak tree than any of them and didn't seem to mind being so close to the big cat, Zak thought he should protect her by being the one to stand closest to the tree. Zak threw the kopis on the altar cloth and moved toward his mother. She held him off with one hand on his chest and with a gentle push said, "We have to resume our former places. Let's not jinx the whole thing by doing something different." For a second, in his disbelief, Zak considered walking away from them all, so disgusted with the whole unsavory mess, he was ready to disown his entire family.

"Holy shit, I nearly wet my pants," Quinn admitted with a quick smile before resuming her unfamiliar gravity and ramrod posture. "Well, here goes." As she recited the prayer, she picked the seeds out of the bowl and sprinkled them over the offering, signifying the cycle of life and death. "Heal us now, oh mighty Zeus. Heal us now, oh powerful Gods of Olympus. Heal Amara Katsaros and all her descendants. Heal all those who share the blood of Ocypete, long known to you as the harpy Swiftwing and heal her lover King Aiolos, divine keeper of the winds."

Once she had finished the Healing Prayer, she dipped her fingers in the blood now pooling around the squirrel and lifted her hand to show her bloody fingers to her family. Instead of following the normal procedure written down by Hera Katsaros, Quinn turned to face the oak tree, hesitated for a moment, squared her shoulders, and marched to the tree trunk. Pretending unconcern at the danger just above her head, she pressed her bloody fingertips into the rough wood smearing the blood and seeds onto the bark.

In a commanding voice, Quinn recited the last prayer, the Invitation to Zeus' Table, "We are ready to sit beside you, noble one. We are ready to sit as equals at your table. As your equals and as your strong arm, we will defend you. As immortals, we will defend you. Blessings on us all. Blessings on the house of Ocypete. Blessings on the house of Aiolos. Blessings on the Gods of Olympus." Visibly shaking, partly from terror at being so close to a wild animal and partly from the heavy responsibility of her position as priestess, she returned to the altar, "We're ready to drink a toast to our ancestors and the Gods of

Olympus." Jule pulled out the wine glasses from the hamper. Luke opened the wine specially selected for the occasion, a wine which had been drunk in the Nerin family since the moment Hera Katsaros stepped off the boat in New York City.

Nobody wanted to linger over the wine. Without ceremony, they all drank the few sips of wine in their glasses, bit off a chunk of bread chewing rapidly, some swallowing the tough bits with a painful grimace and before Zak had to remind them of the hour or the present danger poised to drop on their heads from the thick branches of the oak tree, his mother and Quinn were already blowing out the candles, packing up the crystal bowl and the altar cloth as Luke went back and forth between the walrus rock and the utility wagon dumping the items inside in a haphazard fashion.

Without waiting to escort the family to the cars, Zak left the site. It was obvious his mother didn't need his protection. Disgusted with himself for participating in the whole stupid ceremony and for his family's part in buying into a pagan superstition with such zeal, he had to catch his breath suddenly at the thought that his former sanctuary had become tainted with this memory. It was only when he managed to get to his car that he remembered he'd left his little cooler near the banks of Willow Creek.

In the area near the walrus rock, his family had managed to clear away any evidence of their ceremony. With the moonlight shining down on him and not a sound or sight of any living creature, Zak searched for his cooler. After a few minutes searching for it, he heard the wind rushing through the leaves and looked up in time to see yellow eyes watching him. He decided to come back during the day and search for his cooler. Feeling eyes on his back, Zak took the long way around the Little Serpent Mound and managed to reach his car safely. The rest of his family had left, probably eager to get home in anticipation of all the good things to come from their successful sacrifice.

Surely Zeus would hear their prayers and grant them their rightful place at the table on Mount Olympus? It was when Zak while waiting for the motor to warm up looked back toward Little Serpent Mound, that he thought he saw a woman standing on the top watching him. At first, he moved to open the door thinking the woman might be his sister who in their haste had been left behind. Then with the hairs on the nap of his neck reading danger, instead he locked all the car doors.

540

The rational part of his brain kicked in reminding him that his mother would never leave Quinn behind to fend for herself in the dark, especially not with a wild animal so close by, an animal which didn't seem to be afraid of humans and seemed uncomfortably territorial when it came to the Nerin family. If it wasn't so late and he wasn't so tired, he'd have realized that there was nothing normal about any of the events that had taken place tonight.

By the time he drove back to the Woolly Man, it was nearly four in the morning. The lights were blazing inside the bar. Instead of going straight to his trailer, Zak decided to give his family a second chance. He entered the bar and looked around the room. Everything seemed so normal. Jule was busy boxing up the heavy leather books while Quinn could be heard in the kitchen loading the dishwasher. The fat candles which had been used earlier had been lit and were arranged on the pool table along with the bottle of wine and clean wineglasses.

"Come have a glass of wine, Zak," his brother Luke said motioning him over to the pool table. "Tomorrow we're going to be getting our hands dirty replacing the old wood stove. We might as well celebrate what's left of the night."

"No thanks. I've had enough celebrating," Zak said addressing his mother as well.

Jule had wiped down the bar and was now standing in the middle of the room with her hands on her hips. "Would you take that box up to my room. It belongs on the top shelf of the closet." Without a word, Zak lifted the box and carried it up the stairs to his mother's room across the hall from Quinn's room. Her closet door was still open and there was a spot on the shelf for the box. Once he was finished in the room, he closed his mother's door. Just as he reached the bottom step he heard his brother say to his mother, "If nothing happens, I'm going to blame Zak. His filthy attitude might just have jinxed the whole thing." He couldn't hear his mother's response.

Pretending ignorance, Zak walked up to the pool table and accepted a glass of wine from his mother. He drank the wine down and set the empty glass on the bar. "I'm beat. I'm going to bed."

"I've been thinking about renting out your old room, Zak. You've been living in the trailer for nearly a year now. You wouldn't mind, would you?"

He turned to face the room. Quinn had come out of the kitchen and with the robe gone and her newly shaven head glinting in the light from the ceiling fan, Zak felt suddenly very, very sad. "You're right. Go ahead. Rent out my old room. I'll clear out my stuff in the morning."

"It's nearly morning now," Quinn quipped with a slight smile.

Zak didn't have the heart to smile back. "Well, I'll need a few hours' sleep if we're going to replace the old stove." And with those parting words, he left the bar through the side door and crossed the meadow toward his trailer.

Once he was inside his trailer, he sat down at his little table and started to cry. Like a pipe bursting, all the events of the week came rushing out of him: Jane Smith entering the Woolly Man, a herald of bad things to come, Leona taking over and playing her sick little paranormal parlor games, Acacia beating his brother nearly to death, he and Eve spending the night together in Paris, Nevada, then the hell raising switchbacks from Grants Pass to Antelope Summit. It had been too much. What had put him right over the edge though he had to be honest had been the ceremony at Little Serpent Mound.

The bursting of the floodgates had exhausted him. Yet he wasn't tired enough to sleep just yet. He switched on the television and the early morning news included a story about some poor deaf child discovered at a church in Klamath Falls along with three cellphones and the news that the FBI were looking for three people of interest who may or may not be victims of the kidnapper. Twenty minutes later, he felt tired enough to sleep. Half asleep he thought he heard something outside his trailer. He ignored the warning and turned over gradually falling into a deep sleep.

He climbed down from the branch of the Scarlet Oak and moved toward the altar. In one fluid motion feeling his powerful hind legs lift him in the air, he leaped onto the altar and stretched himself out upon the cold stone. He heard her on the top of the mound and the rattling of stones as she descended into the hollow. When she came into view, he struggled against the instinct to attack. Instead of lunging at her with teeth and claws, he turned over onto his side in a posture signifying trust. The woman, hair the color of a raven's wing which flowed down her back in long undulating waves stood before the altar looking down upon him with a tender smile.

He closed his eyes waiting eagerly for the end. It had been so long since someone had looked at him with love, had touched him with gentle hands and sung so sweetly in his ear. She would keep her promise to him. He was ready, eager for that good rest.

A long time ago, he'd shared her memories and her thoughts, seeing her as she had once been so long ago, a beautiful proud woman living among the native Columbia River people who had trusted her. Unlike the others trapped in the hell that was the cabin on Ruby Mountain, she had trusted him enough to show him an image of herself in all her glory, as a full-breasted woman with a tiny waist and long shapely legs. She had even trusted him enough to show him an image of herself in flight, her magnificent wings stretched wide circling the sky above the tree tops. She shared her view of the world as she flew and together they dreamed of the Columbia River Gorge and the magnificent Amazon before the white man came.

Seventeen years ago, as the orderlies and Mona Lawson pulled him from the burning cabin, he'd seen her in the flesh hiding in the chaparral nearby. The harpy had been naked, newly freed from her coffin, her skin pale and sickly from lack of light and air, so different from the way she'd been as a free woman. No one could see her but him. He remembered how startled he had been to hear her familiar voice inside his head just before the orderlies put him in the ambulance, "Keep your promise to Tessa and Kallan. One day, I will come for you. You are our brother now, a member of our family. Be patient, dear one. Be patient, my good friend."

Now as she stood before him at the altar dressed completely in black from her tight-fitting wool sweater dress to her knee-high boots with skin the color of smooth copper and green eyes alight with purpose, his heart thudded in syncopation with her own. Soon, soon, his suffering would be over.

She leaned down and her hair fell forward warming his body. She whispered in his ear, "I am sorry, my old friend, but it is not your time to leave this good earth. Hush. Stay still. Don't be afraid. I know. I know. I made you a promise. I keep my promises. You will see. Soon, you and I will receive our gift of everlasting sleep. I have seen our deaths and they are good ones. I ask you now for patience and understanding and the will to return to your true nature, my courageous and kind friend. I am here to help on your journey back."

Without warning, she straightened to her full height nearly as tall as himself and pulled off her sweater dress. Then for the first time he saw her wings as she spread them out to their full length effectively cutting off the moonlight and the stars. Before he had time to realize her fingernails had become claws, she lifted her right arm and slashed. He felt the warm blood flowing down his throat. There was no pain just the warmth seeping out of him. Cool fingers wrapped themselves tightly around his throat and squeezed. He blacked out.

When he woke, it was nearly dawn, and his body felt stiff and sore. There was a dull throbbing around his neck where she had slashed his throat and squeezed so tightly. He reached up to touch his throat and stopped to stare at his hand. His hand could claim four fingers and a thumb. He rose to a sitting position feeling the cold rock on his bare buttocks. He looked down at his naked body in wonder. A skittering of stones alarmed him, and he leaped off the walrus rock intending to climb into the oak tree to hide. Amara, still wearing her black sweater dress and boots came around the corner of the Little Serpent Mound with an armful of clothes.

She stopped to admire him, "Here, I've brought you some clothes and boots. While you dress, I will find us some breakfast. We must leave this place soon." Before they left the sacred site, Terence and Amara gave thanks to the Gods by leaving what was left in their cups as offerings. Their offerings were rewarded with the sudden appearance of three Cooper Hawks who settled themselves on a thick branch of the Scarlett Oak. The hawks were too far above them to be caught.

Amara laughed and said, "They are afraid of me."

Terence noticed one of them had prey in its beak. The Hawk dropped the small creature from a great height. Without thinking Terence rushed to catch the pitiful thing before it hit the ground. Amara was quicker. She caught the gift and presented it to Terence saying, "Where madness perverted the ways of nature, nature has made right again."

When Terence just stared at her in confusion, she smiled. Her smile filled with love and compassion may have been the reason for his decision. He would never know for sure because when she smiled his body was already in motion stepping forward with his arm extended. By the time his brain caught up with his body, she'd already dropped the jaguar cub into his palm saying, "When I was born we worshiped the Greek goddess Gaia."

She took a step backward and continued, "We ancient Greeks worshipped her as a part of us and as a guardian of the earth. We were wrong. Our happiness and the earth's wellbeing are our responsibility not hers. She is a symbol, but we are the real guardians.

All my life, I've been told to worship the Gods of Olympus and Gaia among them. And I did and then I didn't. When I turned my back on the Gods, my mother said Zeus punished me. No. He did not. My mother was wrong. I am not an abomination. Zeus did not punish me. I was created on Earth over many generations. I am meant to be here. There are wonders and beauties here, wonders and beauties unforced. I am also unforced. I am a part of the earth and have just as much right to be here as the beetle crawling up the oak.

I trust in that truth. So, I apologize to you now. I manipulated you and you did what was natural as a man, you pushed back. Remember how I smiled at you and you moved forward to accept Gaia's gift. It is the old Greek in me. A big mistake. If the old Greek in me had won, the cub might have suffered. You would have felt used and turned on the little one. So, I say to you now, you must choose. Take the little one or leave him behind."

The cub's eyes were sealed tightly shut. His sleek black body lay quietly in Terrence's palm. The years of rage and futility dissolved as he held the living creature. It lay trustingly in his hand as if the tiny creature knew him well. Absently he heard Amara explain, "He. I forget my English sometimes. He was reborn the moment you became a man again. Do not worry, Mister Hunter. His eyes will open in due time. Keep him warm and safe. Feed him mother's milk."

"Mother's milk? Where? How?" he asked in alarm as the blind cub clawed its way up his arm and clung to his shoulder. Little by little the cub inched closer until he was curled up near Terence's neck. In the cold morning air, the two of them shared body heat and kept each other warm.

Luke refused to allow his brother's sulking to dampen his good mood. Quinn set her empty glass down on the bar first and blew out the candles. Without a word, she left the room climbing the stairs to her bedroom with a steady swoosh of her skirt and the tapping of her heels on the wooden stairs. Automatically, his mother began to gather up the glasses removing all evidence of their night's work.

No. Not yet. Let's linger and enjoy the moment, he thought. It had taken so long to prepare for the ceremony; and now, such a short time later, the ceremony was over. But was it really over? Shouldn't there be more? At least more effort or suffering on their part? He thought of all the preliterate cultures and even a few places in the world today where rituals and ceremonies could take days sometimes weeks to complete.

Someone banged on the front door and Luke assumed the person outside was Zak. On his way toward the door, he glanced at the clock on the wall. He paused to be sure his eyes had read the hands correctly. It was nearly dawn. They had been at Little Serpent Mound for less than an hour. They had spent more time preparing for the ceremony than the time it took to perform the ritual. He felt as if time had raced through yesterday and cruelly dumped him in the present moment. Like liquid fire the reality of his new found power ran through his body and he could hardly contain himself as he rushed to the door. This was it – the person knocking would bring them good news. He was sure of it.

When he swept the door open, he had to readjust his eyes because the person standing on the threshold with his shoulder propping the screen door open was a stranger. The handsome middle-aged black man had to bow his head in order to move beyond the threshold. He must have been seven feet tall. He had massive shoulders. And his eyes. The eyes were incredible. Luke had never seen such large, luminous, brown eyes before, eyes that spoke of so much pain and misery, yet looked at the world with renewed hope.

Luke must have imagined the look of recognition in the black man's eyes. Perhaps they had known each other in college? No, not college, he would have remembered this man walking around the halls of Harvard. Wait. There had been someone years ago. He'd been a kid and Parker Youngblood was involved somehow. Maybe Zak knew this guy?

It took less than thirty seconds for the two men to size each other up. The black man spoke first, "Hi. I'm Terence. I'm here to pick up the Ford Taurus."

"Excuse me?" Luke asked.

"Terence Hunter," the man said.

"How astonishing," Luke commented and then asked. "Did Frankie send you?"

"Yes," the man said with a bright smile. "Frankie sent me."

"Excellent," Luke said and opened the door wider. "She left her satchel behind as well. Mom, Mr. Hunter is here to pick up the Taurus. Where'd you put Leona, I mean Frankie's stuff?"

He watched as his mother set the empty wine glasses on the bar and moved toward them like a sleep walker. As she got closer to the door, her expression changed from a thoughtful frown to delighted surprise. She rushed the rest of the way and exclaimed in a voice Luke hadn't heard in years, "Holy Shit. It's Terence. Terence Hunter. It's so good to see you. Oh my god, it's been years. I was so sorry to hear Sally had died. Parker and I never had a chance to pay our respects. Mona mentioned something about Sally dying and you leaving town. I suppose beings as how she's your neighbor, she would be the first to know these things.

But Parker and me, we expected to see you again. Your house is just the same as you left it. All your furniture is still there and your cloths and Sally's cloths. Even your car is still parked in the garage. When the sheriff showed up for nonpayment of your taxes, Parker paid them. He was sure you'd be back. And when Parker left, my youngest one, you know Zak, he paid your taxes, up until this year. Well, come on in. Sit down and have a beer or a soda with me. I know how much you love my orange sodas."

Luke debated whether to allow the man inside. With one foot inside the room, Terence must have already seen the work they'd been doing on the mantlepiece above the fireplace and the new stonework on each side of the new wood stove insert. There was also candle wax on the pool table where they'd shared a final glass of wine to celebrate the Resurrection of Amara. Hera's Book of Prayers at least had been put away and taken up to Jule's room, but there was still the altar cloth drying on the table near the women's bathroom.

No matter how much his mother tried to remove the bloodstains, they remained stubbornly visible. She'd vowed to give the washing machine one more chance to redeem itself and if a third washing didn't do the trick, then she'd burn the altar cloth and buy another one. Belatedly as he ushered his mother's friend Terence into the room, he noticed through the window that Quinn's ceremonial robe was still on the clothesline outside. Terence must have seen the robe as he stepped up onto the porch. Maybe he thought they were getting ready for Halloween. And how had Terence gotten here anyway? He hadn't heard him drive up to the bar and there were no other vehicles but the ones that belonged to the occupants of the property.

Oddly enough, Terence ignored the signs of cultism and instead seemed more interested in the workmanship of the mantlepiece and the masonry around the pillars. Luke stepped aside, and Terence eagerly examined the mantlepiece. First, he made an initial sweep of the whole ensemble, then he made a second sweep touching what appeared to be a deer leaping over a fallen tree in a slab of stone on the left-hand side. At one-point Terence went so far as to kneel to appreciate the wonder of the images in the stone. It had taken a catastrophic event to create the picture jasper and by design or by coincidence the pictures in the stone looked as if they'd been created by man himself. And once Terence had had his fill of the beauty of the mantlepiece and the pillars, he straightened to his full height and turned to face Luke.

"This particular stone is difficult to find. Where'd you find it?" he asked.

Luke relieved, settled down on a bar stool and shrugged his shoulders, "Sorry. Don't know. My stepfather collected rocks. These are his. Well, no, there my mother's now since he's been gone for nearly five years."

"You've got yourself a nice piece of art here. Very nice."

"Really? You a rock hound or something?"

"I know a bit. I'm just an amateur though. Never found anything as nice as this before."

"My brother Zak put the mantlepiece together. Well, um. Wait a second. To tell you the truth, I don't really know what the pictures represent. Zak sliced them and arranged them. It's a gift for my Mom."

"He a bricklayer or mason?"

"Not really. He's an archeologist like me."

"So, you dig up things."

"Not rocks. No. But we look for artifacts and."

"Yeah. Graves. That's what archeologists do, right? They dig up graves and old ruins. They dig up the past, the dead," Terence said rhetorically rather than with a desire to know the answer.

Luke should have been worried about the man sniffing around the bar, but he wasn't. He wasn't worried about anything anymore. He was at peace. The ceremony was over, surely a success. And soon, all the power would be gathered to him. Anything he could imagine or want would be his. Even if this Terence Bellow's guy suspected anything, the knowledge would never hurt Luke or his family. Not now. The Gods of Olympus would protect them and soon the Nerin family would be just as powerful. He recited the Invitation Prayer to Zeus in his head while Terrence walked around the mantlepiece for the third time obviously an enthusiastic fan of picture jasper.

When Terence knelt to examine the cat image on the side of the mantlepiece closest to the window, Luke thought about immortality. The idea that he would now live forever, that he would never die, never grow old awed him. The average human being would die, even if people were living longer these days, they would eventually die. Whereas he would live on forever. He would shape the future. This man here, this Terence Hunter would eventually die. He felt sad for him. He seemed like a nice guy. His mother obviously liked him. The reason he didn't remember him was probably because he'd been away at school. By the time he was ten, the local schools could no longer challenge him, so he'd spent the school year in Boise and summers at Archeology Camp.

A great calm enveloped Luke, a sense that everything in the universe had clicked into place and all the events so far were a sign he had been meant to achieve everything he desired. Even his nose had stopped hurting. And he could tell that the swelling around his nose had subsided and probably his eyes were back to normal as well. When he heard footsteps pounding down the stairs, he hopped off the bar stool and smiled in the black man's direction.

"Here she comes now," he said and watched as his mother erupted into the room with the satchel over her left shoulder and a small suitcase that he'd never seen before in her right hand. The suitcase looked fifty years out of date. It was the ugliest shade of yellow he'd ever seen. His mother handed both articles to Terence who had walked around the pool table eyeing the candle wax with interest. He accepted the satchel and suitcase from her and even went so far as to bow. Luke snorted. His mother scowled then punished him for his bad behavior by ignoring him and instead focused all her attention on the visitor.

"There. That's all of it. So? She's herself again, hum?" his mother asked having to crane her neck in order to look up at him.

"Of course. She's more than herself these days," he said as he held the items in his hands. Somehow the weathered leather satchel looked as if it belonged to Terence more than to Leona. His mother touched Terence's arm. Her hand looked so tiny against his massive bicep. Terence looked down at his mother with a thoughtful expression in his kind eyes. It was difficult to define what happened next, but Jule took a step back and looked frightened.

They heard her say, "What's wrong Terence? What happened to your family? I haven't seen your brother Travis in years. Did he finally move to Hawaii like he always said he would? It was as if all three of you vanished out of the blue in the middle of the night. You didn't call or give us any warning. I went to your house several times and nobody was home."

Terence bowed his head and thought for a moment. Just as he began to talk, they heard footsteps stomping down the stairs. Terence closed his mouth and waited for Quinn to enter the room. Quinn was wearing her dirty old baggy sweats. Luke still couldn't get used to her bald head. He sincerely hoped she'd let it grow out before the weather got any colder. Jule ignored Quinn and touched Terence's arm again, "Please Terence. Tell us what happened."

"It's been sixteen years. I'm grateful to Parker and to Zak for their concern for me and my property. Seems funny now to think such things were important once upon a time. If I told you what happened to me, I don't believe you'd understand, even if I had the time to convince you. All I can say for sure is that I'm here to right a wrong. A friend has asked me to pick up her car and her satchel and deliver a message to an old enemy."

"Old enemy?" Jule asked her frown changing the beauty of her face into an ugly mask.

The deep bass of his laughter echoed through the room. "You haven't changed a bit, Jule Nerin. Always thinking people are talking about you."

"What really happened to Sally?" she asked.

"Sally and me, we were tricked by a coyote. We should have known better. Sally and the baby paid the price. My brother Travis paid the price. Me. My time is coming. I'm getting old and I'm ready to meet my maker. But not just yet. I promised a fine old lady, I'd make sure my little girl came to no more harm. And that's just what I plan to do."

"I thought you said Sally lost the baby?" Jule asked, a worried look on her face which even Quinn registered with alarm.

"Yes. Sally lost the baby. And the surrogate carrying our baby lost her life too. She was a spunky little thing. And when I say, my little girl, I'm talking about a little girl I've known a long time. Her daddy was my best friend."

"Quintus Rose Ranch," his mother said so quietly Luke could barely hear her. "She's Benjamin and Cara's daughter, isn't she? The first time I saw her, I wondered if I'd met her before."

"I got lots of friends Jule," Terence said with a grunt. "You don't know all of them."

"She didn't die in the fire, did she? Who kidnapped her?"

"I got to go now. You've got a work of art there," Terence said pointing at the mantlepiece and pillars. "Tell Zak he's in the wrong business. Instead of digging up graves, he should be doing that for a living."

As he thought about Leona, Luke couldn't help but ask, "So what do the doctors say is wrong with Jane Smith, I mean Kallan Keys? My brother thinks she's suffering from DID."

"I'm sorry. I don't understand," Terence said as he moved toward the front door.

"You know. Dissociative Identity Disorder. What people sometimes call Multiple Personality Disorder," Luke explained.

"All I was told was to come here and pick up a Ford Taurus and some personal items," Terence explained. "I don't know anything about any DID or that other thing."

"So you don't know Kallan Dilys Fremantle?" his mother asked. He noticed the dawning worry in her eyes. Luke heard his mother pronounce the name Call Lynn and a picture popped into his head of a six-year-old little girl with long thick black hair, bushy black eyebrows and penetrating green eyes.

"Who?" Terence asked.

Luke walked toward him, "I thought you said you were here because Leona asked you to fetch her car? You know, the woman called Navan Keys. Her name's on the papers in the glove compartment of the Taurus. She had to have identification to even drive out of the lot with that rental. If you're not here on behalf of Leona, then what are you doing here?"

In amazement, Luke watched as Terence brushed past him as if he had been an annoying gnat. How dare the man ignore him in his own house? Luke hurried after him wanting to give him a piece of his mind. Eventually, he caught up with the man outside, as Terence paused to fish through the satchel. Before he could find the keys to the Taurus,

Luke grabbed the big man's shoulder. Terence shrugged, and Luke went stumbling backwards. Flapping his arms to keep himself from falling on his ass, he remained upright and embarrassed. The hard muscles beneath Terence's shirt were enough to give Luke second thoughts. What was wrong with him anyway, he should have been able to handle the old guy?

Of course. The truth dawned upon him like a shot of whiskey. The powers had yet to manifest themselves. With the blessings of the Gods, next time, he would crush the man beneath his boot. He'd need to be patient for now. It was all good. They were well rid of the Taurus and any lingering possessions belonging to Frankie and her entourage. With the Taurus gone, everything would go back to normal and the psychotic female from the land of the loony tunes would be forgotten for good. As the Ford Taurus drove away in a cloud of dust and the pinging of flying gravel, Luke waved and whistled and cheered.

When the darkness reclaimed Terence Hunter, Luke noticed that the Camaro was missing. Evidently, Zak had also taken off. Zak's disappearance made him nervous. What was he up to? He glanced toward Zak's trailer. No car parked on the grass. Why was he upset? This was a time of celebration, not a time to get pissed at his brother for no good reason. When he reentered the bar, his sister and mother were sitting at a far table with a shoebox full of pictures. They were pulling the pictures out one by one and looking at them and commenting on them. He heard his mother say, "I know she's in here. All I have to do is find a picture of her mother and one of her and I'll know for sure. I never forget a face. You know how good I am with faces."

Quinn dropped the pictures she had in her hand and stood up, "Well, I don't have any idea what you're looking for, so I'm going back to bed. Last night took so much out of me. Damn I could sleep a week. Maybe I will." By the time Luke found his cellphone and left the bar, his sister was upstairs snoring and his mother was flipping through old photos.

As he walked toward his trailer, the sun had been above the butte for nearly two hours. He heard the wind rustling through the leaves of the willow and didn't so much as twitch. Even the sunshine seemed to hum. The light made him feel drunk. He thought about his mother's reaction. How odd. All her life she'd been thinking about this moment yet, instead of shopping for a new car or a new house, she was flipping through old photos desperately looking for some people she'd known years ago. His mother even seemed disappointed, as if she'd been expecting more, much more. What had she wanted – balls of fire exploding in the night sky above the bar? Or maybe, Amara Katsaros to come swooping down from the sky and plant a crown on her head?

He knew what tomorrow would bring, anything and everything he could imagine, and he could imagine a lot. There would be lots of money, lots of glory, and travel. He'd be traveling all over the world and not have to worry how to pay for the private jets or the private yachts. He might even be turning down offers from universities. Anything was possible. The idea of all the good things to come made him giddy. He stumbled up the steps of his trailer and with a heave-ho threw open the door.

Zak kept his flashlight pointed at the ground as he crested the top of the butte. He paused to catch his breath. Even in the pitch blackness, the faint flickering of lights from the windows of the Woolly Man could be seen from the top of the butte's mesa. He walked cautiously across the ground occasionally tripping over loose rocks and small sage brush. He heard rustling ahead of him then the crash of a terrified animal fleeing in the opposite direction. From the noise it made, the animal might have been a jackrabbit. If he'd startled a cougar or badger, he would have paid for his trespass in painful ways. A jackrabbit, on the other hand, was more likely to run in the opposite direction.

After a minute or two of stumbling and cursing, he managed to find the rocky ledge overlooking the Woolly Man and sat down to wait. He could see their silhouettes against the closed curtains as they played their dangerous game. They were still standing around the pool table. What could keep them there for so long? He checked his watch and then flipped the flashlight off quickly. If anyone looked out the window, they would see the light. And in their present condition, they would assume the light meant someone was spying on them.

His family wouldn't understand why he had chosen to climb the butte and watch them from afar. And even he, didn't quite understand why, he had decided he didn't trust them anymore. Tiny pieces of paper were lost every day. They slipped out of people's pockets all the time. Once they were on the ground or on the street, they were either run over or walked over or eventually collected and placed in trash bins. Therefore, he had no good reason to suspect Luke of theft. Yet Luke might have believed Eve posed a threat to the family. And the family meant everything to Luke. In his present state of mind, Luke might do anything in the false belief he was saving the family from ruin. Before Zak left to find Eve, he wanted to be sure Luke no longer considered Eve a threat.

The large rock embedded in the soil like a toadstool had lost the day's warmth and to add to his discomfort its grooves were cutting into his butt, so he sat on the softer ground further back from the ledge. He debated whether to use the Navaho blanket or just wrap it around his shoulders. No. It had to stay in its protective case. The blanket had to go back to Brent Wade. And thinking of Wade made him think about his promise. He didn't have time to spy on his family. He should be on the road this minute, hunting for Eve and meeting with Brent. Down below in the hollow near the Woolly Man, the air had been stifling and warm, but up here, the temperature had dropped. Up here he was exposed to the cold north wind. He shivered and decided he was an idiot. He might be up here for hours and gain nothing from freezing to death.

Slipping down the butte was easy. When he sprinted for his Camaro which he'd hidden behind the trailer, he grabbed his sleeping bag and a six pack of beer. Then he returned to the butte. Climbing the butte with his sleeping bag and beer took more time, but the beer was worth it. He could still see the Woolly Man and some of the road leading up to the bar. Well, not exactly the road but what he knew from memory would be the road that passed the Woolly Man.

In the dark, the road was indistinguishable from the brush and fields and valley below. In the dark, only the stars in the sky and the lights inside the Woolly Man illuminated the night. From his perspective, if he turned to his right or his left or behind him, he could imagine himself all alone in the world, in a dark chilly place that smelled of damp earth, sun soaked rocks, sage, and the antiseptic smell of deer and cattle urine.

He knew from experience how the deer would make themselves at home up here on the butte and would lie down among the sage to sleep. Up here, they had an excellent view of the terrain and could watch for predators. During the day evidence of deer and the cattle occupying this spot were everywhere. The crushed sage was one indication. And their tracks in the sandy soil another. Yet tonight they had chosen a different spot to sleep. It was lucky for him they had. Zak would have been content to share his watchtower with them but not the cows, not the noisy messy cows.

Zak woke at the sound of crunching. Or was that munching? For a moment he thought a deer had been eating nearby, perhaps nibbling on soft sage or winterfat. As he oriented himself to his surroundings, he realized the crunching came from below. It sounded like a giant in heavy boots crushing the pea gravel beneath his feet. Or maybe it was Sasquatch. The idea of Sasquatch heading his way was alarming enough to slap him into full consciousness.

It was nearly dawn. From his vantage point at the top of the butte, he was the first to see the sun peeking over the horizon. He unwrapped himself from the sleeping bag and crawled toward the ledge. There were no deer or cattle on the hillside below munching away on shrubs and winterfat. Then he listened closely and finally recognized the sound. It was the sound of someone walking down the graveled road, a pair of feet walking purposely toward the Woolly Man. This person might be a patron or a stranded hunter or hiker.

To his right, the road leading away from the Woolly Man held nothing remotely suspicious. But when he turned to his left the direction people usually came from town, Zak saw a man emerge from the deeper shadows of the willow and proceed up the road and onto the path leading to the bar. He was the biggest man Zak had ever seen outside of basketball. The sight of him so composed and sure of himself startled Zak. And what was more disturbing was that there was something familiar about the shape of his head. He had a neat head with dark hair cropped close to his scalp. And his head was just the right shape to match his wide shoulders and long neck. Some big guys had no neck at all, just a head springing from their massive shoulders, while this guy looked as if he had been designed after a Greek statue.

And just to make him feel even more puny and insignificant, Zak noticed the way the big man walked with easy graceful strides, his legs eating up the ground. He might as well have been on skates gliding across the ice, so effortlessly in his movements with his arms swinging in perfect harmony with his body. He had an unusual grace for such a big man. And Zak suspected the big man had some tricky moves of his own. He wouldn't have wanted to tangle with him. He seemed so purposeful that Zak began to wonder if he had a beef with Luke or his mother. He debated whether to climb down from the butte and check him out. The reaction when he knocked on the Woolly Man door reassured Zak. They spoke briefly and then Luke ushered the stranger inside.

Time passed slowly. It seemed forever before the stranger emerged from the bar and headed toward the Ford Taurus. Zak saw his brother run out of the bar and toward the man. He saw his brother put his hand on the man's shoulder and the man shrug him off. He also saw Luke reel backwards nearly falling to the ground. Instead of confronting the big man again, Luke prudently stood back and waited. In disbelief Zak saw the stranger holding Leona's satchel and an ugly yellow suitcase. The man opened the trunk of the Taurus and dumped the luggage inside, then moved toward the driver's side door.

Alarmed, Zak grabbed his sleeping bag and tumbled down the butte, no longer concerned with being seen. Sounds carried on the early morning wind as he slipped and slid his way down the path: the Taurus engine warming up, the car backing out and pulling away as the gears shifted into drive, the slowing down of the car as its tires crossed the cattle guard then the bumpety-bumpety of tires moving over wooden slats from the old bridge, his brother whistling and laughing, boots stomping across the porch making the old boards squeak, the pathetic protest of the screen door opening and finally the whack of the screen door, ever hopeful of hitting something besides the frame. Evidently, Luke didn't seem too concerned about someone stealing Eve's car.

Maybe she'd sent the stranger to retrieve her car and her luggage? If so, then the guy probably knew where to find her. By the time Zak stumbled and skidded down to the bottom of the butte, the man and the Taurus were long gone. He supposed he could have chased after the Taurus, but why, since the road led to town? What if he kept on going? Then he groaned remembering where he'd parked the Camaro. By the time he had managed to reach the Camaro, warmed up the engine and driven to town, the stranger could have taken any number of routes. Even though he longed to chase after the stranger and find out where Eve was staying, he had to wait. He to wait and see what Luke would do next.

When Luke reemerged from the Woolly Man, Zak ducked under the willow and knelt on the ground to watch what he would do. Luke headed across the vacant lot toward the trailers. Zak sat down and crossed his legs and waited. No one else came out of the Woolly Man. He felt foolish sitting on the side of the road under the willow. The damned branches kept brushing against his head and shoulders like ghostly fingers. He crawled out from under the tree and started walking toward the bar. Maybe his mother could tell him something about the stranger who had retrieved the Taurus for Eve. He entered the bar and found it empty. The back table where his mother loved to do her bookkeeping was a mess. There were pictures covering every available surface.

He stopped on the threshold of the stairs and called up thinking his mother and Quinn might have gone back to sleep. His sister's bedroom door opened, and she peeked out and said, "Leave me alone, Zak. Can't you see I'm sleeping?" Then she shut her door and he heard the click of the lock. He walked toward the pool table noticing the droplets of cold wax spotting the green baize. Somebody was going to have fun pulling that crap off without tearing the material. He left the bar through the back exit and circled around the building. Then he saw the Taurus. For a moment his heart leaped thinking Eve had come back to him. Then he saw the big black dude coming out of the barn carrying the footlocker.

"What the hell do you think you're doing?" Zak shouted. He heard an echo of the exact same words and realized he was hearing his brother calling from one of the open windows of his trailer. The black dude ran to the Taurus and threw the footlocker inside. He couldn't shut the trunk. By the time Zak had reached the Taurus, the Taurus was on the move and he had to jump aside before his toes were smashed by the tires.

Futilely he tried to chase the Taurus down. He hadn't heard a thing. The guy must have driven across the cattle guard, then across the wooden bridge, then down as far as the corral. Once he reached the corral, he could take the dead end leading to the Woolly Man or the washboard road snaking its way east up and down the hills and valleys. The washboard road ended at a point a few feet from their barn. Once he knew he was close to the property, it would have been necessary for him to turn off the engine and push the Taurus the remaining fifty yards. The sneaky Ninja had trespassed on their property without wakening his family. And they'd been closer to the courtyard too.

By the time Zak reached the front porch, he had to stop, his side ached and his heart felt as if it might burst from his chest. He heard someone running up the dirt road behind him and turned in time as Luke barefoot wearing a yellow fluffy robe with his hair in a plastic shower cap skidded to a stop and threw his arms in the air.

"Who is that guy?" Zak demanded.

Luke still carrying his toothbrush bent down and held onto his knees gasping for air. When he could speak he said, "That's Terence Hunter. You should know him. Mom says you've been paying his property taxes for years."

The first thought that popped into his head – that couldn't have been Terence. The second thought – you're a big fat liar Luke Nerin. Terence wouldn't steal from anyone. No, the Terence he remembered was the gentlest, kindest man in Woolstone. But seventeen years had gone by without a word.

What's he been doing all this time?

Maybe he was pissed at the town for not doing something about his disappearance?

What could they have done? He and his wife drove to Twin Falls and were never seen again. Mona told everyone Sally had died in childbirth. He and Parker pestered the police for months and were told there were no leads. So they did what they could and paid his property taxes as a way of assuaging the guilt, also in the hopes when Terence returned to Woolstone, he would still have a house to live in.

Then he thought a bit more and realized the guy who resembled sasquatch could be Terence Hunter. Yet, Terence had been a tall skinny guy when he knew him. Or had he been? Maybe he was thinking of his brother Travis? He shook his head. The sleepless night and all the craziness the last few weeks was turning his brain into a head of cauliflower.

"What are you doing?" Luke shouted pointing his toothbrush at the retreating Ford Taurus. "Why aren't you in the Camaro chasing after him?"

Instead of running for his Camaro, Zak walked back to the bar and went inside to wash his face and get a beer. Luke remained outside. After finishing off several beers, Zak started to feel uncomfortable. It was so unlike his brother to go back to his trailer and say nothing more. It was time to beat the truth out of Luke. Zak banged on the door of his brother's trailer several times, but no one answered. He'd seen Luke go in, so either Luke was ignoring him or he was in the shower.

The continued silence pricked his conscience. Something wasn't right. The heavy silence encircled Luke's trailer, the courtyard between the barn and the Woolly Man, every bit of sagebrush and weed. There were no flies or mosquitoes or no-see-ums buzzing about his face. And the mourning dove had yet to call. Maybe she was still asleep? Maybe it was too early for the doves, the meadow larks, the American bushtit, or the sparrows? No, something wasn't right. The birds and the bugs should be swooping from sage to tree to rooftop.

The profound silence frightened him. It was unnatural. It was wrong.

He tried the door and when the knob turned, he walked inside. It was dark. He pushed back the curtain above the sink. The main part of the trailer was empty. He started down the dark hall. The first thing he saw was a pool of motor oil on the floor. He paused wondering why Luke hadn't cleaned up the mess by now. Correction, why would Luke bring motor oil into his precious, pristine trailer?

Then he flipped on the hall switch. The light glistened on a trail of blood. The blood had trickled from under the bathroom door toward the wall and stopped. A thinner stream had created a puddle in the center of the hallway and stopped near the tip of his right boot. Zak stepped over the pool of blood and pushed open the door. He saw his brother with his back resting against the bathroom wall clutching his stomach. He was holding something in his hands. It took a second for Zak to realize that a knife was protruding from his brother's gut.

Luke looked up and smiled saying, "Don't worry. It's just an experiment. I'll be Okay. The bleeding will stop soon. You see, I can't die. I'm immortal."

As Zak with trembling fingers punched in the number for emergency services, he heard someone screaming and laughing. He threw the trailer door open and saw his mother doing a jig on the porch floorboards waving her arms in the air and smiling like an idiot at the sky. "I know who she is. I know who she is. And it's all coming true. Every bit of it. Zeus has forgiven us."

Shutting the door to drown out his mother's crazy talk, Zak talked into the cellphone, "Hello. Yes. My brother's been stabbed. Get someone out here quick," he said as he heard his mother cry out again, her words ricocheted off the butte, coming to him in stereo. He heard her say, "One hundred thousand dollars. Oh my God. The bastard left me one hundred thousand dollars. Oh my God. Oh my God. It's all true. It's all destiny. Oh my God. I can't believe it."

"We're just outside of Woolstone about five miles north of town," Zak told the woman on the other end of the airwaves. "You know the Woolly Man Bar and Grill? Yes. That's right. He's in the trailer, the trailer closest to the bar. What should I do? What can I do?" Zak asked his knees beginning to buckle. The background music was his mother's voice, her laughter, and her ecstatic joy. He would never forget. Her joy and Luke's blood would be seared in his memory forever.

Zak heard the voice on the other end assure him in a soothing voice, "We'll have someone out straight away. Don't touch the knife. Put pressure on the wound. The ambulance is on its way. Sir? Is everything all right? Are you having a party? Is there alcohol involved?"

"No. It's my mom. She doesn't know. I haven't told her yet. She doesn't know."

Zak watched as Quinn stumbled out onto the porch in her pajamas still half asleep. His mother shook Quinn's shoulder and cried out, "Your daddy left me one hundred thousand dollars. He left you the same. One hundred thousand dollars baby. I can't believe it. Five years with no word and now this. Oh, Quinn the powers have restored us. Prepare for more rewards to come."

Then his mother broke down and started to cry. Quinn put an arm around her shoulder and led her back inside. Zak didn't want to leave Luke alone. He ran back down the hall, terrified his brother had died while he'd been on the phone. It seemed like hours before he heard the ambulance. Zak spent the next ten minutes blazing a trail between the front door and the bathroom periodically checking on Luke's condition, all the while with the phone to his ear as he talked to his sister.

"There's nothing you can do for Luke. Your job is take care of Mom. She'd can't know just yet. Keep her away from the cops and the paramedics. Do whatever you have to do to get her calmed down. Quinn are you listening? I'm sorry about Parker. They'll be time to grieve later. Please keep her away from the cops. She's in no condition to be seen by anyone. You hear me?"

Quinn whispered into the phone, "We're not criminals Zak. You act like we've done something illegal. We just had a silly ceremony. It meant a lot to Mom, but nobody died, and nobody got hurt." And then she realized what she'd just said and started to cry. It took Zak another five minutes to get his sister calmed down. When he recognized the Pinto pulling up to the porch, he ran out of the trailer and shouted at Mona, "Get out of the way. The ambulance is coming."

Mona Lawson pulled her 1980 Pinto Wagon behind the bar and parked near the barn where Terence Hunter had carried the mermaid to the trunk and drove away. She came running toward the trailer, "What's wrong?"

"Luke's been stabbed," Zak said and shoved her off the stoop. "You can't go in."

"I'm a nurse," she said calmly and tried again to get inside.

"You stay away from my brother," he said shoving her so hard she fell to the ground like a discarded mannequin, all pasty white and impossibly thin.

He went back inside and closed the door realizing Quinn had heard the whole exchange between them. He said as if their conversation had never been interrupted, "Maybe not. They were just old bones, but some people might see what we've done as perverted. And what Luke and I did is definitely a crime. We robbed a grave for god sake, we robbed a grave on federal land. And you go and grind some of the poor creature's bones into a powder and put it in the wine. How do you think that's going to look? People will think it's sick, that we're sick."

"What are you talking about Zak? I did no such thing."

"What were you grinding up in the mortar?"

"Oh that. Shit. That was chalk, some old chalk from my art tools. I thought it would add realism to the ritual, you know, like those stories you guys used to tell me about African funeral ceremonies. How people ingested the bones of their ancestors to give themselves more power."

"You're thinking of ancient Asian ceremonies. They worshipped their dead and had a totally different culture and belief system than we do."

"Whatever. It was just symbolic."

"Shit," Zak said as he slid down the wall and started to giggle hysterically thinking what an idiot he was. He sat there on the floor of the hall and giggled and watched his brother. His sister hung up. She probably thought he'd gone nuts. He had done what he could. He had packed towels around the knife to staunch the blood and tried to cover his brother's shivering body with more towels. To hell with them all. He wasn't going to just sit and do nothing. He wasn't going to let his brother bleed to death. As he waited, he avoided looking at his poor brother's face, so jaundiced from the blood loss, his nose swollen and his eyes ringed with black and blue bruises.

The sight made Zak want to cry.

When the seconds ticked by and still no siren, he started to cry in earnest, a cry without sound, the hard kind that hurts the chest and can break your jaw. He didn't want people to see him cry. He tried to make it stop. Then he heard the sirens and struggled to his feet holding onto the wall for support. At first the police thought Zak had beaten up his brother and knifed him.

When one of the cops took out his handcuffs with his eyes on Zak, Luke spoke to the EMT, "It was a stranger. Some guy was trying to steel tools from the barn. He saw me. He came in and attacked me." If Luke had been in his right mind he would have known forensics would figure out his fingerprints were the only fingerprints on the knife handle. And Zak had seen enough crime dramas to know those guys would figure out the wound had been self-inflicted.

After all that had happened this week, Zak was long past caring about the possibility of spending time in prison or visiting his brother in a psychiatric ward. All he cared about was that his brother survived. Zak insisted on going in the ambulance to the hospital and to his surprise they let him ride in the back with his brother. He saw his sister and his mother standing together on the porch holding each other like frightened shivering puppies, their eyes round and large and wet from crying. Zak looked away and down at his brother. Then he got angry, angry at Luke for doing something so incredibly stupid, angry at his mother, and his grandparents, and all the damned relatives long dead who had passed on the most colossal lie of all time.

Just before the ambulance doors closed, he and his family were a witness to the arrest of Mona Lawson. A sheriff from Twin Falls and a guy in a suit were forced to wrestle her to the ground so they could handcuff her. As she screamed at them to let her go, an officer read her the Miranda Warning. "I'm innocent. I don't know anything about any cellphones. I don't know anything about people in Oregon."

"Mrs. Lawson, the FBI are on their way to take you in for questioning. We are taking you to TFPD until they arrive. They have a warrant to search your home. They're also aware Dr. Winter is your aunt, so telling us you don't know any people in Oregon is a lie. She never showed up for a medical conference in San Francisco. No one has seen her for months. The Oregon PD are searching for her as we speak. The FBI believe you are connected with a ring of pedophiles and kidnappers. You either come with us quietly or come with us unconscious."

The party was over. Zak watched as Quinn and his mother drove away from the Woolly Man. Mom had invited a few neighbors and her regulars while Luke, Quinn, and Zak sat in silence and watched their elders. Zak had even chosen to drink sodas and just plain water instead of his usual beer. Drinking had only driven a deeper spike into his chest and he had had enough of pain. Zak had planned to forego the party altogether, but in the end, he was glad he had come because one good thing came out of that party. He got to hear the gossip about Mona Lawson's criminal trial.

Even though the FBI had yet to find the owners of the famous cellphones found in the deaf child's blanket, the authorities were proceeding with the trial based on new evidence. A newspaper article had confirmed that the cellphones had belonged to Dr. Violet Euphemia Winter, Ray Millhouse, and Farrah Zee Foster-Koodark, formerly known as Myrtle Zee Foster-Koodark. Mona Lawson's claim that she'd been framed didn't hold water when she couldn't explain how she had paid for the restoration of her 1980 Pinto Wagon or the huge sums of money discovered to have been deposited over the last twenty years in a Swiss bank account in her name. Soon the authorities would be looking for Zak to question him about his anonymous phone calls.

The current party at the Woolly Man was for his mother who was on her way to Montana to visit old friends and relatives. She still had enough money left to live comfortably for the next three years or so, even after paying part of Luke's ambulance fee, emergency room visit, and hospital stay. As for the remaining balance, Luke would have to figure out how to pay it off. Zak turned to look back at the Woolly Man, seeing the windows all boarded up for the first time in his life. Like a sore tooth his eye kept going back to the sign on the door. His mother had written the words, "Closed Indefately" misspelling the word indefinitely. She'd always been a terrible speller.

Zak sensing a panic attack turned to stare at the butte as a means of collecting his thoughts. Everything had changed. Nothing would ever be the same again. And the Nerins had only themselves to blame. Leona had been an innocent bystander. Then Zak looked over at the shed and quickly away remembering the day he'd seen the jaguar. What a fool he had been. A second later as if the universe had chosen to prove him wrong, he heard footsteps approaching from behind the building. He tensed in a moment of superstitious fear, expecting to see the jaguar coming around the building with the intent of killing him. When Nate appeared around the corner with his Caribbean tan and his brown hair gone nearly blonde from all his fun in the sun, Zak relaxed.

"You haven't left yet," Nate said as he walked toward his vehicle and deposited another bag of trash in the back of the truck bed.

"Not yet. I'm just waiting for Luke."

"He's coming with you? Is that wise?"

"No. No. He says he's got something for me."

Nate grinned, "Well, you have a good trip kid. We'll miss you."

Zak shook his hand, "I feel better knowing you're here to watch the place and keep an eye on Luke."

They both turned to watch as the trailer door flew open and Luke in his wheelchair exited the trailer and rolled down the access ramp to the paved walkway. Zak had finished the walkway several days ago. Their constant comings and goings had already made a rough path between the sage and rocks, so he had no trouble perfecting the path with a wood frame and concrete walkway.

His sister had planted hens and chickens and miniature roses along the walkway with a bit of bark and a border of some sort of shrub with white flowers as another accent piece. The path seemed out of place juxtaposed with cheat grass and sage and rock on either side. But the walkway had permitted Luke an illusion, an illusion he had control over his life – even now. Well, at least for Zak the work had turned out to be therapeutic, sometimes even kind of awesome.

As they waited for Luke to reach them, Nate moved the boxes intended for a local charity off the ramp, so the wheelchair would have free access inside the Woolly Man. Luke looked like himself again. The swelling had disappeared and there was no sign he'd ever been punched in the nose. His blue eyes looked up at Zak and Zak relaxed. It would take time, but his brother would be back on his feet again.

He looked sane. Well, as sane as one could be after stabbing himself in the stomach to prove a theory. The doctors had wanted to keep him in the hospital for more testing, but his mother had insisted he be released. Zak wondered if her decision had been wise. Yet to hire someone to watch over Luke would only make Luke angry and perhaps convince him that he was indeed crazy.

Without fanfare, Luke handed Zak a piece of paper. Zak opened the paper. He'd already recognized the note Eve Endicott had left him. Zak heard him say, "You dropped this on the floor of the Camaro a while back. I picked it up and put it in my pocket and forgot about it."

"Thanks. Thanks a lot."

"No problem. You have a safe trip man. You're coming back? Right?"

"Sure. One day," Zak said not wanting to be tied to a promise. "For sure I'll be back for Thanksgiving."

As Luke watched his brother drive away, he waved in the off chance he might be watching. Nate with the weekly garbage riding in the back of his truck followed the Camaro toward Woolstone. Once in in town, Nate and Zak would part company. Zak would continue on to parts unknown chasing after a woman who like a runaway bride wanted nothing to do with him. Nate would deposit the trash at the dump, stop in at the Brown Bottle Bar, and eventually, after he'd had a few beers with the locals, buy groceries for the two bachelors. Once Nate returned to the Woolly Man, he'd make supper and put the cripple to bed. Nate never acted as if he was Luke's nurse and Luke pretended not to care when Nate had to lift him up out of the wheelchair and set him down in the tub like a little helpless baby.

With his back to the Woolly Man, Luke sat in his wheelchair and surveyed his home with new eyes. He saw the world nor longer as just an ordinary collection of rocks and trees, sun and moon, sky and stars, he saw beneath all the familiar shapes, right down to its individual particles. The wheelchair might carry him closer to the ground, but his vision remained up among the stars.

It was just a matter of time.

He'd been too quick to accept his reward. The Gods were fickle sometimes. He must wait for his powers to manifest themselves. They would. He believed in Amara's goodness and power. And the doctors assured him that in a few more weeks he would be strong enough to begin therapy. He'd walk and run and jump and do everything he'd done before the accident once more. It had been foolish to test Amara. So what? He'd survived. According to his medical staff his survival had been a miracle. He was wiser now. He would wait for a sign.

Zak drove through Woolstone and as he paused to wait for the only street light in town to change to green, he noticed a familiar Taurus parked at Drummond's Market. Instead of driving out of town, he decided to stop in at the little store and purchase a few items for his trip. Once inside he walked up and down the aisles pretending to shop. Then in the hardware aisle he found the big black man staring at shovels. Zak walked past the man and the man looked up acknowledging Zak absently, then stopped and turned in surprise as if he recognized him.

Terence just stared at him with an unreadable expression. Zak, steadily growing uncomfortable broke the silence first, "You're Terence Hunter. Hi, I'm Zak Nerin. You used to come into the Woolly Man when I was a kid." They shook hands. It was like shaking a thunderegg.

"How are you doing, kid? I knew your stepfather, Parker Youngblood. We used to go rock hunting together. He loved Sally's apple pie."

"I'm managing. Thanks for asking," Zak said, then extended his hand once again and the man hesitated, eyebrows raised. They shook hands a second time and Zak said all in a rush, "Thank you for taking her away. I hope she's somewhere peaceful where she won't be disturbed. I shouldn't have helped my brother dig her up. It was wrong. Nothing good came of it anyway. Do you know who she was? Were you there? No, that's not right. She's got to be hundreds of years old."

Terence ignored Zak. Zak might as well have been talking to the wall. Terence just kept nodding his head in agreement with a wide reminiscent smile, "Oh Parker Youngblood was a good man, a really good man," then Terence looked up at the ceiling and his eyes widened. He continued, "You said – Parker had. What did you mean by that?"

"Parker moved to Quartz, Arizona about five years ago and just a few weeks ago, my Mom received news of his death. He was so young, you know, only fifty-five. We had a wake for him today at the Woolly Man."

"I'm so sorry to hear it. I planned to visit him after selling my house."

"You're selling the place, huh?"

"Yeah. There's been so many people coming to gawk at my neighbor's house, I can't get anything done. People come from all over the country. They park in front of my house, sometimes, in my driveway. She's almost as famous as Dracula."

"Oh, I wouldn't say she's as famous as Dracula. Maybe that other dude, you know, the nurse, the one who killed all those people in Germany, because he got his rocks off killing them and bringing them back to life. Anyway, it's nice to know you're okay. Parker was worried about you. He looked everywhere for you. Sometimes I'd go with him to Twin and we'd ask people on the streets and in the shops if they'd seen you and your wife."

"Thank you Zak for taking care of my place and paying my property taxes. The neighbors told me you used to come by and mow the lawn and shovel the snow. It must have been hard for you to come up with the money to pay my taxes. Archeology doesn't pay much. Why would you do such a thing? You were just a kid when I. When I left."

"Parker paid most of them. He sent me the money and I'd go down and pay the taxes in cash. It's just been the last year Parker hasn't sent the money. So I paid. No big deal. See you, Mr. Hunter," Zak said unable to come up with the words to explain why he felt he had to make sure the Hunter family returned to Woolstone.

Terence nodded absently in his direction returning to his assessment of the shovels. Since Zak was already in the store he decided to head to the candy aisle and pick up a few things. As he carried his candy toward the cashier station, he noticed Terence in conversation with the owner of the store, Drummond. When Terence stepped away from the man and glanced in Zak's direction, Zak had an odd sensation run through his belly as if something weren't quite right. He soon discovered his gut reaction had been a warning. When he put his purchases on the counter and smiled into Heidi's cheerful eyes, Drummond stepped up to him and gave him the stink eye.

"Zak, would you come with me please?"

"Why? What's up Mr. Drummond?"

"Please come with me."

Why Zak followed the douche bag up the stairs and into his office would puzzle him for years to come. He had every right to refuse the order and could have instead demanded to see a police officer. Drummond's office window was so big, they could see the entire floor of the store. When Drummond demanded Zak strip down to his underwear, Zak threw him against the wall and threatened to sue the shopkeeper for sexual harassment. The sheriff arrived soon after.

The sheriff listened to both sides, then spoke privately with Drummond the Douche bag and Drummond the Douche bag promptly had to apologize. Zak had heard wild stories about clueless employees complying with orders from their bosses to strip down, because security suspected them of shoplifting. Although, he'd never heard of a store humiliating a customer in the same way. If every store demanded their customers strip when they were suspected of shoplifting, stores wouldn't have many customers left.

As Zak hurried out of the store, he vowed Drummond was going to be in a world of hurt once this story hit the press. When he thought back to Drummond's condescending attitude, the whole nasty business made Zak even angrier than before. Evidently, Drummond had wanted so badly to believe in the lies Terence Hunter had told, he was willing to risk his reputation and his livelihood. When Zak left the store, he decided there and then, that his hometown held only misery for him. And the irony of a moment's decision in Woolstone was not lost on him. There was no sense in sticking around because the town would end up dying all by itself anyway.

Most of the young people had moved to Twin Falls and those that stayed behind were becoming less and less adaptable to newcomers and would soon drive away business anyway. Drummond's suspicious nature and intense dislike of the Nerin family finally made up Zak's mind for him. Once back at his Camaro, sans his candy bars and baked potato chips, he noticed that the lid of his trunk was unlatched. He opened the trunk. Nothing was missing.

Even though he felt a measure of relief he still searched the parking lot for Leona's Taurus. It was when he glanced in the Camaro's backseat he got the shock of his life. The box was gone. He'd kept the hybrid rabbit bones inside the box and thought the backseat with all the other junk was the perfect hiding place. No one would bother with a box of rocks and bones. Why hadn't he hidden the box somewhere on his mother's property? The box had caused him so much trouble in Klamath Falls. And now trouble had found him in Woolstone. Since there were no police around eager to arrest him again, the thief had to have been Terence. No big surprise.

The lie to Drummond made sense now. It all made a weird sort of sense. Terence was determined to undo all their efforts. He supposed the remains of the hybrids, the rabbit and the mermaid were going to spend their time sleeping peacefully under the stars, if Terence's shovels were any clue to his mindset. Side by side the mermaid and the hybrid would keep each other company until someone else came along and tried to unravel their mysteries.

In his rear view mirror, Zak glanced back at the town and saw Terence standing on the corner across from Drummond's Market watching him drive away. Zak extended his arm out the window and gave Terence his blessing. The sunglasses hid Terence's expression but Zak figured the cheerful wave in response was the big guy's version of the finger. Yeah, Terence had done a dirty rotten thing. So why couldn't Zak work up enough piss and vinegar to be mad at the guy?

What dangled on the periphery of Zak's thoughts wasn't worth contemplating at the moment. Without enough data, it was useless to speculate. Honestly, he would rather not know the truth just now. He would riather let this new mystery marinate in his mind. Everyone deserved to hold onto their secrets, as long as those secrets did no harm. And as far as Zak was concerned, Mr. Hunter had only returned to Woolstone to reclaim his property and right a wrong.

Zak skirted away from the thought of how many wrongs had to righted. It boggled the mind. He'd only scratched the surface in the crawl space of the cabin. There were probably coroners and forensic staff combing the entire Antelope Summit at this very moment searching for more bodies. And there were probably people desperately hoping to find their lost loved ones and grieving somewhere in America wondering if they were alive or dead.

Terence watched the little fucker drive away and wanted so much to wrap his hands around the pretty boy's throat and choke the life out of him. How dare he take his baby's poor body, the damned grave robber. He walked to the Ford Taurus and climbed inside. He found the cellphone easily enough. It was in the satchel. He dialed the number listed under the name Clinic. A recorded message greeted him each time he tried to get a real person. Then he went home and used his own landline. The phone company told him someone had been paying for the service for the last seventeen years. There were twenty-three messages on the tape recording. It was a fresh new tape too, not a tape from seventeen years ago with thousands of messages recorded and deleted, recorded, and deleted.

By the time he'd listened to more than a third of them, he realized Mona Lawson had been using his phone for her own sick purposes. She must have paid his telephone bill every month and told her aunt to call her at this number. The last message on the tape recorder brought a smile to his lips. At first when he heard the familiar voice, his body automatically jerked as if he'd been stabbed. He listened to the tape over and over and over again. Evidently, Mona Lawson hadn't had time to listen to these messages and delete them which was a good thing.

"Where are you Mona? You should have been here days ago. Myrtle is impossible. I need you. She doesn't have your steady hands. You must be aware I have a medical conference in San Francisco in three days. I told you months ago. I want you here to take care of things while I'm gone. I can't trust Myrtle to do the simplest thing. Ring me straight away." Terence listened in puzzlement. He replayed the message several times and the voice kept speaking into his ear, a familiar voice he hadn't heard in years.

The next message was from a man, "Leland gave me this number. He said this is your private number. Violet isn't taking my calls. I'm going to have a talk with Dr. Frankenstein. She owes me. She took my pumpkin and I'm getting her back. If you hear anything you can reach me at..."

He recognized Mona Lawsons' voice as she picked up the phone in the middle of the recording, "Hi Ray. I don't think it's a good idea to go down there right now. Why don't we meet at the shop and find a nice place to eat and discuss this calmly?"

Before he could hear Ray's answer the recording ended. Then he came to a decision. It was time to find his little girl. It was time to return her rental car and her belongings to her. He locked up the house, got into the Ford Taurus and drove out of town. As he drove along the country dirt roads smelling the newly mown hay he noticed an irrigation ditch filled with water. He picked up the metal monster belonging to the woman who owned the satchel, a metal monster with an evil demon inside and threw it out the window. Then he pulled out the ribbon from his tape recording machine and tore the ribbon to shreds throwing the bits out the window.

Now that the evil had been purged from his house and the rental car, his good humor returned. And just as he figured out the radio, he heard a different tune playing inside the satchel. He dumped the satchel on the passenger seat and found the object making all the racket. It was another metal monster. He flipped the phone open, "Hello."

"Who's this?"

"Terence. Who's this?"

"Terence. I knew a Terence once."

"Hey little one," he began his voice breaking up all of a sudden. "I've been looking all over for you."

"No need. I'm not lost."

"I promised Tessa I'd take care of you Dilly."

"Where's Leona?"

"Who?"

"Is she there? She must be there. You answered her phone."

"I've been at the Woolly Man and heard those Nerin boys talking. The angry one's coming after you."

"Thanks for the tip. I'm sure there's someone here who will be pleased by that piece of news."

"Are you hurt, Dilly?"

The woman snapped, "Quit calling me that name. Listen friend. I don't have time to shoot the shit with you. I'm a busy woman. Do me a favor and mind your own business."

"You are my business, Dilly. I've been reborn, you see. A powerful woman took away all my pain. I still have the sorrow. I haven't forgotten my promise to you. Let me help you Dilly dear."

"Reborn, huh? Good for you. I'm not much into religious mumbo jumbo, so why don't you go find a nice church and tell them your good news."

"I'm not talking about that kind of rebirth."

"Listen Terence, I don't need your help."

"Have you seen Travis? I've been looking for him everywhere."

There was a long silence, he got worried, "Are you still there?"

In a voice he didn't recognize, he heard her say, "My friend tells me Travis died. I'm sorry for your loss Terence. Was he a close friend? I've lost people over the years too. It hurts. It really hurts when a close friend dies."

"He was my twin brother, Dilly. You know that, you used to tease Travis about his cowboy hat. You said it was too nice to be a real cowboy's cowboy hat."

"Keep your nosey nose out of my business. I suppose you're trying to tell me that you're all alone," the woman said in a familiar voice.

"I suppose you think you can just hitch up with me, no problem. Well, sorry Mr. I got enough shit to deal with right now. I don't have time to babysit you."

Then all of the sudden, he knew. "Acacia," he asked in alarm. "Is that you?"

A gentle voice nothing like Acacia's curt twang answered him, "It's good to hear your voice, Terence. All this time, I thought you were dead. Glad to know you're still alive, big guy."

"Eve? Is that you Eve?"

Ignoring his question Eve continued, "Oh, honey. I am so sorry about Sally and the baby. Acacia's mad because she blames herself."

Before he could say anything, another person interrupted their conversation, "Like every young person in the world Acacia is exhibiting adolescent egocentrism. You know how she is, she sees the world only through the prism of her personal reflections in the moment they happen, and she believes that the smallest thing she does influences others in catastrophic ways. I've tried to talk to her about her egocentrism, but she just won't listen."

"What should I do Mary?" he asked growing more bewildered by the second. "Where should I go? I'm driving the Taurus and Navan's satchel and her luggage are in the backseat."

"Oh yeah," a new voice said, her sudden laughter making the phone squeal. With delight he recognized the voice of Navan Leona Keys. She sounded happy which was odd. Rarely did she get a chance to speak because most people interrupted, ignored, or talked over her, "So you do. Well. Terence. Yeah, it's Terence! Yeah, you're alive. I'm so happy. Ok. They're telling me to wrap it up. So, here's what you're going to do, you're going to take the money I left behind, there's about a thousand dollars in traveler's checks in the pocketbook and some papers that give you the right to take a nice two-week Alaskan cruise. You go and have fun. Please! Go have fun."

"Hell no. I couldn't do that. The money and the ticket belong to you."

"I'm too busy right now. You go. And when you get back give me a ring, eh? We'll get together and discuss old times."

"You still haven't told me your real name," Terence reminded her. He decided it was too difficult to talk and drive. He pulled over onto the side of the road under a large elm.

He waited.

He waited some more.

He peered closely at the phone and saw the face of the phone staring back at him. Where had he been that he did not know about these new doodads? Everybody else seemed to know about them. Then he finally figured out the woman on the other end was gone. He searched through the junk in the backseat and found the papers for the cruise, the pocketbook and the money stuffed in a bag and judging from the faint smell detected by his excellent nose the bag had once upon a time held a serving of fries and a large hamburger. His opinion of the Nerin family rose just a notch. They may be off center, but they weren't totally bad; they didn't steal other people's traveler's checks or an expensive ticket on a luxury cruise ship.

He sat in the car for the longest time feeling the fresh breeze on his face. Cars wheezed by him slowing when they realized that the sign said twenty-five miles per hour. He knew where he was now. He was in Horseshoe Bend headed to Boise, Idaho. How had he gotten here? Did it matter? Hell no. Time to move on. A peaceful contentment settled over him. He tried to figure out why. Then it came to him. Someone from the past had acknowledged his existence. Someone had known his brother Travis. And now he knew his brother was finally at peace.

Terence wasn't quite sure if he'd been talking to a roomful of women or just one woman, but he no longer cared. He was convinced he'd been talking to his Dilly. She was alive, alive, and well, now a grown-up lady. In a few weeks, they would meet again, and he would see for himself that there was still something pure and clean and good in the world waiting for him.

29

Leland sat in his brand-new luxury sedan under the cool shade of a maple and waited for James Madison Hughes a.k.a. Oxley to come home from the hospital. According to hospital records, Oxley had been under sedation following the confrontation in the holding pen at the police station. Those same records referred to Oxley as being a man who had suffered from Bipolar Syndrome all his life. Leland snorted and thought better of his response when blood bubbled out of his nose. He wiped the blood onto the surgeon's gown he'd found in a trash bin two days ago.

It had been so easy blending in as he wandered the halls of the hospital disguised as one of the attending surgeons. Leland had wondered if someone might stop him. No one did. Luckily for him, St. John's Hospital had a three-car pileup that day and staff were too busy to notice him.

When a car pulled into the trailer park, Leland scooted down in the sedan and covered his battered and bruised face with a newspaper. At the filling station where he'd bought his gas and purchased food for the trip, the clerk had taken one look at his face and said, "Oh honey. What happened to you?" Any other time, Leland would have grabbed the bitch's throat and told her to save her pity for someone else, but because he had a pressing engagement elsewhere, he accepted her pity with a shrug and said through his swollen mouth, "We had a difference of opinion."

Once he was out of the store and safe in his vehicle, he used his newly acquired map to find Oxley's home. He'd been sitting for nearly an hour near the trailer waiting for him. He was sure he'd read the doctor's notes correctly. Since Leland had signed a waiver absolving the department of negligence and refusing to press charges (which evidently the police department could have negated but chose not to) Oxley was due to be released shortly after Leland left town. Two hours after his assault by the Neanderthal, the physician-on-call in the Emergency Room had shook his head in amazement and told Leland he had a skull made of granite. "You are a very lucky man, Mr. Ansel."

That afternoon Leland received a police escort. Those cops were determined he leave town and never come back. Masking his true intentions with a serenity he didn't feel, Leland drove under the prescribed speed limit all the way out of town. In Grants Pass, he sold his old car to a junk yard and bought himself this sleek awesome luxury sedan. No one stopped him when he returned to Klamath Falls and drove up and down the streets searching for James Madison Hughes' trailer. It was an added pleasure to learn Ricco Banks lived right across the courtyard in what was a twin of Oxley's piece of shit.

That had been yesterday, yesterday when Oxley could be heard screaming and cussing and making everyone's life a misery with his Bipolar Syndrome act. That evening, Oxley had finally quieted down and fell asleep deep in his drugged stupor. Now two days later, Leland was still waiting patiently for the gorilla to come home. The cops were such morons. Did they really expect him to just go peacefully away? Did they really expect anyone to forget two black eyes, a swollen lip, a missing tooth, and bruises all over from a Fuck-Wad like Oxley? No. Leland had something better in mind. They really were morons, those dumb cops.

The Fuck-Wad seemed to be taking his damned time getting home. Had he really heard right? Or were the moron cops even more clueless than he thought? Oxley should have been home by now. He replayed the conversation he'd overheard between the two cops in the hospital corridor.

"He probably had it coming. Sick you know. Messing with kids," the fat cop said.

"How'd he know?" the ugly cop asked.

"You mean the Ox?" fat cop replied. "It was from Ricco. Ricco told Oxley. At least that's what Oxley says."

"Ricco Banks? How'd he hear? I was with him in booking the entire time."

"We had two calls and only two vehicles. We decided to team up. Banks was in the backseat of mine when Ansel was arrested. We couldn't transport the little girl with Banks, so we left Ricco at the motel lobby chained to the chair. When we went to retrieve him, we found Oxley trying to carry Ricco out of the lobby handcuffed to the motel chair. You should have seen him," the fat cop said unable to contain his laughter. "There he was bobbing and weaving as he carried Ricco down the street like Ricco was some sort of King of Siam. It was priceless."

They were not only morons Leland thought, they were proud of their incompetence. No one would be stupid enough to brag about such negligence within hearing of the victim and other witnesses unless they

were major airheads. Ricco Banks had been easy to find. All he had to
do was look him up in the phone book. Along with Oxley, Banks had
been arrested for being drunk and disorderly and upon release had been
given twenty-four hours to dry out before attending a series of ninety
AA meetings. The first thing the Wop did was buy himself a carton of
beer and head for home.

The sound of a car entering the trailer park interrupted Leland's
thoughts. When he was finished with Ricco Banks, the police wouldn't
recognize him. And the best part would be the message the snitch's
beating would have on Oxley. The wait had been worth it. He'd been
prepared for the screams. His past experience had taught him to never
bring his own tools, but to use what was available on site. A person's
home was better than any torture chamber he could devise.

Leland sank back when he realized the vehicle, an old Trans Am
sweeping around the corner included two females in the front seat.
When they pulled up next to Oxley's trailer and climbed out, he watched
them from the holes he'd cut out of the newspaper. Their high-pitched
squeals of laughter grated on his nerves. They looked like little porkers
too. The mother and daughter looked and dressed the same – like sluts.
He wasn't surprised. Like breeds like. With the clinical eye of a butcher
inspecting a dubious piece of meat, he realized that they weren't worth
the trouble. Winter wanted a particular kind of physique and if she didn't
get what she wanted she would refuse to pay him. So, he supposed the
porkers were out.

The women entered Oxley's trailer still chattering and squealing,
the daughter too lazy to help her mother carry the packages inside. That
was the problem with kids today; kids thought they were entitled to
everything, even to be waited on by their parents. And their parents were
stupid enough to grovel at the little monsters' feet. In his day, if a kid
didn't help out, he got an ass-whupping or the back of a hand. If a kid
talked back, he definitely got an ass-whupping. Yep, in his day, kids
respected their elders.

Leland glanced at his watch. His butt was getting numb and his
forehead throbbed. The rear view mirror gave him such a fright; he
turned the shitty thing away, so he wouldn't have to see himself. He'd
be scarred for life. There was no way he could walk up to Millhouse like
this without alarming the sick-turd. Millhouse would assume some angry
parent had done this to him and flee in terror thinking he'd be next. The
thought of his face frightening the neighbors spurred him to action.

Pulling out of the trailer park, Leland drove to the nearest clothing store. Before entering the store, he slipped on his new sunglasses purchased in Grants Pass. Thirty minutes later, Leland had his disguise. He'd tried on several pants and shirts, then chose the baggies pair of pants and an oversized shirt. At the furniture store down from the clothing store, he bought two throw pillows. At a dime store he bought some masking tape. Right around the corner from the trailer park was a busy gas station. He got the key from the attendant and went into the bathroom to get ready for his debut. The throw pillows made him look fifty pounds heavier. The red baseball cap and matching sweater made him look like a clueless hick. And the sunglasses hid his black eyes.

Careful not to smudge his bronzer, Leland avoided touching his face or rubbing his hands on his clothes as he drove back to the trailer park. Instinct told him to park the luxury sedan several blocks from the courtyard. He should have thought of that earlier. Shrugging, he figured at this time of day most people were working and most kids were in school unless they were delinquents. As if he belonged in the neighborhood, he walked up to Ricco's trailer carrying a bag of groceries. Shortly after Ricco Banks opened the door at Leland's initial knock, time seemed to fly by. It was only when he looked up from his work that he realized the lateness of the hour. Glancing out the window, he noticed how the light was fading. It would be dark soon.

Scrutinizing the Banks' living quarters closely, he was reassured to know he'd left nothing incriminating behind. While walking past Oxley's trailer, Leland started thinking about all the trouble Millhouse had been to him lately, how none of this would have happened if Millhouse had kept his promise. He thought about Oxley and began to have second thoughts. After several hours of hard work teaching Ricco manners, he was exhausting. Maybe he should leave town and book a motel room for a week, let things die down before returning. He thought about Celia and her bitch of a mother. She shouldn't have left like that, just up and take the kid like that and leave him all alone in this perverted place.

Then Leland glancing surreptitiously at Oxley's trailer remembered the women inside. Maybe there was something else he could do to pass the time. He looked around. Most people in the park were either napping or at work. When he walked up to the door, he paused thinking perhaps Oxley might appear at any moment. Yet, when

Oxley did arrive, Leland would have the upper hand. Leland rapped smartly on the door. The daughter answered and with her hip resting on the door frame asked in an insolent tone, "Yeah? What do you want?"

Kids these days. No manners at all. Leland smiled wincing at the pain of his still sore facial muscles and said, "Hi. I'm a friend of Oxley's. He said I could crash here tonight until the cops get around to releasing him from the hospital."

The girl called over her shoulder, "Hey Mom. This guy says he's a friend of Dad's and Dad told him he could spend the night here."

The mother showed up at the door peering over her daughter's shoulder. "Oxley didn't say anything to me about a visitor," she said holding a pair of scissors in one hand and a tag in the other.

"We bumped into each other at St. John's."

"Really. I've known Oxley my whole life and he never mentioned you."

"You want to check with him first? I don't mind. I'll just wait out here," Leland said.

The woman hesitated then stepped aside, "Come on in."

Leland stepped inside still smiling. When he took off his sunglasses and his baseball cap, the girl choked on a horrified squeal. The mother, in the act of moving back into the living room, turned in time to see his face. Her hands went up to her mouth. She realized she still had the scissors and set them down on the end table, then said, "Jesus. What happened to you?"

He brushed past her and grabbed the scissors, "I'm not Jesus, but you'll be calling for him soon enough." When the girl ran, he threw his leg out and using his elbow knocked her on the side of her head. She fell to the floor moaning. The mother ran toward the coffee table where her cellphone lay and in the three steps it took for Leland to reach her, he plunged the scissors into her back. He got to the daughter before she reached the door. She was a big girl and it took all his strength to hold her down. When she passed out, he dragged her into the bathroom and threw her in the tub. Lucky for him there was plenty of tape left to tie her hands and feet and shut her stupid fat ugly mouth.

Sanity returned. He would hold off doing anything unpleasant to the daughter until after he overpowered Oxley. It would be so much sweeter to watch Oxley's face as he raped and beat his daughter. When Leland woke from his brief nap, he glanced at the clock amazed at the time. He felt so refreshed. An hour's nap could do that for someone as tired and sore as he was. He stretched his arms up to the ceiling then dropped them down to the coverlet. Oxley's closet was at the other end of the bed and he could see shirts hanging neatly inside. He threw his legs off the bed and wandered over to the closet sliding the door open.

A few minutes of careful study and he found the shirt he wanted. After peeling off his filthy shirt, Leland slipped on a long sleeved white dress shirt with a crisp collar and fine-looking buttons. The shirt was a bit large around the shoulders, but would work in a pinch. He picked up his dirty shirt and peered out the bedroom window. Still no Oxley. What a shame. Then he walked down the narrow hallway to the front part of the trailer and paused to survey his handiwork. Wife lying dead on the floor with the scissors in her back. Daughter lying in a tub overflowing with water, looking like a gray mummy, her mouth and nose, hands and feet tied up tighter than a hangman's knot.

For the last hour, he'd wiped his prints off everything he could remember touching including the scissors. When he heard moaning coming from the bathroom, he paused with the trailer door open. Unfortunately for Leland, just at that moment, the mail carrier jeep pulled into the courtyard. And then a monster from hell flew around the corner of the trailer dragging a chain behind him and charged up the porch steps.

The big dog slammed into Leland's legs and sent him flying backward. Leland hit the screen door so hard he busted through the mesh and slid to the ground landing on his sore butt. With his arms up to protect his face, Leland waited for the monster dog to take a chunk out of his body. Instead the dog disappeared inside the trailer and stood over the dead woman.

With his luck still holding, Leland scrambled to his feet, kicked the ends of the heavy chain inside the hall and slammed the flimsy door shut. The screen door was hanging from a single hinge, so he left the piece of shit and hurried down the steps. The mail carrier remained clueless, never even looking up from her sorting when the pit bull charged. Leland managed to slip by her without being noticed. Once he left the courtyard, he picked up speed and by the time he saw the sedan he was trotting. No one stopped him. No one shouted or screamed in horror. Relieved, he jumped into the sedan and drove away. He didn't realize he was smiling until the old lady walking her dog smiled back at him.

By five o'clock, Leland had managed to pull into Medford, Oregon. He was low on gas, so he turned into a nearby station and waited for his chance to fill up. The man in front of him seemed to be taking his sweet time which pissed Leland off. He'd already been delayed a full morning and most of the afternoon waiting for Oxley. Two days and nothing to show for it. No kid. No cash. No sale. He looked down at his pants. They were wrinkled. He suspected the morons who thought of themselves as cops back in Klamath Falls had dug through his stuff and just thrown everything back inside haphazardly.

The customer in front of him stood there holding the hose as if the damned thing might fly out of the tank on its own. He noticed Leland and frowned. The look on the wetback's face enraged Leland. He had a feeling this guy was milking the situation just to piss him off. Who the fuck did he think he was?

He heard the guy say, "What are you looking at pin day ho?" Leland knew what that meant. He threw his sunglasses on the seat, slipped on his gloves, and jumped out of the sedan. The dipshit fell over the hose and onto his own damned car door in his surprise at seeing Leland holding a baseball bat. Yeah sucker, Leland chuckled, this baseball bat belongs to a skin-head who wants to see your people go back to Mexico. There were so many stupid people in the world and here was one of the biggest ones of them all.

Adrenaline coursed through his body. He felt like superman, larger than life, invincible. And it all began at the base of his neck, that sense of power surging through him. The power ran down his spine kicking his heart up a notch. He took a deliberate step forward with his scalp tingling as if alight with electricity. Even the air he breathed snapped and sparked. He lifted his arm and took careful aim hitting the idiot in the head. The man ducked and fell back against his open door sliding to the ground. People began screaming. Still taller than tall and bigger than big, more powerful than he'd ever felt in his entire life, Leland jumped back in his car prepared to take off.

Belatedly, he realized moving forward would be impossible. The wetback's car blocked his escape. Leland reversed. He heard the shriek as metal struck metal and his neck snapped back sending a wave of pain from his neck up to his eyeballs. The impact with the larger object jerked him forward and only the steering wheel saved him from soaring through the windshield. His car had collided with something huge.

His chest should have hurt, hurt a lot. Mixed among women screaming and men shouting, he thought he heard police sirens. He climbed out of his car on shaky legs and noticed what he had hit. It was a motor home, a deluxe forty-six-footer. "You fucking idiot," he said unaware in the mayhem that no one could hear him especially the old coot in the motor home. The only option left for Leland was to run. So, he ran. And he kept on running until he couldn't run anymore.

It seemed like hours before he felt safe enough to slow down and catch his breath. The sweat nearly blinded him. And when he glanced at his watch, he was amazed to discover that he had only been running for fifteen minutes. It felt like hours though. He was a lousy fucking runner. He realized he had only managed to trot four blocks and walk another two before his legs began to tremble sending messages to his brain – stop, stop, you fucking moron.

When he walked past a wall made of flat stone probably quarried from some place nearby, he found himself inside a tree lined manicured residential area surrounded by manicured lawns and generic middle-class homes with their pampered yards and pampered kids. If Millhouse were here he would think he had died and gone to heaven. All those delicious targets roaming unsupervised just waiting to be coaxed away with treats and promises. Leland heard the police getting closer. He still had his gun tucked inside his pants. He threw the damned thing under a rhododendron. No one had seen him yet. People on the street had paused in their various outdoor pursuits to listen as the wail of the siren became a bedlam of squawking.

Women wheeling babies in carriages stopped and lifted their heads and waited. Neighbors turned off their riding lawnmowers or stopped raking or barbecuing long enough to listen. Children, familiar with the noises of a busy city, traffic whooshing by on the freeway, a helicopter landing on the hospital roof to the west, a plane passing overhead on its way to the airport, and the muffled sound of a fire truck's horn warning motorists to get out of the way, all these sounds were familiar, and the sounds electrified the children into action. Police sirens meant car chases, danger, good guys battling bad guys.

What a crock of flaming bullshit, Leland thought. Cops were just criminals given permission to wear uniforms and carry guns. He watched as children spilled out of houses and backyards to stare in awe at cop cars racing down the street. Some of them remained in their yards clinging to the fence rails while the bolder ones stood on curbs and leaned forward hoping for bloodshed.

Leland moved in among a group closest to the park. He searched his shirt pocket for his sunglasses then remembered he had left them on the seat of the car. He had a pair of cheap ones in his jacket pocket. He slipped them on. He hated this pair the most. They lay crooked on his face and he could feel the bottom rim resting on his right cheek. He hated his skin touching plastic. It felt nasty.

As if his sunglasses could protect him from the cops. What a joke. Everything was happening so fast. At any other time, Leland would have simply followed the bastard home and killed his pet or torched his car. No time for recriminations. Time to zone out. Time to melt into the crowd.

If the people around him and the cops couldn't see the expression in his eyes, then everything would work out for the best. He knew a suspicious move would drew attention to himself, running for one, or grabbing someone and holding them hostage for another, any such obvious sign of guilt would bring the cops to him. No. He had to remain calm, pretend he was just an innocent bystander alarmed by all the noise. With his hands in his pockets, he took his cue from the civilians around him and copied their posture and expressions of concerned curiosity.

As if they were at a Grand Prix race, the group turned their heads in unison as first one, then two, then three patrol vehicles with lights flashing sped by. Some of the dumber adolescents began to chase the retreating cars down the street. Leland heard a parent shout to one of the kids, "Get back here, Scotty."

Leland turned to a young mother pushing a stroller and asked, "What happened?"

The woman eyes politely brushing over his face without really registering him turned to focus her attention on the drama going on in the streets of her neighborhood. Together they watched the red tail lights as the last remaining cop car disappeared around the corner. He heard her mumble, "I don't know what's happened. Maybe someone's sick?"

"Maybe," Leland said. "There should be an ambulance along soon." He pretended to look in the other direction and while she was busy calming her two-year-old, he slipped away from the group and started walking in the opposite direction. He kept his pace crisp, but controlled. No sense in calling attention to himself. It was too early for the cops to have a picture of him yet. He was aware the gas station umbrellas included video cameras directed towards each of the pumps and especially the attendant's booth with its bullet proof glass and cash register. But searching through those videos would take time. And in the amount of time it would take for the witnesses to identify him, he would be long gone from Medford, Oregon.

Instead of hitchhiking which was an amateur move, Leland climbed on a bus and took the bus to Crescent City, California. The four-p.m. bus was just leaving. He would be in Crescent City a little after seven p.m. which would give him plenty of time to ring up Violet and get her to come fetch him from the diner. While on the bus, he kept trying to get a hold of her. She wasn't answering her phone. Leland left his rental car at the diner and walked the remaining two miles to the Winter residence.

When he saw the security gate wide open, he paused wondering if this was her idea of a joke. He walked around the perimeter and found an old trumpet vine growing along the wall. He used the trumpet vine like a ladder, up and over, and climbed down into her high ass' sanctuary. He snuck around the house peering in at windows and found himself in the back facing the ocean. Then he turned to look at the house.

On the ocean side, all the windows were smashed. There were chairs, lamps, pictures, books, candelabra, even a toilet lid dumped on the once immaculate lawn as if some crazy person or persons had taken the contents of the first-floor rooms and anything disposable and chucked them out the windows. Leland didn't bother to go through the mess instead he wandered down to the laboratory spotting the Botticelli Door. He assumed Violet and the others were hiding inside the lab until the intruders left. He shoved at Venus' freakishly vacuous face and heard the door hit the wall. The smell of rotting flesh hit him in the face first, then overpowered every orifice in his body: nostrils, mouth, eye holes, ears, and butt crack. He stumbled outside sucking in clean air.

Determined to fix the problem, Leland held Oxley's shirt to his nose, a shirt which now smelled stale from his sweat which stilled smelled better than the smell of decomposing corpses. He followed the trail of blood from the door down the hall, until he entered the main room where Winter kept her lab equipment and surgical table. He saw Ray's ass first. He was lying on his side.

Leland stepped over him and turned in time to see Ray's face. Ray had tied several strips of his shirt around his head as a tourniquet and beneath the tourniquet to stop the blood flow, he'd packed gauze pads. Leland knelt beside Ray and examined the gauze pads sticking to the dried blood from one eye. The blood had hardened into a thick black paste. Ray looked as if he'd been skewered and the object that had been used to poke out his eye lay in the surgical room's sink.

It was a wicked looking weapon, a thin needle-sharp blade with a slippery notched handle made of the same material. Any prints on the handle would have been wiped off by Ray's desperate attempts to remove it from his eye. At least, Ray had found the fortitude to pull the thin blade out of his eye. From the condition of the surgery, Leland guessed Ray had spent most of his time wrapped in a few paltry blankets which would not have kept him warm for long. The blankets were usually stored in the supply closet. The supply closet included lotions, hand wipes, tissues, scissors, scalpels, respirators, pumps, oxygen masks, a defibrillator and a bunch of other equipment which would not have fed Ray or quenched his thirst.

Most of the prescription bottles strewn about the floor were empty. Ray must have medicated up until the point he died, died of thirst and starvation he supposed. It must have taken a long time for him to die. Every inch of the laboratory had been ransacked. No food here. When Leland turned on the tap, nothing happened. Who had turned off the water supply to the laboratory? Ray must have died recently; his body was still warm.

As Leland stood up he heard a moan and went to investigate.

He stood on the landing hoping he'd find Dr. Winter still alive. She was dead. She'd been dead a long time. He sat himself down on the bottom step and gazed at the women sprawled on the floor between six hospital beds. Myrtle looked as if she'd been choked to death. Dr. Winter's leg told the tale of her death. The six beds with all their fancy equipment would not be accepting any more test subjects. There wouldn't be any more money either. The cash cow had died, died from blood loss. He was clearly screwed.

A disturbing thought made the hairs on the nape of his neck stiffen. So where had the moaning come from if Myrtle and Violet were dead? As if to answer his unspoken question, something buried in the sheets on the bed to his left began to moan again. He scuttled away in disgust. After a long time, he forced himself to stand up and step over to the bed. With trembling fingers, he pulled back the sheet. There was a man lying on the bed. Well, part of a man. He was hooked up to machines, machines which kept him breathing, machines which pumped fluids into his body. Half of his body where his legs should have been was wrapped in urine-and-feces-soaked bandages. The smell made him gag. He'd didn't want to peek under the bandages.

It took him hours to straighten out the mess someone had made of his livelihood. He removed the tube from the test subject, pressed a pillow into his face to cut off the air to his newly freed lungs, and when he was sure the thing was dead, managed to dump it into a body bag and drag the bag to the incinerator in the surgical lab. The incinerator was a twin of the one in Violet Winter's basement. Hours went by as he peered through the glass waiting for the creature to turn into a pile of ash. Of course, not all of him would end up as ash, but Leland was prepared for that set back. He had a canister ready. When the green light came on, he'd shovel the remaining evidence inside the canister and bury the whole nasty shit somewhere no one would ever find it.

Then he heard a stranger calling to him from outside the Botticelli Door.

"Hey, is anybody here? It's Sam from the lawn service. I'm here to turn off the sprinklers. Hello?"

"Hold on," Leland shouted, slipping, and sliding his way on the blood-soaked floor to the Botticelli Door in the hopes he could prevent the man from entering. But Leland wasn't fast enough. The stranger gasped probably hitting the wall of dying flesh as he stepped inside. Leland heard the little fucker scurry away like some frightened mouse. He tried to hold back a chuckle. The air exhaled from his lungs stirred the ash which still clung to his mask. Droplets landed on Venus' face.

Time to go. Time to get the flock out of here. Right quick.

He nearly made it too. Just as he was ready to fling one leg over the wall, strong hands grabbed his ankles and yanked him to the ground. His chin hit the hard concrete of the wall and on the way down he scraped off bits and pieces of skin. When he lifted himself up from the ground, he turned with his fists clenched ready to fight the little fucker. The little fucker wasn't who he expected to see. He stared at the woman blankly. She smiled. Suddenly, he was scared.

He moved to run. Then a pair of Doberman Pinchers came charging around the corner. They looked hungry. The lead Doberman looked at the woman and stopped in his tracks. The other bumped into him. As far as Leland could tell, she hadn't made a move. There had been no hand signals or the sound of a clicker. The Dobie's tail began to wag. The woman pointed at Leland and said, "Attack."

Leland scrambled back to the trumpet vine and tried to climb over the wall. The Doberman got a mouth full of his shoe and wouldn't let go. As Leland kicked the Doberman's head, Leland heard police sirens and ambulance and the heavier wail of fire trucks. Desperately, he tried to kick the dog loose and the dog was equally determined to hold onto him.

The woman spoke again, "Stand down, Rommel." The dog obeyed. By the time Leland was on the ground, several squad cars had surrounded the property and blocked his path to freedom. The woman and the Dobermans waited for the police to come running. Absently, he heard the woman say, "I'm Dr. Winter's dog walker and I caught this man trespassing. The A1 Sprinkler guy says he interrupted this man trying to hide his crimes."

30

The early evening, freshening with a cooler breeze from the west brought the promise of a milder tomorrow. There would be a tomorrow. I wanted to believe there would be one. Nothing had moved in the dark for nearly an hour now. No bums parked under the eaves of the mini-mall across the street. No late-night partiers weaving their way toward their cars. The owner of the tobacco shop which butted up against the right-hand wall of the pawn shop had left several lights on. The lights illuminated his beautifully polished mahogany counter. The cash register, in full view of the window looked brand new and had probably been emptied just before closing.

Robbing businesses had never been my style. There'd been a woman I use to know who couldn't help herself – if she wanted something she'd take it, no matter the consequences. Not me. Maybe I was too cautious. So be it.

Even though life could be harsh at times, there were moments when living had a purpose. Like now. I had a purpose and the purpose made me feel more alive than I had in years. Yet in other ways, the world had changed drastically. People carried cellphones everywhere. Even I had one and I couldn't remember ever having owned one before, but there the cellphone sat, sitting silently on the passenger seat waiting to be used. All last night I'd played with the thing and finally figured out which buttons to press. Manipulating Winter's household accounts had been easier.

A tall skinny guy with a crew cut, wearing a green cotton shirt and green army fatigues, yet, with a slouch which contradicted the tough soldier act instead of continuing down the sidewalk made an unexpected detour. At first, I read confidence in the way he moved and concern on his face, but I quickly changed my mind when he drew closer and I could see his eyes. Once I saw those eyes, I knew I'd been grossly mistaken. His eyes had a veiled thirst. It wasn't just the eyes that told the story. It was in the curve of his lips, a sort of smug self-satisfaction. He wanted something from me and seemed sure he would get it. I had my speech prepared in my head. I would tell him: sorry I'm just as broke as you. I waited for him to speak, not sure if he wanted money or a job.

"You need a hundred bucks?" he asked me.

My first thought: people really have changed if they're offering strangers money. It wasn't until he moved in closer with those glittering greedy eyes full of excitement and began rubbing his private parts and biting his lower lip, I realized the man's true intentions. He wasn't crazy; he was a pervert. I was shocked. How dare he? Anyone who would proposition someone like me must be desperate. I was in no mood to exchange my body fluids with this gross putrid bozo. Just in case the situation turned ugly, I pulled the gun out of my purse and set it on my lap. I knew nothing about guns, but evidently, he did for his eyes widened at the sight.

"If I wasn't busy right now I'd arrest you for solicitation, but I'll be nice this time. Get lost," I told him.

He reminded me of a Promacthoteuthis Sulcus with his mouth resembling the letter O and his teeth beaming whitely in a cheesy-ass grin. The open-mouthed grin didn't scare me. It wouldn't even have scared a passing eel since Promacthoteuthis Sulcus were only an inch long. What would scare me is being so deep down in the ocean, I'd die from the pressure. I tried real hard not to laugh as I watched him stumble backwards, then pirouette and scurry away, moving with just enough nonchalance to look as if he had just remembered an important meeting. Relief made my hands shake as I slipped the toy gun back in my purse and watched the guy pause on the street corner to glance surreptitiously at me.

By early morning, I was still at my post sipping my coffee which had grown cold. A man showed up on the street opposite and paused by the pawn shop door. He tested the door then stepped back. Then he stepped toward my note. I watched carefully ready to run out and slap him silly if he dared to tear the note off the door. I had taken the precaution of folding the note and addressing it to Leland. The man paused for a minute to read the name then turned and searched the streets as if looking for someone. Even though I knew he couldn't possibly see me hiding behind the shrubs with my binoculars trained on him, I still ducked. Stupid.

The stranger walked back to his vehicle and sat in the driver's seat. The car didn't move. He surveyed the area even looking in my direction. It was difficult to keep my hands steady while holding up the heavy binoculars. I had to reassure myself that he couldn't see me. Then he got out of the car and rummaged on the floor of his backseat, retrieved some sort of book, and returned to the front seat. It wasn't until he started flipping through the pages that I realized he had a telephone book. For the first time in eons, watching the people on the street seemed as fun as watching a movie at the cinema. And the man could have been an actor himself. He had the perfect leading-man looks, all six feet or more of him with his spiky black hair and handsome face.

My watch told me I'd been sitting in the same spot for nearly two hours. The only part of me that wasn't numb was my fingers holding the binoculars. They were getting their exercise for sure. But I wanted to wait until Mr. Movie Star finished his business and took off before I stood up and stretched and did a couple of yoga poses I'd seen on late night television. Maybe I should call the police anonymously and tell them a man is missing? Maybe they'd show up and find Leland for me.

Mr. Movie Star started his engine and tore out of the parking lot. I watched as he headed toward the highway. Hum. Maybe I should follow him. No. I might miss Leland. Mr. Movie Star might be going home or to his favorite gym to work on those fine-looking muscles. He might not lead me to Leland, but actually distract me from finding Leland. I couldn't risk distraction. Anyway, I had all the time in the world. I had my friends. I knew they had my back. What more could I ask for? Some people lead lonely desperate lives, but not me. Not me. I have my friends, friends I can trust with my very life. They had already proven their loyalty to me.

When a couple, a man and a woman walked into the tobacco shop next door, I had an idea. Maybe the tobacconist had some answers for me? It took five minutes to throw on a pair of shorts and a shirt and ten minutes to fish through the junk accumulated over the week in the back of the car in order to locate my sandals. When I opened the door, the fresh air hit me in the face, although it wasn't quite fresh saturated as it was with the heat from the asphalt and the smell of exhaust from passing motorists.

All of a sudden, a renewed sense of urgency and purpose washed over me. Now I could act and perhaps find out something useful for a change. I waited until the street was clear of people then circled around the car and out into the street making my way behind the row of arborvitae separating a dental office from the abandoned gas station. Then I walked out onto the street like any other pedestrian and waited for the light to turn green. Unable to contain my excitement, I practically ran across the street and into the tobacco shop.

I heard the trill of the bell above the door; and as I stepped inside, my skin said hallelujah as cool air gently caressed every part of my body. All my senses were pleased with the place. I sucked in the sweet aroma of cherry tobacco and other tobacco blends I couldn't possibly identify, my nostrils appreciating every whiff. My eyes also admired the interior, the way the place reminded me of an early nineteenth century shop with its imitation gas sconces on the walls and a brass spittoon in the corner.

There were also several old wooden barrels filled with umbrellas and walking sticks. The furniture and decorative trappings were too new-looking to be authentic period pieces, but the newness wasn't as critical as the decorator's appreciation of fine wood. I loved wood furniture, and anything made of wood myself. Unlike rocks, wood seemed more alive, warmer, cozier, more willing to bend and be shaped by human hands.

While the clerk helped his customers, I wandered around the room and admired all the objects I saw which represented a period in history familiar to everyone and beloved to everyone – the Victorian era. I studied some of the beautiful wooden pipes arranged inside a display case that ran from one end of the room to the other. I brushed my hand lightly across the gleaming surface of the redwood counter admiring the color and the smooth texture. I craned my neck back to examine the wall of cubbyholes on the shelves, floor to ceiling cubbyholes that had been built behind the counter to store merchandize.

I read some of the names inscribed in imitation gold script under the boxes: McClelland Dark Star, Skandinavik Full Aroma Red, Oliver Twist Wintergreen, and Citrus. Hum. I thought about the faraway places where these tobaccos had come from and wondered what difference the expensive blends made anyway – wasn't tobacco once smoked just a bunch of nicotine in your lungs?

What difference would an expensive blend be over a cheap old leaf? Would a pipe smoker be less susceptible to lung cancer if he smoked a more expensive brand? Did smokers worry about cancer? What was the allure anyway? Might as well sit by a camp fire and suck up the smoke from the burning logs. At least then a person could keep warm and smoke at the same time.

There was nothing worse than a reformed smoker, well, a reformed anything. And me? Without knowing the how, I knew that I had been a smoker – once upon a time. And my cynicism had much to do with the craving eating away inside me now. The body knew. Oh.

Yes. The body remembered, even if the mind had forgotten. The clerk finished serving the couple and when the couple brushed past me, I stepped up to the counter. The clerk wore a crisp white shirt with his sleeves held back with some sort of black band.

I'd seen pictures of men from the early twentieth century wearing those contraptions. They seemed practical, sort of similar to the bands bikers wore to keep their pants from getting caught in the spokes of their wheels. The man had hair the color of my fingernails, a sort of egg white. It looked softer than most old people's hair, baby soft. His hair reminded me of life's magic circle, how as we grow older, we become, once again, that helpless child. Not so bad really if a person has someone trustworthy as a caretaker.

When I looked into the old man's eyes, they were a watery light blue. I must have imagined the look though, the look of sadness behind the eyes. What did this man have to be sad about working in such a pleasant place as this? "May I help you Miss?" he asked and made his way down the counter toward where I stood admiring the gold rings wrapped around the cigars. It was then I noticed his limp and the odd curvature of his spine.

"Yes. I hope so. I've been wondering why the pawn shop next door is still closed. I'm getting worried because to buy back my mother's necklace I have to pay this month's installment. Have you heard anything from Mr. Ansel?"

The old man frowned and looked down at his hands resting on the counter. I noticed how swollen they were from arthritis and the large brown spots that pocked the skin. Hands identify a person's age more than any other part of the body. No one had yet figured out how to youth-in-eyes the hands. I bit my lip to forestall an unladylike bark of laughter – youth-in-eyes. Oh. Yes. Not euthanasia of the hands, but youth-in-Asia of the hands. That's rich. In order to have younger hands a person must be in Asia.

"Don't know the man myself. My son's talked to him on occasion."

As if conjured from a magician's wand, a young man stepped out from behind a red curtain with several boxes in his arms. He stood about six feet tall, yet, he looked much shorter the way he slouched his shoulders and with his eyes permanently downcast as if he had done something terribly bad only just a minute ago. He noticed us down at the other end of the room and paused in the act of shelving the tobacco.

His father turned to see what I was looking at and noticed his son for the first time, "Jasper. This child wants to know about the shop next door. Have you seen the owner lately?" he asked in a shaky voice unlike his soft cultured voice spoken in my presence.

Shouting across a room didn't come natural to this man. His son walked toward us, and I felt the old floorboards tremble as his solid muscled body approached. His dark blue eyes moved across my face without expression then away. A coldness settled over me. Maybe the old man's sadness stemmed from disappointment in his son.

Then I knew. I knew the old guy was lying. This place looked as if it had been around for years, perhaps in business longer than the pawn shop which I had learned had first opened in 1972. I bet the old man knew Leland. Maybe too well. And I suspected that Leland had been as nasty with this man as he could be with anyone else unlucky enough to cross paths with him, especially since Leland had a talent for sniffing out weaknesses in others. Maybe there'd been a dispute between them, a dispute about access to the alley or the parking lot or leasing. It could have been any dispute knowing Leland as I did. Maybe the two had had a confrontation.

This sweet old man wouldn't have had a chance against Leland's foulness. The old guy might have been shocked the first time Leland's dirty mind and even fouler mouth spewed garbage into the air like so much feces. Poor old guy. All his money invested in this business with a monster for a neighbor. He had no recourse, no way to up and leave the business behind. So, he sticks around and endures the unpleasantness vowing to outlive the little feces-eating troll. Yes. This old man was stubborn as hell. What a fool. Peace of mind outperformed money any day of the week.

And what about the son? I thought about Ray and how Ray Millhouse used to work for Leland back in the day. I thought about this block of wood standing beside his father with the coldness in his eyes and the long face and tried to figure out how old he might be – maybe in his early twenties? If so then he might have come across Ray at some time in his life. The thought had to be extinguished. No more images please. Not today. She has a fruitful imagination, someone once said. Poor child and her fruitful imagination.

The son spoke in a voice that made me tremble, the voice of a child. The voice emanating from such a body was disconcerting to say the least. Another victim. And had he become a predator? I made myself look up into his face and studied his expression and listened closely to the tempo of his voice. The lack of inflection disturbed me the most. It was obvious that nothing moved him anymore. Had Leland punished the old man through his son? I had an overwhelming urge to confront Leland and stomp all over his face.

"Shortly after his shop was robbed," the son said and then his eyes lit up for the first time. "He took off. It's been seven weeks and two days now."

"You've kept count," I said with a laugh that never reached my belly. "I wish I had neighbors as observant."

"A guy came in yesterday looking for him. He left a note. You want to see it?" the son asked and without waiting for an answer went to the cash register and punched some keys and opened the drawer. His long white fingers pulled the note out with dainty precision. All the man's movements were rather effeminate which according to cultural stereotyping would classify him as homosexual. I doubted he was sexual at all. Someone had robbed him of the joy of living, much less a desire for intimacy with another human being.

Ray may have begun the process, but someone had completed the desecration of this man's soul. The child within the body of the man handed me the note managing not to touch my fingers in the process. I read the note. It was from someone calling himself Oxley. "Do you have a pen?" I asked the two behind the counter. "I'd like to jot down this number."

The old man handed me what appeared to be an expensive ball point pen. I felt pampered just using the pen to copy down the phone number, yet, I had trouble looking into the old man's eyes as I handed the pen back to him. I made myself speak the thoughts pressing on my mind. It was just the three of us in the room and I hadn't seen any cameras and I really didn't give a damned anyway, "Ray Millhouse is dead you know. I heard he got locked inside a vault or something and nobody noticed for nearly a month. What a way to go, huh?"

"We've heard nothing," said the old man with eagerness in his voice that made me want to smile. "Where did you hear this?"

"This woman I met in a bar, she was sure about the name. Ray Millhouse. A name like Millhouse is hard to forget."

His son walked away without a word and began to pull out the pouches of tobacco from the boxes and stack them in their appropriate cubby holes. The old man looked at me with a perplexed wrinkle between his brows then the wrinkle smoothed out and he did something completely unexpected, he stretched out his arm to me across the counter. At first, I didn't want to shake his hand, but something inside assured me I would not be disappointed. I grasped his hand lightly touching what reminded me of papyrus or rice paper, unexpectedly scratchy almost like sand in solid form.

"My name is Ezra Rosenberg, and this is my son Jasper. Nice to meet you. Miss?"

"Nice to meet you. Thank you for the number. I've got to be going now," I said backing up and trying to navigate my way toward the door without bumping into barrels or tables covered with handkerchiefs and wallets.

"So how do you know Ray?" the son asked me.

I held the coolness of the glass doorknob in my hand for a second then turned to face Jasper Rosenberg. "We were neighbors once."

As the little gold bell above the door rang, I thought I heard Jasper say, "My condolences."

Once outside the shop, the blinding sun and heat radiating from the sidewalk pinned me on the threshold. A customer tried to pass me. I stepped aside, the display window hot against the palm of my hand. Stupid. Why must people be in such a damned hurry? If the guy had had the decency to wait a minute, I would have been out of his way. I fumbled for my sunglasses and shoved them on my face not wanting him or anyone to see my eyes. I started walking. At one point I even jogged. It felt good to stretch my legs to feel the muscles in my thighs contract, to know the blood was pumping through my body cleansing the demons.

When I looked around and didn't recognize any of the buildings, I knew I was lost. It wasn't until I retraced my steps that I realized I'd nearly walked all the way across town. I was back at the rental car before the sun set, thirsty, hungry, and with aching sore feet. I was grateful that the tobacco shop had closed. Maybe father and son were celebrating. The exercise seemed to have helped chase away the tangled thoughts that might have misdirected me.

At least this time, I could see the positive side of one of my blackouts. It wasn't until I'd climbed into the car and drove back to my hotel room that I remembered the note. I fished the note out of the pocket of my sweaty shorts. Lucky for me the numbers were still discernible. Once in my hotel room, I called the number. A man answered. Funny how some voices make an immediate impression on the listener. Like this voice reminded me of a wrestler with too much testosterone and too little mental stimulation.

"Yeah?" he said.

"I understand you're looking for Leland Ansel."

"Who is this?"

"Most of my enemies call me bitch. What's your name?"

"I don't have time for your shit."

"Nor I for your shit. I guess there's nothing more to say."

"Wait. If you know something, then tell me what you know."

"No, not until we meet face to face and I hear what you know first."

"OK. Tomorrow. Burns, Oregon. Rock Gas Station around lunch time," Oxley said, and I could hear the piss in his voice. Too bad. I had a better reason to be pissed. I could barely walk two steps much less waddle to the bathroom.

"Are you crazy? That'll take me half the day."

"The next day then. I'll meet you on the 15th at noon Rock Gas Station in the restaurant."

"How will I be able to pick you out?"

"I'll be wearing leather."

"Lots of people wear leather."

"Jaws will be with me."

"Who?"

"He's a pit bull."

The next day, I drove to Burns, Oregon with a sense of déjà vu. After traveling the same route twice, I'd begun to recognize familiar landscapes. My favorite part of the drive usually took place after leaving Vale, Oregon and before Juntura. I loved the winding road traveling parallel with the Malheur River through those hills, hills which resembled the backs of dinosaurs, a family of dinosaurs snuggled up to each other, and those funny looking hairs on the dinosaurs' backs were the Artemisia species known as sagebrush.

Only in the higher elevations had I ever seen the Artemisia tridentate, tall sagebrush, some as tall as twelve maybe fifteen feet high which grew on War Eagle Mountain, but here in the sagebrush steppe of the northwest where someday I swear the landscape will be nothing, but dunes, there seemed to be plenty of smaller sage and rock cress and occasionally a bunch of little yellow flowers. Someone had told me a long time ago to just call them little yellow flowers.

I remembered we'd laughed at his joke. Yes, his joke, not my joke or my mom's joke, but his joke. In amazement, I saw his face in my mind's eye. I'd nearly forgotten him. It would have been a damned shame to have forgotten such a good, kind, generous man – my father. Those flowers only bloomed for a short time in the spring in the sagebrush steppe. And at present it was early fall and hot and there shouldn't be any little yellow flowers along the way. But I swear as I drove on the road hugging the Malheur River, I saw those same flowers again.

I found myself traveling back in time and I was in the backseat of the suburban with my father and my mother riding up to War Eagle Mountain. We were going to visit Ruby City and Silver City and see the old mining town and the people brave enough and crazy enough to live up there all year long. Now that I'm older, I beginning to understand that the people who live up there on the mountain aren't so crazy. In fact, they may be saner than the rest of us. They just want to be alone, away from the smog of the city and the noise and the traffic.

I saw us again: my mother, father, and me in the old suburban with the windows rolled down on that warm spring day and the dust from the road coating our hair and clothes and getting into our eyes. My mother had been so happy that day. Unusual for her. As a child, I equated beauty with sadness, as if the two were inseparable. Her beautiful face and sad eyes. And the sadness? I was only now beginning to understand the why.

My Dad held the steering wheel as if he were at the wheel of a sailboat letting his hands rest easy, letting the suburban weave from side to side with us bumping and swaying in our seats and sometimes clutching the dashboard or the armrest or the strap above the door in order to stay upright. I saw him turn to me when I pointed to the hillside passing by us. I saw his profile again, the sharp intelligence and the kindness and I asked, "What are those little yellow flowers called Daddy?"

I saw him turn to mother and say, "They're called little yellow flowers, daughter." And we laughed and laughed. I know what people call them now. Botanists call them Bladder-pod (an ugly name for such a pretty plant) or the more scientific name, Lesquerella douglasii, but I prefer to think of them as little yellow flowers. The not knowing can have more significance than the knowing. Sometimes, the mystery in not knowing can be so peaceful.

Before booking into a motel room, I checked out the Rock Gas Station. The station was reasonably clean with loads of travelers stopping every two minutes to buy gas or food or just go in and wander around the gift store. There were few choices as to motel rooms between Juntura and Burns since everyone seemed to be on the road at this time of year.

I spent the evening watching bad television in my room and wondering at the insanity of my selves meeting someone named Oxley who ran around with a pit bull named Jaws. The gas station stood on the outskirts of Burns, Oregon. When I parked near the restaurant, I noticed a Mini Cooper, a Range Rover, and a Harley motorcycle with a sidecar. The plainness of the sidecar looked weird next to the beauty of the motorcycle as if the sidecar had been an afterthought. Maybe Oxley was afraid of me?

Once inside, I saw the pit bull sleeping on the floor next to a big bald guy in the booth by the window. Jaws had more face than body but even the sleek muscled frame looked imposing. From the sounds of his snoring, he had sinus problems. The bald guy watched me walk across the room. Most of the hair which should have been on his head was growing on his chest, an image once this interview was over, I planned to erase from my long-term memory.

He wore a black leather vest and nothing beneath it but bare skin. He flexed his muscles and I almost gagged. He wore leather from top to bottom. On a hot day like today, it must be damned uncomfortable riding a motorcycle wearing all that leather with the sun beating down on you, cooking your body like a gigantic burrito. No thanks. I avoided looking too closely at his tattoos. Too much skin and too little taste.

As I got closer, I noticed the helmets on the seat next to him. Oh, how cute, Jaws wore a helmet too. He nodded curtly in acknowledgement of my presence, "You the bitch?"

"Yes. I'm the bitch. You must be Oxley."

"Yeah. I don't have time for sweet talk. Let's get on with it. Do you know where Leland is?"

"First tell me what you know about Leland."

"Well, he's wanted as a person of interest in a murder. I'm sure he tortured and murdered my friend Ricco while he nearly killed my wife and nearly drowned my daughter. Then there's the cop he beat up in

Medford. He hit him around the head with a baseball bat. It was his way of sending me a fuck-you message. The bat belonged to me. Well, I plan to fuck him good. What do you know?"

"I will. But first give me the details. Where did all of this happen?"

"Why? What difference does it make?"

"Humor me."

"Klamath Falls and Medford. So what?"

"That makes sense."

"Are you tripping or what?"

"I'll tell you in a minute. How do you know about the cop in Medford?"

"I got friends in high places."

"And what else do you know?"

"I'm not telling you nothing until you tell me something, bitch."

"I saw Leland just the other day."

"Oh yeah. Where?"

"You know more than your saying. Come on. Trust me. I'll tell you what I know when I'm satisfied you've told me everything."

"You a cop? Because if you are, you godda tell me."

"Are you sure about that? Sounds like Hollywood to me. Never mind. No. I am not a cop."

"My friend tells me the cops interviewed Leland's former girlfriend and she told them she knows nothing and even if she did she wouldn't tell anyone because she values her life. There's nobody else. Well, except a half-sister and she took off with her kid. So that's it; that's all I know."

"Was he a witness to the crime?" I asked pointing at Jaws in the throes of a doggy dream alternately whining in terror and growling in fear as he lay near Oxley's feet.

"Who Jaws?" Oxley looked down at the pit bull then up at her trying to decide if she was joking and he should be amused.

"Did Jaws acquire any souvenirs like a piece of Leland's ankle or ass while he was in the vicinity?" I asked reassessing Oxley's intelligence. Maybe he'd been raised by someone who valued perfect diction over critical thinking?

The truth dawned upon Oxley and he surveyed Jaws with renewed interest. "The only reason Gail didn't die from her wounds was because Jaws jumped over the back fence, tore up the screen door and made such a racket the neighbors called the cops to complain."

"So maybe Jaws will recognize Leland again."

"I already know the asshole. Why would I need my dog to find the guy, if I already know what he looks like? I spent the night with the fucker in a holding tank."

"But he," I pointed down at the pit bull and smiled at him tenderly as Jaws looked up at me with his flaring nostrils, raisin eyes, and sharp yellow teeth, "has a better sense of smell than you do." From appearances I would say Jaws had been raised by people who adored him and spoiled him rotten. His scary looks were deceiving. Well, scratch that thought, as long as you didn't mess with his family, that is. When I smiled at him, his tail began to wag. I was thinking Jaws might have taken a bite out of Leland and the thought gave me a great deal of pleasure.

With his usual grace Oxley responded by saying, "You're pulling my dick and I don't like it."

"OK," I said. "We're done. It's been a treat." Having had enough of Oxley's thinly disguised sadomasochistic urges, I stood up and stepped away from the booth.

I could cross Leland's family off my list of potential leads. Evidently, Leland's former girlfriend was as afraid of Leland's volatile and dangerous temper as every other person Leland had met in his life. Most likely his girlfriend had been his first victim. Bite the hand that feeds you – a psychopath's first credo.

It was particularly telling how Leland's half-sister knew her brother well enough to snatch her child from his clutches and flee to parts unknown without telling anyone. It would be a waste of time searching for her or talking to the girlfriend. Both probably had a history of survival-ignorance. Besides she was no use to me since the half-sister would know enough about Leland to put him on death row, but not the important stuff like his current whereabouts.

"Hey, where do you think you're going?"

"Home."

"Wait a minute."

"You might find Leland lurking around Crescent City, maybe in the diner or on the beach. I don't know where he's staying exactly, but I know he makes trips to Dr. Violet Winter's home in Crescent City on a regular basis. Bye and good luck in your endeavors," I said and walked out of the restaurant. At that moment the waitress decided to walk over and take our order. Oxley gave me a considering look before we parted company.

He wasn't so dumb. The biker-look and attitude were a ploy. His diction had remained consistently above average and only at one time did he realize his error then make an obvious switch in diction in order to sound tough and semiliterate. The trip had been a waste of time. Oxley knew as much as Jaws. Maybe Jaws knew more, but he wasn't talking.

Leland wouldn't go back to his home or his shop, not now, not after beating up a cop and murdering Oxley's friend. He'd have to be a moron. Unfortunately, he wasn't a moron. If not at home or at the shop, where had he gone? He hadn't been in Crescent City or at home or the shop. Where else could he go? I would sleep on it. Maybe with a restful night's sleep, I might be able to think through the answer to the question about Leland's whereabouts.

In my motel room, I make a ritual out of sleeping. I make sure to eat two hours before bedtime. I take a long hot shower. I moisturize my body with lotions and use a blow dryer and flat iron to get my hair as silky smooth as possible. I wash my face using an expensive moisturizing soap, exfoliate/toner, and final moisturizer. I rub lotion on the bottoms of my feet massaging the lotion between my toes and cramped muscles. And to top off my attempt at finding a way into forgetfulness, I listen to a mediation tape. The spiritual shop was right next to the business that sold bongs, papers and other paraphernalia clearly meant to be used for people who enjoyed pot, weed, Mary Jane, or whatever the hell people called the stuff these days.

Stop.

Only positive thoughts.

Soothing thoughts.

Get into the spirit.

Find your mantra. Speak to God.

I laid back on the queen size motel bed with the smell of stale cigarettes perfuming the air and the lights of passing cars shining through the threadbare curtains and the air conditioner burping and spewing out stale air just a smidgen cooler than the air outside and I tried. I tried real hard to believe in a divine being that had all the time and omniscience to care and look after me and wish me only joy and happiness every second of my life, when it was plainly clear that he had been sleeping on the job for nearly fifteen years.

Someone might excuse god for his negligence reminding themselves he had over seven billion souls to keep track of. Yet. Fifteen years is a long time when you're all powerful, all knowing. Did he have amnesia?

No. Stop it.

Getting mad now.

A moment.

I sat up in bed and ran to my suitcase and rummaged inside until I found the book on yoga. I flipped through the pages until I came to the words and passages I had highlighted. The words rang true to me. A part of me had read the words and thought – "Of course. Of course." I read them again. So, all along there is this me inside this body, a center unchanging, a center capable of reaching something divine. Then why did this divinity seem so elusive? I would rediscover the answer. A long time ago, I had known. A long time ago. Peace, a long time ago. In the midst of pain, I had found peace. I would find it again. I returned to the motel bed and forced myself to lie down. I closed my eyes and saw colors. Black, then blue around the edges followed by yellows and reds in the center. Soon the whiteness spread across my inner thoughts and I was dreaming.

I heard Connie say, "Hush. She's coming."

And we listened to the creak and roll of the trolley cart. One wheel went in the opposite direction from the others and we could hear this wheel protesting wanting to go in a different direction. The old floorboards shook and sagged. Dust filtered between the boards. We heard her slippers, slide and slap, slide and slap against the dried up old wooden planks of what had once been a mighty oak.

The sound reminded me of twin snakes slithering. Then we heard the hinges groan as Mona threw back the trap door of the crawl space. Even I, like the others, drank in the light which radiated down upon us from the opening like the clouds parting on a rainy day. For a brief moment, the light soaked into our bodies warming us and the cold ground. We were starved plants soaking in the light with our faces upturned.

A long time ago, I had mistaken Mona Lawson for an angel. In my fevered dreams, I had even called her an angel. Ever after that mistake, she'd been especially nice to me. Now the long blonde locks of her hair covering her face as she looked down at us signified only food for me, not an angel come to rescue me. Like one of Pavlov's dogs, my mouth began to water. The memory slid away ashamed of itself.

Then I heard Tessa's voice and I began to cry feeling the tears slide down my cheeks. We were having a memorial for Frankie. It had been three days since the last memorial. I scooted up close, so I could touch Tessa and maybe curl up on her good side. "She told me her first had been an Arab businessman who offered her a thousand dollars for one night. She'd been sixteen at the time and on her own. She'd run away when she was fourteen. The usual story, an unhappy childhood with a dysfunctional family. She never spoke about her father, so I'm guessing he was the problem.

"Sweet child. Sweet little girl. You know the bravado and the whiskey voice are just a blind? We all knew the real Frankie, the one she hid from others. You all have a story you could tell, but I'll tell this one. The one right after my fifth surgery. I was in so much pain. I guess I'd been crying in my sleep. I woke up to this man's voice. He was talking fast in a high-pitched whisper and saying, "Hey grandma, I knew a guy once that thought I was Sweet Jesus. Yeah. He'd hire me for the night and call me Sweet Jesus all night long. But I'm not Sweet Jesus. I'm just a fifty-dollar whore with a million-dollar scheme."

And I said, "I thought only women were called whores."

And she laughed and said, "Wait until your bandages are removed and you'll understand I'm an equal opportunity entrepreneur."

And then she kept on talking and said, "You want to hear one of my ideas? You're gonna love this new one I just thought up. It'll make joggers and dog owners happy. Sounds crazy huh? I have this idea for a chain of Pet Gyms. I'll need at least five acres for each one and there will be an outside and inside track. It will have three levels. The first level will be an easy twenty or thirty-minute walk, the second level a more difficult hour-long walk, and the third level will be the toughest at two hours uphill.

And all levels will include a nice graveled path, not the big shit, but the pebble sized gravel. And there will be trees along the walk and trash receptacles where dog owners can deposit the dog shit. In the summer it will be air conditioned and in the winter heated. The idea will be that dog lovers can come anytime of the year and walk their pets without worrying about getting wet or cold or sweaty or sucking up car exhaust. That is a killer right there. You know what I mean?

I think I could swing the deal easy. I checked out the stats on dog owners and in North America alone there are over two million pet owners. Of course, there are pet owners who own cats and gerbils, but a lot more people own dogs than cats, let me tell you. I used to do a lot of walking in my line of work and, honey, I tell you there seemed to be at least ten dogs for every block I walked. That's a lot of dog owners. And what with the physical fitness craze going on right now and owner's ashamed they don't have more time with their pets, it just seems natural to have a pet gym which will benefit them both. If I could get the financing, I figure I could be independently wealthy in two years."

And I asked her when she finally ran out of details, "What about dog fights? Wouldn't so many dogs at one time end up fighting amongst themselves and you'd have to deal with lawsuits and such?"

"I thought of that. No. The owners would have to sign a document stipulating no legal responsibility for injury. And I would include, you see, these walkways which would like cattle shoots, you know, just wide enough for one person and the dog."

"What would you do with all the excrement?"

"The what? Oh. I see. How sweet. Excrement. Well I've thought of that too. The dog owners would fill out a form and one of the questions would be about what they fed their dogs. If they feed them only dog food, they would put the sh…poop in a blue can, but if they feed their dog people food, it would go in the red cans. That way I'd know which …poop to sell to farmers and which to discard."

I asked, "How could you be sure?"

She said, "Test the first sample I suppose. I don't know. I'd have those brainy types figure that one out for me."

I said, "Sounds to me like you got the brains. I like your idea."

And I remember how she said nothing for the longest time. I got sort of worried and then I heard her say in the faintest of voices, 'Nobody's ever told me I was smart before. It's a friggin' shock hearing someone say something nice for a change. You're a nice lady and I'm sorry, so sorry you got caught up in this horror show. How'd you meet him?'

I knew immediately who she meant, so I told her what happened to me. And through the night we talked and tried to comfort each other. And I got through that night because of her. We hashed over her pet gym scheme for hours and hours perfecting the idea until we both could see chains of pet gyms all over the country. It was marvelous to break away and dream."

A voice came out of the dark, "So how did you meet him?"

They just wouldn't let matters rest. They had to be reminded of their pain every so often. At first, I thought Tess might ignore them and continue to memorialize Frankie, but that wasn't her way. "I met him at the Las Vegas airport. It was late. Real late about two in the morning when my flight finally got in. I remember I went to the restaurant and ordered an ice cream. I was so hungry for ice cream with chocolate syrup and nuts. He asked if he could sit at my booth. There wasn't anyone else but us in the place. He told me his flight had been delayed. He showed me this book he was holding, a sort of brochure really, a combination memento and advertisement.

When you open it up there is a picture of a roller coaster ride, I forget the name of it. Anyway, inside is a snapshot of the person or persons zipping by on the ride. And I saw him in the seat. I saw him there, a picture of him strapped in and sitting in the roller coaster with his hair flying behind him. And he was smiling. He was happy. Knowing what I know now isn't that amazing? And I couldn't help, but smile for him."

A voice hissed, "How could you?"

"I can, and I did. I'm tired of hating. I've been hating one thing or another all my life. And now the weight is crushing me. My chest aches with hate. It hurts to breathe with so much hate rotten away inside. It's gone now. It's all gone."

"You're just hallucinating, Tessa. It's the hunger making you talk crazy. You forget I know you're in the placebo group," another voice said barely discernible above the scratching in the walls.

"Maybe. Maybe not. I just feel so good. Remembering that moment when I opened the book and saw him smiling made me happy. I don't know why. I had no idea what was to follow, all I knew was how calm I felt at that moment. Something profound was going to happen to me. My prayers were going to be answered. Then I looked at his companion and I couldn't help but smile at her. Such peace washed over me. It felt so good not to hate. Just for that moment, it felt so good.

And her cute little face, so perfect in its imperfection. I knew what he was, and I knew the little girl needed me. You see he pulled out some cash to tip the waitress and I saw her business card. It was one of her old cards with her picture from when she'd graduated from medical school. It was shortly after that picture was taken, she helped me find a new home, a place where I could disappear and not be discovered. Las Vegas. Then I meet this man at the airport and realize he's working for her and the little girl is not his little girl. She never spoke a word the entire time we were sitting at the booth. He never offered to buy her an ice cream. That's how I knew."

Everyone grew quiet and listened with an intensity I could feel vibrating just below the surface. The vibration reminded me of the humming of a refrigerator. Even the angry one, only a few feet away, listened with all her body with that vibrating intensity. I couldn't see them, but I could hear the way they caught their breath or the rustling of their movements as they tried to stretch their sore limbs.

Tessa, the storyteller, with her imperfect diction and her love and compassion, a voice that sends shivers up and down our spines; she allowed us our brief moments of escape. Her stories moved us away from the dark and into the other world beyond the four walls. I could listen to her all-day long. Unlike the others, she spoke only on rare occasions. That night she spoke to all of us, especially to me and me alone, because we had chosen to co-create a future together. It was Tessa and me and Connie. We had a plan.

I heard her say, "So beautiful. So alive. So happy. You should have seen her face when I handed her a piece of candy. I'll never forget her face. I see it now and I am comforted remembering the inner peace shinning from her eyes. At that moment, she was so happy, and I am happy she had that happiness. You see. All these years, that has been my life's mission. To find security and peace. I used to think I would find it outside myself by getting the respect I deserved from others or winning the lottery or maybe finding the man of my dreams, but now I finally understand. Self-sacrifice, that is what brings me happiness.

I offered my hand to the little girl and told him I would take her to the bathroom. He trusted me. He didn't know me. I knew he didn't know me. His business partner didn't like to share her private life with anyone. So, he lets me take the little girl into the bathroom.

There is a woman in one of the stalls. I convince her the little girl has been abducted and ask her to find airport security. She returns in ten minutes with airport security. They ask the little girl her name. They ask her if she's lost and she tells them a man took her. When we leave the women's bathroom, he is gone. You know how canny he is, canny like a fox.

And as I drive home, I am proud of what I have done. Then I wake in the morning and find him inside my apartment. He is very angry with me. He followed me from the airport. There is a young man with him. I might have had a chance with the old fox, but not the young one. So, I'm taken to my niece and she says nothing to them about our relationship. She tells them she'll take care of me. She drives me to this place and hires two men to watch me.

I don't know what she's told them. They are paid well, so what do they care. I have a nice big room and plenty of food and yet I'm a prisoner. Then the van shows up with all of you. She's building a fancy surgery and a new big laboratory and so temporarily you all have to be placed somewhere secure. That's how I ended up here.

And in all the years I've been a prisoner in this place, I am still at peace. I saved a child's life and I am proud of what I did. Nothing that happens next will matter as much to me. Once I re-remembered how happy I am for someone else's happiness, I am able to dream again. A good dream this time.

And when I woke, I realized peace has been with me all along. It's within us all. I had the most beautiful dream. I saw the lake again. I woke up with the sound of birds calling to each other in the pines and the smell of wood smoke in my nose and the sun on my face. The sun on my face. Can you believe it? It felt warm. It smelled of light and warm earth. Oh, I wish you could have seen it for yourselves. Maybe you can. I'm going to will this dream to you all."

A man's voice came out of the dark. I recognized his voice, but refused to remember his name, so ashamed of myself for leaving him behind. He said, "What lake?"

"Cascade Lake. It's a place I like to call – my little oasis."

"I know the place. I know it well. I've fished there a few times."

"Oh yeah?"

"I was born in Alabama. When I was eight my parents moved up north. They wanted to live in a quieter place, so they moved to Idaho. We lived in a tiny town called Woolstone and eventually my father bought some land and we grew potatoes."

"I've never been to Idaho."

"Times were rough back then and we had to sell the farm. I moved back to Woolstone as soon as I finished school. Spent most of my days rock hounding with my brother and my wife."

"Hey, professor, tell us about your trip down the Amazon," someone asked back in the corner. I recognized the voice, but I wanted to hear Tessa's story first. And like usual, her voice was drowned out by the others. Her fingers found mine in the dark. They squeezed my arm reassuringly and ever after I equated strength and wisdom from their bony dryness, "They need to speak. Let them speak honey. It comforts them."

I dreamed I was a baby again and in my baby chair at a huge table laden with food, so much food. And there were all these faces surrounding me bending down to smile into my eyes. They had plates held out in offering, plates full of food. I couldn't find my arms. I told them I couldn't find my arms and they just grinned and shook their heads.

Then a piece of something that smelled like chicken brushed against my lips and automatically I opened my mouth and accepted the gift. So many offerings, so much love. I cried soundlessly in the dark. I didn't want them to be sad or to think me ungrateful. So much food. Just for me. My empty belly, my growling belly. So much food.

The tunnel pulled Tessa inside its darkness. I could no longer feel her beside me or see her eyes. I panicked. And then Tessa's voice carried back to me, "Don't be afraid, Sweet Pea." I heard the other voice behind me telling us to be quiet, hurry up, and keep moving. I touched the heel in front of me and knew it was Tessa. Her heel reminded me I wasn't alone.

I crawled on my hands and knees, sometimes my head brushing up against a rough ceiling, sometimes against a plant root, and sometimes something softer, something alive like me. I made myself quiet and kept my head down and kept on going because Tessa kept on going. They needed me. We were the three chickadees. We were invincible.

They said they couldn't do it without me. And I wouldn't let them down. Something passed by me. I was scared at first. Then I sniffed again. I smelled fresh air. It was warm. It had been a long time since I had smelled a warm breeze. Up ahead I saw her leading us toward a light. There were three windows and the light streamed through them all. The smallest window was in a door way up high.

We were climbing a rope ladder to the door, toward more fresh air, more sunshine, and another room. I looked up at the face looking down at me from the door. I didn't recognize the woman. Then I thought I heard Tessa's voice, "Come on Sweet Pea. Come on. She won't hurt you." I stretched my arm up as far as it would go, and the stranger grabbed my hand and pulled me into the light. Her hands were rough. Her eyes were cold, hard as the pebbles in the dark below. I felt afraid.

The light blinded me.

The heat burned my skin.

I threw up.

The cabin was on fire. Aunt Connie ran inside the cabin. I tried to run after her. The stranger wouldn't let me go. Tessa resting against a big rock refused to open her eyes. When I touched her, she fell sideways. I broke free and ran for Aunt Connie. The smoke hid her from me. I heard beating on the trap door. The stranger lifted me up into her arms and shook me hard, "We must go."

In the glow from the fire's light, I saw a deer. It lay under a tree near a waterfall. Its eyes were closed. I watched as the warm breeze brushed up against the deer's soft brown fur and made it move. It looked so beautiful. I couldn't take my eyes off the firelight shining down on that beautiful deer. It was asleep too.

I heard the stranger whisper, "Don't be afraid of the sky."

I tried to scream. The stranger covered my mouth and pressed her forehead against my cheek. As she carried me, she whispered in my ear, "You are blood of my blood now."

A passing car lit up my hotel room. With my heart thumping, I tried to orient myself once again, in this, in the here, in the here of this present time I cried out, "Aunty Connie. Tessa. Come find me, please."

31

Zak drove into Twin Falls with a vague idea of stopping at a convenience store or maybe a drive-through and buying breakfast before hitting the Interstate. He drove on automatic and found himself near the mall. He pulled into his favorite Mexican restaurant. They were closed. Of course. It was barely eight a.m. He circled the building and exited the parking lot then cut across the street to Garcia's Take Out. He preferred Café de Olla but he didn't want to wait even an hour to drink it. He had a long trip ahead of him. Six weeks had passed and perhaps she would no longer be in Crescent City, yet, he had to see for himself. She would need him more than ever now.

Dr. Bishop hadn't been any help at all. Mrs. Lawson had given him the doctor's number and the doctor had taken his sweet time returning Zak's call. He understood all the crap about doctor-patient confidentiality, but what about innocent citizens – didn't they have a right to know what sort of person, dangerous or otherwise, might be running around the streets? The woman he chose to call Eve Endicott would be incapable of harming anyone, yet, the other one, now she had the capacity to cause major injury.

All he had to do was think about his brother's poor face. His black and blue eyes had faded to green and yellow and his nose had returned to its normal size and shape. But something inside Luke had changed, something, until yesterday, he'd had difficulty figuring out. Luckily, there had been no broken bones.

Even so, a part of Luke was broken. His obsession over finding Amara kept him motivated and eager. Every morning, he anticipated that would be the day he would find her. Now, nothing sparked his interest; he just sat in his wheelchair and stared at the butte as if he expected nothing. He didn't even look up when a vehicle passed the Woolly Man leaving dust and gravel in its wake.

Now what? What could Zak do to feel better about himself? Desperate to erase his family's humiliation, he thought about yesterday. He'd driven into Boise and bought a disposable cellphone. Then he'd driven to Lucky Peak and parked above the dam and made his phone call. He recalled everything about the conversation with the park ranger at the Bureau of Land Management in Nevada.

"I want to report what I believe is a crime. My brother and I were hiking around Ruby Lake Wildlife Refuge and came across this place where someone had been digging and found what looks like a mass grave. My brother nearly fell into one of the holes. We saw indications that people had been buried in what used to be a crawl space.

I don't know if it's legal in Nevada to bury people that way, but I thought you should know. From the evidence, someone built a cabin up there back in the early 19th century, probably before the refuge became federal land and now all that's left are the foundation stones. I think something bad might have happened there within the last decade because the earth has been disturbed."

"Ruby Lake Refuge is a big area sir. Can you be more specific? And I'll need your name and number."

"We turned onto Ruby Valley Road between Little Antelope Summit and Robinson Summit outside of Ely, Nevada. We intended to stay in Ely, but thought we might check out this back road traveling straight up the mountainside. It was mile marker, ah. Damned. I can't remember. Anyway, I remember passing an old barn, must have been really old and the barn was surrounded by barbed wire. It had only one side left, yet, it was still upright leaning against a chalky cliffside.

You see my brother and I, we're rock hounds. I thought we might find some new stuff along that road. The road looked pretty good at first but wasn't so good three miles up the mountain. I mean we're used to worse roads. You know washboard roads and stuff. Unlike unused back roads, this road had been leveled and someone had laid gravel right up to the foundation stones. Then the gravel road turned into some nasty stuff further up maybe due to spring run offs. There were deep-ruts in the road about three feet deep in some places, so we ended up hiking the rest of the way in."

"How far sir?"

"About two miles. Yeah. It was two miles. From the highway, I'd say the road up to this place must have been five miles altogether."

"And your name sir?"

"Sorry what'd you say? You're breaking up. I can't hear you. What?"

Zak got out of his Camaro, walked down the slope to the reservoir and looked around. It was dark and even if someone had parked on the peak across the reservoir they wouldn't have been able to see what he had in his hand. He pulled the sim card out of the cellphone and stomped on it, then stood looking down on Lucky Peak Reservoir with his hands in his pockets thinking about what he had just done. Maybe the police would find his DNA all over the place and arrest him? Maybe the police would find evidence of a crime? Or not. They'd worn their gloves while digging. Still. You never know what a forensic team might find.

In his mind, the past and all its ugliness, the things he'd been willing to do for his family and for Amara were washed clean by this one act. He owed the dead some justice. And just to be certain his message had been taken seriously, he would check the Nevada papers and the Internet and make sure the Bureau of Land Management had done something about the cabin. He wouldn't let this crime go unnoticed. And maybe someday the sick fucks who'd committed this unspeakable crime would be found and punished.

Eve knew. She knew the murderer, the sick monster who kidnapped and experimented on people. She knew the person's name and the person's face. She must, otherwise, why had she bothered to lead them to the cabin anyway? No one could have found the place in a million years without her help. Sure, Little Antelope Summit had been easy to find and Ruby Lake Road, but the back road to the cabin had been deliberately camouflaged to prevent anyone from stumbling onto the property by accident.

The body of the mermaid probably meant nothing to Eve. It had been just dumb luck Luke had stumbled upon her bones. When Zak found Eve, he would try to get her to talk to him about her past and tell him what happened. Even in the beginning, he'd sensed the soundness and compassion at the center of Eve. His mind refused to dwell on how those people died, but Eve must know more. Part of him didn't want to know the details.

By the time Zak realized where he was, his thoughts were so clouded with anger and loathing for himself and the whole human race, he knew he had to do one more thing to undo the harm he had done. He recognized the street he was on and saw the sign advertising *Around the World Pawn* up ahead. He pulled into the parking lot and climbed out of his vehicle.

He would check on Leland. After all, his day couldn't get any worse. Leland needed therapy for sure. But. Leland hadn't been the one all those years ago who did those ugly things to him. He just happened to be the guy who hired the pervert. He remembered again the way

Leland behaved in the Klamath Falls holding tank. There had been something off about his behavior, as if he were close to a nervous breakdown.

Before approaching the shop, Zak searched the area. There were a few cars in the parking lot across the street which suggested Leland might be back. He walked up to the shop door and tried to open it. The door wouldn't budge. Then he noticed a note taped on the glass of the door. He read the name. He stared at the writing. It looked familiar.

He stepped back and surveyed the display windows on either side of him, then approached the right-hand window peering through the glass at a drum set and several guitars. One instrument caught his eye, a pristine looking steel guitar. The shop looked empty. No one was skulking behind the counter.

Next door, he heard a bell ring announcing a customer. He turned away from the pawn shop window and watched as a man with a salt and pepper beard down to his navel and a few tufts of gray hair on his head exit the tobacco shop. The man nodded curtly in Zak's direction as he strode down the street. Zak watched him head toward the parking lot. The cars parked in Leland's lot were tobacco shop customers. Leland, if he had known, would have been furious.

Zak returned to his vehicle. It took a minute or two to find the note in the glove compartment, the note Eve had left him with the map to Crescent City and the telephone number. He'd already tried the number, and nobody had answered. It had been a land line number without voice messaging. Who would have something that archaic? He had no way of leaving her a message. He wasn't planning to call the number again; he just wanted to compare the handwriting on his map with the handwriting from the note left on Leland's pawn shop door. The writing looked familiar.

Or was it just wishful thinking on his part? No. The writing did look similar. Eve must have been here. His eyes searched the street wondering if she was nearby. He took careful notice of the area next to the pawn shop's parking lot. A rusty van was parked next to the old gas station. The gas station windows had been boarded up a long time ago.

In the weedy area near some pathetic nutrient deprived bushes, he thought he saw movement. He looked away for a second then back to where he'd thought he'd seen something. A bird startled out of hiding flew away from the tallest bush and settled on the roof of the gas station.

The gas station still belonged to his uncle who continued to pay taxes on the property even though he refused to upgrade the station or sell the building or the property. Like his mother, his uncle was stubborn. He'd moved to New York and found his calling – making money by suckering dumbasses out of their life savings. What a guy. Thinking about the gas station got him thinking about his former dream of owning a shop. Back when he was a kid, he imagined himself owning a business selling cars or detailing for a living. That was before he met Professor Constance Wade and discovered in himself a passion for history and archeology.

Convinced he'd seen nothing more sinister than a bird hiding in his uncle's straggly bushes, Zak searched the back floor of the Camaro until he found the old Twin Falls phone book which had fallen on the floor. He opened the book to the yellow pages and found the number to *Around the World Pawn*. He entered the number into his cellphone and then pushed send. As he listened to the ringing, he watched the van from the corner of his eye.

All the van needed was some TLC. A week, that was all it would take to turn the beast into a beauty. He realized his breakfast was beginning to get cold. On the fifth ring the message service picked up and he heard Leland's recorded voice say, "You've reached *Around the World Pawn*. We are closed but will reopen after Memorial Day." Memorial Day had come and gone. Labor Day had come and gone too.

As he waited, Zak thought about Andy Jankowski's presentation only a few days ago. He'd gone above and beyond Eve's aliases and discovered some fascinating facts. Instead of meeting at the Woolly Man, Zak chose to meet Jankowski at a small coffee shop in Twin. He figured Luke had had enough of Jane Smith and he'd rather be miles away from Nate's big ears and flapping tongue.

Everybody thought Zak had forgotten all about Eve and that's the way he wanted them to think. He and Jankowski sat across from each other with old newspaper clippings, Internet documents, printed emails and photographs spread out on the table between them.

In his element, Jankowski began his lecture by picking up the photograph of a middle-aged woman with a sharp nose and sharper chin. Zak was transfixed by the photograph. Here she was, Dr. Mary Ana Evans with her thick white hair piled high on her head and her steely violet eyes assessing the camera critically.

He held her photograph and listened as Jankowski said, "First I searched for Dr. Mary Ana Evans. I got a hit right away. She's a real professor. Or she was anyway. She's been missing for sixteen years. Her sister's still pestering the Idaho police and the FBI to keep Dr. Evans in the Missing Person's Database. She did co-lecture at Boise State for a semester before she went missing. And."

Andy milked the moment by pausing and Zak knew better than to complain. He waited patiently for Andy to continue. "Get this," Andy emphasized his point by leaning forward, "she was a long time very good friend of someone you and your brother know – Dr. Constance Wade. Even more fantastical is the fact that Dr. Evans went to the Director of Anthropology to complain about Krutcher the day she went missing. Weird huh? Evans goes missing and Krutcher goes missing."

When Zak didn't respond to Jankowski's implicit question, his friend with an expression of annoyance settled back into his seat and tossed the next photograph across the table, "Now the name Navan isn't exactly popular in the States. In Ireland its familiar. Although none of the women in the U.K. have the combination Navan Leona Keys. And then I did some more digging and discovered something amazing. There is a woman in the States called Navan Leona Keys and surprise, surprise, she's been missing for nearly twenty years. She'd last been seen driving away from her boyfriend's apartment in Gresham, Oregon.

The missing person's report mentioned Navan and her boyfriend had had a fight. Without family and a recent break-up with her boyfriend, it took three months before anyone figured out she'd gone missing. Unlike the usual urban hipsters in Portland during Y2K, she lived as an avowed Wiccan from the day she was born, at least according to her customers. She charged people for private seances claiming to be able to communicate with the dead. Her flyers claim she has precog, clairvoyant and psychometric abilities. In addition, she advertised herself as a fabulous palm reader and an even better psychic sorceress."

Listening to Jankowski's summary of the woman, he examined the photograph critically, growing increasingly uneasy. Like present day Leona, she had thick black curly hair and large eyes. Yet present day Leona wore her hair short. The woman's hair color in the photograph looked natural. Her eye color did not. Maybe she had worn colored lenses to give her that ethereal quality she would need to convince her customers she was a real psychic? There were differences between the women. Present day Leona had green eyes and a long narrow face. Present day Leona also had thicker eyelashes.

Yet there were disturbing similarities between the two women. While Navan had a makeup free heart-shaped face and full lips, present day Leona also wore no makeup or lipstick. The woman in the photograph's face, hair, and body had probably never been exposed to unnatural chemicals. Zak remembered how fresh and natural Leona had smelled. And the similarity that bothered him the most was in their behaviors and expressions.

Both women looked like the type of people who would have shunned mass-produced shampoos and conditioners and refused to buy any product which had been animal tested. Their eyes had twin expressions revealing heartbreaking sadness. Their sadness reminded him of people who had experienced a great deal of suffering at a very young age.

The final piece which convinced him of how alike the women were was in their choice of clothes. He could only see the top half of her body and the photograph was a bit grainy, yet he recognized the silk tie-dyed shirt with its flowing sleeves. Leona had walked into the Woolly Man wearing a skirt which matched the material, colors, and style of the shirt in the photograph. When he compared present day Navan Leona Keys with this photograph, he had to admit they were eerily alike.

"Earth to Nerin. You awake in there, buddy?"

Rubbing his aching forehead Zak set the photograph of Navan Leona Keys back in the folder marked with her name. Jankowski was nothing if not orderly. A folder marked Frances Margaret Stewart landed in front of him. Zak opened it and looked at the photograph of the black woman. It was a professional photograph. She was wearing an evening gown and she was gorgeous. He judged her to be about five feet eight inches tall. She was what some people liked to call statuesque and others would call Rubenesque. He stopped Jankowski short, "Hold on Andy. You've got the wrong woman. This can't be Frankie."

Jankowski frowned, "Why not? She fits in with the others. She went missing in Las Vegas sixteen years ago. And she'd been seen in the same area as Dr. Wade. I figure they have something in common. They were abducted around the same time in the same city."

"I always pictured Frankie as white," Zak said studying the picture with interest. "Maybe because Jane Smith is white. Wow. This is starting to get really interesting."

"Interesting how?"

"I can't tell you just yet. Someday. Someday I'll tell you everything. I'm still working on how it's all going to end. So just be patient with me Andy. Go on. I'm listening."

"Frances Margaret Stewart was born in Las Vegas. She'd be about fifty-five now. When she was younger she studied dance, and tried to get work in New York. It didn't pan out for her, so she returned to Vegas, went back to school, got a degree in accounting. She worked three jobs, if you can believe it. She worked full-time as an accountant, part-time as a waitress, and she had her own part-time business as a dog groomer.

Then some drunk hit her car and she ended up in the hospital with multiple fractures. She could no longer waitress or groom dogs. It was the pain killers which did her in. Took her years to get off them. But she did. She was off the pain killers and trying to get her life back on track when her husband died in Iraq. She hit rock bottom then and started drinking and taking pain killers. When she lost her job at the accounting firm and was tossed out of her home a few months later, she was arrested for solicitation. The next day they released her, and it was around that time when she went missing. Man, life stinks doesn't it?"

Neither one of them talked for the longest time. Zak kept looking into Frankie's face and wondering if just a day would have made the difference. If the cops had kept her just one more day inside the holding cell, she would have missed being abducted by some lowlife loser.

Jankowski finished his presentation by saying, "So far I haven't found anyone with the names Eve Endicott or Acacia T. Pierce who've been kidnapped or declared missing. It's early days. I'm going to keep looking."

Zak could have told him his conversation with Dr. Caleb Bishop had been a bust. In fact, Dr. Bishop had been no help at all. Instead he told his good friend, "I appreciate all of this Andy. Wow. You should open your own detective agency. I didn't know you had it in you."

Andy's look of horror made Zak laugh so hard he nearly fell out of his chair. The idea of making a living off the misery of others made Andy physically ill. He had few options in today's work force, either he set aside his scruples and worked in a capitalistic environment i.e. any occupation which propagated the ideals of money: banks, schools, department stores, or prisons or continue as he had been doing since high school babysitting and caregiving. He was certainly smart enough to have become a heart surgeon or a neurologist. Instead he chose nursing. Too bad he hadn't been in town the day Luke decided to stab himself in the gut to test his immortality.

When lightning blinded him for a second, Zak returned to the present and looked around for the offending object which had nearly pierced through his eye to the back of his head. He slumped back in the Camaro's bucket seat once he figured out who was to blame for nearly blinding him. He watched in envy as a familiar 1957 Chevy Bel Air in cherry condition with its usual sedate smugness passed by.

Wishing he were in the driver's seat of the Bel Air reminded him of the rusting Bel Air back at Woolly Man which reminded him of the hybrid jackrabbit and the big cat. Thinking about the big cat got him thinking about Leona who'd been sitting in the bar communing with the spirit world. It was a short step from imagining Leona to remembering Eve.

Then he had an epiphany.

Eve Endicott must have known Ana Evans and Leona Keys. Shit, Eve might even have known Constance Wade. Zak didn't buy into Luke's theory of Eve being Wade especially after his stupid stunt to test his immortality. No, his Eve was not a freaking old lady who had discovered the fountain of youth. If he wanted to be sure his Eve was not Professor Wade, he knew he had to visit the Wade house and talk to her sons. He couldn't accept his brother's crazy conclusion based solely on an old photograph. Photographs were deceiving.

That's what he would do. He would meet with the Wade sons and talk to one of them and hopefully find some answers. Never one for waiting around or watching grass grow, Zak tossed the phone book in the backseat of his Camaro and started the engine. It took him no time at all to reach Boise and he had no trouble finding the Wade house.

She lived on what the city called the Central Bench. As he drew near her house, he could tell the area was experiencing a renaissance. Older homes built shortly after World War II were being snatched up by Idahoans and out-of-staters interested in affordable housing. The Central Bench was fast becoming the new North End.

Wade's home reminded Zak of his Great-aunt Marta, a tiny wizened old lady who used to sit in her rocker with her eyes half closed and nap all afternoon on the porch. And sitting between Marta were two beautifully manicured adolescent females proud of their new clothes and expensive accessories. Marta looked short and scruffy between the new skinny homes which were two-stories high and seemed to loom over her menacingly. Wade's xeriscape yard had evergreens, roses, cactus, and rocks. Even the paving stones had been placed strategically so that visitors could either travel straight up to the door under the trellis or circumvent the yard and enjoy the plants before arriving at the door. There was even a walkway leading to the back yard.

He could see in the flower garden weeds just as tall as the rose bushes. When he squeezed between the vehicles in the driveway and the mammoth hedge on the other side, a hedge which surrounded the property like a fortress, he had to draw in his arms to keep broken twigs and decades-worth of cobwebs from sticking to his jacket. The webs weren't intentional, even with the recent Halloween celebrations. The cobwebs were a product of years of neglect by the current owner.

The way the plants had been arranged as well as the paving stones reminded him of a certain shape. What did an oval enclosed in a bigger oval represent? Did the garden represent the symbol for womanhood? Maybe. Yet though he checked through his repertoire of known symbols, an oval within an oval remained a mystery. He blamed the weeds and old car parts carelessly dumped in the front yard. The mess was a distraction and that distraction prevented him from recognizing the symbolism behind the garden's design.

Zak strode up to the porch and searched for the doorbell. He found a couple of wires sticking out of a hole next to the door and figured at one time there had been a doorbell. Either someone had stolen the doorbell, or the doorbell had been removed to be painted or repaired and the owner had long since lost track of it. In any case, the doorbell had the same forgetful attitude as the yard as if everything seemed to wait for the owner's return. He hit his fist against the door several times feeling the house shake and looked uneasily up at the porch roof hoping it would remain standing long enough for him to get out from under it if it did collapse.

He had to knock several more times before the door opened. Zak had to look up and up before reaching the eyes of the man standing in front of him which was unusual for Zak since he was over six feet tall himself. The man had the most incredible green eyes he'd ever seen. Those eyes fairly blazed out of his face with a fiery intensity. The rest of his bone structure reminded Zak of those pictures he'd seen of satyrs, foxlike with big eyes and sharp teeth. The strong jaw and wide forehead suggested strength and stability. He appeared far more mature than he had to be for someone so young. He did look young. Zak would have guessed him to be younger than himself.

"Hi. Remember me? I'm Zak Nerin. I got your text the other day. Thanks for seeing me at such short notice. You've been patient, and I know I could have mailed the blanket to you, but I wanted to deliver it in person. I mentioned my family's emergencies in my text and our video chat last month. What I haven't told you is that your family is also connected to these unusual events. So that's why I'm here."

The man acknowledged him with a curt nod and shook Zak's hand. It was impossible to tell what he was thinking behind that stoic expression, "Yeah. I remember our video chat. Come on in. My brother Chris is on his way. We're anxious to hear your news. Your brother said that if he learned anything new about our mom, he'd let us know."

Before he entered Professor Wade's home, he handed the Navaho blanket to her son. It was still in its clear protective plastic bag. Brent accepted the blanket without a word and ushered him inside. Later Zak would remember how Brent kept the blanket close the whole time Zak was in the house. Zak stepped into the front room and looked around. Once inside he was surprised at the smallness of the rooms. The front room couldn't have been more than ten feet wide by twelve feet long and if occupied by one person would have been considered charmingly cozy, but if by more than say five or six would have been claustrophobic.

The room gave off the impression of abandonment. Its walls seemed to press in on him and the air smelled of decay and unhappiness. Maybe the clutter was responsible for the cramped appearance, a clutter which would have been sweetly eccentric at any other time but just made him long to rush out into the fresh air and soak up the sun shine. The claustrophobia was exaggerated by the piles of books, dusty furniture, and boxes everywhere. There were books piled on chairs and books stacked along the walls like miniature stairs to the ceiling. There were old magazines piled on the coffee table and the end tables and strewn about the floor.

At the opposite end of the room, he saw a blue hanging pot with the ghost of what had once been Wandering Jew barely alive inside. The brothers probably remembered to water it once a month. The dried up brown leaves scattered on the floor testified to the resilience of the plant. There were at least five or six green leaves still clinging to the vine. Zak also noticed a leather couch against one wall and two rocking chairs side by side with a table and lamp between them in the nook of the bay window. Dried dead leaves from the Wandering Jew were scattered on the printed cushions of the rocking chairs. And the wood floor, once a polished cedar, now had several layers of dust covering its surface with impressive cobwebs in the corners of the lathe and plaster walls. Nothing had been moved for at least ten years.

Zak sneezed and said, "Sorry."

Brent Wade started toward the back of the house and Zak followed him through a small library. In here the books had been stacked neatly in their appointed shelves, shelves which ran from floor to ceiling on three of the four walls. A small window looking out upon the front yard interrupted the flow of books stacked on the bookshelves. Through the window Zak could see an empty birdbath. In his absorption with the view, Zak nearly got himself clobbered by whirling fans. He ducked in time to avoid the heavy blades. All the fan did was deposit dust on the books and around the room.

They made their way down a dark narrow hallway and with relief came out into a spacious family room with floor to ceiling windows facing a back yard full of lilac trees, rose bushes, and other plants he couldn't identify, well, one of them looked like a day lily, the kind his mother tried to grow. There was a walkway through the backyard which ended at a wooden gate. The walkway also circled the yard allowing a person to feel as if he or she might be strolling through a secret garden where lilacs grew as tall as trees and their green shade kept the searing heat from penetrating the sanctity of the garden.

At this time of year, the garden looked as desolate as the inside of the house. Leaves covered the ground and the bare lilacs looked like emaciated models. The models were lifting their bony arms to the sky, begging the angry cloud-god for a piece of bread.

To Zak's right was the family room. No, not family room, sun room. Yes, he remembered now. He'd seen rooms like these on television – the glass domed roof and the floor-to-ceiling windows brought the sunshine inside the house while the patio furniture mimicked the outdoors; yet his first reaction on seeing the room was a negative one because the occupants of the room were insulated from the real outdoors. Mosquitos, flies, birds, squirrels, and other annoyances of nature were kept out, so the occupant could admire the view and avoid the reality. Even though he despised the artifice of the idea, he did admire the design. He loved the warm and vibrant colors of the tiled floor and the comfy looking furniture. He could even imagine himself taking a nap on the couch and waking to see a blue sky.

A grunt from his guide woke him to his surrounding and he hurried after Brent's retreating figure into a spacious kitchen with a huge wooden table as its center piece. The table appeared to be the trunk of some mighty tree, maybe a redwood. And on the table, were stacks of books and hundreds of old pictures. Zak looked at the newspaper clippings pinned to the far wall's cork board and the giant map of the United States next to it with hundreds of different colored pins marking towns and cities all over the country. He wondered which one of the brothers had been responsible for the map and the pins.

Brent opened the refrigerator door and pulled out two bottles of beer then noticed Zak examining the map, "That's our record of the places we've been."

Zak knew immediately what he meant. "Why Alaska? What makes you think she's in Alaska?"

Brent handed him a cold beer. Zak took the beer without thinking then felt ashamed to be accepting his hospitality when he had no concrete information to give him. Brent used the bottle opener attached to the side of the refrigerator and Zak followed suit, not knowing what else to do with the bottle other than accept his invitation to sit at his mother's table and share a beer. It was then that he saw the pictures spread out before him, pictures of a woman with hazel eyes, pictures that stretched back in time to when the boys had been toddlers. And in all the pictures, her expression remained the same – one of shy contemplation with a mixture of intelligence and inner strength.

All the tension in Zak's body drained away. Seeing her face in the photographs reminded him of all the times in class she would pace the front of the room and use her hands as another means of communication, unconsciously emphasizing her point with her eyes, her head, her hands, and sometimes her whole body. The best teachers were more like actors strutting about the stage, using whatever means necessary to get their students to pay attention.

Zak slumped back in the chair and looked up in time to see Brent watching his reaction. He'd recognized Zak's discomfort but said nothing. What passed between them remained unspoken. Part of Zak wished he could have brought Brent better news. The sorrow intensified and unable to contain his disappointment, Brent looked down at his bottle of beer. Then Zak heard the front door open and the heavy tread of booted feet marching down the hallway toward them.

Chris had his mother's dark auburn hair and sharp nose. His eyes were bluer than green with thick black lashes. Yet the rest of him reminded Zak of what he imagined a lumber jack, or a Viking raider might resemble, someone seven feet tall with huge shoulders, a massive chest, and thick muscled thighs. If he had a long beard and long hair, he could be mistaken for a Viking raider. Zak also noted how this boy's sorrow had twisted into something deeply disturbed, something fired by rage and mistrust of the world.

Would he have turned out differently if his mother had never gone missing? Maybe the not knowing had led to his mistrust and barely contained rage? Or maybe his mistrust was aimed at Zak? Brent, on the other hand, seemed gentler, as if he had inherited his mother's personality and chose to amplify that side of himself.

Chris and Brent exchanged looks. What passed between them seemed to confirm what Chris had been thinking all along. He'd never expected Zak to bring them good news. It was at that precise moment Zak decided to tell them what he'd found in the Ruby Lake Wildlife Refuge. Constance Wade's sons deserved to know. Maybe she wasn't buried up there with the others? If it was later discovered she had been, Zak would never be able to live with himself if he didn't tell her sons now.

He spent a few minutes trying to organize his thoughts while he watched Chris walk over to the sink and wash the grease and dirt off his hands. The streaks of motor oil on his t-shirt and cheek should have made Zak feel more at home around Chris, yet, Zak preferred Brent's easy-going manner. It was strange to think of a university professor tinkering with cars and willingly getting grease under his nails. Zak wondered if talking about cars might be a way to slice through the uncomfortable silence.

"I noticed the mustang on blocks in the driveway. Is she yours?"

Chris looked over his shoulder, his blue eyes hard and speculative, "No. My Dad bought the mustang and let it rot in his back yard. When he died, I took the mustang and the rebuilt engine and left the rest of his garbage to the Wonky Ones. Since they're skilamalinks anyway who knows what they'll do with the rest of the junk."

Brent spoke up, his quiet baritone a startling contrast to his brother's booming bass, "Chris means Dad's other family. Our Dad died a couple of years ago. He and my mom had been divorced about eighteen years before she disappeared. We'd been real young when they divorced and never saw much of him. He married about eight times. We lost count of all his girlfriends and wives. We figure we must have at least fifteen half brothers and sisters. Anyway, he must have been thinking about us toward the end because we got the mustang in the will."

Chris wiped his hands on a dirty towel and walked over to the table to look down at the pictures then into Zak's eyes, "So the woman you've been following isn't our mother, huh?"

"No, she's not," Zak said.

"Then what the fuck are you doing sitting here in my mother's kitchen drinking our beer and wasting our time?"

"Knock it off Chris," Brent said. "Sorry about that Zak. He's mean when he's hungry."

"I'm still sitting here because I'm trying to decide how to tell you what's been happening the last three months. You may think I'm crazy once I'm finished. I believe the woman I've been following might have known your mother. She took me and my brother to a place where she said," Zak stopped unable to form the words inside his head, all the while with the two of them watching him with the intensity of hungry hyenas. Zak set the bottle of beer on the table and stood up and looked Chris in the eye then turned to Brent which was far more difficult because Brent still had hope.

Zak continued, "About two months ago my brother and I found what appears to be evidence of at least eight people's graves in the crawl space of an old cabin up in the Ruby Mountains. I called the Bureau of Land Management and told them about my conclusions and the fact there are no remains or bones, but plenty of signs that people had lain for some time in the crawl space. I told the man on the phone I thought the markings were recent and a crime might have been committed.

I'm a first-year graduate student of archeology, but I've been on enough digs to know that the evidence on the Summit looks suspicious. I can't be sure if your mother was one of the people left up there and then moved to hide the murderer's crime. So, you're right Chris. I don't know shit. But I thought you deserved to know the little I do know.

The woman who took us up to the summit wouldn't tell us much and she left soon after. My brother and I stuck around and searched the area thoroughly. We came to the conclusion there had been a crime mostly because the woman was freaking out just being there as if it was haunted or something. Before she ran away, she told us there had been a fire. They left the foundation stones behind and everything else was hauled away. My brother and I figure they were trying to get rid of any evidence linking them to the crimes. I talked to a park ranger and he promised to go up and check it out. I can show you on the map where it is?"

The brothers stared at him from across the table without speaking. Zak waited for someone to break the spell. Chris moved first and stepped back with a reeling movement which might have been mistaken for a drunken stupor. He hadn't expected to hear about mass graves and serial killers. How strange? That would have been Zak's first thought. Zak wagered Brent had already considered the possibility. Chris backed up until he couldn't back up any more and used the sink to hold himself upright. Had he believed all these years that his mother deliberately abandoned him? In two strides Brent was standing before the map. He wiped the sweat off his forehead and turned to face Zak with an unreadable expression. He said in an urgent voice, "Show me."

Ten minutes later, Zak found himself walking down the dark corridor toward the front of the house leaving the brothers sitting at the kitchen table trying to absorb the ugly news. As he entered the front room, Zak noticed a decorative wall niche with a scalloped arch in the old lathe and plaster wall which had been placed next to the front door. He hadn't noticed the niche when he first entered because it had been cloudy outside and gloomy inside. Now that there was sunlight pouring into the front room from the big bay window, the light revealed not only the craftsmanship of the original carpenters but also the neglect of the present owners. He could see dust bunnies everywhere and throw rugs covered in dog hair.

He didn't want to think of dust bunnies when he remembered his old professor, so he focused his attention on the wall niche. Unlike the rest of the house, the wall niche had been recently painted a glossy white. It was obvious someone routinely dusted the niche and wiped off any residue clinging to the shelf or the centerpiece on display inside. The niche reminded him of ancient Roman homes where the residents displayed their precious vases or small statues. In the niche stood an 8 x 11 photograph. The photograph showed a young woman and her two children. Cherry wood framed the photograph and cherry wood accentuated their pale faces and brilliant smiles. Those smiles, protected behind glass, remained permanently locked in that moment of innocent happiness.

Zak recognized the eldest Brent standing beside his seated mother with his hand resting on her shoulder and Chris, just two or three years old, with curly blonde hair sitting on his mother's lap. Then Zak stepped closer and examined Professor Wade's face and all the blood drained from his head into his toes. He had to lean over so as not to fall on his face. It was Eve staring back at him with her mischievous eyes, his Eve with the porcelain skin and the perfect teeth and the high cheekbones.

He stepped closer, closed his eyes for a moment, then opened them and looked again just to be sure. The face looking into the camera resembled Eve Endicott's. Although, there were differences. The alignment of the jaw was different and the shape of the nose. It couldn't be Eve. Yet the resemblance was close enough he felt compelled to retrace his steps. Chris and Brent looked up in surprise as he burst into the kitchen. Zak marched to the table and rested his hands on the surface and ran his eyes over the pictures spread out before him. He said, "The picture in the wall niche in the front room back there. Is that your mother?"

Brent rubbed his right eye as if it hurt and said, "You mean the one I enlarged, the framed one?"

"Yes. That's the one."

"Sure. I found the negative a few years back and had the picture professionally enlarged and framed. Why?"

Zak straightened realizing his mistake. Professor Wade couldn't be Eve. Wade would be sixty by now. He couldn't help but ask, "That picture doesn't look like any of these others. Why is that?"

Brent stood up and left the room. Zak waited a minute or two and heard Brent return and look down at the photos on the table, "Well, I guess the reason the pictures are different is because Mom is smiling in the framed one."

Chris growled, "Why don't you tell him the goddam truth? It's not as if Mom's going to care. She probably died in some alley, just like I've said all along. She ditched us and went back to her old ways and got herself killed by some motherfucker who stabbed her for her shit."

"What truth?" Zak asked.

Brent sat down and looked at his hands then at his brother, "Well, there was a period after Dad left when she started to—."

"She was a fucking meth head Brent. Don't sugar coat the truth. She met this drug dealer and got hooked on meth and lost her teeth and her looks and turned into a dried up ugly piece of shit."

The body that leaped up from the table and shoved Chris into the counter no longer had any resemblance to Brent. Zak just stepped out of the way and let the brothers pound on each other. Pictures were falling off the walls and pots and pans crashing to the floor, but the heavy table remained firmly anchored in the center of the room. The table was the referee and when Chris fell forward clipping his forehead on the edge, he dropped like a stone to the ground. At first Zak thought Chris was out cold. Before Zak could move, Brent got to Chris and helped him to a chair.

In the same amount of time it had taken for the fight to begin, it was over. After a bit Chris allowed Zak to examine his wound. Zak managed to stop the blood from flowing long enough to tell the wound needed a couple of stitches only. It was one of those annoying bleeders. All Brent could give him was an emergency kit with a few gauze pads, some leftover tape and a bit of salve to protect the wound. Brent left the kitchen. Meanwhile, Zak grabbed a bunch of paper towels and held them to Chris' forehead. Brent returned empty handed and wiped up the blood off the floor with the rest of the towels. Zak waited until he was sure the cut had stopped bleeding then applied the salve to the gash and covered the wound with gauze and tape.

In the new quiet with only the clock ticking in the background Brent said, "We were taken away until she cleaned herself up. They couldn't find Dad. They separated us then Mom stopped using and went back to school and finally persuaded a judge she was ready to take care of us again. I was ten and Chris was six. Then she goes to see grandma in Las Vegas and never comes home. The police assumed she'd gone back to using again. I knew her better than anyone; she would never have gone back. Never."

Chris touched his forehead, winced, then in a calmer voice asked Zak, "So why all the excitement about the photograph? What's wrong with it?"

Zak had had time to think of a good excuse for his interest in the old photo, "Well, because she doesn't look anything like these other pictures and I wanted to be sure I had the right image of your mother in my head. I also came back because I owe you an explanation about why

I've been following this woman. I believe she knows what happened to Professor Wade. She knew a hell of a lot about the Navaho blanket.

She goes by a number of aliases, so, I won't confuse you with all of them. Back in Chicago they call her Jane Smith. I believe Jane will lead me to your mother. I get the impression they knew each other years ago. Maybe Jane was a neighbor or someone you went to school with or even a family member."

"What's this Jane Smith look like?" Brent asked.

"My brother Luke snapped a picture of her when she wasn't looking. It's on my cellphone." I found the picture and handed my cellphone to Brent. Brent looked at the picture and then handed the phone to his brother, "You recognize her?"

"Nope."

Brent handed the phone back to me, "Sorry. We don't know her."

Zak had been so sure her sons would see the resemblance between their mother and Jane Smith. With regret, he got up from the table, "Well, thanks for seeing me. I hope my news helps in some way. I'd rather I had good news. But."

"We understand," Brent said and crossed the room to shake his hand. "Sorry for the commotion. We didn't scare you any did we?"

"No. Well, yeah a little. It's cool. My brother and I used to go at it too."

"You know she reminds me of Kallan," Chris said. Zak heard Call-Lynn.

Brent turned to look at Chris. Zak watched for a sign he might be on the right track. Brent spoke first, "You mean the woman on Luke's cellphone?"

"Yeah. Doesn't she remind you of Kallan?"

Brent turned to Zak and explained, "Kallan is our cousin. My Aunt Cara and Uncle Benjamin died in a terrible fire. The fire started in the woods behind their ranch house. The firefighters never found Kallan. They think she might have run away and got lost in the woods. There's lots of burrows and old mines around the ranch where she might have fallen in and died. Every spring, Chris and I go out looking for rocks. When we do, we also search for Kallan."

Trying hard to sound disinterested, Zak asked, "Where did they live?"

"In southeastern Idaho."

"Near Twin Falls?" Zak asked already knowing what the answer would be.

"Yeah. About five miles from a dinky town called Woolstone."

"And was the ranch called Quintus Rose Ranch?"

"You know it?" Brent asked.

"Fremantle. Yeah, I remember the Quintus Rose Ranch. They had some cattle but mostly Christmas trees and ornamental landscaping trees. Every so often the owner would try to tame wild mustangs and failed miserably."

"Yeah. That's right. Did you know my Uncle Benjamin?"

"By word of mouth. I never met him. I just heard stories about the fire when I was a kid."

Chris moved to stand by his brother Brent. "He and Aunt Cara worked hard to make Quintus Rose Ranch pay for itself. We called him Uncle Quintus just to bug him; he was cool about it though. He'd invite us to go deep-sea fishing in Oregon with him because Aunt Cara got sea sick. It was in May, wait, yeah, May 25th, 2001, there was a terrible fire. It began as a brushfire. Some people claimed that a couple of teenagers were setting off M80s in the middle of the night and the brush and tall grasses caught fire. It spread quickly burning acres of land including several properties."

"My mom probably remembers more about what happened," Zak said. "Well, I better be going. Thanks. I hope you guys find your mother. I'll keep my eye out for Jane and if I see her again, I'll ask her if she knows anything about Quintus Rose Ranch. Anything I find out I'll tell you. Oh, and I forgot to tell you. I got a text from my brother. The FBI are involved now.

The cabin on Ruby Mountain was homesteaded so the Bureau of Land Management left the owner alone. Now that the cabin's been removed and its been more than a decade since the owner has done anything to the property, the land is going back to the people. After the FBI are finished with their investigation, the courts will decide whether the owner owes back taxes."

The three men stood in awkward silence for a few seconds and then Zak spurred by instinct asked, "So where exactly is the Quintus Rose Ranch?"

"I'll draw you a map," Chris offered scribbling on the back of an envelope and handing the crude map to Zak. Zak looked at the map and tried not to show his sudden excitement. Leland Ansel had made a lot of money when his property and house burned to the ground. People still talked about poor Ansel's bad luck. He had been a rancher for only a few years and hadn't been doing so well. His neighbor had been the Fremantle family. Everybody in town feels sorry for Leland Ansel. Why? He's one of the biggest land owners in the area.

Why do they still feel sorry for the turd? Because people are stupid and Leland is crafty. He pretended to be inept at ranching and told people he was always getting robbed by customers who took advantage of his good nature. And they believed his lies. To this day, he drives a beat-up old Buick and complains all the time about not having enough money. And people don't even question how someone so inept with money could own so much land and afford to pay taxes on that land.

The long con that's what Leland Ansel is all about – the- what was the word Chris used? Yeah. Skilamalink, an old word for something secret, shady, and doubtful.

Brent walked Zak to the door and said quietly with a quick look over his shoulder, "You think maybe the woman you've been chasing all this time is Kallan?"

Astonished at Brent's quick thinking, Zak tried to formulate a response that wouldn't sound crazy. He had no time to think of a good lie, "Maybe. I don't know for sure."

"If the woman is Kallan, there's a strong likelihood of a connection between my mother and her and the person who abducted them. I'll be thinking on it. If I figure anything out, I'll let you know," Brent said and slapped Zak on the shoulder. Brent's deceptive quietness hid a fierce spirit: someone strong enough to topple his huge brother and smart enough to pick up on subtle clues. Brent Wade had already come up with his own ideas about what might have happened to his mother. Zak had no doubt when the Wades confronted the Nevada BLM if nothing had been done by then, Brent would make the wheels of justice spin faster.

The Wade brothers stood at their mother's living room window and watched him leave the property. Every available space on the street was claimed by cars and trucks and vans. What had happened? Was there a football game at Boise State tonight? In the few hours he'd been inside the Wade house residents must have gotten off work or out of school or finished shopping at the mall. And while he'd been preoccupied with an old missing person's case the residents had been playing their own version of musical chairs.

His initial response was surprise, then he got mad. He knew parking was at a premium in a lot of towns and cities in Idaho now. On this street there wasn't even a sidewalk, some homeowners were reduced to parking their vehicles up on their lawns or what passed for a lawn. When he first arrived the Wade family's neighborhood reminded him of the way old Boise used to look. Until the cars showed up that is. Now the neighborhood reminded him of congested big cities and he worried he wouldn't be able to squeeze his way between a truck and a brand-new Honda.

As he tried to figure out how he was going to get out onto the road without damaging his baby, from the corner of his eye, he saw an odd couple moving slowly down the street. From a distance the man looked as if he might be one of the numerous homeless created by the insatiable greed of many, those who were already filthy rich and those who believed by ingenuity or luck or looks, they too would one day be filthy rich. Every time he saw guys like this homeless man, he was reminded once again that hell wasn't some abstract idea – hell was alive and well in America. This man was in hell and when Zak's money ran out, he'd be joining him soon.

What was unique about this guy was his companion and the things he carried. His companion valiantly tried to keep up with the man's long legs, every so often breaking into a run afraid he would be left behind. The clothes were a symbol of the decay of American society. They were cheap imported trash or something somebody had thrown out from several decades ago. The green army jacket circa 1970s looked tight across the man's massive shoulders and loose around his concave stomach. Maybe he'd stashed his traveling companion inside his jacket to keep him warm one too many times?

On his back the guy carried a heavy-duty hiking backpack with a bedroll tied to the top. Across his left shoulder he carried an impressive looking staff made of genuine hardwood. At the end of the staff he'd tied a heavy bundle stuffed with all his remaining belongings.

The man's wild dark hair, bundle of clothes, and tattered blue tarp obscured most of the walking stick. But the little Zak could see convinced him the owner possessed a piece of unique artwork. The staff wasn't just a piece of beautiful art but served a dual purpose as a deadly weapon. No doubt sensible if you ended up sleeping on the streets when

630

there were no beds at the shelters and someone tried to steal your stuff. Zak had read about a homeless senior who woke up and discovered someone'd stolen her dentures. Wow, you'd have to be criminally insane or a scum sucking puke to steal an old lady's dentures.

Seeing this guy walking down the street with his head held high and his back straight gave Zak hope. The cruelty of America had yet to diminish this man's dignity. Zak admired his strength of character and his craftsmanship. The guy had talent. He must have whittled and smoothed the hardwood to a glossy sheen. He'd lovingly scrapped and polished the wood bringing out the shades of gold and sienna inside. And the end piece was awesome. It looked like a wicked hammerhead. Even though the guy was loaded down with all his possessions, he seemed to carry the weight with absentminded ease.

By the time the man and his companion were nearly abreast of Zak's Camaro, he thought he recognized the stranger. As the guy paused to rest for a moment and turned to the Wade house a sudden chill froze Zak near the curb. He studied the face of Terence Frederick Hunter and tried to figure out how he could have followed Zak to Boise so quickly. Then he looked closer. If he was going to pick a fight with the big guy, he'd better be sure he had the right guy. Terence looked straight through Zak as if Zak were nobody worth knowing.

Annoyed Zak called out, "Hey, man, your dog can't keep up with you. He looks tired. Why don't you give him a lift?"

The man looked at the Dobie pup. The pup was using the opportunity as a rest break. He'd flopped down on the grass near Zak's feet. The man addressed the dog, a dog who had the biggest paws Zak had ever seen on a puppy, "You tired Abebe?"

At the unexpected attention, the pup perked up and ran to the man wiggling his butt in delight. The man leaned over and padded Abebe on the head several times, "You're doing great little man. Not much further."

"Holy shit. You're Travis." Zak said. "Travis Wendall Hunter, right?"

The man straightened to his full six feet seven inches and stared coldly into Zak's eyes, "Who's asking?"

"I'm Zak Nerin. I live in Woolstone. You know me. I used to hang around your garage. You taught me everything I know about engines."

"Jule Nerin's kid," the man said. "Yeah. You got her eyes." When he turned away, Zak was disappointed. What was wrong with him?

"You headed to Woolstone?" Zak asked desperate to find out what had happened to him since he went missing seventeen years ago. Back at Drummond's Market, Terence had made conversation impossible, but maybe, his twin Travis might explain what had happened to the Hunter family. A look of annoyance crossed Travis' face then he smiled, and the smile lit up his eyes. At that moment he could have been Terence, just the way Zak remembered the old Terence. If Travis was on his way to Woolstone, he'd be shocked to see how much Terence had changed.

"As a matter of fact, I am. How'd you know?"

"I didn't. I was just hoping you were," he said as he stepped into the street moving a little bit closer. "I saw your brother this morning. He was at Drummond's Market."

"Terence is alive," Travis asked in surprise.

"Yes. I can take you to him if you'd like?"

The twin shook his head, "No need. I've got a ride."

"Really?" Zak looked up and down the street and then spotted Brent Wade coming out of Professor Wade's house. Acknowledging Zak with a friendly smile and brief nod, Brent climbed into his truck and backed out onto the street. In surprise Zak watched as Brent waited patiently for Travis to remove his belongings from his body one by one, then carefully arrange each item in the truck bed, one by one. Oh yeah, it was Travis all right. The staff he'd propped against the passenger door and when he was satisfied with the placement of his personal belongings, he tossed the walking stick inside the truck and dumped Abebe on top of it all.

From far away Zak heard Brent say to Travis, "It's about time you got here, man. I expected you yesterday."

Not caring if he looked like an idiot Zak ran over to the driver's side window and leaned down to look at the two of them, "You know each other?"

Brent looked at his companion in the passenger seat and then back at Zak, "Travis knew my mom. He called right after you called. We got to talking and it turns out Travis isn't just a mechanic, but he used to be a bricklayer. My bricklayer is sick, so Travis offered to help. We're taking care of a small job in Twin and then I'm dropping him off at his brother's house. Sorry Zak but we got to bounce. My other guys are already on the site."

As Zak stepped back he barely had time to say, "Have a save trip," before they were gone. Zak watched until they turned onto the main street and sped away. Before they disappeared around the corner, he saw the pup climb onto the headrest and straddle the cushion between the rear back-dash and the seat. He rested his nose on his paws. He seemed so happy and content inside a warm and dry place with the sun baking his body.

On the walk back to his car Zak debated whether to tell Brent about Leland. At the moment, all he had was a hunch. It made sense though. First the fire kills Leland's neighbors then their child goes missing. He could imagine Leland thinking up some lame excuse to quarrel with Benjamin Quintus Fremantle, maybe over property rights or maybe over water rights. The most contentious disputes were always about water rights.

How had Leland orchestrated the whole thing, the slimy turd?

To get rid of his problem Leland probably hired someone like Ray to set the fire; Leland would never do the dirty work himself. The more he considered Ray as the pyromaniac the more Ray seemed the obvious culprit. Leland must have had plenty of evidence against the pervert. And Leland knew just threatening Ray with exposure wouldn't be enough incentive for Ray to risk imprisonment, years of abuse, and maybe dying horribly. So, Leland knowing Ray's weakness probably dangled a prize he knew Ray couldn't pass up – the Fremantle's six-year-old daughter.

No one had ever found Kallan Fremantle's body on the ranch or in the house.

The plan must have been for Ray to shoot off a few M80s close to the Fremantle home and on the edge of Leland's property. And maybe just in case he got caught, Ray got drunk, so he would have a ready-made excuse for being a criminally stupid scumbag. Zak remembered the images on the news and how the fire consumed the ranch house and part of Leland's property. It had been a sickeningly clever plan. Leland would appear to be just another victim of a drunk's stupid mistake and later, when no one was looking, he'd slither in and buy up the land.

There were all sorts of ways Leland profited from the fire. He made money when the insurance company paid him for the damage to his property and profited a second time when he turned around years later and bought the Quintus Rose Ranch. Zak bet if he searched the county records, he'd discover Leland owned the land. If no living heirs came forward during the probationary period and the investigators determined no foul play had been committed, then the land would be free and clear and up for grabs.

It was so easy to imagine Leland's hand in all this misery and death. If Leland could be perverted and greedy enough to kidnap his own niece in 2017, why couldn't he be just as willing to plan and execute the arson and murder of the Fremantle family? Leland's involvement in kidnapping Kallan made even more sense when he thought about her as the only legal heir to the Quintus Rose Ranch.

On the way out of town, Zak considered whether Eve might be Kallan. The idea gave him such a rush of relief, by the time he reached the Oregon border he'd convinced himself it had to be true. It made sense. Screw his brother's nutty ideas. Like Ponce de León's Fountain of Youth his brother was desperate to forestall the inevitable – his own decay and death.

Once Zak was in his motel room, he took out his notebook and began to write down everything that had happened since the day Jane Smith entered the Woolly Mammoth Bar & Grill. The events had been stirring around in his head making no sense at all. As he wrote down what he could remember, the day by day events began to take shape. Late that evening he finished recording everything he could remember. He threw down his pen and jumped up hankering for a beer. To quiet his own uncomfortable thoughts, Zak switched on the television and tried to plump up the razor thin pillows without success. In frustration, he grabbed the sleeping bag out of the Camaro and reentered the motel room.

Before he shut the door, he heard the news anchor mention a name - Leland Ansel. Zak sat down on the edge of the bed reaching blindly for the remote. He turned up the volume as far as it would go. Still he had to strain to hear the news.

Images flashed before his eyes: an off-duty cop on a stretcher in Medford, a snapshot of a trailer house, and a Christmas photo of a mother and daughter. He heard the woman say, "Four murderous attacks were perpetrated by what some are calling a crime spree believed to have been conducted by Leland Ansel of Woolstone Idaho. Footage shows Leland Ansel beating an off-duty cop with a baseball bat. The baseball bat was stolen from a home in Klamath Falls where a mother and daughter were brutally attacked, one nearly dying from her wounds. Leland Ansel's murderous rampage ended in Crescent City, California at the home of Dr. Violet Winter."

More images appeared on the screen as the commentator revealed the breaking news of the day – an image of twin capes jutting out into the ocean only a mile apart from each other with the camera focused primarily on the peninsula with the weird looking lighthouse. The structure resembled a lighthouse only superficially with its blindingly white tower, fancy lookout disguised as a lantern room and some frilly thing on the very top resembling a bad wedding cake decoration.

The running dialogue from the commentator informed the viewer that Leland Ansel had been caught breaking into the home of Dr. Violet Winter, she of the wedding cake lighthouse. A technician from A1 Sprinkler Systems caught the intruder breaking in during his final maintenance check before winter. Due to a fluke in paperwork, A1 Sprinkler never notified the technician that the company's services had been suspended indefinitely. The technician alarmed by the open gate and the sedan in the driveway which did not belong to Dr. Winter promptly called the police.

But it was Dr. Winter's dog walker who was instrumental in the capture of Leland Ansel when he attempted to flee the premises. The dog walker claimed the Dobermans had been the real heroes of the day. Zak watched as the woman flanked by the Dobermans leaned forward to speak into the microphone, her eyes calm and expression blank as she narrated her part in Leland's capture. She was so cool and composed as if interrupting a dangerous predator was just a routine part of the dog walking experience.

"I pick up Rommel and Wagner every day from the Doggy Motel in town and walk them around the peninsula and down to the private beach. When I saw the A1 Sprinkler van, I stopped to talk to Sam and he told me Dr. Winter's home had been invaded, that someone had trashed the place and the guy was trying to burn evidence. Rommel was the one who led me to the spot where the intruder was trying to crawl over the wall. We got there just before he dropped to the ground. The Dobies prevented him from leaving the premises until the police arrived," she finished giving each one a pat on their sleek backs.

The dogs were unimpressed with all the noise and chaos around them from the news crew to the fire trucks. The dogs impressed Zak so much he wished he could go out and get one for himself. Then the camera panned to the A1 Sprinkler Systems' technician and a microphone was thrust under his nose. He looked at the camera nervously and then at the reporter. She asked the technician, "Tell us what happened here, Mr. Clark."

As he stood near the dog walker and the Doberman Pinchers, the viewers could see he was nervous, probably more nervous about being on national television than being so close to a pair of huge scary looking dogs. He said, "I saw the sedan parked by the front door and thought it was trippy and wondered why the gate was open. Dr. Winter never opens her gate for just anyone. I didn't want to tip him off, so I ran back to the van and called the police on my cellphone just in case he was nearby and could hear me.

Then I went around the house to the garden and saw a door in the wall. I never knew there was a door in the garden wall. I'd always thought it was just some freaky metal decoration. When I stepped inside the door, this nasty smell hit me between the eyes. I thought I was going to puke.

I saw this guy poking at something in an incinerator and then I saw the dead guy on the ground. I was so scared, man. I ran outside and kept on running until I came to the gates and saw the dog walker. I told her about the burglar and about calling the cops. Then her dog started whining and she took him off his lead and he tore out of the gate. She ran after him.

I didn't see what happened next because I wanted to stay by the gates when the cops showed up. It took maybe fifteen minutes tops. Just fifteen minutes since I opened the gate and discovered the guy trying to burn a bunch of bodies. I checked my log, you know. I always write down the time I arrive and the time I finish the job. Fifteen minutes and it was all over. Fifteen minutes and the dog walker shows up and then the cops."

The camera's view returned to the reporter's face and the reporter asked the technician, "In all that time had Dr. Winter been in the house?"

The technician looked up at the house and back to the reporter, "As far as I know, she's in South America."

"You had no idea that all this time, Dr. Winter has been on the property locked away inside a secret chamber?"

"My boss just told me to do the winter maintenance check. So, I did. We all figured she was away in South America. That's what the hospital told us."

"Then why did Shop Mart tell my colleague they've been delivering groceries to this house for two months now?" the reporter asked.

"I heard she'd hired a new house sitter. Dr. Winter sometimes hires people to watch the house when she travels. I knew the old one, but I hadn't seen her in a long time. She used to come into town. Her name's Myrtle something, a tall blonde with scars. I remember when I'd see her in the garden, she'd use her hair to hide her scars. And then there was Dr. Winter's niece. She'd sometimes stay in the house when Dr. Winter was away from home. I can't remember her name."

"Where is she now?"

"I don't know."

"Does anyone know who these people are?"

"Maybe my boss. You can ask him."

The camera switched to the reporter and the reporter looked into the camera with a studied air of someone who had full knowledge of the true situation, "It has come to our attention that Dr. Winter's body and that of two other unidentified persons have been found in what the police believe was Dr. Winter's secret laboratory. That is all the police have been willing to tell us thus far. The strange circumstances surrounding Dr. Winter's demise will be investigated further and we will keep our viewers up to date when more information is forthcoming. Back to you, Jason."

And the focus of the camera turned to Jason, the news anchor for the local news station in northern California. Zak listened as he reported the facts, that Leland Ansel had had nothing to say about the decomposing bodies in the secret laboratory or why he had broken into the lighthouse and trashed Dr. Winter's home. And there Leland was, the final image of Leland walking between two burly police officers through a crowd of curious spectators. In Zak's opinion, Leland looked like a runt, a half-starved, small, and insignificant runt between two hefty police officers. There was no joy in the sight, no joy for Zak in Leland's capture.

In an odd way, Zak felt cheated. Leland would end up in some book, his heinous acts glorified forever in some true crime novel. Most people would remember him as a monster. The psychotic and neurotic would worship him. Like Charles Manson, Leland Ansel would generate a cult of crazies who would worship him as a sign of the coming Apocalypse. And their nasty wet dreams would one day recreate more monsters like Leland.

Some people might pity Leland Ansel and conclude his unhappy childhood was to blame for his crimes. They would ignore the terrible things he had done and instead focus on his pathological childhood. While others would say that he was born a psychopath and society is to blame for not discovering his crimes sooner. Fundamentalists would secretly fear him as an emissary of the devil. Yet no one would acknowledge the fact that Leland's type had been around for as long as humankind had spawned from the oceans. As creatures of the sea, Leland's type – like the shark – would continue to flourish.

It sickened Zak to think Leland would be remembered long after his victims were dead, buried, and forgotten. He would be remembered and feared and discussed ad nauseam. It wasn't right. It wasn't fair. And then Leland turned his head and faced the camera and the illusion of smallness and insignificance faded. Now his true nature had been recorded for millions to see. Now people would remember the real Leland Ansel. Zak shivered at the sight. Nothing looked back at the camera. His eyes were opaque staring fixedly at the camera with a constipated smile. No emotion. No guilt. No shame. No triumph. Yet. Not quite emotionless.

Zak's cellphone rang. With his eyes glued to the screen, he answered the call. On television, Leland appeared annoyed. Yes, that was the adjective Zak had been looking for – annoyance. The little scum sucking ass-wipe. Mildly annoyed. My God. The man had been arrested for kidnapping, murder, and torture and he believed he had the right to be annoyed.

"Hello," Zak said into the phone.

"Do you remember me Mr. Nerin?" a woman asked.

The familiar voice made Zak's mouth water. Freaky. Only after a couple of deep gasps did his heart resume its normal beating. Not quite believing his luck, he asked, "Eve?"

"You do remember me. How sweet. So then, what are you up to now Mr. Nerin?"

Momentarily disappointed by her use of his last name as if they were strangers, he said, "I'm watching the news Ms. Kallan Fremantle. And you? Where are you?"

"You've got me confused with one of your other women Mr. Nerin. You must remember me."

"Well, you sound like the woman I met in Paris. I mean Paris, Nevada. She called herself Eve. Are you Eve? I never did get your last name."

"I told you my last name, Mr. Nerin. It's Endicott, Eve Endicott. You were calling me Eve in your sleep. Remember the game we played?"

"Are you sure about that?" Zak asked hoping he could get her to reveal her true identity. A hopeless task he knew.

"You silly man. Don't you trust me?"

"I'd like to trust you. Then again, you did run off and leave me looking like a fool."

"I knew you could handle it. I'm a good judge of character, you know. A man like you, so educated, so strong and confident. You can handle anything."

"Where are you Eve?"

"Oh, I'm around."

"Here? Are you in Boise?"

"No. Not yet. I'm heading back that way eventually. Right now, I'm looking for someone."

"Well, you've found him."

"Not you silly. Someone else. I'm helping some friends as a matter of fact. I could care less if we ever find him, but they are persistent."

"Maybe I could help."

"So, what are you doing right now?"

"I told you I'm watching the news. Some asshole I shared a night with in a holding tank was arrested today and I'm celebrating."

"No, you're not listening Mr. Nerin. Come on. Play along with me. Please. I want to picture you at this very moment in my head. I got this fantasy going and right now I'm imagining you lying on your couch at home in your bachelor pad with its sparse furniture and incense burning and ancient artifacts in boxes all over the floor and you're wearing nothing but a pair of boxer shorts and an Indiana Jones fedora?"

"You know I don't wear boxer shorts."

"Um hum. Good. Now you're getting into the spirit of things. Now I see you. I see you wearing those soft cotton briefs and the band around the waist rests just below your rippling muscles. And I see you with one arm behind your head and the other hand holding the remote control. I see your spiky black hair resting on the pillow and those gorgeous blue eyes staring at the television screen. You're smiling, aren't you? A sort of cocky smile. Yes?"

"Wow you're a mind reader," Zak said looking down at himself, noticing for the first time the hole in his right sock where his big toe protruded out like a fat worm crawling out of the black earth. Her version of him snapped into focus and sharpened the disparity between her imagination and his reality.

His reality was that his blue jean bottoms were covered in dust and what appeared to be the remains of a cobweb from the Wade house. Another reality was the tank top which should have been thrown out years ago or used as a rag for buffing his car. And more significant and painful, her second sight as to his resemblance to Indiana Jones, a fictional archeologist and vanquisher of bad guys needed fixing real fast.

"Well I wish I was there Mr. Nerin," Eve said with a sigh. "I truly wish I was there to share in your happiness."

"No problem. Where are you? I can be packed and ready to go in ten."

"Like I said Mr. Nerin, I've got obligations. Don't worry. I've got your number and now you've got mine. Let's keep in touch. Okay?"

"When?"

"Soon. I promise."

"Give me a date and a time. Come on humor me," Zak asked. He had never had to beg before. The uncertainty shook him up and made him mad.

There was a long pause and then she said, "How about April 1st?"

"Funny. Come on. No more joking."

"I'm not joking. April 1st would be perfect. It's in the spring. The flowers are blooming. The air is fresher. It's a time of rebirth."

"Why not sooner?" Zak asked disappointed he wouldn't see her tonight. Her continued silence worried him. "That's nearly a year away." The silence stretched on and on. In defeat he said, "Ok. April 1st, it is. Then I get to pick the place."

"I already know. Remember I'm the mind reader."

"I thought you were Eve? I'm talking to Eve, right?"

"You are cute when you're being silly."

"What time?"

"Get rid of your clocks Mr. Nerin. They're just screwing with your head. Time is subjective after all," he heard her say just before he heard the sound of nothing. And nothing sent panic coursing through his body. Where was the click? The click that told the listener he had had a conversation and the conversation was at an end. This nothing might be an illusion. He might have dreamed the whole thing. The sound of a dial tone as from a call disconnected would have helped him to cope. No good-bye. Just the nothing. And she was gone. How could he last six months?

With trembling fingers, he checked his cellphone and found the last call. He dialed the number and after the third ring heard an unfamiliar voice and the recording which announced: *You've reached the Cuddly Kittens. I'm so sad I can't return your call at this time. If this is an emergency, please contact your local veterinarian. Otherwise, if you need to schedule a time for an in house cat sitter, leave a message at the beep. Sweet dreams, my fellow cat lovers.*

32

I woke from a restless sleep and dragged myself out of bed remembering nothing from the night before. The blackouts were making me angry. Drunks and crazy people have blackouts. Not me. I stood in the center of my motel room, a space which had been occupied by so many others and so many more in the future. I considered how many individuals and families might have shared this room, potentially three hundred and sixty-five a year, and then I wondered what I was doing here. What purpose was served by being in this strange hotel in this strange town? Here I was again: in limbo, unable to move backward or forward, just stuck in neutral. How would finding Leland help us? Had anything changed for the better since I'd walked through the Botticelli Door?

A hot shower cured only the sleep in my eyes. My mind pulled this way and that. Go back to the shop. No. Go back to Crescent City. Just drive. Drive anywhere. Forget about Leland. Go back to the Recovery Center? Hell no. There would be no more locked doors and pitying eyes for me. The heat seeping through the hotel curtains suggested another warm day. I peeked through the curtains and looked down at the oddity of a manicured lawn butting up against the desert. For a traveler like me, the hotel surrounded by desert seemed like an oasis.

How absurd. Oasis my asses. The desert with its sagebrush, pieces of jasper and lava rock littering the ground along with knapweed, larkspur, and star thistles, as well as, the ubiquitous rabbit-brush and cheatgrass – now those plants and those things belonged in the desert – not the manicured lawn or the temperamental trees with their infinite thirst for water. Someone said to me, "Correction, my dear, the cheatgrass is just as much an intruder in the desert as this fancy hotel." And then I realized, like the manicured lawn and temperamental trees, I no longer belonged in this place. I needed somewhere open. I needed somewhere safe. But where? There was no such place.

Fifteen minutes later, I was out the door carrying all my worldly possessions. My backpack contained a few jeans, a couple of shirts, some underwear, and socks. On top of the backpack rested my bedroll. Around my waist, I'd strapped a traveling pouch made of special material which was supposed to protect me from would-be thieves. According to the salesperson the material prevented thieves from reading the RFID chips on my credit and debit cards.

My bark of laughter surprised her. I didn't bother to explain why I found the whole idea hilarious. She was so much a part of the paranoid culture today, she didn't realize she was giving up her own autonomy just for the convenience of shopping faster. The chips were efficient trackers. And when dirty dollar bills were replaced with even dirtier chips, no one would be safe. Besides mice and men always find a way inside. I bet there are mice in outer space at this very moment.

My wallet contained a few hundred bucks, credit and debit cards and someone else's driver's license. I paused before opening the hotel door thinking about that person's identification. Why keep something that didn't belong to me? I pulled up my shirt and untied the wallet from around my waist and opened the flap. I pulled the license out and looked down at the picture and the name. Frankie Stewart. She had this sort of assurance I admired, the way she looked directly into the camera with an inquisitive look. I liked her. So I slipped her picture back in the pouch. Just to be sure I was all tucked in I walked back to the vanity mirror near the bathroom and stared at the image reflected in the glass.

The baseball cap signified an allegiance to a team for some people, but for me, the cap signified an attractive contrast between the green felt and my dark hair and the way the green felt made my eyes look even greener. Maybe someone might take exception to the baseball cap and want to pick a fight with me. I smiled at the idea. Yes. Please do. Pick a fight with me. I dare you. Then I turned away from the image in the glass and examined the room carefully making sure I hadn't left anything behind.

I wore a tank top underneath my flannel shirt. Maybe today would be too warm to wear the flannel shirt? Before I changed, I decided to step outside and see for myself. My blue jeans were soft and comfortable, maybe a little too big around the butt and thighs. All the better though. I could crouch down without ripping out the crotch. Before leaving the room, I reached around my backpack to unzip the side compartment. My fingers ran over the disposable cellphone and sunglasses resting inside. I took the sunglasses out. Sunglasses were as important in the desert as my hiking boots. I slipped my sunglasses on and left the hotel room.

Once outside, I paused in the shade of the entryway with its hanging potted plants hovering near my head. Close by I could hear the soothing sounds of a fountain. While I listened as precious water tumbled down a series of basins, I tried to figure out which one of the cars parked in the lot might be mine. The KIA? No. The Mini Cooper? No. And then I saw the white Ranger circa 1990s parked under an ornamental pear tree. The Ranger needed a couple of huskies in the truck bed as they greeted me with wagging tails and slobbering smiles.

I walked over to the driver's side door and dropped my backpack on the asphalt then searched the side pocket for a key. I found a key at the bottom. I was surprised and delighted when the driver's side door opened. I couldn't help but laugh at the idea that I had picked the right vehicle. Someone behind me joined in my delight. I turned, my good mood evaporating.

A man dressed in a business suit carrying his briefcase and walking toward a shiny black sports car nodded politely in my direction and continued on his way. Relieved, I threw my heavy backpack on the passenger seat and climbed inside. I'd never driven a stick before. Or had I? I waited until the sport's car sped out of the parking lot before starting the Ranger moving the stick shift to what I believed was first gear. Simultaneously, I moved my feet into position and gave the Ranger a little gas. The truck moved forward without a hitch as if my body knew how to drive a stick even if my mind couldn't remember.

As I left the hotel parking lot, I thought about the steamer trunk I'd left on the road outside of Juntura, Oregon. Someone surely must have found the luggage by now. I hoped whoever found the steamer trunk might enjoy the silk panties, bras, slips, as well as, the nylons and dress pants and suits more than I had. Disposing of the computer and other devices required more finesse but eventually I found the perfect spot for them. I buried them two feet deep overlooking a butte near a reservoir.

I thought about the town's name. Vale meant valley, but I kept thinking of "vale of tears." Yes. Appropriate I suppose. I had left tears in the vale-of-tears. Now those tears rested in the ground rusting alongside the laptop, the cellphones, the calculator, and all the other accoutrements of other people's lives. Well, perhaps not. Perhaps someone might come along and find the stuff. I had taken the mother board out and stomped on it which was a big waste of time. After a few seconds of searching the ground I found myself a big old rock and using the rock as a hammer pulverized the mother board. The brains of the machine were now dead. I did the same to all the others.

I hoped I'd killed them. How would I know?

I thought about the owners of those dead things. Sure, I felt bad. For a minute or two. At least now, I no longer had to drag the junk up and down stairs and into elevators. What a relief.

When I saw the road signs which told me I could either drive left to Ontario or right to Adrian, I chose Adrian. The name sounded familiar. Someone I had known had been through that town before. And as I drove and saw the farms and smelled the mint in the air with my truck moving parallel to a range of foothills, I knew I had made the right choice. And as the Ranger hugged the curve of a gently rising hill, I saw a road sign offering me a tour through Succor Creek National Park.

I passed the sign and drove until I saw orchards on either side of me, orchards full of pear and apple trees. I had to pull over onto a dirt road because I could no longer concentrate on moving forward. I sat behind the wheel and tried to think of all sorts of reasons why I should keep heading north. But there was a part of me that insisted I turn back. Part of me wanted to explore a place called Succor.

The sunlight burned my shoulder and there was not a lick of wind to be found. It was at that moment I decided to turn the Ranger around and head back toward Adrian and take that dirt road. I turned onto the dirt road bouncing my way up the gentle slope and down the other side. Once on level ground I picked up speed passing a few cows and a farm with acres of tall hay stacks growing in the fields, so tall I could only see the top half of the buttes. I crossed a cattle guard and continued down the road for about a mile then turned to my left and headed north.

It was as if my mind had shut down finally permitting my body to take control. My hands and feet knew the way. I gave in, even when the road became rutted with deep fissures from violent spring rains, even when I saw Angus cows and calves grazing on the grass and winterfat, even as I came around a corner too fast and nearly collided with a calf.

The calf, instead of jumping aside to let me pass, stood in the middle of the road, and stared at my grill. I stomped on the brakes and let the truck idle trying to decide what to do next. Then I pounded on the horn. The sound sent shock waves through me. It was so loud and obnoxious the waves of blasphemy reverberated from one mountain peak to the next probably frightening every living creature for miles.

The calf leaped out of the way. I'd probably frightened a couple of pounds off him. He would never know that he'd frightened a couple of pounds off me too.

I kept on going, moving deeper into Succor Creek National Park. The sweet silence washed over me relaxing the tight muscles in my neck and the prickling along my shoulder blades. As I drove a new sensation took over my body, something I hadn't felt in many years, a peaceful conviction that I was on the right path. I allowed the feeling to take control.

What delighted me the most was the way the little birds, those brownish birds flew in front of my Ranger like dolphins swimming ahead of ships. I had heard their name once upon a time, a long time ago. And as I watched them swoop from bush to bush and cross in front of me, I remembered their name. Bushtit. And the name and the memory made me laugh. I kept on driving my hands practically throttling the steering wheel in an effort to keep the truck from careening down the steep hillside.

At the bottom, I relaxed my grip and felt the blood flowing back into my fingertips. I had to make a choice. Here was a fork in the road. Which way to go? If I stayed on the main road I would have to climb another steep hill. And then I heard someone call out to me and looked around. I was all alone. For miles there was no one else but me and the Ranger.

I chose the path to the right, even though the road looked dangerous. I could see deep ruts where water had rushed down the hillsides and carved crazy quilt paths everywhere. With hands shaking and heart thumping, I made my way over the ruts and around the dangerous curves. At one point I had to put the Ranger in 4wd to make it to the top and over the rocks which had tumbled into the middle of the road.

Finally, I was in a canyon. Not a deep canyon, nothing like the Grand Canyon of which I had only seen pictures. Even so, this was a canyon and as the Ranger reached the top and I put my foot on the break to stare in awe at the cliffs surrounding me with a big fat creek flowing between them, I lost control of my limbs. The engine made one final squawk in protest and then died. Despite the pinging of a cooling engine, the silence took shape. At first the silence scared me. I wasn't used to it. All my life, there had been noise inside and outside my body. Now I felt all alone.

A need to return to civilization washed over me. In my terror, I nearly broke the key inside the ignition. I also realized that my mad pumping of the pedal resulted in zero returns. It was clear I'd floated the engine. I sat back and closed my eyes. "You are an idiot," I said out loud, then I screamed, "You are a fucking idiot." The scream ricocheted off the cliff sides and returned to mock me. Oddly enough, the tantrum seemed to help. I felt drained and kind of sleepy.

In the stupefying silence, I climbed out of the truck listening to the lonely screech of the metal parts rubbing against each other as the door opened and closed. Metal didn't belong here. I grabbed my backpack and hat and started walking the rest of the way down the road, my legs trembling as if I'd jogged all the way here from Vale, Oregon. When I reached the banks of Succor Creek, I saw someone marching toward me. The stranger was tall nearly seven feet tall. She wore her hair loose. It curled down her slim back in waves of ebony. She was dressed all in black from her boots to her sweater dress. Her dress clung to each and every curve. Her eyes never left my face.

When a bitter breeze blew through the canyon, she seemed unaware of the sudden drop in temperature. As she drew close, I saw her amber eyes and froze. I was that calf stunned by the strange predator in front of me. No. I wasn't the calf. I was a deer, a deer long dead, nearly seventeen years dead now. The deer had died to save us. Was this the last thing I would see? She reached out her arm in a gesture as old as time. As if someone else was operating my arm, I shook her hand.

"It's good to see you, Kallan. May I call you Dilly? I've missed you. I've missed all the adventures we shared together."

"Do I know you?"

She shook her head admonishingly, "Dilly? Is that any way to talk to a friend? Come and sit beside me. Don't be afraid."

"Sit where?" I asked watching her suspiciously.

The woman pointed to her left. I looked. There was a thicket of scraggly brush and a few stubborn trees growing close to the water. "We won't be disturbed there. It's a nice quiet spot. Come on, I want to hear all about your trip."

A voice I trusted told me to follow the stranger. The wet sandy soil near the creek made progress slow. Fall was the rainy season in the Owyhee Canyonlands. Once we were settled on a walrus rock hidden from view with the leaves of the trees as a canopy over our heads, the stranger turned to me and smiled. I noticed her beautiful hands. Her nails looked as if she'd painted them black.

We made ourselves comfortable on the rock. Once settled, she looked down into my face with a sad smile and said as if she could read my mind, "You're not crazy, Dilly dear. The voices you hear are real voices from real people. I too share their company. Not every day. But sometimes when I'm feeling lonely." She pointed at her head, her wicked looking nails reminding me of claws.

As she rested her hands in her lap, I couldn't help but stare. I know what fake nails look like and her nails were not fake. Women who wear fake nails have trouble doing the simplest tasks. I could swear the person sitting beside me had the real thing – fingernails made of hardened keratin just like a raptor's talons. The tips were curved slightly looking exactly like thick black hooks.

She must have noticed where my eyes were focused because she said, "Dilly? Pay attention child. We have much time. No. I say wrong. When I'm nervous I forget my English. We don't have much time. You're not crazy. I'm not crazy. The others, our friends, they were not crazy."

"Dr. B says my friends are a way of distracting me from the real healing I need to do. They are an excuse not to remember, because the past is too painful."

"Well, whoever Dr. B is, he's full of Σκατά."

"What's that?"

"In English you say, shit. I say he is full of shit. You are not crazy. You don't have disorders. How you say them?"

"Dr. B calls my problem a Dissociative Identity Disorder."

"Ti?"

"He believes my friends are of my own making, so I can avoid dealing with the past."

"No. He is wrong. He is a very stupid man. You're sane. I'm sane," she said grabbing my hand and holding it prisoner against her breast. I could feel her heart thumping madly. "It's all my fault. Let me tell you what really happened to us. Before you and the others arrived, I was all alone, buried alive in a coffin of pain. I couldn't see the sky. I couldn't feel the sun on my face or the wind in my hair. I thought I would go crazy. And then I hear people. At first, I'm afraid thinking maybe he come back to finish me off.

Then when no one comes for me, I know. The people stomping around above me are unaware of my presence. For weeks, you are so busy in the light and completely unaware of me. I hear you through my prison and I so want to reach you, to warn you about him, to urge you all to get away. But you are beyond my reach. All I can do is listen imagining what you look like and wondering what kind of people you are. Then the stupid one, she puts you and the others under the floor."

"It's a crawl space," I explained trying to be helpful. She frowned irritated by my interruption.

"Now you are close enough I can reach you. I can hear you talking to each other and I can join you when you dream. I join, up here," she pointed at her head again. "Now I am no longer alone. I am the spy listening to you and your friends talk and cry and laugh. You don't sense me. I am good at this. You will be good at this too someday. You and I, we are as one. We are same animal. Remember the fire? I saw their deaths. I knew we had to escape. I wanted to help you. I took you with me and took them too."

"Liar!" I screamed freeing my hands from her tight grip. In my fury, I had jumped up from the boulder and moved as far away from her as I could get without falling into the creek. "They're all dead. They died in agony. Aunt Connie went back for them and tried to get them out. She died. You didn't take them with you. You're a liar."

"No. You don't understand. I not making much sense, yes? I took their ... how you say? Wait. Sense is part of the word. I think," she stopped and stared at the ground. Then she lifted her head and looked at me. I saw Mary Ana Evan's face looking up at me and in Ana's voice through the woman's lips Ana said, "She means consciousness. She took what it means to be us: our memories of our distant past, present, and hopes for the future (albeit flawed memories and hopes); and in the process, she also took our personalities: how we react to situations, our surroundings, and other people. Mind you, she didn't take everyone. There was very little time to scoop up everyone."

"Who are you?" I asked watching in fascination as Mary Ana Evans disappeared and the stranger returned. As if trying to lure her prey closer, the woman padded the walrus rock where I had been sitting. I ignored her obvious manipulation and waited for a response.

"My name is Amara Katsaros. But you know that, you've always known. Remember when I first introduced myself to you? You remember? Yes. I see it in your face. Come now, stop fighting me.

Forgive me, please, Dilys. I know it was wrong of me to take what didn't belong to me. But if I hadn't, you and I wouldn't be alive today."

"Why should they die, just so you and I can live?"

"Come sit beside me. I won't bite," she said with a smile. "Or are you afraid of an old lady?"

"I'm afraid of everyone and everything."

"Now you're lying."

I turned away from her to appreciate the view. It was so peaceful, so quiet and beautiful. My body wanted to sleep. Fighting my sleepiness, I turned back to face Amara. I had caught a look on her face which made my stomach lurch. She had a peculiar expression in her dark eyes. It was difficult to read. Was she finally giving up on me? Or was that grief? Why would her grieving make me unhappy?

I decided to sit beside her. I had nothing to fear from her. She took my hand and squeezed it gently. Then she did an odd thing. She lifted my hand and planted several quick playful kisses in the palm, just the way my mother used to do. Her lips were so soft and warm. When she wouldn't let go of my hand, I didn't fight her.

"I left you with your people believing we would meet again. I tried to find you," she paused and frowned at a new thought. "Oh, that's why I haven't been able to reach you all these years. Your friends have been protecting you."

"Stop it. Get out," I told her fighting against her attempts to read my mind.

She grinned, "Good girl. That's the Dilly I remember."

"The rabbit and the deer," I said. "I see them in my dreams. I'm ashamed and scared."

The woman let go my hand, "I'm not ashamed of what I am. You eat meat. I eat meat."

"Oh, I see. He was your food."

"You think I'm a monster. No. I'm not. I eat meat just like everyone else. You're afraid because you think I eat people too. I don't eat people."

Unable to tolerate being so close to her, I jumped off the rock and moved a safe distance away, "You kidnapped me. You took me away from my aunt. You abandoned Tessa. Tessa was hurt, and you left her to die. Terence was trapped down there, and you let him die. All of them were trapped and you did nothing to save them. I hate you. I despise you. I wish you were dead."

650

The stranger didn't seem to be listening anymore. As I wiped away the tears, I heard her say, "He forgot about me. He left me a prisoner, left me to starve. The stupid one, she fed me dead meat. It made me sick. That one thinks she hears voices. She can't hear voices, because her head is empty. There's nothing between her ears. She threw the dead meat into my prison and ran away. The meat made me sick. When I woke up, I was a prisoner.

I was so lonely, so hungry and thirsty. I slept on filthy mattresses. Sometimes a stupid mouse would creep in and I would eat it. But every time I tried to escape, the coffin would burn my flesh. They fed me through holes like an animal. The food was better. I knew who told her what to bring. Days and days, then months and months went by and no one came. I heard you and the others and hope returned. When the stupid one put you under the floor, I knew the gods were bringing me gifts. Then I see a skinny woman crawl out of a hole and drop into my prison. I am amazed. Then you came next and your aunt followed. I remember your aunt standing beside my coffin and calling it a sarcophagus. She made you help her push the lid off the sarcophagus.

Then I smell smoke and know we are in danger. I try to speak, but my throat hurts. I have not used my voice for so many years. When I climb out of the sarcophagus, you three are piling boxes on top of each other thinking you can reach the door way above your heads. My body is sore, but I manage to pick up the broken staircase and place it against the wall. You remember the door? It was too high for you to reach even standing on your aunt's shoulders? Tessa insisted on going first in case the staircase broke.

You went next and then your aunt followed. I went last. I found Tessa sitting on a box leaning against the rock house wall. She was staring out the window at the trees and smiling. Your aunt tells me to take care of you and runs around the cabin to the kitchen door. She goes in. The fire is spreading fast. I try to stop you from running inside the cabin after your aunt. You remember what happened next?"

As I cradled my arms to my chest, I looked away from her and concentrated all my attention on the cliff face and the birds flying round and round creating a bigger and bigger circle. My chin trembled, and I tried to fight back the tears. The pain traveled from my chest to my stomach. I didn't want to hear her excuses, but the woman kept talking and talking and talking. Where's the mute? Why can't I shut her up?

The last thing I hear is the stranger say, "Before they all died, I took them with me like I took your poor burned body."

For the longest time we sit in silence. I'm standing by the banks of the Succor Creek and Constance is telling me to bend down and touch the water. I do as she says. Tessa tells me to be polite and face the stranger. I do as she says, and I say to the stranger, "I don't understand you."

"I am Amara Katsaros."

"No, I mean I don't understand what you just said. What do you mean?"

"You were so weak like a newborn kitten in my arms. Your body was so burned, and I could hear your heart slowing. I find us food. I feed and chew up the food like a good mama. I give the food to you. I take you to a safe place. The others are with us. They will always be with us. We are one."

"That isn't possible. You can't just go inside someone's brain and steal their thoughts and memories."

"I can. I did. Now you can."

"No, I can't."

"I will show you."

"I don't want to know how to do that. It's not natural. It's wrong."

"Why? We are the βιβλιοθήκη of our time on earth and the time on earth of those we meet, from their first memory to their last. It is an honor to receive such a gift."

"How is it possible?"

"How is it possible to breath? I do it. How is it possible to fly? I don't think about how to fly, I just do it. And when I want something, I take it. I was so alone. Then you came, all of you came so near my prison, near enough I could hear you talking, laughing, and crying. Then you start to fight with each other. I wanted to be closer. I wanted to be a part of you all. So, I did."

"Have you been following me? Are you going to take me back to that place?"

"I am a good huntress. I find you easy. You love your aunt. You share her memory of this place. I knew you would come. I have been waiting for you. When I saved you, Gaia blessed me and forgave me. I have been waiting so long. Only you can grant my wish."

"What wish?"

"I want to be with my mother and my grandmother. I want to join my ancestors."

"How? I'm human. How can I help you?"

"You know what you are. You knew this day would come. Remember the deer?"

I watch in awe as the pentagram woman reveals herself to me. My eyes follow the motion of her great wings as they slowly unfold. They are the color of blood their tips edged in night. She is so beautiful. As she lowers her head to look into my eyes, I smell danger. I have no weapon. Wanting to live, I lash out.

I woke beside my vehicle. How could I have been so stupid as to fall asleep in such a strange place, all alone and unprotected? Anyone could have come up and hurt me. The last thing I remembered was getting out of my vehicle filled with excitement at finally finding this special place. Why had I decided to fall asleep instead of walking down the road to see what was around the bend?

I felt so thirsty as if I'd been asleep for hours. I opened the truck door and reached inside for my water. I drank deeply. Then when I was satisfied, I returned to my original purpose and moved away from the truck. This time I would go down to the water, all the way to the water's edge. It was only a short distance away. And when I finally reached the water's edge, I would sit on the sandy bank and watch the water flow by and find peace at last.

By the time I reached the river, my mind had command of my limbs again. I threw my backpack on the rocky shore and looked to my right. My eye followed the river up to the curve. I looked to my left and saw the Succor Creek weaving its way beside the cliffs then turning a corner and disappearing from view. Up above among the crags there were birds flying in formation, circling the crags as if they were protecting something hidden inside its walls. The air smelled sweeter down here and the sun warmed my head and shoulders. A gentle breeze brushed the sweat from my brow.

Instinct made me turn to the right and walk up the creek. I wanted to see what was beyond the willows and brush ahead. I had to navigate the rocks littering the ground and a few boulders which had tumbled down from the peaks above, but eventually I emerged on the other side of the chaparral and continued to walk west along the winding creek with the water eddying and tumbling over the rocks.

Up ahead I saw an oddity, it appeared to be a boulder resting near the opposite bank, but a boulder covered in a thick coat of ebony moss. And then the breeze lifted the moss and I realized what I was looking at. It was hair, bits of hair stirred into motion by invisible fingers. And then my eyes saw the reality. It was the thick coat of a cow, a cow which looked as if it had curled up and fallen asleep along the bank.

My first thought was that the heavy spring waters must have poured down from the mountains and drowned her while she slept. No. That didn't make sense. It was fall now. More likely she had tried to cross the creek and she had been too heavy and the mud too deep and she had been trapped unable to move forward or backward, unable to finish her journey. The thought of her all alone out here slowly starving, slowly dying, without anyone to mourn her surged over me in waves of nausea.

I stumbled toward her with the wild idea I could save her. Then I stopped with my shoes sinking into the muddy grass. Like her I was trapped in the mud, unable to move forward or backward, trapped in my fear. You stupid idiot. There's no saving her now. It's too late. I heard my Aunt Connie say to me, "There is a place I like to go where the Succor Creek flows through a small canyon. I like to go there sometimes and sit beside the bank and watch the water flow past me. The way the water tumbles over the rocks reminds me of water's paradox; how it can be so destructive at times, yet, how much it sustains life.

And in this place I call home, I imagine the struggle between life and death. My instinct is to want to live forever. I know that's not possible. Death can be a new journey too. I have no idea what's around the bend, but I'm not afraid any more. I used to be so afraid. I'm not afraid anymore."

I fought my way back to dry land and sat down and watched her. All alone. She died all alone. Yes, but I'm here now and I'll be your witness. I thought the ache inside my chest would rip me open from throat to groin. I thought there were no more tears to give. By the time

I had calmed down, the sun was nearly gone. When the peace washed over me, and I could lift my head again, I looked up at the cliffs and then down at the water flowing past me and I thought of her. I want her to find peace. I imagine her safe now. There had to be something beyond the bend for her.

And for me.

I've traveled many strange roads in my life and there has always been something new and exciting beyond the next town, beyond the next horizon, something inspiring beyond the next hill.

I stood up and stretched and looked around. I could see my truck on the hillside waiting for me. Above the truck I could see in the sky a ghost moon. It looked so beautiful, so at peace. There it was – that moon – shining down on us all – shining down on me while tenderly watching over my silent companion.

I walked into the cold water and lifted her in my arms. I carried her across the Succor Creek and into the woods beyond the walrus rock. I gathered brush and leaves and made her a soft bed. When I was finished, I stood back examining her resting place with satisfaction. No one would find her here; I would make sure of that. All the marks of our presence in this place would be gone. I returned to the walrus rock to rest and think and plan for the future.

Someday, I will let go. For now – just to remember the dead is enough. I will remember her. I will remember them. And I will celebrate their lives for the rest of my days.